P9-DTY-686

The Strongest Poison

Also by Mark Lane:

Rush to Judgment
A Citizen's Dissent
Arcadia
Chicago Eyewitness
Conversations with Americans
Executive Action (with Donald Freed)
Code Name Zorro (with Dick Gregory)

The Strongest Poison

Mark Lane

Hawthorn Books
A division of Elsevier-Dutton
New York

THE STRONGEST POISON

 All inquiries should be addressed to Elsevier-Dutton, 2 Park Avenue, New York, New York 10016. This book was manufactured in the United States of America and published simultaneously in Canada by Prentice-Hall of Canada, Limited, 1870 Birchmount Road, Scarborough, Ontario.

Library of Congress Catalog Card Number: 79-87777
ISBN: 0-8015-3206-X

1 2 3 4 5 6 7 8 9 10

To the People of Jonestown, 1974–1978, who left the land of their birth in search of a home. They pursued the American dream in distant Guyana for they had come to believe it unrealizable for them in their own country. As that dream was transformed into a nightmare, nearly one thousand Americans died. We owe to each of them and to ourselves a diligent search into the circumstances to determine why they journeyed from America and why they died in Guyana.

Contents

Acknowledgments

This book has been neither uncomplicated to write nor easy to publish in the United States. I am therefore especially indebted to those who have helped me.

Terri Buford, who left the Peoples Temple three weeks before the massacre, was an invaluable source of information about Jim Jones and the people in the Temple. Her seven years as assistant to Timothy Stoen and Charles Garry—the attorneys for the Peoples Temple—as an aide to Jim Jones, as one of the financial officers of the organization, together with her residence for the better part of a year in Jonestown, provided her with important information and insight into the potential of the troubled movement. Almost all the children, women, and men she loved during her entire adult life perished on November 18, 1978. In order that the truth be known, Terri Buford fought through the tears and pain of remembering and made an indispensible contribution to the historic record.

My law partner, April Ferguson, was a source of strength and support through the endless ordeal following the massacre; she made many contributions as a researcher, editor, and colleague in the preparation of the book.

Once the manuscript was written, Elizabeth Backman, my editor at Hawthorn, offered important suggestions as to style and content. If the complex and paradoxical story can be comprehended, it is in large measure due to her numerous contributions.

Two men, Steven Katsaris of California and Louis Gurvich of Louisiana, each suffered the loss of an only daughter in the tragic event. Each man was committed to an effort to learn the truth about the unprecedented horror, and each man shared his knowledge with me.

I am pleased to acknowledge the work of two women in Memphis: Joan Taylor, who typed the manuscript from my handwritten work, and Crystal Greenwood, who organized much of the research.

My oldest friends, Dr. Ann J. Lane, my sister, and Lawrence Lane, my brother, stood with me during the hardest times.

Dale Timpe, the president of Hawthorn Books, a new aquaintance, had faith in this work from the outset, although that was hardly the fashionable thing to do.

The strongest poison ever known
Came from Caesar's laurel crown.

—*William Blake*

Prologue

Approximately one thousand Americans, most of them poor and black, almost all of them women and children, had died in a massacre on November 18, 1978, in Jonestown, Guyana. They died in a clearing in a jungle in South America thousands of miles from home. A small number of survivors were determined to find out why.

The bitter winter months that followed the Jonestown murders threatened to destroy the few survivors of that unprecedented tragedy. Michael Prokes, who had walked out of Jonestown as the killings were taking place, was unable to live with the special knowledge he possessed. I met with him on more than one occasion in San Francisco after his return from Guyana. I observed his anguish, but at that time I was neither able to gauge its measure nor fully comprehend its cause.

Terri Buford, who had served for several years as an important aide to the Rev. Jim Jones, had defected from the Peoples Temple headquarters in San Francisco three weeks before the massacre and had sought asylum and protection with my family and my law partner, April Ferguson, at my home in Memphis during early November.

Almost immediately following the mass murder in Guyana, it became apparent that agencies of the United States government were at work to obfuscate the relevant evidence. The available information suggested, even at that early moment, that employees of the State Department, the American embassy in Georgetown, Guyana, and the United States Department of Justice had sufficient motive to wish that the truth about the massacre might remain unknown.

Quickly the murders became a multimedia event of enormous proportions, dwarfing the coverage given to other historic events during that nearly exhausted decade. If the essential truth about Jonestown was to remain suppressed in the midst of that maelstrom of fact, rumor, and fancy, the agencies of government needed to act at once and with skill. The royalty in the national news business was receptive. It understood the need for national security and as in past matters of significance, acquiesced. Its members were not unpracticed in that art, having similarly yielded their right to publish the truth through decades of deceit marked by the war in Viet Nam, Cambodia, and Laos and the assassinations of several important leaders.

The possibility that one day the truth might be known seemed to be remote to Mike Prokes, for is not history in most instances only a collection of retold ancient stories? As he viewed what seemed to be irrepressible forces, he was inundated by a sense of hopelessness and he surrendered. Terri Buford and I have not. This book is an effort to present the evidence with which we have become familiar so that it may be evaluated by those interested in learning why the massacre took place.

Mike Prokes was a sensitive, intelligent, and talented young man. He was also a unique resource. When Mike, Terri, and I talked in California in the weeks before his death, our meetings were marked by an unspoken restraint. The national news media had published so many fabrications about each of us (much of the false data having been supplied by the intelligence agencies or the Department of Justice) that we were afraid to trust one another. While none of us tended to accept the news media as a fount of unbiased information, evidently none of us was willing to believe, at that time, that the national news media would publish as fact a stream of damning reports which they knew to be entirely false.

As a result, Mike Prokes was at first reluctant to talk with Terri and me, for he was certain that we had gone to Zurich, Switzerland, together after the massacre to loot the coffers of the Peoples Temple of approximately eight million dollars. Surely he had reason to believe that Terri and I had made such a trip, since Walter Cronkite's CBS-TV news program on December 15, 1978, had made that charge and it had then been supported in a feature story in the *New York Times* the next day.

Under a two-column headline reading, "Cult's Millions Reported Taken from Swiss Bank," the *New York Times* of December 16, 1978, stated, "A government official said today that a bank in Zurich had informed the Justice Department that the Peoples Temple assets, sometimes estimated to total as much as $8 million, had been removed. The name of the bank could not be learned." Evidently, however, neither the "government official" nor the *New York Times* was unwilling to identify the thieves. The article continued, "A Justice Department spokesman said that Mark Lane, the lawyer, and Terri Buford, formerly a business manager for the Jonestown Peoples Temple commune, had gone to Switzerland to remove the secret Zurich assets."

The *Times* identified Robert Havel as the spokesman for the Justice Department. Another Justice Department official, unnamed by the newspaper, was quoted as saying, regarding the presence of Peoples Temple funds in the Zurich bank prior to my alleged visit there with Terri, "As far as I know, the money is still in the bank." The *New York Times* then concluded, "It appears there was newer information reaching the State Department through the Bern embassy to the effect that the money was gone and that Lane and Miss Buford had taken it from the bank."

The same article also reported "attempts to find Mr. Lane and Miss Buford this evening were unsuccessful. Last Saturday they were in Memphis, Tenn., where the lawyer makes his home. Subsequent efforts to reach them were unavailing."

The CBS-TV evening news of December 15 carried much the same information.

Not one relevant statement made in the CBS television newscast or in the longer *New York Times* story was true: Terri and I had not been in Zurich together during December 1978, as CBS-TV and the *New York Times* said, and as the Justice Department and the State Department had charged. Terri had not been in Zurich for approximately two years preceding December 1978, and I have never been there. Terri and I had never been together in any city outside of the United States and Guyana.

On December 15, 1978, the day before the *Times* story, Terri Buford and April Ferguson were working in the kitchen of my home in Memphis when Michael Lawhead, an on-camera investigative reporter for TV station WREG, the CBS affiliate in Memphis owned by the *New York Times*, visited them. Lawhead interviewed Terri about the Peoples Temple.

Terri and April told Lawhead that I was in Paris with several American reporters appearing on a national television program about the international problem of cults. Since Lawhead had proved himself to be an intelligent and honest reporter, we were not even slightly reluctant to share what information we had with him.

Later that day, David Binder, the author of the *New York Times* article, called and spoke with Terri. He then asked for April and told her he had information that Terri and I were in Zurich. April laughed, asked him for the source of his ludicrous story, and assured him that neither Terri nor I was in Zurich.

Two weeks prior to the publication of this false story in the *New York*

Times, I had given two documents to William Hunter, the U.S. attorney in San Francisco. The Department of Justice had informed me that Hunter had been mandated to investigate, for the United States, the murder of Congressman Ryan (the more than nine hundred deaths in Guyana evidently having been distilled by the Justice authorities into one meaningful murder). I had called Hunter in November and arranged to meet with him, Terri Buford, FBI and Secret Service agents, and members of Hunter's staff in San Jose, California. The two documents, dated September 21, 1978, which Terri had provided for me, revealed that on September 21, 1978, all of the Peoples Temple's assets had been transferred from Switzerland to the Union Bank of Switzerland, a Swiss bank in Panama. They also showed that Terri Buford was no longer a signatory on the account: The assets had been transferred to the private account of an elderly woman named Esther Mueller. The documents insured that no one but Mrs. Mueller and Charles Garry, the attorney for the Peoples Temple, was authorized to secure information about the Panama account. Mrs. Mueller's account was established by the transfer of all of the funds from account number 222-00.042-A, which was a Peoples Temple account maintained in the name of an off-shore corporation, the Asociación Religiosa Pro San Pedro, S.A., and was located at the Union Bank of Switzerland at Avenida Manuel Maria Icaza No. 21, Panama City.

I was invited by French national television to appear on a panel discussion in Paris on December 12, 1978. Sharing the live program with me would be Marshall Kilduff and Ron Javers, both reporters for the *San Francisco Chronicle;* Lawrence Stern, an assistant editor at the *Washington Post;* two members of the French Chamber of Deputies; and others. I flew from Memphis to New York on Braniff Flight 118 on December 10, and later that evening from New York to Charles de Gaulle airport in Paris on Air France Flight 70, where I was met by Jean-Michel Charlier, a well-known French film producer and director. We then drove to the Sofitel-Bourbon Hotel on rue Saint-Dominique.

During my stay at the hotel I was interviewed by numerous reporters from newspapers and magazines in France and other European countries, and I received scores of telephone messages from reporters calling from various cities within the United States. After the panel discussion and a series of radio, television, and newspaper interviews, I was driven from the hotel to Charles de Gaulle airport where I flew, on December 15, 1978, on Air France flight 077 back to New York. That same day I flew on Braniff flight 119 from New York home to Memphis to learn that I had been seen in Zurich by operatives of the State Department while I was flying over the Atlantic Ocean from Paris.

CBS and the *New York Times* had published a story which was false in all respects. With the passage of time and events, we were to learn that this pattern was to be oft repeated. The CBS–*New York Times* news axis, after inventing information to meet its predisposed conclusion, intentionally published, as if they were fact, allegations purportedly provided by government agencies, even though the assertions were transparently false and the facts were apparent and easily ascertained. Neither Terri nor I had been to Zurich, nor was the Peoples Temple money in Zurich. The Justice Department and the State Department, in addition to the *New York Times* and CBS, both knew that. The Department of Justice knew that all of the funds of the Peoples Temple had been transferred to Panama two months before the concocted Buford-Lane trip to Zurich became a media event. The authorities also knew that even if Terri and I had been together in Zurich, in the very lobby of a Swiss bank, and even if the funds had been there, miraculously dispatched from Panama, that Terri was no longer a signatory for the account—had in fact never been the sole signatory—and therefore would have been unable to withdraw a franc.

In spite of repeated requests to do so, the *New York Times* and CBS television each refused to publish a retraction of allegations each knew to be false. On behalf of Terri and myself, I supplied abundant proof to representatives of each of the media giants. The *New York Times* reported only that I had denied the charge and then it repeated the original libel. It declined to publish the facts that rebutted its inaccurate speculation. CBS took no action upon our request.

More than half a year later, in an apparently unrelated story, the *New York Times* reported:

> The Swiss authorities said yesterday that $1.8 million held in three accounts in a Zurich bank in the name of members of the People's Temple commune was transferred to banks in Panama and the United States before more than 900 members of the organization died in their jungle camp in Guyana last November.*

Although the newspaper refused to publish a retraction, its later article rebutted the earlier published conclusion that Terri and I could have been in Zurich with the Peoples Temple funds in December 1978, since, as its subsequent article revealed, all of the funds had been removed from that city, according to the Swiss authorities, prior to November 18, 1978. Thus

**New York Times*, Friday, 3 August 1979.

the *Times* inadvertently offered evidence that its falsified story, allegedly based upon Department of Justice sources, was without basis.

On August 16, 1979, I spoke with Robert Havel, who had been identified by the *New York Times* as its Department of Justice source. Havel told me that the *New York Times* had lied when it reported that he had said that Terri and I had gone to Zurich to remove funds. He informed me that he had told David Binder, the *New York Times* reporter who had called him, that neither he nor others at the Department of Justice had any idea of where Terri and I were since we were not under surveillance, and that the Department of Justice had no indication that either or both of us were in Zurich. Havel told me that personnel at the Department of Justice were so disturbed over the *New York Times* attributing the false story to them that on December 20, 1978, Terrence B. Adamson, the special assistant to the attorney general, had sent a strong letter to Arthur Ochs Sulzberger, the Chairman and President of the *New York Times.* Copies of the letter were also sent to Binder, John Crewdson, another reporter at the *Times* who had published similar information, and the managing editor and Washington bureau chief for the newspaper.

In the letter,* the Department of Justice stated unequivocally that "no department spokesman" made the charge attributed by Binder and Crewdson to Havel and that when Binder told Havel that "he had a report that Buford and Lane had gone to Switzerland," Havel replied that the Department of Justice "had no evidence that the report was true, and in fact we had no idea where Buford and Lane were."

On September 4, 1979, Rowland Evans and Robert Novak, two conservative columnists with good lines into the intelligence community, reported† that a disinformation campaign against a Greek expatriate living in the United States was comprised in part of a false story published about him in the *New York Times.* The *Times* reporter said that he had been supplied with the damaging and false information by the CIA. However, Stansfield Turner, the director of the CIA, denied that his agency was the source of the derogatory information. The reporter was David Binder.

The *New York Times* refused to publish the letter from Adamson correcting the untrue article about Terri and me. The original false charges were subsequently republished by the *New York Times* and then widely circulated by both the Associated Press and United Press International.

The fabrication, together with the refusal of the *New York Times* and

*This letter is published in full on the back of the jacket of this book.
†*New York Post*, 4 September, 1979, p. 25.

CBS to publish a retraction was very costly for Terri Buford. The allegation preceded her to each employment interview and was a significant factor in denying her a job. She had been branded by the *New York Times* as a major international thief. Naturally, prospective employers were wary. More than half a year passed after the massacre before she was able to gain employment.

Several days after she did secure a job she was fired due to the *New York Times* article. An employee of the city in which she was employed intervened with her employer, purportedly on behalf of the city administration, to secure her dismissal. The sole charge against her—that the *New York Times* had reported that she had been a participant in the theft of eight million dollars. Thus for Terri Buford the *New York Times* had made its position quite clear in bringing back the McCarthy era. Those who wished to tell the truth about Jonestown would do so at their own, not inconsiderable, risk. On August 3, 1979, not long after she had been fired, Terri Buford was officially notified by Robert Fabian, the court-appointed receiver for the Peoples Temple assets, that his exhaustive examination of the evidence rebutted the early assertion of the *New York Times* that she had taken funds from the Temple. Indeed, Fabian expressed gratitude to Buford for her cooperation in assisting him in his difficult task of marshalling the funds of the defunct organization.

Yet how was Mike Prokes to know at the end of 1978 and during the days preceding his death that the story, vouched for by two of the most respected news organizations in the country and by two departments of government, was a tissue of lies? He reacted to Terri and me with a certain restraint; he viewed us with suspicion that had been planted by the government.

In San Francisco, the remaining members of the Peoples Temple had apparently embarked upon a scheme very different from our effort. Those who continued as leaders in the Peoples Temple seemed committed to selective suppression and even destruction of the evidence surrounding the massacre and its related events. The publication of the CBS-TV and *New York Times* allegations, on the very eve of Terri's trip to San Francisco to testify before a federal grand jury, frightened her, as it heightened the enmity felt toward her by the Peoples Temple leaders. The news story seemed designed to increase the possibility that either she or I, or both of us, might be harmed.

Peoples Temple personnel had evidenced a willingness to kill. They had spoken openly of murdering defectors. They were armed. When the news media and the government conspired in that charged atmosphere to make the false assertion that Terri and I had stolen eight million dollars from the Temple, they knowingly placed our lives in danger. We were vulnerable both to Temple supporters deranged by the deaths of their loved ones in Jonestown and angered by the false stories about us, and by others who seemingly wished to suppress the truth. We particularly feared some form of action from people not associated with the Temple. The government–CBS–*New York Times* project had provided sufficient cover for them to act and place the blame on the Peoples Temple. For the next weeks we moved with an abundance of caution.

Rep. Clement J. Zablocki, chairman of the Committee on Foreign Affairs of the United States House of Representatives, directed that the staff investigative group of that Committee conduct "a comprehensive inquiry" into the murder of Rep. Leo J. Ryan and the "mass suicide/murder" of November 18, 1978.* When the report, dated May 15, 1979, was released it became clear that the committee had marshalled a substantial amount of evidence and had determined to suppress almost all of it. Reports of interviews with witnesses conducted by the committee after the massacre and important documents which predated the massacre and likely provided insight into its causes were placed in "Appendixes II–A–1, II–B, II–C, II–D, II–E–2, II–E–3, II–F–1, III–A–I, III–A–2, III–B–1, III–C, III–D, III–E, III–F, III–G–1, III–H, III–I, III–J–1, III–J–3, III–K, and parts of appendixes I–C–1 and III–G–3"† and "remained classified and are retained in committee files on a confidential basis."‡

Among the questions investigated by the congressional committee were these:

•Was there a conspiracy by intelligence agencies or others against Jim Jones and the Peoples Temple?

•Was there an awareness of danger by federal agencies?

•Could the violence have been predicted?

•Was there a conspiracy to Kill Rep. Leo Ryan?

•What information had the U. S. Customs Service uncovered in its prior investigations of the Peoples Temple?§

*"Report of a Staff Investigative Group to the Committee on Foreign Affairs, United States House of Representatives," May 15, 1979, p. (III). Hereafter referred to as *U. S. House of Representatives Report.*

†*U.S. House of Representatives Report*, p. (VII).

‡Ibid.

§Ibid., p. (XIV).

The answer to each of these central questions as well as to many others, according to the congressional report, was "in classified version only"* and therefore unavailable to the public and the press.

While newspapers, magazines, and the national electronic media have railed with fury against judgments which have limited their access to the facts in ordinary cases, no such complaints were manifest in this instance. For example, while the Gannett newspapers took out a full page in *Time*† to condemn what it called "the doors of injustice"‡ and to report that "Gannett protests vigorously this abridgment of the First Amendment"§ all because the Supreme Court had upheld the right of a court to bar a reporter from a pretrial hearing in a murder case, there is no similar record which reveals that *Time* or Gannett or CBS or the *New York Times* for that matter even requested an opportunity to examine the deliberately supressed record regarding several hundred murder cases in Jonestown.

I have served as counsel in various highly publicized criminal cases over the past quarter of a century. It has long been my belief that the publication of information secured at pretrial hearings may tend to prejudice the rights of a defendant. That published information may reach out and influence a prospective juror although the judge may later rule it to be inadmissible at the trial level. In that instance the whim of a journalist rather than the rules of evidence may determine the fate of a defendant.

Gannett observed that the decision to shield the record from the press "trampled on the people's freedom to know, the cornerstone of our rights as a free people in a free society."‖ It would have been more accurate, in my view, if it had been directed toward the congressional and media determination to suppress forever the facts surrounding the mass murder of the members of the Peoples Temple.

*Ibid.
†*Time* Magazine, July 30, 1979.
‡Ibid.
§Ibid.
‖Ibid.

Part I

Introduction to the Temple

1 Defeat

Very little has been written or said of those events of Friday and Saturday, November 17 and 18, 1978, that preceded and likely provoked the murders in Jonestown that Saturday evening. Although countless newspaper and magazine articles have been written, numerous television specials produced, several books published, and two official U.S. government investigations completed, the record remains almost entirely mute about the catalytic episodes that led up to the massacre, which were perhaps determinant. Probing the mind of Jim Jones is a difficult task that sends one into improbable flights of speculation. Did he arrange for contraband to be sent into Guyana? If poison or weapons or ammunition arrived at the Timehri Airport on Thursday evening, was that an indication that he had already decided upon his final solution? Or had he stockpiled the weapons and the poison, not because he had determined upon the program of death, but rather to keep that option open if all else appeared hopeless to him?

I saw the varying forces operate upon him. I witnessed his reactions as the pressures increased. I saw him tremble, heard his voice break. I watched him breathe and brush away a tear. I believed him then to be either a consummate actor or a man in pain who could bear but little more. I saw the merciless questions and the charges made against him by reporters who, apparently the night before, had agreed to confront him. Perhaps that is to be expected when the nature of the beast is understood. Yet I could not understand the relish they brought to their work as the man, exposed by his own lies, trapped by his empty boasts, and ultimately presented with proof that his own people had betrayed him, withdrew into himself on his couch, and said with enough anguish for all to hear, "I'm defeated. I might as well die." I had never counted upon the mercy of the media to spare him that ultimate humiliation nor upon a refined sense of what is proper. Rather I thought that as we moved inexorably toward the end, a sense of self-preservation might emerge to save us all. Yet NBC wanted their story on video-tape and needed it recorded there for their victory to be fully measured, and some reporters, for mean and private reasons, or perhaps still rankled by imagined personal affronts, were more than anxious to participate in the final exposure.

Late Friday evening, under cover of the consuming shadows, a resident had approached NBC's Don Harris and quickly passed a note to him which said that she wished to leave with the delegation. Richard Dwyer of the American embassy was later to report that another resident made a similar verbal request of him. None of this was known to the Jonestown residents that evening, but early Saturday morning the word began to circulate. During the morning Harris told me that both residents had approached him, that neither had talked initially to Dwyer. The point is perhaps a fine one, but the incontrovertible fact is that Don Harris was one of the first to die.

A charged and hurtful atmosphere had been established during Friday evening. The news the next morning that two residents were to leave with the delegation was to precipitate several more crises, although, ironically, Jones began to rally then. Weakly, but surely, he explained that he had no objection to anyone's leaving, that people had always been free to leave. His arguments were not persuasive, but he was still struggling. At that moment, I believe, many lives still hung in the balance. Congressman Ryan was still engaged in interviewing the people of Jonestown, one at a time, in a patient and methodical fashion. He chatted amicably, asked a background question or two, and then inquired about conditions there. His task was unrewarding, and it settled into a routine to which he had committed himself before he left the United States. Later that morning, to the horror of the leaders, several other residents talked about leaving, but however great a threat the small emigration posed, particularly in view of former Temple lawyer Tim Stoen's threat to make use of each defector, the fabric of the little community seemed intact.

Harriet Tropp, a Temple leader who did not cringe before Jones, came to me as I passed the radio room. She had heard, she said, that some were leaving with Ryan. I said that I thought that would not be a bad thing at all: Those who want to leave should do so; those who remain will be part of an entirely voluntary community. She looked up at me and said, "You don't understand. You're crazy," and then turned and hurried away. At the time, I thought that she was overreacting. Now I suspect that she was reading the signs of the mounting pressures that were being laid upon Jones. Although Harriet was by this time very angry and terror-ridden, she remained active in her defense of Jonestown, which leads me to believe that Jones's fateful decision still had not yet been made.

2 September 1978

Prior to September 1978 I had never heard of Jim Jones, the Peoples Temple, or Jonestown.

In the weeks following the Jonestown massacre, the national news media focused on me, leaving the impression in the public's mind that I had been a longtime friend of Jim Jones, the general counsel for his Peoples Temple, and perhaps even a founding bishop in his church. I never served as general counsel for Jones or his Temple. I met Jones for the first time on September 15, 1978, on my first trip to Jonestown. Jones had just spent some time with his lawyer Charles Garry, and with a man named Joseph Mazor.

Mazor, a former convict with a substantial record of convictions for fraudulent actions, is also a private investigator licensed by the state of California. He had been active in an effort to oppose the Temple and destroy Jonestown for approximately one year. Following a meeting with Donald Freed during September 1978, Mazor ostensibly changed sides and decided to visit Jonestown with Garry.

At the end of the summer of 1978, while living in a small, crowded apartment in Venice, California, just outside of Los Angeles, I was completing the draft of a screenplay with Donald Freed, a California writer, teacher, and director. Freed and Garry had been friends for years. Freed, as the leader of a group of white intellectuals called the Friends of the Black Panther Party, had occasion to spend time with Garry, formerly the counsel for the Black Panther party and its leader, Huey Newton. After Newton had been charged with various violations of the criminal code in California, including murder and a serious assault, he fled to Cuba. Garry stated that his client could not get a fair trial in America. At that point Elaine Brown took over the leadership of the Black Panther party.

As time passed, Newton became inclined and then determined to return home and face the charges against him. During the early fall of 1977, I had dinner one evening in San Francisco with Elaine Brown. She said, "Huey has fired Garry. He's really disgusted with him." She explained that Garry had "ordered" Huey to remain in Cuba, asserting that without any question he would be convicted of murder if he returned to California. Garry was adamant, she said. Newton secured as counsel Michael Kennedy, a talented and able trial lawyer, and returned to the United States. A jury acquitted Newton of the assault and after a sixteen-day trial in Oakland, a jury voted ten to two to acquit him of the murder charge.

In the interim, after Newton had returned from Cuba and before the start of the assault trial, Garry's assistant and close personal friend, Patricia Richartz, quite literally pleaded with Freed to urge Newton to retain Garry. She explained to Freed that Garry cried himself to sleep at night and even talked of ending his life if he could not represent Newton at the upcoming trials. Terri Buford recalls that Patricia Richartz said to her, "I was very worried about Charles' state of mind after Huey fired him. If he didn't have Peoples Temple to represent, he might have jumped out of a window." Those familiar with Ms. Richartz understood that she has a tendency to exaggerate.

During the period before the trial, Freed met with Richartz, Garry, and then with Newton. He told me of his many efforts to convince Newton to retain Garry, and on one occasion he asked for my advice. I suggested that he abandon the effort, explaining, "Huey knows Charles, and he has decided that he doesn't want him. He has a right to an attorney in whom he has confidence." I added that I believed that Kennedy was a more sensible and serious man than Garry and a superior trial lawyer.

According to Terri Buford, who had been assigned by the Peoples Temple to work as a legal assistant to Garry on Peoples Temple matters, Garry told her that his removal as counsel was part of a government effort to capture the Black Panther party. She recalls Garry saying, "I believe that Elaine Brown is an agent. She was sabotaging Huey in Cuba. I learned that she told Huey that I didn't want to represent him, and that's a lie. She worked out a deal with another lawyer so that Huey would come back and be convicted. That way the government could run the party, and I would be out. So would Huey."

Garry's analysis of the events proved to be incorrect. Newton fired Garry because he had no confidence in a lawyer who assured him that he would be convicted. Elaine Brown, who had been a loyal leader of the Black Panther party, left the party before the trials began during the early winter of 1978. Newton was not convicted of a serious crime at either of the trials.

In an affidavit submitted to the office of the attorney general of California and the U.S. attorney's office in San Francisco, Terri Buford recounted one incident in which she had been directly involved in the Newton-Garry affair.* She stated that while she was in San Francisco, she received a message from Jim Jones directing her to give five thousand dollars to Huey Newton to assist him with the defense of his case. She went into the financial office of the Peoples Temple and removed five thousand dollars in one-hundred-dollar bills. She then went to see Charles Garry and asked for his advice about delivering the money to Newton. According to the affidavit, Garry said that he would deliver the money. Garry took the money and then closed the door to his office, explaining that he wanted to talk to her. He said that he "did not believe that Huey Newton was a free agent and that he was not able to call the shots in his own defense," according to the sworn statement. Garry told Buford that he wanted to hold the money until he had determined that Newton "was able to decide for himself." Buford wrote, "Since Garry felt so strongly about this, I agreed."

Several months later, when Buford asked Garry what Newton had said when he received the money, Garry responded that he had not given the money to Newton. The Buford affidavit continues:

> I told Charles Garry that Jim Jones had wanted Huey to have that money for his defense and that that meant a lot to Jim Jones. Charles Garry then said that he understood but that there were a lot of strange things going on around Huey Newton that he was checking into and that he would like for me to trust him to give Huey the money at the appropriate time. Charles Garry told me that if he were to give the money to Huey Newton just then that the money would be given to people who he felt were interested in keeping Huey Newton in jail. I thought that Charles Garry had some inside information from Huey Newton that I was not aware of.

After November 18, 1978, Buford learned that Garry never had given the money to Newton. Newton said that Garry had visited him and offered him a deal. Garry would make a five-thousand-dollar contribution to the defense from Jim Jones if Newton fired his attorney and hired Garry. Newton declined.

After the massacre, a reporter asked Garry about the sum. He said that in September he had returned it to Jones in Guyana. It is a federal felony to carry more than five thousand dollars in any form out of the United States without registering it. Garry admits that he did not register that sum when he said that he carried it out of the United States. It is a felony under

*See Appendix H

the laws of Guyana to state the amount of money one brings into that country falsely. Garry has admitted that he did not mention the five thousand dollars when entering Guyana. If Garry did indeed wish to return the money to Peoples Temple, he could have done so without violating the law by giving it to the organization's office in San Francisco, since it was from that office that he received the sum.

Terri Buford was in Jonestown in September 1978 when Garry claims to have given the money back to Jones. When told of Garry's explanation of the disposition of the fund, she was incredulous.

> I told Jones that I had given the money to Huey. I certainly did not wish to excite him by saying that his white lawyer had ripped off five thousand dollars from Huey. He would have gone through the ceiling and also have been very angry with me for giving the money to Garry instead of directly to Huey. If Garry did return the money to Jim Jones in September, then Jones would have been furious at me for lying to him. Yet Jones never said a word to me and we did discuss the Huey-Newton matter with Garry at some length.

Although I was in no way familiar with the problems that Jones was encountering with his lawyer or the fact that Jones and his advisors had developed a considerable distaste for Garry and his methods, their rapidly developing alienation was soon to affect my life. Garry's desire to control the actions of his client and his almost desperate fear that he might be discharged or replaced so soon after having been fired by Huey Newton and the Black Panther party, was to influence his actions and, in my view, impair his judgment.

During one of Don Freed's visits to the Bay Area to meet with Huey Newton, he had dinner with Charles Garry. Garry told Freed about his client the Peoples Temple and about what he referred to as "a paradise"* in Guyana. According to Freed, Garry spoke of the Temple's socialistic aims and its charismatic aspects. Freed was not informed of the various charges against the Temple and of its serious internal and external problems.

When Freed saw Newton later, he recalls, "I asked Huey if he was thinking of going to Jonestown; he was noncommital. I was later to learn that Jim Jones had visited him in Cuba."

Freed was told that Jones was in the process of inviting writers to South

*Garry had publicly referred to Jonestown as a paradise quite often. Steve Katsaris, whose daughter, Maria, died in Jonestown, later told me that the families of Jonestown residents had nicknamed him "Paradise Charlie."

America to discuss a book about Jonestown. "Radical sociology would be one way to describe it. It would include oral life histories and would tell the story of the Temple's unique social organization," Freed said. He was not told, at the time, of the lawsuits filed by former members and relatives of members against the Temple, nor was he told of the press attacks. "Indeed, no one I knew, with the exception of Charles, ever mentioned the words Jonestown or Peoples Temple or, I think, knew anything about them," Freed said.

Freed met with representatives of the Peoples Temple for the first time in Charles Garry's law office in San Francisco. They escorted Freed to the Temple for a guided tour and a chicken dinner. Freed was "filled in," he said, "not so much about the history of Jim Jones and the Peoples Temple, but basically the ideology, the philosophy; not about the past, but about the future." Then Freed was told about Tim Stoen and the Concerned Relatives, about press attacks by *New West* magazine and the *National Enquirer,* and fears for the future. Freed began to understand that the Temple required in a writer somewhat more than it did in an historian. They wanted a writer who would respond to the attacks. At the next meeting in Los Angeles, Freed was questioned by the Temple representatives for hours as to his ultimate political beliefs. He was asked, he said, "such questions as whether I thought there would be a race war in the United States. I was requested to go on at length. They wanted to know my philosophy, my political point of view." The interrogation to which Freed was subjected had not been authorized by Jim Jones, as it turns out. Jean Brown, coordinator of Temple activities in the United States, had apparently misunderstood Jones and overreacted to his direction that she find out more about Freed before arranging for his visit to Jonestown.

Freed said, "I was asked by them what my response would be if I saw discipline (without that word being defined further) used in Jonestown, whether I would draw the conclusion that it was a tyrannical situation. My response was that regarding any subculture, any community which was building an identity for itself, my inquiry would be whether there was a democratic decision-making process, and whether the decision represented the basic will of the community."

Freed was shown the brochures and other literature which had been produced by the Peoples Temple about Jonestown, and he was impressed. He felt, as a result of this interview, even more strongly that he was not being asked as a writer to present the positive view of Jonestown, but was instead being explored as a possible respondent to the attacks on the Temple.

When he finally got to visit Jonestown and was shown the kitchen and workshops, Freed explains, "I began to see one tableau, one vista after another of highly intelligent, highly organized social engineering, which would have been impressive in New York City or San Francisco, but in the middle of the jungle, were remarkable."

Freed saw, especially in the machine shop, "a combination of apprenticeship and teaching and work going on in an environment of well-cared-for machinery and tools. Creativity and technology seemed to be working hand in hand."

In meetings with Jones and his associates, Freed was briefed in detail about Timothy Stoen, the Temple's erstwhile attorney, who was one of its former leaders and by then thought by Jones to be the chief architect of its destruction. Freed also was told about the private investigator Joseph Mazor. A conference with Mazor, who might be the weak link in the concerted campaign against the Temple, Freed surmised, could be useful.

During September 1978, soon after he returned to California, Freed told me of what he had observed in Jonestown. He said that Jones was interested in inviting me to visit the jungle community and that he also wished for me to deliver a lecture about the death of Dr. King while I was there. Later Don Freed told me of his plan to attempt to interview Mazor at the St. Francis Hotel in San Francisco.

Still later Freed arranged for that meeting. Since I was in the area and might in the near future be in Jonestown, he asked me if, as a favor to him, I might sit in on the discussion and perhaps ask a few relevant questions should they occur to me. I had no knowledge of Stoen or Mazor at that time. I quickly read the material the Temple had published in its newspaper. Freed had given me the appropriate issue. I then agreed to participate in the meeting for a very short time, since I had a reservation on an early airplane from the city.

Mazor, Richartz, Ingrid—an office associate of Garry's—Freed, and I all agreed that the exchange should be tape-recorded. Long before the session was completed I had to leave due to an outstanding commitment.

The meeting was moderately successful. Mazor had broken with Stoen and had begun to provide some valuable information about Stoen's modus operandi. After I left the meeting, according to Freed, Garry had arrived and the victory of Mazor's defection from Stoen was celebrated with a steak dinner. Freed flew back to Los Angeles, having completed the one assignment he had undertaken for the Peoples Temple. At that point Garry assumed complete control of the Mazor file.

3 The Mazor File

On Sunday, January 21, 1979, the *Los Angeles Times* published a lengthy article by Evan Maxwell about a man they alluded to as "Detective Joe Mazor." The puff piece appeared under the headline, "A Private Eye's Uneasy Insight into Cult Insanity," and it embarrassed even some of the more sensitive journalists at the *Times.* As the *Los Angeles Times* saw it, "Detective Joe" was a kind of James Rockford of TV's "The Rockford Files" fame. A decent man who once had a little run-in with the law and now, street-wise and prison-wise, was using his talents in the pursuit of humanitarian aims. The *Times* article never did reveal the cause of Detective Joe's problem with the law except to state that he'd spent some time in Folsom "on a bad check charge."

Now Detective Joe did not just overdraw an account. The record of his arrests and convictions is on public file in California. He was arrested at least eight times in three states for various bogus checks and fraud charges, was convicted six times, and had to be returned to prison on three separate occasions for violating probation and violating parole through the commission of crimes while on release. All of that information was available to the *Times* but not shared by it with its readers.

In spite of his almost lifelong record of fraudulent acts, Mazor was given a private investigator's license by the state of California. He proudly asserts, "So far as I know, I'm the only ex-con in the state with a ticket." He also claimed to be an agent for Interpol.

After Freed and I conducted the St. Francis Hotel interview with Mazor, Jean Brown of the Temple's San Francisco office made radio contact with Jonestown. I felt that the interview had been useful, since Mazor, who had been one of those making wild assertions publicly against the Peoples Temple, was beginning to make contradictory statements. It was clear that he no longer liked Timothy Stoen and even intimated that he knew that Stoen had been involved in improper actions regarding the preparation and notarization of documents without the formality required by the law.

During this period in September I received an invitation to visit Jonestown from Jim Jones, who radioed his request through the San Francisco office of the Temple. I was informed by Jean Brown that the organization was very poor and that it would be unable to compensate me for my time traveling there and back and staying with them for two or three days. She said that they would be able to furnish an economy-class airplane ticket. I was anxious to see the home that so many Americans had carved out of a jungle, and I began to rearrange my schedule to accommodate a trip to Guyana.

I did not know at that time that Jean Brown, evidently very excited by the Mazor interview, had made almost immediate contact with Jonestown. Harriet Tropp, a recent law school graduate who resided in Jonestown, and Terri Buford talked with Jean via radio. Brown informed them that Mazor had told Freed and me that he had proof that Timothy Stoen was employed by the Central Intelligence Agency and that he had shared that proof with us during the tape-recorded interview. Mazor had made no such assertions and to my knowledge he never even indicated that he had proof of such a connection.

Jean Brown had in her possession the audio tape of the entire interview as well as a transcript typed from it by personnel in her office. It remains unclear to me now why she had made such unwarranted assertions. The effect of that report in Jonestown was electric. Terri Buford hurried from the radio room to the large pavilion where the residents of Jonestown were holding a meeting.

As was almost invariably the case, Jim Jones was speaking. Terri interrupted Jones to report that Jean Brown had said that there was available proof that Stoen was working for the CIA. Jones broke into tears. He began to sob, unable to control his weeping. A stunned audience sat quietly, wondering what Jones had learned that had affected him so profoundly. Finally, Jones was able to speak. He said hoarsely into the microphone, "I have been waiting for this day all my life. We now have proof—real proof—that Stoen is working for the CIA. We have cracked the other side. Now the lies about us, the attacks on us will stop. Now we can relax and begin to build our lives and our community without fear of any more government attacks."

As the audience listened, many began to cry. They had, all of them, felt that they had been under a terrible pressure for so long. That unrelenting fear, together with all the problems of a difficult pioneer life—long working hours and less than satisfying food, a difficult climate, and a strange environment—had taken its toll on Jones and all of the other residents. Now part of the oppression was to be lifted.

Almost immediately Jones told his aides, including Harriet Tropp, Eugene Chaikin, and Terri Buford, that Mazor had to be protected. He was fearful that efforts might be made to frighten, coerce, or even kill the man he was told was the source of invaluable evidence. Jones suggested that Mazor be invited to stay at the Temple in San Francisco, that the Temple personnel provide security for him while he remained in California, and that arrangements be made to invite him to visit Jonestown where he could be thoroughly debriefed and protected. Jones also felt that it would be useful if I were asked to visit Jonestown at the same time that Mazor was to arrive, since I'd been present at the Mazor interview at the St. Francis Hotel. He said that he did not think Garry had the wits to handle the situation. Accordingly, coded instructions were sent to Jean Brown via radio to arrange for "Mazor and Lane to come to Jonestown immediately. Do anything you have to do to get them to come. Beg them."

Jean Brown called me and asked when I might be available. She said that Jones wanted me to fly to Guyana with Mazor. I did not understand why Mazor was being invited, since I believed that while he had offered interesting and intriguing insight into the Stoen operation, he had offered no evidence, and had not agreed to sign an affidavit regarding his relatively limited role. In addition, I thought that Mazor's word, even if given under oath, might not be universally respected. On the basis of the meeting which I'd attended as a favor, I told Jean Brown of my doubts about Mazor and cautioned her not to pay him any money, for to do so, I suggested, would be to cast serious doubt upon any subsequent revelations and would convert him from a source into an agent of the Peoples Temple.

Subsequently, she invited Mazor to go to Guyana at a time when I was *not* available. She paid him $2,500 for the trip, in addition to covering his expenses. Several days later, Garry, who was in Jonestown at the same time as Mazor, as arranged by Jean Brown, demanded that Mazor be paid an additional $2,500. Garry threatened to resign as counsel if the payment was not made. A check in the amount of $7,500 was sent to Garry during September 1978 by Peoples Temple to cover his fee of $5,000 a month and the additional $2,500 that Garry demanded for Mazor. In the January interview with the *Los Angeles Times,* Mazor said that he had been paid only $2,500 for his trip to Jonestown.

I did not receive the impression from Jean Brown that Jones and his aides were very anxious for me to be in Jonestown while Mazor was there. Since so much has been made by the national news media of the sums of money allegedly paid to me by the Temple as an inducement to secure my support, it is perhaps relevant to disclose that I was neither offered nor did I request any fee for the week I had agreed to devote to the Jonestown trip. Further, I never was offered, nor did I seek, compensation for the services that I rendered related to the St. Francis Hotel interview.

In Jonestown, the gloom that had settled over the encampment during a good part of its existence dissipated almost at once after the news about Stoen's CIA ties had been revealed. Those who survived the massacre remember still that week in September as the most relaxed and constructive period in recent Jonestown history. The community readied itself anxiously and with growing enthusiam to greet Mazor and to hear his full report. I was to arrive, as it turned out, as Mazor and Garry were leaving Guyana. Jones and his aides urged Brown to delay Mazor's visit until I could arrive. She replied that it was too late to change the plans.

One week after the news of Mazor's proof had been broadcast by Jean Brown, a messenger from San Francisco arrived in Jonestown carrying a briefcase containing the long-awaited tape-recorded interview with Mazor and a copy of the transcript dutifully typed from the audio cassette.

Gene Chaikin, Harriet Tropp, Terri Buford, Richard Tropp, and Mike Prokes hurriedly assembled in a small room in a wooden shack adjacent to the radio room. Eagerly they read through, then dissected, the transcript, at first racing through the pages in an effort to locate the elusive proof of Stoen's CIA connection. And then they cautiously examined each phrase. Finally, not believing, hoping that the transcript was woefully inadequate, they listened to the tape-recorded interview on the verge of tears brought on by their confusion and anger. Mazor had never offered proof that Stoen worked for the CIA. In fact, he had never even made that charge.

Terri Buford and Harriet Tropp quickly communicated with Jean Brown. She apologized for her error, said that she had not read the transcript (which had been prepared under her direction and in her office), and said that she had never really listened to the tape either. When asked from where she secured her information, she responded that she thought that Donald Freed had told her that. Later, when I asked Freed about the matter, he said Jean had the tape and the transcript. "I told her that everything that Mazor had told us was present there," he said. "I told her that there were no off-the-record statements. I believed then, as I believe now, that the Mazor interview raises questions which should be explored —I did not tell Jean Brown that Mazor said Stoen was CIA or that Mazor offered proof to support that conclusion. How could I have said that while giving her a tape on which Mazor did not say that?"

The festive spirit was gone. Jones felt betrayed but was unable to determine the cause. He had little time to ponder the matter because Joe Mazor and Charles Garry had arrived in Jonestown. Mazor had made enough admissions in the interview about the activity he had engaged in to destroy Peoples Temple, along with his public record of unfair attack upon the Temple, to cause some concern when he arrived. Jones and his advisors now began to worry that Mazor might be armed or that he might be carrying a tape recorder hidden on his person. Jimmy Jones, Jr., and Johnny Jones, both adopted sons of Jim Jones, together with Lee Ingram, all three of whom were black, approached Mazor and politely asked him if he would submit to a search. Mazor refused. The two sons explained that they were concerned about their father's safety and earnestly requested that they be permitted to search a man who, after all, only a few days before had been a sworn enemy of the Temple. Garry said that he trusted Mazor and that the Jonestown residents were paranoid. Finally, Mazor agreed to permit Garry to search him. Later Mazor was to tell the *Los Angeles Times* that "Garry conducted the search, but the attorney missed two knives and a can of Mace" which Mazor contended he "had hidden in the tops of his leather Wellington boots."

After spending two days in Jonestown, Mazor and Garry returned to the large house that the Temple maintained in Georgetown. I arrived early that morning in Georgetown and was having breakfast at the Temple house when Mazor and Garry emerged from the sleeping quarters they had occupied. Mazor told me that he had known for some time that Timothy Stoen was not the father of John John Stoen. He said, "Grace Stoen, my own client, told me that Jones was the father." Then he said, "Now that I have seen the boy, I know he's the son of Jones. He looks just like him." I asked him under what circumstances he had seen John John and he answered, "I saw a group of children walking down a path. I said to one of the people, 'That's John John right there?' pointing out the kid. They answered, 'Right. How did you know?' It was simple—the kid looked exactly like Jim Jones."

That little vignette was quite convincing. However, it probably did not happen that way. Jones, knowing that Mazor had been employed by Grace Stoen in an effort to capture John John, was exceedingly careful to see to it that John John was never anywhere near Mazor. John John was secreted in a building in Jonestown far from where Mazor was permitted to visit. Only after Mazor had been thoroughly debriefed did Maria Katsaris, in whose care John John had been placed, appear on Jim Jones's orders at the room adjacent to the radio shack with her ward in tow. John John was introduced to Mazor and said, "Are you going to make me go back to Grace?" This carefully rehearsed little speech moved the hardened former con man and he replied, not quite wiping a tear from his eye, "No, son, I'm not." Mazor may have devoted many years of his life to confidence activities, but he was ill-prepared to take on the master, Jim Jones, on his home ground.

At the debriefing session preceding Mazor's first meeting with John John, Mazor made a number of startling disclosures. He had agreed to talk only if his words were not electronically recorded. Jones agreed to that condition. This meeting took place in the open air pavilion at the center of the community. One Peoples Temple member gave a small tape recorder to another member in the radio room. He placed it in a pocket of his baggy fatigue trousers and joined the group already in discussion. Maria Katsaris, who sat across the table from Mazor, also had a concealed tape recorder on from the moment the meeting began. Those tapes, bearing revelations from Mazor, are now no doubt in the hands of the FBI officials in San Francisco. Crates of documents, tapes, and other evidence were shipped from Guyana to the Special Agent In Charge of the San Francisco office of the FBI. The bugged conversations were in fact twice bugged in a literal sense as well. When the eager agents began to open the crates, huge and strange insects from the jungle of Guyana fled from the previously sealed boxes, no doubt in dubious pursuit of safety and sustenance. Agents fled from the room, scrambled onto desk tops, and jumped onto chairs. Eventually the insects were defeated, after a valiant battle, and the agents were left with the tape-recorded words of Joe Mazor.

In Jonestown, Mazor told a frustrated and susceptible Jim Jones, Carolyn Layton, Lee Ingram, Charles Garry, Terri Buford, Eugene Chaikin, and others that he had been to Jonestown previously. The members of the select audience exchanged startled and questioning glances. Mazor explained that he had, in the recent past, undertaken an assignment to liberate or kidnap all of the children from Jonestown. He refused to disclose the name of the principal on whose behalf he had agreed to act. Mazor confirmed major portions of the story that he told that night to Jones in a tape-recorded interview with me (he had given permission to record his words) in San Francisco after his return from Guyana. He also spoke to the reporter for the *Los Angeles Times* during January 1979.

In substance, Mazor reported that during September 1977 he had led a group of men armed with rifles and bazookas (in one version he referred to the weapons as "rockets," in another as "a rifle equipped with grenade launchers"). He said that a huge jet was standing by to carry all of the children back to America. "The Force," as he referred to it, consisted of four Americans and "two Venezuelan poachers."

In the *Los Angeles Times* version, which is similar to the version he related in Jonestown, Mazor said, "The men walked at night, holing up in the brush during daylight to avoid detection by the few residents of the area. The group reached Jonestown not knowing what sort of place they would find but having been fully conditioned by the horror tales of the defectors.

"What they found was about ten buildings and a clearing—no barbed wire, no guards with automatic weapons, nothing like what they had been led to expect. For two days, the invaders watched the compound and tried to figure out what the hell was going on. The only guns they saw were shotguns used to kill snakes."

Mazor, a fat, out-of-condition middle-aged man, apparently in less than good health, had walked forty-three miles through the unexplored jungle of Venezuela and Guyana carrying weapons, grenades (or rockets or bazooka rounds), and provisions including board and water for several days. He then camped out for two days observing conditions in the clearing from the bush. This brave handful of men had taken on boa constrictors, jaguars, ocelots, tarantulas, scorpions, piranhas in the streams, and an almost impenetrable jungle to get a look at the community. Only Jim Jones, inclined to accept the tale due to his well-developed fortress mentality, not to mention his early stage of paranoia, and the reporters and editors of the *Los Angeles Times* with their own odd predisposition could have accepted the fantasy as fact.

On the second day of his September 1978 trip, however, Mazor was invited to walk a mile and a half to the piggery. He was barely physically fit enough to walk down the deeply rutted road, although he had, according to his account, had a full year's rest since his last and longer ambulation in Guyana.

Yet Mazor was not through with his startling revelations. He had in fact hardly begun. He told the *Los Angeles Times* and the Jonestown gathering a similar story. The *Times* article read:

> At the end of two days, Mazor said, the expedition encountered another armed group in the jungle. He said the other group consisted of either Venezuelan bandits or "ultra-leftist Guyanese intent on harassing the colony." Whoever they were, the expedition decided to let discretion be the better part of valor. They got the bloody hell out, in other words.

In other words, Mazor never did explain to the *Times* how he was able to ascertain the politics of the assailants when he never talked to them and could not even determine their nationality. The version he proferred to Jones and subsequently to me was just a little different, evidently, from the one tailored to the needs of the *Los Angeles Times.* To me and to Jones he said that the group had been sent by the American embassy in Georgetown to assassinate Jones. Garry had previously been quoted in the San Francisco press as having said that during September 1977 a group, determined to assassinate Jim Jones, had fired at him from the jungle. Although to Terri Buford, Gene Chaikin, and others it appeared that Mazor had perused the press clippings and then manufactured a story to support the public allegations, both Jones and Garry accepted the Mazor account as accurate and could not be dissuaded from that conclusion.

Safely back in Los Angeles, Mazor added a bit that he had not shared with the residents of Jonestown. The *Times* reported:

> But before the expedition left, according to Mazor, they were able to locate two teen-agers, the legal sons of a couple whom he refuses to identify but who he says helped to finance the trip.
>
> Because that was part of the plan, the kids were grabbed physically, out of a small hut where they slept. They were chloroformed and taken out, eventually back into Venezuela.
>
> They were taken back to the U.S., deprogrammed at a clinic in Texas and are presently happily living with their parents. There is no reason to make them part of this episode by name.

Unlike most of the Mazor allegations that were apparently based upon some actual occurrence, this one appears to be made of the whole cloth. After discussing the allegations with numerous former residents of Jonestown, I am quite certain that no teen-agers were ever kidnapped from Jonestown. Perhaps the reason that Mazor does not wish to reveal the names of his clients in this one instance is that they do not exist.

Mazor then told Jones that he had gone to the American embassy in Georgetown before making the trip to Jonestown. While there, he said, he was shown the Peoples Temple file and that it was "more than two inches thick." He said he had seen some very interesting things in the file but that he was not at liberty to reveal the contents.

Mazor impressed Jones because he had been involved in the struggle against the Temple for some time, was a duly licensed private investigator, had served as an ally of Tim Stoen and an investigator for Grace Stoen, and had secured the absolute support of Charles Garry. To a badly shaken Jim Jones, Mazor then made other, more threatening assertions. He assured Jones that Tim Stoen had been involved in various questionable activities but that he was not a CIA agent. Mazor frustrated Jones with the charge that there were CIA spies in Jonestown that he knew of but that he could not disclose to Jones who they were. Chaikin, Buford, and Dick Tropp began to ask questions about Stoen. Part of the evidence that led them to the conclusion that Stoen had a government connection, they said, was that he had spent so much money in his obsession to destroy Jonestown. If the government was not funding the Stoen operation, they inquired, who was? Mazor had no answer at that time except to assure them that Stoen had not worked for a government agency.

Later, after Mazor and Garry arrived in Georgetown, Mazor thought of an answer to the question that had been posed in Jonestown. He decided, he told Garry, that Stoen had stolen one million dollars from the Peoples Temple and that he had done it so cleverly that the organization had never even noticed it. When I arrived the next morning, Garry was ebullient. "We've cracked the case," he told those of us (including Tim Carter) seated around the breakfast table. Mazor and Garry then told us their theory about Stoen's thievery.

Garry and Mazor contacted Jones by radio from Georgetown and asked that Terri Buford be directed to give to them all of the available financial data in her possession, including bank account information, safe deposit box material, and Tim Stoen's social security number. She was reluctant to share that intelligence with Mazor, since she and the others, except Jones and Garry, felt that he was untrustworthy. Jones insisted, and she remained at the radio giving the requested information to Mazor and Garry for several hours.

About two weeks later, Mazor presented Garry with a computer readout which he said proved that Stoen had stolen substantial funds from the Temple and concomitantly that he was not an agent of the government. Garry was so impressed by Mazor that he insisted that the Temple pay him an additional $2,500. In addition, the lawyer insisted that Mazor be placed on his payroll, but that the Temple underwrite Mazor's fees and expenses.

Mazor demanded $300 per day, plus an expense account for his services. I again urged Jean Brown and Terri Buford not to hire Mazor, explaining that his operations were apparently not based upon fact and that if he were retained by the Temple, he might well oblige the organization to spend a great deal more than anticipated. Mazor would draw a salary of approximately $15,000 per month (including expenses; he was just then on his way to Paris to look into some secret Stoen-related matter, he said) and potentially greater sums might be incurred by the Temple in defending and paying off libel suits based upon his allegations.

Garry delivered an ultimatum. In Georgetown, he had insisted that "Joe is my partner. I don't want to hear anyone badmouth him." In San Francisco he threatened to resign as counsel if Mazor was not paid twice the sum that had been agreed upon. When Terri Buford saw Mazor's readout, she told Garry that Mazor had merely fed back to the Temple the information they had given to him. Garry insisted that Mazor's computer had "corroborated the Temple material." Buford pointed out that where she had given Mazor incomplete and outdated information, his computer readout did the same. Logic aside, Garry's threat carried the day.

In Jonestown, a crushed and frightened Jim Jones contemplated a bleak future. He had been told, and he believed, that the American embassy had sent an assassination squad to kill him and that CIA agents were there in his compound. I cannot say, because I do not know, what the objective of Mazor's mission to Guyana was. However, the result of his visit was clear. He had cleverly convinced Jones that his life was in danger, that his group had been infested by an enemy willing to kill, and that his situation was very likely hopeless. He had made one other point as well. He had been introduced to Jonestown with one credential which had overcome the original aversion to him. He could, Jones had been told, provide proof that Stoen was working for an American intelligence agency. He left after trying earnestly to convince Jones that Stoen was in no way associated with the CIA, even going so far in an effort to clear him of that charge by inventing a major theft for which there was no evidence except that which he himself manufactured.

He left behind a confused and terrified leader in an isolated jungle outpost. The next day I arrived in Jonestown.

4 Jonestown, Guyana

I met Jim Jones for the first time on September 15, 1978, in Jonestown. Two months later, he and most of those who had lived there with him were dead.

While I had been invited to discuss the assassination of Dr. King, and I did deliver a lengthy lecture on that subject during the evening of September 16 to more than one thousand residents assembled at the pavilion, I now believe that I had been asked to Jonestown for other reasons as well.

Jones and his community were under severe attack. He and the leading members of the commune had been isolated for more than a year and were rapidly developing a siege mentality. Their attempt to withdraw from the structures of American society by escaping from the United States had not been successful. They were unable, even in fortress Jonestown, hidden deep in the bush of Guyana, to elude the American news media. Not long before my arrival, the *National Enquirer* had begun work on a lurid story focusing exclusively upon the sordid details of life in Jonestown. The article, which was never published but which I have seen, was in essence an unremitting tale of degradation; not a word was wasted upon the numerous positive accomplishments of the community.

The *National Enquirer* team had flown low over Jonestown, frightening the residents. Jones, Chaikin, Harriet Tropp, and Prokes told me that they had learned that the publisher of the *National Enquirer* maintained close relationships with the State Department and had worked with American intelligence in the past. They were suspicious, they said, of the prolonged stay in Guyana of the *National Enquirer*'s employees, particularly in view of the apprehensive attitude that the Guyanese government had adopted toward foreign journalists. Jones and Chaikin said that they believed it possible, although they had seen no real supporting evidence, that the American embassy had intervened with the government of Guyana on behalf of the *National Enquirer* team. Long after the massacre, the evidence proved that they were correct. The American embassy had interceded with the Guyanese government on behalf of the authors of the story, including Gordon Lindsay, a British subject, to extend their visas so that they might complete the attack on Jonestown.

While Jones and some of his aides, including Harriet Tropp, Sharon Amos, and Michael Prokes, were filled with fears and suspicions during our initial meeting, many of which seemed to me to be unfounded or exaggerated at that time, it would be unfair in retrospect to report that I carried away a negative impression of the settlement. The beginning of an investigation on my part confirmed the accuracy of some of the charges the Jonestown leadership had made. After the massacre, official documents not previously available proved that some of the fears that Jones had expressed about persecution were rational and were based upon circumstances deliberately contrived by elements within the United States government.

During my brief stay in Jonestown (I had arrived there during the early evening hours on a Friday and left early Monday morning), I was favorably impressed with much that I saw. I had not gone there to investigate the project or to interrogate the residents but to deliver a lecture. On Saturday and Sunday I walked through the agricultural fields, visited the brick factory, saw the medical facilities functioning, spent a little time in the kitchen, and observed the machine shop in operation.

Because I was there during the weekend, I did not have an opportunity to see the elementary, junior high, and high schools in operation, although I did meet with the principals and many of the teachers. The "toddlers program" for infants up to the age of three years was in session over the weekend, as was the nursery for children from three to five years old. The children were obviously happy, clean, well-fed, cared for, and loved. They seemed exceptionally bright and outgoing.

I met a number of elderly people, called "seniors" in Jonestown, who had learned to read and write after having arrived there. Although there was substantially more work to do than the residents of the community could accomplish, no senior was required to work if she or he wished to attend school instead. Jones said, and meant, "Everyone has the right to an education. That is sacred."

During the early evening hours I observed large numbers of people—children, teachers, and seniors—gathered together in a large outdoor schoolroom, studying Russian. Many of the residents were developing a working knowledge of Russian and just about everybody could speak a few phrases in that language. Later I learned why the community had turned its attention in that direction.

I talked with various residents, many of whom had been ghetto dwellers all their lives, casually inquiring about the culture shock which I believed must have ensued upon the arrival in the middle of the jungle community. I asked one black woman who had lived in Watts, the black community in Los Angeles, what brought her to Jonestown. She said, "I have three children; one of them is about high school age now. I figured if we stayed in Watts, my children would never graduate from high school. What with drugs, high crime rate, high unemployment in Watts, it would be a miracle if my children got through school. And if they did, it would be a greater miracle if they would be able to read and write even with a high school diploma." Unfortunately, the most recent studies of schools in disadvantaged communities provide very strong support for her conclusions. Then she said, "Here in Jonestown my children attend the best school we would ever be able to find. They have teachers who really care about them." In fact, the ministry of education in Guyana had granted accreditation to the Jonestown school system. Very likely the schools in Jonestown were superior to their counterparts located in the center of the large cities in the United States.

I asked one elderly woman how she liked life in Jonestown, and she said, "Well, I have high blood pressure. I was pretty sick with it in America, for the charity hospitals made me wait all day whenever I went there and did nothing for me. My blood pressure is checked here three times a day and I've been given a special diet. I'm almost cured now." Then she added "Back in the States, I didn't get my blood pressure checked three times in the sixty-five years that I lived there."

Complaints about the refusal of the American government to provide adequate health care for the elderly and poor tended to dominate my discussions with the seniors about societal failures which motivated them to leave the United States. Younger people talked about the ravages of racism and the debilitating result of high unemployment. Often the two subjects were combined as one, as black youths said that jobs were just not available for them in the cities of their birth.

In a constant struggle against racist terminology, even the most subtle kind, the people in Jonestown adopted new words and phrases. Instead of referring to a "black day" or "dark hour" to designate a troubled time, they called such a period a "white night"; in the same manner, they renamed *blackmail* "whitemail."

During the first evening that I was in Jonestown, a variety show was presented at the pavilion. The skits were original works, as were the lyrics and music. The orchestra, jazz ensemble, singing, dancing, acting, and humor were all of professional quality. Diane Wilkinson, a young black woman, sang a moving work which she had written, "Guyana Is So Beautiful to Me." Her voice possessed a rare and beautiful quality, but she had turned down offers to be a professional entertainer. She wanted to be, she said, a diesel mechanic, and she worked on the tractors, trucks, and farm equipment in Jonestown.

An elderly black woman called "Moms" by everybody in Jonestown, who was a schoolteacher there during the day, presented a rather unique stand-up comic routine, in which she interspersed musical works. Her humor was captivating. The Soul Steppers, a remarkable group of acrobatic dancers, reminded me of a similar group that I had seen perform in Peking years before.

Later that night, alone in a beautiful cabin maintained for guests, East House, I contemplated the meaning of the program I had seen. I realized that in the slums of the decaying city centers of America there is a well-spring of talent that can be temporarily diverted, oppressed, and crushed; I had been reminded that evening that when the irrepressible human spirit is given time and space, its creations may be breathtaking.

The next day I visited the medical center and met the doctor and some of the seventy medical personnel. They served the eleven hundred residents of Jonestown and the scores of Amerindians, the indigenous population, who walked, some of them, miles to secure free medical treatment.

While it was clear, particularly in meetings with the leadership, that a fortress perspective had developed and was certain to color their view of external and internal events, and thus possibly diminish the free expression of ideas at Jonestown, it was also clear that a physically healthy and well-educated community was functioning well in the middle of a jungle. In view of the terrible end of the community, it is difficult not to want to readjust one's earlier impressions about Jonestown. It is possible now, in retrospect, to see the fatal flaws that would eventually help to produce disaster.

In September 1978 I saw a brave group of Americans, many of them children, many of them elderly, most of them black, many of them women, trying to build a new life and a new community under very difficult conditions. During my visit, Jones often excused himself on various pretexts; Terri Buford agreed that when I did see him, he was "coherent and speaking in full sentences." Thus my impression of the colony was much more favorable than it might have been.

But one of the difficulties confronting the community was the mind-set of its leader. He was, by then, beset with troubles, some of which were of his own making, and deeply frustrated by the inability to answer the charges which had been made against him, some of which were false.

The reason that the charges could not be answered, Chaikin, Tropp, and Jones told me, was that Charles Garry, their lawyer, was adamant on that question. Garry had told them that he alone was to be the spokesman for the Peoples Temple. Chaikin said that Garry insisted upon developing strategy for the Temple and serving as its only voice in the United States. Jones wanted to return to answer the charges against him, but according to Chaikin and Jones, Garry had ordered him to remain in Guyana, assuring him that he would be arrested upon setting foot in the United States.

Jones and his aides said that while they resented their lawyer's directions and strongly disagreed with his instructions, they were powerless to act. They explained that Garry, who had just left Jonestown, had made it plain to them that if they did not accept his suggestions or if they discharged him as counsel, that they would suffer. In exploring this matter with them, Tropp and Chaikin, both advisors with legal training, agreed that Garry had not made a direct threat, but they didn't trust his attitude toward former clients. Later Jones said to me, "Garry is so vindictive about Huey that if we fire him he will attack us. This is the worst time for us to be attacked by our own lawyer." As Jones and his colleagues described to me a government plan to destroy them, for which they were able to offer some evidence and a great deal of reasoning and intuition, I saw that they were genuinely fearful of that prospect. As more evidence mounted, including allegations about the ubiquitous Timothy Stoen, I realized that there was more evidence to support their contention than I had previously appreciated.

I agreed to their request that I file a series of applications under the Freedom of Information Act, so that they might learn if accusations of government informants within Jonestown and elsewhere in the Temple were accurate. Before I left Jonestown, the leaders there told me of the admissions that Mazor had made about his own efforts to destroy Jonestown, the allegation made by Mazor that the American embassy had played a part in sending an armed force to Jonestown to attack Jones, and the most painful declaration of all for Jones, that the CIA had infiltrated the community.

I knew of no evidence to support those charges, and I was informed that Garry had failed to secure the charges in writing or under oath. I cautioned Jones and the others against accepting the bad news as proved unless there was some corroboration. However, I agreed to commence actions about those and other charges as soon as Chaikin, Tropp, and their assistants sent to me a vast number of affidavits, memoranda, and other documents which we had agreed were a prerequisite to filing an effective application under the Freedom of Information Act. When I told Jones and the others that we would, in due course, be able to learn about government efforts toward them, they expressed genuine feelings of relief.

I was soon to learn why Jones was so desperate. For a number of reasons, including improperly evaluating in advance special hardships imposed upon an agricultural community set in a rain forest, and the mounting propaganda and legal assaults from the United States, Jones had decided that the Peoples Temple should leave Guyana. It was believed at first that if they could accomplish the heroic task of clearing hundreds of acres, the sun and rain in the tropical area would be more than sufficient to help them grow crops and sustain life. However, the torrential rainfall washed away seeds, the earth was not sufficiently fertile, parasites killed the cattle, bats attacked the pigs, and the people struggled to overcome one natural disaster after another. Rice was imported from Georgetown and became the staple food, the centerpiece of each meal, and too often the meal itself. It cost more than half a million dollars per year to feed and clothe the residents and to provide medicine for them. Jones began to view his great experiment as a project that had failed.

At the same time, the attacks upon the community were increasing in intensity and volume. Jones feared that his son John Victor Stoen would be taken from him. He feared, as he repeated to me, that a "stigma" would be attached to Jonestown by some overt act of the American government. As a result of all these things, Jones had planned to move with the community to the Soviet Union. That question had been raised with the Soviet embassy in Georgetown more than once. The community was preparing in November to send the first contingent of fifty Jonestown residents to Moscow in December 1978.

Jones dreaded the publication of the *National Enquirer*'s devastating article, and feared that his arrest for failure to yield John Stoen might make the community unacceptable to the Russians. The "stigma" that so frightened Jones was an action, sponsored by the government, that would discredit his community, thereby making emigration to Russia impossible.

At that time, Jones saw the move to the Soviet Union as the only possible escape from a difficult situation. Earlier that year, he had instructed Terri Buford to write to the directors of the FBI, CIA, and other government officials. The letters informed the officials that the residents of Jonestown wanted to return to the United States and were seeking assurances that those who had followed Jones to Guyana would not be unfairly treated or harassed as were the members of other radical organizations, such as the

Black Panther party. In exchange for such a promise, Jones was willing, the letters stated, to conduct himself as had Eldridge Cleaver. He too would say that socialism did not work, that the United States was the greatest country in the world, and that Americans would be well advised to appreciate their country and remain at home.

No response to letters were forthcoming. Jones felt that a return to the United States would, in the absence of a positive reaction, place the members of his flock in jeopardy. He then began negotiations with the Soviet embassy in Georgetown, and he saw the flight to Russia as the only escape for the members of the commune.

As the anxiety level rose at Jonestown, the conditions became worse. Jones wanted no one to leave until a solution was found for all. His refusal to permit the residents who wished to leave to do so changed the atmosphere at the commune dramatically and adversely.

At this same time, Jones was becoming more ill each day. He said he was physically sick, and perhaps he was. His reliance upon drugs for his ailments, real or imagined, created additional problems.

Although a blatant United States governmental intrusion into the affairs at Jonestown seemed most unlikely, a devastating media attack upon Jonestown seemed less unlikely. There was no doubt Jones was upset about the *National Enquirer*'s yet-to-be-published piece.

Based upon the assertions made by Jones and my evaluations of his deep concern about the article, I made radio contact from Jonestown with Donald Freed, who was in Los Angeles. I asked him to contact the *National Enquirer* and inform them that if Mazor was the source of their article, they should know that he had for some reason undergone a metamorphosis and was now pro-Jonestown. I asked Freed to tell the *Enquirer* that I would arrange for them to have an opportunity to secure information from the other side so that they might publish a more balanced work and to inform them that Jones was prepared to bring legal action against them if they published a false report.

It was late in the evening, during the weekend, and I knew that Jones would rest more easily if I communicated that message to Freed so that the *Enquirer* might receive it early Monday morning. I took that unusual method of reaching Freed because I was troubled by Jones's apparent despair. Terri Buford expertly handled the shortwave radio transmissions whose methodology was and remains a mystery to me. Freed dictated a strongly worded telegram to the *Enquirer.*

Buford and I reported the conversation with Freed to Jones. Jones seemed relieved, and he told me that if I was able to secure a copy of the

Enquirer article that it would be worth anything to him for me to read it and try to halt its publication. I told him that the only way I could try to counter its impact, if I was able to read it, would be by analyzing it and investigating each of the charges it contained so that I could rebut those that were wrong. Jones told me that he would pay me any sum, "the sky is the limit," for investigating the charges and preparing a reply. However, he said, he feared the wrath of Garry and did not wish him to know that the Temple was paying me a fee. Accordingly, he suggested that he would talk about sending a fee not to me, but for the *National Enquirer* article, in all subsequent radio discussions. He told Terri Buford to pay me whatever sum I said was required for the job and to tell no one else in the Temple the real purpose for the fee. Buford was returning to San Francisco to work with Garry on pending cases and to assist me with the Freedom of Information Act applications. Jones made it clear that he did not fully trust Jean Brown, who would soon be on her way to Jonestown, and asked me not to discuss the real nature of the *Enquirer* project with her.

Later I was able to secure a copy of the *National Enquirer* article. I showed it to Jean Brown, who was then in San Francisco, having left Jonestown for the last time, and I began an inquiry into the charges it contained. In accordance with my client's request, however, I did not disclose to her the fee arrangements. I did ask for her assistance in an effort to determine which of the allegations were false. She insisted that they all were. During the course of that investigation, I was told by two men who worked for the publication that the State Department had urged that the article be suppressed, and for that reason it was not published. Eventually, I was paid a fee of $7,500 for my investigative work, but by Jean Brown, since Terri Buford had by this time left the Temple.

In any event, Jones and Jonestown had been spared the publication of an extremely hostile article. The trip to the Soviet Union was not to be interfered with by the news media, it seemed.

Then, early in November 1978 I was told by Jean Brown that Jones had just been informed that there was to be a congressional investigation of Jonestown later that month. My thoughts raced back to that little American community in the clearing in the jungle. I feared that Jim Jones was likely to be more desperate than ever. I was afraid that Jones would see this unprecedented action as the ultimate provocation designed to attach a stigma to Jonestown that would foreclose the last hope for the community's survival: the move to Russia.

Part II
Jim Jones and His Peoples Temple

5 Jim Jones

Jim Jones was not satisfied with many of the social conditions he encountered early in life. Unlike most, he tried to bring about substantial change. Unlike others, he sometimes fantasized change, and then accepted and acted upon his fantasy as if it were real.

Jim Jones was a white male, born in a depressed industrial area of Lynn, Indiana, in dreary poverty. His father was a member of the Ku Klux Klan and suffered painfully from having been gassed during World War I. Very little is known about Jones's early life because he told those around him so many contradictory stories, but we do know that he began his career as a right-wing fundamentalist preacher.

Much of the national news media has reported that he was part American Indian. It appears likely that when Jones decided that his mission was to work with and lead blacks, he understood that an anomalous situation was being created. Therefore, in an innovative moment, he established himself, as he was years later to say to aides Lee Ingram, Jean Brown, Sandy Bradshaw, and Terri Buford, as "an ethnic." He explained, with evident candor on that occasion, that "I needed an ethnic background or blacks would not have trusted me at first. I thought of all the possibilities. I couldn't say I was part black; I couldn't have passed. But with this jet-black hair and these high cheekbones, I could say I was part Indian. So I did. Actually, I am Welsh and I have dark hair and very light skin from that background."

This example is illustrative of the wisdom of not accepting as established any stories about Jim Jones without first subjecting them to some scrutiny.

Jones used his vaunted powers to heal as the major drawing card at services held in his California Temples and at large meetings organized by the Temple's advance team and Staff in various cities throughout the country, including New York, Chicago, Detroit, Houston, Philadelphia, and Seattle. Many of the members of the audience sat through his long, politically oriented sermons in order to witness the miracles at the end of the service. Jones never confessed to most of his aides that the healings were concocted. Even to the Staff (the information-gathering unit of eight to ten members of the Temple who prepared the faked faith healings) he insisted that the information they provided helped him to "build the faith of the afflicted" in order to facilitate the healing process.

It is true that many people who were in pain and who were not involved in the healing chicanery did say that Jones had eased their pain or healed them of their afflictions. Many people who had not been out of wheelchairs in years did rise from their chairs and begin to walk. Certainly those with psychosomatic ills may have been relieved of symptoms and cured. I have no doubt that some of the methods that Jones employed are but ancient tools in an act that is still practiced today in revival tents and on television programs broadcast throughout the United States to millions of viewers.

Jim claimed that he hated the healing concept but that he saw it as a method to bring huge crowds to the Peoples Temple. He said that if he could move thousands of people in the black community to the cause of socialism by using the tradition of the church and the healing powers that had been given to him, he was obligated to do so. He used the Bible, his belief in God, and the assertion that he was Jesus Christ reincarnated to move thousands to him. To others, he said that he was an atheist, despised the Bible, and scorned reincarnation, but that he was willing to utilize any viable concept to bring about social change. Though he began healing the afflicted in the name of Christ, on later occasions he healed the ill "in the name of socialism." One has to admit that Jones, an ordained minister conducting spurious healings in the name of socialism, was unique.

At the peak of his powers, Jones was a most charismatic healer, with churches functioning in Los Angeles and San Francisco. Thousands would throng to his services held in both cities each week. Saturday and Sunday were often devoted to the San Francisco Temple, and Thursday and Friday to the Los Angeles Temple. For each person who attended a Temple service or had written to the Temple, a chart was prepared. The chart bore a name, address, photograph, and all of the details about each person that could be garnered, including the person's place of employment, and relatives and friends.

The information for the chart was secured by the Staff through telephone surveys in which the real purpose for the telephone call was never divulged;

shifting through the person's garbage; reading stolen mail; visitations to the home of the person, ostensibly to pray and pass out fundamentalist literature, but really to examine the contents of the medicine cabinet with particular attention to the prescribed medication and the date of the prescription; and "overnights." A Temple Staff member would ask the subject if they might spend the night in the person's home. By morning, a wealth of details would be noted, including the layout of the house, the description of photographs in each room, the type and color of clothing in the closets. Casual chitchat after a service, questioning next-door neighbors, and driving past the house also provided valuable tidbits of information.

In short, Jones operated a wretched information-gathering organization, in much the same way that national intelligence agencies operate, except that the Peoples Temple organization was limited in scope (primarily to two cities) and size. In fact, Jones learned most of these techniques from reading FBI documents and manuals; he had adopted the "fight fire with fire" theory and the principle that the ends justify the means.

Once the information was gathered and placed on a chart, Jones, armed with the charts as he ascended the pulpit, was prepared to appear extraordinarily gifted. Various techniques were devised to give the impression that Jones possessed not just psychic powers but the power to heal as well. Cancers, consisting of human blood mixed with oysters, were cleverly concealed by a nurse, and the patient was induced into believing that he had eliminated it through a bowel movement or thrown it up. The ersatz cancer would be carried through the church and displayed to a stunned audience.

Jones rarely removed cataracts, apparently because the trick was difficult to accomplish. Egg whites were placed on the eyes of a young white woman disguised as an elderly black woman. Jones then walked up to the person who was in a position to truthfully testify that she could not see too well at that moment. With a tissue he removed the albumin and thus restored her sight.

He was especially skillful at mending fractured bones, particularly when the bone had not been broken. The victim, usually an elderly woman who was not very alert or a young child, was given a Quaalude while under the impression that it was a vitamin tablet. When she was sufficiently out of touch with her senses, she would be told that she had broken an arm or leg. She would then be rushed to the nearest city hospital in a van staffed with women dressed as nurses. The patient was then carried or assisted through the Emergency entrance to the hospital and taken into a hospital bathroom where a cast would be placed upon the appropriate arm or leg. The patient, wearing the cast, would be removed from the hospital and taken to a place to rest. A few days later, at a public service, Jones healed the patient, and the nurses then removed the cast.

Major hospitals throughout the county were used as a backdrop to the scheme. The fact that such odd adventures were never noticed or considered unusual is indicative of the lack of standards and security found in many hospitals.

Some of the healings were performed with less sophistication. A young white woman made up to look like an old black woman would pretend to suffer from a disabling disease. She was cured on the spot and became remarkably spry and active. This spectacular event was often the highlight of the service. Harriet Tropp had played that role on more than one occasion, although she never liked the concept and disapproved of the deception.

Two key Staff members who cooperated to a high degree with Jones's healing deceptions were Jean Brown and Carolyn Layton. Brown had been an English teacher in the public school system in Ukiah, and then when Jones served as chairman of the Housing Authority in San Francisco, Brown served both as a Temple official and the recipient of a $19,496 post with the Housing Authority. While there, she supervised the work of her subordinate, Carolyn Layton, who was paid $14,420 by the Housing Authority for her daytime work and who in turn supervised the Staff members who prowled through the black ghettos at night preparing future miracles.

Since Jones was living with Carolyn Layton (who engineered the broken limb-hospital healings) at that time and was the father of her child, one of Jean Brown's assignments was to cover for Layton and explain away her frequent and prolonged absences. The salary Layton received went directly to the Temple, and Brown consequently was placed momentarily in a severe conflict of interest. She resolved it at once by claiming that Carolyn Layton was in southern California as a result of medical problems, when Layton was actually working in the church or with Jones. Brown reportedly even provided a false story to cover Layton's absence after she had left the country to reside in Guyana.

On another occasion Jean Brown's assignment was supervising the Door* at the Temple. She once interviewed and admitted a person who then became mildly disruptive during the service. Jones turned from his pulpit to Brown, who was seated on a chair on the platform. He said, "I hold you responsible for this. How did that woman get in here?" Brown's answer was evidently considered to be less than adequate if one can judge from the next

*Brown was the head of the "greeters" who controlled the Door, or access to the Temple services.

proclamation from Jones. Looking directly at Brown, he said, "Drop dead." She fell forward from her chair, rolled over on the platform knocking over chairs, and performed what might be called, with charity, a James Cagney death scene from a very early melodrama. Then she "died." Jones, his painful duty accomplished, returned to the business at hand. Some of the more sensitive or more easily distracted folk of the hundreds in the church, however, were disturbed by the lifeless body on the podium. Jones commanded them not to look at the body, since the cause of her death was contagious and they too might perish.

Several minutes later, Jones, proving that his awesome power was tempered by his bountiful mercy, decided to give Jean another chance. He raised his uplifted arms in her direction and commanded her spirit to return to her body. The spirit apparently responded, because Jean began to stir. She moved stiffly at first, but as life returned, she thanked her savior for his love and promised to do better in the future. Jones allowed as how she had better.

After the massacre, many of the jaded and skeptical reporters who wrote about the Temple stressed the fact that Jean Brown was a sincere and decent person with the finest of instincts and motives. They wondered how a person so committed to human values could have been fooled by Jones for so long. Even after the facts about the Temple were known, and her leadership role in the events leading up to the murders could no longer be disguised, the reporters spoke of their respect for her. She had indeed been an effective instrument. If she was able to confound the press corps whose brothers had died in Guyana, one can only begin to ascertain the effect that she had had upon the poorly educated and less informed ghetto dwellers who had, in their desperate moments, turned to the Temple and Jones and Brown for help.

The standard method of having younger white Temple activists appear to be older and black caused a serious problem at one particular faith-healing service. A blue-eyed, fair-complexioned young woman was assigned the role of impersonating an older black woman at a large auditorium called the Blue Horizon in Philadelphia during a fake faith-healing session that the Temple had organized. Before the imposter's moment to perform arrived, Vera Young, a young black woman assigned as a security guard noticed the black person with pale blue eyes in the audience. She reported that there was an imposter at the service. Jack Beam, a powerful white man who enjoyed a close friendship with Jim Jones, was chosen to resolve the matter. Since he was a member of the Staff, he understood the ramifications of the problem. He arrived at an ingenious solution.

The blue-eyed person was forcibly removed from the auditorium, carried out by Beam and an assistant. Sometime thereafter, her face scrubbed and clothing changed, she reentered the auditorium as herself. Jones and Beam later confidentially told a number of activists in the Temple that the person who had been removed was a white man dressed as a black woman and that he had been armed with an automatic weapon. The "man" had confessed to Beam and others that he was a hired assassin on a mission to kill Jim Jones. He had been disposed of, said Jones, in a fashion that guaranteed that the body would never be found. Beam filled in the lurid details. The body had been placed in a box and the box fed into a garbage truck compressor.

In the following years, Jones said that the Temple "is not afraid to kill" and reminded members to "remember Philadelphia." This apocryphal legend became a useful tool for stifling dissent.

Jones's attempt to convince his followers that he suffered from cancer was not his first effort of the kind. Jones utilized complaints of physical illness as a weapon against others and as an excuse for his otherwise unacceptable conduct. During the summer of 1977, when harsh media criticism of Jones and the Temple began to surface in California, Jones, who was in Guyana, affected a serious ear ailment. This illness, he explained, thwarted him from realizing his desire to return to the United States to face the charges. When he felt betrayed by those who mildly protested against working up to twelve hours a day in the fields or against the diet at Jonestown, which consisted mostly of rice, Jones affected a heart attack or an insulin attack brought on by his rage and disappointment. The offending party felt humiliated, saddened, and often was ostracized by the community for causing the pain.

Thus Jones manipulated his followers through pain and guilt. His pain was counterfeit; their guilt was real. If anyone thought to ask Jones how it was that he possessed powers to cure others, yet suffered disabling and prolonged illnesses himself, Jones was ready with not one, but two answers. This great gift was not bestowed upon him so that he might aid himself. He was a servant of others. In addition, the very process of curing others resulted from the transferral of the pain from the afflicted to the healer.

Jim Jones was many things; among them, he was a master confidence man. His life and his Peoples Temple must be examined with care in order to avoid reaching inaccurate conclusions which, through his conscientious plotting, he had foreordained.

For years, Jones carefully cultivated the press. Through ostentatious good works, he aspired to be known. After the massacre, the *Washington Post,* through its reporter Charles A. Krause, two of its editors, Lawrence M. Stern and Richard Harwood, and its staff members, published a book which it referred to, perhaps a bit immoderately, as "the definitive record of the most bizarre tragedy of our time," written by the award-winning *Washington Post* news team.*

In attempting to fix blame, the authors explored the postmassacre evaluations of various newspapers and agencies, from the Soviet Union to Manila. It failed, however, to inform its readers that the *Washington Post* had nothing but praise for Jim Jones and the Peoples Temple long prior to the tragedy.

In August 1973 the *Post* had extolled the Peoples Temple and had proclaimed it to be the winner of its first annual tourist of the year award. In an editorial, the *Washington Post* had ebulliently printed this panegyric to the Temple with these words:

"The hands-down winners of anybody's tourists-of-the-year award have got to be the 660 members of the Peoples Temple . . . who bend over backwards to leave every place they visit more attractive than when they arrived."

The editorial was manipulated by Jones. He traveled from one city to another to hold fake faith-healing sessions which invariably secured many thousands of dollars. He was accompanied by hundreds of Temple members transported in bus caravans. The Houston "church service" had been rewarding, and Jones and his members had a little spare time before the Philadelphia service. He ordered the buses to stop in Washington, where he directed the members to begin cleaning up a public park.

As soon as the work was under way, his press aide called the Washington news media, posing as an interested resident of the capital, and remarked at the public-spirited contribution being made by the "out-of-town church group." A reporter, sent to verify the allegation, would have seen many people, many of them elderly black women, on their hands and knees, scrubbing public toilet facilities, picking up litter, and acting as servants. To the editors of the *Washington Post,* these activities neither warranted some modicum of investigation nor raised questions; these actions were praiseworthy.

Yet Jones knew that all of the news media were not so easily captured. Some of them had to be influenced by more direct means. During 1973, Jones "awarded" several thousand dollars to various newspapers in California. He also "awarded" cash to a television station and a magazine. The two

Guyana Massacre. "By the reporter who saw it all happen, Charles A. Krause," et al. (Washington, D.C.: A Washington Post Book, Berkley, 1978). Krause did not "see it all happen." He was at the airstrip at Port Kaituma, miles away from Jonestown at the time of the massacre.

newspapers, arguably the most important in California, the *Los Angeles Times* and the San Francisco *Chronicle,* each received the largest cash prizes. The publications were urged to use the funds, the Peoples Temple directed, "in defense of a free press." A contribution of two thousand dollars to the Patricia Hearst ransom fund was certainly not calculated to cause a deterioration in the relationship between the Temple and the Hearst newspapers. The Associated Press ran a very favorable article about the Temple after Jones sent almost one thousand members by bus to Fresno in a demonstration of support for the "Fresno Four": four reporters employed by the Fresno *Bee* who had been jailed for declining to reveal their sources.

In 1976, Julie Smith, a reporter for the San Francisco *Chronicle,* wrote a favorable article about Jones and the Temple. She was flattered and wooed while working on the story and was flooded with effusive and complimentary letters after it was published. My own investigation revealed only one newsperson who rejected the flattery and refused to accept an "award" from Peoples Temple. A former financial aide to Jones recalls that a letter was sent to Jack Anderson offering him a "grant" of one thousand dollars. This followed and preceded a series of letters to Anderson praising him for his work. Les Whitten, Anderson's associate, recalls that the letters were "flattering to such a degree that they were nothing but fulsome praise. I know he was courting us," Whitten told me. Another Anderson aide confirms the award offer. "It was for $1,000, I believe," she told me. "Jack sent back a letter rejecting the money and suggesting that Reverend Jones donate it to his favorite charity. The letter was polite but it was firm."

In his last moments, Jones wanted the world to believe that all of his followers voluntarily took the final step with him. That fantasy was just one of many of Jones's fantasies that were widely accepted and promulgated by the national news media in the days following the massacre. The *New York Times,* for example, devoted a very long story to him, beginning on page one, eight days after the deaths in Guyana. The article of November 26, 1978, appeared under the headline, "Jim Jones—From Poverty to Power of Life and Death"; at the outset it stated, "He began teaching a brand of Christian goodness as pure as that preached by Jesus himself in the Sermon on the Mount." The subheadlines running throughout the piece called Jones a "Champion of Free Press," referred to Jonestown as "Utopia in South America," stated of Jones that "he worked very hard," and added that the people who knew him said, "We all called him Doc." It would be difficult for any reader of the *Times* to surmise that the subject of these anecdotes was responsible for the murders of over nine hundred people.

In one short column, the December 4, 1978, issue of *Newsweek* stated that "Jones' own health was unravelling. His lungs were racked with a fungus infection. . . . Just before he put a bullet through his head, Jim Jones cried out to his mother." *Newsweek* speculated that although his mother had died the year before, "perhaps in his last moments" Jones "believed that he could speak to a spirit."

Jones did not have a fungus infection in his lungs. In Jonestown in early September 1978, at three o'clock in the morning, he suddenly dispatched Terri Buford to find his wife, Marceline, and have her report to him. He instructed his wife to secure a sputum specimen from Lisa Layton, a woman who was suffering from cancer of the lungs. He said he needed the sample to prove that *he* was suffering from lung cancer.

Marceline, or "Mother" as he almost always called her, was a skilled and sensitive nurse; she was bemused by the plan but deeply disturbed that she had been instructed to awaken a dying woman to secure a specimen which was not related to her treatment. She explained, "It's very difficult at this time of day to get a sputum specimen. I'd have to force fluids to get it." Jones dismissed her objections by asking rhetorically, "Where's your socialist conscience?" After the specimen was secured and the slide properly packaged, Jones instructed an aide to label it with a code name that had been previously used by him.

The labeled package was given to Charles Garry, who carried it back to San Francisco and delivered it to Jean Brown. She sent it to a doctor for examination, and he determined that the patient had a "fungus infection of the lungs." Actually the patient, Lisa Layton, was afflicted with lung cancer in the terminal stage. Jean Brown, Garry, and others knew that the code name "Henderson" meant Jim Jones. Now they had proof that Jones was very ill and that he had taken steps, including the use of a code name, so that his followers would not be burdened with the news of his illness. In reality, he had planned the charade to give both of these impressions. He was satisfied with the effectiveness of his little scheme but angered by the inability of the doctor to diagnose terminal cancer correctly.

Before he died (the evidence suggests that he did not "put a bullet through his head," as *Newsweek* reported, but rather that he was killed by another), he was apparently trying to silence Marceline Jones, who was speaking out against the murder-suicide. Jones drowned out her objections with the loudspeaker system, through which he spoke the words, "Mother, Mother, Mother . . ." in a disparaging and patronizing tone. There is no evidence to suggest that he was, his lungs racked with pain, attempting to communicate with a spirit. His purpose was apparently less ethical and decidedly more pragmatic.

With his talent, charisma, organization, and riches, Jones could have lived in luxury in a palace near the French Riviera, instead of spending his last days in a wooden hut in the middle of a jungle clearing. It is difficult to know who Jim Jones was and what it is he tried to accomplish. He said he sincerely loved poor black people and deeply sympathized with them, and perhaps in his way he did. Yet he exploited, controlled, and abused black men and women and utilized them as his power base.

Were the healing fiascoes, and indeed the Peoples Temple, confidence operations designed to win masses to his concept of socialism, or was his adherence to socialism, as he so imperfectly understood it, a play to win the allegiance of young political activists whose talents he required for building his empire? His personality betrays a new layer of information with each expended effort at further exploration; like an onion, each layer may be removed and examined. Likely, however, we may never know which of the contradictory bodies of evidence reveals the true Jim Jones or even if there was one. He often said that he did not wish his death to "dirty the name of socialism." Yet the sentiments he expressed most often were regularly the reverse of what he meant.

One of his closest aides, who survived the end of the Peoples Temple, said, "When under the influence of drugs in Jonestown, he claimed that he was a true, loyal, and patriotic American and that it was a terrible shame that he was obligated to remain in Guyana. He said people would never know what a real patriot he was. He said that socialism could never work; that man is not perfectable. He read and quoted from two books which asserted that socialism could not work. Those books were his Bible."

6 The People

Less than two weeks after the deaths in Guyana, President Jimmy Carter, speaking at a nationally televised news conference, said, "I obviously don't think that the Jonestown cult was typical in any way of America." He also pointed out that "It did not take place in our own country . . . and I believe that we also don't need to deplore on a nationwide basis the fact that the Jonestown Cult, so called, was typical of America, because it is not."

President Carter's geography was impeccable. The deaths did not occur on American soil any more than did the deaths at Mylai. However, as we have learned through recent painful lessons, the situ of a murder does not always absolve those who live elsewhere.

President Carter's conclusions supplemented the reports of the national news media to the effect that those who died in Jonestown had committed suicide. The evidence does not support that contention. The evidence, including statements from eyewitnesses and earwitnesses, the last words of Jim Jones recorded on tape and suppressed by the FBI and the attorney general, the testimony of the one medical examiner who studied the bodies in place, and the statement of the one independent American private investigator who examined the bodies soon after the deaths, led to the conclusion that the overwhelming majority of those who died in Guyana had been murdered.

For those searching for answers as to why more than nine hundred Americans died thousands of miles from home, the government offered a simplistic conclusion. First, it suppressed the relevant evidence under its control, for it explained that the strange breed of humanoids who had banded together in the suicide cult* was not typical of Americans and did

*Newspaper articles, television broadcasts, and magazine feature stories referred to the Peoples Temple as the Suicide Cult in a rush for rights; the *Washington Post*

not reflect American problems. According to most of the government and media reports, an odd assortment of mesmerized sycophants followed their leader across land and sea and, when told by him to do so, they willingly laid down their lives as an eternal remembrance of him. This was indeed the line that Jones and a small band of his fanatic adherents offered. The facts reject this fanciful and self-serving notion. The United States government accepted it and published it.

In the chapter entitled "The Massacre," there is a full discussion of the available evidence regarding the deaths in Jonestown.

This chapter is devoted to a discussion of the people who lived and died in Jonestown. Who were they? Why did they leave homes, turning their backs upon the American promise and their faces toward a new dream in a strange land? Are the stories of their lives and their deaths American tragedies, and does the country from which they fled bear no responsibility for their demise?

During August 1978 Terri Buford suggested to Jim Jones that a few people residing in Jonestown should undertake the responsibility of establishing records about the history of Jonestown, its accomplishments and problems, and especially its people. Jones approved of the idea and Buford, Richard Tropp, and Jann Gurvich began to collect short histories of the people of Jonestown. Carolyn Looman and Tim Carter started work on the history of the project and a description of the various work assignments there. Some of the residents wrote out brief stories of their lives. Others dictated their stories which were directly taken down on paper for them. Others, including elderly people who could not write, gave tape-recorded interviews.

Terri Buford and Dick Tropp were very moved by what they discovered. They began to tell Jones some of the details of the residents' tragic past lives. Jones interrupted them by saying, "Their problems are nothing compared to mine." When Tropp handed him a particularly sad first-person recitation by Elsie, a sixty-year-old black woman, Jones scanned it, put it down, and said, "If all I had to do in life was suffer and die, life would be easy." Jones had become so self-involved at this time that he had passed the point where he could empathize with others. When Marceline Jones read the Elsie story, she began to cry. She said, "Sometimes I think I've suffered until I read something like this and then I'm embarrassed to even have to face these people—they have suffered so much."

---

and the San Francisco *Chronicle* each had books written in four days and published within a week. The *Chronicle* titled its work *The Suicide Cult.*

When I arrived in Jonestown during September 1978, Tropp, Buford, and Jones told me about the stories of the Jonestown people. They were attempting to develop in me a sympathy toward the residents so I would be more willing to help them file under the Freedom of Information Act. They gave the material to me and attached but one condition to its use: They asked that I delete any admissions that were made about a crime being committed if it meant that the person might be prosecuted.

Here, then, are the lives of the people of Jonestown. They built the community, and almost all of them died there.

JANN GURVICH was born in New Orleans, Louisiana, in 1953. In Jonestown she taught English and political science at the junior high school. She was perhaps the most popular teacher among her students at the school. In discussions, she invariably supported Marceline Jones, whose humanitarianism conflicted with the sterner approach of Jim Jones. Those who knew Jann in Jonestown considered her to be a constant voice for sanity. Not long before her death on November 18, she drafted this autobiographical sketch:

"In March 1976 I walked into the courtroom of the San Quentin Six trial. I was twenty-two. Mary Sundance, who urged me to come to the trial, was my writing and research tutor in law school. She was pretty heavily steeped in leftism, as she was the daughter-in-law of David Dellinger and the law clerk of Charles Garry. I was in my first year of law school at a so-called progressive school—Golden Gate University School of Law. The school couldn't have been too progressive, for I remember the ostracizing comments made when I answered the property professor's first question, which was the usual existential query on the lofty subject matter, 'What is property?' I couldn't help quoting P. J. Proudhon's mid-nineteenth century proclamation that 'Property is theft.' Anyway, whatever progressive factors may have existed in the school could have in no way prepared me for the reality of and the utter failure of the justice system in the U.S. that I would observe in the courtroom, and, later in San Quentin, as a relationship with Johnny Spain, the Black Panther defendant, ensued.

"Actually, the picture of the terrible and barbarous San Quentin Six defendants that was carefully staged by the California Department of Corrections and the Marin County officials began shaping up long before I walked into the courtroom. There was the Patty Hearst trial, which was going on in San Francisco just across the Bay. The Flee (F. Lee Bailey) and Patty were getting daily press coverage (actually minute-by-minute, change-of-clothes-by-change-of-clothes coverage). The Six were ignored.

The calculated media image of the Six defendants would further be heightened by the contrast between the decorum, civility, and general niceness of Patty vs. the subhuman image of the Six. They were chained at all times in public—chains on their feet, their arms, and their waists, even chained, I think, to their chairs. They were transported in a special San Quentin bus with bars keeping the defendants in cages.

"I remember entering the Marin County Courthouse. I started to notice something peculiar. If you went down one corridor there was no metal detector, but if you chose the other one going in the opposite direction, you had to go through the metal detector. I had to go through it all the way down to the end of the corridor until I came to a podium-type structure with a man behind it who demanded to see my California driver's license. I didn't have one. I had a battle with him and finally won—promising to get a California I.D. card. He took my name and address and gave me a number; I waited in line. We all went through a pat-down and emptied purses and bookbags into plastic containers which the guards picked through.

"Another requirement was to have your picture taken by the Marin County Sheriff's Office right there. They lined you up on the wall and snapped it—'for security purposes only . . . we promise it will be destroyed as soon as the trial is over.' There was one more metal detector after having your picture taken. We went through it and waited. The guard approached and read from his penal code: 'It is an offense punishable by law to communicate with a prisoner at any time during the courtroom proceedings' or some unreasonable facsimile. Finally he unlocked the courtroom and we entered.

"Before proceeding with my reaction to what I saw, I should produce some relevant details on my background that helped shape that reaction. I was educated at Newcomb College (Tulane University), Vassar College, and the University of California at Berkeley. I had studied Latin, French, German, and Italian all before I was nineteen years old. My interest was literature. I had become an Oscar Wilde fanatic when I was in my early teens and loved Shakespeare (looking back now, I'm sure I didn't comprehend either in much detail).

"I had attended the same school for thirteen years. École Classique was the presumptuous name of the three houses situated on either side of Napoleon Avenue in New Orleans. Carefully admonished never to play with or talk to the black kids on the playground in front of our school, all the little *petit bourgeoisie* kids followed instructions perfectly. I graduated from École with a gold medal in French from the school, a First Prize from the City of New Orleans, and a Fourth Place award from the state competition in Baton Rouge, Louisiana, in French. I also received honors in Physiology and History and graduated with an honors diploma. (I learned that not all whites join the KKK. The higher their social caste, the less likely they are to be vigilante, cross-burning types. They practice their racism in a much more insidious fashion.)

"In 1973 I came to the West Coast to go to school. I came only for the summer to study Comparative Literature at Berkeley. I was to return to Vassar in the fall. But by August, I knew there was no return to Vassar, and on an acid trip I symbolically threw my Vassar college ring into the Pacific. I had run into a burgeoning West Coast triangle of worshiping the Upanishads, being a hippie, and dropping LSD, and I ran off with a Canadian hippie who was talking about love and living in weird places. (We ultimately settled in a pile-driving barge in Sausalito built in the shape of a woman—it was called 'The Madonna.') In three weeks we hitched from Berkeley to Toronto and Quebec to New Orleans, just spending enough time to see my parents.

"Interestingly enough, at this stage you could look at the languages I was studying and figure out what I was doing. I had really gotten excited by the Upanishads and started studying Hindi and Sanskrit at Berkeley. I was later to get enthralled with Maoism and study Mandarin for a year and a half.

"It was when I was studying Hindi and Sanskrit and planning to go to India that I met Jim Jones. I remember distinctly that I was in search of a teacher—*the Teacher*—and from all I'd read, I expected to find him in India. Instead I found Jim Jones at a school called Benjamin Franklin [in San Francisco]. Coming from the South, I had never seen blacks and whites doing anything harmoniously together. But here there was no racial animosity—instead there was an unswerving loyalty to the principles of love, of harmony between the races, and of commitment to change. I cannot say though, that I wholeheartedly embraced the Temple when I came. Jim taught about worldwide suffering and of the possibility of change, but the Temple, at that time (in 1974), was not able to show itself for what it really was without losing its religious following.

"For two years, I came to the Temple but I was not really with it. I had this Che Guevara image of change and I did not understand the importance of the church as an institution for fomenting change in the black community. I would spend my time checking out the Communist party, going to Panther gatherings, and generally window shopping the Bay Area leftist movements, and it was in this way that I found out about the Six trial and Johnny Spain.

"The trial of the Six would ultimately convince me of one thing: that Jim

Jones and the Peoples Temple provide the most effective movement for change in the United States and certainly the only viable alternative I could go with. I was to see that 'justice,' even with the best lawyer, was no justice at all.

"When I walked into the courtroom, one of the first things that happened to me was Johnny Spain turning around and looking at me. Finally he said, 'What's your name?' I didn't know what to do since this huge plexiglass partition separated defendants from spectators and supporters, and I knew I wasn't supposed to speak through it. He sent me a note through Charles Garry, who was representing him, and we began corresponding on tiny slips of paper that Charles would take from Johnny to me and then from me to Johnny during recess.

"Finally I was approved on Johnny's visiting list in San Quentin. Ericka Huggins, Elaine Brown, and I were his most frequent visitors. I shall never forget as long as I live what it is to visit a hated and feared black revolutionary author and former tight friend of George Jackson's. San Quentin was afraid of these men and did their utmost to destroy them psychologically as well as physically. This is what I wrote about it at that time:

> When you love someone, you want to touch him. I have never been able to touch Johnny Larry Spain. When I visit him in San Quentin, his arms are chained to his waist and his legs are chained together. We see each other through an uncleaned plexiglass partition that reaches from wall to wall and ceiling to floor. We are locked in a tiny room divided by this partition. We are not alone. On his side is a guard who watches us, there is an unseen electrical device that monitors our conversation, and the real conspiracy, the conspiracy to deny the humanity of these who "live" in San Quentin, goes on.

"From March 'til April 1976, I watched this trial with critical eyes. Judge Henry Broderick was no more an arbiter of justice than the judge in the Rosenberg trial had been. He was profoundly and unmistakably partisan. What the D.A. didn't know how to do, this judge did for him.

"The rest is history now. Johnny got convicted of conspiracy for trying to escape from prison and for the killing of two guards. Yogi got one conspiracy to escape count, I think, and Jap got an assault beef.

"What was the effect of all this on me? I left the States on August 21, 1977. A year after the Six trial ended, I came to Jonestown with one guiding thought in my mind: that there should be a place where no more murderous executions of leftists take place; that there should be a society where people live free of oppression and exploitation. Let there be no more executions or political frame-ups—not of Johnny Spain, or George and Jonathan Jackson, or Victor Jara. Jim Jones is building that society and there is victory in that fact alone."

RICHARD D. TROPP was born in Brooklyn, New York. He was a brilliant student, won a Woodrow Wilson Fellowship, was an outstanding teacher and a very talented musician. He served as the principal at the high school in Jonestown. He organized the high school quickly and well and taught English there. His younger sister Harriet was part of the leadership group in Jonestown; he was not. The Tropps were involved in numerous arguments which later became loud and public affairs. The quarrels resulted from his opposition to the most radical programs and suggestions either initiated by Jones or opposed by him.

During the afternoon of November 18, 1978, Dick Tropp rushed up to Jim Jones just after Jones had ordered Charles Garry and me to go to East House and remain there.* Tim Carter, who left Jonestown with his brother Mike and Michael Prokes just after the killing began, remembers the final confrontation between Dick Tropp and Jim Jones: "Tropp was telling Jones that it was murder, that there was no reason for people to die, that they were committed to life."

Dick Tropp died that afternoon in Jonestown. His autobiographical notes follow:

"I started out in Bedford-Stuyvesant, grandson of Jewish immigrants from Eastern Europe, lower middle-class upbringing in suburbs on Long Island, and did very well in school. Deep interest in music, and studied cello from age nine. Went to the University of Rochester where I majored in English and Comparative Literature, and developed intellectual interests. Studied with Norman O. Brown, Hayden White, other excellent teachers. Interests in existentialist philosophers, drama, history of ideas, mysticism. Graduated with highest honors, went to Europe on a travel scholarship. Lonely, depressed a lot, and felt that all I had learned was somehow an exercise in futility.

"I was seeking for something else. All intellectual friends, everything, seemed to be poised at the verge of total failure. Studied Beckett with Ihab Hassan, which had deep influence over me. Consumed with idea of apocalypse, and found my life directionless. Tried to pursue academic route at Berkeley, 1965–66 on a Wilson Fellowship. I was supposed to go 'to the top'

*This matter is fully discussed in the chapter entitled "The Escape."

in my field, but somehow I had profound dissatisfaction with it all. I equated academic life with death. After I received Master's, I had been experimenting with psychedelic drugs, had drifted into the 'hip' culture of Berkeley, and my outlook became that of a confused radical Utopian.

"I lived on several communes, all disappointments. I was torn between several poles of intellectual, social conscience (I was a participant in civil rights demonstrations and marches, and by the mid-sixties, I was attracted by revolutionary ideas), transcendence (the urge to overcome, to become 'enlightened,' to have supreme awareness-type experiences). Also hedonistic side of personality that kept me from concentration anywhere.

"I found no people around me who I could relate to—they were either in one world or another—I was in several.

"In late 1967, I accepted a teaching position at Fisk University in Nashville. I became involved in everything from radical politics, supplying some of the kids there with good marijuana from New York, to teaching very offbeat (for Fisk) classes that got me in trouble with the faculty and administration. I ran in a lot of circles, and finally, when the year was up, the administration decided that they had enough of me.

"I had planned to leave anyway. Back to Berkeley to study classical Indian music with Ali Akbar Khan. The other pole. Music-culture-search for transcendence. I was seeking for something. Berkeley was a nirvana supermarket, and I was a shopper. Very unhappy. Taught part-time at Merritt College, ran around with all kinds of losers. Couldn't get a handle on my life.

"I was accepted in a teaching post at Santa Rosa Junior College (back to the nipple of knowledge). But a few weeks before I was to start, I went through some kind of change—I again feared that I would 'die' in the college. I made a spur-of-the-moment decision to move to Mendocino County and mine jade with a friend of a friend. The jade business lasted two months. I was unemployed, drifting. Looking for people with whom to buy land and start a community. I had some plans—fairly Utopian, but never could seem to find the right people. They were either too far one way or another, yet at the same time (typically) I was too far from them. I met Jim Jones in the spring of 1970.

"In the Peoples Temple, I have found the synthesis I was always looking for, personified in Jim Jones. At once a spiritual teacher, a down-to-earth human being, a person who represents to me the Nietzschean 'overman' who builds that bridge of transition between the human animal and the human being and who is not one to transcend for himself, but who has sacrificed himself for the cause of human overcoming on a myriad of levels.

never met any person who brings those seemingly disparate and mutually exclusive worlds together. He is a psychic technician, a person with a strong, extraordinary imaginative/mind/power, who uses that power for good. I could go on for a long time.

"To be brief, I have found a place here to serve, to be, to grow. To learn the riddle of my own insignificance, to help build a future in the shadow of the apocalypse under which I felt I was always living. All these controlling metaphors that were kicking around my subconscience during the 1960s have again been reshaped, synthesized.

"I look back on the past as if to another world, a dead and dying world. I could have achieved success in the knowledge-empire. I was unable, however, to fit in there. I wanted something else, something *more.* I knew somehow that there was light at the end of the tunnel. Now I am in a struggle that consumes my time and energy. I feel very grateful to be working with a man who I consider to be a higher, more evolved type of being. A savior, in the most profound sense of that much-abused word. I don't mean this in some cheap 'religious' sense, but in terms of the evolutionary/spiritual direction of humanity. The conditioning I received as an intellectual had a lot of influence on the development of my ego-structure. Sometimes I look back, I sometimes look at things in terms of the parameters of the 'dead' world. But a new center of gravity has been established in my life—and, to my great relief and happiness, it is not *me.*"

VIRGINIA TAYLOR or "Mom Dean" was a friend to just about everybody in Jonestown. She died there at the age of ninety-two:

"I was an unwanted child but I enjoyed a fairly good life. I went to good schools, such as Frederick Douglas School in East Walnut Hill, Cincinnati, Ohio, where I was born in 1886. I sang all kinds of songs and tried to cover up everything that would break a little child's heart. I didn't have the love of my father and mother. My mother didn't really want me and she didn't allow my father to hardly pick me up or touch me, and I craved so much to be loved and picked up as other children were. I never had that blessing. But I made the best of it. I swung in an old rope swing outdoors and got jolly and rolled old hoops and old tires and made the best of my childhood. I was the only child. It's a cute little thing that happened to me: I hooked a piece of chalk from school and I hid it on some of the rafters in the basement and I measured myself everyday to see how fast I was growing up so I could get out of that mess I was in. I lived three blocks from Howard Taft's mansion. His mansion was on Grandon Road. Three blocks over where I lived was called the ghetto, you know. The rich people, Alice

Longworth lived on one corner. I passed by Howard Taft's house every day going to school and you know he became President of the United States. But I'm glad for that experience because I can understand people better this day. I can know people's problems and things. I can relate to people because I went through quite a bit of it.

"And when I was seventeen, I ran away with the show called 'Holliday in Dixie.' I stayed with that show two years. At that time, I had a pretty nice voice and I sang. And after I came out of the show business and had to be forced back home, I was eighteen then and they couldn't keep me. And I later married a man by the name of Harrison Taylor from Columbia, South Carolina. We had a fairly nice life for about twenty-eight years and then he started drinking and running around as most men do and then it got kinda dull. I promised him without a shadow of a doubt, if he ever hit me . . . that would be him. And I meant that from the bottom of my heart. I kept my old trusty .45 where I knew it was at and I had been taught to shoot by shooting tomato cans and corn cans off of the fence. I was a pretty good shotsman.

"Finally Harrison worked with the Pittsburgh Coal Company. The company needed an airway drilled and cut through for the miners in Kentucky and they moved him down there and I moved with him. And I had took training as a nurse and I was signed up with a nursing group. My husband had sent back to Pennsylvania and got fifteen black men to come and help load coal because they were short on coal loaders.

"But one night the whites of that community decided that the black people were getting all the money. We heard an expression one day, 'We're gonna run all the niggers out of town tonight.' And right back of my house on the top of the hill was the Company Powder House. I only had the .45 and I had those ten men as boarders and there was a German among them named Mike. He and my husband kind of buddied together. He was a good fellow. He said, 'I'll tell you what we'll do Taylor, we'll go up here and break in the powder house and get the dynamite out. We don't have a lot of bullets and we don't have a lot of ammunition, we'll get some.'

"So he and my husband broke in the powder house and brought down three cases of dynamite, what they call moneybelle, and the fuse that went with it. So I had a little girl there about seventeen who was my little dishwasher and my little helper and I sat down there on the floor and taught her how to cut that fuse in two small pieces, four to five inches long, and stick it into that dynamite, and cut that dynamite half in two, and pack it in the boxes. I gave my husband and this man Mike two boxes to take up on the hill. These men were shooting into all the black people's houses and as they came up the road four or five miles down the road, we could hear them shooting as they came. When they got to the turn of our road, my husband and Mike set off this dynamite on the hill and it was just raining rocks. One right after another—*Loom, Loom, Loom!* It sounded like cannons going off.

"There was about ten families above my house and a lot of little children and I says to this girl, 'We can't let them hurt those little children and those women up there.' When they turned the fence to get to me, we started pouring that dynamite at their feet and everywhere. As I looked over to the road, I saw this man coming out way by himself and I figured he was going to try and overpower us or do something and I shot the .45. Later the next morning, I learned that I had shot through the superintendent's hat, to my great surprise. He called himself trying to make peace with the men. How was I to know that? I had already shot him right through that felt hat he had on. This happened about 1920 and I was about thirty-three years old. I had saved those ten families that lived above me.

"The next morning my husband went down to the company store to see how they felt about what happened. He heard an old man eighteen miles from the county seat and had never been to town. And with his country hillbilly twang, he says, 'I'll just tell you there ought to be something done to those niggers up on Red Row, they run my son last night till his tongue was hanging out!' Of course we got a kick out of that. My husband immediately went to Jenkins, that's a company town and bought a little box car and we loaded it that morning with all our belongings and put a padlock on it and got the 9:45 train on out to West Virginia. They tell me that the judge said if he ever got his hands on me he was going to make an example out of me. But I certainly blew that town that night.

"Many years later, long after my husband was gone and I had come out to Los Angeles, California, a friend of mine came to me and says, 'C'mon, I want you to go with me to hear a man named Jim Jones.' Well I want to say I had long since fell out with all religion. Those preachers weren't doing nothing. They were preachin' the Bible but living everything they wanted—drinking and running with women and breaking up people's homes—everything he's big enough to do and telling me to be good. I was fed up with that mess, sick of it. I'd listened to Oral Roberts and all those evangelists and there wasn't nothin' to none of it. I didn't want to hear of it. She begged and persuaded me to go and told me he was different. 'That's what they all say,' was my reply.

"She convinced me to go one day just for the ride. So there I went to meet this man Jim Jones. I went there specially to pick him to pieces. I went there with my mind to see everything in him that was crooked. So I was sittin' down and he came out, I looked him up and down and through and through to see was he real. I had seen so many crooks and pretenders. So I looked and looked and I saw nothing. I turned to my friend and said, 'I'll tell you something, that man is a man of God.' She said, 'You think so?' I said, 'I sure do.' But that day in the Embassy Auditorium in Los Angeles, I was the first one dressed ready to go back the next morning and I been coming and going ever since.

"I am grateful to be where I am at in Jonestown today, because I lived under fear all the time when I lived in the States. I always thought when there was a stranger around, he was always looking for me. But I am so happy today because I am ninety-two years old and I'm active and able to get around and go and have my right understanding. I have my right mind, I'm not senile, and I just love it down here where I'm at in this lovely place in the wonderful air and sunshine. It's perfectly beautiful to me. I admire the beans and the banana trees and everything is growing so fine. I have flowers growing in my window. I'm just enjoying myself immensely, and I believe anybody that would be down here in Jonestown ought to be happy too. And I am now revising a song in the tune of 'Is It True What They Say About Dixie?'. . . . 'Is it true what they say about Jonestown? Does the sun really shine every day?'"

ELSIE was born in Eudora, Arkansas, in 1918. She died at the age of sixty in Jonestown:

"I was born in the country. I belonged to my grandmother and my grandad. I had no clothes. Had to make them out of adult underclothes. I was illegitimate; I don't know who my father was. My mother was in college when she got pregnant. She rejected me and my grandmother accepted me. Another sister was born in 1923. My mother had two children by her legal husband. That's where my problems started, because I was resented. My grandmother had been a slave and had twelve children.

"My stepfather began to molest me from the time I was very small. I was made to take care of the other children by my mother. If I let the children cry, my mother would beat me with a buggy whip. These were terrible beatings. If I did any little thing wrong, I would get beat. Only my grandmother intervened. I was light, the other children were dark. If I was dark maybe I wouldn't have gotten beat so much, because my mother wouldn't have hated me so much. The older I got, the more my stepfather would molest me. My grandmother moved out of the house in 1928. She fell dead on August 1, 1929, while carrying two buckets of water. I asked God why he did this to me. I was totally alone. There was misery all around me.

"Where I lived blacks were getting shot. We would find their bodies in the woods. From age ten to fifteen, things got worse. I finally got pregnant by my stepfather. My mother wanted me to be turned out of the house. It was a nightmare. I had never been out in the world. I was fifteen and pregnant, had no education. Didn't know a thing, if the baby was going to come out of my mouth or what. I had to work like a dog. My mother threw me out pregnant and said that I was not good enough to be around people.

"I bore the child alone, with no midwife and no doctor. I was in labor for twelve hours. I didn't know about womanhood. I screamed and screamed. It was a beautiful boy child.

"I was sent away from the house when my mother's church friends would come. That is why I hate churches and preachers and 'church people.' I would never go to church or Sunday school. My stepfather was not through with me after I bore his child. He got me back in the house to be his servant until I ran away at seventeen.

"I met a man who was forty-five years old. I married him and he took me to Vicksburg, Mississippi. I had a child and he took her away and left me. I got pregnant again by another man, and he left me at the altar. Then I met another man (all of these men are old enough to be my father). I never had the life that young people normally have. I never saw a school until I was eleven years old.

"I married while pregnant, but my husband kicked me out of the house. I was nine months pregnant when that happened. I walked for weeks with no place to stay. Church people who knew me wouldn't take me in. I was only allowed to stay on the porch. On the night my child was born I walked twenty-five miles to get to a hospital. My husband knew where I was, but he didn't come for four to five days.

"I had seven children before I was out of my twenties. I got a job for ten dollars a week. I had to do ten people's work—scrubbing pots. I didn't have enough money for a babysitter. I was forced to give my children to my husband. But he only wanted his *own* children. I kept the five-year-old with me. I had to sell myself to get enough money for food for the children. Then my husband got a lawyer and said I was an unfit mother. I had no money for a lawyer. I had no recourse. I had to give my children up. Then he goes and gets him a sixteen-year-old girl to care for his children. They almost burned up in a fire.

"I had to give up my son. And he rejected me even though I prostituted to get money to feed him. I also got a daughter out of Mississippi and slaved for her, yet she has turned and rejected me. When my son was twelve years old, a white woman said he whistled at her, and he was sent to reform school. He went for three years, but I didn't have the money to get him out. But when I finally got him out at eighteen, he was a totally different person. He drank heavily. When he was twenty-one, he was charged with rape. He is in Los Angeles now, constantly in and out of jails. I feel he was ruined in that reform school—it was a mental hospital, actually.

"Light-skinned people. I can't say how much I detested them. I had to work for them. My son was destroyed by whites. But Jim Jones told me, taught me that all whites are not the same. I am glad I met him.

"My mother went to California and I wanted to come out there to see her and my son that my mother took, the one born from my stepfather. I still loved her even after what she had done to me and what she had said —that I would never be any good for nothing. The boy died at nineteen years of age in 1954. She never allowed me to see him.

"I came to California and saw my mother for the first time in twenty years. She treated me like she saw me yesterday . . . like a low-down dog. Finally, one day, I saw her for what she was. I left the house in Los Angeles in 1960.

"I had a stroke in 1968. I thought I was going to die. I said I can't die. My daughter needs me. I am much improved since I joined Peoples Temple. Jim Jones got plastic surgery done on my face and it was done beautifully. I've been married to the same man since 1951. He has been the best of my husbands.

"I love roses. I like all kinds of plants. That does something. I like trees, gardens, and I like to read. I read about animals and herbs. I belonged to the Audubon Society. I have listened a lot, thought a lot. I am a very good cook, first-class, and I am a good housekeeper; I can make things look beautiful. I make cosmetics in the kitchen. I know a lot about cosmetics, sewing. I think I am an expert in that. I can create beautiful dresses, gowns. All this is self-taught. I am also an amateur painter and have done portraits. I like to write about things. I have written about Jonathan Jackson and the Gary Tyler case. I had to discipline myself a lot. I don't say I am a perfect socialist but I am trying to be a good socialist.

"I see in our adult education classes people, old ones, who cannot read or write, who want so bad to be able to write. I feel the pain, the pain. They wanted to learn. I look at these women. At their hands that have worked all their life. It upsets me. They had to work, they could never go to school. They didn't have a choice, a chance. I look at children here. Black children. They won't have to suffer what my son suffered. They won't have their lives exploited and destroyed. Given drugs.

"I heard Jim on the radio. I began listening. I wanted to see him. I came to the Embassy Auditorium in Los Angeles very early on March 17, 1971. I was the first one there.

"Words cannot express what I think about Jonestown. It's the greatest thing. I went through so much with racists, and always hoped to be in a place where there were no racists. I always wanted to go to a black country. I am satisfied. I am happy. I am grateful. Everybody's equal here.

"As I listen to Jim informing us what is going on in the black liberation struggle, it takes my mind back to things I knew about in my life. I remember my grandmother's baby was buried alive at the age of three. It is not hard for me to identify with the black struggle in Africa and in the USA. I am so grateful for Jonestown, for all my comrades, and a great leader.

"I myself could not live in the capitalist world anymore. I just could not. We are not going to be like the Jews. We will fight if we have to. If we die, we will die with honor. My idol was Mary McLeod Bethune, cotton picker, educator, White House advisor. She lifted herself from the cotton fields to the White House. I lifted myself from the cotton fields and the ghettos to socialism and a principle to live by and a great leader whose idea will never die.

"I have always wanted to leave the United States. That was my dream. I did not think it was possible. I had given up on the idea. I am grateful to be out of that place."

TOM GRUBBS was the principal of the elementary division and junior high school in Jonestown. He was born in Bremerton, Washington, in 1941. He died in Jonestown on November 18, 1978.

"My life before the age of twelve can be summed up as: oldest of four children, born seventeen days before the declaration of World War II, Dad served in Navy during the war then spent a year in Alaska working on construction, so I did not know him as a young child. There was continual hostility between my parents, as far back as I can remember. I had rheumatic fever between the ages of six and twelve, bedridden most of the time, cooped up in an upstairs room away from children, radio, or television, and unable to read. I essentially began school in the sixth grade but after two years of intensive study, I made honor roll the second semester of the eighth grade.

"Age twelve found me in Wyoming with my mom, brother, and sisters (my parents had been divorced), trying to earn board and room working nine hours a day hoeing in the fields during the summer and holidays and doing chores and odd jobs in the evenings. This living situation lasted about a year because of conflicts between my mom and the proprietor of the rest home where we were living.

"When we left there, we moved to an abandoned itinerant farm worker dwelling. It had no door, furniture, lights, or water. We ate what we could scavenge from its land: lamb's quarters, young tumble weeds, sugar beet greens, field corn we could steal from the fields, stolen fruit, garden produce given by neighbors, and sugar beets that had bounced off passing trucks.

"We got another abandoned house late in fall. It had doors, windows, water, and a heater but no furniture. The winter that year was the coldest in fifty years. Water pipes and toilets were frozen over solid for three weeks at a time. All that winter we ate boiled sugar beets and boiled potatoes.

"I remember that school year sharply because of the hate I still have for the teacher. I had virtually no academic skills, was shy and bashful, insecure, I only had two changes of clothes and there was no washing machine. I can remember sitting through the Christmas party looking down at my desk top because it hurt too, too bad to watch the party the children were having. My religion and finances did not permit me to participate. But the thing I remember most was the teacher, Mrs. Starkey. She many times sent me to the chalkboard in front of the class, gave me a problem she knew I could not perform, then mocked me until the whole class got their jokes and laughs at my expense. I got so upset that I got flatulence. When I passed the gas, she said she would take me down to the rest room to wipe my ass. I learned a lot the year I was in her class because I stayed in my desk all day and studied. I did not go out to recess, P.E., music, or lunch. I stayed in my desk and learned. But the thing I remember learning best was how to hate.

"The year I turned fourteen, we moved to Kermit, Texas. This was close to Odessa, Texas, the headquarters of the fanatical religious sect my mom belonged to. The housing situation was better, but the food got worse because there were no farms to forage on. We resorted to pilfering garbage cans and trash bins behind grocery stores to eat.

"The most significant aspect of this period of my life was my mom was very emotionally unstable. We had to learn three scriptures before every totally raw meal and quote all twenty-one without prompts on the Sabbath before we could eat anything. She was determined to save our souls if she had to destroy our bodies. She tried, very hard. She inculcated in us a trembling fear of people not in our religious group as the agents of the devil determined to lead us to destruction. In this she succeeded.

"By the age fifteen, the stage was set. All the rest was predictable. I was terribly afraid of people, very insecure, a bundle of anxiety, and I had a huge inferiority complex.

"When I met Jim Jones, I felt a sense of immense relief. He was then and remains wise beyond belief. He knows what make people tick. He was able to verbalize my thoughts and feelings better than I could. He could help me look at myself without embarrassing me. He helped me to explore and understand my thoughts and my responsibility, not as a psychiatrist but as a friend. He made sense out of my muddled emotions.

"Perhaps even more important he gave me opportunities to earn my own self-respect. He gave me responsibility and challenges. He provided situations which called for my best and made it better. And his own personal stability gave me stability when I needed it. Almost strangely, I became sensitive to others and their life predicaments and past experiences. I learned to see how we were alike victims of vicious early lives.

"In 1973, I began teaching children with psychoneurological learning disabilities. I could relate to their frustration, their fears and anxieties. I worked and studied with a fervor in order to help these tormented little people that no one seemed to understand or know how to help. By 1976, I had a special education credential, was granted super maximum pay scale, and was a recognized authority in the area of diagnosis and remediation of learning disabilities.

"But strangely, when I had money and status, the substance of most compensations, I did not need it anymore. I had found a great challenge and personal fulfillment helping to give children a better beginning than I had, striving for the type of beginning that everyone should have.

"However, had it not been for the friendship, the example, the opportunities, the trust that Jim Jones provided, I would have destroyed my life either by suicide or by imprisonment. Jim Jones became my friend and it made all the difference in the world."

HENRY MERCER died at the age of ninety-three in Jonestown.

"I was born in Jessup, Georgia, April 3, 1885. I went to school to the sixth grade. My daddy died when I was thirteen years old and I had to go to work to help my mother. I considered then that there was something wrong at that young age because I knew that I seen the white kids had something that I just couldn't have. I seen the oppression of all people, white and black. When I was around sixteen years old, I joined the Marcus Garvey movement and quite naturally started to learn a lot about the revolutionary struggle.

"But to go back a bit first, one thing I can tell you, when I got to be a young man, I was working one night at the ice plant and a honkey picked me up in a car and said, 'I just got to kill me a nigger tonight.' And I was scared to death. So he put a pistol to my head and drove all around. And he came back, he brought me back and said, 'Well, you're a good nigger, go ahead and go to work. You ain't the one I'm looking for.' That was in Georgia—Wayne County.

"We used to go out and pick cotton. This was before I worked on the railroad, you know, to help along with the family because my dad wasn't making but a dollar and a quarter a day. There was four of us in the family to feed and he somehow or another managed to provide a place and pay for it. He worked in a freight house and I used to help pick cotton from the time I got out of school at two o'clock to into the evening.

"There was a time, if you was a black man, you couldn't come through there on the train, and if you did, they'd throw rocks at the train. I was working down at the depot one night, and we had a white fellow kill a black man on the train and nothing was done about it. Another time, there was a bunch of blacks working in a little town about five miles from Jessup and this white woman hollered rape, and they arrested the gang of the boys, drove 'em in, and put 'em in jail.

"The train was coming around 2:19 and I worked on the train, but I noticed that it turned around and didn't come back. Well, I didn't get off work until about four o'clock and when they came back they was loaded with honkeys and they had every kind of gun that you wanted to see. Well the blacks all left there and I was scared because I had to stay on my job. So they went down to a little place across the river in a little thicket and they stayed there until that night, until twelve o'clock and they blowed their horns at eleven o'clock and they went to the jail but the sheriff kicked them out.

"I never saw a lynching but I saw it after it happened. It's an ugly looking thing. What they do, they hang you up on the trunk of a tree and they'd cut your penis off and put it in your mouth. I went away from there. I stayed away twenty-six years and I went straight from Jessup to Philadelphia. All of us blacks used to keep guns.

"One thing I can say, that we were all for one and one for all—we stuck together. That's what kind of kept it down. I don't know how many guys I shot, I don't know how many guys I wounded, but I know I got away from there.

"Another thing, we got rid of a lot of Uncle Toms too. Got rid of them. I know one fellow there, I was working on the job and he used to tell the boss everything he did to his wife, and everything, so we took him out that night and whipped his ass good. And he came back the next day and he was very quiet, he didn't do it no more. That's one thing I always did hate—a sneak and a stool pigeon. I never was one myself, I wasn't an Uncle Tom myself and I *hate* that, I hate that, just like I hate a defector, a counter-revolutionary. I hate an antisocialist and all that. I tell you, I feel like going out and chewing them up when they do anything against the working class, against the poor people. Sometimes, I cry about it [his voice breaks] the hurting things, to think about it, until Jim Jones came and rescued me. [sobbing] You don't know until you go through it. People say 'I'm a socialist, I'm a socialist.' But they don't know. [There were things that Mr. Mercer felt were too painful to discuss in his life, things he had witnessed.] It takes more than you know to be a socialist. [sobbing] I got many a beating by the police. [pulling himself together] I beat many of them too—don't you think I didn't do that. I know many tricks about fighting in the revolution. In fact, I went to a revolutionary school for two years. I was designated to go to Moscow, but I didn't go.

"In 1929, I joined the Unemployment Movement in Philadelphia. We got to have jobs, everybody was unemployed and nobody was employed and nobody knew what to do. There were many days I was hungry, there was many days I didn't have food to eat. They was giving us soup, watery soup, and we had to go to the station house to get it. During this time we were in line and some communists came along and distributed leaflets and I take one of the leaflets and read it and it said, 'meeting tonight,' at a place they had in Philadelphia called 612 Brooklyn Street. And we went that night there, we had a discussion on strategy. We were going to organize the workers. So we had a meeting that night and decided to collect food for the workers which we did.

"The spring of 1930 it was, and sometime in the middle of May we met there with a hunger march. We carried around one hundred fifty of us to Harrisburg, Pennsylvania. But we had to struggle to get there. We were denied entrance to many towns. We negotiated and went through, and we went to Harrisburg and they wouldn't even give us a place to stay, they wouldn't rent a hall to us. We had a meeting the next day on the Capital Plaza. We had communists come from west of Pennsylvania, miners and different unemployed workers. At that time we had three hundred thousand people unemployed in Philadelphia and the government was not giving one nickel of relief, not one cent of relief. So we went and pressured the state and they gave us some form of relief. All channels are exhausted and that was the onliest way we could get anything, by pressuring the state government.

"The Democratic Convention came off somewhere about 1931. Roosevelt came out, and in his speech he said, 'One third of the people are unemployed.' After he was elected he went to Congress and called for billions of dollars for the first work program that we had. It lasted about six months because the politicians stole all the money. Then came WPA. They worked ten thousand people in Philadelphia, it was the biggest project that we had. We had some miserable conditions on the WPA job. We decided we'd call a strike, and the leaders were singled out as communists and they were immediately transferred away from the project to other projects that was much tougher. I was one. They transferred me to a stone quarry. Well, that was pretty hard work—I didn't have no experience about breaking stones. I worked there about eighteen months, and during that time I was in an accident and we didn't get paid for that. Around 1939, I got a job at a naval yard but I never did sign the denial that I was a communist because I was a communist and I never did sign it.

"I was Chairman of the Propaganda Committee, and I had a tough time. If you was a Communist at that time, you had a tough time. After that we had Joe McCarthy, in the 1950s. They called us subversives and I was arrested for that but we had a good law department and I came clear of that.

"I had other jobs and then I went to work for the Board of Education. During that time I was a Union Steward in the Union and we got along pretty good. That was around 1968 we was have little skirmishes but no strikes. But it was at this time that we called this strike, and that's when I got it—I got my eyes blinded from tear gas.

"In the winter of 1973 I was sitting down on the corner one night, and I had WCT radio station on and I heard this song and I heard this Peoples Temple Christian Church with Jim Jones as minister. I was impressed with the message. I called the station and asked for the address, and the man said, 'The best I can do for you is Redwood City.'

"We took a bus to Redwood City and I called a taxi. The taxi driver took me around looking for the church. We went to the police station and I asked the desk sergeant about Peoples Temple. I called the secretary and they said they would come and get us, but I said, no, we will stay in a hotel and you can get us in the morning. When I got to the Temple, I got up to speak. I said I'd never liked preachers all my life, that I'd been a revolutionary for forty years and I never did like preachers, because they didn't want to do nothing but eat chicken and buy Cadillacs. The congregation went wild and cheered for a good while and I went back to sit down. Jim said to me, 'You don't know how you thrilled my heart when you talked about the preachers.' And I laughed. I seen some things I never seen before. I seen a dog up there with Jim, and a cat came up and sat on his lap. I said, 'My goodness, there's some love going around here, even the animals are loving you.'

"I'll never go back to the U.S. again. Jonestown is the most beautiful place I've been. It's the onliest place you can relax, it's the onliest place you can be safe from robbery, rape, and I love it out here. I wouldn't go back to the States if I had the best room in the best hotel with a silk suit and a pocket full of money, eating beefsteaks every meal—and that's just how I feel about it. And I hope someday my boys will come over; I hope someday my sister will come over. I'm glad for the care we have here for all of our comrades, for seniors, and all of us—and I'll do everything I can to help the revolution.

"I've been a communist a good many years. I did a lot of study with the *Daily Worker* when I first got started, and I got the *Moscow News.* To me, Russia was the only country that gave workers inspiration that they could rule themselves, and conduct their own business without the fatbellies.

"I believe that everyone should be equal. That the wealth of the world should be distributed among the workers who produced it. The fatbellies didn't do nothing. You take the farmers—they worked the ground, produced it, gathered the food, and carried it to the tables. So that son-of-a-bitch didn't do nothing, so I think we're entitled to all of it—not him. That's being fulfilled here in Jonestown and I'm glad I lived to see it."

PAT GRUNNET worked with the emotionally disturbed children and other children with special problems in Jonestown. She was widely respected there for her good work, and people marveled at the results her approach was able to achieve. She too died in Jonestown.

"When I was born, they didn't expect me to live; they didn't even make out a birth certificate. They said I'd never talk and I surprised them again. In fact, I had to learn to talk several times after different surgeries. I learned early not to trust; people said it would hurt and it did—people said they would be back (when I was two years old at the hospital) and they didn't come. When I was a kid, I did a lot of thinking. Most of what I saw people doing didn't make sense to me—particularly what adults were doing. And as I didn't trust anybody and didn't confide in anyone, I had a lot of stuff inside. I came off confident because I had to and I learned to have confidence in myself because there wasn't anyone else. My family had so many sicknesses and tragedies, I didn't feel I could burden them with my worries.

"I loved school because I learned to read and could escape the craziness of real life and living people. I read animal stories and all about people who had suffered. Every time I got to feeling sorry for myself, I always knew or read about somebody who was worse off—like the guy who cried because he had no shoes until he met a guy who had no feet. I had little patience with folks who talked about their troubles and didn't do anything about them or weren't aware of other's troubles.

"I was real young when I secretly read *Hiroshima* and of the American concentration camps we put the Japanese in—and I lived one mile from Santa Anita Race Track. I thought about it when I heard the crowd holler at the horse races. I knew the government had done a lot of awful things to people but couldn't understand why more people weren't angry or wanting to do something—like on the Indian reservations or the San Joaquin Valley farm workers or the city problems.

"I wanted to do something but I didn't know where to start. Too many problems. I always wanted to be a pediatrician but the counselors said to pick something else to be because poor kids can't go to college and so why didn't I go to junior college and be an X-ray technician in eighteen months. I was convinced although I was an honor graduate in high school. I was ready to do that—because my dad was an invalid and I could sooner go to work and help at home. Then, a youth group leader gave me one hundred dollars and said go to college. I got a teaching credential in four years—I really enjoyed school and being away from home.

"While still in college, I spent vacations taking groups of middle-class white kids to Indian reservations and San Joaquin Valley depressed minority areas to work with the people in order to expose them to the culture of poverty. We painted, planted, built, played, and worked with the folks there, said we'd never forget them, and then went right back behind the white picket fences and birch trees in our own communities.

"I knew I couldn't handle teaching in public schools in suburbia with bridge clubs and PTA's, so I put off trying to find a place in the U.S. scheme of things by going to Tanganyika to teach with the Peace Corps for three years. They had recently got independence and were setting out on a nation-building course that was exciting to be a part of. That was the early days of the Peace Corps with the Kennedy kids, a medical team, and a library.

"I reluctantly left after three years and traveled throughout South Africa to see how anyone could live there with a conscience. I saw a lot that angered me and felt there would be a bloodbath within five years. Basutoland, the Congo (Zaire), Senegal, then New York to Florida and the Migrant Ministry Research Project to investigate programs for farm workers. I left for California.

"I sought out a depressed area in San Joaquin Valley in which to teach for money while getting involved in the farm labor struggle. The summers were spent going to Europe campaigning and then working with the Migrant Ministry with Cesar Chavez.

"From there, I went with a couple of friends to Cuernavaca to attend school at C.I.D.O.C., a center for 'intercultural studies'—a very curious place indeed. Ivan Illich brought folks who were into 'revolution' in many areas from all over the world to listen to them and write about them. Others came to take classes from them in addition to Spanish. When I was there, Jonathan Kozol, Paulo Freire, and others were there telling about changes happening throughout South America and elsewhere. I never had quite figured that place out. Andy Young was there too trying to figure out what his place would be.

"I went from there to Stockton to a multimillion dollar open school run by closed minds in a depressed area. It could have been an exciting experiment, but politics kept it from developing into something of value. Through these years, I involved myself with things that seemed 'terribly important'—the farm worker struggle, the war resistence, prison reform, school politics. But through all of these efforts, as a matter of fact, all my life, I felt alone—and worse than that, ineffectual. I felt deeply about struggles but didn't have a good sense of strategy and had no trust in others. Whenever things weren't right, I knew it was because the power (the decision-making) was not in the hands of the people; but how to effect that change was beyond me.

"I needed a community that when the going got rough, wouldn't take their liberal selves on a vacation. By 1972, I had decided to go back and work full time for Cesar Chavez. I thought perhaps at least I could accomplish *something* if only on a limited scope. And then I met Jim. I was directed there for legal help for my federally imprisoned Chicano companion. The whole church rallied to us, and the moral support we received from letters and assurances meant a great deal to us. Jim spoke of all the things I'd wanted to be a part of in an effectual way. *Here* was the community. They were accomplishing what I wanted to be a part of, led by the most incredible strategist I'd ever heard of. My days of playing at changing things were over. Now we're doing it."

MATTIE GIBSON did not want to talk about the past. She told the interviewer she was a seventy-five-year-old black woman born in Blevins, Arkansas. She died on November 18, 1978.

"When I was a child I had very little schooling. No shoes, no proper food or clothing. I never went past the third grade. We lived in a country area and sharecropped. We didn't really have anything of our own. I worked in the fields. My mother did domestic work for fifty cents a day.

"During the Depression, I worked for seventy-five cents a day, and I had to feed seven kids. My mother was a very smart and shifty woman. She had to be. I remember how we had to carry wood to keep the school warm. I remember a boy who was a friend of my brother. They said he was looking in a window. They took him out and castrated him. The people were afraid to talk. The doctor didn't do anything about it. There was no hospital. He died.

"My father had his horse taken from him that he had worked and saved for because my sister rode it to town during work time. We had to work extra hard to get money for the barest essentials. They only gave Dad fifty dollars to get his crop started. I had to walk five miles each way to school. I had to wade through icy water—there was no way around. In school, I remember brutal beatings. There were lynchings. I have blocked it out."

SHARON AMOS was born in San Francisco in 1936. I met her in Jonestown in September 1978 and saw her again in Georgetown in November just before I left there for Jonestown. She was one of the members of the Peoples Temple who was present when Charles Garry and I met with Congressman Ryan the day before the massacre. She and her three children died in Georgetown as the result of murder, suicide, or a combination of both at about the time the massacre was taking place in Jonestown.

"I was part of the 'beatnik' movement in North Beach in the 1950s. It was a period of nihilism, complete rebellion against all middle-class values. I wandered around, disillusioned with the political left. I found nothing to belong to or make any commitment to. I had dropped out of college. My marriage was a failure. I didn't know how to play the role of middle-class mother.

"I became involved in group therapy and communal living, and scrounged my food. Then I got involved with a man who was a real 'mindfucker.' A feudalist. He took an exploitative protecting role over others. I wanted attention. I hung around searchers, the Big Sur Crowd, Kundalini yoga enthusiasts, Eric Nord, Robert Chrisman.

"I had some political involvement. During the 50s I had gone to the California Labor School. There was an excellent atmosphere there, and I did work in improvisational theatre. The place was finally closed down, a victim of McCarthyism. Earlier, I had gone to socialist dance school. Earlier, I did work circulating antiwar petitions and identified deeply with the Rosenbergs. My mother, though, was apolitical. My aunt was a bourgeois socialist. During those years, as a teen-ager, the FBI came to our house and threatened my career if I wouldn't cooperate concerning investigations of left-wing performers. I wouldn't.

"After I got married, I dropped out of college. I worked, had a child, and proceeded to go back to school a course at a time to get my degree (I finished after ten years). People I knew at that time started taking a lot of drugs, freaking out, even committing suicide.

"By the late 50s, I was deeply into the North Beach scene. I came to conduct groups in therapy sessions. I always talked and gave advice, talked out problems with people—ever since high school. I like to play the 'little mother' role.

"I 'dropped out' when living with my second husband, Deneal Amos. I was working on a Master's at California. I was tear-gassed in Berkeley in 1965. Marched at the People's Park protests. But there was never any *real* involvement. Just ad hoc work. I recognized that there were special 'in' groups in leadership that were closed to me.

"I worked with the American Friends Service Committee in a program for the mentally ill at Napa State Hospital. I worked at the San Francisco State Psychiatric Ward with psychotic patients. I went to a Zen Buddhist temple for a while. My husband taught meditation. 'Everything is really nothing.' I wanted to commit my life to something. I was strangling under this repressive relationship, this passive meditation.

"I went to communal meetings. A sociologist interested in communes, Ben Zablocki, told me about Peoples Temple. He called Jim Jones 'a prophet.' I wanted to go. I visited the Temple with a friend from Mendocino State Hospital and liked it, even though Jim was not there at the time. I later met him at a demonstration in Ukiah.

"My interest in Peoples Temple resulted in my breaking with my husband, who demanded absolute obedience. He had sold my car, took me out of the Master's program I was in, and burned my poetry. It was total oppression.

"When I came into the Temple I felt I had nothing to offer. But I got right into the work—a lot of organizational work. I did everything: psychological counseling, communication groups, individual and group discussions. I went to work for the very provincial Mendocino County Welfare Department, a city person in the midst of archconservatives. I must admit that in 1967, when Peoples Temple was still largely made up of Midwesterners, it was hard for a San Francisco hippie to fit in. But it worked out."

FORREST RAY JONES was born in Kentucky in 1931. He was a talented country and western musician. He married Agnes Jones, the adopted daughter of Jim and Marceline Jones. He was one of the founders of the Jonestown Express Band that entertained Congressman Ryan the night before the massacre. He died in Jonestown.

"I was born in the Bible belt, on the edge of Appalachia in Monticello, Kentucky, Wayne County. That's halfway between Louisville and Nashville. That was 1931, and I was brought up in rural surroundings raising livestock and tobacco. I was an only child and I took life quietly and simply. My parents forced me to go to church, but they couldn't force me to be religious. My parents were hard-working religious people.

"I was always a loner. I didn't associate with too many people. I've been learning guitar ever since the age of eleven. The music I played was country and western. I played in a high school talent show and when I won first prize they sponsored me on television in Knoxville. My specialty was Elvis Presley improvisations like, 'Baby, Let's Play House.' After I graduated from high school, I went to work in a sheet metal factory. In 1955, I married and moved to my wife's hometown, Albany, Kentucky, where I worked for one and a half years at unskilled labor. There wasn't much for us there.

"A musician I met liked my playing and invited me to join a band called Kentucky Boys, so my wife and I moved to Dothan, Alabama, to give it a try. We did one record together called 'Cotton Fields,' it was pretty popular then. We had some fine musicians with us then such as Lamon Morris who is now Hank Williams's lead guitar player. I was a singer with the band, and we did a lot of radio and television jobs.

"I played banjo with a group called the String Beans with June Carter. I had the chance to meet many country and western stars like Mel Tillis, Leroy Van Dyke, Billy Walker, and Benny Martin (violin player). At that time I was always on the road. It was really depressing work. All the people I met in show business were selfish and cutthroat, especially the musicians. They just plain lack character.

"I returned home to Monticello in 1963, discouraged enough to give up my life as a musician full time for a job in a hardware store. It was hard to get work then. The band members—none of us were doing very well—and we had to share a small apartment to get around money problems. Going through life as a small-time musician had no security in it at all.

"I made a switch to selling insurance and that lasted for one and a half years. My wife and I separated and divorced during this period. Life was falling apart. Opportunities were bad, real bad.

"I met Agnes, Jim and Marceline Jones's adopted daughter, in 1969 and we got married. She wanted to return to Ukiah, California, where she had family and friends. Anything sounded good to me. I had no idea where this move would lead me, but I was just about willing to try anything. We moved to a small apartment and I took on some odd jobs. Then through the help of Peoples Temple, I got a much better paying job at Masonite where I worked for three years.

"I was Jim Jones's son-in-law for two years before I met him. In his first sermon that I heard, I was very impressed. He exposed contradictions which were easy for me to understand and accept. I came from a racist background with all the misconceptions and stereotypes that my family and friends had taught me. But I was so impressed with Jim's dedication to oppressed people and the fact that he could have anything that he wanted but chose to wear ill-fitting secondhand clothes. I felt for the first time in my life that there were people who could actually care for you instead of using you. I gave up both drinking and smoking though I was hooked on both.

"I feel that seeing this community in actual practice is the best thing that could happen to anybody. I have learned through Peoples Temple to do semiprofessional plumbing, carpentry, repair all major appliances, farming, and cattle raising, and currently I am the assistant supervisor of our sawmill. My most recent endeavors are experimenting with solar heaters and playing in the Jonestown Express Band and helping to organize it. I've really found a rewarding place in my life after all. If you had told me that I'd spend the best years of my life with a group of integrated people (when I was back in Kentucky) I would have called you crazy."

RUTHIE was raised as part of a sharecropping family in Mississippi. She ran away from that life at the age of twelve to a job as a dishwasher in a restaurant in Greenville, Mississippi. Seven years later, she went to Los Angeles. She became a prostitute there, became a heroin addict, and was arrested, convicted, and sentenced for several crimes, including robbery and prostitution. She had spent several years in jail and was being sought for a series of crimes when she met Jim Jones. He urged her to surrender and then arranged for her to be bailed out. His interviews with the court, after she pleaded guilty, resulted in an unusual sentence. A substantial prison term need not be served, the judge concluded, if she agreed to move to Guyana. That judicial ruling became a death sentence. Ruthie died in Jonestown, Guyana, on November 18, 1978. I met her two months before she died. She was a strikingly beautiful woman. She seemed happy at last, working in the field, and supervising agricultural field work. She said she was still working the crops just as she spent her childhood. "But now it's for us, for all of us," she told me. "Now I'm not a victim any longer."

"I had some real bad beatings when I was a prostitute. If I wouldn't get this three hundred and fifty dollars every day that he wanted to get, if the police kept messing with me and I be hiding—go sit down at a bar—get them off my back, then I couldn't make that money. When I get ready to go home, he would get me. He'd ask how much money would you make. And I'd tell him I couldn't get the amount because the police was after me. It's better to not get the amount today then we have to get a case and to have to spend money to bail out of jail. We was ending up putting all our money to the jail, bail bondsmen, and the lawyers, and the fines and things. So he would give me a real good beating if I wouldn't bring in the amount. He would take this coat hanger and beat me 'til blood just ran out of my ass and throw me right back out there on the street and tell me I better get it.

"At first, he tried to hook me on drugs and I would refuse to take them, they would make me too lazy or too sick. Then, I found out that he didn't care nothing about me—all he wanted to do was to use my body for experiments. So I would just go on and do it—and I got hooked on heroin. But I wasn't shooting it—I never would do it. I snorted it for two years but I seen it wasn't doing me no good. So I got off of it by myself.

"But it was really cold, you know. Like now, I look at what Jim has did for us and how many young people he have saved from those players in the streets. They be riding down the streets and it's some real fine little girls around there, and the players ride down the streets and say to them, 'Hey baby, you want to ride with me? I'll take you out to a movie.' That's how they catch you. They pick you up and tell you you look fine until they get tired of you. Until they get tired of you and then they throw your ass on the street and get you hooked on them.

"She thinks this is the only man can make me feel good so I'm going to do everything he tell me to do. This is the kind of thing they do to you. She would feel worthless except when she's around the guy. He's blowing smoke up her ass—telling her she's fine and he buying her all kind of fine clothes with the same money she be making off of the street.

"So I was up in the thousands—I went up in the thousands. Sometimes two thousand dollars a week. It was a lot of money for a girl to be using her body day and night. It's terrible, it's really terrible. I didn't, you know, I didn't have nobody to turn to. I just didn't know no better. And I was in this for eleven years. I was trapped in it. The only way I could get out would have been to get killed cause it was just like a game.

"O.K., you get into it. If you want to get out you tell this guy. If you tell him, he going to put some more mens they call henchmen out there to watch you everywhere you go. You can't go nowhere—you can't get away. I tried. If you go to somebody else's house that guy going to be right behind you but you won't know it. He follows you on the other streets.

"I had friends to get killed doing that. How did they get killed? They would snitch on their pimps or they would tell somebody what the guy was doing to them. They either would tell where they dealing at or how much they were selling—kind of drugs they were selling to different ones. They were trying to get him busted, but who they was telling would go back and tell him what was happening. It was a mafia game like you get mixed up in—and the ladies they would have to go along with the thing until they just dropped dead or they get killed, you know.

"Past thirty-five is old for the streets. They like people nineteen up to twenty-one. When you get old, they start over and get somebody young. The old ladies just stay out there and work for their time. The young girls they got everything. Their body is good, built up and everything. Especially they like them young if they going to spend money and I don't blame them.

"I was in that life for eleven years and I didn't know how to get out of it. I ran away three times and I came back because I had nobody to turn to. I was hooked on that life—anything to do something that I was sure that I could do and that I was sure that I was pleasing somebody because I wasn't pleasing myself. But I was pleasing a lot of those people out there. And I was thinking about the little young girls that were getting raped by these different mens. A prostitute saves a lot of those little girls from getting used like that. I was doing good in a way. I was taking a rapist off the streets and giving him some feeling that he could give satisfaction.

"I couldn't get no kicks. They couldn't have got me off into it, you know? I couldn't do nothing. My sexual life was just gone. It just messed me up. I just made a job out of sex. So I don't have no desire for none.

"Little girls was getting raped. Guys used to come up to me and say I'll give you this, a grand, if you get me a ten-year-old-boy, or if you get me a thirteen-year-old girl. If I takes this money and I go and pick somebody's child up, how could we even get ourselves together? You and me both would be totally assholes if I would go and get somebody's child and let you rape them just for the love of money. I don't care much about money—that much to hurt a child. I say this is why I'm out here so I can avoid this shit happening to children.

"I was a slave—yeah, I was a slave. I worked for the same pimp for eleven years. He was a sadist. He liked to bring pain to a lady's body. He would like to watch you in pain. You know like when he whipped me with this coat hanger, my whole body had big gashes of cuts, bloody cuts. And he would just take his hand and rub in there and he would try to rub me up and make me feel good. But he couldn't make me feel good—I hated his guts, I hated him, he was a lousy man. He was a punk otherwise—you know one of those kind that liked men and he tried to play on me like he liked the ladies. But one night I came home and I had made all this money. And I seen him laying up with this man in the bed—this king-size bed I had bought with my body.

"He was this kind of man who liked to dress clean with his pretty fingernails sticking out. Clear fingernail polish. White suit. Hair laying on his shoulders from a process. He drove Cadillacs, Lincolns, and Rolls-Royce. He had about twenty whores, prostitutes. He was living out of ladies' bodies. He was just a greedy man. All I could see—he didn't do nothing but turn into a dope fiend. After getting all of that money, he fell down to a pile of shit—he didn't have nothing. Before I left, everything he had, I hocked it. I hocked the diamonds, I hocked the house—we had a $57,000 house. I sold his car for $1,600 which was a Lincoln. I sold it all because he was fucked up on dope. He got five to life for selling dope.

"In the last end of it (so he went to get these five years in the penitentiary), I chose this Muslim man. And he used me too, but he didn't use my body —he made me use my brain. I used my brain for forgeries. I forged checks from Inglewood, California, to Kansas City, Missouri, and I cashed them all and didn't get busted.

"This is the way I did it. I would get real sharp—I put on a clean dress every day. A cute dress, short. Maybe stockings and boots. Some perfume and my hair be combed real good. I'd stop at liquor stores with this I.D. I have and all kinds of credit cards like high-class people. So I'd get into the liquor store and I'd observe this man. You can look at a person and tell whether he's the right one. I would check him out, I'd say, 'Would you cash this check for me please?' He'd say, 'Yeah, you have to show me some kind of identification.' We'd go ahead and pull out a driver's license, credit cards, and whatever. We'd go up and down the highway stopping at truck stops cashing these two- and three-hundred-dollar checks.

"I had a friend who worked in a bank in Los Angeles. Every time I wrote a check and they called in, she would okay it. No problem. All my checks went through her. She got a part of the check. I didn't get no money out of the deal. I just messed up my I.D. I was the biggest nut.

"I knew the cops was after me—they had been after me for about three or four years. Around this time, I had been over to these friends' house.

They had been to some of Jim's meetings. They told me how good Jim Jones was. So, I wrote him a letter and he answered my letter. Then, he sent for me. He told me to turn myself in, that I wouldn't do no time in jail—that he could help me. I didn't believe him. He said if you go on like this, you'll lose your life. He said trust me and won't nothing happen to you.

"Okay, so I trusted him and I went to turn myself in. He called the FBI from this Temple that he was in and he told them that I come to him like a daughter that needed a father—which I did. I didn't know nobody I would like to be around but him. He told me to turn myself in and I would be out in three days. He spent $4,500 to bail me out and I got to court and the judge kicked the whole thing out and gave me three years in Guyana. All through my life, it was just me being used—I was a guinea pig. He gave me three years probation because he knew I'd been used.

"It's the best thing that ever happened to me—being here in Guyana. Nothing's bothering me. You don't have to worry about no pimps driving down the streets taking up with our little kids. Nobody getting killed. We sleep with our doors open. Nobody come in and plunge something into our heads.

"But I look back at my life story, my life history and it just scares me to death. I know I'm in good hands now.

"I didn't exist in the United States because they didn't know nothing about me. They didn't even have my birth certificate. They don't know when I was born. They don't know if I went to school or not. This show you how much they care about black people there. What if I didn't have Jim Jones as my leader? What if my leader wasn't strong as he is? I could have never gotten out. I couldn't have got nothing done. I would have just been sitting over there without a free life. I would just be lost. My little boy Nouye wouldn't have nothing either. I would like to share this story with others because some peoples look upon a prostitute as being no good. Just a lousy bitch, you know. 'I wouldn't do that if it took the rest of my life,' that's what some ladies say.

"Once I met this man—he had sex with his momma. He don't know how to have sex with another lady. He said, 'I goes home and I eat my momma's box out.' Then, I had another one would tell me he was the first one to have sex with his daughter. If a daddy love his daughter, you know he ain't going to do that.

"I was seventeen. My momma worked at night. My stepdaddy just determined to rape me. He come into my bedroom. I would wake up with his big old cock hanging out with his hand on it—he'd be standing over me. He'd be telling me, 'Wouldn't you like this up your vagina?' I said stick it up my momma's vagina. It would be low for me to go behind her back and make it with her old man. I wouldn't go to bed with him, so one night he just strong-armed me. My momma walked in the door and she tried to kill him. He was on top of me and he didn't even know she was behind him. I cried out, 'If you shoot, you're gonna kill me too.' He jumped up. He never looked right to me again. My momma would be sleep and he'd walk by and he'd feel all between my legs.

"My life is completely different now. I am the supervisor of one of the agricultural crews. We plant Cuban black beans, banana suckers, citrus trees. I also teach some of the high school students how to farm. I enjoy everything I do here. It's exciting when you know what you're doing and you see what you're doing is growing. Like the fast life I was doing, I was running from myself. Couldn't look back and see nothing I had did but something wrong. Now, I can look back and see plants growing. I can be sure that there's going to be some food in this place and we can pick it off, cook it, and eat it the same day. My life once was in a mess, but it's straightened up now—it's clear. Now I'm free, do you understand what that means?

"We don't have no pollution put in our water. Everything is fresh here. When we go home at night, we take a shower and crawl up in our bed and the air just blow through like.

"When I was in the States I was running from something that was behind me that's been behind me all of my life—fear. Over here it's beautiful because I don't have nothing to look back and be afraid of. But here, I can't find the words to say how beautiful it is."

TERRI BUFORD, too, was a Jonestown resident. Her autobiographical sketch was prepared after the massacre. She was born in 1952 at the naval hospital in Newport, Rhode Island. Her father was a career naval officer, now a retired naval commander. By the time she was sixteen years old, she had attended thirteen different schools. In spite of the transient life forced upon her as a military dependent, she became a brilliant student, and was graduated in 1976 with an "A" average from the University of California at Berkeley, where she majored in journalism.

In 1971, believing in nonviolent political change, she organized a Quaker center in Indiana, Pennsylvania. She did voluntary work in black communities wherever she lived when she attended various high schools and colleges. For her, life was filled with societal contradictions. She was a navy dependent, yet she opposed the war in Vietnam. She benefited from a middle-class life, yet sympathized with and worked for those required to live in

America's black ghettos. In a recent interview, she said:

"When I was nineteen, I left Pennsylvania for California. I began to audit classes at San Fernando State College and read extensively about American Indian history. It was an important experience for me. I realized that America did not become a racist country overnight. Blacks did not have anything approaching an equal opportunity. That I had seen with my own eyes. But studying Indian history just showed me that this country was built on racism and genocide. I began to wonder what I could do to change it.

"Kent State, too, was a turning point for me. The students were murdered because they were demonstrating against other murders done in our name. In my name too. I knew that I had responsibilities as an American—some very serious obligations that came with being born here and watching your own government kill people in Southeast Asia even though most of us wanted the war stopped.

"Being an honor student just had no real meaning for me any longer. It was too self-directed for me in a time which demanded that we speak out against the war and racism or be guilty of an unspeakable silence. I had some very unfortunate experiences while hitchhiking, and I was tired and weary of searching. One person, who gave me a ride to Redwood Valley, California, told me about the Peoples Temple. He said it was an interracial, interaged group of working people who supported the same general political beliefs that I did. And it was. I understood that it was less of a church than a political organization which opposed the war, opposed the persecutions of Black Panther party members, supported freedom of the press, and fought racism. I felt at last that I had found a work with some meaningful purpose.

"It seemed to me that the leaders espoused socialism, as I did, but felt that the status afforded to a church made it a lot easier for them to operate. I was intrigued with the idea of a socialist organization functioning through an evangelistic type of church.

"I have a lot of respect for my great-uncle, James Agee, who was a very sensitive author. When he was asked if he was a communist on one occasion, he answered, 'I am a communist by sympathy and conviction.' That meant a lot to me."

These were some of the people of Jonestown. About eighty percent of those who lived—and died—there were black. Even a higher percentage were women. Most of the people who made Jonestown were elderly or children. President Carter may believe that the people of Jonestown were not typical in any way of America, as he observed soon after the massacre. No doubt they were not typical of those who dined at the White House. Many of them found it difficult to find adequate food to feed their families. Some suffered disabling physical disorders and were sometimes unable to secure decent medical treatment. The members of the Senate and of the House of Representatives who denied to them and to another two million Americans a comprehensive medical program as a matter of right are themselves the recipients of excellent, free general and specialized medical care.

The crimes they committed, some of these Americans who died in Jonestown, were the crimes of survival. Prostitution, stealing food, shoplifting, robberies to sustain a drug habit were not designed to make them wealthy or powerful but to maintain life. They did not pervert justice from a position of power, destroy evidence, erase tapes, manipulate banks for specialized treatment, or use elected office for private gain. In a sense, they were not typical of the people with whom President Carter and his predecessors most often find themselves associated.

They were born in America, but young and old they fled their country in search of a dream which they felt could never be realized for them at home. Privileged white middle-class teachers and students rejected a society which insisted upon waging war against the people of Vietnam, a war in which their brothers suffered and died while the battle they had enlisted to fight—the previously approved domestic war against poverty and racism—was abandoned. For the residents of the ghettos of Watts in Los Angeles and the Filmore in San Francisco, no unjust foreign adventure was needed to demonstrate to them that much was wrong with the society in which they lived. They had seen Dr. Martin Luther King, Jr. murdered as he directly confronted evils of war, an unfair economic system, and racism. They had seen Malcom X murdered as he began to build an interracial alliance for radical change. They had seen the government-sponsored murders of leaders of the Black Panther party, which drove its remaining leaders into exile in foreign lands.

Millions of other Americans, who never left home as the people of Jonestown did, continue to live in the rat- and roach-infested tenements in the ghettos and in mud and log huts on Indian reservations, in shacks in Appalachia, and in the special degradation reserved for migrant agricultural workers, Americans and Mexicans. They are ill-fed, ill-clothed, ill-housed, without adequate medical care and often without hope. President Carter should not forget that they exist.

7 The Paradox of Jonestown

Donald Freed said that one of the problems with Jonestown was that the community had been organized, was working fairly well, and that it really did not need Jones anymore.

Terri Buford also has said, "Jonestown would have been a nice place to be without Jones."

Jones was restless in his jungle exile; he was anxious to return home to the United States but repeatedly warned by his lawyer Charles Garry not to do so. Jones had many conflicting plans; at this point he pleaded with Garry to permit him to return, if not to California due to impending legal problems, at least to Miami or Philadelphia where he could quietly set up a business, perhaps a nursing home. Garry assured Jones that he would be arrested if he set foot in the United States.

Trapped in Guyana, utilizing various drugs to help him escape from the community he had planned and in which he had become ensnared, Jones became progressively irrational. He was sustained by a morphine substitute, injectable Valium, various barbiturates, and codeine. He became addicted to drugs which tranquilized him, put him to sleep, or woke him up. In addition, he drank cognac in moderate amounts. Both he and Jonestown were agonizingly deteriorating; a move back home for Jones would have provided the beginning of a solution for the man and the community.

He was troubled, besides, about his still sizable but dwindling fortune and the inability of the project to produce the food it needed to sustain itself. He found imaginative ways to reduce the food ration. He held lengthy meetings at the pavilion where attendance was compulsory. He spoke for hours at some of the meetings. Often the marathon sessions lasted until three or four o'clock in the morning, and on occasion until six. The residents were then permitted three and a half or four hours for sleep.

Breakfast consisted of rice with two teaspoons of sugar or a scoop of gravy. On occasion, a cup of tea was also available. When there was to be no lunch, breakfast consisted of biscuits with syrup. On Sunday mornings breakfast was comprised of doughnuts and rice.

When lunch was available, it was usually bread and soup. Dinner was a portion of greens; fruit, if it was available; and rice; or eddoes or cassava with a meat or cheese sauce. Flavour Aid, a powdered fruit-flavored soft drink, was available two or three times each week. At the Sunday dinner, each person was served half a chicken. Sunday evening, Jones personally gave a cookie or a piece of fudge to each resident.

Jones himself did not live in the style of a millionaire, although he was one. However, his comforts were considerably more grand than those enjoyed by the population. He ate several eggs each day, and his regular diet consisted of chicken, pork sandwiches, canned chopped beef, canned fruits and vegetables, diet Pepsi-Cola, a variety of candy and cake, and expensive cognac. This is not the fare of the affluent, but because it was so dissimilar from the food available to others it caused serious rumblings of discontent.

Jones established a new policy. If the meetings lasted into the early morning hours, a late breakfast would be available at eight o'clock instead of at five-thirty A.M. In that event, no lunch would be served, since dinner would be ready at six-thirty in the evening. During August 1978 a group of the residents met together and prepared and signed a petition, stating in essence that they did not wish to be deprived of the noon meal; they would prefer to sacrifice time to sleep rather than give up food.

Pat Rhea, a young black woman, handed the petition to Terri Buford to give to Jones. In remembering the event, Buford said, "When I read the petition, I was afraid that Jones would become enraged if he discovered that so many people had gotten together to talk negatively about the project. Pat was a friend of mine, and he would have dealt with her first since her name was the first one on the petition. All of the others that signed it would have been in trouble too."

Instead of presenting the petition to Jones, Terri discussed the substance of it with him. She said, "I would bet if people weren't afraid to say so, they would prefer to give up their sleep, work the extra hours, and eat the noontime meal." Jones began to scream at her, saying, "We can't afford to give people that much food! I have good reason for letting them sleep in, and that is to cut out the lunch. If I start to give in to this kind of pressure, the people will eat up all that I have worked for. Don't these people have any socialistic consciousness? Don't they know you have to make some sacrifices to build a community? They must think that there is an endless supply of money out there."

Almost consumed with rage, he demanded of Terri, "Give me the name of anyone who has said anything like that and I'll deal with them publicly. They will be glad to eat what they can get." At that point, Terri said that her request was the result of an impression she'd picked up and that she knew of no dissenters.

The people in Jonestown were rapidly becoming the victims of Jones's tyrannical rule. They were powerless to change the quality of their lives without acting violently against him. They looked toward the San Francisco leaders as potential allies in an effort to improve their living and working conditions.

In San Francisco, Jean Brown, the coordinator for the Temple in the United States, and Charles Garry, the attorney for Jones and the Temple, were conducting the Temple's affairs. Brown knew everything about the terrible problems in Jonestown; she had lived there on two separate occasions and had been in constant radio communication with Jones when she was not in Guyana. Garry knew about many of the ordeals faced daily by the residents there, although he did not possess Brown's specific information.

During May 1978 Deborah Layton Blakey, who had lived in Jonestown for some months and had served as the Temple's financial secretary, defected from the organization. Her detailed complaint against the Temple, filed with the American embassy in Georgetown and the State Department in Washington, D.C., was well publicized in San Francisco.*

Garry was very upset that the serious charges about his client had been so widely circulated in the city in which he practiced law. He ordered Jean Brown to examine Blakey's eleven-page affidavit and to write a memorandum that answered each charge. She did so and then submitted it to him.

Brown's act of writing the five-page document entitled "Refutation of Deborah Layton's Affidavit" and Garry's act of denying that he knew about the severe problems in Jonestown after reading the refutation make one question Brown and Garry's credibility. To Blakey's charge that Jones had become a tyrant who proscribed disagreement, a charge which was by then sadly demonstrated true, Brown wrote, "Untrue. JJ [Jim Jones] encouraged disagreement—he always has." To Blakey's charge that Jones broadcast over a loudspeaker system on an average of six hours a day, Brown wrote, "Ridiculous—maybe he has spoken one hour at the most."

Terri Buford suggests that six hours a day is a most conservative estimate. "You would hear Jim Jones's voice, either live at a meeting or broadcast over the loudspeaker system, approximately sixteen hours a day. It was

*Deborah Blakey's affidavit appears in Appendix C.

against the rules for residents to speak to each other while Jones spoke. Jean Brown knew this to be true because she was there. She never stayed in Jonestown very long because she couldn't stand it there. Charles Garry knew this to be true because I told him about it." To the charge that the food was "woefully inadequate," Brown responded, "The food is tremendous. Excellent, nutritious—so much food we don't know what to do with it."

Perhaps the most important charge in the Blakey affidavit was the allegation that there were fifty armed guards, each with a rifle. Probably the most damaging statement that Brown made to Garry was contained in her answer to that allegation: "Never fifty armed guards—not half that many." Brown's admission to Garry that there might be a score of armed guards in Jonestown, in the context of her obviously false denials to other charges, is astonishing. Garry later denied that he had any idea that there were any weapons in Jonestown, or as he described it, "in the province in Guyana."

When Buford returned to San Francisco during September 1978, Garry met with her at his office. He said, "Come here a minute," and beckoned her from his own office into the receptionist area. It was early evening and the office appeared to be deserted. He explained, "I'm afraid my own office is bugged." Then he said, "Just between you and me, how much of this crap that Blakey is saying is true?"

"To a greater or lesser extent, it is all true," Buford said.

"How does Jim Jones expect me to represent him if he's not going to tell me the truth?" he asked.

"Well, you know it now," Buford responded. "Gene Chaikin told you what the situation was."

Garry said, "Yeah, he told me Jim's flipped his lid. Well, I'm fed up with Jean Brown always lying to me." Brown and Garry, with their arsenal of relevant information about the plight of more than one thousand Americans in Jonestown, had before them a most important decision. They could press for desperately needed medical care for Jones; or through their silence and inaction become allied with those who denied human rights.

The people of Jonestown, victims of their leader's growing mental aberrations, received no relief from the Temple's directors in the United States.

The paradox of Jonestown can be vividly illustrated by examining the lives and deaths of two of its residents through stories told by Jean Brown to San Francisco leaders. Shanda Oliver, an attractive nineteen-year-old woman, was infatuated with Jim Jones; Eugene Chaikin, an intelligent lawyer who loved Jonestown for its people and its promise, despised Jones for betraying both. Shanda Oliver and Eugene Chaikin died in Jonestown, very likely together, in the intensive care unit of the hospital.

Bruce Oliver and his wife Shanda lived in Jonestown. One day, while Bruce was on assignment in Georgetown, Jones, who was living in a cabin with Carolyn Layton, entered into a sexual relationship with Shanda. He then asked her not to live with her husband any longer. She acquiesced; when Bruce returned to Jonestown, he found his possessions packed and in front of his house.

As was usual for Jones in these matters, he began to complain publicly about his latest relationship. At meetings, he reverted to his theme that he was tired of women—in this case, Shanda—putting sexual pressure upon him. He said that he was a revolutionary and could not take the responsibility of solving women's sexual problems. He said, "If you men (referring to Bruce Oliver) would treat your women right, I would not have to go through this." In that process of public humiliation, through which Shanda wept copiously, he announced the termination of the relationship. By then Bruce had begun a relationship with another young woman, Tina Grimm.

Shanda subsequently developed a close friendship with another young man, Al Smart. Jones told her that he required her to end her new friendship. "It reflects badly on me," he said, "since everybody knows that we were together." That evening, at one of the interminable meetings, upon orders from Jones, Shanda announced that she disliked Al, and that she was ending their relationship.

Shanda Oliver's life had been manipulated to the point of destruction by Jones. He had broken up her marriage, begun and ended a sexual encounter with her, forced her to destroy a new relationship, and placed her in a situation where she knew she never could be with another man. Since Jones had done all of this rather openly, although he sought to cloak his own responsibility in revolutionary rhetoric, no other man at Jonestown would dare to become intimate with her.

She became an embarrassment to Jones, and toward the end of September 1978 he had her placed in the intensive care unit under heavy sedation.

When Jean Brown returned to San Francisco from Jonestown during October 1978, Terri Buford, who had not been in Jonestown since the middle of September, asked about Shanda. Brown said that she had not seen Shanda during her visit of more than one week. She explained that "she was being kept in intensive care and Karen Layton was assigned to talk to her." Brown said that she "felt very sorry for Jim for having to put up with this kind of emotional pressure from women."

Buford recalls, "Jean Brown did not say one word to express shock at the idea that Jones had seduced a black teen-ager who was emotionally immature or that she was then being isolated and drugged. Jean said that Shanda had 'attempted suicide by trying to run into the jungle.' Jean Brown and Jim Jones may call that a suicide attempt; it seems to me more like an attempt to escape."

During the fall of 1977, Terri Buford asked Eugene Chaikin to go to Jonestown from San Francisco because Jones was moving into spasms of irrationality. Tim Stoen, aided by the State Department and the American embassy in Georgetown, was increasing the pressure on Jones to force him to relinquish John Victor Stoen. Chaikin arrived in Georgetown in time to learn that Jones was then in the process of planning to murder all of the five hundred Americans then residing in Jonestown as a response to a legal decree requiring him to give up the child.

Chaikin fled to Grenada. From there he telephoned his brother Ray, who resided in California. Then he talked by telephone to Charles Garry. Chaikin told Garry that Jones was insane. He said, "I've been with him during some difficult times, but he has really flipped his lid now." Chaikin said that he intended never to return to Jonestown due to Jones's madness.

He had been one of its earliest pioneers, helping to plan the community and clear the jungle; he had lived and worked at Jonestown long before Jones had decided to reside there. Now he told Garry that there no longer was hope that the Temple might evolve into a decent and progressive organization. Chaikin was heartbroken that the potential which had encouraged and sustained him for so many years had turned to ashes.

Garry advised Chaikin to remain with the Peoples Temple; he remonstrated him, telling him that it was his duty to remain. "Just because the captain of a ship is sick," said Garry, "that is no reason to desert a ship. You got to stick with it. Don't let him down now that he needs you most." Garry then told Chaikin that he had continued to represent a well-known leader who had "cracked up."

Chaikin returned to Jonestown. At that same time, in September 1977, Terri Buford, who was in constant radio contact with Jones, told Garry that she might leave the Temple since she could not carry out the irrational orders that Jones was giving her. He had told her to smuggle half a million dollars in cash into Grenada at once by strapping one-hundred-dollar bills to her body. One of Jones's many plans was to emigrate with John John to Grenada, where extradition laws are very lax; the money Terri was to smuggle out would provide them with funds once they arrived. She told him that it was not possible for her to conceal such an amount and that she would be required to change planes in Trinidad where they conducted a thorough search. Jones answered, "What are you complaining about? What if there is some risk for you? We are all going to die here. Do it."

Buford told Garry of the impossible assignment and that it seemed to her that the only alternative was for her to leave the Temple.

Buford remembers Garry's response quite well. "Just because a captain is sick, you don't desert the ship. Stay on board and try to make it work." She too took Garry's advice. She did not attempt to smuggle the money to Grenada for a number of reasons. "It was a kamikaze mission, and I was afraid that Jones wanted to use my arrest in Grenada as a pretext to kill everyone in Jonestown if he failed to come up with another excuse." She was afraid he'd tell the residents that the authorities were out to destroy the Temple through Terri's arrest. She did leave the Temple one year later, at the very end of October 1978, just three weeks before the massacre.

Chaikin accepted Garry's advice and returned to Jonestown. Later, because he again had doubted the leader during a time of crisis, it seems that he was given tranquilizers. I believe that he was drugged and placed in the intensive care unit just before Congressman Ryan visited Jonestown in November 1978. Charles Garry and I asked to see him on that occasion, and we were given various cover stories regarding his whereabouts on Friday afternoon and evening and again on Saturday morning, hours before the massacre.

I later learned from Ray Chaikin, with whom I spent an afternoon in California, that Ray had talked with Richard Dwyer, the representative of the American embassy who entered Jonestown with Ryan. Dwyer told him that Gene Chaikin's name was on the first list of residents that Ryan wanted to interview. Since I had seen that list in Jonestown, I knew that Dwyer's statement was true. Dwyer said that when Ryan learned that Chaikin was in the intensive care unit, he asked Dwyer to interview Chaikin. Dwyer reported that he saw Chaikin at the intensive care unit the evening before the massacre and that he interviewed him then. Very likely Shanda Oliver and Eugene Chaikin were murdered, probably while they were in a tranquilized and helpless state.

When it became clear to the people of Jonestown that neither Garry nor Brown was interested in efforts to liberate them from the conditions imposed upon them, they moved slowly toward revolution.

During August 1978 Diane Wilkinson, the gifted singer who was also a diesel mechanic there, said that she saw serious trouble ahead. "It's the same old story of whites telling blacks what to do and blacks having to do all the dirty work." She said that the performers were very upset and angry that they had to sing and dance for the visitors and watch them, Jones and the leaders, eat decent food which was denied to them. Diane became outspoken in her criticism of the leadership. She criticized Carolyn Layton, telling her that she did not know how to communicate with black people and that, due to her relationship with Jones, she placed herself far above the ordinary people in Jonestown.

Some months prior to that time, Diane and Terri spent time in San Francisco exploring ways of improving life in the project. Jean Brown saw them together and immediately reported them to Jim Jones. Terri was called to the radio to talk with Jones who told her that her conduct was "treasonous."

Because of Brown's action as a spy for Jones, Diane was never thoroughly trusted again when she returned to Jonestown. While that fact interfered with her effectiveness as a voice for change at the settlement, it soon became clear that she was not alone in her feelings. At the machine shop, rumblings of discontent became vague demands and ethereal plans. At night a number of the residents, who had in the past quietly complained about hardships, began to speak less softly about the deterioration of the leader and the concomitant retrogression of the community. Individual residents admitted after the massacre that they had given thought but not words to the idea of liberating the community from Jones.

The most serious threat to Jones's hold came when word circulated that the security guards had begun to express their discontent. Jones had armed guards stationed around his cabin ostensibly to protect him from external assaults. Toward the end of 1978, it was unclear if the guards were there for that purpose, or because the people had become painfully aware that Jones and his small entourage stored canned goods in the cupboard and fresh food in his refrigerator. The guards began to ask among themselves, "Is a milkshake worth a .22?" Even they were weighing the risk of being shot against the value of a milkshake.

When Jones spoke of the disadvantages incumbent upon leadership, the guards stationed at the perimeter exchanged meaningful glances. They sardonically referred to the cabin where Jones worked as "the White House." Their discontent was a new and important factor; they held the guns. Jones, his senses dulled by drugs, was probably unaware of the depth of the acrimony and the widely shared feelings of rage and mutiny that flowed through the community. He was able to sense the feelings of despair, possibly because he, himself, had developed similar feelings.

There was hope he said, and he believed it. He proclaimed that salvation was near. The community would move to the Soviet Union. The suggestion was unanimously cheered: Life in Russia would be infinitely more satisfying than life under their demented leader. They would enjoy a new liberation there. Among the rights that the Jonestown people would acquire in Moscow would be the right to leave if they wished. For those who desired to return to the United States, the trip to the Soviet Union was the solution. And for the many who wanted to live in a society that seemed to have a more rational approach to socialism, the move to Russia seemed ideal.

A move to overthrow Jones was postponed pending the outcome of the plan to migrate. During December 1978 either the move to the Soviet Union was to commence or Jones would face the possibility of a coup led by his security guards or a revolution with many residents participating. Early in November, it seemed as if the Peoples Temple experiment in Guyana might not last out the year. It seems likely that this was known to both the American embassy and the intelligence forces.

All that was required was a short period of official benign neglect so that Jones, the Soviet embassy in Georgetown, and the Soviet government might resolve the matter in one fashion, or failing that, the people of Jonestown might resolve it in yet another.

Part III

The Last Days

8 The First Days of November

After I returned to the United States on September 18, 1978, I began to assemble evidence for the Peoples Temple in support of lawsuits to be filed with the federal district court under the Freedom of Information Act.

Eugene Chaikin and his staff were also hard at work in Jonestown securing affidavits and preparing memoranda. Chaikin wrote to me about his progress, and wrote to the Temple in San Francisco saying that there had been some delay, but his documents would be forthcoming. He asked the San Francisco office to secure various newspaper stories that had been written about the Peoples Temple, which he said would assist him in his work. His mood was hopeful and the letters evidenced a real commitment to our task, which he believed would save the Temple from unfair attacks in the future. I met with Joseph Mazor in San Francisco twice after returning from Jonestown and at the second meeting I interviewed him at some length.

The documents from Jonestown still had not arrived when I received a telephone call from Terri Buford during mid-October. She'd arrived in San Francisco the month before. She said, whispering into the telephone, "Do you agree that a lawyer should have all of the facts in order to represent a client?" I said that I did. When I asked why she asked me that question, she paused for a moment; someone had entered the room. She changed the subject abruptly, and shortly thereafter said good-bye.

Terri Buford called me again in a day or two. She said that our telephone call was confidential and she wanted to know if I could accept such information from her and agree not to tell Jim Jones about our conversation. I told her that I presumed she was seeking my professional advice. She said that she was. I assured her I could never reveal any information that she might give me, unless it was about a contemplated crime or something related to that. She laughed weakly and said she was not considering committing a crime, that if anything, quite the reverse was true.

I reminded her that I was not the general counsel for Jones or the Temple, that my brief was quite limited. But, I advised, if she had any information that would reflect adversely upon the Freedom of Information Act lawsuits that I was preparing, perhaps she should not discuss it with me as I might be obligated, due to a prior commitment, to discuss that matter with Jones. She said that she thought it very important that I continue to work on the cases and that her information was in another area entirely. At that point, I said I would be glad to talk with her and that the matter would remain privileged and confidential until such time as she waived our agreement. "When can we meet?" she asked, adding, "Not in San Francisco. I'd like it to be far away from here."

We agreed to meet in New York City at the Gramercy Park Hotel later that week, on Saturday, October 28. She asked me to promise that I would not tell Jim Jones or Jean Brown or anyone else in the Temple that we were to meet. I agreed, then called her back a little later and asked if it would be inconvenient for her if we postponed our meeting for one day. She acquiesced and we set the time for eleven on Sunday morning at the same place.

I arrived at the hotel at ten-thirty A.M. After eleven, Terri Buford called. She seemed very nervous, and she asked me if I was alone. I said that I was. "Are you sure?" she asked. I assured her I was.

Ten minutes later, she arrived. She looked around the room and when she was satisfied that no one else was there, she said, "I've left the Temple. I might as well tell you that at the very start, so you'll know where I stand. If you pick up that phone and call Jean Brown and tell her where I am, they will probably be willing to pay you one million dollars cash to learn."

I asked her why they'd pay for the information, and she said, "They will be very concerned because I know where all the money is—how to withdraw it—and I know all there is to know about the Temple and Jim. I don't want to cause trouble for anyone. I just want to get out. Are you going to tell?" I told her that the potential offer did not tempt me and that my whole life had gone in a very different direction.

We had lunch and then she began to tell me that some of the charges made by the press and Blakey against the Temple were true. She was afraid to give me very much factual information due to her extreme caution. She was very nervous, and I did not feel it appropriate to press her for details at that time.

Approximately three days later I called the Temple and spoke with Jean Brown, who said, "Terri has left the Temple. She called me after she left and made, I hate to tell you this, Mark, but she made derogatory statements about you and Don Freed which Jim just does not believe. During that call, she [Terri] said she had left a note for me. I found it. [In the note] she said she went on a mission to infiltrate Stoen's group in Berkeley. Jim is very worried. If she contacts you, please let me know. We will do anything we can to find her."

Later, I told Terri what Jean had said. "I never made derogatory statements about you and Don," she responded, "Jim has made that up so in case I contacted you or Don, you would be more inclined to turn me in. In fact, I never called Jean." Terri said:

> On Friday morning, the 27th of October, at 5:45 in the morning, I asked Phyllis Houston to drop me off downtown at Charles Garry's office. I said that I had some work to do there and that I had a dentist's appointment at 9:30. I went to Garry's office, leaving behind a message at the Temple that I was going to infiltrate Tim Stoen's group. I left such a message because I wanted them to waste a few days looking for me in the Bay Area so I would have time to get to New York to talk to you. That morning I went to Garry's office and picked up a small briefcase of clothing that I had hidden there the night before and from there went to the airport.
>
> Five minutes before the plane was to take off, I called Pat Richartz and told her that I was going in for an early dentist appointment but that she should call Jean Brown in about an hour. I had not wanted to wake Jean, I said, to let her know I had some messages for her, and I told Pat where the messages were. I then boarded the plane and went to New York, and stayed for a few days at my sister's house. She thought I was exceptionally nervous but I did not breathe a word of the problem to her.

Recently I asked Terri to draft a statement for me about her motivation for leaving the Temple and why she had not left earlier. This is her answer:

> I had decided to leave the Peoples Temple definitely while I was in Guyana. I had been toying with the idea off and on for several years, seriously for the past year, and made up my mind to take the chance while I was in Guyana. My reasons for wanting to leave were:
>
> a) I hated Jim, not for personal reasons, but I had come to believe that he was at best a sick tyrant.
>
> b) I no longer believed that Jim Jones believed in socialism which was my original reason for joining the Temple.
>
> c) I no longer could follow his instructions. I believed that his instructions were not only tactically weak but morally wrong as well.

My reasons for not wanting to leave were:

a) I believed, and still do, that the majority of the people in Jonestown, with the exception of most of the leadership, were a principled, hard-working, sacrificing crew of people who had given up everything to build a community. I was therefore reluctant to walk out on them.

b) I liked living out of the country. I loved Guyana. I liked the feeling that I wasn't paying tax dollars toward the destructive things that the United States government used taxes for. We had a sense of pride in building a community.

c) All my friends were there and I was unable to communicate my feelings to them about why I was leaving and I knew that I would never be able to tell them why I had left after I had gone. I finally made the decision to leave when I realized that by staying in the organization, I would have to follow instructions from Jones which in the long run would be detrimental to the people. Therefore my staying was no longer beneficial to anyone I cared for.

Upon arriving in the United States, I had tentatively planned to remain with the organization until December, and then "get lost" in the Christmas rush traffic. I chose Christmas time because I thought that during the madhouse of airline flights the Temple would have a harder time finding me, and secondly that it would be harder for them to secure an investigator to follow me during the Christmas and New Year's holidays.

However, the whole plan was shot when Jean Brown came back from Guyana and told me the Shanda Oliver story. I just wanted to leave and leave fast. I wanted no part of contributing to the kind of degenerate behavior that she was talking about. I called my sister and let her know I was coming out that way. Daily, I went to the post office and mailed off a little more of my possessions.

I made airline reservations under the name Kim Agee, the name of a cousin of mine, and paid for them with money that I had kept aside, through the years, that my parents had sent me. I called Mark Lane and told him that I wanted to meet him in some city far from the West Coast; that I needed to talk to him. I asked him to keep this meeting with him in confidence until such time as I could talk to him. We agreed to meet in New York City.

Tim Stoen and others have publicly alleged that Terri is still part of the Temple hierarchy. They base this conclusion on the assertion that she would not have met with me, but rather with Stoen, if she had genuinely made the decision to defect.

I asked Terri Buford, just as I asked Timothy Stoen and Patrick Hallinan,* to prepare answers to relevant questions. I assured all of them that any answer they submitted would be published in full and unedited.

Terri Buford asked for an opportunity to answer the assertions made by Stoen and various publications, such as the *New York Times* and *Newsweek*. This is her response:

"Since so many people in the press have asked me why I would pick a lawyer who was then working for Peoples Temple, and since they insist this is a conflict, this is my answer.

a) When Mark and I were coming from Jonestown to Georgetown, we flew back on a plane together. While waiting for the plane in Matthew's Ridge, Mark and I went for a walk. He talked about the Temple and asked several questions which I thought to be not critical of the project, but critical of the leadership. This made me think that if I were to talk to Mark about some of the problems in the Temple, that he would be able to see that there were in fact problems.

b) I did not believe that there would be any conflict of interest because I was very worried about the well-being of the people in Jonestown. The fact that I disliked Jim did not mean I wanted to harm the organization in any way. I had no intention of connecting with Stoen, for I sincerely believed, and still do, that Tim Stoen was working for the government, and for the destruction of Jonestown.

c) I did not feel that Mark could be corrupted by the desire for money or position. This was important to me because I believed that Peoples Temple would eventually find out where I was and that I had met with Mark and I knew that they would pay probably as much as a million dollars in cash to him to get him to disclose my whereabouts.

d) Jim had told me that if I ever left the organization I would be killed. I believed him. I wanted to tell someone who would be in a position to help of my impressions of Peoples Temple before I died. I chose Mark because he didn't always see things as just 'good guys and bad guys.' I wanted someone to know that Peoples Temple was a decent place, but it was under attack, and Jim Jones was running Jonestown like a concentration camp. I wanted someone who would understand that both Jim Jones and Tim Stoen were equally destructive to the Temple and the people and that the combination of the two of them was explosive.

e) Mark had been to Guyana and was better able to judge what I was telling him. Unless one had been there and seen it, the situation would have been impossible to describe.

*See Appendix J.

f) Mark was in a position to talk to Jim. Jim hated Charles Garry; he felt that Charles was blackmailing him. I believed that also, and I also suspected that Charles Garry had stolen money from the Temple—which was something that Jim did not know about. I had hoped that with Mark knowing some of the facts that he would be able to help the people in Guyana. Charles Garry knew all the facts and much more than Mark did. However, whenever I talked to Charles about the problems he would not listen to me. I believed that Charles was making decisions for the Temple on the basis of what looked good for him politically in San Francisco without regard for the real situation in Guyana. I also believed that Charles would not give proper attention to the problems because his first loyalty was to Jim Jones. For Garry, it was the old story of he who pays the piper calls the tune, and not for the people of Jonestown. On one occasion, after the massacre, Charles said that he represented Jim and the Temple, but not the individual people.

"I believed that the government was out to destroy Peoples Temple. I had what I believed to be substantial documentation which led me to that conclusion. I believed that were I to go to the government, they would use me as another pawn to destroy the Temple, and I would not be used in that way. I believe that Debbie Blakey, when she left the Temple and went to the press, thought that she made the right decision. Legally, she did, but when she did that, Jim went almost completely insane and conditions that were bad in Jonestown before became suddenly worse. Jim used Debbie's defection as an excuse to establish martial law. He was determined that no one else would have the opportunity to defect; he was determined to be sure of that.

"I did not go to the government because I believed that, sick and corrupt as Jones was, the government was trying to aggravate his illness. I told Jim before I left Guyana that I believed Tim Stoen wanted him to commit mass murder, as he had threatened, and that Tim would see that as a victory. At the time, Jim agreed with me and promised he would not do it—ever.

"I could not take a chance on giving information to the government, not when I believed it would have just been a matter of weeks before the Temple went to the Soviet Union. I did not want to do anything that would hinder their getting there.

"Once they got to the Soviet Union—I would have been able to have made contact with some of the people there and helped deal with the problems as we had not been able to in Jonestown."

It was never the thought of Jones, the people in the Temple, or officials in the Soviet Union that the Peoples Temple would exist there. The members were just going to live in various cities throughout Russia as American dissenters, not as Temple members. Those who did not wish to remain there could arrange to go home. Those who liked it could stay there.

Our family invited Terri to stay with us in Memphis and she accepted the invitation. When she contacted her sister to request her to ship the clothing she had sent to her home, she learned that the Temple personnel had called there saying that they were in the neighborhood and looking for Terri.

Later Jean Brown called me. She said that Jim Jones had sent Tim Carter to Berkeley to infiltrate the center there and meet with Tim Stoen. His purpose was to find Terri Buford and persuade her to return to Jonestown. She said that Buford was not there and had not attempted to join Stoen's group. She said, "Jim said that if you can find Terri, he would do anything for her. He wants her to go back to Jonestown at once."

Early in November, while in Memphis, I received another telephone call from Jean Brown. She informed me that Jim Jones had just been notified by Congressman Leo Ryan of California that he would be leading a congressional investigating team from the House International Relations Committee into Jonestown.* She said that Jones was very upset by the news and wished for me to respond to Ryan's letter. She made it clear to me that Jones did not want Ryan to visit the community and that instead of refusing him entrance, Jones was establishing conditions for the visit.

During the next days, Brown told me of various conditions precedent, firm requirements set by Jones, she said, which were offered as non-negotiable. Some of them were so absurd that I could not forward them to Ryan. The notion that members of the congressional black caucus must form a substantial portion of the delegation was presumptuous, since those being investigated are not entitled to choose those who investigate, and impractical since I did not know if there were any black members of Congress on the committee. Though that information might be ascertained easily, it certainly seemed unlikely that any member would be willing to take so arduous and unrewarding a trip on such short notice.

Jean Brown said the delegation must consist of a number of members of Congress who support the political aims of the Peoples Temple and its leader. Since Jones had proclaimed himself to be a Marxist, I pointed out that it seemed unlikely, unless the committee was to be comprised of members of foreign parliaments, such as a number of deputies from France or

*The letter from Congressman Ryan dated November 1, 1978, is published in Appendix F.

Italy, that such a balance could be achieved. From my one philosophical and political exchange with Jones, I had concluded that his scholarship in Marxist ideology was so deficient that he might have experienced difficulty in distinguishing between the works of Karl Marx and Groucho Marx.

At nine o'clock in the morning on November 3, 1978, I placed a telephone call to Congressman Ryan's office in San Mateo, California. I suspected that the congressman would not be in Washington, since Congress was not in session during that election week. I was informed that Ryan was not in the office, and when I told the aide that Jones had asked me to discuss arrangements for the trip with him, she said that he would call me "very soon."

Later James Schollaert, an attorney on the staff of the International Relations Committee of the House of Representatives, called me from Washington on behalf of Ryan. He said that Ryan was to be accompanied to Guyana by Congressman Edward Derwinski of Illinois and that each representative would be assisted on the trip by an aide. Schollaert said that he would be traveling with Ryan. In the course of several conversations during the next days, he informed me that the delegation was to arrive in Georgetown on November 14 and would leave for Jonestown on November 16. He assured me that the delegation would be comprised of two members of Congress and two aides.

On November 6, I wrote a letter* to Ryan stating that I wanted to meet with him to discuss his proposed visit and to tell him "of my experiences in Jonestown and with Jim Jones and with the Peoples Temple." I pointed out to him that his visit "might result in the premature evacuation of Jonestown and cause an emigration to a nation with which our government did not enjoy entirely friendly relations."

I concluded with "I hope that this matter can be resolved in an amicable fashion and I continue to wait for a telephone call from you so that we may discuss this matter more fully." Ryan never did call me, and each time I called him I was referred to Schollaert.

I told Schollaert that Jones was "quite ill and under very heavy medication." I told him that "this is the least propitious time for an official visit." I said that, due to Jones's condition and his attitude toward the delegation, I could foresee no favorable result from the visit, and therefore suggested that Ryan might learn a great deal from interviewing people then in the United States who had lived in Jonestown, before he embarked upon such a difficult trip. I made a similar suggestion in my letter to Ryan, saying, "It would seem to me both fair and appropriate for you to seek information

*This letter is published in Appendix F.

from the other side as well before embarking upon a trip to Jonestown."

On November 10, Ryan responded to my letter.* He made it clear that he did not wish to meet with me or with any other person who was in the United States to discuss conditions in Jonestown. He wrote, "I intend to go to the source and to allow those 'on the other side' the opportunity to speak for themselves. In this case, I have offered Mr. Jones and his supporters the full opportunity to speak for themselves."

As to my statement that the residents might flee to another country, Ryan wrote:

"I am even more puzzled by your further vague references to one or two other countries that have offered 'refuge' to the 1200 Americans in Jonestown. Am I to understand, then, that all 1200 have already been asked if they would be willing to travel to yet another country and begin their lives, under what must already be difficult conditions at best? Perhaps we can learn more about that after we arrive."

Jones, Chaikin, Tropp, and Prokes knew that I had worked closely with members of the Congress in establishing the Select Committee on Assassinations of the House of Representatives. They expressed the view that it would be useful, in the event that they decided to allow Ryan to visit the private settlement, for me to be there at the same time. However, the Select Committee on Assassinations decided that my client James Earl Ray was to testify before them on November 16, the same date that Ryan had decided to visit Jonestown. Therefore, in my letter of November 6 to Ryan, I said:

> I have been informed that you wish to tour Jonestown during the middle of November. My client has asked that I be present while you make that tour. It seems entirely appropriate and proper that I should be there on that occasion. Accordingly, I placed a telephone call to your San Mateo office at 9 A.M. on Friday, November 3, 1978, to make arrangements for your trip to Jonestown and to discuss the entire matter with you. Your aide stated that you would return my telephone call but I have not as yet heard directly from you. However, I did receive a telephone call from Jim Schollaert, who told me that he was a member of the Committee's staff. I informed him that I would be engaged during the middle of November in that I would be representing several witnesses who were to appear in public testimony before the House Select Committee on Assassinations in Washington, D.C., from the middle until the end of November. I suggested to Mr.

*Ryan's letter is published in Appendix F.

> Schollaert that if you called me, we would no doubt work out a date which would be satisfactory to all of us.

Ryan responded:

> I regret that you will not be able to be in Guyana this next week, but I understand that Mr. Jones has other legal counsel available in the event he feels such counsel is necessary. In a situation where the Committee schedule does not coincide with your own personal schedule, I must obviously resolve such a conflict for the United States House of Representatives. I hope that you will understand."

During that week, Don Harris, a television newsman working for NBC, called me. We had worked together for a series about the assassination of Dr. Martin Luther King, Jr., which NBC-TV had aired. When I first met him I found his manner to be sharp and incisive. I was pleased with the interviews that he had conducted with me, but I felt that he had taken unfair advantage of an elderly woman whom he questioned. I do not object to difficult and fair questions when directed toward me; the difficult and, I thought, unfair questions which he asked the woman, who was an important witness in the King murder, riled me and I told him so at the time. Later, he was assigned by NBC to present the defense view on network television in the case of the People against James Earl Ray while James Polk was chosen to present the government's view. It was not exactly a new role for Polk, but it was, Harris told me, unprecedented for him. Harris did an excellent job; I told him so, and we became friends who shared a drink or two in Memphis and later in Washington, D.C.

When he called me in November, he said, "Are we going to do another one together? Are you in this one, too?" I asked him what it was he was talking about. He said "Jonestown. I'm flying in there with Ryan; I thought you knew." I told him what Schollaert had told me. Harris said, "Listen, Mark, I'm going in with a television crew and there are a lot of other reporters going too. They are not leveling with you."

Harris then asked if I could arrange an interview for him with Jones. I told him that I did not know if anyone would be allowed in, that Jones would be outraged when he discovered that he had been lied to, and that he could be counted on to overreact. I said I did not believe that I would be present in Jonestown with Ryan and that even if I were there, I could not guarantee that Jones would consent to an interview. Finally, I said, "I don't think you should go all the way down there expecting an interview with Jones, because even if you got one, it would not be much good." Harris asked what I meant. I said that I understood that Jones was under very heavy medication and that a one-on-one interview with him might disclose a drugged man's rambling.

Harris asked me if Jones was physically ill, or dying, or if he was just on drugs. I said that I did not know the answer. I told him that I had given him information similar to information that I had given to Schollaert and that I expected him to use it quietly. I said that if Jones decided that I was betraying him that matters could worsen.

I also asked him, should he actually conduct an interview with Jones, not to be nasty or accusatory but to be fair, even if he did not like Jones or his answers. Harris told me that he had heard many attacks upon Jones and had also heard from supporters who greatly admired Jones. Then he asked, "Who are the guys in the white hats, Mark?" I said, "I'm afraid there are none."

Harris took a long pause, and then said, "Wow!" I asked what that signified and he said, "You are the most committed advocate I've met. You insisted that there was a conspiracy in the King case. I can't believe you just said that." I told him that I considered him a friend who called for a briefing about a serious question and that I felt that it was wise to tell him what I could."

I called Ryan's office, identified myself, and was told that he would call back. Instead Schollaert returned the call. I told him that I had learned from Don Harris, who had placed no restriction on the use of the information he had given me, that it had been arranged for the news media to accompany Ryan to Jonestown. Schollaert said he did not know anything about a Don Harris and reiterated his position again, assuring me that no media representative would be on the trip. He said that the Pan American flight from New York to Georgetown was a public carrier and that it was obvious that anyone could purchase a ticket and make a reservation. He speculated that perhaps the media had somehow learned of the trip that the congressman was planning and thought of joining him. He insisted however, without qualification, that the trip from Georgetown to Jonestown would be in transportation controlled by the congressional team and that only Congressmen Ryan and Derwinski and two aides would be making that trip. Schollaert said that he could assure me that there would be no media people on that last and decisive leg of the journey to Jonestown.

I told him that I accepted his assurances and that I wished to stress my strong feeling that it would be an error to try to trick Jim Jones, that he was ill and under heavy medication, and that I was afraid he would become very angry if he felt he had been lied to by the congressional committee. I knew that Ryan must be familiar with Debbie Blakey's affidavit disclosing just how dangerous Jones's anger could be. She had also disclosed that the camp was armed with semiautomatic weapons and rifles.

I again asked Schollaert if he could arrange for me to speak with Ryan. He said he would inquire.

During this period, Ryan's letter to me arrived. In it, Ryan said that it was his "policy" in these matters "to deal with the principals in a given situation" and that "it is for this reason that I asked Mr. James Schollaert, as an attorney on the staff of the committee, to respond to your telephone inquiry, to which you make reference." Ryan had invoked a nonexistent protocol to prevent us from discussing the matter.

In the past years, I had met scores of members of the House and of the Senate, as I walked to and from my home/office on Capitol Hill. Not one of them had ever declined to talk with me and many of them had been most hospitable. While his reasons were obscure, there was no ambiguity about his decision. Ryan would not talk with me.

I discussed Ryan's odd letter with my law partner, April Ferguson, who had also worked on Capitol Hill as an officer of the Citizens Commission of Inquiry, which had successfully lobbied for an investigation into the murders of Dr. King and President Kennedy. We puzzled over it and decided that it seemed to be written by someone who had little experience with these matters, or that Leo Ryan was a very unusual representative. Later, months after the massacre, Steven Katsaris told me that members of the Concerned Relatives group, established with Stoen's assistance, had drafted the letter to me from Ryan. Ryan's office had furnished them with my letter, he said, and they agreed to prepare his response.

The posture that Ryan adopted and adhered to was contrary to proper procedure.

A report filed with the House of Representatives* stated that "on November 5, the U.S. Embassy advised Mr. Ryan that the Peoples Temple wanted Mr. Ryan to work with Peoples Temple legal counsel, Mark Lane, on the appropriate arrangements for the Ryan CODEL [Congressional Delegation] to visit Jonestown."

Ryan's refusal to talk with counsel was improper, and it is improper to insist upon speaking with the principal once a party has learned that the other principal has selected counsel for that purpose.

The congressional report stated that Jones had by then established three conditions for the visit. The report reads:

**U.S. House of Representatives Report*, p. 2.

"The Embassy also relayed to Mr. Ryan that the Peoples Temple had informed an Embassy official that Mr. Ryan could visit Jonestown, provided: (1) that the CODEL was "balanced"; (2) that there would be no media coverage associated with the visit; and (3) that Mr. Lane be present during the visit."*

The evidence now available discloses that Ryan had planned to violate the provisions that Jones had set. The delegation was not to be balanced; its chairman and sole member had already enlisted in the crusade on behalf of Tim Stoen.

On May 15, 1978, Ryan had written in a letter, on his congressional stationery, to Reverend Guy B. Young:

"Please be advised that Tim Stoen does have my support in the effort to return his son from Guyana. In addition, a long time friend of mine, Bob Houston, a wire service photographer, has told me his granddaughters are being held in Guyana."

Ryan knew that Stoen had previously confessed that John Victor Stoen was not "his son." He also knew why Bob Houston's granddaughters were in Jonestown: their mother had sent them there voluntarily and later joined them. Their father was dead.

While Ryan agreed with the second condition, stated in the report, that there would be no media representatives on the trip, he had planned to bring at least one reporter with him from the very outset. His office, in fact, had solicited participation from the print and electronic media. In retrospect, it seems possible that Ryan refused to talk with me because he was reluctant to make false statements to me, preferring to have Schollaert handle that chore for him.

The State Department report on the massacre disclosed that on September 15, 1978, Ryan and an aide met with State Department officials and told them of Ryan's plans "to visit Jonestown sometime after November 10, 1978, with a party of about eight persons, including a member of the press and possibly some relatives of Temple members."† On October 18, 1978, Ryan sent letters to other members of the House International Committee inviting them to accompany him to Guyana.‡ In that letter, he advised the members that "we have to take at least one newsman."§

When Jones learned that a number of reporters, including Don Harris

*Ibid., p. 3.

†State Department, "The Performance of the Department of State and the American Embassy in Georgetown, Guyana, in the Peoples Temple Case." [May 1979], p. 11. Hereafter referred to as *State Department Report*.

‡*U.S. House of Representatives Report*, p. 46.

§Ibid.

and his NBC-TV news team, were planning to accompany Ryan to Jonestown, he became enraged. John Burke, the American ambassador to Guyana then, informed the government of Guyana that "it was the Embassy's clear understanding that the Congressman had not invited the [NBC] team to come and that San Francisco had only become interested in covering the story when news of the Congressman's prepared trip became known."*

While Schollaert was asserting to me that no member of the press would accompany Ryan, and the American embassy was offering similar false assurance to the government of Guyana, Tim Carter was learning the real purpose of the Ryan visit, as Timothy Stoen saw it. Stoen told Carter at the meeting in Berkeley that he had masterminded the congressional trip.

Jean Brown called to tell me that Tim Carter had learned directly from Stoen that members of the press and the Concerned Relatives, possibly including Tim Stoen, would be going into Jonestown and that my assurances to the contrary, based upon my talks with Schollaert, were considered by Jones to be valueless. Carter, it seems, had infiltrated the Stoen group in Berkeley and was learning directly from Stoen about the plans for the congressional delegation. I told her that Schollaert did say that members of the press might be on the flight to Georgetown, but that he guaranteed that they would not go into Jonestown with Ryan, and that Ryan was in charge of ongoing transportation to Jonestown from Georgetown. I said that Stoen might have misunderstood or exaggerated about the trip to Jonestown. Brown said that she would tell Jones what I had said.

Stoen was right and I wrong, as it turned out. Stoen was part of the planning group for the trip, and Ryan and his staff were open with him about their plans, while they embarked upon a program to deceive me—and through me, Jim Jones—about the reality of the trip. This effect of their scheme considerably lessened my influence with Jones and thereby reduced my ability to calm matters in Jonestown on November 18. It also convinced Jones that the government and Stoen were working together to destroy him.

It was apparent that Ryan was planning to be in Jonestown while I was in Washington, D.C. I was bemused by Ryan's statement in his letter to me in which he wrote, "I understand that Mr. Jones has other legal counsel available." I did not know then that Ambassador Burke had already notified the State Department that "PT representatives also informed Consul that their response to Congressman Ryan's cable would be communicated through Attorney Mark Lane."† At that time, I had no knowledge that the

*Ibid., p. 51.
†Ibid.

Ambassador had notified the State Department that Jones had established as a condition "that attorney Mark Lane be present for CODEL visit to Guyana and Jonestown,"* and I did not know that Ryan's representative in San Mateo arranged for my letter to Ryan and his response to be delivered by hand to Charles Garry. Garry then called Jean Brown and threatened to resign as counsel if he was not invited to accompany Ryan. He insisted that he be the only attorney on the trip. Jones, frightened that Garry would attack him and place his confidential and damning files into the street, as Garry had previously threatened to do, told Garry through Brown that his demands would be met.

Before leaving for Washington on November 12 to represent the interests of Grace Walden, a witness in the King murder case, and James Earl Ray, I met in Memphis with Terri Buford and April Ferguson to discuss the Ryan trip. At that time it seemed very unlikely that Ryan could be persuaded to postpone his visit. However, I was concerned that if he did agree, I would have to decide whether I too should go to Jonestown. That is the matter the three of us discussed.

April quite firmly suggested that I simply withdraw from the entire affair with the exception of meeting my commitments to bring appropriate actions under the Freedom of Information Act. She explained that those lawsuits might very well uncover evidence that would assist Jones by relieving the pressure upon lives and restoring to him a sense of hope. I agreed with both her analysis and her conclusions.

Terri Buford offered another perspective. She had known many of the residents of Jonestown for many years. She loved and respected many of them. She said to me, "If you don't go and Garry does go, he will just make matters worse. I'm worried about the people there. If some incident takes place, I think you might be able to resolve it, because Jones has some respect for your judgment. He hates Garry and is suspicious of him and afraid of what he might do." I was persuaded by her plea and I said so.

I told April that in the unlikely event that the plans were changed to permit me to make the trip, I would go.

April was alarmed, and I sought to comfort her and said that I believed that Ryan was unalterably committed to November 16.

Ryan, his aides, the State Department, and the embassy together quite effectively concealed from Jones the real nature of the trip. He had been assured that Stoen would not be in Georgetown, and did not know that

*Ibid.

Stoen and his associates, working together with Ryan, had arranged for the presence of the news media.

At the same time, Ryan and his aides did not know of the dangers that awaited them in Jonestown. The State Department and the embassy had effectively concealed much of that information from them. Ryan was not even informed that the consul had confirmed my statement to Schollaert that Jones was, then, mentally incapacitated. With the State Department and Stoen both misleading Ryan, subjects discussed in detail in chapter 21, and with Ryan relying upon Stoen and consequently, even brashly misleading Jones, the series of events that would lead to the tragedy were already well under way.

Just before I went to Washington to appear before the Select Committee on Assassination with Memphis attorney Duncan Ragsdale on behalf of Grace Walden, I was informed that the committee had decided not to permit James Earl Ray to testify. He would be denied the right to answer his accusers.

When I arrived in Washington, Jean Brown told me she had informed Jones that I was now available for the trip. She said that Jones was very anxious for me to be there and that she felt he needed me at that most difficult time. I told her that I would go.

I called April, told her of my decision, and asked her to request someone to bring suitable clothing to Washington the next day. In an attempt to lighten her mood, I said that one must dress appropriately for whatever jungle one appeared in. The effort was not successful. She just said, "I don't think you should go. Jones sounds unstable to me, and we're only researching for them. Why do you need to go?"

Terri was in hiding, in fear of an assassination team of the Temple or someone operating under that cover. She was using a different name and staying as a guest at our house in Memphis. She volunteered to go to Washington, reside in the building on Capitol Hill that we maintained, and make some discreet inquiries about an aspect of the King investigation for us. I introduced her to a fine investigative reporter, briefed them both, and left for Guyana.

I stopped off at a department store to buy several white undershorts. I do not intend to burden the reader with such uneventful details in my life, especially my shopping or laundry lists. The purchase of the shorts, however, becomes relevant later; in fact, even the color of the shorts was to become crucial.

Upon my arrival at JFK International Airport in New York, I purchased a new watch because the one I had been wearing persisted in stopping regularly. Then I bought several books and a small package of cough drops. In September, I had developed a bad cough, no doubt encouraged by the fact that I had played basketball in Jonestown before becoming acclimated to the heat. Our game had been postponed briefly several times by sudden tropical rainstorms of limited duration, which had drenched us all. When I had journeyed back to Georgetown from Jonestown on my way home in September, I had searched in vain at two large pharmacies for cough drops. I could not locate that simple medication anywhere in the capital of the country. Then, at the airport, I had been disappointed to discover that paperback books were not sold.

So after buying several paperbacks, I ran into Charles Garry, who had just passed through an electronic gate into the departure area. He was discussing a matter with the security guard as I came upon him. He wanted to know why his briefcase, a very large, old-fashioned one, had to be subjected to physical scrutiny after it had already been screened electronically. The guard explained that a suspicious, large metal object in the bag had to be examined. I was to discover what this article was, and it would, like my shorts, my new watch, paperbacks, and cough drops, take on added significance forty-eight hours later in the jungles of Guyana.

9 November 17—Georgetown

I greeted Charles, who seemed genuinely surprised and not at all pleased to see me. Apparently Jean Brown had assured Garry that I would not be going to Guyana. She had told me that Garry would be going, but on a different flight. She also told me that she had informed Garry that the Temple was not paying me a fee for any of the work that I was doing on its behalf, and she asked me also to tell this to Garry. (Although I had not been paid for my work with Mazor, the Temple was to pay for my help with the Freedom of Information filing.) She said, "Garry will quit and really hurt Jim and the Temple" if he learned that I had agreed to help. In that atmosphere lacking candor and mutual trust, our trip to Guyana began.

In spite of my many apprehensions and forebodings about the imminent confrontation between the congressional delegation and Jones, I was happy to be returning to Guyana. The newness and strangeness of the place, which was so much a part of my experience two months earlier, had dissipated. The austerity program, as Guyana struggled to transform itself from a colonial outpost into a collective democracy, was severe, but that, too, had lost much of its dire impact upon me. I hoped that as a result of this visit, the Jonestown community would become a more open place. I knew that I was going to do everything in my power to reduce the possibility of confrontation and try to assist the process of reform.

Garry and I were greeted at the airport in Georgetown on Thursday evening, November 16, by members of the Temple staff. There we were delayed, however, because Garry had brought with him an enormous amount of luggage which was not his own: Duffle bags and various boxes had been dispatched by the Temple in San Francisco, in Garry's care, for Jonestown. Garry probably did not know what was contained in the baggage, and I puzzled over his cavalier attitude. Previously Terri Buford had told Garry that weapons, ammunition, and other contraband had been smuggled into Guyana by assigning the luggage to a well-known professional who was traveling from California to Guyana and whose credentials seemed above reproach. I never agree to carry even an envelope from one country to another as a friendly service until I am permitted to open the package and look at the contents. I could not imagine why Garry would do so.

Eventually, we were taken to a spacious two-story house at 41 Lamaha Gardens, which served as a residence and office for the Temple members. One of its ground level rooms housed the radio which provided communication between the Georgetown cadre and Jonestown, and between Georgetown and the San Francisco office of the Temple.

When we arrived at Lamaha Gardens late that Thursday evening, we were told that an American reporter had climbed over the backyard fence and had walked into the house unannounced earlier that evening. The reporter was part of the Ryan entourage, the Temple members said. They also said that Ryan had himself visited the house without having made an appointment. At that time, Ryan informed them that if he were not permitted access to Jonestown he could make charges against Jones and the Temple for violations of the Social Security law and various finance and tax laws. He said that if he were denied entrance to Jonestown, he "intended to pursue that through every area of the U.S. government." Ryan had sought out Charles Krause, a reporter for the *Washington Post,* and had asked him to drive to the Temple building with him. Of course, all of that information had already been communicated to Jones via the radio, and the tension level and fear quota in Jonestown were high and rising.

The presence of the news media as a de facto part of the Ryan delegation was particularly rankling to the Temple members. It was their position that while they were willing to accept the presence of the congressional delegation, albeit with great reluctance, they were unwilling to open the gates of their private refuge to hostile or even probing reporters. That especially was true since they believed that Tim Stoen had proclaimed to the media that their role during the Ryan visit was to try to destroy Jonestown.

If Jones knew how the press had learned of the Ryan visit, he would have been even more driven. Will Holsinger, the son of an aide of Ryan's, Joseph Holsinger, and an attorney hired by Ryan to research the Peoples Temple, also notified the news media of Ryan's plans to visit Jonestown. He gave the information to Gordon Lindsay, the British journalist who had been writing the unbalanced horror story about Jonestown for the *National Enquirer* during September. Although Lindsay was a British subject, the

American embassy had interceded on his behalf with the government of Guyana to extend his visa so that he might complete the attack upon Jonestown. Lindsay contacted NBC-TV, told them of the Ryan delegation, and arranged to join the NBC team headed by Don Harris. Later, Holsinger also called David Perlman, the city editor at the San Francisco *Chronicle,* a publication which had published a series of hostile articles about Jones and the Temple and which had recently assumed a protective stance regarding Timothy Stoen.

Perlman, having been invited to send a reporter to accompany Ryan, met with William German, the newspaper's managing editor, and Richard Thieriot, the publisher. They agreed to send a reporter. Although Marshall Kilduff was the most likely candidate, having written a number of derogatory stories about Jones and the Peoples Temple, both for the *Chronicle* and the magazine *New West,* Perlman later said, "Frankly, we thought it might not be safe for Marshall down there. At the very least, he might be harassed. It was also possible that his presence alone might be enough to keep the whole party out of Jonestown." The newspaper sent Ron Javers. Perlman explained that the Temple did not know Javers. "That was an important factor in choosing him for the assignment," he said.

Had Jones known that the media was notified by Ryan's associate and that he had chosen, at the outset, two of the most notorious publications insofar as the Temple was concerned, he would have, I believe, canceled the visit in spite of Ryan's warning of serious consequences. By concealing these machinations, his own role in them, and the guiding hand of Stoen, Ryan was able to gain access to Jonestown. By then, however, Jones began to understand that each of the promises to him had been betrayed. His reaction was swift and merciless.

At Lamaha Gardens, Thursday evening, I tried to diminish the expressed fear and anger of Temple members by examining Ryan's actions in the most sympathetic light. I said that his spontaneous visit was not an evil act and that the reporter's furtive entry should not be considered as a hostile act. I suggested that Ryan's informality might be indicative of a relaxed, open attitude and the reporter's antics could be explained by the architectural ambiguity of the building: It was difficult to determine the front entrance from the side entrance, and no easier to discover that a stairway to the second floor was considered by the Temple personnel to be the public entrance, rather than the more immediate doorways which greeted visitors on the ground level. As to Ryan's threats of action, contingent upon being turned away at the Jonestown gates, I submitted that he might have been demonstrating nothing more than excessive zeal, clumsily put, in a sincere effort to visit the settlement.

I would have been considerably less sanguine had I known that Ryan had been personally meeting with the newsmen and saying "Trust us. We'll walk you through." Later, Joseph Holsinger said, "Leo thought the press was his best protection and the press thought he was their protection." The deception they practiced together, however, tended to undermine their already fragile credibility with Jones, engage his wrath when he discerned their betrayal, and ultimately endanger both their mission and their lives.

I also learned Thursday evening that earlier that afternoon, a group from the Concerned Relatives had also tried to enter the Temple's house at Lamaha Gardens. They, too, it seemed, had come to Georgetown with Leo Ryan.

On Friday morning, November 17, at my request, Ryan was called and an appointment was made for Garry, a representative of the Temple staff, and me to meet with him at a place he might designate and at his earliest convenience. Ryan agreed to meet with us a little later that morning. He suggested the Pegasus Hotel, where Jackie Speier, Ryan's aide, was registered. Ryan had been staying at the residence of the American ambassador.

Sharon Amos and Debbie Touchette—representing the Temple staff—Garry, and I set out for the Pegasus. The twenty-minute ride was memorable. Garry asked the two women, "Who do you think should speak for the Temple at the meeting with Ryan?" Debbie, a bit more sophisticated than Sharon, and decidely more relaxed, quickly picked up on the tension created by Garry's tone and question.

An attractive woman with a lovely smile, she looked at Garry and said, "Charles, I don't think we need one spokesperson. All four of us will be there and we can all participate."

Garry was not to be denied. He said that there must be one person chosen to speak for the Temple. Sharon agreed. Garry then asked Sharon, apparently a new ally, who she thought should be the "spokesman." It would be best if, said Sharon, she was the one. Garry, his voice rising in anger said, "I'm the lawyer for Jim and the Temple. The only lawyer for Jim and the Temple. If you don't want me to be the spokesman, then you might as well drive me to the airport and I'll go back to San Francisco. I have other things to do."

Sharon explained that the political position that Jones had adopted should be presented by a Temple member. She said she had just recently talked with Jim and knew his position very well. Garry was adamant. Debbie and Sharon yielded to his anger and an implied threat to withdraw as counsel, conceding that he could lead the discussion. Garry, then relaxed, began in a conciliatory fashion to explain why the decision, already made, was a proper one. He said, "I've worked with these turkeys before. I know how to establish rapport with them."

I remained uncharacteristically silent throughout the exchange, studying Garry's techniques. When we arrived at the hotel lobby, Don Harris came forward to greet me warmly. He took me aside for a moment and asked if he was going to be able to get into Jonestown. I told him that the matter was already complicated and, I feared, growing more so. I said that I had to meet with the congressman and at the conclusion of that meeting, I would be happy to brief him. He asked if we had a date for a drink or lunch and I answered affirmatively. Numerous other reporters were in the lobby also.

I caught up with the Temple delegation, and together we walked through the lobby to an outdoor patio and garden. Ryan was seated at a table with his aides. I shook hands with Ryan, since he recognized me, and then I introduced him to the others in our group. Reporters who were in the lobby drifted over toward Ryan's table as did some of the members of the Concerned Relatives. Harris hovered in the background, discreetly observing from a distance. Garry asked Ryan where we could talk. Ryan said, "Right here." Garry objected to the members of the press being present. Ryan said that as chairman of the delegation, he was not empowered to preclude the press. I told Ryan that I found that assertion to be absurd and that I knew of no House rule that prevented him from retiring with his aides to a room where we might discuss arrangements for the Jonestown trip. He insisted that we meet either with the press present or not at all. Garry exploded, and called Ryan a "dumb son of a bitch." He spun around and hurried away from the short-lived meeting, saying, "That cocksucker. Fuck him. There's going to be no trip to Jonestown."

Debbie, Sharon, and I caught up with Garry in the lobby. Sharon said, "We must tell Jim what's happened." Garry, still fuming, agreed. It was his advice, he said, that Ryan and his party be barred from the settlement. I said that I thought we should make another attempt to meet with Ryan privately, so that at the very least, we could determine what his plans were and what requests he planned to make of us. Debbie agreed with me.

Meanwhile, at the patio, Ryan was talking with most of the reporters. Don Harris approached me in the lobby and asked if I thought that a meeting with the congressman sans the reporters might be useful. When I said that I believed that it might be, he said he would get the newsmen to withdraw.

Ryan asked the reporters if he should meet with us privately. He said, "It's up to you guys." The reporters, influenced by Harris, said they didn't care where the negotiations were conducted and whether they were in public or private.

Schollaert approached our meeting in the lobby with word that we could meet with Ryan in Jackie Speier's room. Garry was reluctant to attend the meeting. Sharon expressed the view that we should drive back to Lamaha Gardens, report to Jones what had taken place, and ask him if we should meet with Ryan. I said that we could not expect to take minute-by-minute directions from Jones, and furthermore, he had asked us to meet with Ryan and learn what it was the congressman wanted. As we started to move toward the elevator where Schollaert was waiting, I turned to Garry and said "Charles, I don't think you established rapport with them." The attempt at humor failed with Garry and Sharon. Debbie smiled.

Garry, Sharon, Debbie, and I sat on beds and chairs facing Ryan, Schollaert, and Speier in the latter's room. The meeting began acrimoniously enough and then, marked by growing rancor and anger, became openly belligerent. We agreed to tape record the informal proceedings. It was about the only agreement we reached in the crowded room and, as it developed, a concordat that was technologically beyond us. The congressman's tape recorder was not working. The Temple's model worked sporadically at best.

Ryan said that he and an aide would be leaving for Jonestown shortly. He said that the embassy had secured an eighteen-seat plane for his use and that he had reserved two seats for use for the Temple's lawyers. Debbie and Sharon asked if there was to be room for them on the plane. Ryan's response was in the negative. He explained that all of the seats, with the exception of the two for Garry and myself, had already been assigned. I asked, almost afraid to hear the answer and being very much aware that I would soon be required to repeat that answer to a frightened and angry Jim Jones, "Who will be on the plane?"

Ryan said that he was taking nine members of the news media into Jonestown with him. I looked at Schollaert and was about to remind him of his direct and unqualified assurances to me that the media would not be brought to Jonestown by Ryan when I realized that the mathematics were also imperfect. I said "Who else will be on the plane?" Ryan said, "I'm bringing in four members of the Concerned Relatives." I asked if Stoen was going to be one of the four. Ryan said that Stoen was in Georgetown, but that he would not disclose the names of the four who would accompany him.

I asked Schollaert if he believed that Ryan was violating the commitment given to me by his office. Schollaert said that he did not believe so. He said that he had told me that the congressman did not "plan" to have reporters or relatives on the plane with him when he left Georgetown for the interview, but that "the plans had changed." I asked Ryan why the plans had changed and he said, "I expected to have a six- or seven-seat plane. But the embassy got us this eighteen-seat job. It's expensive. Five thousand dollars for the trip.* So I'm selling tickets to the media to cover the cost. My committee will really be on me if I saddle them with the whole bill."

We pointed out that he had placed the success of his mission in jeopardy with this maneuver. The congressman seemed unconcerned about the possibility. It struck me that his cavalier attitude resulted from a prior determination that he had made. I believed then that he probably had not expected to enter Jonestown but that he envisioned a televised and heavily reported scene of his spurned efforts at the Jonestown gate. With the NBC-TV news team grinding away, with the dramatic events captured on tape recorders and witnessed by reporters from the *Washington Post* and the two San Francisco dailies, the story would be known in America. A congressman seeking to unite children and parents in a remote setting in the midst of an impenetrable jungle had enough gripping elements to generate widespread interest.

In the State Department's report, the conclusion was reached that "even the staff members on the Congressional Delegation had been unaware of the extent of media participation in the trip until they boarded the airplane in New York."† This explanation is inadequate, I believe, in view of the

*Later Ryan said it cost two thousand dollars for the round trip. Charles Krause wrote in the *Washington Post* that the chartered airplane cost three thousand dollars a day.

†"The Performance of the Department of State and the American Embassy in Georgetown, Guyana, in the Peoples Temple Case," p. 82. The relevant portion follows:

> The question of media participation came to a head on November 14, 1978, the day of the Delegation's departure for Georgetown. The Embassy cabled that it had been informed that, in addition to the NBC team from San Francisco, two and perhaps three other journalists from Bay area newspapers might be accompanying Ryan. The Embassy was getting its information on possible press participation from the Peoples Temple, which seemed to have fuller and more accurate information than either the Department or the Embassy. As it turned out a few hours later, a total of nine media representatives arrived on the same airplane with Congressman Ryan all of whom, with the exception of the NBC team, had no Guyanese visas.
>
> There are indications, however, that even the staff members on the Congressional Delegation had been unaware of the extent of media participation in the trip until they boarded the plane in New York. If there was more precise information on media plans available in Congressman Ryan's district office in California, it was not fully shared with the Washington office.

invitations offered to the press by Ryan's California employees and Ryan's own letter written on September 15, 1978, to the other members of his own committee stating his intention to involve the media in the visit.

Garry and I urged Ryan not to confront Jones with a fait accompli. I reminded him that Jim Jones was ill, under medication, and that he would see this effort as a deliberate betrayal of the promises that had been made. Ryan said there was nothing to discuss. "I'm leaving here in fifteen minutes for the airport," he said, "and the only decision for you two to make is whether or not you want to be on the plane with us."

Garry and I asked Ryan if he would at least delay the trip for two hours so that we might return to Lamaha Gardens and tell Jones of the current situation via radio. I added, "You don't want to confront him at the gate. You don't want to surprise him with the press and relatives. That would be a mistake."

Ryan replied, "Well, now you have ten minutes to decide if you want to go. We're leaving then."

Garry, Debbie, Sharon, and I left the room. The lobby was filled with reporters, who immediately surrounded us. Of course they wanted to know the outcome of the meeting. I told them what had happened. And I said I believed that Ryan, by denying Jones an opportunity to learn of the new and threatening plans, was establishing a confrontation at the gate and that I thought he was making a serious error.

As the reporters, especially Don Harris, began to appreciate the logic of our modest request, Jackie Speier appeared on the scene. Javers, later writing of the incident in the lobby, recalled that she said, "You're stalling, Mark, you're stalling. Let's get the show on the road."* I did not understand then what she meant, nor do I now. The issue was resolved when Speier said, "All right you have your two hours. We're leaving from the airport then with you or without you."

We drove back toward the Temple's building in a silence broken only by a suggestion, which found immediate agreement, that Garry and I would talk to Jones as soon as possible. Radio contact was quickly made.

Jones wanted to know the facts. I presented them to him. I tried both to calm him and to tell him who would be visiting Jonestown. He was very much agitated and declared that he would never allow that group into Jonestown. I told him that I understood his feelings, but that there were so many positive aspects of the Jonestown community that it would be

*Ron Javers and Marshall Kilduff, *The Suicide Cult* (New York: Bantam, 1978), p. 146.

worthwhile for the American people to learn of the experiment there, and that if the project could be seen by Americans, flaws and all, there might be genuine sympathy for the struggles of the people in Jonestown. He seemed unimpressed and nervous. I told him that the alternative would be a well-publicized scene of the relatives and the congressman being turned away at the gate and that this might well result in congressional hearings being held by the committee.

Both Charles and I tried to convince him that if he viewed the opening up of the community to the outside world as a positive experience, it would, in fact, become a positive event. Jones kept repeating, "This is terrible. It's terrible." He wanted to know which relatives were going to be on the plane. "Is Stoen going to be on the plane? Is Cobb going to be on the plane?" I told him that we were unable to secure that information.

He asked for my advice. I told him that a decision had to be made and that I was in no position to make it for him. I said that as an attorney, I could tell him only what I already knew. Since he resided on rented private property, the congressional delegation, reporters, and relatives could not enter as a matter of right. If a full-scale investigation by Congress in the future was not a problem, he might want to decide to bar the group. If a fast-breaking news story showing the group being turned away at the gate was a problem for him, perhaps preventing the emigration to the Soviet Union, he might want to admit them.

Garry said that to deny admission to the group would be a "catastrophe." He told Jones that if the group was not allowed in, then he, Garry, might just as well return to San Francisco from Georgetown. Jones seemed frightened of the "stigma" that would be attached to him if the group was turned away and Garry returned with some of them to San Francisco.

Jones began to ramble. He said that "the people"* had taken a tractor to the Port Kaituma airstrip and were going to park it in the middle of a runway so that the airplane could not land. It occurred to me that the airstrip was public property and that Jones was involved in a serious and senseless violation of the law: senseless because Ryan had planned to land at the airstrip only if it was suitable. As an alternative, he was prepared to land at Matthew's Ridge approximately twenty-five miles from Jonestown and cover the rest of the distance by surface transportation. I pointed that out to Jones. He seemed terribly indecisive and I could not guess what his final determination would be. He was about to end our discussion saying that he would think about what to do, when I reminded him that if he

*Jones often referred to spontaneous actions of "the people" when, in most instances, those who undertook the maneuver in question were following his orders.

wished for Garry and me to be on the plane, he would have to decide very soon.

After a pause, Jones said, "All right, you two should be on the plane." Then he added enigmatically, "But the tractor will be blocking the airstrip." I would have been amused if the matter had been less serious. I said, "Listen, Jim, either Charles and I will be on the plane because you plan to let the delegation in and you want us there during the visit or you won't let them in, which is why you may leave the tractor on the airstrip. But it makes no sense to tell us to be on the plane which you won't let land." Jones seemed puzzled. Garry again insisted that the delegation should be allowed to enter. Jones, painfully, reluctantly, and hesitantly, said, "All right, Charles, they can come in. Will you both be with them?" We said we would.

Garry and I were driven to Timehri Airport. We said good-bye to Sharon Amos, not knowing that it would be for the last time. We arrived at the airport after the one-hour ride, a few minutes early. Ryan and his party had not yet made an appearance. They were about twenty minutes late. Grace Stoen was at the airport, as were many of the relatives. All nine journalists boarded the chartered airplane. They were Don Harris, Bob Flick, Bob Brown, and Steve Sung, forming the NBC crew; Charles Krause of the *Washington Post,* Ron Javers of the San Francisco *Chronicle,* Tim Reiterman and Greg Robinson of the San Francisco *Examiner;* and the ubiquitous Gordon Lindsay of the *National Enquirer.* In addition, Neville Annibourne, an official from the Guyanese Ministry of Information, Richard Dwyer of the American embassy, Leo Ryan, Jackie Speier, Charles Garry, and I climbed on board. For reasons unknown to us, Ryan had apparently decided to take Speier into the settlement rather than Schollaert. The four relatives who joined the group were Beverly Oliver, Carol Boyd, Anthony Katsaris, and James Cobb. Cobb, who had an active lawsuit pending against Jones and the Temple and was asking for millions of dollars in damages, was being represented in that suit by Tim Stoen. Katsaris's sister Maria was high in the Jonestown hierarchy. His father, Steven Katsaris, also represented by Stoen, was suing the Temple and Jones in a very substantial action at that time.

On the plane I sat next to Charles Krause of the *Washington Post.* He appeared to be totally uninformed about the facts and even ill-informed of the charges against the Jonestown community.

Many of the charges had been published in magazines and newspapers and many of them were a matter of public record in sworn complaints and affidavits submitted to various courts in lawsuits then pending against the Peoples Temple and Jim Jones. *New West,* the Santa Rosa *Press Democrat,* the San Francisco *Chronicle,* the San Francisco *Examiner,* and various small publications in California had published numerous articles and stories dealing with the horrors of Jonestown. Charles Garry himself had been quoted in the California press as having said that there were guns in Jonestown, and Deborah Blakey, a former leader of the Jonestown community, had talked of the large number of automatic weapons that were there. I believed then, as I believe now, that the *Washington Post* was criminally negligent for sending a reporter to that scene without briefing him about the problems which might lie ahead.

Krause asked me if I thought that all of the people in Jonestown were content to remain there. I told him that I thought that ninety percent of those there would not wish to return home under the present circumstances. He looked at me with concern and asked if I meant that perhaps ten percent were being held there against their wishes. I told him that he was an investigative reporter and that he had the obligation to raise those questions in Jonestown with the people who were there. He said that my tone indicated to him that there were problems ahead and that he was surprised that I was so critical of my own client's cause.

The pilot announced that he could not land the craft at the airstrip in Port Kaituma because the dirt appeared to be too soft and too wet. We circled over Jonestown, and for some reason the pilot changed his mind and decided to attempt a landing. We landed without incident and then found ourselves surrounded by a number of very grim-looking men from Peoples Temple. They were led by Johnny Jones, the adopted son of Jim Jones. One of the men carried a weapon. Later, I learned that the man with the rifle was a Port Kaituma police officer, but since he was dressed in a short-sleeved shirt and slacks, as were the members of the Temple on the airstrip, he appeared to be a member of the Peoples Temple "welcoming team."

Johnny Jones announced in a firm and angry voice that "only Lane and Garry come ahead; the rest stay here." Then to me, Johnny Jones said, "I want you to order those people back onto the plane." I told him that I had never previously ordered a congressman to do anything and reminded him that the airstrip was public property not owned by Peoples Temple. I also said that it was very hot in the plane while it was on the ground. I told Johnny Jones that I believed it would be a terrible error to try to herd the invited guests, albeit reluctantly invited, back onto the plane.

Ryan quickly evaluated the dour and foreboding temper. He did not strenuously object to being left at the airstrip. I told him that I would talk with Jones and as quickly as I could, I would let him know the result.

Garry and I entered a large heavy truck and were driven across the airstrip toward the muddy, deeply rutted road to Jonestown just seven miles away.

10 November 17—Jonestown

We had traveled perhaps one mile on the narrow road to Jonestown when we observed a tractor moving directly toward us as quickly as the condition of the road would permit. The driver brought our vehicle to a halt. A young woman jumped from the tractor just as it was in the process of stopping. She ran toward the truck we occupied and shouted to Johnny Jones, "There are new instructions." By then I recognized her as Harriet Tropp, a young law graduate I had talked with in September. Now, however, her distressed countenance suggested a person involved in a front-line struggle.

Although she knew Garry and me, and was quite warm and modestly friendly in meetings with me two months earlier, now she did not acknowledge our presence. She reached Johnny Jones and said, "Ryan, the people with him, and Dwyer can come with Lane and Garry. No one else."

I said hello to her after she had delivered the message. She gave me a horrified look, said "Hi," and added, "It's goddamn bad. The whole thing."

She jumped upon the running board of the truck and the driver reversed the vehicle a good part of the way back to the airstrip. An intersection, created by a road crossing the one we were laboring on, provided an opportunity for our driver to turn the truck around and drive in forward gear to the airstrip.

I told Leo Ryan that he, Jackie Speier, and Richard Dwyer were invited to join us on the trip into Jonestown. Ryan was hesitant at first; he asked if the reporters could come also. Garry and Tropp both told him that they could not. When Ryan asked me why Jones would not allow the press to enter, I told him that I had not yet talked with Jones and that I would ask him to allow the reporters to visit as soon as I saw him. He seemed resigned, although not satisfied, and together with Speier, at my invitation, entered the cab of the truck. Garry, Dwyer, and I, as well as various members of the Temple climbed onto the bed of the open truck. It was suddenly obvious that Neville Annibourne, the one Guyanese official at the airstrip, was being left there as the truck begun to pull away. The truck was stopped and after a moment of frantic scurrying about, which involved, as I recall, both Harriet Tropp and Johnny Jones, as well as two others, Annibourne was invited to join us in the rear of the truck.

Ryan and Speier, whom I observed in the cab, rode in silence. Annibourne and Dwyer chatted with Garry and me, while the various members of the Temple who shared the truck bed with us remained stonily silent. Johnny Jones glowered. Mike Prokes, the director of public relations for the Temple, seemed nervous and fearful. Harriet Tropp was frenetic.

In contrast with my first visit two months earlier, this journey on the road to Jonestown seemed especially ominous. During that first drive, my hosts had enthusiastically pointed out the endless rows of cassava plants and the lush banana trees that lined the path. The sun had been shining and the Temple people had been outgoing and showed obvious pride in their accomplishments. They had heroically fought and tamed a jungle, clearing acres for their settlement. They had built, with their hands, a school, hospital, meeting halls, wood and metal workshops, and homes for their entire collective. They pumped their own water, generated their own electricity, and for the Amerindians, who were their only neighbors, they regularly dispensed medical assistance and occasionally provided schooling and food. Away from the highly developed society which had denied its advantages to them and others of their color and class, they had created a sanctuary. Now, they quite justifiably sensed that their refuge was about to be invaded for the first time by hostile forces.

Ryan and Speier, bouncing on the lumpy seat in the cab of the huge truck, looking at the miles of a most primitive and almost unusable road ahead, must have sensed the growing tension and the white-hot anger of those who were compelled, through threats and intimidation, to be their hosts. At the same time, they probably felt that although they were on an uncomfortable mission, its results would provide both truth and liberation. To each group, the other must have seemed an alien and hostile force.

I spoke to Johnny Jones and Prokes. "Why don't you tell Ryan about how this road was built? Tell him what's growing there." Johnny Jones answered, "Fuck him. We don't want him here." I said that I understood his feelings, but since the decision had been made to permit the congressional visit, we were obliged to make it as positive an experience as possible. Johnny shrugged and looked away. A moment later he climbed from the truck bed onto the running board on the passenger side and began to brief

Ryan and Speier. He was businesslike. He shouted over the sounds of the huge, laboring engine which seemed to reverberate his anger.

As we rounded a curve and neared the settlement, we saw a trailer in the center of the roadway. A wheel had been removed from the conveyance and it sprawled across our path like a lame and abandoned creature. The truck came to a stop. The silence was broken by Charles Garry, who said, "Johnny, if I didn't know better I would say that that thing was put there on purpose." At his words, the old silence—created by the thoughts of men and women who wondered at the meaning of the obstacle and what was to follow—that old silence died, and a new, awkward moment came into being.

In time the carrier was dragged away, and our little party began to move slowly ahead until we reached the first buildings of Jonestown. A small delegation stood together there to greet us. I climbed out of the truck bed by stepping first onto one of the truck's massive tires, then down to the slippery red mud in the road. Marceline Jones and I hugged each other, and then I introduced her to Leo Ryan and Jackie Speier. She was, as always, outgoing, and possessed of an apparent dignity and inner beauty. Jim Jones was nowhere to be seen. Gene Chaikin also was absent. Marcie said, "Welcome, Congressman Ryan. We're glad that you're here," adding, "I hope you will be comfortable here after that dreadful trip. It's almost impossible to improve that road because of the torrential rain."

Speier remained reserved. Ryan, in response to Marcie's warmth, seemed to relax and become somewhat affable.

As we walked together toward the center of the village, Marcie said, "Congressman, I would like you to see our school and our nursery and our health center. We're really proud of our medical facilities. I'm a registered nurse and I'd like you to see how we try to care for the health problems of our seniors."

Ryan had previously told the press that he was not going to settle for "a two-dollar warden's tour" and that he was going to insist upon carrying out the investigation in his own manner. He declined Marcie's offer with grace, saying that he would like to see the facilities she spoke of "a little later." As for his present intentions, he said, "Now I want to talk to a few people. I have their names here," he said, indicating an attaché case which he carried. His terms were simply and bluntly stated. He wanted to be alone with each person whose name he would submit. He asked for a place, an office, where with his aide he could meet privately with individual residents.

Marcie led them toward the pavilion, a large open building comprised of a roof held up by timbers. There were no walls but there were chairs, tables, and, in two places, raised platforms. Ryan and Speier sat down at a table which had been placed on one of the platforms. Marcie offered them coffee and soft drinks and talked with them.

I asked Johnny Jones where his father was, saying that I wished to speak with him. He answered, "Dad is not well. He's sick. He's in his cabin." Then he led me to the little wooden building which served as the communications center. A moment later, Mike Carter handed the telephone to me, and Jim Jones, who was in his cabin, began our conversation by saying, "This is just terrible. It is a terrible thing. We're being invaded. They're trying to create an incident to keep us from moving to Russia."

I assured him that I did not think that that was Congressman Ryan's intention, but that even if it were, as long as we were all calm, relaxed, and open, there need be no incident. Jones said, "Wait till you talk to Tim Carter. He'll tell you what Stoen is planning." I told him that the relatives and the news media were being kept waiting in the hot sun at the airstrip. He said, "You don't know Stoen like I do. This is to destroy us. He's behind the whole thing. Mark, this is the stigma they're going to attach to us so that we can't go to Russia. I've worked my whole life for these people—now look at what they're doing to us. It's terrible, Mark. It's terrible."

When I tried to reassure him about Ryan's intentions, he said, "You don't know, Mark. My God, they lied to you about everything. About the damn reporters not coming. And now the relatives. They're coming to destroy us and we just let them come in."

Since he had led our conversation back to the reporters and relatives, I pursued the matter. "Jim, you will have to decide about them fairly soon. It's hot and they have no shelter there." He said, "You mean you want all of them in here?" I told him that I believed that since the matter was to be decided sooner or later, in any event, it would be wise to make that determination now. He asked, "What do you think we should do? You are the only one I trust. Garry is such a goddamned fool. What do you think?" I said that some of the reporters appeared to be fair. Regarding the relatives, I said, "I think relatives should always be welcome at Jonestown to see the members of their family."

Jones said, "You don't know what they are planning. They want to destroy us. That's Stoen's plan. He's behind the whole thing. Talk to Tim Carter. He'll tell you about it." I told Jones that Gordon Lindsay, the journalist for the *National Enquirer,* had been on the airplane and was at the airstrip. I advised against inviting him to Jonestown. I suggested that the other reporters and the four relatives be admitted. I saw Lindsay's presence as a provocation which might endanger him. Although no Temple member had ever spoken in my presence of committing an act of violence against Lindsay or anyone else, the fact that there was a general distrust of the media was very apparent; so was the fact that Lindsay was particularly despised by many of the Jonestown residents.

Jones sighed and said, "All right, Mark, if you say so. Tell Johnny to send the truck for them." I suggested that he talk directly to Johnny instead. He agreed and then said, "Well, you had better put Garry on so that I can talk with him, too." I have no doubt that Jones also told Garry that he trusted only him and wanted to secure his invaluable advice.

After Garry spoke for a minute or two with Jones, he handed the telephone to Johnny, who listened silently but impatiently and with a controlled but visible rage. Johnny most reluctantly agreed to follow his father's instructions. However, he delayed sufficiently so that the truck was not dispatched for some time. Eventually, the skies darkened and a brief torrential rainstorm struck. Johnny Jones and Jack Beam laughed when the sudden storm hit. Beam said, "I hope those bastards on the truck get drenched." Johnny Jones replied, "I hope their cameras are ruined."

Meanwhile, Harriet Tropp had agreed to assist Ryan in his efforts to locate residents to be interviewed. He had handed her a small piece of paper with five lines of names written down it. Two of the lines contained two names; the rest had one each. Harriet left Ryan and Speier, who were planning to interview the residents in private, and walked out of the pavilion toward the small boardwalk which led to the residential cabins and larger living quarters. At the exit from the community meeting room, she stopped and showed the list to several of us who were standing there. I noticed that the last name on the list was Gene Chaikin.

Harriet was tense and, as she looked up from the list, she flashed a nervous smile and said, "There are no problems here." I was gratified to hear her comment, because I had been wondering about Gene's whereabouts as well. I also wondered who might, in her mind, constitute a problem. Joined by a few other trusted Temple aides, she went off to find the seven residents.

While waiting for the first listed resident to arrive, Leo Ryan talked casually with those who were in the vicinity. His demeanor by now was becoming informal and open. He had seemed a trifle reserved and cautious at first, in what for him was a new and very different setting. In a short while, he began to relax. This was even more apparent after the reporters had arrived; Ryan remained affable and his approach was decidedly nonthreatening.

After Ryan indicated that he and Speier had completed interviewing those whose names appeared on the list, he withdrew from his case yet another list, with several more names. The Temple leadership watched apprehensively. Ryan must have reasoned that he was not breaking new ground, but merely following in the footsteps of Richard McCoy, the former American Consul in Guyana, and the other American officials who had advised him that they too had conducted private interviews in Jonestown. However, since McCoy always furnished the names of those he wished to see well in advance of his visit, each prospective interviewer could be, and in fact was, subjected to a series of drills in which the necessity of providing appropriate answers was stressed. In addition, many of McCoy's interviews were conducted in the presence of those who were loyal to Jim Jones.

If Leo Ryan and Jackie Speier felt that they were repeating a time-honored tradition, the Jonestown leadership knew otherwise. By reaching into his case and extracting a second list, Ryan was actually exacerbating the fear and near-hysteria of the leadership. Any observer could have easily determined that something new and very threatening was transpiring, yet Ryan continued to obtrude as no other person had done in the compendious history of the community. Obviously, the obscurant evidence given to Ryan by stateside bureaucrats meeting with him in Washington, D.C., almost on the eve of his departure, had altered Ryan's initial perception of Jonestown, for he pushed on ahead, asking for additional residents to interview, seemingly without fear of any consequences. I watched as the fear grew among the leaders, and I wondered where Gene Chaikin was and why Ryan seemed satisfied that his first list had been fully exhausted when Chaikin had not appeared.

Long after the massacre, that mystery was solved for me, but from its resolution grew another enigma. According to Ray Chaikin, Gene's brother, when Ryan was informed that Gene was too ill to be interviewed at the open pavilion, the congressman asked Dwyer to visit him at the medical unit. Dwyer interviewed him there and reported to Ryan, and later to Ray Chaikin, that Gene had no complaints to make to him. I now believe that Chaikin had been placed on tranquilizers in preparation for the Ryan visit and maintained as a possible dissident in the intensive care unit.

Ryan kept producing more names. Those who were sought were found and interviewed and almost all of them gave favorable accounts of life in the community. Some gave grand and glowing reports.

Early in the evening, the truck that had gone to the airstrip to pick up the rest of our party, returned to the community, sliding through the mud, bouncing from rut to rut. The drenched reporters and the four relatives disembarked from the truck. Some of the newsmen began unloading video equipment. Don Harris, smiling as he bounded from the truck, seemed in good spirits, as if challenged by the adversity. He walked over to me and said, "Thanks, I'm sure you're the one who got us in." I said, "Welcome to Jonestown, Don, and take it easy here. You can cut the tension with a knife, so please let's have no Mike Wallace interviews." He smiled and said, "You know I'm fair. I'm going to edit it all myself." I explained that I was less interested in the finished product and more concerned about a hostile interview which could provoke an incident. Don smiled, held up his right hand, and said, "I promise."

Marcie greeted the newcomers and invited them to dinner at the main pavilion (which served as Jonestown's community center) where Jim Jones stood waiting. The *Washington Post* reporter, Charles Krause, later wrote, "I noted immediately that, contrary to what the Concerned Relatives had told us, nobody seemed to be starving. Indeed, everyone seemed quite healthy." Krause said that his first impression was that "considering everything, this little place was pleasant. I could see how someone might want to live here."*

Ron Javers, the reporter from the San Francisco *Chronicle,* recalled the dinner.† "They offered us coffee, and later we were given a dinner of barbecued pork, collard greens, potato salad, and coffee."

Javers conceded that "an excellent rock band performed for us" and that "the show was lively and entertaining." He added, "The emotional content was thick and heavy—and unreal. We watched, but we were isolated from the rest of the audience. It seemed forced and unnatural for elderly people, many of them middle-class whites, to be stamping their feet, yelling and clapping their hands to music that only a younger generation could understand." Javers concluded, "I thought they might be under orders to be enthusiastic."

He continued, "Then several young Jonestown men and women and a comedienne, an old woman they called Jonestown's Moms Mabley, sang for us. All of them were surprisingly first rate." If the music and humor so blended to create a beautiful and entertaining program, as indeed was the case, why was Javers so surprised that others might respond to it? Why was he surprised, in fact, that the artists, almost all of whom were black, one of whom was Korean, would be, as he put it, "first rate?" Why did Javers feel "isolated" from the audience when he was seated at a table in the midst

*Charles Krause, *Guyana Massacre,* with exclusive material by Lawrence M. Stern, Richard Harwood, and the staff of the *Washington Post* (Washington, D.C.: A Washington Post Book, 1978), p. 41.
†Javers and Kilduff, *Suicide Cult,* pp. 152, 153.

of the group? And who were those "many" elderly middle-aged whites who he observed acting as if they were black, of a different class, and younger? Of the more than one thousand people who filled the open air pavilion and overflowed onto the boardwalks and meadows, I do not believe that ten could be so described.

The emotional baggage that Krause brought with him to Guyana made him particularly unfit for the assignment. He was, however, unburdened by any factual data. After the event, he wrote that on November 13, the *Washington Post*'s foreign editor, Peter Osnos, had assigned him to the story. He said "Osnos, like me, knew nothing about Jones."* Krause also spoke of the terrors of his first experience in Guyana.† It took place at the airport, where, he wrote, "I promised myself that the *Washington Post* is not going to spend the night in a crummy airport." When he was, as he wrote, "free at last," he journeyed into the capital city, "But I did learn," he wrote, "that it's not safe to walk the streets of Georgetown, day or night." He had discovered, through research done on the spot, that "thieves, using a technique they call 'choke and rob' and I call mugging, were all over the city, waiting to steal rings, watches, money, or anything else of value."

Krause reported that upon his arrival in Jonestown, "there to greet us as we got off the dump truck was the white Mizzuz [sic], Marceline Jones."‡ Krause had worked as the *Washington Post*'s South American correspondent for eight months, but his racism is unmistakable and classically illustrated by his fear of attack by the black and East Indian population (whom he refers to as muggers), night or day, in the lovely and friendly city of Georgetown. As Krause walked into the Temple village, he was greeted by Tim Carter, who introduced himself and then, according to Krause, smiled and said, "Mark Lane told us about you. He said the reporter from the *Post* seemed sensitive and fair. It's good to have you here." No further comment need be made upon my judgment, as no defense seems tenable.

During dinner and the entertainment, Ryan and Speier remained seated near one of the far sides of the pavilion, continuing to interview residents one at a time. Many of the reporters crowded near Jim Jones and engaged him in conversation. Garry sat two seats from Jones and participated in the talks. I chose a place at a table perhaps twenty-five feet removed from the head table at which Jones, a few of the reporters, and Garry were ensconced. I wanted the reporters to hear Jones answer their questions, and

*Krause, *Guyana Massacre*, p. 3.
†Ibid., p. 14.
‡Ibid., p. 14.

I did not wish for my silence during those talks to be considered agreement with Jones. Accordingly, I did not hear the exchange. Nevertheless, Krause wrote that "Jones, who was talking to the other reporters, was flanked by his lawyers."*

I noticed, and was mildly disturbed by, the absence of Don Harris during substantial portions of the evening. I knew him to be an inventive and creative reporter and I presumed he was prowling about somewhere in search of a story that those who were dining, talking with Jones, or watching the show were likely to miss. I hoped that his unorthodox actions would not create an incident. Later, he returned and directed the filming of some of the artists who were performing.

At one point, I went over to Jim Jones and suggested that it might be appropriate for him to introduce Leo Ryan to the group formally, welcome him publicly, and perhaps invite him to say a few words. Jones thought for a moment and then agreed that this would be a good idea. However, he asked me if I would request Marcie to introduce the congressman, saying that he did not feel well enough to handle the chore. In view of subsequent events, I would later reflect upon what seemed at this time to be an inexplicable response, for Jones did not retire. I would wonder later if Jones was even then contemplating the possibility of mass murder, to be ignited by the murder of Ryan. Perhaps he was reluctant to say a kind or welcoming word about the man he would soon condemn to death and berate publicly, for fear of compromising his subsequent stance. Jones surely knew that if he did decide that a massacre was the solution, his wife Marcie would try to oppose that decision by rallying forces of sanity in opposition. It is very possible that Jones thought that if it were Marcie who was openly welcoming Leo Ryan, this action would tend to negate her credibility later, if she had to oppose his decision for death. After months of research, reflection, and study, it still seems unlikely that I will ever completely understand what was operating at that moment in the mind of Jim Jones. And since that moment occurred during only our second meeting, I understood even less during that evening in November than I do now.

About midway through the formal program, Marcie offered a mellow welcome to Ryan, who rose and walked forward to cheers of the audience.

He spoke briefly, stating that he had come to look into charges that had been made. Tape recorders registered his words, reporters jotted them down. The NBC-TV team video-taped his entire speech. In the book written by Javers and Kilduff† from the San Francisco *Chronicle,* Ryan was re-

*Krause, *Guyana Massacre,* p. 46.
†Javers and Kilduff, *The Suicide Cult,* pp. 153–155.

ported to have said "I am sure there are *some* people here this evening who *believe* this is the best thing that ever happened to them in their whole life." (Emphasis added.) Krause, in his book, asserted that Ryan said ". . . there are *some* people who *believe* this is the best thing that ever happened in their whole lives."* (Emphasis added.)

The "Report of a Staff Investigative Group to the Committee on Foreign Affairs" quoted, I believe with accuracy, the words that Ryan spoke. "For some of you, for a *lot* of you that I talked to, Jonestown *is* the best thing that ever happened to you in your lives." (Emphasis added.)

Two great American newspapers, one on the East Coast and one on the West Coast, managed to come up with basically the same quotation, but although each had a reporter present jotting down Ryan's words as they were spoken, each, in the retelling of the incident, substantially reduced the impact of his words and meaning.

Kilduff and Javers reported that there was an ovation for "three solid minutes."† Krause and his team, being a part of the *liberal* establishment, more liberally wrote, "The crowd cheered for nearly twenty minutes."‡ Javers was right. Krause may have been distracted, looking about for the local "choke-and-rob" squad.

Ryan responded with laughter and smiles and allowed as how he was sorry that all of the folks in Jonestown could not vote in San Mateo. There was an additional round of applause following that remark, and the entertainment resumed.

Following dinner and the performances, as the group began to melt into the darkness, I walked toward Jackie Speier and asked if she had enjoyed the evening's festivities. She said, "Yes. They've got a lot of rhythm." I immediately regretted having talked to her and hoped that her answer had not been overheard. However, Diane Wilkinson had caught Speier's response. As she walked by, Wilkinson froze and turned with a look of disbelief toward Speier, a look which soon transformed itself to one of hatred. I thought how humiliating it must be for the black people of Jonestown to be evaluated as objects by Krause and Speier and Javers, the people from whom they had fled.

Johnny Jones arrived with word that the truck was ready to take the reporters and the relatives to Port Kaituma to spend the night. It would be dispatched, he said, to pick them up in the morning. Harriet Tropp said that arrangements had been made so that Congressman Ryan, Jackie Speier,

*Krause, *Guyana Massacre,* pp. 45–49.
†Javers and Kilduff, *The Suicide Cult,* pp. 153–155.
‡Krause, *Guyana Massacre,* pp. 45–49.

Neville Annibourne, Charles, and I could sleep at Jonestown. Javers reported the matter in this fashion: "We are told we would have to get out. Ryan and the two lawyers could spend the night at Jonestown, but we were informed there was no room for us in the entire settlement."* Harriet had mentioned Speier and Annibourne, even though Javers had not. Javers continued:

> We argued. We wanted to lay out our sleeping bags in the empty pavilion or on the ground outside it. Anywhere. But this was impossible, we were told. The Peoples Temple had reserved space for us at the home of a man named Mike who ran a discotheque in Port Kaituma. We would be picked up at 8:30 the following morning to continue our visit.
>
> There was nothing we could do. We climbed into the truck and arrived at Mike's house at midnight. The women in the group were offered the bedroom, and the men were told they could sleep in the living room and on the kitchen floor.†

The suggestion that they might sleep on the ground was not made in my presence. If it was offered at all, it could hardly have been taken seriously. No one sleeps on the ground near the bush if there is any possible and less dangerous alternative. The Amerindians build their simple huts on stilts off the ground out of respect for the animals in this area. Can one believe that Charles Krause, afraid to walk in Georgetown at high noon, would face the perils of the night on the jungle floor?

Javers continued to discuss the discomforts imposed upon him:

> The press retired to the disco, a corrugated-tin-roof affair with a small, rickety record player and five or six reggae records. The walls were painted with iridescent paint and slogans like "Hey-O, Baby," "Soul Time," and "Play That Music."
>
> We drank some beer out on the patio and talked. We were deeply discouraged.‡

Why were the reporters deeply discouraged? They had come thousands of miles, ostensibly to learn the truth and liberate those in need of their help. Yet as the first day passed, their primary concern and the one issue upon which they took a stand revolved around their own material comforts.

*Javers and Kilduff, *The Suicide Cult,* p. 154.
†Ibid.
‡Ibid.

Krause also devoted almost three full pages of his article-length paperback to a discussion of the problems with the sleeping accommodations. He writes:

> The lights were turned on and Jones, obviously tired and ill, asked if our lodgings had been arranged. One of his aides assured him that the reporters and relatives in our party had arranged to spend the night at Port Kaituma, that there was a dance we wanted to go to in town.
>
> I was infuriated. No arrangements of any kind had been made. I told Jones that he had no obligation to put us up for the night, but it simply wasn't true that we had a place to sleep.*

Krause continues with his complaints,

> It bothered me that after an earlier display of ostentatious hospitality, Jones was now sending us out in the dump truck in the middle of the night. But I said nothing more to him.†

But he did say a great deal more about where he wished to spend the night in discussions with Richard Tropp, Harriet Tropp, and me.

I had previously urged Ryan's office to postpone the trip for several reasons, among them that it would take time to make appropriate arrangements for food and shelter for the guests. This request, oft repeated, was rejected by Schollaert on Ryan's behalf. The Jonestown community was told that a maximum of four people would visit there: two members of Congress and two aides. Instead, sixteen arrived, including reporters and relatives, whom Ryan's office had specifically said would not accompany the delegation once it left Georgetown.

Special arrangements were made to provide some comfort for the delegation. Congressman Ryan was given a room at East House. In the past, a fifteen-member team of a Guyanese women's organization had visited the community and shared that relatively small and very crowded room without complaint. The press came, uninvited, bullying their way into the project behind the open threats that Ryan had uttered and which they were prepared to exploit. Then they bitterly expressed their deep disappointment and their fury that the last-minute accommodations were not up to their standards.

When the social aspect of the evening ended, Don Harris walked over to

*Krause, *Guyana Massacre,* p. 48.
†Ibid., p. 49.

me to say goodnight. I asked him where he was going. He said "We've got some plans at Port Kaituma. A dance at a disco. Do you want to join us?" I declined, saying I was tired and that I wanted to talk to Jones and Garry that evening. I asked Harris where he was going to spend the night. He winked, then smiled, and said that he had made plans.

When Krause heard Johnny Jones's report that the truck was ready to take the reporters to Port Kaituma, he began a campaign to reserve a room at Jonestown. He appealed to me. I asked Marcie Jones where the reporters were to go. She said that Don Harris had told her that arrangements had been made in Kaituma. Krause said that he had not agreed to go there and had not been informed that he would have to leave. I walked over to Don, who was packing up the video equipment in order to carry it to the truck. I told him about Krause's complaints and asked for his advice and guidance.

He said, "That little prick is so unready for this story, I can't believe it. On the truck coming in here, I pointed out the cassava growing in the cleared area and he said, 'What part of it do you eat?' The staff of life in Latin America, he's the *Post*'s South American correspondent, and yet he's never heard of cassava. Pay no attention to him. Nobody else does."

As I moved back to him, Krause was already appealing to Marcie Jones and Harriet Tropp. Finally, realizing that all of the other reporters and visiting relatives were climbing onto the truck, Krause left the pavilion. I asked Marcie if she could find a bed for him at Jonestown. I said, "He's just going to cry about this for days and be a pain tomorrow otherwise." She agreed to find a place for him. Harriet and I walked quickly toward the truck and called out to Krause. We said that he could stay. The other reporters called to him from the bed of the truck. Although he obviously wanted to remain in Jonestown, the jeers of the other reporters were just too much for him. He said, "Well, thanks, but I'd better go with them. What will they think if I stay here now?" With that he waded through the mud to the waiting truck.

The anger that Krause and one or two other reporters had generated with their personal demands was resounding among the Jonestown residents in the pavilion when I returned there. Later, every bed and almost every square foot of cabin space had been utilized to capacity. Seniors doubled up in narrow bunks so that the guests who remained might be adequately housed. Garry and I slept on canvas cots in a tiny office.

Jones said to me when I reached the pavilion, "They won't be satisfied. Don't you see that, Mark? We can't do anything to satisfy them. They want to destroy us."

I said that I knew he was tired, ill, and under a severe strain, and I was sorry that he had to go through this. However, I added, "They are not out to destroy Jonestown. They are just competing with each other for a story." While I was offering those assurances to Jones in an attempt to pacify him, Javers later would write of that moment: "We [the reporters at Port Kaituma] were all highly competitive by nature, but we had decided by this time that we were competing with Jones, not with each other."

Still later, other reporters would charge that Jones was paranoid, offering as proof Jones's protest that there was a media conspiracy or agreement to expose or harm him and his organization.

After the media left, we sat around a long wooden table near the center of the pavilion, Jones, Garry, Jack Beam, Harriet Tropp, Tim Carter, Mike Prokes, Jim McElvane, Carolyn Layton, Johnny Jones, myself, and one or two others. Speaking to Carter, Jones said wearily, rubbing his eyes, "Tell them what Stoen told you. That son of a bitch. Tell them what he's said he's going to do to us." Our heads turned toward Tim Carter.

Carter said, "During the first week in November I went to the so-called Human Freedom Center in Berkeley to see if I could find Terri Buford. That was my only reason for going there. I said I was a defector from the Temple."

When Carter was asked who he saw at the meeting he said, "There were just three people there besides me. Stoen and Elmer and Deanna Mertle."

Carter told us that Stoen had outlined his strategy to destroy the Peoples Temple. He said, "Stoen announced that they had arranged for Ryan to lead an investigation into Jonestown. He said that one of Ryan's relatives had joined a cult and that Ryan was very upset by it. Stoen said that, therefore, Ryan was a 'good guy' to investigate Peoples Temple because he had a 'special interest' in the project. In fact Stoen told me that his wife, Grace, was then in Washington, D.C., meeting with Ryan and the State Department."

Carter then outlined the Stoen plan to destroy the Temple and Jonestown. He said "The plan Stoen presented and Deanna Mertle agreed with was what they called a 'no-win' strategy from the Temple's viewpoint. Stoen said that Ryan was going to take the news media with him to Jonestown. If they were turned away at the gate, it would be a big media event, and they would launch a media blitz. Stoen said the reporters had all been briefed by him and that they were ready. If Ryan and the media were allowed in, Stoen said, 'We can get at least one person to defect for sure.' Stoen estimated that ten people would leave with Ryan and the press. He said, 'We can use them for a big media event. A real exposé of Jonestown. It's a media blitz either way, and either way we can do a great deal of damage to the Temple.' Stoen made it clear that they were working closely with the reporters. They knew which reporters were going to Jonestown, and they were meeting with them."

Carter continued, "This trip to Jonestown is expected to be just the first one. Stoen said they are planning another trip which will be 'even bigger.' He made it very plain that the Ryan trip was part of a whole campaign to destroy the Temple. This is their whole life. This is their entire commitment."

Jones sat through the meeting in despair. On occasion he sighed and interjected a comment. He said, "You see. They're going to destroy us. We are in a no-win situation." Toward the end of the meeting he said, "How can I be sure that one person won't leave and betray us?"

After the meeting I tried to reassure him. I said that Stoen's strategy was obviously meant to upset him. He said, "Mark, while you were telling me that Ryan was not going to bring the press in here, Stoen was planning the whole thing. It's terrible." Jones walked off toward his cabin.

Later I talked with Tim Carter alone, who told me, "Stoen kept insisting through the meeting that they could count on Jim's overreacting. He said, 'Jim Jones will overreact. We can count on it. We can base strategy on it.' "

11 November 18—Jonestown

The sun was warm and fine, the hearty breakfast far more than adequate, and the coffee hot and rich. In any other community, these factors, once combined, would have created a pleasant morning. In Jonestown, a sense of foreboding hung heavy over the settlement. The anger of those in the Temple's leadership was carried in their posture, in their stride, in their voices, and in their faces. They spoke not only of the invasion of their home but of the rudeness of the strangers, who, seemingly unsatisfied with the dinner and the entertainment, were infuriated and petulant that not enough elderly people had doubled up with others to provide beds for all of the visitors. A few reporters had not even expressed their gratitude for the meal before they began to make their demands for special sleeping accommodations.

Rumblings were reaching deep into the community as well. Ryan was not disliked, for he was likable and warm. But the all-white media invasion he led had left an indelible enmity. Don Harris had assured me, in response to my request, that he would videotape no one without securing permission from the subject. The night before, as the NBC crew lit the pavilion with its searing lights, the camera focused upon a couple who asked not to be photographed. The cameraman persisted, and when I asked him to desist, he continued, and without even looking up, he said, "Don't talk to me. I'm working. Talk to the director." I quickly sought out Don Harris; he intervened, apologized, and promised that it would not happen again. But it had happened already.

Diane Wilkinson, who was not in the Jonestown hierarchy, had told a number of other young and militant blacks of Speier's gaffe, and as Speier walked by, they turned away.

Krause, and the most arrogant among his companions, had accomplished what Jones was no longer able to achieve: They had created a fragile unity of Temple members behind Jones in opposition to the media.

I was told that morning by an elderly black woman that Jackie Speier was "sticking her nose into our kitchen and what do you think about that, Mark?" I smiled and said that she was doing her job and that if the people had been starving, they would be pleased to know that someone cared. Several people seemed upset about Speier's aggressive inquiry, particularly Harriet Tropp, and others asked why she was there. Harriet said that she had been informed that Ryan was bringing "a man named Schollaert from the congressional committee." She asked why Schollaert, who had been transported at government expense from Washington, D.C., to New York City to Georgetown, Guyana, and put up in the most expensive hotel in the country for several days, had not even bothered to visit Jonestown. I said weakly that there were only eighteen seats on the plane, which prompted the next question. Harriet asked, "Then why did he bring that bitch instead?"

The report to the House Committee on Foreign Affairs raised, but did not answer, a similar question. The report noted that "Miss Jackie Speier, of Mr. Ryan's personal staff" was part of the delegation and that unlike Ryan and Schollaert and the other members of the delegation, her "expenses were not paid for by the U.S. Government."* The report did not disclose who did pay her expenses or why she, rather than Schollaert, accompanied Ryan into Jonestown.

When the reporters arrived, Marceline told them that a breakfast of pancakes and coffee had been prepared for them. Krause wrote, "That raised my spirits briefly. But Don Harris and the other newsmen vetoed breakfast."†

Krause reported that the reporters had been told that Jones was sick "and we might not see him that day. Don Harris vehemently protested, and demanded of Lane that Jones appear for a filmed interview." In actuality, Don walked over to me and said, "Mark, I found out something last night that you must hear. I can't tell you now, but be sure that before I leave, no matter how hectic it gets, that you talk with me. I think you'll want to leave with us." I said that I would remind him before he left. He made no mention to me that Jones was reported to be sick and he did not demand an interview vehemently or in any other manner. Jones, mean-

**U.S. House of Representatives Report*, p. 2.
†Krause, *Guyana Massacre*, pp. 65–68.

while, was sitting in a chair toward the center of the pavilion.

Hours later, as the visit neared its conclusion, Don Harris found me chatting with Ryan. He said, "Mark, I got to get Jones on tape. Do you think you can arrange it?" His tone was neither demanding, nor vehement; he adopted a mock, somewhat overstated, imploring manner.

Marceline led the reporters to the day-care nursery and later to a classroom for disabled children. She was a registered nurse, and she said that "here in Jonestown, we can care for each child individually. In California, when I was a state hospital inspector, it was not possible."

Krause wrote that "All of us were getting a little restless about Marceline's guided tour." He decided, he said, to "go off on my own to look for places where people actually lived." It turned out his decision was to invade the private residences without asking for permission to do so. He observed three buildings which he thought to be, he said, "residential dormitories."* He approached one with a sign reading "Jane Pittman Gardens." He no doubt presumed from the name on the sign and from the fact that senior women outnumbered the men in Jonestown by overwhelming numbers that he was advancing upon a residence for elderly women. He reported his conduct: "As I got closer to Pittman Gardens, I could hear muffled coughs from inside. I knocked on the back door and no one answered. I tried to pull back a shutter for a look inside but someone inside was holding on to it."† Had this event occurred in the United States, Krause might have been charged with an attempted burglary, robbery, or breaking and entering. Perhaps a lenient officer might have, under the circumstances, merely booked him as a Peeping Tom. Knowing that women were inside and that they declined to welcome him, he had sought to force open a shutter and peek inside. Had some black person approached his house in America in a similar fashion, one can hardly imagine what his response might have been.

He continued his attempt to gain entrance by trying the front door. Krause continues with his narrative:

> A young woman walking by came over and asked what I was doing. I told her I was curious about the dormitory and would like to see the inside. She said people might be resting but that she would find out. She told me to wait on the front porch while she went to the back. That seemed curious.‡

*Krause, *Guyana Massacre*, pp. 66–67.
†Ibid.
‡Krause, *Guyana Massacre*, p. 67.

Why it was curious to Krause is curious to me. A man was asked to wait outside of a woman's dormitory while a woman inquired of resting women if they wanted a man to enter what was their large, shared bedroom. Krause reported the next event:

> It was no surprise to me when she came back and said the people inside didn't want visitors. I smiled and she suggested that I go back to the main pavilion. She said she was sure I understood and I didn't answer. What I was thinking was that I had probably stumbled onto a warehouse for people the commune wanted kept out of sight, maybe people who had been tortured, beaten, or otherwise abused, as the Concerned Relatives had claimed.*

What evidence Krause evaluated that would make him conclude that "probably" the dormitory, now transformed into a warehouse containing recalcitrants, perhaps tortured and beaten or even "otherwise abused," is not apparent.

I was, at that moment, not far from the pavilion, answering a question from some of the younger men and women about the assassination of Dr. King. A woman ran toward me and said, "The reporters claim that people are being held at gunpoint at the Pittman Gardens." I rushed toward the dormitory to witness another confrontation that Krause was instrumental in building. Krause wrote of the event,

> I returned to the pavilion and told the other reporters there that we had to go back to Jane Pittman Gardens to find out what was going on there. Sarah [Harriet] Tropp, my friend of the night before, suddenly became very angry and said I had no right to invade the privacy of people in Jonestown.†

Krause reported that Mike Prokes

> [Agreed] to go back and see if whoever was at Jane Pittman Gardens would let us inspect the building. All the newsmen, including the NBC crew, came along with Prokes. He identified himself, knocked on the door and it was opened by a frail black woman who looked to be at least 70.‡

*Ibid.
†Ibid.
‡Krause, *Guyana Massacre*, p. 67.

She said that the people did not want to meet the press and closed the door. While Prokes felt the matter had been resolved, Krause elegantly dissented. Or as he himself put it, "Prokes said this proved that the people inside wanted no visitors. I said 'Bullshit.'"* The discussion had continued for a short time before I arrived at the building. Moments later, I saw Garry there also. Krause has written:

> While we argued, Mark Lane and Charles Garry showed up, saying we could go in the building immediately. No one had asked the people inside but we entered anyway.†

His account is at this point almost entirely inaccurate. Each of the other reporters who was present can substantiate the history of that possibly decisive encounter.

When I arrived at the dormitory, Johnny Jones was standing with his back against the front entrance to the building. He was directly confronting the reporters, some of whom were standing below the narrow deck which was contiguous to the large shelter, while Krause was still on the platform. I asked Jones, who was clearly very angry, what the issue was. He pointed to Krause and said that he had been trying to force his way into the building where some of the senior women were sleeping and probably not dressed. Krause said, "We were told we could go anywhere we wanted."

The reporters may have been told by Ryan, Dwyer, or even those associated with the Jonestown community that they would not be restricted to a guided tour and that they would be free to look about. Yet even if such assurances had been given to the unwanted and uninvited guests, the invasion of a women's dormitory, over the objection of the women who were occupying it and resting, could not have been contemplated as an exercise in reportorial propriety.

Krause later wrote that "I was the only journalist aboard who was not based in California," that "the others were a fraternity apart," and that "I was the outsider."‡ It seemed at that moment that Krause was attempting to force his way into the club from which he felt excluded and to demonstrate through personal pique, which perhaps he confused with perseverance and perception, that he too could uncover a serious problem in Jonestown. The conflict which Krause had developed was viewed as a deliberate provocation by Johnny Jones and others associated with the leadership.

*Ibid., p. 68
†Ibid.
‡Ibid., pp. 4, 5.

Jones said, "These are people's homes; you have no right to insist upon looking into their homes and interviewing them if they do not wish to see you."

Krause, who has a low-key manner, remained at the door, stating that he wanted to talk to the residents. Johnny Jones was vehement in condemning the media for insensitively probing into private homes where they were not invited. I explained his position to the media, and the media's position to him, in an effort to alleviate the strain.

At that point, Tim Reiterman of the San Francisco *Examiner* made a suggestion. He asked Jones if the people would object to "Mark asking them if they want to talk to us." Jones remained silent. Rieterman said, "If Mark tells us that there is no problem and the people don't want to see us, I'll be satisfied." Jones looked at me. I said nothing. Jones paused for a moment and said, "Okay." I knocked at the door and a woman's voice said, "Go away." I identified myself and asked if I could come in for a moment. A woman's voice said, "Of course, Mark, you're always welcome."

Many elderly black women were lying in bed; some were sewing, some were resting. I walked around the room and asked each of those present if she wanted to talk to the news media and each declined. Some said, "Why don't they just leave us alone?" Or, "Why can't they let us rest on a Saturday afternoon?" Some of the women were not fully dressed, just covered with light sheets. There were no weapons and there were no keepers. None bore the signs of having been tortured or beaten. Most seemed resentful that their privacy was being invaded and that their home was being laid siege to by a pack of reporters. The newsmen continued to argue loudly under their windows after one of them had tried to force his way into the building and was asked to leave after he had tried to rip open a shutter to stare at them. "We're not animals, Mark, and this is no zoo, don't they know that?" a soft-spoken elderly woman said to me. I apologized for the intrusion and said good-bye.

In a sentence or two, I told Reiterman, in the presence of the reporters who remained, what I had done and of the response. He seemed, if not entirely satisfied, willing to accept the result of what had been his own proposal. He began to walk away, jotting down some notes. Krause, however, remained. He wanted to know why he was not allowed to enter. He smelled a big story, one which he had personally uncovered. The bruised and bleeding captives within, would, when he liberated them, lead to the downfall of Jonestown, no doubt via the front page of the *Washington Post.*

Reporters who had begun to drift away took a step or two back toward Jane Pittman Gardens. At that time, Garry and I agreed that the matter probably could not be ultimately resolved unless the reporters were permitted to inspect the interior of the premises. I told Johnny Jones what he already knew; the reporters, especially Krause, had reached certain conclusions from which they could not be dissuaded without an examination which invaded the privacy of the women. He grimly indicated his reluctant agreement by nodding his head as he looked at Krause with unmasked fury. Jones knocked at the door, gained entrance, and asked the women if they would be willing, at his request, to put up with one more indignity. They agreed. The reporters then toured the premises. Krause described the room:

> The big room was filled with at least 100 bunk beds in long rows, with two or three feet between each bunk. Every bunk was occupied with an elderly woman, most of them black.*

Javers was with Krause when they entered the dormitory. He wrote that "there were sixty bunks or more" and that he observed "thirty old women sitting on them,"† and that some other women were leaving the building as he entered. Krause had not found the warehouse of the damned he had just a short while before believed he had "probably" stumbled onto. In retrospect, he concluded, "The room was clean. The women seemed to have been well enough cared for and had been resting." He continued, "I was told later that we had not been admitted originally because of the Temple's embarrassment at the overcrowding in the dormitory. I told Lane I understood the concern and could also understand the overcrowding."‡

I have wondered since if Krause has also come to understand the part that his arrogant behavior could have played in the mass murders that were soon to follow. I think not, for introspection and self-criticism seem not to be his forte. After there was an attempt to murder Congressman Ryan, Krause and others left Jonestown. He wrote that as he approached the airstrip at Port Kaituma, he thought of his newspaper story and

> [My] mind was also on the trip back to the hotel where I would get a good meal and my first shower and shave in more than 24 hours. I thought maybe I could leave the next day for Trinidad, check into a good hotel with a beach, write my Peoples Temple saga, and try to leave for the States on Wednesday, November 11. [sic]. That would get me home for Thanksgiving.§

*Krause, *Guyana Massacre*, p. 68.
†Javers and Kilduff, *The Suicide Cult,* p. 158.
‡Krause, op. cit., p. 68.
§Ibid., p. 86.

A number of people from the Pittman house and others who were passing by stopped to remonstrate reporters who were preparing to leave the area. They wanted to know why their privacy was considered unimportant, why their living accommodations in Jonestown were fair game for media ridicule. One woman said, "When I lived in Watts in a ratty slum, you didn't care. Now we come thousands of miles to build our own place and look what you do. You follow us here." She waved her hand in disdain and walked away. The resentment of the media that Jones and his predominantly white leadership had felt was now reaching deeply into the souls of the gentle people of Jonestown.

Edith Parks saw Don Harris and asked him if she and her family could leave with him that afternoon. Harris led her to Ryan, and her family soon gathered around while the congressman interviewed them. In addition to Edith, the group consisted of Gerald and Patricia Parks and their two daughters, Tracy and Brenda. Dale Parks, a young man who worked in the Jonestown hospital, was there also, as was Chris O'Neill, a youth who was Brenda's close friend. The Parks family was white, as were almost all of those who decided to leave Jonestown.

Unlike most of the residents, they had not maintained a relationship with the Temple for years before journeying to Guyana. They went to Jonestown only after Jones had arrived there. Krause reported that on the trip from Jonestown to Port Kaituma, Edith Parks told him that "she would probably return to Jonestown after seeing her family in California."*

Some of the reporters, and Jones, viewed each decision to leave as a betrayal of Jonestown and as an act of personal defiance directed at Jones. Both Ryan and Dwyer assured me that they did not share that view. Each said to me that he did not intend to make much of the fact that several of the one thousand residents had chosen to leave. Earlier, Don Harris had told me that if half of the residents who had founded Jonestown remained there for a year or two, he would consider the project a resounding success. Ryan walked over to where I was standing. He said, indicating the Parks family, "That family wants to leave with us. Now Jones should not see this as a reflection on the community." By then, Jones had heard of the planned departure. He walked toward the bench at the edge of the pavilion where they were gathered, and he began to talk with them.

As that discussion, led by Jones, who seemed to be imploring them to stay, continued for some considerable time, Ryan, who had been discussing

*Krause, *Guyana Massacre*, p. 85.

the crops, the weather, and the housing facilities with me, interrupted himself to look at Jones and say to me, "Jim Jones is the genius who built this place and it has many positive aspects. He is Jonestown's greatest benefactor." And then he added, "But he is also its greatest enemy. His desire for absolute power can destroy this place. He demands too much." I was struck by the objectivity and accuracy of Ryan's assessment.

Approximately one hour after Jones began his conversation with the Parks family, he asked me to join the discussion. He said, "Mark, they have decided to stay, but they want you to do something for them." Jim looked exhausted but somewhat victorious as he walked away. Dale Parks spoke to me. "We are willing to stay another week if you will give us a letter in which you personally guarantee that we will be allowed to leave in one week. Will you give us such a letter?" The letter, he said, must be signed by me and by Jim Jones. Jones had the power, Gerald and Dale Parks said, but I was the person they trusted.

Jones had told them that they could leave at any time, but if they chose this occasion to leave, they "would be lining up with the U.S. government against the people of Jonestown." He said that their departure at this time with the American embassy representative and a member of Congress would be seen as a victory for Tim Stoen against socialism. He urged them to stay just a short while longer and said that they could leave any time they wished in the days ahead. The two young girls in the family had begun to cry. Chris O'Neill began to resist Jones's coaxing. Finally, though, they had agreed to stay for a few days, pending receipt of the letter from me.

Their earnest request placed me in a most difficult situation. In the cause of ephemeral tranquility, I could have fashioned and signed the document and observed while Jones affixed his signature to it and handed it to the family. I now know that had I adopted that course of conduct, the six members of the family, and young Chris, almost certainly would have died in Jonestown within hours. I chose instead to discuss the matter with them so that we might analyze this request in terms of their objective.

I replied that I would freely give them such a letter but that I felt obligated to tell them that I thought it valueless. I said, "If you are free to leave at any time, the letter adds nothing. On the other hand, if you are not free to leave, the letter signed by me will not get you out of here." I told them that I would not be there a week from that day and that even if I were, that I could not then guarantee their ability to leave.

Patricia Parks asked what could be done. One of the daughters began to sob. As Dale began to speak, Chris O'Neill interrupted to say he wished to leave then. Dale asked me who might be there in a few days or a week to ensure their departure. I replied that I did not know but that the representative of the embassy might be able to answer that question. They agreed and we asked Dwyer, who was perhaps twenty yards away, to join us. I told him of the dilemma. He listened sympathetically and said, "Oh, yes. I can arrange this when I come back." O'Neill asked, "When is that?" Dwyer said, "In about three months."

O'Neill, who had planned to leave that afternoon, and who had slowly adjusted his thinking to accommodate a few more days at Jonestown before returning to the United States, was not able to contemplate so long a delay. He raised his voice and almost shouted, "Three months! I will not wait three months." Dale and Gerald Parks both looked at me and said, "What can we do?" and "What should we do?"

I did not wish to add to the anguish and sense of betrayal that Jim Jones had been experiencing. I did not want to take any action which might drive him, however imperceptibly, toward a decision which a rational man would not make. Yet here were seven people who had said to me they wished to return home, had asked my aid, and now were seeking my advice. They were, for that moment, my only clients. I said to the family, "If you really want to leave, then leave now."

I looked up to see Jim Jones looking directly at me. He had been attracted by O'Neill's outburst and he had stood there, a few feet from our little group, when I offered my last advice to them. Jones looked at me in a way I had never seen before. I did not experience a comfortable moment in Jonestown thereafter.

The family remained at the pavilion for a few moments. One of the women said that it was a shame that they could not get their clothing. When I asked why that was so, Gerry Parks said that he wasn't sure that it would be safe to walk into the area where their cabins were. I agreed to accompany them and Dale, Gerry, and Edith and I walked to the two cabins together. I carried two of their suitcases back toward the pavilion and on that long walk, I asked Gerry why he wished to leave. He said that they did not want to hurt Jim Jones, who they liked and respected, "but the food isn't what I'm used to. It's mostly rice." He said the working hours were long and that he did not object to that except it all seemed so hopeless: "The crops don't really grow well here. We can't grow enough to eat." He said he didn't resent the long meetings. "I guess they are good, you learn things at them." But, he added, "I'm always tired here." He worked two different jobs, and he told me he did not see any possibility of real progress in the future. "It was Jim's dream and he's sincere," Parks concluded.

We had reached the center of the community. The Parks family was reunited and they waited together at the pavilion with their luggage for word that the truck was ready to take them home.

Ryan called me over toward the table and chairs on the little platform that had served as his interviewing office the night before and during a good part of that day. His interviews were finished and he wanted to talk. He had seen me leave with the Parks family and return with some of them and the suitcases. He asked how it had come to be resolved in that fashion. I told him what had happened.

He asked, "Is Jim Jones sore at you?" I said that I hoped not, and that I believed that people should be free to come and go as they wished. I said that it would be easier to accomplish that end if Stoen and the press had not encouraged Jones to believe that each person who left was a defector and had defied him personally. Ryan said that he and Dwyer had taken great pains to demonstrate that they did not hold to that view. I said, "It would have been better, Congressman, if you had come without the press." He said, "Maybe you're right."

Later, Ron Javers, in writing of those who decided to go home, said, "Finally about twenty were ready to defy Jones."*

As I crossed the pavilion, Don Harris called to me. He walked over and told me that there were automatic weapons in Jonestown. A police officer in Port Kaituma the previous evening had told him. Don asked me to assess the mood in Jonestown and I told him that I was very worried. He asked me, "Do you think Jones may try to pull off a 'mass suicide?' " I could only answer, "I hope not." Don then put his hand on my shoulder and said, "Why don't you come back with us now?" I answered that I came knowing there were risks involved but I thought that I would exercise a calming influence upon Jones and the other leaders while assisting those who wanted to leave. I said, "I think I have to stay and help process those who want to leave tomorrow morning."

When it appeared that most of the visitors who were planning to leave had reached the truck, another great commotion erupted on the path in the heart of Jonestown. Al Simon, a resident, was hurrying toward the truck carrying one small child and dragging two others with him. A woman ran toward him screaming that he was stealing her children. I ran after them, as did a number of others. As we reached the area where the truck was parked, I saw Garry, carrying his briefcase. He was about to board the truck when he too observed the active scene moving toward him.

A brief discussion held in the muddy clearing revealed that Simon had

*Javers and Kilduff, *The Suicide Cult,* p. 159.

just decided to leave, taking his three children and without informing his wife, who was the mother of the children and who wished to remain. Jackie Speier told Simon that he could not leave without first being interviewed by Congressman Ryan. Reluctantly, Simon, still holding the children, made his way back to the pavilion where Ryan was waiting. I asked Garry to join us, pointing out that this was a legal conflict. He hesitated until Speier insisted that he should join us.

I explained the matter to Ryan, and he said, "I'll be damned if I know what to do." Then he said to me, "I'm not even a lawyer, what do you think?" I said that he was the federal presence there, albeit probably without authority or jurisdiction. I said, "Custody matters are settled by courts but there is no court here." Ryan questioned Mr. and Mrs. Simon and asked if they could work out the matter together. Simon said that he would not leave if he could not take the children, at which point each spouse accused the other of not caring for the needs of the children. The question was temporarily settled, with Simon agreeing to stay a little longer.

Later, while Ryan and I were talking, we were joined by Karen Layton, an attractive young woman in her late twenties. A few moments later, a young man brushed past Karen to the congressman and said, "I wish to make a declaration." Ryan walked with him toward a table and began to fill out a form. He was arranging for the departure of Larry Layton. As they sat there talking, we could not know that within two hours, Larry Layton would be charged with the murder of Congressman Ryan, nor could I suspect that Dale Parks, whose release from Jonestown I had just arranged, was to disarm Larry Layton at the Port Kaituma airstrip after Don Harris, Leo Ryan, and three others were murdered there.

Karen Layton seemed astonished that her husband was planning to leave. She said, "Larry, are you leaving? Why are you leaving? Why haven't you told me about this?" He didn't answer her. He signed the papers that were before him and walked away silently.

Ryan stood up and walked back to where I was standing. He said, "The worst part of this whole thing is the pain of watching families split up." As we talked, a tall and powerfully built man came behind him and placed an arm around Ryan's neck from the rear. As he held him in a headlock, he said "You motherfucker, I'm going to kill you!" Ryan, apparently believing that his assailant was not serious said, "Okay, that's enough fooling around, you can let go now."

The man's other arm encircled the congressman from the rear. He spun Ryan to his right, away from where I was standing and held him fast. Still the representative gave the impression that it was not a matter for concern.

He said, "Do you think the joke is over now?" I tried to see who the aggressor was. It seemed to me that since Ryan was so unconcerned about so unconventional a situation, he probably knew who the would-be desperado was. I wondered if Schollaert had arrived somehow from Georgetown; I could not imagine who else might act so familiarly with the congressman. Whoever it was, I thought, was a fool to act in such a violent fashion, even in sham, in an atmosphere so charged.

Then Ryan looked at the hand which completed the encirclement of his chest. He looked up toward me from his position, an enforced crouch, and cried, "Help me." At that moment, his hand went to the assailant's hand held near to his chest and as I reached his side, I saw that a knife was pressed alongside his chest, near his heart. I grabbed the wrist that held the knife. I was aware that many people were standing around watching the struggle that consumed the three of us and I cried out, "Hit the son of a bitch. Stop him." But for a time, just the three of us remained in combat. I held to the wrist with all my strength, and Ryan's power, combined with mine, kept the knife from plunging into his chest. After an eternity, which may have been but a few moments, other hands joined ours, and the assailant was pulled from behind backward onto the ground. Ryan fell backward upon him and I, still joined hand to wrist to hand, fell with them. The knife, at last, dropped harmlessly aside, and the man who'd wielded it disappeared into the shadows. I had never seen him before, so I did not know who it was. Tim Carter quickly picked up the knife.

Leo Ryan was lying prostrate upon the earth. His shirt front was spotted with blood. I was kneeling above him and I said, "Are you all right, Leo?"

"I don't know," he said.

"Have you been wounded?"

"I don't know."

He tried to rise, and I said, "Should you get up?"

Again he said, "I don't know," but as he said that, he struggled to his feet and I helped him to a nearby bench where he sat down heavily.

"Is that your blood?" I asked him, indicating a portion of his shirt drenched with blood.

He said, "Is it? I can't tell."

At that point, I ripped open his shirt and discovered that he had not been wounded; he had in fact not even been scratched. For the first time, as I held his shirt open, I saw that my hand had been slightly cut in the melee, but it was clear that the blood on Ryan's shirt had come from a much more free-flowing wound.

I saw Jim Jones seated a few feet from Ryan. He seemed calm for the first time since we had arrived. He looked directly at the congressman, and said "Does this change everything?"

Ryan, in a state not far removed from shock, his shirt wet with blood, and blood visible on his trouser leg as well, said quickly, too quickly, "Yes. It changes everything." Ryan then rallied. He paused and said, "No, it doesn't change everything. It does change some things though." He looked around nervously. He appeared to be scanning the vicinity for the man who had attacked him.

I asked Jones where the assailant was, and he responded, "When you break up these families it's a terrible thing. The people are very upset. I try to do what I can but this is a terrible thing." Jones then told Marcie, who was standing alongside him, that he was experiencing a heart attack. She said that she would get the pills. I asked Ryan if he needed medical assistance, and he said that he did not. I nevertheless told Jones that the doctor should be called. Jones agreed, and said to someone in the small crowd standing around us, "Get Larry."

Ryan asked for the whereabouts of the man who had assaulted him and then said, "Is he in custody? He must be in custody." I told Jones that the police at Port Kaituma must be called.

He sighed and said, "I suppose so."

"Jim, we're dealing with a very serious charge," I said. "The police must be called at once."

Jones took some pills that Marcie offered to him, and then drank from a glass of water. He said, "Yes, yes, we'll call the police." He gave instructions to someone in the group to call the police by radio, and when I reminded him of the need for a doctor, he added that request to his instructions also. Neither the doctor nor the police arrived.

Harris and Dwyer came running toward our group. They had apparently been at the truck and were preparing to leave when circles of excitement radiating from the pavilion had reached them. Harris saw the blood-drenched and open shirt. He quickly turned to his right, back toward the area from which he had just come, and said, "Get the camera." I called to him. He looked at me and I said, "Don't bring a camera here." He quickly assessed the situation and called back, "Forget it. We don't need the camera." Dwyer joined the group centered around Ryan. He inquired about Ryan's injuries and Ryan answered, "I'm all right. I'm not hurt."

The committee investigating the tragedy for the United States Congress offered this recitation of the facts:

> It was at this point that an unsuccessful knife attack was made on Mr. Ryan's life. The attacker, identified as Don Sly, was fended off by Mr. Lane and others but cut himself in the process and Mr. Ryan's clothes were spattered with blood. After receiving Mr. Jones' assurance that the incident would be reported to local police, Mr. Ryan assured Jones that the attack would not substantially influence his overall impression of Peoples Temple. Despite the attack, Mr. Ryan reportedly planned to remain in Jonestown and eventually left only after virtually being ordered to do so by DCM* Dwyer. In turn, Mr. Dwyer planned to return to Jonestown later in an effort to resolve a dispute between a family who was split on the question of leaving Jonestown;†

Dwyer was apparently the source for the allegation that Ryan was insistent upon remaining in Jonestown one more night after the attack upon him. When I testified before the body empowered by the Congress to investigate the matter, I was told by the investigators that Dwyer had testified that he had told Ryan moments after the knife attack that his conduct had been provocative and had created the conflict. Dwyer, drawing upon his authority, reportedly then said that as the senior federal officer present, he was ordering Ryan to leave. Dwyer added, according to the congressional committee, that I joined with him in the effort to persuade Ryan to leave.

Krause published a view which corroborated part of that story: "Lane and others persuaded Ryan to leave Jonestown after the incident, although he wanted to stay on and help resolve the Simons' [sic] dispute."‡

Javers saw an aspect of the aftermath of the assault and reported it in this fashion:

> The newsmen scrambled down onto the muddy roadway to see what was happening. The frightened dissidents, hoping to ride to freedom with us, stayed aboard.
>
> We dashed toward the assembly area. A bunch of tough-looking young security guards blocked the way. They ordered us back on the truck.
>
> Then we saw Ryan, blood all over the front of his shirt, being led briskly back to the truck. Lane was holding him by the arm. Ryan's face was as white as his hair.
>
> Lane helped Ryan climb aboard and told us he and Garry would stay behind with another batch of dissidents who hoped to get away.

*Deputy Chief of Mission
†*U.S. House of Representatives Report*, p. 5.
‡Krause, *Guyana Massacre,* p. 73.

He said they would try to calm the enraged members of the Peoples Temple.

"Get out—fast!" Lane shouted.

But our driver was from the Peoples Temple too, and he was in no hurry. The yellow, ten-wheeled dump truck moved slowly from the scene. We could see Lane waving at us as we reached a bend.*

Javers wrote that as the truck lumbered toward the airstrip at Port Kaituma, "we knew we had to get out as fast as we could. But we weren't fast enough."†

The Javers account was far more accurate than the version published by the congressional inquiry and the Krause version, both of which apparently relied upon Dwyer. I do not know why Dwyer is reported to have said that he ordered Ryan to leave after berating him for causing the attack through improper conduct. Ryan's conduct, after he arrived at Jonestown, was exemplary and did not warrant such a rebuke. Furthermore, no such admonition was given to Ryan at Jonestown after the assault, and no such statement was made to him in my presence at any time. I never left his side from the initiation of the attack upon him until I assisted him as he boarded the truck.

It appears that the State Department, by focusing upon imagined misconduct by Leo Ryan, is attempting to shift the responsibility for the massacre to the actions of one lone man. If Ryan, acting alone as an unwitting provocateur, was responsible for the assault upon himself, then possibly the State Department may be spared criticism for the massacre. The congressional report concluded, "The evidence of the Staff Investigative Group has indicated that very shortly after the Ryan group left Jonestown, Jones was in a highly agitated state."‡

If Ryan, through unpredictable conduct, caused the assault, and the assault created a highly agitated state which led, the report suggests, to the "mass suicide/murder ritual,"§ then no culpability need attach to the State Department, the American embassy, and the American intelligence organizations.

The most serious flaw in the chain of events as woven by the agencies of government is in regard to the integrity of its first and essential link, the charge that Ryan had provoked the attack by misconduct on his part.

*Javers and Kilduff, *The Suicide Cult*, p. 73.
†Ibid., p. 167.
‡*U.S. House of Representatives Report*, p. 6.
§Ibid.

When Dwyer learned that Ryan had not been wounded, he said to Ryan, "Maybe you ought to go back." I said, "Leo, that might be a good idea." Dwyer then said, "If Mr. Lane will stay with me, I can remain here tonight to help process those who want to leave." Dwyer looked toward me and I said, "Yes, I'll stay another day." Ryan rose, relieved that it was no longer necessary for him to remain, and walked with me through the pavilion and toward the waiting truck. Jim Jones approached Ryan and offered him a chance to change into other clothing. Ryan accepted the proffered shirt and trousers but said that he would change later. Garry approached Ryan and offered profuse apologies for the attack.

Leo Ryan and I walked together to the truck which was to take him back to the airstrip at Port Kaituma. He thanked me for my help and said he hoped that his presence had not created a problem. "I hope you're not mad at me for coming," he added. I told him that although I had originally felt it would have been better if he had not come, his conduct was so open and friendly that perhaps it would all work out well. I said, "It is as if you opened a window to a room which had been sealed off for years. Most people here, I'm sure, were pleased at that opening. I hope it does not drive the leadership into a fit of paranoia."

As Ryan and I approached the truck, Jim Cobb leaped from the truck bed and hurried toward us. I was to Ryan's right and Cobb joined us, walking to the congressman's left, until we reached the parked vehicle. One of the people in the truck reached out a hand to help Ryan into the rear of the dump truck. I asked if the passenger seat in the cab was available, and learning that it was, I walked with Ryan to the cab and helped him enter it.

He grabbed my hand and then hugged me and said, "You saved my life, Mark. You know, I'll never forget this." He asked if I expected to be on the West Coast in the near future, and when I said that I might be, he made me promise to call him when I had made specific plans for a visit. "We'll have dinner, okay?" I said that I would be really pleased. He said, "Tell Jones that I do not consider this attack to be an act by Jonestown. There are assaults in every city in America and I don't judge Jonestown by one crazy person." He told me that in his report he would refer to the attack, "because it happened," but that it would be a balanced report incorporating his positive and negative impressions.

"Jim is very upset," I said.

"I know."

I asked, "Can I tell him that you will not recommend that there be a full-scale congressional investigation?"

Ryan hesitated and then said, "Yes, tell him that."

It was my impression that the congressman meant that while I could relate that decision to Jones, it did not necessarily reflect a final determination.

I walked back alone to Jonestown and saw Charles Garry standing near the pavilion. At that time, I did not know how much he knew or suspected about the problems in Jonestown. As we walked together I told Garry of my conversations with Dale and Gerald Parks. I told him how poor the daily food was, how many long hours the people worked, how crowded the living facilities were, and how little sleep the residents were allowed. I swore him to absolute secrecy about these observations. I said, "If Jones ever found out what we have learned about this place, he might become enraged." Garry assured me that he would not reveal the information which I had confided to him.

Then he remarked that he had not seen Chaikin. I said that I then believed that Chaikin might have been deliberately kept out of sight because he was not trusted.

As we walked together on a path through the village, we were called by Jim McElvane. He was with Jack Beam. We waited until the two men reached us. McElvane, a mountain of a man, stood approximately six feet nine inches and weighed not much under three hundred pounds. He said, "What do you think the situation is?" Garry answered, "I think you ought to get better food for the people here. Rice is not enough." McElvane impatiently interrupted Garry and said, "I didn't ask you about that. What is your evaluation of the situation now? What do you think?" Garry still did not grasp the question. He said, "People should not have to work so many long hours in the field and they don't get enough sleep. That's why they're complaining."

As Garry spoke, a voice over the loudspeaker announced that a meeting was being called at the pavilion. Soon a few people reached the place at which we stood on the narrow path. The few became a river of humanity and the four of us left the path to continue the discussion at a clearing a few yards away. Garry continued to advise the two men that the quality of life at Jonestown required enhancement. Beam, frustrated by Garry's long and irrelevant answer, broke in, "Charlie, what do you think the situation is *now? Now!*" Garry said, "I've been trying to tell you. You need better conditions here—" but before he could complete the sentence, McElvane said, "Both of you come with us to see Jim. Now!" This was the first time that a command had been addressed to me and I was aware then of a rapidly changing situation.

In retrospect, I believe that Jones sent the two emissaries to learn of our response to the deteriorating conditions. I am quite certain that by then, Jones had decided to order the death of those at Jonestown and was likely concerned that Garry and I would forcefully oppose that plan. Having failed to secure our view, his agents brought us to him.

We were taken into a building across a walk from the pavilion where most of the residents had already gathered; a few stragglers, mostly elderly people, were slowly wending their way on the slippery path. Several of the leaders attempted to enter the room with us, but Jones turned around and spoke sharply to some of them, including Tim Carter, stating that it was not a public meeting. Carter and several others withdrew.

On the table were two sandwiches made with toasted bread. I recalled that earlier in the day, as I was rushing about from one potential crisis to another, that Marcie had inquired of me if either Charles or I had eaten lunch. I said that I did not know about Charles; that I hadn't eaten and wasn't hungry. She said that she would have sandwiches made for us in case we were hungry later. Now, sometime later, we apparently came upon the food at our final meeting with Jones.

Jones began by stating that he had been defeated. He said that he would be blamed for the attack upon Ryan. "I didn't do it, but it will be blamed on me." I told him that Ryan had himself told me that he held neither Jones nor Jonestown responsible. I related to him my recent talk with Ryan and reported that there was to be no full-scale investigation. Jones then abandoned that subject and said, "The men who left here on the truck did not betray me. They left out of love for me. They all left to kill our enemies." He sighed and said from behind his large sunglasses, "I will be blamed for that even though I don't want them to do it. When you divide these families, it's a terrible thing. That's what happens. I can't keep the people from doing this. I try. But I can't keep them."

I said that I had talked to Gerry and Dale Parks, two of the men who left. I said that they made it clear to me that they had left to enjoy material possessions, not to kill enemies. I said, "Jim, they told me that they would never attack you, that they will always defend Jonestown at press conferences, but they have no intention of killing anyone."

Garry broke in and said to me, "Tell him what they said about just eating rice three times a day." Jones looked up angrily and asked me about that comment. I tried to assuage his fury by saying that the Parks family was not up to the rigors of pioneer life. Garry continued, "Tell Jim about the long hours." I tried a similar approach, indicating that possibly the problem lay not with the objective circumstances but with the subjective response to the normal difficulties associated with founding a new society. I never did understand what Garry thought would be useful about his interjections, but believing that the setting was not appropriate to explore that matter, I changed the subject. I assured Jones again that Gerry and Dale Parks and Chris O'Neill would cause no violence which might be later traced to him.

Jones paused then and said, "Larry Layton gave me a cold embrace. When he did I knew he was going to kill the enemies." I responded that we were not mystics, pointing out that Jones was a Marxist. I said, "We are rational men, Jim," which perhaps at that moment tended to overstate the matter. In my desperate effort to present the facts in the best light, I said that it would be wrong to presume that there would be an act of violence elsewhere and base an action upon that speculation.

Jones looked at me, and said, "We have proof that they are going to shoot down—shoot up that plane." Until that moment, I had thought that I had perhaps defused each potentially explosive assertion which Jones had made. I knew then there could be no answer to his final statement. He had proof, I believed then, because he had given the orders.

Jones said, "The people demand it. You can't divide up, separate families like that." At that moment, almost as if on cue, an elderly woman began to scream and chant irrationally. Jones said, "You see, the people are hysterical. What can I do? They demand action."

Maria Katsaris entered the area and walked up behind Jones. She bent down and whispered into his ear. He rose, turned, and said, "Excuse me," and talked with Maria while Garry, Johnny Jones, Marcie, McElvane, Beam, and I waited.

Then he turned toward us and said to McElvane, "Take them to East House." He had pointed toward Garry and me. Jones then addressed us: "The people are very angry with you for bringing Ryan. Go to East House and stay there." As McElvane escorted us from the area, I asked him if Charles and I could pick up our belongings which we had left in the room where we had spent the previous night. The result of that request was later to save our lives. McElvane agreed and we walked a few yards to the room. As we reached the cabin, we saw Lew Jones dart out of the room. Garry picked up his large and heavy leather briefcase. I grabbed a light plastic shoulder bag and we walked to East House.

Don Sly, the man who had assaulted Ryan, was dispatched to East House. He sat outside on the wooden porch, his hand heavily wrapped in bandages. The choice of Sly to guard us was ominous.

Garry and I entered the cabin. I heard Jones begin to broadcast over the public address system. He spoke of death.

Part IV
The Last Hours

12 The Escape

Several minutes later, a group of perhaps eight to ten men came running from the direction of the pavilion toward our cottage. They were shouting, "Let's get them! Let's bring them up! Let's get them now!" Since Charles and I were the only apparent "them," I turned to Charles and observed, "This does not look good." However, the men ran past the cottage in which we were held and into a small guard shack a few feet away, from which they removed large numbers of semiautomatic rifles. One man carried three, others carried two each. Two young, strongly built men struggled with what apparently was an ammunition case, which they carried up the path and over a narrow footbridge toward the community center. The other men, carrying numerous weapons, ran up the hill toward the community center.

I heard Jones broadcasting over the loudspeaker system. We were some distance from the pavilion; therefore, I could not hear every phrase or understand all that I did hear. I did know he was speaking of death. He said there would be a catastrophe. He said that they had better not have "our children left." He spoke of death as "a revolutionary act." I heard a woman's voice speak out for life and the possibility of flight to Russia. Jones answered that Russia would not accept them due to "all this stigma." He spoke of forces about to "parachute" in on them.

East House was the cabin built upon the easternmost boundary of the improved property. It is located many hundreds of feet from the main pavilion. I believe I could only hear the words that were spoken directly into the microphone. While I could not hear the reaction of the people in the audience, I could partially assess their mood from Jones's efforts to calm them, to persuade them, and finally to order them to act. Within minutes, two young black men came running down from the community center toward East House. One of them told Sly that he could then report to the community center. Sly rose and walked with long strides up the path toward the pavilion. I stood at the window of the cabin and said to Garry, "When they all cross over that bridge, lets get out of here." He asked, "And go where?" I said, "What's the difference? Let's just go."

One of the men began to move toward the cabin as Sly passed him. He carried a long weapon and was followed by the other man, who was similarly armed. I believe the weapons were semiautomatic rifles. The one in the lead came close to the cabin and said, "Charles, Mark, come on out!" Garry whispered to me, "I'm not going out there." I understood and shared his feelings, yet I was painfully aware that the frail structure in which we stood, a cabin made of soft wooden slats, offered little protection. By hiding there silently, I sensed that we would have squandered the strength of any dissent we might wish to offer had we been seized. I had, in any case, prepared a few remarks earlier in the day in the event of a calamity. When the squad had come down the hill to collect weapons, I thought that we were to be brought before the meeting. Again, I tried to compose some words which could, if but a moment were given to me, present another view.

I then decided to leave the cabin. I walked up to the armed man. In the background, I could hear Jones urging the populace to relax. Later, I noticed that Garry was outside the cabin too, standing to my right at a distance of several feet. He did not leave the cabin with me, but he apparently came outside soon afterward. The man with the weapon was familiar to me.

At that moment, the voice of Jim Jones seemed loud and clear. He was urging the people to "die with some dignity." The man kept his weapon pointed at me, though not raised to eye level with me in his sights. Rather, he carried the weapon at waist height, with its barrel pointed at me casually, although at that moment, I would not have chosen that word to describe his stance. Behind him and to his right stood the other man, his weapon carried in a similar style. I recognized the first man as Poncho. He had been the master of ceremonies at Friday evening's entertainment, and he'd sung a moving song beautifully as well. I said, "Hello, Poncho."

He said, "Man, we are all going to die. There is dignity in death. This is the way to struggle against fascism."

I responded to him with what I would have said to the group at the community center had I been present at the final meeting. "There is no dignity in suicide. Suicide is the absence of struggle; worse, the denial of struggle." He stood there smiling at me as I continued. "Poncho, killing children is not a struggle against facism. It is facism." Nothing I said appeared to register. He seemed to be calm, determined, and not open to a contrary suggestion. He repeated, "Man, it's beautiful to die; we are all going to die now."

I remembered that in September after I had spoken in Jonestown about the assassination of Dr. King, that Poncho seemed particularly interested in the subject. I had spoken with him informally about the mystery and later had arranged for some copies of the book on the subject which I had written together with Dick Gregory to be sent to Jonestown.

Now I was particularly concerned with Poncho's use of the word "we," and wondered if he intended to encompass both Charles and me in that pronoun. I decided not to put that question to him directly for fear that the answer might be terribly disappointing. Instead, I said, "Well, Poncho, if you have made up your mind, I guess there is nothing I can do, but at least you will know that Charles and I will be able to tell the truth about the last minutes of Jonestown." I had injected a new thought into the discourse and he raised his head and looked directly at me for a moment. Then he said, "Mark, you are a good writer, that's right. Tell the truth about it."

He stepped forward and held his rifle in his right hand in an upright position. He and his fellow guard were both stripped to the waist and both glistening with sweat. Poncho threw his arms around me. We embraced each other as two friends who knew that they would not meet again. He stepped back and said, "Good-bye, Mark." Then, as he moved to his left to bid Garry good-bye, the other man came forward and he and I embraced as well and said good-bye.

The two men walked back toward the center of the community. I called to them. They spun around, their rifles pointed once again at us. I said, "Poncho, how do we get out of here?" He said, "When it's all over in a few minutes, just call a plane." I said, "I don't have a plane and you don't have a phone; I don't know how to work the radio. How do we walk out of here?" Poncho thought for a moment or two. Much later, when I was to analyze this episode in retrospect, I realized that I had inadvertently tested Poncho. Had Jones not ordered him to kill Garry and me, he could have merely told us to walk up to the pavilion and from there cross over to the road to Port Kaituma. I knew that route. Every visitor to Jonestown understood that simple geographical fact in a moment. Yet Poncho decided we were not to find the road the easy way. He said, "Go there," and he pointed to an area almost directly opposite from the route to the pavilion. "Walk up that hill, then you'll find the Jonestown road." I said, "Thank you." He said, "Remember Poncho from San Francisco!" His companion said, "Johnson from Los Angeles!" Then Poncho held his rifle high in the air and said, "Jim

Jones is the greatest man who ever lived." Garry held his fist in the air and shouted, "Right on."

Poncho and Johnson ran up the hill toward the pavilion. Garry and I slipped into East House for the last time. I picked up my small plastic bag, threw the strap over my shoulder, and moved quickly toward the door. Charles picked up his heavy briefcase and followed me. I said, "Do you need all that, Charles? We have a tough hike ahead." He answered that he did and we almost ran from the cabin into the rough terrain leading to the hill.

The area was a good deal more difficult to move through than it appeared from a distance. We were not in the jungle but in an area that appeared to have been cleared of trees some time before. There were small holes and rivulets and thick underbrush and treacherous yawning gaps in the earth. Soon we reached a ravine with a jungle stream running through it. I had been warned during my last visit that the voracious and sharp-toothed piranha abound in the rivulets. Under ordinary circumstances, I would have ventured forth with the greatest diligence and caution—if at all—but now I plunged into the stream with abandon and pulled myself up on the other bank by grabbing onto some heavy but thorn-encrusted vegetation. My hands stung and began to bleed.

I turned and saw that Garry was having serious difficulty negotiating the bank since he had but one free hand and the weight of his briefcase threw him off balance. I reached out and took the case, ran up the bank and dropped it there, and then returned to give Charles my hand as he labored up the embankment. He said he needed to take a break, and he sat there trying to catch his breath. He told me that he could not overtire himself without suffering severe physical consequences. I heard Jones speak, more faintly now for the distance we had covered, but suddenly distinctly. He said, "Mother, Mother, Mother, please," and then repeated, "Mother" and "please." He told her to "lay down your life." I did not hear her response but I did hear several volleys of rapid fire as if from a semiautomatic or automatic weapon.

I said to Garry, "We can be seen here from Jonestown." I urged him to use all of his energy to cover the ground until we reached the crest of the hill. I said once we get there, we can rest, out of sight. I knew that Charles was seventy years old and that it would take all of our combined energies and skills to get us both through the jungles of Guyana and back to America.

The bush just alongside us had been described as the last completely unexplored jungle in the world, and I knew that among the terrors in that jungle were large cats, including jaguar and ocelot, and that scorpions, tarantulas, and vampire bats abounded. I knew that many snakes with deadly venom slithered about and that boa constrictors were prevalent. I suspected that the hours ahead were to be crucial for us. For the moment, however, the greatest threat seemed to emanate from man rather than beast, and I was afraid that if we lingered much longer, we might be observed.

I also thought that, just as we sought the road to Port Kaituma, others too, perhaps armed guards in search of those who might have escaped, might set out in much the same direction. Charles looked weary and still out of breath. I swore to him I would never abandon him. "We will walk out of this together, I swear to you." I felt odd and my words seemed a trifle unnatural when I heard what I was saying. Yet the sentiment was sincerely meant and Garry looked up and said he was ready to walk. He got to his feet and said, "Thanks."

I carried his case for part of the way. As we moved up the hill away from our right where the bush encroached upon the cleared area, we headed directly for a cassava field. The stalks were high and rather thickly planted, but the going was much easier. In time, hot and sweating, we reached what seemed to be the mountain's crest. From that pinnacle, we did not take even a moment to look back at Jonestown. I plunged ahead, through the cassava plants, toward the shade and dubious security offered by the edge of the ominous bush. I fell upon the ground a foot or two into the jungle, dropping Garry's case and my shoulder bag. Garry sat heavily beside me.

I looked at Charles. I was astonished by what I saw. His hair, ordinarily worn in what appeared to be a normal style, was not what it seemed. He was almost completely bald, with hair growing just from the fringes and at such an enormous length that when twirled about his head, patted down, sprayed, and dried it gave a different impression. Now it hung limply down his back and onto his shoulders while almost all of his head remained bare.

When I dropped his bulging briefcase, it popped open. A large metal object protruded. I reached over to examine it and once I had done so, I said, "Charles, we are carrying a hair dryer through the jungle." He nodded affirmatively and said, "It's a good hair dryer." I said "Throw the fucking thing out, Charles. Buy a new one if we get back." He refused. I asked what else he had in the case. He said that he had the legal files for the Peoples Temple. He added, "I'm still the lawyer for the Temple. I need those files." I said that while he had not been formally fired, I thought that the dispatch of a firing squad to dispense with us could be said to have released him from further obligations. I observed that he should toss out the briefcase, hair dryer, files, and all. He said he would not.

I looked into my own shoulder bag and found that I had two paperback books, now drenched. I threw them into the bush. We stood up and I asked Charles if he knew where the road was. He looked about and saw a tall lone tree standing high above the rest on the horizon. He pointed toward it and said that the road was there. I asked him how he knew that and he said that he remembered passing that tree as we drove up to Jonestown in the back of the truck from the airstrip yesterday. We headed for the tree through terrain that became rough and difficult to move through. Eventually, as we came closer to the tall tree, we saw rows of cassava plants ahead, and beyond the plants, the road to Port Kaituma. Garry had been correct. His memory had confirmed Poncho's directions and we were at the road which might take us home.

He wanted to walk on the road, for although it was deeply rutted and awash with red mud, it was by far the best surface that was available. I suggested that we stay off the road and walk between the bush and the cassava growth. I said I thought the road dangerous, that it might be patrolled and that walking down it would make us visible and therefore vulnerable. Garry yielded to my concerns but did so reluctantly and unhappily.

We began to move, slowly making headway near the bush and using the cassava for light cover. Suddenly we saw three men on the other side of the road. Two were carrying wooden footlockers on their backs. Charles later told me that he thought they had been armed with long guns. I whispered to Charles to follow me and I dived headlong into the bush. We fought with vines and were cut by plants with razor-sharp spikes, as in panic we forged deeper and deeper into the jungle. We were by then almost exhausted and it was too dark to see more than a few feet ahead. I changed direction and walked until it was too dark to see where we were. Charles and I then fell on the jungle floor. It was just seven P.M. and we knew that that first light was almost eleven hours ahead.

As the rain dripped from the hundred-fifty-foot canopy formed by the treetops, it seemed as if someone or something was moving inexorably toward us. Suddenly I saw a flashlight coming toward us. We hid behind a fallen log and waited. The flashlight came closer, then flickered out, and then on again. It was a giant firefly. We knew that the jungle was home for many creatures that crawled and prowled, that slithered and flew, and that many of them had the ability to kill us as they killed Amerindians who ventured into their domain at night, and often during the day as well. Yet, with human killers roaming the area, the bush seemed more hospitable than the road from Jonestown. In the total darkness which enveloped us, in which my sight was no more impaired with my eyes closed than open, I began to consider our hopes for survival. What should our response be if attacked by a cat? To strike out with all possible force, particularly with the feet, I thought, although I was not sanguine about our chances for surviving such an encounter. As to the poisonous snakes that darted about, the best defense, I thought, was to remain absolutely still so as to avoid the possibility of rolling over on one and thus inviting its attention.

The recurrent terror that engulfed me came from the thought that we might never find our way out of there to the road. In the dark, Charles reached into his bag and found some multivitamins which he shared with me. Then he produced a vitamin C pill for each of us. He also located penicillin tablets after foraging at the bottom of the bag for a time. I reached into my case and located a few cough drops. We each had one, and a little later, another.

As he delved once again into his briefcase, he said that he was looking for some aspirin. "I've got a splitting headache," he told me. Just as he located the bottle, I said, "Don't take one, Charles." He asked why and I said, "I just remembered that we saw Lew Jones come out of our room just after Jones sent us to East House." I pointed out that the room we shared had not been occupied by Lew Jones before. "What was he doing in that room?" I asked.

Garry became extremely agitated and began to search through the files in his briefcase although it was so dark, he could see nothing. He said, "I'll bet that son of a bitch took that file. He was after that file." I did not care about that matter and I never did inquire about it. I then suggested that we consume no more products in the dark. I said it seemed unlikely, but possible, that our possessions had been laced with poison. Garry agreed and did not take the aspirin until the morning when at early light he was able to identify the tablet. He seemed much more troubled, however, about the possibility that the file might be missing.

We talked quietly through the night, often jolted into a panic of silence by the sound of something approaching, hesitating, and at last retreating.

Charles seemed confident that as soon as the sun rose he would lead us directly to the road. He said that he had an excellent sense of direction. My reason told me that we were lost, perhaps hopelessly lost. I blamed myself for having led us so deep into the jungle in a panicked response to those men on the road who may not have even seen us and who, even if they had, might have been more intent upon escaping than harming us.

Now we were alone. I was strangely comforted by Charles's certainty that he knew exactly where the road was, and at the same time annoyed by what was projected as his contempt for the hazards of the bush.

It was dark; so dark that I literally could not see my hand before my face. The watch I'd bought at JFK was the first one I'd ever owned that had a light switch. It was more than a little reassuring to be able to clock the time and see some small light every few minutes through the night.

Charles said that he had to urinate and he stood up and took a few steps. I urged him not to walk around, as he might step on a snake or we might be separated. It was then that I knew how important it was to me that I was not alone, although my reason told me that my companion's presence in no real way increased my chances for survival. Yet when I talked to Charles about simple matters, and he answered, the cold sweat, the rapid heartbeat that I was so aware of experiencing subsided. It was as though panic began to give way to reason because there was another human being present.

I thought of my father, about to celebrate his eighty-seventh birthday within a week, and how the news of my death might affect him. In nature, as it was intended for us, children bury their parents. In war and in the violent society that we had become, all of the rules for life and death had been rendered inoperative.

I thought of my two daughters, living in Paris with their mother. I thought they might never understand what mission had brought me to Guyana.

I thought of my lady, April, and how the quiet terror that I had lapsed into on the floor of this beautiful and deadly place would be outdone in Memphis by her anxiety and fear. I thought how I just wanted to see her one more time to say the things that I should have said long ago.

I remembered clearly then how she had begged me not to go to Guyana, saying that my life would be in danger if Jones ever was driven by madness to action. At that time I told her that I felt an obligation to so many good and decent people that I had met in Jonestown. She smiled and asked me if I was not interweaving my sense of adventure with my obligations. I denied it then. Now in the jungle I wondered if she was right. I know that whatever thirst for adventure I might have had by then had been satisfied. I just wanted to be home.

The stars came out and we could see them through the trees, then the moon. The light was sharp as it contrasted with the darkness, and was scattered on the jungle floor in odd patches by the swaying treetops. Too soon the moon and the stars were gone and two urban lawyers were again enveloped in total darkness.

Mosquitoes attacked us, biting through our clothing and buzzing in formation about our heads. It was only much later that the possibility of malaria was brought to my attention. Ants and flies bit us as well. As annoying and painful as those bites were, it was the thought of snakes and large cats that terrorized me in the darkness. We could see nothing. We were vulnerable to any attack. We were completely defenseless. The last time I had felt such an absence of control over my own destiny was when I was placed in a southern jail for demonstrating for equality some years before. Then, too, I had known that I was entirely at the mercy of events I could not control, could not begin to influence, and could not even understand.

Panic and hopelessness returned with the blackness. I struggled to use reason, to conjure up a method which could take us out of there. I prayed that Charles knew the way. Part of me believed that he could not be so sure and yet wrong. But logic told me that even those who knew the bush well would probably now be lost if they were with us.

I asked Charles how far from the road he thought we were. He said that he thought we were not more than 150 to 170 yards away. This confirmed my own belief. I had not long ago read of a plane that crashed in New England. The survivors were but half a mile from a road which would have taken them to safety. They died in a forest after having circled in vain for days.

I felt sympathetic toward Charles and I decided to share the information that I had secured from Terri Buford with him. Of course, since he had been counsel for the Temple for a year and a half and I had learned of the existence of the Peoples Temple only two months before, Garry certainly knew far more about the odd organization than I did. But he was so determined to maintain the Temple as a client that I wanted to brief him about the possibility of additional potential problems.

Before telling him about my frank exchanges with Terri, I swore him to absolute secrecy. He asked if he might share the information just with Pat Richartz, his legal assistant. Since she was not noted for discretion, I was firmly opposed to that proposal. I said, "Charles, a human being's life may depend upon your absolute commitment to secrecy." He agreed to tell no one. He kept his promise only until he returned to San Francisco and there, at a large press conference, he announced, "Mark Lane's source was Terri Buford." He described her as a defector who had been the second in command of Peoples Temple. He thus endangered her life and mine when he violated the attorney-client rule regarding privileged information.

As we sat or reclined on the jungle floor, Garry said that he wished that he had the ability to sleep there. I marvelled that our approach to the subject was so different. I was tired and afraid of dropping off to sleep. I fought sleep for fear of becoming even more vulnerable. I began to focus my mind upon some logical method which might help us to escape from the jungle in the morning. The trees towered one hundred fifty feet above us. When the sun finally rose, I would not know above which horizon it was first visible. There were no horizons there. On which side of the tree does the moss grow, I asked. Neither of us knew. It mattered little, I decided, since we did not know whether the road was east or west, south or north of us.

I was not able to share this problem with Garry. He insisted "Look, the road is right over there. We can go there right now." I asked how he could be so sure and he said, "I've been in the forest before." I reminded him gently that we were not in a forest, but we had gotten lost after dark in an unexplored jungle.

I suggested that we discuss developing a methodology for solving the problem, or failing that, a technique which might be serviceable when the morning came and we began to look for the road. Invariably Charles scornfully rejected this approach as "a waste of time" since "I can walk right over to that road now." After one occasion, when he seriously proposed that I follow him in total darkness to the road, I abandoned the matter as a subject for discussion.

Using the faint light from my watch and taking advantage of the moments when the moon lightened the sky, I began to search through my bag. I came across a soaked passport, a wilted airplane ticket, another small paperback book which I had previously overlooked, a toilet article kit, and nestled in at the bottom, a plastic-wrapped package containing three pairs of white undershorts. As I examined each item in the toilet article kit, I felt a toothbrush, toothpaste tube, a pair of cufflinks, a nail file, and then a small smooth object which seemed unfamiliar. It was a little leather container with a flap that had been closed and snapped. It seemed familiar, yet I could not recall putting it there or what it was. I opened the case and felt a smooth metal object. Suddenly I remembered having purchased the folding precision scissors about one year before at JFK Airport in New York City. I was between flights and had wandered into a favorite store, Hoffritz, where an effective salesman convinced me that the device would be very useful. He was expecting me to trim my moustache with it regularly, he said. I had tried it once the next morning, and then tossed it into my utility kit where it had remained until that moment. I discontinued the process of taking inventory and began to assemble my thoughts around the meager possessions which might be made to serve our desperate need.

Charles stretched, and said, "Do you really think there was a conspiracy to kill King?" I snapped back, "Yes." He asked "What do you base that on?" I said that I did not wish to discuss the subject then. He said that he had been under the impression that I lectured on the subject at college campuses. I said that I had done so but was at the moment thinking of something else. He rolled over and said, "If you're still worried about getting out of here, it's ridiculous. I have an excellent sense of direction."

As my mind returned to the problem which I had never wholly forgotten, Garry spoke again, "Mark." I answered in a tone that left no doubt that I was annoyed. He continued, "The one positive thing to come out of this for me is that we have gotten to know each other for the first time. I'm glad that we are friends now. After this experience, we'll be friends for life." I was strangely moved by his words and I hastened to tell him that I felt the same way.

"The white cloth," I said, "the underwear." Garry asked what I was talking about. I said, "I can cut the underwear, fortunately—it's white—into thin strips, a hundred or more if need be. I can cut it into strips with these scissors." I explained that if we were truly less than two hundred yards from the road, which seemed likely, we could find our way out eventually if only we could always return to our starting place. "This place," I said "is our base camp. If we see it as a hub to which we always return, we can strike out in every direction, like spokes on a wheel, until we find the road. If we string up white cotton markers as we go, when we conclude that we have gone too far, we follow the markers back, picking them up on the way until we reach the base camp and strike out in a new direction." I was elated. I felt as if a great weight had been removed from me. It was just a question of getting through the night and avoiding the armed killers the next day once we found the road.

The silence was broken by a gentle rain which turned almost at once into another torrential downpour. It was four-thirty. The jungle floor became soggy, then wet, and then a sliding shallow lake. We stood up and shivered in the surprisingly cold rain. In forty-five minutes the rain stopped, but from the canopy of leaves and vines, the drops continued to fall. At five-fifteen, another thunderstorm burst upon the bush. Still we stood and shivered until at last it stopped.

As we once again lowered ourselves to the ground, in the total silence and oppressive darkness we heard an eerie sound. It began as a muffled wrenching noise and consumed the night with a loud and urgent whisper. We both sat up and Charles was able to explain the phenomenon. A giant tree had fallen. A little while later another tree fell much closer to us in the dark.

I expected the morning to begin at six o'clock, for on Friday night I was present when Don Harris asked Johnny Jones about first light in preparation for his plans to film Saturday morning. Yet at six, the solid darkness had not cracked. Forty-five minutes later, a grayness began to infiltrate the black. As I began to cut the shorts in strips, Garry's attention turned to his briefcase. He searched through his files one by one and then exclaimed, "The bastard. He took that file. That's what the son of a bitch was after."

He stood up and said, "For Christ's sake, lets go. We don't need that shit." He began to walk into the bush. I asked him to wait until I had manufactured enough strips. He refused. I handed him half of the strips and followed as he plunged through the heavy underbrush, the prickly vines, and the thorny vegetation that tore at our clothes and skin. I paused to place a marker on a tree or across a low-hanging vine, calling out to Garry to move less quickly lest we be separated. He moved on resolutely, a display of absolute and almost inspiring confidence. He drove on until he faltered, indicating his unsureness by a slight change in direction, a sudden spurt ahead, and then, at last, the realization that he was lost. He spun around, betrayed by a sense upon which he had gambled both of our lives. He looked hopelessly bewildered and then he said it, "I guess it was the wrong direction." I do not suffer fools gladly and if there is some small virtue associated with that weakness, it is perhaps that I recognize it as a failing. My anger that early morning in the jungle was divided: A good portion was squandered on Garry, but a substantial force was inner-directed for having followed him. He had, we soon discovered, placed only one white strip on a branch, and I, in my desire to keep up with him, had placed too few to mark the trail back.

Then, at 7:45 Sunday morning, we heard running through the bush. In the green, dripping rain forest, overgrown by vines and undergrowth and covered by a canopy draped across hardwood trees, it was impossible to determine from which direction the sounds came. We heard cries and screams. It seemed that women and children were being pursued, perhaps hunted. We froze and listened. Within moments, I heard the reports of some fifteen to twenty shots being fired. I heard more screaming and more sounds of people thrashing about in the jungle. We were afraid to move, for it was impossible to move quietly. Moving there meant crushing fallen branches, breaking vines, repelling plants with sharp thorns. Often it meant stumbling and falling. We remained still. We were both lost and in danger of being found. I felt my anger surge against Charles; his false confidence might cost us our lives. I considered calling out; notifying the hunted and the hunters that we were there. At that moment, the knowledge that we were lost was more oppressive than the fear that killers might find us.

Instead, together, patiently, we searched for the cotton trail. I found one marker and then another; Garry found one. The cloths were darker now, muddied by contact with our hands and clothing and more difficult to see in that dark green and brown prison.

Twenty minutes of desperate searching intervened before we found the next marker. Slowly, with a false patience firmly rooted in panic, we found our way to the base camp.

At that moment I took full charge of the escape plan. I carefully cut the remaining shorts into one-inch-wide strips. I set off in the opposite direction from the one from we had just returned. I gave Charles a number of strips, but I did not rely upon him to mark the trail. As I looked back there was not a moment or a place from which I could see fewer than five cotton strips in a row. On occasion, I could see almost a dozen. Employing that system, we found the road.

Charles suggested that we walk down the road. Again I argued, with success, for the rough area between the cassava plants and the bush. We rested at intervals. The sun was bright and steam was rising from the ground. We heard the unmistakable sound of a helicopter. Then we heard and soon saw a fixed-wing plane. A little later, we saw the helicopter. It was circling over the village of Jonestown. For the first time, we felt quite sure that the world had heard of whatever had transpired at the settlement in the midst of the jungle.

Until then we did not know if our spotty information and rampant speculation comprised the entire body of knowledge regarding the event. We had not seen a person die. We had not seen a body. Given the bizarre mind of Jim Jones and his history of threats made but not carried out, it seemed possible that our fears, magnified by a night spent in the jungle, had been enormously exaggerated. Garry held to the theory that quite possibly nothing much had happened. It all seemed quite real to me, however, and I feared for the safety of so many warm and beautiful people. I was certain that Garry knew Jones and his operation intimately and was an integral part of it. I believed, therefore, that his knowledge would better prepare him to interpret the events. I had met Jones just one time before that weekend, and, until earlier that month, had no idea of the real problems that his actions had created.

As we rested near the bush, Charles and I discussed our differing views about how we should proceed. Charles favored a fast walk down the road to Port Kaituma. While I was as anxious as he to get out of there, I foresaw the possibility of danger in that approach. I suggested that we crawl back a few feet into the bush, always keeping the road in sight and our path back to it marked by strips of cloth. I said, "If we spend tonight here, by tomorrow, we will see an abandoned muddy road transformed into a United States military highway." I said that a thousand Americans had lived down that road just the day before, that many were probably dead, and others lost in the jungle. Garry said that he would not spend another night there under any circumstances. My analysis was entirely inaccurate. Not a single vehicle was dispatched by the United States government to rescue those who were lost. As a result, I am certain, many Americans, mostly children and women, perished in the jungle.

Garry and I reached a compromise. We would wait one hour to see if any public or military authorities arrived. With the exception of the airplane and helicopter, no such presence was manifested. He then insisted upon walking on the road. My position, that we choose the rougher but safer terrain, prevailed for a short time; then he headed for the road. It was hot and muggy. My glasses were steamed and dirty and nothing we possessed was clean or dry. I could see as well without my glasses as with them, differently and not too clearly in either instance. Garry insisted that his eyesight was so sharp that he would be able to observe gunmen hidden in the jungle and awaiting us from an ambush before they could spot us as we walked down the open road. Suddenly he halted. He said that he saw two men, one a tall blond with a rifle, standing at the side of the road. The other man also held a weapon, he said. We crawled into the cassava fields and slowly approached the scene. We saw, as we drew closer, two trees, one a banana tree with a twisted brown broad leaf. My fragile feeling of security could not withstand the error. The tree was three times the height of a man.

We proceeded as cautiously as my poor eyesight and Garry's swollen confidence would allow. We passed a final long bend in the road and then we saw a small guardhouse at the end of the road. Beyond it, if we could reach it, was the main and lightly traveled road to Port Kaituma. Garry was sure the guardhouse had been abandoned. I was less certain. I suggested that we circle around it by returning to the bush. Garry dropped his briefcase, picked up a pole that had been used to prop up a banana tree heavy-laden with fruit, and looking like Don Quixote, he bravely rushed the guardhouse. He tore open the door, prepared to spear anyone who might be there. No one was there. A few small piglets rooted about the shack. I picked up our luggage and together we ran for freedom toward Port Kaituma, three miles away.

Garry was certain that a left turn would take us past a road marked with a large chain. He said that he remembered seeing that landmark on the trip from the airstrip on Friday. We walked to the left and soon came upon the chain. Feeling vindicated, he said that soon we would pass an abandoned wooden house on the left of the road. We did and we believed then that we were closing in on Port Kaituma. We saw several figures moving toward us from ahead. They came closer and were recognizible as four young Guyanese women. I asked them the way to Port Kaituma. They stared at us almost in astonishment and then said we were on the right path. Garry and I looked at each other. We were scratched, bleeding, and wearing filthy and wrinkled clothes that looked as if someone had slept in them on a jungle floor during a torrential rainstorm. Garry's bald head reflected the sun, while his long, tangled hair trailed behind him.

A helicopter flew above us, and then it circled over Jonestown, by then far behind us. As we reached the outskirts of the little village of Port Kaituma, a community without a regularly operating telephone line and with but one on-duty police officer, a military truck belonging to the Guyana Defense Force (GDF) overtook us. I waved it down, Charles and I jumped on board, and I asked to be taken to the police station.

At the station I told the officer that we had just come from Jonestown. I asked him if he knew what happened there. He said that many people had died, perhaps hundreds, that there were practically no survivors who had made it out. I told him that there were people lost in the jungle. He said that the authorities were looking into that.

I asked if there had been any problem at the airstrip. It was then just twenty-four hours after Ryan and his group had been driven back to the airfield. He said, "Oh, yes. Five people were killed." I asked if he meant injured or killed. "Many others injured but five killed," he said. When I asked who had died he said, "Ryan, the woman with him,* and three cameramen." I asked him if he knew the names of any of the reporters and he said that he did not. I asked, "Don Harris, do you know that name?" He said, "Yes, Harris was killed."

As we sat in the office of the police station a man, locked behind a wooden door, asked to speak with me. I approached the door to see who there knew my name. At the same time Garry asked the police officer if there was a place where he could plug in his hair dryer. The officer seemed surprised and said that he could not help him with that problem. The policeman then opened the locked cell door and I saw Larry Layton for the first time since he had told Ryan that he wanted to leave. Layton told me that he had been arrested in connection with the murders at the airstrip. He spoke to me in the presence of a police officer, who in fact stood between us. Therefore, no

*The reference here was to Jackie Speier, who accompanied Congressman Ryan and served on his personal staff. Although she was not killed during the attack at the airstrip, she was seriously wounded.

confidential attorney-client communication was initiated. I asked, "What happened there?" He said, "I need a lawyer." I repeated my question, and he said, "I think I may be innocent." When I asked him how it came about that so many decent people had died, he said, "Maybe you're too tired to talk about this now." I think that his observation was astute.

Garry and I were flown from the airstrip to Georgetown by a military airship, where I made a full statement to the national police authorities and a representative of the American embassy. I implored the American authorities to search for the survivors in the jungle and to preserve the existing evidence at Jonestown. The embassy representative said that the authorities had determined I was a "genuine political refugee" and that as such, the embassy had reserved a hotel room for me in Georgetown and would cover all of my expenses while I was there. Later, I arrived at the hotel to discover that no reservations had been made, and when I checked out, I was told that I would have to pay, since the embassy had not agreed to do so.

While I was speaking with the Guyanese justice officials, I was told that the minister of justice wanted to see me. He welcomed me to his office and handed the receiver of his telephone to me. I said "Hello," and April said, "It's you, thank God." I asked her to call my father, my sister, and my brother and to tell them that I was fine and would be home soon. I gave her Garry's home telephone number and asked her to tell his wife that he too was fine.

Later, I discovered that the State Department had regularly made false statements to April. She had flown to Washington as soon as news of the massacre had reached the United States. The State Department issued false public statements and, as a matter of course, refused to release reliable information in its possession to relatives of the victims and instead gave them information it knew to be untrue. Further, efforts by relatives of the victims and Guyanese authorities to learn the facts and to investigate were impeded by the State Department. The concern and kindness shown to the survivors and the relatives of the victims came primarily from the people of Guyana and their representatives.

I went to the hotel in Georgetown to which the embassy had directed me and took a long hot bath. My body, I saw for the first time, was covered with literally hundreds of scratches and insect bites. The cut on my hand had become infected.

By early morning swarms of reporters had discovered where I was staying. I did not wish to talk to them or anyone. I was still struggling to comprehend the enormity of what I knew had occurred. Hundreds of my newfound friends were dead. So many children and so many old people had died there. They were such a gentle people and they had sought to find a place of peace. My anger found its focus on Jim Jones, whose twisted standards and devious conduct had made the massacre a possibility. Yet it seemed that others, for purposes then unknown to me, had acted so that the possibility might be transformed into a reality.

A dozen American major media forces had called to meet with me, including the radio and television networks, the major newspapers, and news magazines. Only when it became clear that they were accepting the United States government's handouts, which classified the mass murder as a "mass suicide ritual" and were slavishly following that lead, did I decide to talk with them.

Part of the reason for my reluctance to encourage the press was that Terri Buford had taken refuge in our home. Neither she, nor the members of our family, wanted it known that she was with us.

As I contemplated the best course to pursue, other forces determined that the truth about the massacre, including the knowledge of what caused it, should never be known.

13 The Massacre

In the United States, as in most countries in which the requisite skills and techniques are available, the body of a victim is subjected to an autopsy when there is a question as to the cause of death. Many prosecuting attorneys consider the report of the forensic pathologist to be essential in a trial in which a defendant is charged with having committed a homicide.

Upon hearing the news reports that hundreds of Americans had died in Jonestown, Guyana, leading American forensic pathologists, among them Dr. Sydney B. Weinberg, medical examiner for Suffolk County, New York; Dr. Cyril Wecht, medical examiner for Allegheny County, Pennsylvania, which includes Pittsburgh; and Dr. Leslie I. Lukash, medical examiner for Nassau County, New York, urged that the bodies be subjected to examination by forensic pathologists.

Dr. Lukash said that the single most important step in determining how many of the members of the Peoples Temple died voluntarily or were murdered would be the performance of autopsies. He continued, "Everything is presumptive about the cause and manner of death without autopsies having been performed."*

Dr. Weinberg said that it was crucial that autopsies be performed and tissue samples be secured for toxicological tests before the embalming of the bodies.† Dr. Wecht said that a number of pathologists suggested that the government send a team of specialists in forensic medicine to Jonestown immediately upon learning of the deaths. They stated that the team should have the responsibility for photographing the victims as they were discovered, collecting tissue samples, and beginning the process of performing

**New York Times,* 3 December, 1978.
†Ibid.

autopsies. The doctors suggested upon medical and humanitarian grounds that the bodies be flown immediately to a military mortuary in Oakland, California, close to where the relatives lived. They explained that the proximity to the relatives would be of invaluable assistance in the medical investigation.

Early in 1979 I met with Dr. Cyril Wecht, a forensic pathologist, lawyer, and an appointed consultant by the Select Committee on Assassinations of the U.S. House of Representatives in its investigation into the death of President John F. Kennedy. I asked him to explain what he would have done had he been given the responsibility for the medical investigation into the Jonestown deaths. Wecht said, "The first thing that should have been done was that each of the bodies should have been photographed. There should have been close-up photographs of the face and photographs to show the location of the bodies and their relationship to other bodies. Diagrams and sketches of entire areas should have been prepared and numbers arbitrarily assigned to the bodies should have been noted on the sketches and diagrams which would fix the place of death and the relationship of one body to another permanently. With the photographs, sketches, and diagrams, a great deal of valuable information would have been preserved.

"In addition, I would have stakes prepared with numbers which corresponded to the numbers assigned to the victims, and the stakes would be placed in the ground indicating where each body was as it was removed. In that fashion, a subsequent examination of the death scene might be more useful. After these preliminary steps had been accomplished and before each body is removed, teams of forensic scientists would be assigned to make a cursory examination of each body.

"I am not suggesting that a complete postmortem examination could have been accomplished under field conditions, but certain steps should be taken at the outset. A member of the team would dictate to a tape recorder a full and complete description of the body so that a permanent record would be established, revealing the condition of the body at that time. An attempt would be made to withdraw blood for a toxicological analysis. For that purpose, long large-bore needles of at least fifty centimeters would be required. This should be done in the field and quickly before decomposition.

"It would be necessary in the field to determine if there were injection sites from a needle and where such sites were visible. A portion of the skin, underlying fat and underlying muscle should be excised and placed in bags without fixative. No Formalin should be used for those tissues and they should be maintained in a frozen state for subsequent toxicological studies. In that fashion, the nature of the material injected into the body could be ascertained through biological and chemical studies. Portable X-ray units should be brought to the scene so that wherever there was evidence of injury, such as a possible bullet wound or an indication that someone had been beaten or injured in another way, that area could be examined by X ray. I do not believe that it would be possible to take routine X rays in the field, but X rays for suspicious areas could be extremely useful."

I asked Dr. Wecht if he knew whether or not doctors might be available for the kind of investigation which he suggested. He said, "The Armed Forces Institute of Pathology has available several forensic pathologists. In addition, the U.S. military, including the air force, army, and some naval bases, have numerous pathologists. All that would be required would be a relatively small number of forensic pathologists in charge of the operation who would supervise the work of other pathologists. The pathologists who were not forensic would certainly be qualified to open the body and to collect relevant materials from the body. They can perform those tasks as well as forensic pathologists can. I believe that the U.S. government could have secured from military and civilian sources all the forensic pathologists and photographers and others required almost immediately."

Because I was aware of the fact that the bodies in Jonestown were subjected to conditions on the floor of the jungle which would accelerate ordinary decomposition, I asked Dr. Wecht how quickly the teams could accomplish their objective in the field. He said, "I believe that twenty-five to thirty teams could have been established in a very short period of time. With each team handling thirty to thirty-five cases, conducting the preliminary examinations that I made reference to, I believe that in a matter of several hours all of the preliminary examinations could have been completed. I do not mean that the toxicological studies would have been completed, but in that short period of time the bodies could have been photographed, described, an external examination made, the initial incisions made, and body fluids and tissues obtained.

"With such teams it would certainly be possible to secure and preserve from each body, body fat and muscles, urine and bile from the gall bladder, a large portion of the liver, one kidney, a portion of the brain, and gastric contents. While these tissues would be placed in small plastic bags and frozen, a small portion of each tissue could be placed in Formalin which is the most common fixative. Those tissues would be valuable for subsequent microscopic study or what we call histopathology. Examination of the tissue would, of course, make it possible to determine if the deaths were caused by cyanide poisoning or cyanide and some other substances—gunshot wounds—or as the result of an injection of cyanide or other poison as opposed to the victims having ingested it orally."

I asked Dr. Wecht if he believed that autopsies should have been conducted in Guyana or if the bodies should have been subjected to pathological examinations after their return to the United States. He said, "That decision would have to be made based upon a study of the law, logistics, and perhaps other matters of overall investigative strategy. If it was not going to be possible to conduct autopsies in a suitable place in Guyana, then perhaps it would be necessary to preserve the bodies by placing them under refrigeration immediately and returning them to a suitable facility in the U.S. If the bodies were to be returned to the U.S., it would be wise to place them on the West Coast close to where those who could identify them reside. The most crucial matter is that the decision as to where to conduct the autopsies be made immediately and the bodies preserved and examined as quickly as possible."

I was impressed with the speed, skill, and thoroughness with which Dr. Wecht described the procedures which should be employed to preserve evidence. He said, "What I have told you is neither profound nor brilliant; it is just routine. While the deaths of so many Americans in Jonestown was a unique experience for America, there have been other disasters, including airplane crashes, in which large numbers of bodies are scattered around. On occasion, these bodies fall to earth in jungle areas where decomposition takes place quickly. Therefore, forensic pathologists throughout the world understand and have established routine procedures to deal quickly with these matters."

Almost immediately after the United States government learned of the deaths in Jonestown, arrangements were made to send Colonel William Gordon to the area. Gordon is the Director of Operations for the United States Army Southern Command. In November 1978 he was stationed in the Panama Canal zone and was responsible for all U.S. activities in South America. He was placed in full charge of the American action in Guyana.

The initial position taken by the United States government was to urge the Guyanese authorities to dig a large trench in Jonestown and bury all of the bodies there in a mass grave. The State Department and the American embassy in Georgetown, both of which favored that final solution, did not suggest that an effort to identify the bodies precede the mass burial or that tissue samples be taken. Officials in the government of Guyana were offended by the suggestion and stated that they would not comply with it. The United States government made no arrangements initially to remove the bodies from the floor of the jungle. After several days they began to decompose and identification was quickly becoming unlikely.

Three days after the massacre on November 21, 1978, the Associated Press* reported that, "Douglas Davidson, an officer with the U.S. Embassy, said the bodies are in an advanced state of decomposition and authorities are considering burying them in Jonestown." The AP dispatch quoted, "An Embassy official, Peter Londoner," as having said, " 'The bodies are starting to swell and some seem ready to burst.' " The American officials again suggested a mass burial in Jonestown, since the bodies were hardly suitable for transportation to the U.S., and again the Guyanese officials declined.

To assist the American authorities with any investigation they wished to make, including the removal of the bodies, the Guyanese government waived its own law, which required autopsies in homicide cases. While the American authorities declined to act at first, the Guyanese police arranged for many of the bodies to be identified by Peoples Temple members who survived the massacre, including Tim Carter. The bodies which were identified were maintained by the Guyanese authorities in family groups wherever possible.

A number of autopsies were performed upon the bodies by Dr. C. Leslie Mootoo, the chief medical examiner of Guyana. Although he had been in contact with Dr. Robert Stein, the medical examiner of Chicago, and had requested assistance from American forensic pathologists, none was forthcoming. Later, when Dr. Mootoo was asked why the American pathologists were not dispatched to assist him, he said that he wondered if American government officials had made the determination that forensic pathologists from the United States were not to be sent to Guyana.

Finally, after the bodies had lain under a tropical sun for four days, the United States government acted. Forty of the badly decomposed bodies were placed into plastic body bags and flown from Jonestown to Georgetown in military helicopters. They were placed at the Timehri Airport in a holding area and kept there while arrangements were made to secure military cargo planes to fly them to the Dover Air Force Base in Dover, Delaware. While the bodies were maintained in the tropical climate at Georgetown, no effort was made by Colonel Gordon or those under his command to preserve them by refrigeration or any other means. Many of the bodies did not reach the Dover Air Force Base until ten days after the massacre. During that entire time, no tissue samples had been removed by American technicians, no autopsies had been conducted, and no effort toward identification had been made. The Dover Air Force Base was chosen over military bases in California because, as the government authorities

*New Orleans *States-Item*, 21 November 1978.

stated, they wanted to keep the bodies as far away from the relatives as possible.

On November 26, the *New York Times* reported, "Pathologists interviewed said that embalming bodies before an autopsy would adversely affect the ability to detect cyanide and other toxins." The *Times* also reported in the same issue that "Pathologists familiar with other disasters said that legal problems could arise in the next few years in cases where the cause of death had not been firmly established." Although it was clear that in the absence of an autopsy it might be difficult and perhaps impossible to determine the cause of death, the *Times* reported that, "A spokesman at the Delaware Air Force Base said bodies had begun to be embalmed without autopsies." Both AP and UPI reported that as the bodies began to arrive at the Dover Air Force Base, teams of morticians and fingerprint experts worked around the clock to process the bodies and to begin the identification process.

The U.S. government had arranged for autopsies to be conducted upon Jones and six other members of the Peoples Temple. The autopsies were performed by military pathologists under the direction of the Deputy Director of the Armed Forces Institute of Pathology, Colonel William Cowan. Dr. Rudiger Breitenecker, a civilian pathologist at Greater Baltimore Medical Center, acted as a consultant to the military pathologist. In the March 1979 issue of *Lab World,* * a respected journal read by directors of laboratories and forensic pathologists throughout the United States, Dr. Breitenecker suggested that if the mission of the federal government was to effectively return the bodies of the more than nine hundred American citizens to the United States, "then the investigation should be centered on the two cardinal questions: (1) identification, and (2) cause and manner of death." Dr. Breitenecker said, "This could have been aided substantially had it been handled by following current standards which are routinely used by all good medical examiners—identification, tagging location of bodies, and noting surrounding family members. So in this particular case of families dying together, we could have gained a lot by identifying one member of a family. It would have been easier to identify the rest. Speed of procuring and securing toxicological samples would have allowed rapid and definitive determination of the cause of death."

In the same article in *Lab World,* Lt. Col. Brigham Shuler, public information officer in the Office of the Secretary of Defense, admitted that "samples were not taken." Lt. Col. Alfred Keys, logistics operation officer

*Manley Witten, "Guyana: The Autopsy of Disbelief." *Lab World* 30(3):14–19, 1979. Article hereafter referred to as *Lab World.*

for a support group which recovered the bodies, said, "No attempt was made to identify the bodies." He explained, "It was hot and we were three days behind." The government directed Dr. Lynn Crook, a forensic pathologist from the University of South Carolina Medical Center, to fly to Jonestown. He was accompanied by Col. Bruce Poitrast, a military surgeon stationed in the Canal Zone. They arrived three days after the massacre and stated that they had been the first Americans on the scene. Dr. Crook was an expert in the treatment of rat poison victims and for reasons not subsequently explained, the United States government was at first under the impression that the victims had been poisoned by rat poison.

(Terri Buford surmised that there was some confusion over the fact that she and Terry Carter had ordered rat poison some weeks earlier for the large number of rodents attacking the fields at night. The coded message had been misconstrued by Temple members, who thought the message had to do with "enemies" as well; this message may well have been intercepted by government monitors in Panama.)

When Dr. Crook was asked by *Lab World* why he did not take specimens from the bodies, he said, "I didn't even have a pocket knife, no equipment and no preservatives for specimens." He said he had not brought any equipment with him.

Lab World also conducted an in-depth study of the various medical failures by American authorities regarding the deaths in Guyana. In the study written by associate editor Manley Witten,* it asked "why a professional [Dr. Crook], who had traveled hundreds of miles to attend to the medical needs of fellow Americans, carried no equipment with which to work." Witten reported that "the securing of toxicological specimens was not even mentioned in Guyana," according to Col. Gordon. Gordon said, Witten reported, " 'I don't know of any discussion that took place about samples. No one mentioned it to me as being critical or necessary.' " Col. Cowan, who was in charge of the bodies in Dover, said that the embalming of the bodies was done by contract morticians and no body fluids were saved for analysis. *Lab World* reported that Col. Cowan explained, "We raised the question of obtaining fluid samples but we were told we had no authority."

Dr. Breitenecker was among those most critical of the autopsy procedure. He said, "Embalming prior to the autopsies is a serious strike against any appropriate medical legal examination. One of the cardinal sins in a medicolegal examination is to embalm the body before the examination since this

**Lab World*.

destroys a large number of toxic substances and poisons. It often makes chemical analysis useless." He added, "I don't think I've ever done a major examination of a case of national interest or otherwise where I had less information to go on than in this particular case. The communication between the on-site investigations and the team at Dover was deplorable. So little information was provided to us that it was appalling."*

The seven autopsies were performed on December 15, 1978. More than two months later, Dr. Mootoo addressed a meeting of the American Academy of Forensic Sciences in Atlanta, Georgia, where he presented the findings of his medical investigation. According to the *New York Times,*† "His one-hour presentation stunned many in an audience of eight hundred experts, including members of a team of the Armed Forces Institute of Pathology in Washington." The Justice Department had asked this team to do the autopsies in this country last December on the seven bodies from Jonestown. At the meeting, Dr. Breitenecker said, "Those of us on the front line knew nothing about Dr. Mootoo's scientific findings until today." He said, "We shuddered about the degree of ineptness." Dr. Mootoo reported that although he had examined a small number of the bodies in Jonestown, he had discovered that eighty-three people had been injected with cyanide. He said that his investigation was unable to continue because of fatigue, insufficient supplies of equipment, and lack of assistance. In summarizing the medical work done by the American military, *Lab World* concluded:

> The contradictions, inconsistencies, and questionable truths related through these interviews leave many unanswered questions. In fact, the entire episode suggests government mismanagement or a coverup of the true facts. The statements given by various government officials lend fuel to accusations made by people like Mark Lane, who served as legal counsel for Jones' Peoples Temple. Lane proclaimed that a U.S. conspiracy existed to destroy the cult and its leader. The totally unprofessional and questionable handling of the bodies and the failure to establish cause and manner of death do not dispute Lane's charges. Unfortunately, his claims are strengthened because there are so few facts about what actually happened. It is regrettable that professional medical personnel failed to do what the newest member—fresh from college—of a clinical medical laboratory would have known to do.

**Lab World.*

†Lawrence Altman, in the *New York Times,* 18 February, 1979.

Dover Air Force Base had been chosen by the government for two reasons. It was far from the families of the victims who lived in California and since it was on federal property, military authorities could establish total security. Reporters were not permitted access to the base and civilians had no way of knowing what procedures were employed at what was referred to by the military as the "base mortuary." However, an existing contract obligated the government to employ the services of the Andrew W. Nix Funeral Home in Philadelphia, Pennsylvania, for the embalming of the bodies. Two dozen FBI agents and a substantial number of top-ranking military officials were present when the bodies were brought to the base. The funeral home personnel were instructed not to release any information to reporters of the news media or to in any other way violate the iron security surrounding the bodies that had been established by the military authorities and the Federal Bureau of Investigation.

However, I was able to interview Theophilus Nix, Jr., who is presently a student at Ithaca College in New York. Before attending Ithaca College, Mr. Nix attended the Cincinnati College of Mortuary Science for one year and then served his internship in Philadelphia with the Nix Funeral Home. He was subsequently licensed by the state of Pennsylvania as a funeral director and embalmer. When his uncle, Andrew W. Nix, was commissioned to establish a team of embalmers for the work at Dover Air Force Base, he chose his nephew Theo Nix as one of the team.

In an exclusive interview with me in early 1979, Theo Nix described the condition of the bodies. "They were in really bad shape. They were bloated, the top skin was slipping from the adjoining skin. You couldn't even tell what sex they were because of the condition they were in, so we had to cut the clothes and look down into the pubic area to determine what sex they were. The bodies were covered with maggots."

He told me that he was instructed as to the security measures that had been established and he was ordered not to talk with anyone about what he had observed. He said, "They had officers all over the base and security was very tight. They had a master list of people and if your name was not on the master list or if you didn't have a mortuary sticker you could not get into the compound." I told him that witnesses who saw the bodies in Jonestown soon after death said that there were substantial abscesses on the faces, foreheads, chests, and arms of some of the victims where they had been injected with cyanide. I asked him if he had observed any such marks. He replied, "I couldn't tell if there were abscesses, because in most cases there were no faces. Many times there was nothing left but a skull. Many times there was nothing left but bones."

I asked him to estimate the number of bodies with faces sufficiently intact so that identification could be made. He said that in more than seventy-five percent of the cases he would have been unable to make an identification even if he had known the person. He described for me the method which was employed. He said the bodies were delivered in black body bags secured with a zipper. The zippers were opened and the bodies were sprayed with gasoline to kill the maggots.

The FBI agents then tried to make identification of each body, and then each was given to the embalmers, who removed it from its body bag, put lime on it, wrapped it in cloth, and then placed it in a new body bag and into a casket. He said the caskets had been specifically designed with a rubber gasket so that they would be permanently sealed when closed. I asked him how the FBI attempted to identify the bodies. Nix said, "They photographed them and took fingerprints." He estimated that although the photographs would have been useless in more than three-fourths of the cases, "The pictures could have been more help than the fingerprints, because in so many cases, there were no fingers or the skin had so badly decomposed that you couldn't take fingerprints."

One mortuary publication described the fingerprinting process as particularly gruesome: as the hands and fingers were too decayed to handle, the skin on the ends of the fingertips was scraped off, an FBI agent would place the scraped skin on the ends of his own fingers, and then attempt the fingerprints.*

"I believe," Nix said, "that in the more than nine hundred bodies, only sixty had been identified." He said that after the FBI had attempted and failed to make an identification of the body, the embalmers assigned a letter and number to the body.

Although the media reported that all of the bodies had been embalmed, Nix described that procedure:

> We couldn't embalm those bodies intravenously as we normally do because they were in such bad shape. We couldn't remove the blood and put in the embalming fluid because some times there were no arms or faces. The bones were there, sometimes the flesh was gone and they were in various stages of decomposition. The bodies were sprayed with gasoline. Embalming fluid usually kills maggots but that process takes too long and we did not have the time. We injected cavity fluid into the trunk of the body and then we put a jellylike substance on

**American Funeral Director*, published by Kates-Boylston Publications, Inc. January 1979, p. 27.

the remaining skin and on the bones. That kills any organism that might have been there. This was to halt the decomposition process."

The first American reporter to arrive at the scene following the massacre was Charles Krause of the *Washington Post.* Krause reported, "From the air it literally looked like a garbage dump where someone dumped a lot of rag dolls." He said that the bodies apparently were lying where they fell and had not been touched. He also said that many "were holding one another." That early and erroneous report gave further support to the false assertion that the victims had all committed suicide. A more scientific examination, however, was conducted by Louis Gurvich, whom I had first met in New Orleans more than a decade ago. I saw him in Georgetown soon after the massacre. In the following months we exchanged information on a regular basis.

For thirty years Louis Gurvich has been running the largest private detective agency in New Orleans, Louisiana. His daughter Jann was a Jonestown resident when he last heard from her. Gurvich was in bed on Sunday morning, November 19, when his former wife called to tell him that a radio news broadcast had just reported that two hundred people had died in Jonestown. Gurvich immediately made arrangements for the first flight to Guyana, and in Georgetown on Monday evening, November 20, he talked with Douglas Ellice, the American Consul who had recently replaced Richard McCoy. Ellice said, "There is nothing we can do for you here and there's no way for you to get to Jonestown. It would be best if you went home now." Gurvich pointed out that his skills and experience as a detective might be useful in investigating the deaths. He said that he had not the slightest intention of going home until he had been to Jonestown and had an opportunity to search for his daughter. Ellice responded, "I guarantee you, you won't get to Jonestown."

Gurvich then said, "Do you know if my daughter is among the survivors?" Ellice answered, "I can't tell you that because of the Privacy Act." Gurvich ridiculed that answer, and Ellice admitted that he had seen a list containing the names of twelve known survivors and that Jann Gurvich's name was not on that list.

Gurvich met with Police Commissioner Lloyd Barker of Guyana, who gave him a letter authorizing him to enter Jonestown. Gurvich had permission but he still did not have transportation to the interior. The Guyanese then made a seat available to him on a flight from Georgetown to Matthew's Ridge. From there, however, no transportation was available that day into the airstrip at Port Kaituma, near Jonestown. The following morning a plane arrived at Matthew's Ridge and body bags were unloaded. An American military helicopter arrived soon after that and Gurvich asked the pilot, a lieutenant, to take him to Jonestown. The pilot said, "Sure, we have two empty seats and we're going in there now." Gurvich was told, however, that he would have to get Colonel Gordon's okay.

The colonel, who was in charge of the entire operation for the United States government, said, "I can't let you go in there. You have no right to be in Jonestown." A lieutenant of the Guyanese army said, "He [Gurvich] has as much right as you do. This is Guyana and he has a letter of authority from Commissioner Barker." Gurvich showed Gordon his letter. Gordon said, "Okay you have a right, but I don't have any gas. I can't take you or anybody."

The Guyanese lieutenant called over an enlisted man and said, "Fill that chopper up with gasoline, man." According to Gurvich, the lieutenant stood with his hands on his hips, "as if to say to Gordon, 'What is your next excuse going to be?' " Gordon said, "Mr. Gurvich, I know how you feel, but I can't take you in." Gurvich said, "Why can't you? You're in charge of this whole operation!"

Gordon answered, "This is a military helicopter, and you're a civilian." Gurvich reasonably pointed out that the situation constituted a unique type of emergency, that his daughter was in Jonestown, that he was a licensed detective with the authority from the highest police official in Guyana to enter Jonestown. "I can't take you," Gordon said. With that he turned his back on Gurvich and strode away. The Guyanese lieutenant said to Gurvich, "This is a fine government you have. Man, don't you worry, I'll get you there on a Guyanese helicopter." A little while later Gurvich did board a Guyanese helicopter and was flown to Jonestown. If Colonel Gordon understood his assignment to be: Take no steps to preserve the bodies; gather no valuable evidence; remove the bodies haphazardly and slowly from the jungle floor; and keep out all serious and trained investigators, even those with credentials from Guyanese authorities, then he acquitted himself effectively. Under his command, the evidence vanished, the bodies decomposed, and no trained investigators were assigned to record the available evidence.

Perhaps the most tawdry result of the intrusion of the American military operation in Guyana was the wholesale looting of the valuable documents in Jonestown carried out by the American military. They were sent in to remove the bodies. According to one American reporter in Panama, knowing that the documents, particularly those stored in the cabin that Jones had occupied, were of some value, the American soldiers stole them and smuggled them to Panama. In Panama, a number of reporters gathered to purchase the stolen property. Some of the documents, after highly selective editing, were published in America's leading newspapers, including the *New York Times.* Thus in the final American intervention in Jonestown, our soldiers became thieves, and our newspapers recipients of and profiteers through the use of stolen property. Much of the evidence was gone when Gurvich arrived at the death scene four days after the event to see what his practiced eye could discern.

He had not gone to Jonestown to probe the cause of the deaths but rather to learn of his daughter's fate. Yet, in addition to discovering that his daughter had died, he found other evidence as well. Gurvich told me what he saw in Jonestown.

"I saw the body of a man who was obviously fending off somebody and he died in that position. The odor was overwhelming. People with me began to vomit. But I just kept on, looking around, fighting not to be overcome by what I saw and the odor. There were bows and arrows still lying around.

"And I saw guns there. A number of guns. I am sure that more than six hundred of the bodies showed evidence that they had been murdered. Now people who were brainwashed or forced to drink the poison were murdered too, but in a different way.

"The evidence I saw convinced me that at least two-thirds of the people had been murdered more directly. Bodies were dragged after death, and laid out. Their bodies were stretched out from having been dragged. Jim Jones had been shot. I found out later that the authorities never even did a nitrate test* on his hands. Can you believe that?"

Gurvich said that he saw evidence that a number of the victims had been injected with poison. "They were punching them with the needle wherever they could. They injected some people in the back. Some in the foreheads. Some in the arms.

"Then I walked over to what looked like a family that had died together. There were injection marks on the man's body. Then I realized that I was looking at the result of a family being murdered. If you ever saw a mute scene of a man who died trying to defend his family, this was it.

"I told McCoy that at least they had to designate each area by letters or numbers and make a record of which area the body had come from when they removed them. And I said to him, for the U.S. government to allow American citizens to lie this long decomposing in the Guyanese

*A simple chemical test can detect the presence of nitrates on the skin. If Jones had shot himself, nitrates should have been present on one of his hands. The absence of nitrates would be strong evidence that he was shot by another person.

heat and rain is so staggering. And he said, 'Well what were they gonna do?' I said, 'You know that the Guyanese would have let them fly any number of teams down here and they could have been on the scene.' McCoy was defending the government. He said that after the Guyanese notified the U.S. government about what had happened, that he became a minor cog in the wheel, that it was really being handled in Washington. I did hear that the State Department wanted to dig a trench and bury them all in the same trench in Guyana. I said, 'You mean you were actually gonna bury my daughter in Guyana without my permission?' Of course he had no answer."

Two eyewitnesses, Odell Rhodes, Jr., and Stanley Clayton, offered evidence that confirmed the conclusions reached by experts, the Guyanese medical examiner, and the American investigator.* Both men had survived the massacre by quietly slipping out of the area where Jones and his aides were stationed. Each man found the road from Jonestown to Port Kaituma. And each man spoke of what he had seen.

Rhodes had found his way into the police station at Port Kaituma and said, "They're killing everybody at Jonestown!" He had witnessed a number of murders at Jonestown.

Clayton had seen what happened to those who protested. He told reporters, "One old lady was saying she didn't want to die. Then she said she had already taken the poison. One of the medical staff called for the security people. Two of them held her while she was injected with the poison."

Clayton saw many women and children murdered. He added that "The bodies were arranged neatly in the field behind the pavilion by members of the security staff."

Clayton said that the "heavily armed security squad" was then in force to see to it that anyone who did not drink the poison as directed by Jones would be injected with it. Clayton said that the "people were shaking with fear. Old people were weeping. The children were screaming." When mothers refused to surrender their children so that the poison could be squirted into their mouths, the armed guards and the nurses "just murdered the children." Clayton said, "Nurses took babies right out of their mothers' arms."

And through the nightmare, Jones, in complete control of the public address system, exhorted his flock to kill themselves. His words were preserved on a reel-to-reel tape recorder at the pavilion.

After the massacre, reporters were given a handwritten petition that was

***Washington Star*, 25 November, 1978.

later picked up by the wire services. It was apparently prepared by mothers in Jonestown, directed to Jones, and read:

> We the undersigned mothers have been shown a dream. We left our homes to follow it. Now we fear that it is about to turn into a nightmare.
>
> You want to end this because you see a threat from the outside. Do you not realize that we are strong enough to meet any challenge.
>
> Jonestown has become our haven and our strength. We can defend it. Not with arms or the terror of wholesale death but with the truth of our accomplishments and the strength of your vision.
>
> Dad, our Dad, we beg of you don't finally embark upon the step that you have spoken of.
>
> Please spare our children. If we must die, let them live. There is nothing noble in dying, nothing fine about killing our children.
>
> They have trusted us and you. Their lives and their deaths are the true tests of Jonestown.
>
> They are setting out on life free from racism, free from the pressures and the betrayals of modern society. Please do not force us to curse that future, the hope, with the bitterness of mass slaughter.
>
> We have seen Jonestown as a beacon of cooperation. Please do not insure its place in history as a symbol of horror, terror and futility. We face a period of danger but we can and must overcome it.

In spite of the overwhelming evidence of murder, the major news media in America called the tragedy a "mass suicide." On November 21, 1978, the *New York Times,* in a four-column headline on its front page, referred to "An Apparent Mass Suicide Rite." As the evidence of murder, rather than suicide, became available, the *New York Times* responded by erasing the word "apparent." Thus on November 22, its headline read, "Explaining the Mass Suicide: Fanaticism and Fear." The Associated Press story began with reference to "The Jonestown Suicide Cult" and then referred to "the site of the mass suicide."

Almost one month after the massacre, Attorney General Griffin Bell answered that the Federal Bureau of Investigation had in its possession the last recording made at Jonestown. He said that the evidence would be withheld from the public, since, in his view, disclosure would serve no purpose. The attorney general said that he had reached that conclusion, although he had not examined the evidence. "I do not suffer from morbid curiosity," America's chief law enforcement official explained.* The *Wash-*

**Los Angeles Times,* 16 December 1978.

ington Post ran a story about the tape recording on December 9, 1978, referring to the "mass suicide" of November 18, and on December 16, 1978, a *Los Angeles Times* headline read, "Bell Forbids Public Release of Guyana Mass Suicide Tapes."

Apparently the original tape recording has been placed in the FBI archives. It seems that a rather poor second generation copy was given to the Guyanese authorities. A cassette copy of that copy was made and ultimately became available to Beau Buchanan, the president of International Home Video Club, Inc., a New York corporation. The *New York Times* published excerpts from the tape in May 1979, and credited Buchanan as its source. Buchanan also furnished me with a copy of the cassette. In making the copy for the government of Guyana or in the production of a later generation, the tape was crudely edited.

The Staff Investigation Group to the Committee on Foreign Affairs of the House of Representatives began an investigation into the assassination of Congressman Ryan and the Jonestown tragedy. George Berdes, the staff consultant, told Buchanan that he had been unable to secure a copy of the tape recording for the congressional investigation from the FBI or the attorney general. Accordingly, he acquired one from Buchanan.

Buchanan is an outspoken critic of censorship. He said to me, "I'm opposed to censorship in any form. This tape is important evidence. It should not be suppressed. In the tape is the possibility of knowledge and understanding which can help people to avoid mistakes made out of ignorance. A great deal of human suffering comes from ignorance. Censorship prevents us from gaining that understanding."

Buchanan said the *Newsweek* reporter who interviewed him told him that the ghastly cover picture in full color of the bodies at Jonestown "sold more magazines than any cover in recent history." Since it is likely that the bodies were placed in order by Jones's security team, the picture was deceptive.

The portions of the tape selected by the *New York Times* were not representative of the entire tape and the transcript published by that newspaper contained serious errors. The *New York Times* interjected the word "applause" throughout the tape and the phrase "music and singing" at one point. The music and singing apparently did not come from the residents during the massacre, which was the impression created by the *New York Times,* but from a record. Among the obvious errors was this phrase attributed to Jones and published in the *Times*—"Jack Dean Maufin said —I don't know where he's at right this moment—hi, Jack." The list of those at Jonestown (which was published by the *New York Times*) revealed that there was no Jack Dean Maufin there. There *was* present an aide to Jim

Jones named Jack Beam. And, on the tape, Jones quite clearly said, "As Jack Beam often said—"

This and other similar errors, although innocuous, were indicative of the scholarship which the *New York Times* brought to its task. These mistakes were dwarfed by the *Times*'s biased editing of the tape. Throughout the latter half of the tape, beginning with what appears to be the time when those assembled realized that they were not attending another suicide drill but had been assembled to die—shrieks, screams, and cries of protest and despair predominate. Jones can be heard in angry tones excoriating those who are attempting to thwart his scheme. He orders them to "stop this nonsense." He calls upon them "to quit exciting your children." Yet nowhere in what the *New York Times* refers to as "Portions of a transcript of tape from Jonestown" is there an indication that many of the people are screaming and protesting.

In one other matter as well, it appears that the newspaper exercised poor judgment in selecting portions of its flawed transcript for publication. Terri Buford had already testified before local and federal grand juries that the Peoples Temple had authorized an assassination team to kill defectors from the Temple as well as political figures upon the death of Jim Jones. Her remarks were widely published as well as her statement that this plan might proceed only if the remnants of Temple activists in San Francisco felt that Jones wanted them to act. It seemed that they might never learn of their fallen leader's final position on the question. Then the *New York Times* selected for publication from its lengthy transcript these lines:

> Jones: The people of San Francisco will not—not be idle. Or would they? They'll not take our death in vain, you know.

Jean Brown, who emerged as the Temple's spokesperson after the death of Jones, said that the dying requests of the martyred leader should be honored. Given those circumstances, it is difficult to understand why the *New York Times* chose to become the conduit for his last homicidal instructions.

The appearance of a sympathetic, not to say identical, analysis of the evidence by the newspaper and the Department of Justice surfaced once again. As the *Times* published segments of a transcript wrenched out of context and replete with its own subjective and inaccurate interpretation, apparently to support its discredited theory that a mass suicide had taken place, Michael Abbell, coordinator of the investigation for the Department of Justice, said, "I would say the transcript indicates a collective will by the majority."

Published here for the first time are substantial excerpts from the last minutes at Jonestown.

The transcript is but a partial record of the event. The transcript is a stage of evidence once removed from the tape recording and is, therefore, less valuable. It is devoid of the screams of protest and anguish. Yet if the transcript is understood in the context of the events, it has some validity.

The setting is the pavilion in the center of Jonestown. An audience, consisting to a large extent of black children, women, and elderly people, is surrounded by scores of guards armed with semiautomatic weapons, shotguns, pistols, and crossbows. Jones has control of the microphone. He knows that Christine Miller is probably one of the most despised members of the commune. During the months that she lived in Jonestown, she demonstrated lack of concern for the welfare of the other residents. Her antisocial behavior in a difficult pioneer setting earned for her the least enviable reputation in Jonestown. He calls upon her to speak for the opposition, thus attempting to solidify support for his position. Others, including Marceline Jones, who try to protest, are denied access to the microphone and must try to shout from the floor. Jones is supported in his decision by a voluble claque, especially huge Jim McElvane, who prevents dissenters from being heard. Jones silences Marceline, drowning out her protests with, "Mother, Mother, Mother."

JIM JONES: It was said by the greatest of prophets in time immemorial—no man takes my life from me, I lay my life down. So to sit here and wait for a catastrophe that's gonna happen on that airplane, it's gonna be a catastrophe. It almost happened here, a congressman was nearly killed here but you can't steal peoples' children; you can't take peoples' children without expecting a violent reaction.

What's gonna happen in a few minutes is that one of the men on that plane is gonna shoot the pilot; I know that; I didn't plan it, but I know it's gonna happen. They gonna shoot that pilot and down comes that plane under the jungle and we had better not have any of our children left when it's over cause they'll parachute here in on us. I'm praying just as plain as I know how to pray. I've never lied to you, never have lied to you. I know that's what's gonna happen. That's what he intends to do and he will do it. He'll do it.

It oppresses on my brain seeing all these people behave so treasonous.

It was just too much for me to put together but I now know what he was telling me and it will happen, if the plane gets in the air even. So, my opinion is that we be kind to children and be kind to seniors, and take the potion like they used to take their infant [inaudible] and step over quietly because we are not committing suicide. It's a revolutionary act. We can't go back, they won't leave us alone, they are now going back to tell more lies, which means more congressmen. There is no way, no way we can survive.

CHRISTINE MILLER: Is it too late for Russia?

JONES: Looks like it's too late for Russia. They've killed. They've started to kill. That's why I think it's too late for Russia, otherwise I'd say [inaudible] that you're right but it's too late. I can't control these people. They are out there. They are gone with the guns. It's just too late. Once we kill anybody, at least that's the way I learned, I just put my lot with you. If one of my people do something, it's me. I don't have to take the blame for it but I don't live that way. If they deliver up [inaudible] who tried to get the man back there. The guy whose mother has been lying on him and lying on him and trying to break up his family and they've all agreed to kill us by any means necessary. You think I'm willing to let them get ya'll? [*crowd roars, "No!"*] Not on your life. No, you're not going, you're not going. I can't live that way. I cannot live that way. I've lived for all and I'll die for all.

MILLER: I'd say let's make an airlift to Russia. That's what I say. I don't think nothing is impossible.

JONES: How are you gonna airlift to Russia?

MILLER: Well, I thought they said if we got in an emergency, they gave us a code and to let them know.

JONES: No they didn't. They gave us a code that they'd let us know—not us creating an issue for them. They said if they saw the country coming down, they'd give us a code. We can check on them and see if it's on the code. Check with Russia to see if they'll take us immediately, otherwise we die; I don't know what else to say to these people. But to me, death is not a fearful thing. It's living that catches it. I have never, never, never, never seen anything like this before in my life. I've never seen people take the law and do—in their own hands—and provoke us and try to purposely agitate mother and children. There is just no future. It's just not worth living like this.

JONES: What's gonna happen when they don't leave? I hope that they could leave, but what's gonna happen to us when they don't leave, when they get on the plane and plane goes down?

MILLER: I don't think they'd do that.

JONES: You don't think they'd go down? I wish I could tell you why but I'm right. There's one man there who blames, and likely so, Debbie Blakey for the murder of his mother and he will stop that pilot by any means necessary. He'll do it. That plane will come out of the air. There is no way you can fly a plane without a pilot.

MILLER: I wasn't speaking about that plane. I was speaking about a plane for us to go to Russia.

JONES: To Russia? Do you think Russia's gonna [inaudible] want us with all this stigma? We had some value but now we don't have any value.

MILLER: But I don't see it like that. I feel like that as long as there's life, there's hope. That's my faith.

JONES: Why then is everybody dying? Some place that hope around God but everybody dies. I haven't seen anybody yet that didn't die. And I'd like to choose my own kind of death for a change. I'm tired of being tormented to hell, that's what I'm tired of. I'm tired of it.

ANOTHER WOMAN: Not that I'm afraid to die, by no means, but I look at our babies and I think that they deserve to live—you know?

JONES: I agree but also they deserve nothing more than to be at peace.

WOMAN: We also live for peace.

JONES: Have you had it?

AUDIENCE: NO!

JONES: I tried to give it to you. I laid down my life practically. I've practically died every day to give you peace. And you're still not having peace. You look better than I've seen you in a long while but it's still not the kind of peace that I want to give you. A person is a fool to continue to say that you're winning when you're losing. Win one and lose two [inaudible]. No plane is taking off. Suicide [inaudible] Stoen has done it. I've talked with San Francisco to see that Stoen does not get by with this infamy. That's infamy. He had done the thing that he wanted to do. To have us destroyed.

WOMAN: When you—when you—when we destroy ourselves, we're defeated. We let them, the enemy defeat us.

JONES: I'm speaking to you not as your administrator; I'm speaking as a prophet today. I wouldn't have said these things and talked so serious if I didn't know what I was talking about. If anybody calls back—the immense amount of damage that's gonna be done—but I cannot separate myself from the pain of my people. You can't either, Christine, if you stop and think about it; you can't separate yourself; we've walked too long together.

MILLER: I, I know that, but I still say, as an individual, I have a right to say what I think, what I feel and I think we all have a right to our own destiny as individuals and I think I have a right to choose and everybody else have a right to choose theirs. You know? I still have a right to my own opinion.

JONES: If anybody else wants to speak—what did you say, Louise? You'll regret this very day if you don't die. You'll regret it. You'll regret it.

WOMAN: [Inaudible] so many people?

JONES: I saved them, I saved them but I made my example, I made my confession, I made my manifestation and the will was not ready—

JONES: I'm gonna lay down my burdens, down by the riverside. So we lay 'em down here in Guyana—what's the difference? No man didn't take our life by now . . . but when they start parachuting out of the air, they'll shoot some of our innocent babies. I'm not gonna, don't want to see that—they gotta shoot me to get through to some of these people. I'm not letting them take you. Dorothy, will you let them take your child?

AUDIENCE: NO!

WOMAN: John John—

JONES: What's that?

WOMAN: You mean you want to see John, the little one—

JONES: I want to see—

AUDIENCE: [*much excitement*]

JONES: Please, please, please—

WOMAN: [Inaudible] John's life above others?

JONES: You think I put John's life above others? If I put John's life above others, I wouldn't be standing here with you at all. I'd save John out and he could go out on the driveway tonight . . .

WOMAN: [Inaudible] John [inaudible]

JONES: He's just no different to me than any of these children here. He's just one of my children. I don't prefer one above another. I don't prefer any of you above John. I can't do that. I can't separate myself from your actions or his actions. If you'd done something wrong, I'd stand with you. If they wanted to come get you, they would have to take me.

JONES: You're just as precious as John and I don't know what I'd do—wait and judge the things I do. I've waited against all evidence.

JONES: Stay at ease, stay at ease, stay at ease. Take Dwyer on down to the East House.

WOMAN: Everybody be quiet please.

JONES: We've got some respect for our lives . . .

JONES: I've tried so very hard . . .

JONES: Get Dwyer out of here before something happens to him. Dwyer? I'm not talkin 'bout you [inaudible] I said Dwyer. Ain't nobody going to take your [inaudible] I'm not letting them take your child. GET IN FOLKS, IT'S EASY, IT'S EASY . . .

JONES: It's all over—all over. What a legacy. What a legacy. The Red Brigade's only ones made any sense anyway. They invaded our privacy, they came into our homes, they followed us six thousand miles away. The Red Brigade's showed them justice; the congressman's dead.

Please get us some medication. It's simple, it's simple, there's no convulsions with it, it's simple; just please get it before it's too late, the GDF [Guyanese Defense Force] will be here, I tell you, get moving, get moving, get moving.

Don't be afraid to die; we're guilty if these people land out here, they'll torture some of our children here. They'll torture our people, they'll torture our seniors, we cannot have this.

Are you gonna separate yourself from whoever shot the congressman? I don't know who shot him. Speak of peace and those had a right to go and they had a right to—how many are dead [inaudible] My God Almighty—God Almighty . . .

JONES: I don't know how in the world they'll ever write about us. It's just too late, it's too late. The congressman's dead, the congressman's [inaudible] dead, many of our traitors are dead, they're all laying out there dead.

AUDIENCE: [Inaudible]

JONES: I didn't but my people did, my people did. But—they're my people, and they've been provoked too much. They've been provoked too much. What's happened here has been an act of provocation.

JONES: Can we hasten, can we hasten with that medication, you don't know what you've done. I tried. [*applause*] [inaudible] [*music*]. I guess they saw it happen and ran in the bush and dropped the machine gun [inaudible] my life. But there'll be more.

You wanna get that medication here, you've got to move.

JONES: Give them a little rest, a little rest. I do hope that those attorneys will stay where they belong and don't come up here. [inaudible] It's hard only at first. Only at first is it hard. It's hard only at first. When you're looking at death, it's—living is much, much more difficult; raising up every morning and not knowing what the night's bringing. It's much more difficult. It's much more difficult.

WOMAN: I'm looking at so many people crying. I wish you would not cry and just step over. Just take it.

JONES: Please, for God's sake, let's get on with it. We've lived as no other people have lived and loved; we've had as much of this world as you're gonna get. Let's just be done with it. Let's be done with the agony of it. It's a lot harder to have to watch you everyday die slowly from the time you're a child to the time you get gray, you're dying. It's honest and I'm sure that they'll pay for it. They'll pay for it. This is a revolutionary suicide. It's not a self-destructive suicide, so they'll pay for this. They've brought this upon us and they'll pay for that. I leave that destiny to them.

Who wants to go with their child has a right to go with their child. I think it's humane. I want to see you go, though—they can take me and do what they want—whatever they want to. I want to see you go, I don't want to see you go through this hell no more. No more, no more, no more.

We're trying. If everybody would relax. The best thing to do is relax and we'll have no problem. You'll have no problem with the thing if you just relax.

JONES: It's not to be feared. It's not to be feared. It's a friend. It's a friend. While you're sitting there, show your love to one another.

Let's get gone, let's get gone. There's nothing we can do. We can't separate ourselves from our own people. For twenty years, lay them in some old rotten nursing home. They've taken us through all this [sic] anguished years. They took us and put us in chains and that's nothing. There's no comparison to that, to this. They've robbed us of our land and they've taken us and driven us and we tried to find ourselves we tried to find a new beginning but it's too late. You can't separate yourselves from your brother and your sister. No way I'm gonna do it. I refuse. I don't know who fired the shot. I don't know who killed the congressman but as far as I'm concerned, I killed him. You understand what I'm saying, I killed him. He had no business coming. I told him not to come. [*music*] [*pause*] Die with respect—die with a degree of dignity. Lay down your life with dignity. Don't lay down with tears and agony. It's nothing to death, it's like [inaudible] said—it's like stepping over into another plane. Don't be this way. Stop this hysterics. This is not the way for people who are socialistic communists to die. No way for us to die and let's die with some dignity, let's die with some dignity. Then you'll have no choice, now we have some choice. You think they are gonna allow this to be done and allow us to get by with this? Must be insane. It's just something to put to the rest—oh, God. Mother, Mother, Mother, please. Mother please, please, please, don't do this. Don't do this. Lay down your life with your child but don't do this. Free at last. Keep your emotions down, keep your emotions down. Children, it will not hurt if you'll be quiet, if you'll be quiet.

JONES: I tell you I don't care how many screams you hear, I don't care how many anguished cries, death is a million times preferable to ten more days of this life. If you knew what was ahead of you. If you knew what was ahead of you, you'd be glad that you're stepping over tonight. Death, death, death is common to people—the Eskimos, they take death in their stride. Let's be dignified. If you'd quit telling them they're dying—if you adults would stop some of this nonsense. Adults! Adults! Adults! I call on you to stop this nonsense. I call on you to quit exciting your children when all you're doing is going into a quiet rest. I call on you to stop this now if you have any respect at all. Are we black, proud, and socialists or what are we? Now stop this nonsense; don't carry this on anymore. You're exciting your children. No, no sorrow—that it's all over. I'm glad it's all over. Hurry, hurry, my children, hurry. All right, let's not fall into the hands of the enemy. Hurry, my children, hurry. They're seniors out here I'm concerned about. Hurry. I'm not leaving my seniors to this mess. Quickly, quickly, quickly, quickly. [Inaudible] No more pain now. No more pain. I said no more pain. Jim Cobb is laying on the airfield dead at this moment. [*cheers*] That Oliver woman said she would come over and kill me if her son wouldn't stop her. These are people, the peddlers of hate. All we're doing is laying down our life. We're not letting them take our life, we're laying down our lives.

JONES: Stop it all this nonsense. Stop this screaming. All we're doing is taking a drink and going to sleep. That's what death is—sleep. You can have it, I'm tired of it all.

JONES: Where is the vat, the vat, the vat, with the green sea in it? The vat with the green sea in, please?

Lay it here, so the adults can begin. Don't follow my advice, you'll be sorry. You'll be sorry. Better we do it than they do it. Just trust me—you have to step across. You used to think this world, this world is not our home; well it sure isn't. As we were saying, it sure wasn't.

WOMAN: [Inaudible]

JONES: [Inaudible] telling me [inaudible], sure [inaudible] some people are sure these pilgrims, are for the [inaudible] of stepping over into the next plane. But it set an example for others. We've set one thousand people—said we don't like the way the world is . . . [inaudible] take our life from us. We laid it down, we got tired. We didn't commit suicide, we committed an act of revolutionary suicide protesting the conditions of an angry, mean world.

Jim Jones, the *New York Times,* and the Department of Justice agreed. The people of Jonestown had committed suicide. The evidence, however, disputes that conclusion.

In Matthew's Ridge, a coroner's jury, after hearing testimony for six days, concluded that Jim Jones and others were "criminally responsible" for almost all of the deaths at Jonestown. The presiding magistrate, Haroon Bacchus, said that the evidence disclosed that Jones and his armed guard "murdered those persons."

Bacchus pointed out that Jones had been killed by a shot fired into the side of his head from a weapon that was discharged at close range. The gun, however, was found twenty yards away. The jury found that Jones had been killed by "person or persons unknown" and that "James Warren Jones and others unknown are criminally responsible for the deaths of nine hundred ten persons."

An ominous report, largely ignored by the news media, came from the Venezuelan authorities. Jonestown was located in disputed territory claimed by both Guyana and Venezuela. The leadership at Jonestown had, on previous occasions, made plans for crossing the border into what was clearly Venezuelan land in the event of a crisis in Guyana.

The Venezuelan border patrol revealed that its aircraft had observed thirty to forty people moving in a group toward Venezuela shortly after the massacre.

Part V

The Unquiet Death of Michael James Prokes

14 The Suicide

Michael James Prokes was born in Modesto, California, in 1947. He died in a motel on Kansas Avenue just off U.S. Highway 99 in Modesto on March 13, 1979. He was a soft-spoken, kind, and gentle young man. He attended Modesto Junior College where he studied journalism and starred as a quarterback on the football team in spite of his modest size and slight build. He was graduated from the University of California at Fullerton, earning a degree in Communications. In 1970, Prokes was employed as a reporter for station KXTV-TV in Sacramento, and was also the Stockton bureau chief for the station. He was a devout Christian Scientist.

During October 1972 Michael Prokes joined the Peoples Temple in Ukiah, California. He quit his television job and, in doing so, rejected the advantages that often fall to the upper middle class in America, including his home near a country club, a better than average income, a fashionable automobile, and the respectability that accompanies such an accepted lifestyle. Prokes soon assumed the position of media spokesperson for the Temple. He became acquainted with San Francisco media personalities when both he and the Peoples Temple moved headquarters to San Francisco during 1975. When publications in the Bay Area began to attack Jim Jones in 1977, Herb Caen of the San Francisco *Chronicle* rejected those attacks because of his acquaintance with Mike Prokes.

I met Mike Prokes in Jonestown toward the middle of September 1978. He was eager to show me around the agricultural experimental project and was proud, he said, of a society that was struggling to eliminate racism. I think people who knew Mike Prokes could not doubt his sincerity. He was an enthusiastic supporter of the positive aspects of Jonestown. He told me that he was very fearful of government's efforts to destroy Jonestown and to infiltrate agents into it.

I saw Mike again in Jonestown on November 17, when Congressman Leo Ryan arrived to begin his investigation. It was the day before the massacre began. Mike was worried and fearful. He told me then that he saw the Ryan visit as a method of preventing the emigration of the Jonestown commune to the Soviet Union. When I tried to reassure him that the investigation, as far as I knew, had nothing to do with the emigration, he told me that it would be a mistake for me to underestimate the duplicity and cleverness of the American intelligence agents. He said, on the eve of the destruction, "I wouldn't be surprised if they have agents infiltrated in here and in San Francisco [at the Peoples Temple building]."

Four months later, on March 13, 1979, I had finished giving a talk to the students at the University of Iowa in Ames, and retired to my motel room for a few hours of sleep before a morning flight home to Memphis. I was awakened by a telephone call. April told me that there was bad news. Still fighting sleep, I realized from the tone of her voice that the news would be very bad. She told me that Jerrold Ladar, a San Francisco attorney, had just called to say that his client and our friend, Mike Prokes, had shot himself in the head and was not expected to live. She said that Jerry was afraid that Terri Buford might learn of the event through the news media and he felt that April or I should break the sad news to her. In the midst of that new tragedy, I was moved by Ladar's concern and his immediate effort to communicate with us.

I called Jerry at the motel where he was staying while he prepared for a trial in northern California. He said that he had little factual information: Apparently Mike had called a press conference in Modesto, California, where, after addressing those present, he'd distributed copies of a statement he'd written. He then went to a nearby bathroom and fired a bullet through his head. Jerry said that the doctors believed that there was almost no chance that Mike could survive.

In Memphis, after Terri learned what had happened, she became frantic to talk with Tim and Mike Carter. She wanted to reassure them as well as to secure assurances from them that they were all right.

Although she knew they lived in Boise, Idaho, she didn't have their telephone number. So April and Terri called the Boise police department and various other officials and supervisors at the telephone company. Finally, after hours of frantic calling, Tim telephoned Terri, and she and Mike and Tim began to talk through the night, each offering the others support, friendship, and love.

The next morning we learned that Mike had died during the night. He had called his press conference for 7 P.M. in room 106 at Motel 6 on Kansas

Avenue. To the many reporters who crowded into the room, he made available a forty-two-page statement, a portion of which he read for the electronic news media. When a reporter demanded to know, "Did Jim Jones order the killing of Leo Ryan?" Mike looked at the reporter, silently rose, and entered the bathroom, which was behind him. He closed the bathroom door and fired one shot from a .38-caliber Smith and Wesson revolver. By 7:43 he had arrived at Doctor's Hospital in Modesto and was pronounced dead there three hours later.

Near his body, reporters found a one-page suicide note in which Mike had written, "If my death doesn't prompt another book about the end of Jonestown, my life wasn't worth living."

15 To Die in Vain

Mike Prokes wanted to talk about the causes of the Jonestown massacre. When he was initially approached by federal authorities, his inclination was to tell everything that he knew. However, Charles Garry strongly advised Prokes to remain silent. It soon became apparent that Garry, who had been deeply associated with the leadership of the Peoples Temple for almost two years, could not continue to represent himself as well as the remaining leadership of the Peoples Temple and Prokes. Prokes then sought other counsel.

He retained Jerrold Ladar, a former assistant U.S. attorney for San Francisco. Ladar, an experienced and able defense attorney, had no objection to his client's speaking freely about the events surrounding the massacre. However, Charles Garry telephoned Ladar to discuss the representation of Prokes. Ladar properly reminded Garry that he, Ladar, was counsel for Prokes and that it would not be proper for the two lawyers to consult about the matter.

Ladar sought a grant of immunity for Prokes from William Hunter, the U.S. attorney. When Prokes appeared before the United States Grand Jury meeting in San Francisco in January 1979, he requested immunity as a precondition to testifying to the facts surrounding the massacre at Jonestown. Either Hunter opposed the grant or the Department of Justice failed to process a request from Hunter for immunity. In any event, immunity was not granted and Prokes was effectively silenced.

Prokes continued to visit with former members of the Temple living in California, and then evidently decided that he could most effectively reveal what he knew at a press conference which was to be dramatized by his death.

The *New York Times* did not report the press conference or his death.

Newsweek, the *Los Angeles Times,* CBS-TV, NBC-TV, ABC-TV, the *Washington Post, Time,* the Associated Press, and the San Francisco newspapers all published similar, homogenized versions of the news conference and the suicide.

Some of the news media ignored the most illuminating point that Prokes had made: that the United States government was out to destroy the Temple. The remaining news organizations quite simply lied about that point. For example, on March 14, 1979, the *Los Angeles Times* wrote of the calm presentation made by Prokes: "He ranted against the U.S. government and accused the Central Intelligence Agency of conducting a 'witch hunt' against the cult." The *Washington Post,* in its story filed with a Modesto, California, dateline, and not credited with a byline or to a news source, said: "He ranted against the U.S. government, and accused the CIA of conducting a 'witch hunt' against the cult." The *Los Angeles Times* continued its story with, "The former television news reporter joined the Temple six years ago after setting out to prepare an investigative story on the Temple and Jones." The Los Angeles *Herald Examiner* wrote: "Prokes' involvement with the cult began six years ago when he was a news reporter with a Stockton television station. He started to do an investigative piece on the group and instead fell under the spell of Jones, eventually joining him 'for idealistic reasons.' "

The San Francisco *Examiner,* in an article written by John Jacobs on March 14, 1979, asserted, "In 1972 he went to Ukiah to do a story on Jim Jones and wound up joining the Temple, attracted by the political idealism and racial integration Jones espoused." In a preface to that article, the *Examiner* explained that Jacobs following the massacre "spent nearly two months in Guyana covering the Peoples Temple tragedy, during which time he had extensive interviews and conversations with Michael Prokes, who last night committed suicide."

Newsweek, on March 26, 1979, reported that "Prokes was a former television reporter who set out to do an exposé of the Peoples Temple in 1972 and stayed on as a true believer." ABC-TV ran three sentences from the videotaped conference. The viewers could hear some of the last words that Prokes spoke and note his calm and restrained manner. CBS and NBC ran the same tape but omitted the sound. CBS stated that Prokes "again defended the cult" and that he "had left a suicide note which said he wanted to die, as he put it, for the same just reasons as those who died in Jonestown."

Terri, April, and I monitored the radio and television broadcasts and studied the magazine and newspaper accounts in an effort to determine why Mike had killed himself—what he had said in his last hours. Yet the public record was barren; no answers could be gleaned from what the media had published.

During the afternoon of March 15, 1979, a bulging plain manila envelope bearing no return address was delivered to me. It contained a brief personal note from Mike Prokes to me and a copy of the forty-two pages from which he had read at the conference. The note was dated March 13. Judging from the postmark, he had mailed it to me shortly before he committed suicide.

There were eight reporters at the press conference that Prokes held, including a journalist with tape recorders and a media tape camera. Although the media reported almost unanimously that Prokes had said that he joined the Peoples Temple after setting out to do an investigative story on Jim Jones and his followers and that he decided to join the Temple for reasons of idealism, Prokes had not made those statements to the assembled reporters. Indeed, he had said something quite different.

In both his oral and written statement to the press, he asserted, "The truth about Jonestown is being covered up because our government agencies were involved in its destruction up to their necks. I am convinced of this because, among many other reasons, I was an informant when I first joined Peoples Temple."

Prokes attached to that statement a four-page document in which he detailed his role as a government agent. In that report he revealed his salary, his assignment, the name of the government agent who had recruited him, and the method he employed when making his regular reports to the agent who served as his control. All of this information was available to the reporters at the press conference and to many others as well, for I had not been the only recipient of that mailed press package. Mike had also sent a copy of the material to Tim and Mike Carter. Among those Mike mailed his final statement to were: the *New York Times, Newsweek,* and *Time.* They, however, did not print a word from the statement.

During the early evening of March 13, Prokes had concluded his formal remarks to the news media by confessing that he had been a government informant and then stating,

> I didn't remain one, however, because I came to realize that the Temple was probably the only hope for the many people it was helping off the streets, off of drugs, out of crime, and out of mental institutions, jails, and prisons. I learned to identify with these people until they became my brothers and sisters and then I understood what it meant to be black and old and poor in this society—the hell of living every day in fear.

> The people of Jonestown died—as one suicide note said—because they weren't allowed to live in peace. They died because they didn't want to be left with no choice but to come back to live in the rat-infested ghettoes of America. They died for all those who suffer oppression. I refuse to let my black brothers and sisters and others in Jonestown die in vain.

As this is written, more than six months after the death of Michael Prokes, not one national newspaper, magazine, radio or television station, or news service, to my knowledge, revealed what Mike Prokes actually said during the last minutes of his life. Instead, the national media have apparently published a uniform statement attributed to Prokes.

I believe that if Mike Prokes was willing to die so that his words about the destruction of Jonestown could be heard, we should be permitted to read those words. If Prokes entered the Peoples Temple as a government informant,* one can imagine the anguish he suffered after the death of his family and friends in Jonestown. He was a sensitive man who tended to accept too easily a burden of guilt which he rightfully should have been spared. After surviving the massacre, he might have contemplated and possibly magnified the damage that his early reports had done to the settlement. Published below is Michael Prokes' covering letter to me along with the entire four-page preface that Prokes released to the media on March 13 and which he mailed to others earlier that same day.

"In October of 1972 I called Jim Jones' house at the number listed in Redwood Valley to try to set up an interview with him for the news. I talked with a woman, a senior named Esther Mueller, who Jones had taken in. I told her of my interest and she suggested I call the San Francisco Temple where Jones was at that time. I called but was told to call back on the weekend. A few days later I received a call at my office from a man who asked if I would meet with him to discuss the Peoples Temple. I found the request very curious; I said o.k. and we met the next day in a Stockton restaurant. The man told me his name was Gary Jackson. I asked him what he did and he said that he worked for the government, but I couldn't get him to be more specific. He asked what prompted my interest in Peoples Temple. I asked him how he knew that I was interested in the Temple. He paused for a few moments, then said something to the effect— 'There are

*I have already initiated actions under the newly amended Freedom of Information Act in an effort to secure documents from the CIA, FBI, and other intelligence agencies to determine if any existing records are available to confirm the allegations that Prokes has made.

Mark--

I just thought you might be interested in reading through the enclosed materials, which you may use in your work if you think it would be at all helpful.

There's got to be a "Deep Throat" somewhere.

Take care and good luck, Mark

Mike Prokes

ways if you think about it.' The answer was obvious—Jones' phone was tapped. I told him that a series of articles in the San Francisco *Examiner* prompted my interest. I said I wanted to look into some of the things the articles said about Jones and the Temple, and if I found them to be true, I was planning to do an exposé for our TV news program. Jackson (somehow I doubt that was his real name) said there was a lot more to the Temple than what the *Examiner* wrote. He said it was a revolutionary organization led by a dangerous man, bent on destroying our system of government. He talked to me a while longer, telling me various things Jones had supposedly said and done; then he made a proposal. He said if I could be successful at joining the Temple full time as a staff member and report regularly on what was going on inside the organization, he would arrange for me to be paid two-hundred dollars a week.

"In thinking back upon it, I must have been checked out and considered to be a good prospect since I had been a dedicated Christian churchgoer, attended college in conservative Orange County, good student with no involvement in any kind of organization or activity that could be considered 'questionable.' I told the man that I found his offer intriguing but that I first wanted to pay a visit to the Temple. He agreed, saying I wouldn't be able to join on the first visit anyway. But he said I wouldn't be able to get a good picture of the organization until I was inside it, because the public meetings were only so much posturing. I arranged to attend a service at which I heard Jones preach. Later, I got to talk with him privately. I was surprised to hear him speak so openly against the system in my presence, particularly so soon after the negative publicity about him. But I was fascinated by his ministry and I thought it would make great stuff for a book or screenplay, which I thought I might like to write. I talked with Jones for at least two hours. I asked him if he needed more staff. He said he could use as many as were willing to work voluntarily with the Temple providing only living expenses. I told him it was something I wanted to give serious thought to, and he said he would be thrilled to have me.

"Jackson called me a couple of days later and I told him I was going to quit my job and accept his offer. I didn't tell him I wanted to write a book about the Temple. Arrangements were made for me to be paid (the payments were left for me at various predesignated locations, always in the form of cash enclosed in plain white envelopes). My reports were made verbally (from pay phones at which I was called) because it was too risky to write anything, as there was a lot of suspicion in the Temple (as one might imagine) of a reporter who quit his rather prestigious job as a bureau chief to join an organization that didn't pay any salaries.

"As time passed, I gradually began to feel conflict over my role as an informant, even though I wasn't providing what one might call valuable or sensitive information. I was starting to identify with the problems and sufferings of the members. As I observed various ones' troubles being resolved by the Temple's program, the conflict I was feeling turned to guilt. I had been watching Jones for some time, as closely as possible without drawing attention to myself. His schedule was unbelievable. He was up at all hours calling people on the phone, consulting, reading reports, and staying in touch with every phase of the organization. It was obvious he worked harder than anyone—but I questioned his motives. Personally, I didn't like the man after the first few months I was in the Temple. But I recognized that it was for reasons that were subjective and which I didn't want to affect my judgment of his character. One thing I was noticing was that he was almost always the first to notice someone's need and point it out—a senior in a packed auditorium without a chair, for example, or interest in someone's health who lived alone. He was always dealing with needs and often ones that weren't that obvious to others. He seemed unusually sensitive. Every time I saw him he was expressing concern, or doing something for someone or asking that it be done. But he didn't leave it at that. He was keen on following up on whether the thing he had asked be done for someone was actually carried out. Still, in view of all this, I *didn't* give him the benefit of the doubt. I had to be sure about him.

"One day I had taken some letters to his apartment in the San Francisco Temple just as he was coming out the door. He was late for an appointment, so he told me to put the letters on a table inside. He left and then I went out. I started back to my office and then changed my mind and went downstairs to get a drink from the water fountain. Down the hall I noticed Jones had stopped and watched for a moment as an elderly woman moved slowly up another staircase. Jones didn't see me as he was facing the other way, and there was no one else around. Even though he was late for his appointment, he was going to take another five minutes to help that woman up the long flight of stairs. (She could not have seen Jones as her back was to him.) He went up and began assisting her and then I intervened and told him to go ahead to his appointment. That act of kindness did it for me. I had become virtually convinced of Jones' sincerity. I had finally seen him do something in private that I had suspected he only did in public or when others were around to see it. I became even more convinced of his basic integrity on subsequent occasions in which I observed his actions—for example, toward animals—when he was unaware that I (or anyone, for that matter) was around.

"But that first occasion was enough for me. I could no longer justify informing on Jones and his organization. During my next contact, I told Jackson what I thought of Jones and he desperately tried to convince me I was wrong. I told him I had to act according to what I had seen and experienced, and my conscience simply wouldn't allow me to continue selling information that might be used against an organization I believed in. I told him that even though I didn't particularly care for Jones and I didn't agree with some ways in which his organization was run, I felt it was making tremendous achievements in terms of human rehabilitation and improvement in the quality of people's lives and character. He asked me what I planned to do. I told him I was going to stay with the Temple and possibly write a book about it. He urged me not to tell Jones about him and I told him I saw no reason why I should do that unless I suspected someone else was taking my place."

16 The Last Will and Testament of Michael James Prokes

The major portion of the forty-two-page document released by Mike Prokes dealt with his analysis of life in Jonestown and the reasons for its destruction. I publish here, for the first time, his entire written evaluation (the rest was composed of newspaper clippings and documents), not because I am in agreement with all of the points found therein, but because I believe that the perspective of Mike Prokes, an intelligent and perceptive newsman, must not be ignored. Here, then, is his last testament.

The Peoples Temple
by Michael Prokes

Jonestown

Jonestown had nothing to hide. Most of its visitors went there unannounced. The project was talked about far and wide in Guyana and, thus, anyone who had heard about it would inevitably drop in if they were anywhere in the area. Often we had visitors almost every day of the week. Some nonhostile relatives came to spend time with members of their family, and others were scheduled to come, including my own mother and brother. But the positive testimonies about Jonestown from such persons were not enough to halt the organized efforts of those determined to destroy Jonestown. Neither were the visits of the President of the National Newspaper Publishers Association (the "Black Press of America"), Dr. Carlton Goodlett, or the former Methodist superintendent from the Bay Area, the Rev. Dr. John Moore, who found "every aspect of the work and life . . . impressive." Dr. Goodlett wrote in the Jonestown guestbook, "I have lived today in the future." But, unfortunately, the black press is not the white press, and we realized something more had to be done to get the harassers off our back. Thus, a request was made to the United Nations to send a team to Jonestown. But our communication received a negative reply.

At that point we were left with little choice but to take a chance and let the same press in which had carried on a relentless attack against the Temple. (Feelers had already gone out to Bill Moyers, David Wolper Productions, and a number of other journalists and filmmakers, without success.) Finally, an agreement was reached to allow in one of the Temple's biggest press enemies—the San Francisco *Examiner*. But for some strange reason (which will never be revealed by the paper), the *Examiner* decided to back out of it at the last minute. What had happened? Were they afraid their man wasn't prejudiced enough against the Temple or that he might get there and discover that he couldn't do a decent smear job? It is just a bit incredible that after all the clamoring about the goings on in Peoples Temple, the *Examiner* decided it would stick with secondhand reports and innuendo from such sources as Tim Stoen's lackeys. The *Examiner* didn't want to take the chance that it would not be able to confirm its yellow headlines of the past because it would hurt its credibility and, more importantly, it would mean fewer bucks from the sale of other headlines in the future. After all, the *Examiner* created some of its most sensational banner headlines using the Temple.

One got the feeling, in Jonestown, of being backed up against the wall—not being able to win for losing. But when Congressman Ryan—whose May 1978 letter to us declared his sympathy for Mr. Tim Stoen—announced his intentions to come, with media, the feeling of being entrapped turned to belief—it had to be a setup. Paranoia? I doubt it, but even if it was, the key question in all this is—who created it? Who tapped the Temple's phones in California? Who was blackmailing Dennis Banks to get at us?* Who was putting up all the money for the Stoen–Mazor operations? Does Joseph Mazor now deny that when he came to Jonestown last year he told us that he was hired to come there months earlier with sophisticated arms and mercenaries on a mission to "get the children out" and that if he had to wipe out hundreds of adults in the process, he was prepared to do that. But the plan was abandoned, he said, because he saw no evidence—such as gun

*Dennis Banks is a prominent Indian leader. He served as one of the officers of the American Indian Movement and played a major part, along with Russell Means, in the 1973 occupation of Wounded Knee, South Dakota. Evidently an effort had been made by a person acting under the color of law to bring pressure on Mr. Banks to make a false and incriminating statement against the Peoples Temple. That matter is discussed in some detail in this book in chapter 17.

towers, barbed wire, and armed patrols, which he was told existed—that anyone was being held against their will. (A Ukiah *Daily Journal* article or editorial once mentioned a "concerned relative's" desire to use mercenaries to get people out of Jonestown.) Was that venture what turned Mazor against Tim Stoen—because Stoen had lied to him about Jonestown? (Both during and after Mazor's subsequent visit to Jonestown, he said, on at least two occasions, "I hate your politics, but I love what you're doing here.") *If there wasn't a conspiracy to destroy Jonestown, why did Mazor insist on getting Jones a bulletproof vest and offer to train the community's security personnel in the use of weapons?!*

I believe Tim Stoen was a CIA operative, if not from the beginning, then certainly long before the end. Where was the money coming from to keep him on the Temple's case full time with an office, to hire a private detective (Mazor), and a prominent San Francisco public relations firm (Lowery, Russom, & Leeper) to work against the Temple. Where was the money coming from to send relatives and attorneys to Guyana and put them up in the best hotels while they did their dirty work? There was too much money behind Tim Stoen. And why did he suddenly decide he wanted his wife's son back, who he knew was fathered by Jim Jones—a fact both he (Stoen) and she acknowledged publicly and privately in the Temple. Moreover, Jones had no reason for claiming the child from virtually the time of his birth, if the child was not in fact Jones'. But suddenly Grace and Tim Stoen were back together again, in public, acting as if they were reconciled, after literally hating each other for years (since 1972, in fact, when I lived with them near Redwood Valley) and during a period when Grace was living with another man. But Stoen's announced goal was the destruction of Jim Jones and the Temple. He realized the child was a point of vulnerability because he knew Jones wouldn't give him up even if a court directed him to do so. Stoen knew he had an advantage, being the husband of the child's mother, and he also knew it would be virtually impossible to prove he was not the father since he and Jones had the same blood type. But when the Guyana courts failed to make a decision in the case, Stoen applied more pressure on another front. Using the so-called "Concerned Relatives," Stoen kept the pressure on by hitting again at what he knew to be Jones' most vulnerable area—his loyalty to his members. He promised never to give up anyone who didn't want to leave. So all these "Concerned Relatives" show up in Guyana with Congressman Ryan (supposedly on separate missions)—some of whom were so concerned that they hadn't bothered to even call or write their Temple relatives in years. They suddenly show up and discover that *all* of their relatives in Jonestown are happy and don't want to leave. But unfortunately, in the process, about twenty persons (only one of them black) did want to leave, triggering the tragic incidents that Stoen and the forces backing him were hoping for. And now Stoen has quietly disappeared from the scene.

For clarification: I am convinced beyond all doubt that there was no conspiracy from within Peoples Temple to kill Rep. Congressman Leo Ryan. Tim Carter was sent to the States to deliver some legal documents. While he was there, Terri Buford left the Temple and said she was going underground to get information about the conspiracy against the Temple. Jones and others around him (i.e., Harriet Tropp, Carolyn Layton, & Maria Katsaris) doubted that her real intention was to get information for the Temple. They thought her letter was a smokescreen for getting out altogether. According to Harriet Tropp, Jones instructed her to give a message to San Francisco to have Carter infiltrate the "Concerned Relatives" to see what he could find out about Buford. That was Carter's mission. It was already known that Ryan was planning to come to Jonestown. When Carter returned to the project, he told Jones that Stoen & the "Concerned Relatives" were counting on an overreaction on the part of Jones and the Temple to Ryan's visit. From that point on, *Jones desperately tried to keep Ryan from coming in.* Jones feared that Ryan was coming to deliberately provoke an incident and that he was bringing the media to record it. One thing in particular that added credence to Jones' and others' fears was that Ryan showed up totally unannounced at the Temple's Georgetown headquarters late one night (just prior to flying out to the project). Then the next day at a press conference, it appeared evident that he was attempting to set the stage for the type of investigation he would seek to make into Jonestown. He said he was concerned about a church that had no signs of religion at its headquarters. He also made deprecating remarks about members of the Georgetown household because they appeared to be stand-offish. After Ryan's press conference, Jones and his staff were convinced that the community was in for a rough time with Ryan. Then Ryan announced that he was coming in, welcome or not, with the media. That was the worst thing he could have said. *It came across as a virtual threat, made by an arrogant white person representing the American "establishment" which had failed the blacks and the poor who—for that very reason—were attempting to build a new life where they had found an opportunity to do so.* Ryan's actions only served to confirm the suspicion that he was coming to discredit Jonestown by provoking an incident which, if it didn't serve to preempt the planned move to the Soviet Union, at least would lessen or eliminate the propaganda value for the Soviets. (The State Department was well aware of the Temple's plans to move and that Sharon Amos was meeting regularly at the Soviet Embassy. The American Embassy called the Temple's Georgetown, Guyana, headquarters after the first two meetings and asked why were we visiting the Soviet Embassy. Deborah Blakey, who later defected, also informed the American Embassy and the State Department of the Temple's plans.)

A final effort to prevent Ryan's visit came via instructions from Jones to block the runway at Port Kaituma so that his plane couldn't land. The instructions couldn't be carried out, however, because members of the Guyana Defense Force were at the airstrip repairing an airplane. It was felt by Johnny Jones and Jim McElvane that the GDF would have interfered with any attempt to prevent a Guyana Airways plane from landing. So the plane landed, and after much discussion, it was decided that it would be better to let Ryan come in than to have him go to the entrance of the project with the media and create a scene for the benefit of the cameras. Thus, Ryan and his aide were allowed in and, later, Jones succumbed to the pressure to allow the media in also. The rest is history.

I don't believe the knife attack on Ryan in Jonestown was ordered. Ryan had announced that he was still going to give a favorable report on the community even after the twenty or so people chose to leave. The individual who attacked Ryan was a machismo-type ex-Navy man. Some of the young guys he worked with in Georgetown would make fun of him because he was always trying to outdo the others in their work, such as loading the Temple truck and boat. Also, this man admitted during a catharsis meeting that he fantasized being a hit-man. I believe this man, Don Sly, was acting on his own.

I don't know how the final attack at the airport came about. But I do remember hearing Jones say, following Ryan's departure from Jonestown, something to the effect that the lid was off or he didn't see how he could keep the lid on any longer. (I took this statement to be in reference to those who always wanted to answer the Temple's problems with violence.)

Miscellaneous Reflections

When speaking during a service in one of the California Temples, Jones would usually trace the oppression of blacks and other minorities to current times. It was almost like a history lesson. He would give long and specific accounts of how blacks, particularly, have been victimized by racism and capitalist exploitation. He would rattle off relevant statistics and examples in meticulous detail. For many blacks who came with no education to speak of, often blaming themselves for conditions they didn't understand, having little sense of self-worth and actually feeling inferior because they had been beat down by white standards and white institutions for so long—for them, Jones was a hell of an eye-opening experience. It wasn't brainwashing that Jones was engaged in—it was more like deprogramming. Jones was educating and the effect was therapeutic for thousands who heard him and whose lives were in a state of confusion from feeling imprisoned in a society they were told was free. He liberated many minds out of their confused states by demonstrating why there are huge ghettoes in every large city of America and why those ghettoes are populated mostly by blacks. He laid the blame squarely at the feet of white racism and a socioeconomic system that clearly puts profit motives above human values, resulting in the lack of opportunity necessary for blacks to enter the mainstream of American life. This was not a demagogic approach Jones was taking, either. He had too much of a grasp of his subject; he was too concerned about minute details—details that a demagogue need not bother with in order to achieve his objectives. Not that emotion wasn't involved—it was. But it was aroused by the sheer logic of his presentations which were backed up by an impressive array of facts, statistics, and documentation gathered from a massive amount of reading.

There was no way anyone could dispute what Jones said about the social ills of the society and how blacks were the victims. Others, far less progressive than he, were saying the same things. It was Jones' lucidness that made him effective—what he said made sense. When he would spend hours attempting to show how the system was to blame for the conditions of blacks in the United States, he was convincing. He became even more convincing when the government, in spite of itself, gave credibility to his thesis. For example, in 1968 the National Advisory Commission on Civil Disorders, a bipartisan committee formed by the Johnson Administration, concluded its report with a searing indictment of our system, which declared, "This nation is moving toward two societies, one black, one white —separate and unequal." It put the basic blame on "white racism" which it said was created, maintained, and condoned by white institutions. Here was a respected commission, made up of respected public leaders who were charged by the President with determining the root causes of civil disorder, and it laid the blame right where it belonged. Not surprisingly, however, its recommendations for remedying the situation were not carried out and thus we are still left with conditions akin to urban apartheid and the danger of blacks taking to the streets again, as moderate voices (such as Vernon Jordan and Benjamin Hook) warn us. The American system continues to fail its black citizens, and not from any lack of prompting by black leaders.

The significant thing is that it is this failure that allowed Jim Jones—no matter what perception one might have of him—to do what he did with Peoples Temple. There is no getting around it—Jones jumped into the vacuum created by this system's failure to meet the needs of its people. And that may well be the key lesson to be learned from Jonestown.

Healings and Power

It is with reluctance that I discuss the healing aspect of Jones' ministry because it will doubtless take away from the credibility of things I say about other areas, at least in some people's minds. First of all, some don't believe in the paranormal at all and will automatically use this to discredit other items they choose not to believe. While there are those who believe in its possibilities, they've been so prejudiced by news stories portraying Jones in the worst possible light that they won't allow themselves to be open to this aspect. Thus, I'm left with appealing to perhaps a few persons who can realize that I have nothing to gain by getting into this area. I'm doing so because I don't want to be accused of avoiding it; moreover, I want to tell what I know to be the truth. The last impression I would want to give anyone was that Jones was some superhuman being because he had the ability to heal. On the contrary, he was only too human. But somehow he was able to utilize a dimension of the mind that most people haven't tapped.

There were times when Jones would request that everyone in the particular service he was conducting, who had some form of crippling affliction, form a line. Usually hundreds of people would respond on such occasions. It wasn't only people who were crippled in some way who got in line, however. People with all kinds of physical problems and infirmities—thinking it might be their only chance—also got in line.

The healing session was usually the last part of the service, coming after Jones had spoken anywhere from two to four hours. But when he called for people to line up for healing, it would usually take at least several hours more to get through the line because he worked with each person individually. After it was over, virtually every person said they had received some measure of relief, if not total healing. It was too much to be denied even by the most hardened skeptic. Some of it was no doubt psychosomatic (which Jones said himself)—but not all of it. One could observe actual physical transformations take place with hands or fingers crippled up with arthritis, for example. Elderly persons who were familiar to everyone and who for months and sometimes years had moved painfully slow, suddenly walked at a more brisk pace after Jones had attended to them. There can be no question that Jones possessed a phenomenal ability to heal. Normally, he would call people out from the pulpit, one by one, for healing. But on those infrequent occasions that he allowed people to get in line, the visible results would convince the most cynical observer. Also, Tim Carter and Laurie Efrein were among those who handled hundreds of letters a month containing expressions of gratitude and testimony from persons who said they were healed through Jones.

The significance of all this to me, however, is not that Jones could heal, but rather that if he had wanted power in terms of gaining the largest number of worshippers and raising the maximum amount of money, he knew that all he had to do was limit his ministry to healing. This is an area where those who have accused Jones of being power-hungry are misguided. He could have had hundreds of thousands of followers and raised many more millions of dollars than he did, because the vast majority came to Jones' services to get healed, not to hear his social-political message. If he had just stuck to healing alone, he could have had tens of thousands of people in idolatrous worship of him, and he knew it. But his main thrust was socialist politics and the struggle for civil rights and social justice, and when he got into it, most of the healing crowd was turned off. His message was what kept people from returning, but he kept on with it knowing full well the effect it was having. He would often say, "If I would just keep my mouth shut and stick to healing, I could pack out the largest auditoriums."

People didn't want to hear Jones' message because it required something of them. It made them feel responsible to do something to help improve or correct the conditions they were hearing about. They didn't want to hear the message because it upset their lives by pricking their consciences, particularly those who were living rather well off and were looking for ways to feel good about themselves. But they came to the wrong place to feel good because Jones always spoke about a world filled with inequities and the myriad injustices that created them. He spoke in a manner that compelled people to face themselves in terms of viewing their lives in relation to such a world (populated by "have" and "have-not" nations and peoples). That's no doubt why few people of means (or those who aspired to it) stayed with the Temple. The only thing they understood about equality was that it meant sacrifice—something they were not prepared to do.

The Community

If you can believe anything anyone says about Jonestown, you can believe this: For an integrated community, populated by a virtual cross section of the human race, it was the most racially harmonious I've ever seen or heard about. Its value system was different. It was based on a code of consideration, respect, and concern for people, and the progress being made along these lines was remarkable considering the number of so-called misfits and outcasts that were there. The children were learning how to share and to be concerned as much about the welfare of others as they were about their own welfare.

The vast majority of the people (well over ninety percent I would estimate) loved Jonestown, and there was a tremendous will for it to succeed, against all the odds. And it *was* succeeding. It was an incredibly productive and creative community that was viewed as a cooperative model by virtually everyone who visited. Not that it was without faults; however, its bad points were *nothing* compared to the way it was portrayed by those who left the Temple—individuals who simply did not like living in the jungle under an extremely structured program, most of which was essential in dealing with the various types of people there.

It is important to realize that Jonestown had ex-cons, former drug addicts, individuals who were classified as social deviants, youths who came or were brought to the Temple as emotionally disturbed, maladjusted, and hyperactive (not to mention those who were physically handicapped and mentally retarded)—you name it and they were there. Why did they end up in Peoples Temple? Obviously, because U.S. society and its institutions had failed them. With these types of persons, there had to be a tight structure. Sure there were some excesses, but nothing like the fabrications and exaggerations made up by those who decided to leave because they considered it too much of a sacrifice to make. (The vast majority of them were selfish whites.) They had to justify to themselves why they were leaving, in order to be able to live with their consciences. That's why they made Jonestown out to be something it was not. Well, it may not have been paradise to them, but it was paradise to those who suffered the day-to-day struggle of life in America's slums.

All kinds of people came to Peoples Temple and with every kind of problem. For many it was their last resort. Seeing their problems made my worst ones seem petty. I became conscience-stricken and, realizing there was nothing more worthwhile that I could do with my life, I decided to stay on indefinitely. Somehow, as difficult as it may be to believe, I don't regret that decision. The experience made me a realist about life and about people. It gave me as much insight into myself as I had the courage to face. (I know the same is true of others, as I have heard different ones make similar statements.) Beyond that, it gave me about as accurate a picture as a white person can hope to get of what it means to be black in America. It also gave me a unique perspective and insight into the nature of the American system, and how that system functions.

Except for the first few months in the Temple, I never really liked Jim Jones. I guess it was his authority that bothered me, although I often saw the necessity for it. I recognize that my dislike for him stems from feelings that are purely subjective and which I don't want to color my portrayal of him. One thing about the man that I had to respect was that he did practice what he preached. Despite how some have portrayed him, he really didn't live above the people. (Maybe he did in minor ways but he always had a very modest life-style, even in the U.S.) In Jonestown, he spent most of his time in his quarters which consisted of one approximately 12′ x 18′ room. Basically the same thing was true of him in San Francisco where he lived in a small apartment inside the Temple. And, in fairness, I know that the vast majority of Temple members did not feel the dislike for Jones that I felt.

Why was the move to Guyana made? Perhaps the answer is best stated by former Methodist District Superintendent, Dr. John Moore, who now pastors his own church—First Methodist of Reno, Nevada. Rev. Moore had two daughters in the Temple, and he and his wife, Barbara, visited them in Guyana. He was familiar with Jim Jones, the Temple, its programs, and a number of its members. In a statement to the House Committee on International Affairs, Rev. Moore wrote:

> The people went to Jonestown with hope, hope which grew out of a loss of hope in the U.S. There can be no understanding of movements such as Peoples Temple and Jonestown apart from this loss of hope. They migrated, because they had lost hope in any commitment of the American people or the Congress to end racial discrimination and injustice. They had lost hope in the people and the legislatures to deal justly and humanely with the poor. . . . Older people went to Jonestown hoping to become free of purse snatchings, muggings, and the harshness of the urban scene. Some young people hoped to learn new skills, or to become free from pressures of peers in the crime and drug scenes. People went to Jonestown to find freedom from the indignity our society heaps upon the poor. They went with hope for a simple, quiet life. . . . They saw themselves leaving a materialistic society where things are valued more than people. Many went as pioneers to create a new community in the jungle. Still others saw in Jonestown a vision of a new society, a wave of the future.

It's interesting that Rev. Moore says the people went to Jonestown to escape indignity. The President of the Southern Christian Leadership Conference, Rev. Joseph Lowery, has never met Rev. Moore, but came up with the same assessment after doing his own investigation. Rev. Lowery went to Guyana in the aftermath of the tragedy out of concern that Jonestown represented a failure of American churches to meet the needs of the "hopeless." After visiting the project and interviewing a number of survivors, he concluded that it was "dignity-creating programs" that drew the people to Guyana, and he expressed surprise at the "incredible progress" Temple members had made in developing the project.

It is true, the Temple had lost all hope and faith in America. Jones saw no hope for changing the basic profit-greed system. Capitalism was too entrenched, there was no strong socialist movement, and the working-class consciousness was misdirected. Additionally, in light of what was happening to other progressive groups and organizations, Jones knew that Peoples Temple would come under increasing scrutiny and harassment, particularly in view of the way the Temple was operated. Its activism brought too much notoriety. And already the Temple had suffered damaging publicity; already the phones had been tapped; already the San Francisco headquarters had been destroyed by arson; and already a number of persons had left who had shown themselves to be active enemies. It was obvious to Jones that his organization would not be allowed to survive in the United States as a socialist entity. He saw no choice but to build an alternative community in another country.

Jones didn't think it would be possible to move everyone en masse to the Soviet Union, which he would have preferred doing particularly for reasons of collective security and protection from U.S.-based enemies. The information that he was given from persons supposedly knowledgeable about Soviet affairs was that the Soviets would not take in such a large group directly from the U.S. Thus, Jones concluded that he would have to establish in some other country first, and Guyana was it.

Finances, Communal Living, and Life-style

In 1975, a push toward communal living began in San Francisco and Los Angeles. The Redwood Valley Temple already had most of the members in that area of the state living communally, as it was the original headquarters of Peoples Temple in California. After San Francisco became the headquarters, approximately seventy communal residences were organized in that city alone. Virtually everyone who lived communally planned on moving to Guyana. Actually, communal living was an understood requirement for those who wanted to make the move to Jonestown. The members understood that becoming a communal member meant, by its very concept, turning over all of one's financial assets, including homes and property. The Temple, in turn, would then provide for the person's housing, food, medical-dental, and educational needs, and living expenses, such as transportation, clothes, toiletries, etc.

It was through the communal process that the Temple ended up with so much property. It wasn't a matter of coercing people into giving it, as has been charged. It was something the members knew was a requirement if they expected to stay in the Temple and go to Guyana. Many people stayed in the Temple, right to the end, who never tithed, much less went communal. *And most people who did go communal had no property or savings to give.* The ones who did turn over assets were given no special privileges. Once communal, everyone lived on the same basic level. (The finances were being kept in reserve in preparation for another move, which would have meant starting all over again after Guyana.)

In Jonestown, the vast majority of the people loved their new life. They were building their own community, their own future, and their children's, with their own hands. They took great pride in the fact that the Guyana government considered it a model cooperative project in line with the country's own goals.

Although living conditions were crowded, the people were reasonably comfortable, particularly when you consider that this was truly a pioneering effort. A sawmill had been built for lumber production, and some 70,000 board measurements of lumber was on its way from Georgetown for use in the construction of over one hundred new houses.

Although the food was limited in variety and consisted mainly of vegetables, cassava (the main crop), and rice mixed with pork, chicken, or fish, it was adequate in meeting the nutritional needs of the community. Anyone having a special dietary need (e.g., protein deficiency, diabetes, pregnant mothers, etc.), was put on an appropriate diet. I, personally, was ordering one thousand chickens every three weeks, a process that was to continue until there was enough production for everyone to be served eggs daily for breakfast. In addition, the diet was supplemented regularly with pork from the piggery and fish which was brought in every two or three weeks on the Temple's boat. Temple agriculturalists said that we would have been self-sufficient in food production within a year to a year and a half from last October. Thus, despite what some press reports have stated, the land was productive—it just took some trial and error to learn how to farm in a tropical climate. Guyanese agriculturalists who were familiar with the area, including visitors from the government Ministry of Agriculture, were surprised to see the farming achievement in Jonestown. Information and techniques were exchanged regularly. Visitors were particularly amazed at the amount of land that had been cleared and either developed with facilities or put into agricultural-livestock production, in light of the fact that the project was entirely covered by dense jungle growth when it was begun. More than one visitor referred to the project as a "labor of love," which is perhaps the most apt description given to it.

On only one day of the total time period I was in Guyana (which was a year and three months), did a fight break out in the community, which I find remarkable considering the number of members who had been violence prone. (Ironically, it was two fist fights that broke out in that same day—one of them was between two young men who were friends, and the other was between two girls over some petty difference. The participants, incidentally, were all of the same race.) During the last five months of Jonestown's existence, violence was totally banned from the meetings, where it had been used on occasion and in extreme cases, as a last resort. However, not once did I witness any brutality, nor did I hear of any.

It is sadness beyond tears to think of my brothers and sisters from Jonestown, hundreds of them, not only unidentified, but still unburied. It is significant and tragically symbolic that they have laid for so long, in coffins piled up like so many matchboxes, waiting for a final resting place. They are back in their homeland, but they have no home. Peoples Temple was their only home, their only family, their only life. They are nameless and alone—forgotten by America. They died courageously—as one of their sisters wrote—because outside forces wouldn't let them live in peace. Is it any wonder that officials didn't want them all buried together, fearing their place of interment would become a shrine—and an all too painful reminder of a tragic American failure. Though I'm white, when I die, I belong with them, for their struggle was mine also.

17 Was Prokes an Agent?

The fact that Prokes declared, just before he killed himself, that he had been a former government agent or informant does not prove that he had functioned in that capacity. It is possible that he fabricated the allegation because he believed that there had been a government conspiracy to destroy the Temple and because he knew that proof of such activity might be difficult to secure.

At the law, deathbed or dying declarations are generally credited with a status that tends to elevate them above other unsworn statements. Under certain circumstances they may be admitted into evidence at a courtroom trial, although they do not meet the ordinary rules of admissibility. The theory which controls this exception to the hearsay rule is that a witness, just before death, and knowing that death is imminent, is less likely to make an untrue statement. However, the statement, whether admitted into evidence or not, is not subject to cross-examination. It is the technique of cross-examination that is essential to our concept of a fair trial.

For example, if any of the reporters at the March 13 press conference had either the intelligence or curiosity to ask probing questions, we might now have a physical description of Gary Jackson, the alleged contact, discovered how long Prokes had worked with him, learned if Prokes had deposited his weekly sum of two hundred dollars in a bank, and the specific locations where he picked up the money, determined the telephone numbers Prokes had been called at, when he received those calls, and whether he had ever been given a telephone number to call in the event of an emergency.

However, the failure of the reporters to ask the obviously relevant questions and the subsequent death of Mike Prokes have conspired to preclude the possibility of a serious examination of Mike Prokes regarding his very serious allegations. No doubt, government files hold the answers to many of the questions that surround the most recent of American tragedies, the massacre at Jonestown. Yet the relevant files of the police and spy organizations remain inaccessible to the American people and even beyond the reach of the members of the United States Congress, as the recent experience of the Church Committee of the U.S. Senate and the Select Committee on Assassinations of the House of Representatives demonstrated.

Without a record disclosing the cross-examination of Michael Prokes and without access at present to government files about the major figures in Peoples Temple, the search for the truth about Prokes must be directed toward existing and available facts even though that body of evidence may be somewhat peripheral.

It is apparent that the government was deeply concerned about the Peoples Temple. A significant part of this book, chapters 20 and 21, are devoted to considering the evidence in that regard.

In view of the developing political power of the Peoples Temple, its effectiveness on the local political scene, together with the assertions of its leaders that it was a communist organization, it defies logic and a sense of recent history to believe that the intelligence agencies ignored the burgeoning movement. Certainly, it is likely that the agencies ran one or more agents in the Temple. The admission of Prokes, painfully made in the last hours of his life, that he had for some time betrayed his newfound friends and may even have played some small part in the chain of events which led to the death of his loved ones, must have been difficult to make. It deserves serious evaluation.

It is logical to presume that if Mike Prokes were an informant in the Temple, he would not have confided in his colleagues there. His operation was, as he described it, necessarily shrouded in total secrecy.

The very background which likely made Mike "a good prospect," as he put it—"a dedicated Christian churchgoer," a good student in "conservative Orange County," and "no involvement in any kind of organization or activity that could be considered 'questionable,' " although he was on a California campus in the midst of the widespread and powerful movements against the war in Vietnam, for equal rights for blacks, Chicanos, Indians, and Orientals—might have created suspicion about his sudden conversion. Mike was aware of the doubts about him at the outset. He wrote of that period, "There was a lot of suspicion in the Temple (as one might imagine) of a reporter who quit his rather prestigious job as a bureau chief to join an organization that didn't pay salaries." Yet Mike died never having learned that after the first wave of doubt about him had abated, there was very strong evidence which led leaders in the Peoples Temple to conclude that he was still a federal agent during 1977. Jim Jones rejected the evidence at the time, primarily due to reasons of ego. He felt certain that he had genuinely converted Prokes and that the evidence to the contrary should be discounted.

On March 23, 1977, Dennis Banks, a leader of the American Indian Movement and a friend of the Peoples Temple, was approached by David Conn. In a declaration,* Banks swore that Conn had identified himself as "working with the Treasury Department." Conn also told Banks that he was working with an agent of the Treasury Department and with two men from the San Francisco Police Department. Conn was part of an inter-agency task force designed to "destroy the Peoples Temple," according to Banks. Conn explained to Banks that the goal of the coordinated effort was to discredit the Temple through the use of the news media. Banks quoted Conn as stating that he had been investigating the Temple for seven years and that he was associated with Grace Stoen, the wife of the former Peoples Temple lawyer, Timothy Stoen, and various other persons. Art Silverman, a reporter for the *Berkeley Barb,* wrote in the September 23–29, 1977, issue of that publication, "When reached by the *Barb* this week, Conn admitted that he had been investigating Peoples Temple for seven years." Conn denied that he was working for the government, stating that he had devoted part of the past seven years to the investigative project "on his own, as a private matter." According to the *Barb,* "Conn also admitted that he sought out Dennis Banks and arranged a meeting with him." Conn explained, "I wanted to talk to Banks because I respect the guy, and I was afraid that he was going to discredit himself through his association with the Peoples Temple without really knowing what they were about." Conn has not offered his denial under oath facing the penalty for perjury.

In his affidavit, Banks stated that "Conn was obviously making a deal with me." Banks concluded, "I was being blackmailed." He swore, "These agents all knew that I had a lot hanging over me. Besides the extradition,† I also had a case in federal court in which the Treasury Department was

*The declaration is published as Appendix A.

†The state of South Dakota was seeking to extradite Banks from California to imprison him for participation in a human rights demonstration on behalf of Indians. That matter was peripherally related to the confrontation at Wounded Knee, South Dakota. During the major trial in the Federal District Court for South Dakota (the trial having been moved to St. Paul, Minnesota, once the Hon. Fred Nichol, the senior federal judge of South Dakota, had determined that the two defendants, Banks and Russell Means, could not get a fair trial in South Dakota), all of the charges against the defendants were dismissed. This was due to the misconduct of the federal government agents, including the Special Agent In Charge

involved. I have often made it clear that if I am extradited to South Dakota, that it is like a sentence of death, because I am certain I will be killed there."*

According to Banks, Conn, after having identified himself as working with the Treasury Department, offered to assist Banks to resist extradition to South Dakota in exchange for "a public denunciation" of Jim Jones and the Peoples Temple.

Conn is ostensibly employed as a "surveyor" by the Standard Oil Company. He admitted to the *Berkeley Barb* that together with George Klineman, who described himself as a free-lance journalist, he met with various police and governmental agencies during the fall of 1976 and that both men helped to write, place, and promote hostile stories about the Peoples Temple.

Banks was accompanied at the meeting with Conn by Lehman Brightman, a leader of the Indian rights movement. Brightman supports the assertions made by Banks regarding the statements made by Conn. Conn has described himself as a longtime friend of Elmer and Deanna Mertle,† who were both ostensibly loyal members and leaders of the Peoples Temple for many years. Conn now admits that he was secretly investigating the Temple, for the purpose of exposing it and destroying it, during all of the years that his close friends were active members of the organization.

When Jones and the Temple leadership group learned from Dennis Banks of the coordinated government program to destroy them, according to Terri Buford, they initiated a counterintelligence program to learn more of the details. They discovered that David Conn spent a considerable amount of time at the home of his former wife, Donna Conn. Peoples Temple members thoroughly probed the house of Mrs. Conn and determined that by entering the garage they could squeeze through a trap door and gain access to a crawl space under the house. Christine Lucientis and a young man entered into the crawl space under the house. Two blocks away, a woman was seated in a getaway car. She remained outside the house with a flute. It was agreed that if she began to play the flute, Christine and her partner would escape

---

of the Federal Bureau of Investigation for the three-state area. I represented Dennis Banks at that trial.

*Dennis Banks's codefendant at the federal trial, Russell Means, returned voluntarily to face prison in South Dakota. He was attacked, stabbed, and almost killed in a South Dakota prison.

†Mr. and Mrs. Mertle now call themselves Al and Jeannie Mills. They left the Temple approximately six months before Conn surfaced as an open opponent of the Temple, and since that time played a major part in efforts to bring about a confrontation with the Temple.

from the crawl space, reenter the garage, and run toward the getaway car.

After Christine and her partner were in place, two other members of the Peoples Temple placed a telephone call to the home of Donna Conn from a nearby telephone booth. When she answered the telephone, a tape recording was played into the mouthpiece of the public telephone. The purpose of the tape-recorded message was to create a climate of concern in the Conn house in order to encourage the occupants to discuss relevant matters so that they might be overheard by the two members under the house. Believing that federal agents were in the house and fearful that the conversation might be monitored or recorded by the Conns, the Temple members were careful not to record their own voices. At first they considered attempting to disguise their voices, but Jim Jones was afraid that voice print technology was sufficiently advanced to overcome that simple effort to deceive.

The tape that was played to Donna Conn that spring evening in 1977 did not bear the voice of a member of the Temple. That tape had been prepared, as had so many others, on the streets of San Francisco in that section where homeless alcoholics wander about. Temple personnel created a script and other members asked derelicts to audition for a radio play by reading from the script into a tape recorder. Those auditioning were modestly paid for their trouble. The tapes, when judiciously excerpted, presented the points that the Temple wished to project but in the voice of a person who, in the unlikely event that he could be located, would in all probability be unable to lead an investigator back to the Temple. This operation, marked by an abundance of caution, was not illegal. In most instances the quasi-threats were cleared by in-house counsel for the Temple to ensure against a valid charge that a real threat had been made.

The tape-recorded voice that Donna Conn heard that evening informed her that the caller knew that "you and your friends" are "working for the government" in an effort to destroy Peoples Temple and "to blackmail Dennis Banks."

Christine and her partner were astonished at the acoustics provided by the crawl space. They could, they said, hear every sound spoken. They reported that Mrs. Conn became almost hysterical. She condemned David Conn for having parked directly in front of her house. "That's what gave it away," she said. "They saw you park your car here." She demanded that when he visit in the future, that he park his car some distance away. She was frightened by the call. She said to David, "Call the agent right away. Tell him what happened. I want protection now." David replied, according to the two eavesdroppers, "The agent can't help us. We can't call him."

Another man in the house began to speak. The two eavesdroppers froze.

They recognized the voice. They were certain that in the house with David and Donna Conn was Michael Prokes, one of the trusted aides to Jim Jones. At that point Prokes had been a member of the Temple for five years and had become a major spokesperson for the Temple to the outside world. The two members listened closely. The unnamed man was never referred to by name, but they were quite sure that it was Mike Prokes. Jones had arranged for the operation to go forward under an NTK (need to know) status. Only those directly involved in the project were to be acquainted with it. They could not understand what Mike was doing in the house. It did not occur to them at that point that he was an agent. They presumed that Jones had sent him there in another NTK mission which they had been excluded from and that the projects had unfortunately fouled each other by becoming inadvertently interwoven.

Christine and her partner left the crawl area, thinking they had heard a flute, and then all three returned under the house when they discovered their error. The three of them were dressed in black and all wore oversized tennis shoes. The sneakers were worn so that they might move more silently. The larger than necessary size was to reduce the chance that the tracks they were to leave behind could be traced to them.

After a while, David Conn left, as did Mike Prokes.

The three heard Donna make a telephone call and also greet a man who entered her house and whom she addressed as Bruce. They heard Donna say, they state, that she was in a position to make a telephone call and have weapons in her home in "five minutes flat." They heard Donna draw a bath and then apparently begin to take a bath. Then they heard Donna speak to Bruce. The three agreed that she said, "David has a Treasury card" and that "we both have high priority numbers" with the Treasury Department. She talked, they said, about a conservative member of the San Francisco City Council. She expressed concern about how the Peoples Temple had located her telephone number. She speculated that a television reporter was responsible. "Probably Van Amberg tipped them off," she declared angrily.*

Mrs. Conn, her daughter, and Bruce were in the house. The daughter's small dog ran out of the house and began to bark at the three interlopers under the house. Bruce and Mrs. Conn searched for the dog with flashlights and finally located it and returned to the house, never noticing the cause for the dog's action. Later that evening, Mrs. Conn again talked to Bruce

*The television reporter was not the source for the telephone number. Peoples Temple personnel who had searched through the garbage cans at Mrs. Conn's house three days before had found a discarded telephone bill which bore the telephone number.

about Jim Jones. She began to explain to him how David had started working with the Treasury Department.

It was not until approximately four o'clock in the morning that the three members under the house felt that they could exit from there without being heard.

The group reported back to Jim Jones. He asked them if they were sure that they had heard Prokes in the house. They said that they were certain he had been there. Jones had not assigned Prokes to visit the Conn house. For the first time it occurred to them that Prokes had not been there on Temple business. No one in the Temple recalled having seen Prokes all evening. He was finally located, sleeping in a little-used room. Jones and others agreed that someone who had sounded very much like Prokes visited the Conns the previous evening. He was not told then, or ever, that he was regarded as a suspect. But some Temple leaders were convinced from that night on that Prokes may have been working against the Temple and for the government.

Prokes began to drink heavily and often returned home to the Temple drunk. His friends in the Temple covered for him so that very few people knew that he had developed a drinking problem. Terri Buford, who tried to help Mike during the period of his obsessive drinking, has said,

> I knew that Mike was in great conflict then. He never would say what the problem was. I thought it was a personal matter, but I knew it was something he could not talk to any of us about. It was clear that the conflict was literally destroying him. In retrospect, I think it may very well have been the fact that he was an agent, informing on us, and that he also respected a lot of what we were doing and had very good feelings about some of us he was betraying. During that time, I guess he made the decision, perhaps subconsciously, that he would rather destroy himself than destroy all of us. We were just about all the friends and family he had, whatever his assignment might have been.

Unlike others in the Temple, Prokes often was not able to account for his time. The standard method of operation in the Temple called for the members, including the leadership, to work with a partner. Unlike most of the rest of the leadership, Prokes often found an excuse for working alone. He also was very wary about breaking the law, even when he agreed with the purpose of the action and when it was a low-risk operation. For example, the one time he was asked to carry money into South America, he refused to do so.

Jim Jones watched Mike Prokes closely after the incident at the Conn house. He made it plain to others in Temple leadership that he did not trust him, but that it was important to manipulate him and that it would be harmful to the Temple if a person so publicly associated with the organization defected.

After Jones arrived in Guyana he evidently decided that Prokes, who was a media specialist and quite effective for the Temple in San Francisco, should be in Jonestown. Jones spoke to Prokes from Jonestown by radio and urged him to visit upon the pretext that there were important matters regarding public relations that the two men had to discuss in person. The affairs were too delicate, Jones assured him, to be considered in a public medium.

After Prokes arrived in Guyana during the fall of 1977, ostensibly for a short visit and a long talk, he was coerced into staying by a trick that Jones had arranged. From various sources I have pieced together the facts about that maneuver. Some years before, a young teen-ager named Curtis Buckley had died in San Francisco from an overdose of drugs. The foster parent with whom Curtis was living had no legal right to the child. She panicked and called Mike Prokes in.

Prokes apparently knew that medical aid was not immediately sought for Curtis Buckley and there were signs that he had been beaten. Prokes did not reveal to the authorities what little he knew about the negligence that may have contributed to the death of the young man. After Prokes arrived in Guyana, he was informed by a Temple lawyer (Eugene Chaikin) that the authorities in San Francisco, armed with a grand jury subpoena, were seeking him in connection with the cover-up of negligence in the death of Curtis Buckley. Both Jones and Chaikin told Prokes that if he returned to the United States he would be in serious trouble. Resigned, Prokes remained on in Jonestown until the killings began on November 18.

There had been no grand jury subpoena for him. It was a device that Jones had created to keep Prokes close to him until the last hour.

Part VI

The Lawyers

18 Timothy Stoen

I believe that it is not possible to understand what happened at Jonestown or certainly why it happened without examining the unusual career of Timothy Stoen. During 1969, Stoen, a thirty-two-year-old graduate of Stanford Law School, married a young woman who had graduated from Lincoln High School in San Francisco the previous year. Grace and Timothy Stoen were married by Rev. Jim Jones in the Peoples Temple, then located in Redwood Valley, a very small farming community near Ukiah, California. Until that time, Stoen was practicing law, wearing very expensive clothing, and driving a Porsche. According to Jim Jones, Stoen had approached him while Jones was serving as the foreman of a grand jury in Ukiah. Stoen decided, Jones said, to give up his possessions; he sold his Porsche, closed his law office, and he and his new wife became members of the inner core of the Temple. Stoen became the chief legal advisor to Jones, his closest confidant and partner in running the affairs of the Temple. Jones and Stoen soon became extremely close personal friends. Speaking of that period, Stoen later said of Jones, "I guess I almost saw him as the Second Coming." Stoen also became an assistant district attorney for Mendocino County. At that time, the office exercised criminal jurisdiction over Redwood Valley and Ukiah.

On January 25, 1972, an event took place which was ultimately to adversely affect the lives of hundreds of members of the Temple almost seven years later and in another continent: John Victor Stoen was born in the Santa Rosa Memorial Hospital in Santa Rosa, California. Before the child, who was affectionately called John John, was two weeks old, Stoen prepared, wrote, and then signed, "under penalty of perjury"* a three-para-

*In certain instances under California law, a document signed under penalty of perjury need not be witnessed by a notary to enjoy the same official status as an affidavit.

graph document which was then witnessed by Marceline Jones.

The Stoen Statement, signed on February 6, 1972, emerges diacritically even in the eclectic archives of the Peoples Temple. Stoen, who has subsequently conceded that he did write and sign the statement, wrote:*

> TO WHOM IT MAY CONCERN:
>
> I, Timothy Oliver Stoen, hereby acknowledge that in April, 1971, I entreated my beloved pastor, James W. Jones, to sire a child by my wife, Gracy Lucy (Grech) Stoen, who had previously, at my insistence, reluctantly but graciously consented thereto. James W. Jones agreed to do so, reluctantly, after I explained that I very much wished to raise a child, but was unable, after extensive attempts, to sire one myself. My reason for requesting James W. Jones to do this is that I wanted my child to be fathered, if not by me, by the most compassionate, honest, and courageous human being the world contains.
>
> The child, John Victor Stoen, was born on January 25, 1972. I am privileged beyond words to have the responsibility for caring for him, and I undertake this task humbly with the steadfast hope that said child will become a devoted follower of Jesus Christ and be instrumental in bringing God's kingdom here on earth, as has been his wonderful natural father.
>
> I declare under penalty of perjury that the foregoing is true and correct.
>
> /s/Timothy Oliver Stoen
> Timothy Oliver Stoen
> Post Office Box 126
> Ukiah, California 95482

Dated: February 6, 1972

Witnessed: /s/Marceline Jones
Marceline Jones

Although it may have seemed at the time, as Stoen was later to insist, that Stoen had given Jones a weapon to utilize against him and to hold him, his wife, and the child hostage in the church, quite the opposite was apparently true. Stoen gave Jim Jones a false sense of security regarding the permanence of Jones's relationship with his son. To know Jones even casually was to appreciate the fact that he would never abandon the custody of John John upon pain of censure, disgrace, or even death. Stoen knew Jones

*Patrick Hallinan said to Herb Caen in the San Francisco *Chronicle,* "I think that when Tim signed that affidavit, he really believed Jones was the father."

well, and often said that he was quite certain that Jones was capable of killing John John, himself, and others if his tenuous legal hold upon the child seemed threatened. He said that one could be optimistic that Jones would likely overreact if sufficient adverse stimuli were introduced into his life.

Grace Stoen recalled her first impressions of the church, "When I first went, it was beautiful. All races and religions in one room. People with no schooling and people with eight years of college, people with money and people with none. There were lots of children. It was great. I always had a feeling for community."* Grace Stoen secured a job in a convalescent hospital, attended college four nights a week, spent some time with John John, and devoted the rest of her time to the Temple. Soon she dropped out of school, quit her job at the hospital, and devoted much more of her time to the Temple. Both Grace and her husband were notaries public and each formalized documents involving transfers of property from members to the Temple.

Grace Stoen accompanied Jones and others across the country on revival meetings, featuring faith healings magically and regularly performed by Jones, in city after city. The healings resulted from the hard work done by a secret group in the Temple called the Staff. They searched through garbage cans, interviewed those thought to be in need of salvation, without revealing their association with the Temple, ranged through homes looking for letters from friends and prescription drugs in medicine cabinets, and then provided Jones, prior to the revival meetings, with hard background evidence about people in the audience. Jones then appeared to be mystically in touch with some force which mysteriously provided the information to him. The entire operation was so effectively carried off by the charisma and organized brilliance of Jim Jones, and so well contained within a small elite group in the Temple, that members and leaders, including intellectuals with advanced college degrees, were convinced that Jones had special powers. These continual demonstrations of his exceptional gift were responsible for much of the awesome strength that Jones employed to maintain the respect, love, and worship of his followers. Many genuinely saw him as a holy man. Grace Stoen, however, should have known better. She was married to Timothy Stoen and apparently there was nothing of importance that he did not know.

Grace Stoen visited the Jonestown mission during its incipient stage at the end of 1974. She was impressed with what she saw and had only kind words to say about the experimental project upon her return to the United States. As the Stoens undertook leadership responsibilities, friction began to develop between them. With the passage of time, Grace became disen-

*San Francisco *Examiner*, 7 October 1977.

chanted with the Temple, with her dwindling relationship with Jones, and concerned about the closeness that was developing between her husband and Jones. Finally, she decided to leave both the Temple and Tim Stoen. Later, she said, "I didn't trust anyone, including Tim." She left without telling her husband that the marriage and her membership in the Temple were concluded. She also left her son, John John, behind. During September, 1976, she visited John John at the Peoples Temple in Los Angeles. She said that she was prevented from taking him home by Tim Stoen and Jim Jones. She never saw him again.*

But Tim Stoen did visit John John, who had accompanied Maria Katsaris to Jonestown. He saw him early the next year on a trip to Jonestown and again during a subsequent visit. Stoen remained voluntarily in Jonestown for many weeks during 1977. When he left Jonestown for the last time in the spring of that year, he left John John behind. He made no effort to take the child with him. He also left Jones with very strong advice as to how to contest any custody action that Grace Stoen might initiate. Indeed, it appears that Jones had quickly arranged for John John to be taken from California to Guyana specifically to thwart possible legal action by Grace Stoen and upon the advice of his lawyer, Timothy Stoen.

Terri Buford, serving as a trusted aide to Jones and as liaison to Stoen, was present at numerous meetings, public and private, which commenced shortly after Grace left the Temple and continued almost until Stoen left. When asked how many such meetings there were, she replied, "Scores and scores; over a hundred." She explained, "Jim was obsessed with the fear that John John would be taken from him. He discussed the matter every day with Stoen, often several times a day. It was practically the only thing on his mind. It was boring, to the point of tears. Stoen said, 'Grace is a cold-hearted bitch. I would never trust her with the child.' Stoen told Jones that he would 'do anything' to see to it that Jones could keep his child. He said 'I will die fighting for your right to keep John John.' Jones didn't want Stoen to die as much as he wanted him to develop a legal program to protect against a custody action by Grace."

According to Buford, Tim Stoen originated the concept that the most effective defense against a suit by Grace Stoen for John John's custody would be the physical transfer of the child to another country because a California court would be inclined to grant custody of a minor to the mother. Grace and Stoen had already signed statements authorizing Maria Katsaris to take the child to Guyana and authorized Joyce Touchette to serve as the child's guardian there. Therefore, reasoned Stoen, Jones could never be charged with kidnapping if he sent the child to Guyana.

*Ibid.

Stoen, according to Buford, advised Jones that he had thoroughly researched the extradition treaties between the United States and Guyana and had examined the history of those treaties. He told his client that although there was a treaty "of sorts" between the two countries, it had never been enforced and that he was certain that the United States government would not be able to force Guyana to surrender custody of the child. Stoen told Jones that the State Department was not authorized to interfere in a domestic matter or in child stealing, and that question could never come up since the biological father, Jim Jones, and the husband of the mother, Tim Stoen, both wanted the child to be reared in Jonestown. Again, Stoen pledged his life, if need be, to protect the relationship between father and son. Stoen said that no court in Guyana would ever state that life in that socialist country was inferior to life in America and that, under the circumstances, he was satisfied that Grace would never be able to dislodge John from Guyana and the supervision of his real father.

Upon the first indication that Grace Stoen might bring legal action to secure custody of her son, Jones sent Maria Katsaris and John Victor Stoen to Guyana.

Terri Buford remembers the event clearly: "Maria and I visited Tim Stoen in his office in the San Francisco District Attorney's office. Tim decided to speak with Grace that evening by telephone at about eight o'clock. Stoen took out his cassette tape recorder which he had kept in his desk drawer and attached it to the telephone with a small microphone in a rubber suction cup. An earphone was placed on his tape recorder so that Maria could listen in on the conversation. Grace told Tim that she wanted to visit her child. He answered, 'That will be quite impossible, because I myself took little John to Guyana and he is there now.' Grace began to cry and carry on and she may even have begun to threaten legal action. Stoen then offered to provide a ticket for Grace to Guyana to visit the child. Grace, still crying, said that she could not quit her job. She was also probably afraid to go there, although I don't believe she said that. Stoen then made many suggestions. He said he was so sorry she was upset and that he felt it was a very good environment in which to raise a child. She became even more upset, stating something like 'I just want John to grow up like a normal little boy. You're such an idiot that you were trying to teach a two-year-old to speak Russian. That's not what I want for my son.' "

Stoen visited the Temple later that evening. He brought the tape of the conversation, which, according to Terri Buford, he had made without his wife's permission or knowledge. He gave the tape to Jones, who played it in the presence of Gene Chaikin, Carolyn Layton, Maria Katsaris, Tim Stoen, Mike Prokes, and Terri Buford. Jones listened to the lengthy tape-recorded discussion carefully. It had already been decided by Jones and Stoen that John John would be taken to Guyana in the event of an emergency. The matter for determination was not where, but when. Jones felt that Stoen's telephone call to Grace had presented him with a fait accompli. He said that the child should leave for Guyana the next day. Stoen agreed. Jones wanted Stoen to take John to Guyana, but Stoen begged off, saying that he could not leave the next day, since he was in the middle of an important investigation.

The next day, Maria Katsaris and John Stoen flew from San Francisco to Miami. After spending that night in a Miami hotel, they left the next day for Guyana. John John Stoen was in Jonestown. If Buford's account of the events proves accurate, then we can only ponder what action Grace Stoen might have taken if she had been told the truth by her husband. It seems likely that she would have tried to enjoin Jones, Stoen, and Katsaris from taking John to Guyana and that she would have hastened to revoke the statement she had signed which gave permission for such a trip. Had Stoen revealed that there were plans to take John to Guyana and not presented her with a faked fait accompli, John might never have been sent to Guyana. Before the legal, political, and extralegal efforts which swirled about his presence there and which were ostensibly devoted to returning him to the United States were completed, he died there at the age of six, as did many others.

Timothy Stoen was later to recount in magnificent detail during attacks he led in 1977 and 1978 against Peoples Temple and Jones how he had been taken in by Jones. Since many others also had been, Stoen's exposition rang with a feeling of truth. Stoen, however, knew from his earliest days in the Temple that fraud was being regularly employed to bilk substantial sums of money from the poor people, most of whom were black, at meeting after meeting as the traveling miracle makers moved from city to city. Unlike Gene Chaikin, who felt constrained to set aside his scepticism in the face of what seemed to be a growing body of evidence that Jones possessed a rare ability, Stoen was not fooled. His wife later said that she was at one time on the Staff, but I have not been able to find evidence to corroborate that allegation. Sandy Bradshaw, Karen Layton, Carolyn Layton, Sharon Amos, Patty Cartmell, her daughter Patricia (Tricia) Cartmell, Steve Addison, Rita Tupper, Christine Lucientis, and Jack Beam made up the backbone of the Staff. They were given a private meeting room in each city where the Temple revival meetings were to take place. Almost no one else in the Temple had access to those rooms, which were locked and guarded when Staff work was taking place there. However, Tim Stoen had access to the rooms, and Jones subsequently told Terri Buford that Stoen knew all about the work of the Staff. Patty Cartmell gave this account of a potentially serious problem she had encountered while on a Staff assignment:

"Jack [Beam] and I were doing a stop/by* on a house in Los Angeles. Jack was in the car and I was in the yard. The cops came and Jack, the yellow-bellied coward, took off, leaving me holding the bag. I was arrested and taken in."

Cartmell was a very large white woman, who in the manner of the Staff members had put on black stage make-up as camouflage as she prowled around black neighborhoods. The police who encountered her, due to a telephone call from a neighbor who had noticed her strange behavior, were struck by her black face, arms, hands, and calves—and her white thighs which were visible when she leaned over. She later admitted that she panicked when placed in a jail cell; she was claustrophobic and was unable, quite understandably, to come up with an acceptable and reasonable explanation for her actions and appearance. Patty Cartmell later explained, "I didn't know what to do so I called Tim and told him I'd been arrested." She said that she had reached Stoen at his office in the district attorney's office in Ukiah.

Stoen explained to Terri Buford how the Cartmell matter was resolved. Buford recalls, "Stoen said that Jim came up with this brilliant idea that Patty should be told to say that she was having an affair with a man and had put on this disguise; she was meeting him in a black neighborhood, and she didn't want her husband to find out. Stoen said the story was so incredible that the police believed it and released Patty."

While the church was located in Ukiah, according to Jones, a telephone operator wrote to advise him that the telephones at the Temple's law office maintained by Eugene Chaikin were being monitored. The writer asked that her name not be divulged. She said that she feared for her safety. This incident helped to convince Jones, Chaikin, Tropp, and others that efforts were under way to destroy the group; Stoen said that he, too, was certain. Jones told Buford that it was important that the members of the organization know that the Temple was under attack, but, at the same time, he felt reluctant to share the facts with the membership out of fear that so wide a publication of the evidence would impair the ability of the leadership to secure more information. Jones then hit upon the idea of inventing a purported assault. He asked a Temple member to call Mike Cartmell so that he could claim to have been shot. Unable to reach Cartmell at any of his known haunts, the member then called Tim Stoen at the Mendocino County District Attorney's office and told him of Jim's plan. Stoen agreed to play the part of the wounded martyr.

A telephone call was placed by Edith Kutulas, who was in the Temple's

*A stop/by or S/B describes a Staff approach to the exterior of a house. It includes peering through windows, examining the contents of garbage cans, noticing the placement of the mail box, observing the landscaping, and determining the hours that the house is unoccupied.

third-floor office, to a pay telephone located on the main floor of the church. She disguised her voice and reported that Tim Stoen had been shot. She gave as her first name that of Stoen's secretary at the district attorney's office. Coincidentally, Grace Stoen had answered the pay telephone. She became frantic. She ran to Jones and told him of the message. He assured Grace and the others that he intuitively knew that "Tim is all right. I feel it. I know it." He instructed Grace and Terri to call Tim. Tim confirmed that he had been shot on the trip back to the district attorney's office where he had planned to work that evening. He said the shot had been fired by an occupant of a passing vehicle. He said that although the bullet had struck him in the chest and he fell to the ground in pain with what might have been his last breath, he called upon Jim and he was healed instantly. The graphic description by Stoen was broadcast live over the public address system and was heard by hundreds of people who also had gathered in the auditorium of the Temple in San Francisco. The next time Stoen went to a meeting of the Temple in San Francisco, he gave witness to the miraculous powers of Jim Jones. He described in detail the attempted assassination of the committed Marxist, himself, and how it was foiled by the Father, as he called Jones. Ultimate proof of the healing powers could be discerned by examining Stoen's chest, which showed no trace of the bullet wound, so perfect was the touch of the master.

After my return from Jonestown during September 1978, I met at the Temple's Georgetown building with a Catholic priest, Father Morrison. I had been told that he had written of his negative impression of Jones and the Peoples Temple in a nationally distributed newspaper, the *Catholic Standard,* which he published and for which he served as a journalist. I asked him what it was that he found distasteful about the Peoples Temple. Father Morrison said that during the winter of 1974, Jones had arrived in Georgetown with a number of church members. Jones had conducted a faith-healing service there. The priest then told me, "I am a believer in the 'Charismatic church.' I do not oppose healing by faith, but I do oppose trickery designed to give the impression of faith healing." I said, "Father, do you know that there was fraud during the service?" He said that he did know that. He explained that after the service, one of those purportedly healed had confessed that he had not been ill. I was reluctant to doubt Father Morrison, since he seemed so sincere. While I could believe, I am afraid, that the Temple leaders, resting upon their philosophy that the ends justify the means, might have indulged in sharp practices, it was harder to believe that any of the leading members would have betrayed that secret so quickly.

An investigation into the matter reveals that Father Morrison was correct and that I owe him an apology for having doubted his report. At a meeting in Georgetown which was held two weeks before the aforementioned service, the Temple leaders discussed the efficaciousness of such an event. Jones expressed his hesitancy, expounding his opposition to a faith-healing service in a socialist country. Stoen, it is reported, favored the idea and was persuasive and flattering enough to prevail.

After the massacre, Stoen said that he had faked a stomach ailment at this service in Georgetown.* He said that he "faked it through the whole meeting. I never was much good at that." Stoen said that he also pretended to be "cured" when Jones approached him. As Stoen reviewed the event later, he said, "The journalists there were very sharp and got onto the healing thing right away. They gave us a lot of bad publicity." The most influential journalist who wrote about the event was Father Morrison. His articles did give the Temple a great deal of adverse publicity. In retrospect, Stoen has said, "It was a major blunder and it made me doubt him [Jones] for the first time."† Yet Stoen, as we have just seen, was to participate in a second faked healing episode—the one in which he was allegedly wounded by an assassin's bullet—even after he began to doubt Jones.

When Terri Buford testified before the Federal Grand Jury in San Francisco and met with local, state, and federal law enforcement personnel, she made a series of statements about Timothy Stoen and his method of leadership in the Peoples Temple. The following pages are devoted to an effort to recapitulate her charges fairly, which have in most instances not been previously published or referred to in detail but which have, in most cases, been submitted to authorities after the appropriate warnings were given about the penalty for making false statements.

One of the major threats to the good image of the Temple was the fear that members of the organization might reveal its secrets to the public at large. Since the Temple was structurally schizophrenic, in the classical sense, that fear was not delusional. The reality was that the Temple held itself to be a religious organization devoted to sound social work principles as well as transforming society into a more compatible place for the poor, the black, the brown—the disadvantaged of America. Its leader, Jim Jones, was presented as a self-sacrificing man whose goals were identical with the stated aspirations of the Temple. That image did not badly distort the real situation. However, the methods which the Temple employed, ostensibly in search of those objectives, made a mockery of their goals; in order to create an organization that could effectively struggle against cruelty in the world, the Temple leaders would engage in some cruel conduct themselves.

Many of the younger members who had joined the Temple through selfless motivation, responded to the professionally trained leaders, who explained tactics and strategy to them. Jones and Stoen, the minister and

**The Suicide Cult,* p. 95.
†Ibid.

the assistant district attorney, were an effective team. Together they established priorities, instructed as to the moral and legal implications of the acts, and placed their analysis in the context of a superior understanding of Marxism and a total devotion to revolution. If Gene Chaikin had moral and legal reservations about a proposed act, Stoen condemned his bourgeois background and attitude after Chaikin had left the room, and Jones, impressed by Stoen's revolutionary commitment, relied more heavily upon him and less upon Chaikin. Stoen's actions were divisive; Jones, quick to suspect the absence of sufficient revolutionary ardor in others, was reinforced. Thus, in relatively short order, a Jones-Stoen partnership emerged.

During a meeting in the fall of 1973, at which Tim Stoen, Jim Jones, and Carolyn Layton were present, the Diversions Department was evidently created. Its purpose was to ensure that the Temple's secrets be kept. To divert skeptical attention away from the Temple, the newly formed unit publicized other faith healers, alleging and attempting to prove that the others employed tricks. In addition, telephone calls were made to various opposing political candidates by representatives of the Temple Diversions Department pledging support to each and stating that the Temple was mobilizing its legions to elect the candidate. When the result was in, the Temple called the winner to give the kudos and called the losers to express solidarity and concern.

The work of Diversions underwent a metamorphosis, however, as members began to resign from the Temple; Stoen and Jones feared that these former members would inform about the methods used by the organization. Diversions was no longer primarily devoted to political and media fun and games. It took on a deadly serious character.

Buford states that Stoen prepared and drafted letters to former members. The letters were carefully written and although they contained implicit threats, they were designed to avoid criminal liability. For example, one defector, while a member of the Temple, had stated that she achieved an orgasm while watching children being beaten. The letter to her, while purportedly coming from another source, clearly made reference to the incident, stating that the writer had just heard a tape recording of her admission. On another occasion, Stoen designed a letter to his wife after Grace had left the Temple. For reasons now obscure, in the Temple lexicon, the phrase "a trip to New York," was a death threat. Stoen, apparently concerned that criminal responsibility could be attached if the coded threat were used blatently, prepared a letter in which the threat was conditional. Buford recalls that the letter, which she saw many years ago, contained a phrase of this nature: "If you are still around [on some date] you will receive two tickets to New York."

Perhaps the most aberrant episode in the history of Diversions centered around James Cobb, Jr. Unlike others who left the Temple because they felt the Temple asked too much of its members and had embarked upon an unrealistic revolutionary program, there is evidence to suggest that Cobb left in part because the Temple demanded too little of him and was insufficiently bellicose. According to Terri Buford, Stoen suggested that Cobb be threatened by means of a telephone call. In his own hand, Stoen wrote out the threat and ordered that a member of the Temple telephone Cobb and read the threat to him, Buford states.

After Stoen left the Temple in the spring of 1977, he agreed to represent Cobb in a lawsuit against Jones, the Peoples Temple, and all of the alleged members of the Diversions Department with the exception of himself. The multimillion dollar suit was filed by Stoen in the San Francisco Superior Court on June 22, 1978. In the suit, Cobb complained about the receipt of the threatening telephone call and the establishment of a Diversions Department. Stoen, who as his counsel had to draft the complaint, spelled out in detail the responsibilities of Diversions. Since the department was a well-kept secret within the Temple, known only to the Diversions Department members and had not even been established until just after Cobb had left the Temple, it appears that the intimate knowledge of the department's nomenclature that Stoen demonstrated does little to refute the charges of Stoen's complicity. In the lawsuit, Stoen said that "On or about June 23, 1977,"* the Temple established "the Diversions Department." He said that the Department was to be divided into three "de facto divisions" and was to "engage in the following 'dirty tricks.' " He then displayed a rare familiarity with the modus operandi of the newly formed department. He wrote:

> a. Defectors & Critics Division: To divert individual persons, particularly ex-members of PEOPLES TEMPLE and outspoken critics thereof, from publicizing and from organizing in opposition to the practices of defendants JONES and PEOPLES TEMPLE, by threatening such persons with death and injury to their persons and properties, including threats that their homes will be burned;
>
> b. Government & Media Division: To divert agencies of government and of the media from investigating the practices of defendants JONES and PEOPLES TEMPLE by:

*The date chosen by Stoen in the sworn complaint is not accurate. The Diversions Department was formed by Stoen, Carolyn Layton, and Jim Jones during the fall of 1973. Since Stoen was no longer involved in Temple operations during June 1977, one can readily understand why he chose a date which tended to exculpate him. However, that effort seriously jeopardized his client's cause, for if the "threat" to Cobb, complained of in the lawsuit, predated the establishment of the Diversions Department, how can Stoen and Cobb expect to fix responsibility upon the Diversions Department of the Temple for the alleged threat? Perhaps if Stoen were to listen to the tape recordings of two meetings of Diversions at which he was present, both of which took place prior to June 1977, his memory might be refreshed.

(1) "Bombarding" them with continual mass volumes of letters written in longhand by PEOPLES TEMPLE members conscripted as part of "letter-writing committees" which allege various types of unjustified harassment; and

(2) Making anonymous telephone calls to agencies of government and the media which accuse totally innocent persons selected at random of heinous crimes and immoral acts (particularly crimes and acts related to those for which defendant JONES feared he was about to be accused); and

c. General Public Division: To divert the public from focusing upon the questionable practices of defendants JONES and PEOPLES TEMPLE by publishing press releases and other communications which falsely accuse the critics of such practices as being sexual deviates, terrorists, drug traffickers, or child molesters.

When Buford read the complaint that Stoen had written for Cobb she was astonished that Stoen had remembered the details, including the alleged date of the first meeting, with such precision. She did not challenge Stoen's recitation; she was surprised that he was capable of it and of such an indiscretion. She said, "He remembers it well as I suppose only its creator could. Stoen told the members of Diversions what to do. Now that he has exposed his master plan for Diversions in writing I can see how each of the assignments that he gave all fell under that plan. I don't think that anyone in the Temple, except possibly Jones, had ever seen the Stoen master plan for the Diversions Department until Stoen put it together for the Cobb suit."

Buford asserted under oath with supporting documentary evidence, including a note handwritten by Stoen directing that a threat be made, that Stoen ordered the threat and then sued on the basis of the threat. If this is true, his conduct has been less than exemplary. Indeed, he stands to earn a very substantial sum (he is asking for several million dollars as a result of the threats received by his client) for actions which he improperly initiated.

Other than the threat to take John John away, one can hardly conceive of actions more likely to drive Jones to an extreme response than the defection of his lawyer-partner and his sudden transformation into an unending fount of incriminating data delivered directly to what he conceived as the enemy camp. The canons of professional responsibility, stressing the sanctity of the attorney-client relationship and the privileged nature of statements made by clients to attorneys were designed, it seems, to prohibit such conduct. Jones felt that he had been betrayed. He saw Stoen, whom he said had established the Diversions Department, telling the whole truth about it, except the nature of his own role in its creation and direction. Jones knew that he had been effectively stopped from rebutting the Stoen attack. If Jones responded that the threats had been sent under Stoen's leadership, then the massive lawsuit would have been lost and the $22,-900,000 in compensatory and punitive damages sought by Stoen could have put an end to the Temple.

While Stoen asserted that the Diversions Department was set up "in order to institutionalize the tactics of terror," Buford adds, "The entire time that I was aware of the work of Diversions, there was not a single death threat or other threat mailed or telephoned to former members which had not been initiated or cleared by Stoen. He directed the work of Diversions, he wrote out threats, he ordered that the threats be communicated, and he alone had the authority to clear each threat before it was mailed or called. This he often did without Jim Jones's knowledge or consent. He had the authority to act in this area without supervision and he had that authority because he set it up that way."

Stoen told Buford that he had met with Jones and advised him that to protect the leader, Jones should not be involved with the workings of Diversions. He said, Buford recalled, that Jones had agreed and gave full authority to Stoen to run the department autonomously. Normally, it is the lawyer who may care to isolate himself from too close a contact with the dubious actions of his client. Here, according to Stoen's account, the lawyer who was employed by law enforcement authorities was attempting to shield his client.

Later, when Stoen gave assignments to Buford which called for improper conduct, bordering on illegal conduct, she consulted with Jim Jones in any event. In those instances Jones did agree that he had given Stoen authority to act on his own, stating, "I trust Tim completely." He never conceded to Buford that Stoen's authority was a play to protect him. Buford explained, "Jim always came on as the most honest and most committed of leaders. I knew he would never admit that he had agreed to let Tim make the Diversions decisions out of concern for his personal protection. Yet he did say that Tim had the authority to act. He said he was too busy running the operation to get involved in all the details."

The circumstances surrounding the Cobb defection were, as indicated, unique. When Jim Cobb was an active member of the Temple, he was an extremely athletic and powerful man. For a period, he attended Santa Rosa Junior College in California with a number of other Temple members. He emerged as the leader of the Santa Rosa Temple Community and there he taught survival techniques. Cobb left the Temple with seven other members. The defectors were known in the Temple simply as "The Eight." Cobb's mother, sister, and the two younger brothers remained in the Temple. The Eight left behind a declaration stating that they did not disagree with the tenets of the organization, but rather with the failure of the Temple to carry out its stated objectives.

Sometime thereafter, at a Planning Commission meeting in San Francisco, Stoen sent a note to Jones stating that he believed that Cobb should be threatened by telephone. Jones handed the note to Buford and said, "This is too risky. I'm really nervous about this kind of thing." Stoen then sent another note to Jones, through Buford, who was sitting near Jones. Since a number of questions were being discussed, Buford states she wrote at the top of the note the words "RE: COBB" and then passed the note to Jones.

Re: Cobb

I still think it advisable to proceed: Person who does it should be unknown to subject and should try to disguise voice and speak to the point.

Annie Moore probably good.

I don't think that the authorities will go to all the trouble to make a voice print since nothing illegal involved.

It's rare that such a "natural" opportunity will present itself.

Terri

Later, based upon new instructions from Stoen, a telephone call was made, which Cobb said he considered to be threatening.*

According to Buford, who now views her several years of working with

*Terri Buford's affidavit in the case of *Peoples Temple v Timothy Stoen,* which presents the relevant details of the instructions leading up to the telephone call, is published as Appendix H.

Stoen in a perspective sharpened by hindsight, "It seems that there was a pattern to his actions. It is almost as if he operated from a larger plan which either he or others developed but which we were at the time unaware of." Buford described the first meeting she attended where Stoen laid out a plan to kill defectors should Jones die. Once there was a general acceptance of that broad principle, based upon a contingency which hardly seemed imminent and therefore the application of the principle did not seem likely, Stoen moved on to the next phase. Having secured consent, or at least the absence of protest to his general program, Stoen suggested at a subsequent meeting that an enemy should be killed. No longer was there the unexpected contingency to cushion the decision-making process from reality. When that plan was rejected, he suggested that an enemy be assaulted.

The facts, as Buford recounts them, relate to the first meeting she was aware of in which an enemy list was discussed. The meeting took place in August 1973 in a cow pasture in Redwood Valley at a ranch owned by one of the Temple members and operated by the Temple. Stoen, Sandy Bradshaw, Buford, and others were present. Stoen chaired the meeting. He opened the meeting by stating that the result of the meeting was to be reported to "Jim." He said that it was his opinion that Jim should not be present at meetings for tactical planning because Jim was vital to the leadership of the organization and if anything were to go wrong, "We want to be able to say that we were acting independently and Jim had not been advised of our actions." Stoen said that the group should come up with some contingency plans. The first contingency to be considered, he said, was what the reaction should be if Jim was killed. Stoen then wrote on a piece of paper a "hit list" comprised of Temple defectors and critics that "should be made to pay if anything happens to Jim." On that list was the name Lester Kinsolving, a man who had written a series of articles critical of the Temple. Stoen then suggested that a kidnap list be compiled. He thought, he said, that if Jim was arrested, political figures should be punished by being kidnapped, not killed. This less drastic approach was not dictated by a merciful instinct but by pragmatism. The kidnapped officials were to be held hostage until Jones was released. No one could think of a prominent person who could easily be kidnapped given the Temple lack of expertise in the field. Patty Hearst, one participant reminded the others, had already been taken. Stoen then assigned a task to each of the members present: "Before the next meeting, come up with the names of likely people to kidnap."

Stoen then proposed a program for "simultaneous political action" in which some members of the Temple would perform "political activities," while the church as a whole moved forward with its regular program. The "political activities" Stoen suggested included the establishment of a bomb factory and poisoning the water supply of Washington, D.C. He suggested that Jim McElvane be assigned to secure the plans for the water supply system of Washington, D.C., and that someone should take on the responsibility of researching the kind of poison that could effectively be used for that purpose. He asked for volunteers. Stoen reported directly to Jones about the proposal. There is some evidence that Stoen, together with Sandy Bradshaw, visited the law enforcement library at the district attorney's office in Ukiah to look into the various kinds of poison. Whether or not he recommended to Jones any particular type of poison will remain an enigma unless the thousands of documents of Peoples Temple files in Jonestown, those stored in Charles Garry's law office, and those that were in the custody of Jean Brown at the Temple's San Francisco building, are brought forth and no longer suppressed, as they have been thus far.

At this same meeting, when another member proposed the idea that they take over a National Guard Armory to steal weapons, Stoen agreed. He added that all of those present at the meeting were required to learn to fire weapons.

On various occasions since that meeting, Terri Buford said, Stoen asked her if she had learned to fire a weapon yet. She said that she had not, that she had never fired a weapon. Stoen lectured her, she recalls, telling her that she had a "cavalier attitude about revolution" and that a "real marxist cannot go through life believing that there will never be a confrontation." He told her that her attitude was indicative of the fact that she did not really "care about the movement." When Terri was twenty years old, Stoen instructed her to register with personnel in the sheriff's office in Mendocino County. Stoen's office in the district attorney's office was located in the same building in Ukiah. He told her that if she registered at that age, she could be hired as soon as she became twenty-one. She recalls that shortly before she became twenty-one years old, Stoen told her that there were three essential reasons that he had assigned her to register. They were, he said:

a) "As a deputy, you will be licensed to handle weapons."

b) "As a deputy, you will be trained to handle weapons."

c) "As someone in that office each day, you will have access to the information there and you will be able to report any activities of the office to us."

Following his directions, she went to the office and filed an application. Stoen, she said, continued to discuss the matter with her and repeatedly urged her to learn how to fire weapons. She was nervous about weapons. She was aware of the fact that she could discharge one in error and injure someone. Buford also had serious reservations about firearms as a mechanism for social change.

One evening, in desperation after a Wednesday evening church service, she appealed directly to Jim Jones. At that point, she did not know him well enough to approach him at any other time. Buford waited in line until Jones was free, then asked him, "Is it absolutely necessary for me to apply for the job at the sheriff's office? I do not believe that I am emotionally, physically, or psychologically equipped to handle the job of fronting as a deputy sheriff for socialism. I don't think I have what it takes." Jones seemed stunned by her statement. He said, "What gives you the impression that you should take a job like that?" Terri said, "Tim Stoen told me that that's what I'm supposed to do." Jones answered, "Well, I told you I want you to get your degree, and I never gave any orders that you were to go into police work."

Stoen urged other members to secure weapons and to learn to fire weapons. At one time, it was decided that weapons should be collected from the many members of the Temple. Ostensibly this was in support of an anti-crime crusade. Weapons were to be gathered and then turned in to the local law enforcement authorities. Numerous people surrendered their weapons to Stoen. Many Saturday night specials, other handguns, and various long weapons were collected. The program was effective and, in its initial stage, in conformity with the statewide program. However, since the Temple kept all of the weapons for its own purposes (it later sold some, keeping the proceeds), the program tended to deviate from the established standards in its second and determinative phase.

Just after Terri's twenty-first birthday, and after she had made plans to complete her education at the University of California at Berkeley, Stoen instructed her to change her major to chemistry. He explained that with that background she could learn to manufacture bombs. Stoen also suggested that Tom Adams, another Temple member, drop out of school (he was a history major at Berkeley) and apply for a job in a pharmaceutical company. Stoen said that Terri and Tom should rent an apartment together, get married so that no one could accuse them of living in sin, and set up a bomb factory in San Francisco. Again, Terri Buford in panic appealed to Jim Jones. She again sought out Jones after a Wednesday night meeting and shared her concerns with him. He took off his glasses and looked her straight in the eye, a mannerism of his to determine if the person he was speaking with was being truthful, and said, "That's crazy. You'll blow your head off." Jones was amazed that Stoen seemed more concerned about the young couple being accused of living in sin and less concerned about them being arrested for possession of bombs. He said, "There's something wrong with that man."

According to Buford, Stoen had more than a passing interest in the idea of explosives. On several occasions, he gave her books and pamphlets which described the process for manufacturing bombs, booby-trapping doors, and demolishing automobiles. Stoen said that he had secured the literature from "the office," in reference to the district attorney's office in Ukiah where he was still employed. He urged Terri to study the material and then to pass it on to Jim Jones. Later when Buford showed the books to Jones, he told her to keep them locked up in her room as a precaution against the church's being raided.

Later, Stoen informed Buford about a bookstore near the California-Oregon border which sold technical and advanced works on the manufacture and use of explosives. He said he had learned about the store from discussions "at work" and that law enforcement agencies secured reference material from that store. He instructed Terri to "get dressed up like a school teacher" and purchase a good selection of the technical manuals on bombs, weapons, and other explosives from the store. She was to secure "false I.D.," Stoen said, and to explain to the salesperson at the store that she was going to teach some kind of course on "safety." The project and the ill-fitting cover story made no sense to Terri. Where could she get false identification that would pass that kind of scrutiny, she wondered. How could anyone believe that a school teacher, instructing on safety, would require or even be interested in acquiring technical and expository works on the technique of assembling explosives? When Buford discussed the proposal with Jones, he told her not to go. He said, "We're too busy; we don't have time for that kind of stuff."

Stoen kept up his fetish for bombs "and the like for as long as I can remember talking to him or listening to him," Buford later said. She continued: "He was very impressed, he said, with the Mafia, especially with its tactics and organization. He urged me to read about the Mafia as he was doing, and said that there was a great deal of technical information that we could learn from them. He said that the idea of the horse's head in the bed [as illustrated in *The Godfather*] was 'brilliant.' During one of the last conversations that I had with him, not long before his last trip to Guyana, he was stressing the need for me to read about the structure and strategy of the Mafia."

After Stoen had prevailed upon a unit within the Temple to accept his leadership rather than Jones' in the area of contingency planning for terrorist activities, and after the members of the Temple had found his long-range plans, which conceivably would never be implemented, acceptable, Stoen apparently moved the group further in that direction through his distribution of books and pamphlets and his effort to involve others in the process of securing additional literature. Clearly Stoen, as a Mendocino County assistant district attorney, could easily have obtained the literature he said he sought without attempting to involve Buford in a scheme so poorly contrived that it was likely to fail. His efforts to involve others in machinations which he devised and which through his concept of intrigue and deception, he had made almost self-defeating, raise serious questions about his motivation.

During the fall of 1978, Sandy Bradshaw signed a statement under the penalty of perjury in which she described a visit to the library at the district attorney's office. Bradshaw, a Temple activist, was at that time employed in the sheriff's office. In her statement, Bradshaw said that the purpose of the visit to the library was to research various kinds of poison. The written statement had been given to the attorney for the Peoples Temple, Charles Garry. Later Bradshaw confirmed the accuracy of that written statement to Buford in a conversation.

Toward the end of Stoen's association with the Temple, he became more insistent that action should be taken against the Temple's enemies. During his last visit to Jonestown in the spring of 1977, Stoen, Jones, Patty Cartmell, and Terri Buford met outside the warehouse in which the communications center was located. Al Touchette had been working the radio and Stoen, Jones, and Buford had been exchanging messages with the Temple personnel in San Francisco. They had lost radio contact and Touchette went to bed. The others were walking toward their sleeping quarters when Stoen announced a plan for dealing with the enemies of the Temple. Buford recalls that he said that "the media needs to be taught a lesson." Recalling the effectiveness of the horse's head in the bed, Stoen suggested that one member of the news media should be punished in a similar fashion. He suggested that Lester Kinsolving be captured, a burlap sack then placed over his head, and that he should be badly beaten but not killed.

Patty pointed out that Kinsolving would be able to see through a burlap sack. Jones said that Kinsolving would be an enemy for life if he were beaten. Since Kinsolving had already claimed that his house had been broken into and that Peoples Temple had probably done it, it appeared likely that he would strongly suspect that an anonymous beating had been arranged by the Temple. In fact, Stoen knew it would be assumed that the Temple was responsible. If not, how could the assault be instructive for other members of the media? Since Kinsolving was at that time an inactive opponent, he had not written about the Temple for years, his selection by Stoen is curious.

When Kinsolving had, years earlier, asserted that his home had been entered and his papers gone through by Temple leaders, at whom the finger of suspicion was then pointed, they believed that the break-in story had been fabricated, for they knew that they had not been involved. Later, after a series of similar events, it became clear that someone very familiar with the Diversions work of the Temple, was leaving behind a trail which appeared to lead to the gates of the Peoples Temple. After Stoen left the Temple, the Diversions Department was slowly phased out of existence. Immediately upon his leaving, the high-risk adventures which he had urged and directed were ended. Yet someone familiar with the high-risk proposals and the methods that the Temple had employed under Stoen's directions evidently carried forth those projects. In every such instance, Jones and the Temple were publicly branded as the culprits, and Jones, frustrated and panicked by the unfair and untrue charges, became angry and then increasingly frightened by the invisible trap into which he sensed that he was falling.

When I first met Jim Jones in Guyana during September 1978, he said to me, during a rambling monologue: "It all started, these insane attacks, they all started with those Kinsolving articles. If only Tim Stoen had not made up that crazy story then maybe Kinsolving would not have written the articles. I don't know why Tim said that to him. It didn't make any sense. I never would have let him say anything like that if I had been there." That portion of the Jones exposition made no sense to me at that time, for I did not then possess the factual background in which to understand the Kinsolving/Stoen association.

Later, I discovered that Kinsolving, a writer with government credentials,* had decided in 1972 to write a series about the Temple for the San Francisco *Examiner.* In preparation for the series, Kinsolving spent some time interviewing Stoen. Stoen described in lucid detail how Jim Jones had raised the dead in his presence. This assistant district attorney vouched for an event which had never taken place. He described the lady Lazarus to Kinsolving as a woman whose face had gone ashen grey, with eyes rolled back and tongue hanging out. She was, Stoen assured Kinsolving, dead, quite dead. According to Stoen, he witnessed the miracle as Jones com-

*In 1976, Lester Kinsolving, an Episcopalian priest whose syndicated column appeared in twenty newspapers and who was host of four radio shows, lost his credentials as a journalist after the National Council of Churches complained that he had acted as an agent for the South African government.

manded the woman to return from death to life and she did so. Since this description predated Jean Brown's performance, Stoen could not have been referring to that event. According to Jones, Stoen had not informed him that he had fabricated the story for Kinsolving. Therefore, Jones was astonished to read the hostile series which featured the Stoen invention. Later, Jones said that he thought it "incredible that Stoen did not realize that an assistant district attorney could not be quoted saying that he witnessed the raising of the dead." Jones believed at that time that Stoen "had just been trying to be helpful" but he said, "often when he tried to help his efforts were damaging."

The efforts of Lester Kinsolving, utilizing Tim Stoen, resulted in the initial important attack upon the Temple. Had Stoen's proposal to assault Kinsolving been supported by Jones, then Stoen's efforts, utilizing Kinsolving, might have resulted in the last important attack upon the Temple.

In retrospect, Buford now believes that if an assault upon Kinsolving had led to the arrest of Temple activists, that "Jones would have said to the authorities, 'release those people or all of us in Jonestown will die.' " When asked why Jones might have responded in that fashion, Terri Buford said, "You have to remember that since the time of the Stennis affair, Tim had completely convinced Jim that there was a government effort to destroy him. Jim, I am sure, would have seen the arrest as another part of the government's plan to destroy Peoples Temple. Stoen knew that, since Jim had often said to him and everyone else in the Temple, 'we have the trump card; we are not afraid to die.' "

The "Stennis matter" was the first serious investigation, initiated in part by Stoen, which led to the conclusion that a wide-ranging federal government effort was under way to place the Temple under surveillance. This astonishing conclusion resulted from Stoen's use of facilities made available to him through his work as an assistant district attorney in San Francisco. After the Temple moved from Ukiah to San Francisco, so did Stoen. He also moved from being assistant district attorney in Ukiah to the same position in San Francisco. While in that office, he worked with and was befriended by another assistant, William Hunter, who later was to be appointed United States Attorney for San Francisco. After the massacre, when information about Stoen's activities began to surface, those charged on the local and federal level with the responsibility for examining the evidence were Stoen's friends, former employers, or former co-workers. Hunter had been so impressed with Stoen that he had offered him the position of chief criminal assistant in the United States attorney's office.

According to Stoen, Joseph Freitas, the District Attorney for San Francisco, had offered him the position in charge of investigating terrorist activities in the city. These offers were made after Stoen had publicly attested to the special and divine powers of his leader, Jim Jones.

During a regular service held by the Peoples Temple in San Francisco on Sunday afternoon, November 7, 1976, two white men who appeared to be in their late twenties or early thirties were observed outside the Temple between the church building and the Kentucky Fried Chicken restaurant next door. Most of the members of the Temple were black; the church was located in Fillmore, San Francisco's predominantly black community, and the few white members were well known. The two men appeared to be listening to the guest speaker, whose voice was electronically amplified. A Temple member approached them and asked what they were doing. The two men ran to a car parked nearby on Geary Boulevard and sped away without answering her. She alertly wrote down the license plate registration number, 412 PTK, noted that it had been issued by the state of California and described the vehicle as a two-door, brown Granada. Jones ordered Buford to give the number to Stoen so that he could look into the matter. After she did so, she forgot about the matter.

Two or three days later, Stoen telephoned Buford from his office. He seemed very excited, she reported, and he said, "It looks like a government operation to me." He said that he had a man in his office check out the registration—the automobile had been rented from a Budget Rent-A-Car office in Sacramento. Stoen instructed Buford to "tell Jim right away. I predict that an investigation will show that these men are government." Buford asked for the basis for that conclusion and Stoen responded, "I know how the government operates. The M.O.* for surveillance by government agencies is often to require people doing surveillance activities to rent vehicles in a city other than where the surveillance is to take place." That Stoen's prediction was proved accurate by a subsequent investigation does not resolve, but rather heightens, the mystery. All Stoen said he knew at that time was that two men had rented a car in Sacramento, driven it to San Francisco, and fled when found loitering outside the Temple. There was neither proof of governmental spying nor evidence for such a prediction at that moment. Budget, Hertz, Avis, and National would all be surprised to learn that if two men rent a car in one city and drive to another that a law-enforcement officer may presume that they were on an official mission. As it developed, people from the San Francisco District Attorney's office

***Modus operandi.*

had been used as spies in what appears to have been a federal mission.

When Buford told Jones of Stoen's conclusions, he immediately sent Harriet Tropp, Patty Cartmell, and a driver to Sacramento to determine the identity of the two men. Harriet Tropp presented a most imaginative and complicated story to the clerk at Budget's office there. It revolved around a diamond ring which she had lost on a double date in the back seat of a car. Fortunately, while she had forgotten her escort's name, she had recorded the license plate of the vehicle that he drove. The clerk checked her records and gave Harriet the name and address of Thomas Dawsey of Biloxi, Mississippi. Patty Cartmell, upon returning to San Francisco, called Dawsey's family, pretending to be a local baby-sitter. She tape-recorded the extended telephone discussion. Stoen, Jones, Buford, Tropp, and Cartmell listened to the tapes later that day and gleaned certain facts. Dawsey had achieved the rank of EMC-13; his job required him to move from city to city quite often; his base was Keesler Air Force Base; he was involved in international radio and radar problems; part of his work was to ensure that radar in the United States was not interfered with by radar originating from elsewhere. He was "very high up" and he "got his orders directly from Senator Stennis."

A check into the meaning of EMC-13 revealed that, in this instance, it designated a highly ranked person, possibly a civil service employee assigned to a military unit with advanced training in the use of sophisticated electronic equipment. Jones wondered why two white military men would fly from Mississippi to Sacramento, rent a car there and drive to San Francisco to stand in an alleyway in a black community. "We've got them now," Stoen said.

On November 16, 1976, Jean Brown sent a letter* to Senator John Stennis complaining of the harassment and stating that "we will defend these rights with our lives, if necessary." Brown also sent a letter to Representative Phillip Burton, a San Francisco congressman, asking him to discover what interest the United States Air Force had in the Temple. At the end of January 1977, Burton received a letter† from an official of the United States Air Force stating that Dawsey was permanently assigned to Keesler Air Force Base, was on temporary assignment to Mather Air Force Base in California during the time in question, but had been off duty on Sunday, November 7. Dawsey's duty status record was sent to Burton who, on February 8, 1977, sent it to Jean Brown.

*The letter is published as Appendix G.
†The Burton letters are published as Appendix G.

Other members of Congress expressed concern as well. On November 30, 1976, Representative Patricia Schroeder wrote to Jean Brown, "I am very much concerned about the kind of surveillance and would like to be kept informed of further difficulties you experience in this area."

Representative Paul N. McCloskey, Jr. wrote to Brown on December 9: "I have contacted Congressman Burton's office regarding some of the allegations you raised and they are presently investigating the matter with the Air Force and, if necessary, the CIA. Their response should determine whether any further action, legal or otherwise, should be taken by your organization.

"I would appreciate your keeping me informed of any new developments."

The speaker at the church upon whom the two men were apparently eavesdropping was Unita Blackwell Wright, the black woman mayor of Mayersville, Mississippi. She had recently returned from a well-publicized trip to China and was discussing her observations at the Temple that Sunday. Jones expressed the belief that she had been the target of the surveillance activity. He was concerned about her safety and instructed Temple personnel to locate her and warn her. Stoen disagreed: He insisted that the Temple, a most important force on the Left, was the object of the federal surveillance, not some local black mayor. Had not he been accurate in predicting the result of the investigation before it had barely begun? What more was required to demonstrate his expertise in these matters? Stoen was successful in convincing the leaders that the Temple was under siege. Years later, a State Department Report published in May 1979 emphasized that a contributing cause to the massacre was the fact that Jones believed that the Temple had been under siege.

One day Stoen informed Jones that most of the lines coming into the office were not safe as they were monitored by tape recorders. He gave Jones three numbers at the district attorney's office and the sheriff's office, which he said were not monitored. Soon afterward, Jones decided to file a complaint at the sheriff's office against someone he suspected of wrongdoing. Since he was concerned about the legal implications inherent in that action, he instructed an aide to call Stoen to ascertain the legalities. The aide discussed the matter with Stoen, who assured her that the complaint was justified, proper, and could result in no adverse ramifications for the Temple. The aide briefed a Temple member, and he called in the complaint. When it was discovered that the aide had not given the Temple member one of the discreet numbers, both Stoen and Jones abused her verbally for several hours. She had believed that since the complaint was lawful and proper, it should have been communicated officially to the sheriff's office on a listed number. She was concerned that by using one of the other lines she would inadvertently expose the Temple's knowledge that some of the lines were monitored. However, so overwhelming was Stoen's anger that she merely apologized for the error. She then gave the reasons for her action. Stoen said that her excuse was not acceptable and that he was convinced that she was lying. She was instructed, therefore, not to offer her explanation before the Planning Commission, where she was again verbally attacked by Stoen that evening. Stoen accused the aide of being counterrevolutionary. He said she had sabotaged the organization. Stoen said that it was clear that her actions resulted from "her subconscious hostility to Jim." Stoen pursued a policy of complaining to Jones about his subordinates, with the exception of Jean Brown, whom he regularly praised to Jones.

Apparently, Stoen was so concerned that the sheriff's office had a tape-recorded record of the complaint called in by the Temple member that he arranged for the tape to be altered. According to a witness, he told Phyllis Houston, who was then employed by the sheriff's department in Mendocino County, to "swap the tapes so that the one in question will be erased." Houston duly substituted the tape-recording which bore the complaint for the blank one that was to be used that day. Thus the offending document was erased slowly as it recorded the day's conversations.

The entire episode raises more questions than it answers. If Stoen's advice to Jones had been sound, why would he be disturbed that a record of the complaint had been made? If his advice were flawed, why did he give it with such assurance? In either case, why did he make such a fuss about so minor an incident when he, himself, was suggesting the possible kidnapping of officials, assaults upon a journalist, and ways to poison the Washington, D.C., water supply? His behavior increased the level of fear and suspicion among Temple members, and involved another Temple member in an illegal overt act.

The Congressional Investigative Committee later stated that "Peoples Temple defectors were frequently frozen in fear and severely hampered in their efforts to counteract Jones."* In support of that contention, the committee wrote:

> The problem is illustrated in the following example which points up the desperate lengths to which opponents of People's Temple were driven as well as the degree to which officials in San Francisco appear

**U.S. House of Representatives Report,* p. 22.

> to have been involved. Afraid to contact any public officials for fear that they were tied-in or friendly to Jones, one individual went to the length of writing consumer advocate Ralph Nader because he could not think of anyone else he could trust. The letter to Nader outlined many of the allegations against People's Temple which were later proven true. It also indicated that the letter writer feared for his life. It closed as follows:
>
> If you want to help us, please write in the personal column of the Chronicle to "Angelo" and sign it Ralph and then we will respond and talk to you.
>
> Rather than do that, Nader sent the letter to the District Attorney's Office in San Francisco. By some means, the letter filtered back to People's Temple and the writer soon thereafter received a threatening phone call that said "We know all about your letter to Angelo."

The phrase "by some means" indicated either that the committee did not discover the method by which the Temple had infiltrated the district attorney's office in San Francisco, or that having secured the information, declined to publish it. Since Stoen was an assistant district attorney at that time, and was also the general counsel for the Peoples Temple, I submit that there was a clue, which, if pursued, might have provided the solution to the mystery. The committee questioned Terri Buford at length and learned at the outset that she had functioned as a liaison to Stoen and as his assistant. Yet she was not asked about the incident. Stoen's testimony before the committee is secret and may not be seen.*

According to Terri Buford, Stoen rushed into her room at the Peoples Temple one afternoon and dropped off a letter in a large manila envelope. He said, "I couldn't discuss this on the telephone. This is very important. I caught it in the incoming mail in the office. Tell Jim I want to discuss it with him this evening." Stoen left, apparently to return to the district attorney's office. In the envelope was a letter from Nader to Freitas, and the letter from the defector which Nader had enclosed. Buford told me, "Stoen had brought the original letter from Nader. It was not a photocopy, which led me to believe that probably there was no other record in the D.A.'s office."

That evening, Buford recalls, Stoen and Jones decided that a telephone call should be placed to the defector and that the code word "Angelo" should be used to frighten the person and expose his vulnerability. Stoen,

* *U.S. House of Representatives Report,* pp. 22, 23.

Buford states, cleared the language that was to be employed during the telephone call.

Grace Stoen said of her husband, "Tim used to remind him [Jim Jones] all the time to get rid of the money, and told him where to put it so it wouldn't get the church in trouble."† Stoen later conceded that he was the financial mastermind who established foreign corporations and opened foreign bank accounts for the Temple. "There was $1 million that I had in my name at one time in an account of the Bank of Nova Scotia in San Francisco."‡ That, however, was not the entire story. Stoen went to Panama, and together with a local lawyer whom he retained, established two corporations which he referred to as "off-shore" corporations. They were Briget, S.A., and Asociación Evangelica de las Americas, S.A. For the former, he opened an account with the Swiss Banking Corporation in Panama. For the latter, he established an account with the Union Bank of Switzerland in Panama. Several months later, Stoen and two other Temple members went to Panama. Stoen and one other member carried with them more than $1 million in cash. The third person carried various legal documents, the plan being to segregate the carriers of the money from the papers that could identify the Temple. The cash was placed in the account of Briget, S.A., and Debbie Blakey, Maria Katsaris, and Terri Buford were the signatories on that account. A check for several million dollars was deposited into the account of Asociación Evangelica de las Americas, S.A., during the same time, with the same three women as signatories.

On one occasion, Stoen entered a private room of the Swiss Banking Corporation in Panama City to deposit the contents of several suitcases. He was not a signatory on the account. Hr. Stocker, the bank official, and Sr. Lima, the bank's attorney, met with Stoen. In introducing himself, Stoen presented a card that showed he was an assistant district attorney under District Attorney Joseph Freitas of San Francisco. Stocker and Lima blanched: The suitcases were open on the table before them, each well packed with hundred-dollar bills. After a moment of silence, in which the stunned banker and his equally astonished lawyer looked from the suitcases to the official card in Stoen's hand, one of them asked Stoen to leave the room. Quite clearly, they believed that Stoen was there in his official capacity and that something unpleasant was likely to occur. After a considerable delay, the cash was accepted. Later, when Stoen was called on to explain

†*The Suicide Cult,* p. 79.
‡Ibid., p. 80.

his gaffe to Jones, he said, "I thought that it would add to my credibility and they would be less likely to think it was a laundering operation if they knew my official position."

Stoen told Buford that he had previously smuggled a large sum of cash from the United States to Switzerland. He explained that Swiss banks in Switzerland were reluctant to accept large sums in cash from United States citizens because "the Mafia has a bad reputation." He said that when he and Carolyn Layton had carried the huge sum to Geneva, it was rejected by each of the banks they visited. Carolyn Layton had planned to fly to London to meet Jones. This left Stoen holding the bag, so to speak. Stoen apparently described to Jones and Layton, and later to Buford, his travail at the U.S. Customs desk upon his return. "I looked like Porky Pig, I was so fat with money," he said. He said that he had distracted the customs officer by directing his attention to a tape recorder and inquiring as to whether he had to pay duty on it.

During a previous trip to Panama, Stoen studied the customs practices at the Panama City airport to see if he could smuggle substantial quantities of money into the country. He then reported to Jones that the customs checks were "superficial," and would not constitute a problem.

Stoen later said that he and another Temple member had forgotten the vaccination record or "shot card" during a trip to Panama, but explained, "I paid off the public health officer." He added, "In South America, a little money will buy you anything."

During March 1979, a series of feature stories appeared in the *Los Angeles Times* and the San Francisco *Examiner.* These stories all referred to the arrest of Jim Jones in a Los Angeles theater on December 13, 1973. The newspapers claimed that the case against Jones had been handled in a most extraordinary fashion. In a copyrighted story by Tim Reiterman and Ken Kelley, the San Francisco *Examiner* said "the mysterious dismissal of a lewd conduct case against the Rev. Jim Jones five years ago has raised questions about whether the Peoples Temple successfully pressured the Los Angeles Police Department, the city's attorneys office or the judge."* The *Examiner*, charged that the case against Jones had been dismissed at the request of the city attorney's office for lack of evidence, but that the reasons for the dismissal had not been stated in the records at the time, as the law required. The article pointed out that the judge who sealed the records also took the "highly unusual step of ordering the records of the law enforcement agencies to be destroyed."

*San Francisco *Examiner,* 22 March, 1979.

Since the records were ordered sealed and destroyed in a session which did not take place in the court, and since the files of the city attorney's office on the case are missing, no record reveals whether or not a prosecutor was present when the judge ordered that the records be sealed and destroyed. The arresting police officer, Arthur Kagele, said that he had filed a departmental appeal of the dismissal and that his appeal went to Deputy Chief Daryl Gates, who is now Los Angeles Chief of Police. Assistant City Attorney Ward McConnell said, "The investigation by his office into the matter reveals that there was no statement made in court at the time of dismissal as to why it was dismissed. The law requires that the court's minutes and docket state the reasons for dismissal." The city attorney's office stated that it had not yet determined which prosecutor had evaluated the case.

Jones had been arrested on December 13, 1973, after he allegedly made a homosexual overture to two police vice officers in the balcony of the West Lake Theater, which is located approximately one mile from the building which then served as the Los Angeles Peoples Temple. According to the arresting officer, Jones came out of a stall in the bathroom, masturbating. The officer then summoned his partner, and the two of them handcuffed Jones, arrested him, and took him to the Ramparts Division Station. An examination of the court's records reveals that the Municipal Judge Clarence Stromwall, who had been a police officer, directed the sealing and destruction of all case records, including arrest records, in an order dated February 1, 1974. In addition, he ordered that the police, Federal Bureau of Investigation, and other law enforcement agencies destroy their records. As the 1979 press review of the case progressed, the Chief Assistant City Attorney, George Eskin, indicated some reluctance at criticizing Judge Stromwall's action. He did say, however, that "there should have been representatives of the City Attorney's office and of those law enforcement agencies he's ordered to destroy files. Our Office, the L.A.P.D. and the FBI should have been there and given the opportunity to oppose such a motion."*

The Los Angeles and San Francisco news media embarked upon a campaign which compelled that the court and police records be unsealed. Toward the end of March 1979, the records were made public for the first time since 1973. The records, however, did not supply answers for the key questions in the case: Why was the case dismissed and why were the records ordered sealed and destroyed? The San Francisco *Examiner* asked, "Did pressure from Peoples Temple—or bribery—result in special handling?"

**Los Angeles Times,* 29 March, 1979.

The arresting police officer, Arthur Kagele, said that he had written a memo expressing concern about the seal and destroy order at the time and about the disposition of the case. The police records show no trace of such a memorandum.

During 1979, Kagele complained to the California press that a solid case had been thrown out of court. He also said that he had been involved in a campaign to have the case reinstated since he was afraid that the method of dismissal for the arrest, "no stipulation as to probable cause," would leave him open to a false arrest suit. Kagele revealed that two or three years after the arrest, he approached the Los Angeles Chief of Police, Ed Davis, to complain about the disposition of the case. He was told that nothing could be done because the case had been sealed years before by the judge.

In the light of the publicity surrounding the case four months after Jones' death, Kagele held a press conference during which he said that he had not known who Jones was when he arrested him in 1973, that the suspect had not identified himself as a minister until he was being booked at the station, and that even after the massacre in Guyana, he had no idea that the Rev. Jim Jones he had arrested was the same one who was associated with the Peoples Temple tragedy in Jonestown.

The California news media had several field days throughout the month with the publication of several sensational stories designed to appeal to the readers' prurient interests. The *Examiner* mentioned Tim Stoen in one article, stating that just after the arrest, "Tim Stoen, then a Mendocino County assistant district attorney and a high Temple official, asked police officials and State Justice Department officials to do everything possible to prevent public access to the records to protect Jones' reputation."* The *Los Angeles Times,* in its series on the case did not refer to Stoen in feature articles published on March 2, March 13, March 27, and March 29. Yet the evidence suggests that Stoen was an active participant in the drama.

The newspapers that reopened the question earlier this year devoted a great deal of space to the matter but apparently not a substantial amount of research and even less thought. A casual reader of the stories might be prompted to ask a number of questions that apparently did not occur to the authors. For example, if the case were nothing more than a simple arrest for a minor misdemeanor, why was there an FBI record? Why did a low-ranking member of the vice squad keep the matter alive by personally protesting its disposition to two different Los Angeles chiefs of police? His explanations that he feared a lawsuit and that the dismissal was a mark

*San Francisco *Examiner,* 22 March, 1979.

against his record are difficult to accept at face value. The matter had been settled as far as Jones was concerned. He wanted the case buried, forever far away from public attention. Clearly he could not file a lawsuit without making the matter public. Kagele would have been in jeopardy, only had he succeeded in reinstituting the charge, for Jones then probably would have sued him, claiming that the original determination was res judicata and the resurrection of the charges was personal harassment. Had Kagele reopened the case, Jones would have felt constrained to bring an action to protect his image, and might well have won it; in any event he would have had little to lose from filing a suit, since by then the matter would have been a question of public discussion. Kagele's claim that he wanted his own record cleared is more spurious. Charges made by police officers are dismissed every day. Officers shrug off such regular occurrences—especially low-ranking vice squad cops.

Months before Jones's arrest in the theater, an event occurred that was to make Jones and the Temple infamous in the eyes of the Los Angeles Police Department and well known to every police officer in the Ramparts Division. In view of this event in the history of the Temple and its relations with the local station house, it is difficult to accept officer Kagele's subsequent denial that he knew the person he arrested to be Jones.

During a regular weekend service at the Los Angeles Temple, a woman in the congregation became ill. An ambulance was called by nursing personnel at the Temple. Johnny Brown, whom Jim and Marceline Jones later adopted, and Cleveland Jackson—two black men—assisted the stricken woman to the ambulance in an alley between the Temple and the annex to the Temple. According to witnesses at the scene, a white ambulance attendant handled the woman very roughly, was criticized for his lack of sensitivity, and then said to his partner, while pushing the patient into the ambulance, "Get this nigger bitch in there." Johnny Brown demanded that the woman be allowed to leave the ambulance. He said to the attendant, "We'll take care of her ourselves, and a lot better than you will." The attendants refused to let the woman leave, and Brown grabbed one of them to keep him from driving the ambulance away. The attendant pushed Brown and pulled away. Brown struck the attendant and a fight was under way.

During the fight, the woman left the ambulance and returned to the Temple. The police immediately arrived in force. Several police cars stormed the area with sirens wailing and lights flashing. A dozen policemen charged into the few black churchgoers, who were outside the Temple dressed in their Sunday best. Brown and Jackson were arrested, and when they resisted brutal treatment, they were charged with assaulting a police officer. Marceline Jones gently asked if so much force were required against both men. The white police officer looked at Marceline, a proper, attractive white lady in her forties, and at the two young black men, and arrested her for interfering with an officer in the performance of his duties. Police helicopters arrived above the scene, circling the area and hovering above the Temple. Witnesses saw what appeared to be barrels of several long guns pointed downward toward the group outside the Temple.

The services were shattered by the noise of the helicopters, yet the Temple leadership kept the thousand members of the congregation inside the church to prevent the conflict from becoming more serious. Jones went to the police station to support his wife and the other members of his congregation, and was arrested as he arrived.

While the California newspapers published stories during 1979 alleging that Jones had offered a $5,000 bribe to the Ramparts Police Station after the December 1973 lewd conduct arrest, the leader of the precinct house, Captain Joseph Marchesano, has denied that allegation. He also said that early in 1973, long before the arrest, while the captain visited the Temple, a church member offered a contribution of $250 to a youth fund maintained at the station.

Approximately two weeks before the arrest of Jim Jones in December, Jones returned to the Los Angeles Temple with Lew Jones, his adopted Korean-American son. Both men reported to those then at the Temple that Lew had almost been arrested in the bathroom of a theatre. They said that Lew had visited the rest room and a man whom Jim Jones thought to be a police officer began to "hassle" Lew. After Jim Jones entered the room, the man presumed to be a police officer, perhaps seeing that there were two witnesses present, withdrew from the room.

From the time of the helicopter-assisted assault upon the Temple members and the arrest of Jones in the station house until the arrest of Jones in the bathroom months later, there was an apparent concentration upon Temple personnel by police officers. People were ordered out of their cars when attempting to drive to or from the Temple. Others were stopped and searched when walking to or from the Temple. Many of the members complained bitterly that they were harassed only upon attending Temple services.

Knowing the propensity of police officers at the Ramparts Station, Jones was reluctant to travel without the protection of witnesses. Yet he was caught in a dilemma of his own making. He had proscribed members from attending films. Yet he himself enjoyed motion pictures. He compromised by taking Lew with him two weeks before, as we have seen, no doubt believing that his secret was safe with his son. To Temple members, he excused his attendance when speaking of Lew's close call by explaining that the pressures upon the leader are great and that "people are always pulling at me so I thought that the only place I could go to be alone with my son was to a movie."

Two weeks later *Jesus Christ Superstar* was playing in the neighborhood. This was irresistible for Jones. He reasoned that if he sneaked off and told no one where he was, no advance plan could be established to frame him. He told his aides that he would be gone for a time and left for the theater alone. He told only Tim Stoen of his plan, he later said, in case an emergency developed. After the arrest, but long before Stoen left the Temple, Jones continued to puzzle over how the police knew where he would be.

Jones was the victim of an embarrassing affliction. According to his doctor, Alex J. Finkle, and several close friends in the Temple, Jones suffered from a prostate problem that had resulted in a urinary outlet obstruction. In short, he had great difficulty in urinating. He spoke about his problem at Planning Commission meetings. Those who knew him well —and no one knew him much better than did Tim Stoen—knew that in order to urinate, Jones would jog in place, jump up and down and manipulate his penis with his hand. His physician, a prominent urologist, confirmed that circumstance in a letter for the court* and added that in view of the physical problems that Jones suffered, "I am stunned to learn of the preposterous allegations against Rev. Jones!"

During September 1978, Gene Chaikin told me that he and Tim Stoen had paid a very substantial sum to have the case quashed. I indicated my disapproval prematurely, I fear, for Chaikin then gave me no additional information except allegations which placed his action in the best light. He then said that Jones had been framed. He also told me that with Stoen he had found a lawyer and paid him a great deal of money. "As to what he did with the money," Chaikin said, "I can always say that I don't know." By then, of course, Stoen was an avowed enemy of the Temple and Chaikin had adequate motivation to charge him with improper conduct.

Stoen actively pursued the case, using his contacts and his position as an assistant district attorney to have the records sealed and then destroyed. Stoen pointed out that the Mendocino County District Attorney's office was not officially involved, but he identified himself as an assistant district attorney and a church member in his numerous efforts. To the other leaders

*Letter quoted in *Los Angeles Times*, 27 March, 1979.

of the church, Stoen explained his trips to Sacramento, the state's capital, as part of "the other work"* he was involved in. However, it now seems that at least part of that time was spent by Stoen trying to cover up the facts of the arrest of his leader. Jones was terrified by the charge against him. It seems, in retrospect, that had it been tried in court, Jones would have been acquitted. Yet the methods used to seal and then destroy the records (which, as it turns out, were not destroyed) permitted those who wished to destroy Jones to use the threat of reinstituting the humiliating case at any time.

During the late summer and early fall of 1978, an official effort was under way to reopen the case. A motion had been prepared to unseal the records of the case, and Charles Garry, counsel for the Temple and Jones, was opposing that effort. The timing of the motion was particularly insidious. We see now in retrospect that as the last days of Jonestown were approaching, Jones was being tortured once again by the fear of public exposure. I can attest that this matter was very much on his mind, for he spoke to me of his fears when I met him in September. His voice and hands were trembling as he begged to be spared this one additional humiliation.

By then, Jones strongly suspected that Stoen had a hand in the recurring trouble. In 1973, Stoen had met with Dean Speck, now the director of the law enforcement divisions of the office of the Attorney General of California. He introduced himself as an assistant district attorney from Ukiah and expressed his concern "about the possibility that someone other than law enforcement personnel would penetrate the privacy barriers," Speck now recalls. At that time, Speck was the Assistant Chief of Police in Los Angeles.

Mike Franchetti, now the Chief Assistant to the Attorney General of California, said that Stoen had visited him because "I was an expert in records law; how they were sealed." Franchetti recalls Stoen's saying, "Jones was improperly charged," and that he'd been arrested because in order to urinate it was necessary for Jones to "look like he was masturbating."

Franchetti said that Stoen asked him to have the criminal record pulled and thrown away. Franchetti remembers he told Stoen "we couldn't do that." According to the San Francisco *Examiner,*† in its one story that made reference to Stoen, "another source within the State Attorney-General's office" said Stoen contacted him. "He said to me, 'Here we have a

*"The other work" was a phrase that Stoen and Jones both used to describe "revolutionary activity" they said they were involved in.
†San Francisco *Examiner,* 22 March 1979.

wonderful person and he's made a mistake. And what can be done?' " Later Stoen claimed that "I was simply a character reference." However, it is not within the purview of character witnesses to travel repeatedly to the state capital and to cajole and implore various city and state officials to destroy official records. In this conflict, it is Stoen's record against the statements of several other disinterested persons.

In this conflict, the statements by the state officials support Terri Buford's recollection that Stoen reported back to her in San Francisco with the message, "Tell Jim that I'm back from Sacramento and that everything went O.K. He'll understand." He told her merely, "It was a special mission for Jim."

After the church began moving their headquarters to San Francisco from Ukiah late 1974, Temple members went through boxes of material that had been stored in an otherwise empty room in a building in Ukiah that the Temple was planning to sell. There were approximately half a dozen boxes filled with various kinds of documents. As they sorted through the material, they made several startling discoveries. Among the documents, they came upon two copies of an official Los Angeles record. That afternoon at a meeting of the Planning Commission, they passed the documents to June Crym, who was a legal secretary. Crym read them and quickly passed them to Buford. Crym said, "This is Jim's arrest record. I don't think I'm supposed to see this." Buford then read the document carefully. Stoen had made two copies of the official police record of the Jones arrest for lewd conduct and had squirreled the records away among letters from his family.

Terri passed the copies to Jones. Jones halted the meeting and shouted at her, "Where did you get this shit? Come up here, I want to talk to you!" When he learned where the copies came from, he privately asked Stoen why he had made copies of a record they had worked so hard to seal. Stoen said he thought they might need them some day. He assured Jones that no other copies of the document existed. When Jones demanded to know why Stoen had not asked him if copies should be made and had not even told him that he had made them, Stoen said, "I don't know." He again assured Jones that there were no more copies. Later that day, as they continued to go through the boxes of material, they found six more copies of the arrest record in different places.

At that time, Jones decided not to discuss the matter with Stoen again. He said to Buford, "This is not an accident from neglect or overwork. This is an action. He had to make those copies and hide them away for some reason. I wonder how many more he has, and where."

Several months later, very likely due to another discovery of more frightening significance from the Stoen cardboard file, Stoen fled from the Temple. Jones did almost everything in his power to maintain Stoen's neutrality. He offered him money, he declined to criticize him publicly, and he withheld from the public the statement that Stoen had signed regarding his request to Jones to "sire" his wife's child. In these matters, Jones was acting neither from compassion nor mercy; he was terribly frightened that if he criticized Stoen, or failed to send large sums of money to him, Stoen might release information about the lewd conduct charge. Stoen knew, I believe, that Jones was no longer emotionally able to cope with that charge. In Guyana just before the massacre, according to Charles Krause, Stoen told him that Jones was "a classic paranoid schizophrenic." Not long before that, Stoen had predicted at a meeting in California that Jones was sure to overreact when pressed and frightened. In due course, and at the appropriate moment as the events were building to a tidal wave, the news came to Jones that the information was to reach the press. The motion that had been filed to unseal the record had in fact accomplished that very purpose. It had attached to it the record of the arrest. It was an exact duplicate of the documents that Stoen had so carefully secreted. In the weeks before his death, Jones said, "Well, now I don't have to guess. I know now that Stoen kept at least one more copy."

Jones was often absent from the Temple in San Francisco, at first without explanation. He would leave alone in an automobile stating that he was off on "a mission." As his mysterious sorties became more frequent, he evidently felt constrained to confide in his supporters, or at least create the impression that he had. He told Mike Prokes, Terri Buford, and some members of his security team that he was secretly engaged in the "other work." He said that the only Temple member who participated with him, who they would recognize, was Tim Stoen. Jones said that the "other work" entailed dangerous activity carried out by the revolutionary cadre of the Temple. Sixteen women, Stoen, and Jones were a trained urban guerrilla unit. They had, Jones said, blown up an ammunition train at Roseville, California, to protest the war in Vietnam. Later, Harriet Tropp, Gene Chaikin, and Johnny Jones told me the same story. Jones said that one of the sixteen, an Asian, was very likely a spy. In retrospect, Terri Buford believes that there was no "other work;" that Jones and Stoen had developed the story to explain repeated absences, including Stoen's frequent trips to Sacramento to cover up Jones's arrest record, and pleasure trips that Stoen and Jones took together.

Stoen told Buford that in the "other work," Jones was fantastic and displayed a remarkable ability to handle and work with those in the group. One day, as Terri looked back upon that period, she marvelled over the attention to detail demonstrated by Stoen and Jones, and in regard to the apocryphal group and its nonexistent suspected traitor, she observed, "even in his fantasies, Jones was a racist." The commitment that Jones and Stoen said they had demonstrated by endangering their lives as secret urban guerrillas placed a very substantial burden upon those whom they cajoled to undertake dangerous and illegal work. If Stoen, a lawyer, and Jones, a minister, had offered their lives to the movement, how could Tropp, Chaikin, Bradshaw, Buford, and the others object to longer hours, dangerous missions, and hard and tedious work? If the "other work" was as Stoen and Jones described it, which seems unlikely, then they should be judged for having undertaken such adventurous and counterproductive activities. If it was merely a deception for relatively mild misconduct, it nevertheless became a tool with which to manipulate the others through feelings of guilt, and was calculated to move the organization in a dangerous direction. How could a Temple member, knowing what Stoen and Jones had risked for the movement, decline to make a modest contribution when asked to smuggle a weapon into Guyana so that the project might be protected? Weapons Stoen collected and the atmosphere he helped to create came together one sad day in Jonestown.

As a leader of Peoples Temple and as its counsel, Stoen was in the position of promulgating policy, carrying it out, and then defending it. He served a legislative, executive, and legal function for the Temple. Often the interests of the Temple came in conflict with the interests of the other people who lived in Mendocino County. On some of those occasions the local district attorney's office was asked to represent the public interest in actions against the Temple. Stoen was then caught in a classic conflict of interest. An examination of the record reveals the method he chose for resolving that conflict.

Dennis Denny became the director of the Mendocino County Social Services Department in 1969. The Peoples Temple had moved from Indiana to Mendocino County four years earlier. Many of the members of the Temple had moved from San Francisco and the Bay area to Redwood Valley to join the Temple and to live in one of its crowded communes. Jones and Stoen arranged for many of the members to apply for welfare benefits. Denny felt that the local resources were being unduly strained. In a short period of time, Denny and Jones were locked in conflict.

In matters which involved questions of welfare-cheating and related questions, the county district attorney's office served as the attorney for the county social services department. Too often, Denny complained, when he sought help from that office, Tim Stoen chose to represent his other client, Jim Jones and the Temple.

Denny recalled a serious problem that arose in May 1975. An elderly man had been improperly transferred from a local nursing home to a home in Los Angeles by Temple personnel. Actually it appears that he was taken without the permission of the director of the local home and over the strenuous objections of the man himself. The act was tantamount to kidnapping. The woman who directed the local home sought assistance from the district attorney's office. She was shown into the office of Tim Stoen, she told me, and knew that she could get no help. She fled from there without asking a question or filing a complaint.

Later Stoen called Jones triumphantly to describe the flight of the woman from his office. Denny called Jones about the matter. Later, Denny said, "I immediately got in contact with Jim and told him that we wanted that person back." Jones replied, "I don't know anything about those things. You'll have to deal with Tim Stoen."*

Denny operated in his continuing conflict with Jones from a distinct disadvantage. Eight of his employees worked for the Temple and regularly reported to Jones and Stoen about what they learned on the job. According to the Ukiah *Daily Journal,* † one of the eight was Grace Stoen, Tim Stoen's wife. Denny later revealed that one of the eight—he would not name her—was a double agent reporting back to him about the Temple's plans.

Denny had learned, perhaps through his still secret agent, that two truckloads of federal surplus food missing from a San Francisco warehouse may have been stolen by the Temple. With a social service investigator, he visited the Temple property in Redwood Valley on March 5, 1971.

Denny recalled the event later. "One of the things that was terribly disturbing to me that day was that myself and the investigator were standing there talking to the Reverend Jones. While we were talking, who should come up but the assistant district attorney." At that point Denny asked Stoen, "Whose counsel are you today, Tim?"

Stoen replied, Denny said, that he was the attorney for Jones and the Temple in that matter. As Denny put it, "and at that point in time, to my displeasure and disappointment, Mr. Stoen reflected the fact that he was Peoples Temple's counselor. That, needless to say, brought about strained

*Ukiah *Daily Journal,* 6 March, 1979.
†Ibid.

relationships between the department and the district attorney's office, and especially Mr. Stoen."

Denny was asked by Eric Krueger, a reporter for the Ukiah *Daily Journal* during March 1979, if Stoen "impeded the investigation of foodstuffs." He answered, "In my judgment he did." When Krueger asked Denny to offer other specific examples where Stoen placed his "allegiance to Jones before his duty to the county," Denny said that he had to "hesitate because those questions are being asked by a grand jury investigation. Of course there are answers to those things, and they will be answered in the proper arena."*

Denny, however, said, "Tim had a severe, tremendous conflict of interest." When the reporter sought to secure Stoen's response, he was referred to his lawyer, Patrick (Butch) Hallinan. Hallinan said that Stoen has "no comment" on any question related to the Temple. Hallinan said "I'm advising him not to talk." He said that Stoen's case is "messy and bizarre." He added that to answer questions about "Timmy" and the Temple "you have to literally put yourself in an Alice-in-Wonderland world." He complained that everybody was "looking for a scapegoat," so they look at "Timmy."†

Stoen's actions resulted regularly in creating a series of conflicts of interest. His passive presence in the congregation was also valuable to Jones. At church services attended by hundreds of members, Jones tangentially addressed himself to the widespread but silent discontent with the harsh methods of discipline used by the Temple. At services in Los Angeles, San Francisco, and Redwood Valley, Jones said, "We are a family and we handle our own problems here. We have people in the district attorney's office." On occasion, Stoen would raise his hand and wave it at this point in the oration. Jones, after having paused for a moment, would continue, "Yes, we have people in the district attorney's office, the sheriff's office, and the police department. So if any of you have a mind to take your complaints elsewhere, we'll find out about it. And you will be severely dealt with." Those Temple activists in law enforcement willingly allowed themselves to be used to hold other members hostage in the Temple.

Evidence suggests that Stoen used his position as a prosecutor and counsel for the Temple to arrange for a couple, considered to be enemies of the Temple, to be required to leave town. In this scene, reminiscent of the abuses of one-man rule in old Western towns, Stoen told the couple that

*Ibid.
†Ukiah *Daily Journal*, 6 March, 1979.

they should be packed, ready to go, and on the way out of town. The couple, Marvin and Jackie Swinney, had charged that they had been swindled out of their property. Marvin Swinney had been chief of security for the Temple. The couple said that in June 1973, they gave an abstract of the deed to their property to a leader of the Temple because they were pressured to do so. "We didn't think there was any danger of turning it over because we hadn't signed anything." The couple said they left the Temple two years later and then discovered, upon visiting the Mendocino County Recorder's Office, that their signatures were on a grant deed recorded on September 22, 1975. The document revealed that Stoen had notarized the signatures in June 1973. They have since sworn that they never signed the document which Stoen swore that they had signed in his presence.

After leaving and discovering that the church no longer owned their home and the nine-tenths of an acre on which it stands, the Swinneys made efforts to regain their property. They felt vulnerable because their son was in Jonestown. They said that their efforts were met by responses which they considered to be threats.

During 1975, Marvin Swinney called Timothy Stoen in a first effort to resolve the matter. Stoen agreed to pay off the Swinneys if they agreed to release the property to the Temple and agreed to leave town at once. According to Mendocino County records, the property was sold for $30,000 two years later. Stoen offered Swinney $2,000 for the property. Eventually Stoen agreed to pay to them $10,000 in cash and to send $3,000 later. The Swinneys say that they never received any sum other than the $10,000, although others state that additional payments had been mailed to them. Marvin Swinney, in looking back upon the discussions with Stoen, said, "At that time we didn't care if it was a bribe or not. We just wanted to get out what we could and get our son back." Swinney tape-recorded the first telephone conversation with Stoen. The tape discloses that Swinney asked an operator in the prosecutor's office for Stoen. Stoen, who had previously notarized the deed asserting that the transfer to the Temple was a gift by the Swinneys, then began to negotiate with Marvin Swinney for a new document stating that the Temple had purchased the property. Swinney said that he had given everything he had owned to the Temple and that if he were to move far away from the area, as he had been ordered to do, he would need some cash.

Stoen agreed that the cash would be delivered to Swinney on his way out of town. On the tape, Stoen says, "It's my understanding that you were told that you would have it on your way out, which would be, you know, when you're packed and ready to go." Stoen continued, "Therefore, I can't make a promise to pay you anything until you're in that situation."

Stoen added that Jones "just wanted to make sure you had enough to start with." Stoen then told Swinney that Jones had never been so generous with other members of the church. He said, "I know that Father's only doing that out of love for you."

A number of other former Temple members have made similar complaints. Elmer Mertle, for example, said that when he signed documents giving his home away, he believed that the property was being given to the Temple. However, documents on file at the recorder's office disclose that the property was transferred to a business partnership operated by Temple leaders, including Stoen.

Grace Stoen said publicly after she left the Temple that her husband had notarized some questionable property gifts to the church. In 1977 she said that a piece of property she had owned jointly with her husband was given to the Temple. The deed to the property indicated that Grace had signed it before a Temple notary in Mendocino County on June 20, 1976. At that time, Grace said, she and several hundred other members of the Temple were in New York City.

During that year, various former members of the Temple said that they had not previously complained about misconduct because they had been warned not to complain to the authorities and told that Stoen would, in any event, quash all investigations. In all, more than thirty pieces of property in San Francisco County and Mendocino County, worth approximately one and one half million dollars, formerly belonging to Temple members, ended up as Temple property. Many of the deeds transferring the property to the Temple were notarized by Stoen.

A few months before Tim Stoen left the Temple, another Temple member, Gene Chaikin, an intelligent and astute lawyer, had begun to wonder if Tim Stoen was a government agent. Chaikin prepared a two-page memorandum for Jones in which he raised a number of questions that inclined him to question Stoen's intentions.

Chaikin addressed himself to Stoen's role as the Temple's legal advisor. He pointed out that Stoen had advanced a number of suggestions for illegal conduct and that those high-risk programs were capable of but minimal yield. Chaikin noted that when others proposed adventurous and counterproductive ideas, Stoen was quick to support the plan. Chaikin reasoned that the responsibility of the lawyer for the Temple was to caution the group about the problems that might befall the organization if a high-risk scheme should fail. This, Chaikin said, Stoen did not do. "It is not the lawyer's job to advocate that his client commit crimes," Chaikin said, "Rather it is his obligation to discuss with him the possible adverse effect of such conduct."

Chaikin noted that Stoen acted with alacrity when he felt the need to advise others to commit crimes, but that he was most reluctant to become personally involved in carrying out the proposals himself. One exception, of course, was Stoen's willingness to carry cash out of the country. Chaikin always opposed that idea. His position was that there was no need to smuggle money out of the United States and that the chances of being caught were unacceptably high.

After a meeting in which the smuggling of currency was discussed—Chaikin, as always, voting against the proposal—Stoen told Jones that Chaikin was still "caught up in the system" and that he was demonstrating "reluctance to take risks for the cause."

Ostensibly to reduce the risk to the Temple, Stoen had told Terri Buford that if, while being questioned by customs, it became clear to her that she was a suspect, she should commit suicide. Stoen, who regularly said that he supported the idea of mass suicide as the final solution, as an alternative to direct confrontation, had audaciously taken that notion and sought to apply it to an individual as well.

On the last overseas trip that Terri Buford made before Stoen left the Temple, she ran into a serious confrontation with customs. At Stoen's direction, she traveled from San Francisco to Panama, then to London, to Switzerland, back to Panama, and then to Los Angeles. Stoen had advised Buford to carry a substantial sum, which he knew to be in violation of the law. Just before leaving, Buford, who did not wish to smuggle money across national borders, discussed the proposed trip with Jones. He advised her not to carry any cash out of the United States or into it. He reasoned that since she was traveling alone, she would be too vulnerable and might not be able to notify anyone in case of an arrest. Stoen did not know that the plan had been altered.

Upon her arrival in Los Angeles, the customs authorities were evidently waiting for her. She was interrogated at length, then sent to another room and subjected to a thorough search conducted by two matrons. The law provides that such a search may be justified only in the event that there is probable cause that the person to be searched is violating the law. In almost every instance, proof of probable cause is provided by an informant.

In Chaikin's analysis of this event, he pointed out that Stoen had been eager to travel on each of the other overseas trips but refused to accompany Buford on this occasion.

Chaikin also observed that Stoen had given away his real feelings in other ways that were meaningful when seen as part of a pattern. He said that Stoen was reluctant to assist Temple members with legal problems; that he lost their papers, deeds, checks, and claims. He said that poor black women and men, the very people Stoen pretended to care about, were badly abused by his failure to follow through on his undertakings on their behalf. These members, Chaikin concluded, would have been better served by seeing outside counsel even though they would have been required to pay a fee. Chaikin, who was thoroughly responsible in the matters he accepted, ended up trying to handle the matters that Stoen had accepted and neglected.

Chaikin contrasted Stoen's attitude toward the real legal needs of the members of the Temple with his aggressive posture when as a prosecutor he opposed trade unions, blacks, and progressive organizations with unflagging zeal.

On March 10, 1961, Rotary International awarded a Foundation Fellowship for International Understanding to Timothy Stoen, according to a six-page letter to Stoen signed by George R. Means, the general secretary for the organization. The fellowship stated that Stoen was to study at the University of Birmingham in England. A nine-page document attached to the letter listed the recipients of the Rotary awards for the 1961–1962 year. That compilation disclosed that Stoen was the only recipient designated to attend the University of Birmingham. A newspaper account of the event revealed that Stoen had "spent a semester at American University in Washington, D.C., on the Washington Semester program."* These documents, the Rotary letter and compilation, and the newspaper clippings were discovered by Terri Buford as she examined boxes of data shipped to Georgetown from the Temple in San Francisco. This material was with the other documents which had been found abandoned in the Temple-owned building in Ukiah. In Georgetown, during the late spring of 1977, Buford found the opportunity to look through all the papers for the first time. Together with the letter, its attachments, and newspaper clippings was another clipping describing Stoen's arrest in East Germany and many handwritten notes by Stoen describing that event.

The article stated that Stoen had spoken before a Rotary Club upon his return to the United States. There is no explanation in the article as to why Stoen, an anticommunist student scheduled to study in England, was in East Berlin, except for his statement, "I thought I should go to East Berlin

**Arapahoe Herald,* [Littleton, Colorado] 14 March, 1961 (now the *Arapahoe Independent*).

and see what it's like behind the Iron Curtain." He noticed, he said, "blank expressions on the faces of everyone" in East Berlin. "You could tell they were just waiting for the day that they might have some freedom," Stoen observed.

Stoen told the members of the Rotary Club that he was arrested when he took a picture of "a sign being erected near the newly-built wall." Stoen and his associate, whom he took pains to describe to the press as his "newfound friend" were seized by police officers. Stoen said that he was imprisoned for fifteen hours and then finally released.

In his private notes, however, Stoen did not refer to a "newfound friend" but to his "source." Throughout the notes he referred to the information that he had received from his source about the inner workings of the Communist party in East Germany. Stoen wrote that even in his private notes he could not reveal his source, for if the notes ever fell into the wrong hands, the life of his source would be placed in jeopardy. Stoen also wrote that his source escorted him about East Berlin and was with him when the pictures were taken in an area known by the source to be a restricted area, clearly off limits to photographers.

Buford later flew to the airstrip at Port Kaituma to share the evidence with Jones. Buford said Jones concluded that Stoen was likely an agent working with a government police or spy organization. Jones said, "Why hasn't Tim said anything about this all this time? He must be still with them." Jones focused upon a portion of Stoen's handwritten notes in which he had committed himself to the destruction of communism wherever he found it and at whatever cost. Jones said, "He joined us, knowing we were communists, and he wanted us to be much more militant. Now I understand all his crazy ideas. What a fool I have been, what a fool."

Jones, feeling very vulnerable, tried to develop a plan to counter the Stoen effort. Jones contemplated having Stoen killed, but was dissuaded from the idea, since the community might be destroyed in response, and in any event a new agent would very likely be sent to take Stoen's place if another one were not already in place.

Jones also considered passing false information to Stoen. Then he sighed and said, "But what is there to lie about now? We've given up the healing services. We're just running a farm and medical program and he knows all about that."

Jones finally decided to meet with Stoen to try to convince him that it would be cruel to take any action to harm the people of Jonestown. For the better part of a week, Jones talked to Stoen. They spoke from eight to fifteen hours a day. Together they took long walks, they sat side by side outdoors.

They continued their discussions indoors when it rained or when the sun seemed oppressively hot.

Later, Jones said, "I poured my heart out to the man. He said that he would never hurt Jonestown and that he would never let Grace take my son John John from me."

Stoen, confronted with his own handwritten notes, according to Jones, was constrained to admit that he had been arrested in East Germany. He told Jones that he had forgotten to mention it.

After Terri Buford testified before the investigating committee for the House of Representatives regarding Stoen's various overseas trips for Peoples Temple and his earlier trip to East Germany, Rep. Clement J. Zablocki, the chairman of the Committee on Foreign Affairs of the House of Representatives, wrote to the State Department asking for information from the record about those trips. Zablocki said that he regarded such information as important to the Committee inquiry.* The State Department responded.†

> Apart from his most recent passport application, which was filed in February 1977 and which stated the purpose of this travel was to visit Guyana, the Department has no other record of planned foreign travel by Mr. Stoen. Previous passport applications have been retired and are not readily available. Our former Consul in Guyana recalls that People's Temple members told him that Mr. Stoen had visited the German Democratic Republic sometime between 1973–75. They gave the Consul some poorly reproduced handwritten notes that were illegible and allegedly made by Mr. Stoen during this purported visit. Mr. Stoen did not discuss any previous travel when he met with the Consul in January 1978.

At the first available opportunity after Jones confronted Stoen about his assignment in East Germany, Stoen went to ground. He just disappeared from Georgetown without having uttered a word of his plans to his colleagues with whom he had shared so many adventures and so many secrets for many years. Soon a telegram arrived from Trinidad to a Temple leader in Georgetown. It had ostensibly been sent by Stoen and asserted that he had gone to Trinidad to check out a law school there. He would return, the telegram said, in ten days.

Stoen had gone to London. He had planned never to return to Jonestown.

*Letter from Zablocki to Douglas J. Bennet, Assistant Secretary, Congressional Relations, U.S. Department of State, 13 March, 1979.

†Letter from Bennet to Zablocki, 28 March, 1979.

From London, Stoen contacted his old friend, William Hunter, with whom he had worked in the San Francisco District Attorney's office. President Carter had just appointed Hunter United States Attorney for San Francisco, the most important federal law enforcement position in the city. Stoen had written a letter of recommendation on Hunter's behalf, vouching for his good character. Stoen had also been in contact with Hunter before embarking upon his last trip to Jonestown. He had secretly stored a suitcase at Hunter's home. The luggage contained clothing appropriate for the climate and fashion of London.

For approximately two weeks the leaders of the Temple wondered where Stoen had gone. They did not know of his continuing relationship with Hunter and they did not suspect that Stoen had developed an exit plan even before his last journey to Guyana. Chaikin had raised questions about Stoen, but it was presumed that Stoen had no knowledge of his suspicions. After Stoen disappeared, and it was quickly determined that he was not in Trinidad, Chaikin wondered if there might be another informant in the group who had notified Stoen of the developing questions. Jones rejected that possibility, stating that so few people knew about the Chaikin memorandum that Stoen could not have been informed.

Both Jean Brown, who had worked closely with Stoen on occasion, and Debbie Blakey, who later entered into a secret relationship with Richard McCoy of the United States Embassy in Georgetown, had access to the information contained in the Chaikin memorandum. She was in control of the massive files of the Peoples Temple, including the documents which implicated Stoen in serious misconduct. Although Stoen waged a media war upon the deceased Jones and some Temple survivors, he did not criticize Jean Brown. She reciprocated; she refused to release any documents that raised questions about his actions.

Stoen's flight from Georgetown had taken him to London. From there, he sent a message to Hunter asking him to send his suitcase to him. Hunter apparently had not been briefed about the reasons for Stoen's leaving, and the message had been so incomplete that Hunter did not know upon which flight the baggage was expected.

Hunter communicated with Tim's friends at the Temple in San Francisco to determine if they knew when Stoen expected the suitcase to arrive. Maria Katsaris was the first Temple loyalist to learn that Stoen was in London, had secreted his clothing with Hunter, had planned his quick and deceptive leave-taking for some time, and expected to pick up his clothing in London in the near future. She said that she would be glad to undertake to get Stoen's bag to him.

Jones sent Sandy Bradshaw, known to Stoen to be the head of the Temple's Assassination Squad, and Mike Prokes to London instead of the suitcase. Bradshaw had a license to carry weapons in California and, as Stoen well knew, she possessed them. When Stoen arrived at the baggage claim area at Heathrow Airport in London, he was greeted by Bradshaw and Prokes. Mike Prokes said, "Stoen saw us and he turned white. The blood had drained from his face. He looked at Sandy and gave up. He said 'All right. Get it over with.' There was no doubt in his mind; he expected Sandy to kill him. I said to him, 'Jim wants to talk with you.' He had an attaché case with him."

Stoen agreed to return to Jonestown to meet with Jim Jones. He was met by Temple personnel at the Timehri airport, which serves Georgetown. He was still carrying his briefcase. He was taken to the Temple house in Georgetown, where he met Jones. The next day Jones, Carolyn Layton, and Stoen flew to the airstrip at Port Kaituma and from there they were driven by truck to Jonestown. Jones and Stoen engaged in marathon talking sessions. Stoen said that he would die before he would let Grace take John John from Jim. He pledged that he would never do anything to harm the Temple. Jones did not trust Stoen, but he pretended to believe him. He believed by then that Stoen was a government agent and that he carried the ability to destroy Jonestown and the Temple. But Jones was not ready to kill; he was rational and he was deeply worried.

Meanwhile, in Georgetown, Stoen's attaché case was discovered hidden under a bed. The lock was carefully picked and the attaché case opened. Two Temple members examined the papers that it contained. One member said, "Tim had a detailed diary in which he had noted everything that he was to do or did. He always wrote everything down, even the most incriminating details. I was not surprised to see the detailed statements. In the past, I had read his notes to himself about the steps to smuggle money out of the country. He was so obsessive that he would write 'put money in envelopes, tape envelopes, place legal documents on top of envelopes.' "

As they examined the documents in Stoen's attaché case in Georgetown, their despair grew. Stoen had written, possibly after meeting Bradshaw and Prokes at Heathrow Airport and before leaving London on the flight to Georgetown, "Pass letter to customs' official upon exit." What was in the letter? With whom was Stoen establishing contact through British customs?

Other items in the diary disclosed that Stoen had left keys to safety deposit boxes with a contact in France. Various London banks were noted with their addresses, telephone numbers, and in some instances, the name of a contact. No Temple accounts had ever been established at those London banks. Another note reminded Stoen to "call Billy H."*

Stoen had evidently led three lives. Jones had known about two of them. Stoen had been employed as a prosecutor in Ukiah and later in San Francisco. He had served as a leader of the Peoples Temple at the same time. His diary revealed a glimpse of possibly yet another life.

They made copies of the material in Stoen's diary, returned the locked attaché case to its hiding place, and flew to Port Kaituma to brief Jones in Jonestown.

Jones read the material and finally, after slowly digesting it and discussing its implications said, "I'd bet on Kimo's† life that man is working for the government."

Stoen, Jones, Carolyn Layton, and Terri Buford boarded the *Cudjoe,* a fishing trawler owned by the Temple. The trawler took them downriver to the ocean and then toward Georgetown. Stoen spent most of his time sleeping or throwing up, although for the *Cudjoe* the trip was quite pacific.

Several weeks after Stoen left the Temple permanently, a telephone call was placed to the San Francisco office of the church. Terri Buford answered the telephone with her standard, "May I help you?" A man's voice replied that he wished to talk to either Terri Buford or Carolyn Layton. When Terri asked the caller to identify himself, he refused to do so, stating that he had an important message to deliver from Tim Stoen and that he would have to remain anonymous. Terri asked the caller to wait a moment. Fearing that the message might be a threat or constitute evidences of criminal conduct, she secured a cassette tape recorder, attached the device to the telephone, and identified herself. The anonymous caller said that Tim Stoen knew there was going to be trouble and that he was working desperately to avoid it. He said that Stoen would contact the Temple in two weeks. When Buford again asked the caller who he was, he said that he was not free to reveal his identity and that he was not authorized to say anymore. Terri Buford told Charles Garry about the call; he told her to report to his office at once with the tape. At Garry's office he listened to the recording and asked Terri

*Stoen and most others who knew William Hunter called him "Billy." When Hunter became United States attorney he offered Stoen the position of Chief Assistant U.S. Attorney. After the massacre, the United States government placed Hunter in charge of the investigation of the Peoples Temple. Hunter told me that Stoen was not a target of his investigation. When I asked Hunter if he had considered excusing himself since Stoen was his friend, he denied any association with Stoen except for having been in the same office with him when they were both assistant district attorneys in San Francisco. Later, when disclosures revealed that Hunter had offered a position to Stoen in his office, Hunter did step down. He turned the investigation over to Robert Dordero, an employee of his.

†Kimo was Jim's youngest son, the son of Carolyn Layton Prokes.

to type a transcript from it at once. She did so and then made a photocopy of it, which she took back to the Temple, leaving the tape recording and the original transcript with Garry. Jean Brown was ultimately given the Temple's copy of the transcript.

During August 1977, Garry told Buford that Patrick Hallinan had called to inform him that he was representing Tim Stoen. Garry said, "Hallinan says that Stoen is in need of money; he's living on credit now." Some local newspaper articles were appearing, primarily in Ukiah, about Stoen's irregular conduct as a notary public in reference to deeds which had transferred property to the Temple. Stoen was apparently thinking of a trip abroad. However, through his attorney, he was letting the Temple know that he required funds. Garry told Buford that Hallinan had said that Stoen needed $5,000 from the Temple. Garry advised Buford, "If you don't want any trouble from Stoen I think you better give him the money. Also give it to him in cash. Don't do it by check."

When Buford spoke to Jones by radio, he was not sanguine about the suggestion that Stoen be paid off. Jones had previously authorized Debbie Blakey to pay a substantial sum to Stoen, but she never was able to find him to offer the cash to him.* Upon consideration, however, Jones saw the policy as self-defeating. He said, "Once you start with whitemail, it never stops. We give him $5,000 today and what is to stop him from asking for more the next day. When it was our idea to pay him, even then it was dangerous. But it's worse now that he's demanding it."

Jones asked Buford to ask Garry if he agreed that the payment of $5,000 might not be just an initial payoff to be followed by additional demands. He told her to ask Garry if he agreed that responding to threats, even though they may have been unspoken, was a show of weakness which might make the Temple even more vulnerable. Jones's message to Garry was, "Aren't we admitting to Hallinan that we have something to hide by paying Stoen?"

Buford reported the message to Garry at the latter's office. Garry was seated behind his desk. Impatiently, he interrupted Buford, shouting, "Are you all crazy? You do have something to hide. You have a lot to hide." Then pounding his desk with his fist, he shouted, "Goddamn, pay him the money. Pay him the money or get yourself another lawyer."

Garry arranged with Hallinan for Terri Buford to deliver to Hallinan $5,000 in cash the next morning. Jones had accepted Garry's advice, partially because of the explicit threat that Garry would withdraw

*In *Suicide Cult,* the allegation is made, "Stoen could not be bribed, however." The allegation no doubt resulted from rushing the book into print approximately one week after the massacre.

as counsel at that sensitive time if his recommendation were not heeded.

Terri arrived at Hallinan's office at about nine-thirty in the morning. A secretary told her that Hallinan was not in and was not immediately expected. Buford said that she would wait. She held the oversize manila mailing envelope, bulging with the cash. The secretary asked her if she could accept a message or anything else on behalf of Mr. Hallinan. Buford declined, saying only that she would wait for his arrival. After a short while, Hallinan called his office, and upon learning that Terri Buford was still there, asked to talk with her. Hallinan told Buford that he would, after all, not be at his office for quite some time. He inquired, "Did you bring the stuff?" When she responded affirmatively, he said, "you can leave it with my secretary. You can trust her." Buford reluctantly left the package.

Several weeks later, Hallinan began to speak to Marceline Jones at the Temple in San Francisco. He told her that Stoen wanted his file cabinet* and his suitcase. Marceline reminded Hallinan that Stoen had sufficient funds to purchase whatever he needed. Hallinan said that Stoen had spent all the funds, explaining that "travel is expensive." Marceline said that Stoen could pick up his belongings at the Temple. As it turns out that would not have been easily accomplished; in the weeks after Stoen had left the Temple and before any word had been received from him or from his lawyer, the clothing in the suitcase had been distributed by Mike Prokes to various church members.

Marceline Jones, Terri Buford, and the others in the Temple later remarked that in the telephone calls to Garry, Buford, and Marceline Jones, and in the meeting with Buford, Hallinan had never asked about John Victor Stoen.

Long after the massacre, I met with Steven Katsaris to share information in an effort to determine the cause of the tragedy. Since Katsaris and Stoen had been active together in the Concerned Relatives organization and had together visited Congressman Ryan, I asked him to explain Stoen's motivation. Katsaris, of course, had been committed to securing the release of his daughter. One could ascribe similar motivation to Stoen only if it appeared that John John was his son and that he cared for him. Katsaris said, "I think it is possible that he could have been Jim Jones's child, but it is possible that he was Tim's." He said that he had better insight about Grace Stoen. "You might cloud Tim's motive with either having some intelligence connections or something like that, but in my mind, Grace's motives were never

*Stoen had previously authorized the San Francisco District Attorney's office to release his personal file cabinet to the Temple. An examination of that cabinet revealed that Stoen had kept a file of the Diversions operations.

clouded. Grace loved that child. She had spoken to me frequently and at length about how she had made a mistake and not walked off with the child when at one time my daughter, Maria, gave her a signal. I didn't believe that Grace felt that the child would be killed when the congressman went to Jonestown."

Katsaris told me that in considering the possibility that "Tim Stoen masterminded this, I'm going to make some allowance in my own thinking for my resistance to having Tim Stoen use and manipulate me because, at many points along the line, I felt that I had to kick Tim Stoen in the ass to move." He added, "I'm all for exploring the question of who Tim was initiating these things for." Katsaris said that in his numerous meetings with federal agents in the period preceding the massacre, "Everybody I ever talked to on the agent level believed me and was concerned that there was something wrong." He said that FBI agents and others were "as frustrated as I was." He said that since no action was taken, "I don't know if that equates to a conspiracy. I'd like to find out." Katsaris at first rejected the idea that Stoen was something other than he held himself out to be. Katsaris observed that "Stoen even defended Jones after he [Stoen] got out [of the Temple]." He said that Stoen had told him, after leaving the Temple, "Steve, when I got out, my only concern was to trade my silence for my son; to get my son back. I thought by just being quiet and not presenting a threat to Jim, he would give me back my son."

Stoen's explanation rested upon the foundation that Stoen was pressing for the return of John Victor Stoen. There's no evidence to support that assertion. The explanation, which caused Katsaris to accept his sincerity, would have been less effective if Katsaris knew that Stoen had not sought to secure the release of the child—had not even inquired about him immediately upon leaving the Temple—but focused his efforts upon securing cash, a suitcase, and an old file cabinet instead. Had Katsaris known the circumstances of Stoen's departure from the Temple, he might have adopted a more critical posture toward Stoen.

The $5,000 payment constitutes the last effort by the Temple to buy Stoen's silence. In a relatively short time, Stoen underwent still another metamorphosis. He insisted that he was the father of the child and apparently spent enormous sums on legal actions to confront Jones on that question. A leading lawyer in Georgetown, for example, told me that Stoen had paid another Georgetown lawyer $25,000 in effort to secure a court decree ordering Jones and his aides to relinquish the child. He became counsel for various former Temple members and their relatives and instituted lawsuit after lawsuit against Jones and the Peoples Temple, demanding millions of dollars in damages in each action. In interviews with

Grace Stoen, she insisted that she not be asked who fathered her child. When asked that question by one newspaper reporter, she declined to answer.

I am confident that Steven Katsaris was accurate in concluding that Grace Stoen would not have pressed for a confrontation with Jones if she believed it likely that her child might die as a result. The case of Timothy Stoen presents a somewhat different set of circumstances. Stoen evidently expected to die at the hand of Sandy Bradshaw in London. He, better than anyone else, knew of his connections. He knew, and said that he knew, that Jones was capable of murdering the residents of Jonestown if confronted. He had purposefully or inadvertently let Jones know that if one resident of Jonestown betrayed Jones by leaving with Congressman Ryan, Jonestown would be destroyed. He labored industriously to arrange for the congressional visit to Jonestown and then briefed the representatives of the news media, especially the uninformed *Washington Post* reporter, Charles Krause, so that embarrassing questions might be asked of Jones. Earlier he had helped to collect weapons, some of which were smuggled into Jonestown. He smuggled funds into the United States, some of which may have been used to purchase additional weapons and ammunition later shipped to Jonestown. He had suggested that violence be used against enemies of the Temple. He favored threats to enemies. He drafted the first enemy hit list for the Temple. Acting on his own initiative, he researched the question of the most effective poison to be used.

After the carnage in Jonestown, Stoen began to emerge as a media-created hero. Terri Buford, who had defected from the Temple almost three weeks before the internecine event, was profoundly affected by the slaughter. All of her friends and many of those she loved had died in that tragic moment. She felt constrained to speak about the events which led to the slaughter. As she presented what she knew from her years of work under the direction of Tim Stoen and Jim Jones, she made allegations about Stoen that had not previously been published. After she had asked me to represent her, she made a lengthy and specific statement to the news media gathered at that time in the Federal Building in San Francisco. Stoen went into hiding. It was rumored that he had left the state. His attorney, Patrick Hallinan, was quoted in the press as responding, "They're lies and damn lies, and there's no truth to them."* Although the intensity of his rhetoric seemed to diminish as he neared the end of the sentence, he made a sudden

**Los Angeles Times,* 22 December, 1978.

comeback in his next effort: "Mark Lane and Terri Buford are moral degenerates, and I'm not going to get out in the press and sling mud with them." That dazzling display of judgmental restraint made one puzzle over what the distinguished attorney might have pronounced had he been willing to "sling mud," as he so eloquently put it. Until that moment, I had in fact not mentioned his name, offered no public statement as to my own observations of his client, and Terri Buford had merely presented a relatively brief digest of the testimony she had just offered to the United States grand jury which had required her presence through the process of a federal subpoena. The following day, Tim Stoen himself may have responded: the Associated Press reported that "a man who said he was Mr. Stoen telephoned the Associated Press yesterday to deny charges made by Terri Buford." The voice, which declined to leave a number where Stoen could be called to answer specific questions, stated that Buford was "following a script written in detail by Jim Jones and is still working for Jim Jones." The man said that Jones had set up a plan to "make false charges against Tim Stoen should he ever defect and if he couldn't be crushed emotionally or destroyed legally, he was to be physically killed."

Since I was not present at meetings of the Planning Commission with Stoen, I cannot be certain that all of the allegations made about him are accurate. I do know that the charges he has made against Buford are not true. Since Stoen defected more than a year before Buford revealed what she knew about him and she made the revelations after the death of Jones, it does not seem logical to suggest that she did so upon orders from Jones. Stoen did not explain why, if Jones wanted him destroyed, one way or another, he took no action to accomplish that during his own lifetime. Far from following a preordained script, Terri Buford painfully struggled with her conscience for some time and discussed her concerns at great length with April Ferguson, my law partner, and with me before deciding that she should disclose what she knew. That process, which I witnessed, does not establish the accuracy of her remarks; it does, however, establish the inaccuracy of Stoen's response.

Stoen has steadfastly refused to answer questions proposed to him by the news media. He has insulted reporters who persisted and even verged upon threatening one, to my knowledge. He has failed to come forward before the institutions that are investigating his conduct to make his answers under oath and under the penalty of perjury. Various documents support some of Buford's allegations, including documents signed by Stoen.

Buford, on the other hand, has made her statements under oath and with full knowledge of the penalty for perjury for each allegation that she had made. She volunteered to testify before the Federal Grand Jury in San Francisco and was thereupon served with a subpoena to testify. She answered every question asked of her there. Prior to that testimony, she had met with the United States attorney for San Francisco and members of the staff, FBI agents, and a secret service agent at a hotel chosen by the FBI in San Jose, California. There too, every question was answered. Later she met with the assistant attorney general of California, Timothy Reardon, on more than one occasion and in my presence, mailed material to him, and talked with him many times over the telephone. She answered each question he asked her.

She testified fully before the San Francisco city grand jury; she answered numerous questions asked of her by an investigator for the Los Angeles District Attorney's office.

She met with special agents of the Federal Bureau of Investigation and agents of the secret service in Memphis in my presence and answered each of their questions, and then met with other FBI agents in San Francisco and again in Memphis in my presence and answered all questions put to her on those occasions. Stoen has, during the last six months, refused to answer any questions. Nevertheless, in an effort to encourage Stoen to respond to the allegations which have been made against him, on May 7, 1979, I sent him a letter* by certified mail asking him to respond in person, and if he wished in the presence of his attorney and a tape recorder, or in writing, to the charges contained in this book. I agreed in advance, and in writing, to publish in full whatever statement he wished to make. I also agreed not to edit his answer in any fashion. Stoen did not respond to my letter; he returned it unopened. I then sent the same letter to his attorney, Patrick Hallinan, with a covering letter. Hallinan, on behalf of his client, threatened to sue me and my publisher if I so much as mentioned the name Timothy Stoen in this book. However, on behalf of Stoen he specifically declined my request that his client present his view of these serious questions.

During 1976, a Bay Area television reporter told Mike Prokes that an investigation of the Temple was being conducted by the San Francisco District Attorney's office. Jones immediately called Stoen at the prosecutor's office and summoned him to the Temple. Stoen appeared that day for a meeting at the church at which Harriet Tropp, Terri Buford, Mike Prokes, and Jones were present. Stoen said that he had not heard about any investigation of the Temple by Freitas, but that he would check it out at once. The next day Stoen discovered that a complaint had been filed by a black

*The letter to Stoen is published as Appendix J.

minister, Hannibal Williams, charging Jones with being the Antichrist; the complaint was not limited to the type of allegation that ordinarily fell within the purview of the prosecutor's office. Some time after Stoen informed Jones of the nature of the complaint, a Temple member threatened Williams. Robert Correia was assigned by the district attorney's office to investigate the Williams complaint, including allegations of a death threat.

During 1979, San Francisco District Attorney Joseph Freitas said that he had conducted a recent in-house review of Stoen's conduct for the period in which he had served as his deputy.* Following the initiation of an investigation by the office of the attorney general of the state of California under the direction of Deputy Attorney General Timothy Reardon, Freitas said that he discovered that Stoen had acted improperly in attempting to use his office to interfere with Correia's investigation into allegations of death threats made by the Peoples Temple against Williams. Freitas concluded that the improper conduct was "a firing offense."†

Stoen did not comment directly upon the statement made by his former employer. Patrick Hallinan told the San Francisco *Chronicle* that Stoen denied any improper actions while he was a deputy district attorney and said he had never discussed his job with Jones. However, Correia said that Stoen had confronted him two days after the investigator had interviewed Williams, saying that Jones was a "fine guy" and asking why Correia was investigating him.‡

The Williams complaint of death threats was not pursued "because of a lack of leads."§

During May 1979, the report of the inquiry conducted for the Committee on Foreign Affairs of the House of Representatives revealed that before the massacre, Stoen had been able to secure the intervention of twenty-eight members of Congress on his behalf in his struggle against Jones.‖ The members of Congress had not known that Stoen had previously used his official position to shield himself and Jones from discovery and prosecution. One of these twenty-eight was Leo Ryan.

*San Francisco *Chronicle,* 21 January, 1979.
†Ibid.
‡Ibid.
§Ibid.
‖*U.S. House of Representatives Report*, p. 215.

19 Charles Garry

This chapter has not been an easy one for me to write. Charles Garry is a brother lawyer who has valiantly participated in many cases important to the rights of the oppressed over many years. I admire and respect his past accomplishments. I respect the truth as well.

One cannot present an accurate history of the Peoples Temple or of its troubled leader without examining the important position that Charles Garry occupied during the most crucial period. Soon after Garry became counsel for the Temple and Jones, he said, and then repeated on numerous occasions, that he was certain that there was an organized government effort to destroy his client. His words were employed to highlight a six-page document widely distributed by the Temple. The document was prepared with Garry's approval and with the approval of his associate Pat Richartz. Several thousand copies of the document were given out in San Francisco. Filling the top of page one are the words, "VICTIMS OF CONSPIRACY—'This is an organized, premeditated government campaign to destroy a politically progressive church. . . .' Charles Garry." The end of the brochure asserts, "Charles Garry lived with us several days and nights at the Temple project in Guyana. He is a man known to speak the truth all the time—and he called Jonestown 'PARADISE.' " Yet after the massacre, when Garry appeared before a congressional investigating body, he said, "I want to unequivocally tell you in the year and a half since July 1977, with the years of experience I had had with governmental wrongdoing, particularly with regards to the FBI, I found no evidence to support any of the charges that were made by Peoples Temple. I found no evidence to support any of that."*

**U.S. House of Representatives Report*, p. 21.

Since Garry's position and memory on this and other related questions have shifted so dramatically since the massacre, it is necessary in this chapter to determine his earlier stance from statements which he made at the time to Jones, Tim Carter, Terri Buford, Congressman Ryan, reporters, and others, including me.

Terri Buford, who had been assigned as liaison to Tim Stoen, became liaison to Charles Garry after he was retained by the Peoples Temple. During the summer of 1977, just as Stoen was departing, the Temple learned that *New West Magazine* was about to publish an exposé of the arranged "faith healing" meetings. Jim Jones, who was then in Guyana, realized that the organization was definitely in need of a general counsel. He communicated by radio with Terri Buford, Harriet Tropp, Gene Chaikin, and Mike Prokes, who were in San Francisco. Jones favored an effort to retain William Kunstler, a talented and experienced defense lawyer. Tropp adamantly opposed that suggestion, relying upon hostile news accounts of Kunstler's work. Gene Chaikin suggested that since Garry had attended a testimonial dinner for Jones and had spoken at the Temple in San Francisco, he might be more willing than Kunstler to represent the Temple. Jones and all of his aides agreed that Garry's location (he maintained a law office in San Francisco) was much more convenient, since the Temple's officers were in that city and communication with Jones was facilitated through the shortwave radio there.

Accordingly, Buford, Tropp, Chaikin, and Prokes called upon Garry and retained him. Terri Buford recalls the day. "We were all prepared to urge Garry to represent us, since we knew that with the *New West* article about to come out, we were in desperate need of counsel. Garry agreed at once and accepted a substantial retainer. He never did inquire at that time about the facts upon which the *New West* piece was based."

A few days later, Patricia Richartz, Garry's assistant, called Buford to tell her how important the retainer was to Garry. Buford, upon reflection, said, "I think that part of the problem was that Garry wanted to fill the void that was left after Huey Newton of the Panther party fired him. He wanted us to become another Panther party so that he could be counsel for a militant, revolutionary organization."

After the *New West* article* was published, the Temple leadership feared that Garry, who had developed an image as a principled lawyer for the Left,

*Marshall Kilduff and Phil Tracy, "Inside Peoples Temple," *New West Magazine,* 1 August, 1977, pp. 30–38.

might resign. Reluctantly, after conversations with Jones, who had instructed the group to tell Garry the entire truth about the Temple, Tropp, Chaikin, Prokes, and Buford met with Garry at his office. There they confessed that many of the outrageous allegations in the *New West* article were true. They admitted that Jones had arranged for people who he had convinced were suffering from cancer to enter a rest room and then emerge from a stall believing that they had "passed" the cancer. Marceline Jones and the cured patient then returned to the faith-healing meeting to display the miraculously passed malignancy. In reality, the diseased organ was composed of oysters soaked in human blood that Marcie Jones had carried with her into the bathroom. In their panic and while struggling through feelings of shame and guilt, the Temple leaders never noticed that the authors of the article, Marshall Kilduff and Phil Tracy, had carefully refrained from publishing the most serious charges against Timothy Stoen.

After having made the painful admissions to Garry about the fraudulent methods that Jones had utilized, the leaders, who had themselves but recently been informed that the healings had been faked, awaited his response. Garry broke into a smile, leaned forward in the chair that he occupied behind a table in the conference room, and said, "I like that man." The Temple members were bemused. What man? Why was Garry smiling? In a sudden eruption of ebullient chatter, Garry effusively praised Jones for his courage and his commitment. "I like that man," Garry repeated. "He's got balls." To the astonishment and relief of his audience, Garry continued, "The one thing I really like about Jim Jones is that he's not afraid to get his hands dirty. He's not afraid to look like a charlatan to support his cause. Some people on the Left think that they're too good to get their hands dirty. But not Jim. I like that kind of man. He's my kind of man."

The effect of Garry's words had considerable impact on Gene Chaikin. Chaikin also was a member of the California bar. Unlike Stoen, Chaikin's advice to Jones had often been cautious and relatively conservative. Before the meeting with Garry, Chaikin, who had exercised a restraining influence upon Jones, had expressed his discomfort upon learning that the healing sessions had been fraudulently conducted. Jones had confessed that only Stoen, and those actually involved in the arrangements, had been informed about the preparations for the faith healings. Although Chaikin continued to maintain serious doubts about the wisdom of combining religion with chicanery, Garry's enthusiasm for the organized deception helped to temper Chaikin's dubiosity. Chaikin was a talented lawyer with few movement credentials; however, his commitment to a movement for social justice and change was almost absolute. Garry was a venerable movement lawyer whom Chaikin, at that time, respected. Chaikin accepted Garry's judgment. As the four members left Garry's office, Chaikin shook his head and said, "Garry has chutzpah. I never thought of looking at it that way."

Since Buford was given the responsibility of maintaining an ongoing regular relationship with Garry as liaison from the Temple, she began to brief him about the actions, legal and illegal, in which the Temple was engaged. Soon after Garry was retained, she began to share with him information about the shipment of weapons to Guyana, foreign bank accounts, and other crimes that Temple leaders, including Jones, had committed. "Garry said," Terri Buford reported, " 'I'm not critical. I'm a revolutionary and I know that these things have to be done.' "

When Temple leaders told Garry that Jones required members to sign blank sheets and to confess to crimes they never committed, Garry, according to Terri Buford, instructed the Temple leaders to store those documents in his office. Immediately after the *New West* article was published, three truckloads of Peoples Temple files were delivered to Garry's law office; if the incriminating evidence were in his office, he could protect it under an attorney-client privilege from civil or criminal seizure.

Garry also knew that Jones maintained those files to prevent Temple members from defecting; these allegations had been published in *New West* and later confirmed to Garry by Tropp, Chaikin, Buford, and Prokes. Instead of urging Jones and the other leaders to dispose of the documents which held unwilling members as hostages, Garry acquiesced by providing a safe place in which to secrete the false confessions. According to the statements made to me by a number of Temple leaders, including Jones, Chaikin, Tropp, Prokes, and Buford, Garry later used his control of those files to exert influence over the Temple. They each told me that when the Temple wished to discharge Garry or exercise judgment independent from his, he often threatened to place all of the files out into the street where anyone could get them. Some of those conversations, I was told, were tape-recorded. If they were correct in those assertions, then the signed confessions, originally intended to coerce members into remaining with the Temple, were used to coerce the Temple into remaining with Charles Garry.

Throughout 1977, the Temple stored weapons and ammunition in substantial quantities in private lockers which were leased from a commercial locker firm. The lockers were located on Bryant Street in San Francisco, within sight of the district attorney's office. Buford had just returned from an overseas trip and planned to store some documents in one of the lockers. When she arrived at Bryant Street, she discovered that the lockers which had held the weapons and ammunition were empty and open. She rushed back to the Temple in panic and informed Jean Brown and Tim Clancy, another Temple leader, that the weapons were missing. They all presumed that the police had seized them. "As I recall it now," Buford said recently, "the lockers were rented to Jack Beam. I never wanted us to have the guns anyway and that fact, and our panic, came together. I told Jean and Tim that the police would be able to locate us through Jack Beam and that they should take any rifles, pistols, and ammunition that were stored in the Temple and throw them into the Bay."

Jean Brown and Tim Clancy did dispose of some of the weapons in that fashion, but Brown stored a number of weapons in the trunk of an automobile parked in a lot behind the Temple until the crisis passed, and then returned them to the Temple.

Believing that the police might be moving in shortly, Buford tried to contact Garry to prepare a legal defense. She now knew how far Garry might go to aid the Temple. Since Buford only visited the Bryant Street lockers after sundown, to minimize the chance of being observed, by the time she had returned to the Temple and dispatched Brown and Clancy to disarm the church edifice, it was well into the evening. It was raining and dark when she dialed Garry's home telephone number. Louise Garry, the attorney's wife, answered. Buford said that it was essential and urgent that she speak to Charles. Mrs. Garry replied that her husband was out of town on business and that she did not know where he could be reached.

Buford then called Pat Richartz, hoping that she could locate Garry. Richartz was not at home either, but one of her children took Terri's emergency message. A few minutes later, Richartz called Buford and asked about the emergency. Buford said that a serious event had just happened and that she would rather not discuss it on the telephone. Richartz said that if it was that important, they should meet at once. She told Buford the name of the large hotel at the San Francisco airport at which she was staying, gave her the address and her room number and told her to come over at once.

When Terri Buford arrived at the hotel room, Pat Richartz greeted her. When Terri entered the room, she saw Charles Garry there. Quickly, she briefed him about the missing weapons and ammunition. He said, "So what's the problem? It's okay to have guns." Buford said that she was afraid of repercussions if the police found them. If they were stolen, she said, the thieves might use them to commit crimes. She reminded Garry that the weapons bore the fingerprints of Temple members.

Garry was apparently unconcerned about the removal of the weapons. He adopted the same position that Jean Brown later adhered to: Weapons were required by revolutionaries, and storing them—pistols, rifles, or other weapons—was not a crime. He told Buford not to worry about problems related to weapons, and then asked her why so many weapons were being stored in the locker. Terri explained that it was possible the arsenal would be sent to Jonestown. Garry was curious about how weapons were smuggled out of the country. He asked Terri how the weapons in Guyana arrived there and how additional weapons were to be transported. Buford told him that weapons were placed in false bottoms of crates that were manufactured in the woodshop at the church in San Francisco. Then various belongings of those on the way to Guyana were placed in the boxes. In some cases, she said, a rifle, broken down into components, was placed in a duffel bag that contained sheets, towels, pillows, or clothing. Garry smiled and raised his right fist in the air, as if giving a power salute.

Garry made keys of his law office available to Terri Buford and Gene Chaikin. Later, Jean Brown took charge of the keys. Although the Temple group in San Francisco had made a collective decision not to store weapons in Garry's building, Jean Brown, relying upon Garry's statement that it was not illegal to keep weapons, placed several of them in the basement of the building occupied by Garry's law firm, Garry, Dreyfus, McTernan, Brotsky, Herndon & Pesonen, Inc.

According to Temple members, Garry was so concerned with securing all available publicity for himself that he insisted that he direct and control all press conferences given by the Temple. A conference at which a movement organization expresses its goals and methods is primarily a political act, and generally is not controlled by counsel. Yet Garry saw himself as more than a lawyer for the group. He neither participated in collective meetings at which policy was hammered out, nor subjected himself to the discipline of the organization, often explaining with a smile, "I'm an elitist." Yet, he strongly influenced the direction of his client by insisting that all matters were potential legal cases. He asserted, as an example, that a defamation case could flow from an ill-framed phrase spoken at a press conference, and that therefore, in almost all matters, he, as the general counsel, should make the ultimate political decision for the client.

During a speech delivered at the University of California in Berkeley, long after the massacre, he stated clearly what his approach was: "I did not know exactly what was coming down on the Peoples Temple, but I issued them an ultimatum. I said I would not condone any form of publicity or press conferences on their part." He added, "I said if there are any press conferences that are going to be given, I said I want to be able to direct it and be a part of it."

During June 1978 Garry explained to a reporter* why the Peoples Temple maintained weapons in Jonestown. According to the reporter, Garry "claimed credit for the elaborate security system at the Temple's jungle outpost in Guyana."

Garry said to the reporter, "While I was there (in Guyana) I set up the security system because Jim Jones had been shot at. I worked out a system where there was a twenty-four-hour watch on the gate." Garry added that he "encouraged them [Temple officials] to get weapons."

When Garry was asked if he knew where the weapons came from, Garry responded, "I did not inquire. I assume they bought them somewhere like people do in this country."

When Jones discovered that his lawyer had publicly announced that there were weapons in Guyana, he was outraged. The weapons had been stored in California illegally; smuggled out of the United States in violation of federal statutes; smuggled into Guyana in violation of Guyanese law; and kept at Jonestown without permits, in violation of the law of Guyana. Jones could hardly believe that his legal advisor had publicly announced and defended the continuing violation of the law and then took credit for it.

Jean Brown, who was in San Francisco, read a copy of the article to Harriet Tropp and Terri Buford, who were operating the shortwave radio in Jonestown. Buford recalls the event clearly: "We flipped. We couldn't understand Garry's behavior. We knew we were going to have to tell Jim about it at once, but we dreaded the effect it was going to have on him. Our immediate concern was that Jean Brown had read the article over international air and had admitted that it was true. She had read it in a somewhat coded manner, but it was quite clear that she was vouching for the accuracy of the report. Harriet immediately tried to cover for her, saying that Garry had gotten his facts wrong, but Jean, as she would invariably do in these matters, kept on insisting in public that Garry was correct about the guns. This was one of the reasons that Jim never felt sure that he could trust Jean."

Tropp and Buford told Jones about Garry's statement to the newspaper. Jones said, "Doesn't he know that we are trying to build a farm there? We are not trying to get ourselves blown up. Doesn't Garry know it's against the law to smuggle guns here and to keep them here? Tell Garry we have learned something from what happened to the Black Panthers. We don't

*Santa Rosa *Press Democrat,* 22 June, 1978.

want to be killed here. We don't want black soldiers from a socialist country coming in here and attacking us. Oh my God, doesn't he see what he's done? Tell Garry that I demand that he call the newspaper and take it back. Tell him that he can say he was mistaken."

Tropp and Buford communicated the message to Jean Brown. Brown later said that Garry had refused to issue a retraction, telling her that "the people in Jonestown should quit panicking. Tell them that I'm calling the shots from here."

Later, when Terri Buford met with Charles Garry at his office, she tried to persuade him to retract his statement about weapons, or at least to agree not to make similar statements in the future. She told him that Jones was concerned that he would not know what to do if Guyanese soldiers came onto the property in search of weapons. Buford said, "Garry listened impatiently, then got up from his desk and said, 'Horseshit! Jim Jones can't call the shots from the jungle. I've got to be in a position to call the shots. I've got to have the authority to call them from here without worrying about Jean running to the radio and telling Jim everything I do and say. He can't possibly know what to do in the middle of the jungle about the press here.' "

During that meeting, and in numerous other meetings in San Francisco, including statements to the press, Garry established a three-point program for running the affairs of Peoples Temple: 1) Jones would run the operation in Jonestown and Georgetown; 2) Garry would run the operation in San Francisco; 3) Jones should not return to the United States. If he did, Garry said, he was certain Jones would be arrested at once.

Garry pointed out to Buford that he believed that Jones was "nuts" and that if she or Jean Brown or others in the Temple listened to Jones, rather than to him, Garry, then they were nuts also.

Garry regularly told the San Francisco news media that he and he alone was the only authorized spokesman for the Peoples Temple. He told Art Silverman, a reporter for the *Berkeley Barb,** that Jones remained in Guyana on "Garry's orders."

Returning to his public statement that there were weapons in Jonestown, Garry told Buford, "I did you a favor telling about the guns there. They'll think twice about messing with anyone who they know has guns."

Six weeks after Garry had been retained as counsel for the Temple, he told the San Francisco media that the charges against the Temple and Jones were "an organized, orchestrated, premeditated government campaign to

**Berkeley Barb,* 23–29 September, 1977.

destroy a politically progressive organization." The *Berkeley Barb,* in the September 23–29, 1977, issue, devoted a great deal of space to Garry's charges under a massive headline—"A Conspiracy Behind Peoples Temple Exposé?" The reporter, Art Silverman, had in fact dug up some evidence to support Garry's contention and he concludes that there are "a number of unusual circumstances" which "can't help but raise the suspicion that there's more going on than first meets the eye."

Silverman refers to evidence of a federal conspiracy to frame Jones which he encountered at a press conference that Charles Garry had presided over in his office earlier that month. During that conference, at Garry's request, Dennis Banks, a leader of the American Indian Movement, offered a statement in support of Garry's contention that there was an ongoing government conspiracy to destroy the Peoples Temple.*

At numerous meetings with Temple members and leaders in the United States and Guyana, Garry spoke of the "orchestrated and premeditated government conspiracy against the Temple." He adhered to that line at press conferences, public meetings, and private sessions.

After the massacre, as the news media persisted in referring to the tragedy as a "mass suicide" committed by deranged individuals who felt that there had been a conspiracy against them, Garry quickly moved to isolate himself from any charge that he had ever believed or said that there had been a conspiracy. In his effort at self-vindication, Garry denounced all who had suggested that agents of the government played some part in the debacle. The media overlooked many of his past statements. They featured Garry's condemnation of those who believed there was evidence to the effect that various unexplained actions by federal employees had helped to bring about the tragic end to the Jonestown experiment. Garry insisted that Jones was paranoid and that he had seen conspiracies against him when none existed.

At the University of California at Berkeley early in 1979, Garry said:

> I went there (to Guyana) in September 1978. I said to Jim Jones, who in my opinion, was highly paranoid by me. His paranoia was that every governmental agency of the U.S. was out to destroy the Peoples Temple in Jonestown and in California, and very frankly, since July of 1977, when I was engaged to represent the Temple, I looked for all the things that the Temple was worried about. Namely there was an attempt on the part of the FBI, CIA, or whatever other federal

*The charges that Dennis Banks made, which apparently involve an undercover agent for the United States Treasury Department, are discussed in chapter 17, and his full statement appears as Appendix A.

> organization or the IRS to destroy that worthy organization. Very frankly, I found none. I found nothing in the way that any governmental agency was either directly or indirectly involved in the People's Temple. We have since found out that Jim Jones when he was in Ukiah was an established member of the Republican party.

Garry continued to describe his search for evidence that some government agency was concerned about Jones or the Peoples Temple. He said that in spite of his thorough investigation, no such evidence was ever discovered. He concluded, "What I'm trying to say is there is no evidence whatsoever that the FBI even knew anything about the Peoples Temple and obviously the CIA was not involved in any way at all."

Garry said that he had completed an extensive examination of all relevant government files. He had investigated, he said, under the provisions of the Freedom of Information Act. After studying the evidence, he concluded, "I did not find one single member of the Peoples Temple who had any relationship to the FOI files. Jim Jones himself," Garry continued, "was not once mentioned in the FOI files."

However, the FBI itself, speaking through its director William Webster, had conceded that the FBI not only knew about the Peoples Temple, but its agents had conducted interviews after having received a complaint that Jonestown residents were not free to leave the project.* In addition, the State Department and the American embassy in Guyana had compiled files about the Temple and about Jim Jones, as had the Federal Communications Commission, the Internal Revenue Service, and other agencies of the government. Indeed, although Garry continued to insist that his thorough FOI investigation proved that "not a single member"' of the Temple had been the subject of government scrutiny, his office had received various documents pursuant to an FOI request about Eugene Chaikin, revealing that Chaikin had been the subject of an intelligence watch.

Far more significant, however, is the fact that Garry had never brought a single action under the Freedom of Information Act on behalf of his clients, although he had been requested to do so. Terri Buford had been given the responsibility to monitor his efforts for the Temple, and has claimed that Garry never showed much concern with the inquiries, and that he did not file any actions under the law for the government files. She explained, "Two Temple members, June Crym and Jean Brown, visited Garry's office and were given a large number of copies of the letterhead from Garry's firm and envelopes by Pat Richartz. June then typed form letters

**U.S. House of Representatives Report,* p. 21.

to various agencies on behalf of Jim Jones and several other people in the Temple, including me. Many of the letters were, I believe, typed at the church in San Francisco."

Since the letters bore Garry's address, the replies were sent to his office. June Crym took charge of the replies and gave them to Terri Buford who sent them on to Jones. Many of the agencies denied having information about the Temple and its leaders. Jones told Garry and others that he presumed that the agencies were deliberately withholding information, but Garry indicated that nothing more could be done.

The federal statute providing for access to government files has been a source of great irritation for the government agencies. The directors of the FBI and the CIA have opposed it regularly and routinely failed to meet its provisions, and have called for its abolition. Lawyers who seriously expect to secure information under the act know that the three-phase procedure established by the statute is almost always necessary in order to secure relevant information. The initial letter to the agency is often ignored for some time, in clear violation of the law. The ultimate response to the letter is often negative. The inquiring party is then provided, under the statute, with an opportunity to appeal the ruling until all administrative remedies have been exhausted. At that point, it is possible for the first time to institute an action in the relevant federal district court for full disclosure. The court then has the obligation to examine all of the files and determine if any of the exemptions found in the authorizing statute apply. It is primarily through this full procedure that relevant information is secured.

When I informed Jones and his aides of the provisions of the law during my first visit to Jonestown in September 1978, they were astonished to discover that it was not necessary to accept as final a nonsworn letter of disclaimer from an agency.

One of the most bizarre aspects of Jones's personality, manifesting itself in an effort to maintain control over his followers, was his sexual extravagance. Jones harbored doubts about the wisdom of his policy of using sexual relations with numerous women and men as a method to "build the movement," as he put it. At a meeting with Garry, during which Chaikin, Tropp, Prokes, and Buford were present, Jones confided in Garry about his multifarious sexual encounters and his incertitude in that regard. A sensitive counselor might, at that point, have told Jones that such actions would not be constructive for Temple members or their leader. Garry inquired about the specifics of the myriad sexual acts, requesting names and details, or what might be referred to as "clinical data." Jones asked Garry if he thought it right to "play with people the way I have." Garry told Jones that he thought it was great. He reassured Jones, pointing out that not only was it not unusual for a leader to "fuck the following," but that it was in fact "a historical tradition." Garry told Jones that he respected him for his sexual exploits. He pointed out with approval that, "in the early days of the Communist party, white women would fuck black men in order to get them to join the party."

Garry then confided in Jones and the others who were present that a very well-known American actress, whom he named, once "fucked a man for fifty thousand dollars and then gave the money to the Black Panther party." Garry, who had been counsel for the Black Panther party at that time, vouched for the accuracy of the story.

Terri Buford later commented, "With Garry overtly supporting Jim's sexual politics, and the actress and the early communists inadvertently condoning this kind of activity, Jim then began to think of himself as a communist hero, rather than a sexually overdriven pervert. From that moment on, any effort to persuade Jim to change his ways was doomed. Until then, a number of us had been critical of Jim's actions and we thought we were making some progress with him. But Garry had reinforced Jim's belief that his bizarre conduct was normal for a revolutionary leader and that those of us who disagreed were not sufficiently radical. Garry kept saying, 'Remember I'm not just a liberal, I'm a radical.' "

Toward the end of the summer of 1978, Jones became seriously concerned that property owned by the Temple was vulnerable to legal attachment. Jones told Gene Chaikin, Harriet Tropp, and Terri Buford that he had decided to maintain a minimum bank account and to acquire and keep large sums of cash in Jonestown, and in the Temple in San Francisco. In order to accomplish that end, he decided to sell substantial portions of the Temple's holdings in California and thus generate a cash flow. He knew that the property, valued at over one million dollars, might not be easy to sell at market value if the Temple were required to dispose of it all too quickly. He therefore concluded that some of the property should be transferred to Charles Garry or to his law firm, then sold at leisure with the proceeds, of course, going to the Temple.

In an interview with me, Buford said, "The first piece of property that Garry and his firm accepted, sold, and returned the proceeds to the Temple was an apartment building owned by the Temple located just behind the Los Angeles Peoples Temple on Hoover and Alvarado. With Garry's consent the property was transferred to his firm and then sold for cash. Jean Brown handled the sale."

Buford said, "The underlying motivation for this procedure was Jim's belief that there was a conspiracy against the Temple and that in support of that conspiracy, our property might be taken away through lawsuits developed by Tim Stoen. Garry agreed that there was a conspiracy against the Temple and used his law firm's name to help the Temple convert the property into cash."

The first deal worked so well that Jones asked Brown to see if other properties could be transferred to Garry or his firm as well. Instead of merely exploring the matter with Garry, as Jones had instructed, Brown and Garry actually transferred additional property to Garry's firm. Jones became very angry. In Guyana, he said, "If Garry should quit, we might lose the property and there would be nothing we could do about it." Later, Garry requested documenting support for his ownership of the property. Jean Brown contacted Harriet Tropp and Terri Buford by radio and informed them that Garry wanted a letter which would provide cover for him in case of an inquiry. The requested letter from the Temple was to state that the property had been transferred to the law firm as payment for legal expenses. Jones adamantly refused to send such a letter, telling his aides in Jonestown that he could not trust anyone with such huge sums of money or parcels of property and that Garry might "desert the Temple at any time" and thus leave them without legal recourse to regain the property.

During September 1978, when Charles Garry and Joe Mazor were in Jonestown, Jones decided that Garry should be told the "Philadelphia story."* During a small meeting held in an office next to the radio room, Jones told Buford to find Jack Beam and have him report to him. Jones whispered to Beam, and Beam and Garry left the room together. Jones said, "Jack's telling Charles the 'Philadelphia story.' " Ten minutes later, Garry returned from the walk with Beam. He was smiling broadly. Beam winked at Jones.

Later, Beam said that he had told Garry how "he had killed an agent in Philadelphia," and that Garry was quite excited by the description of the event. Beam said he had tape-recorded Garry's reactions so that "Jim would have some leverage in dealing with him if he decided to attack us."

On various occasions thereafter, according to Terri Buford, Garry observed that "that Jack Beam is quite a guy. He's quite a man."

*See chapter 1 for details of the "Philadelphia Story" incident.

Just after Garry and Mazor departed from Jonestown in September, and just before my initial visit there, I met Garry at the Peoples Temple house in Georgetown. In the presence of Mazor, who had been working against Jones and the Temple for some time, Garry insisted that Jones was paranoid. Tim Carter, Leona Collier, and other Temple members were surprised and angry to hear Garry insist, over and over, that Jones was paranoid and dangerous. He said that it was paranoid of Jones to insist that Mazor be searched upon entering Jonestown.* He gave various other examples of Jones's paranoia, and insisted that Mazor was trustworthy. "He's my partner," Garry insisted.

Soon after my arrival in Jonestown, Jim Jones and his legal advisors, Gene Chaikin and Harriet Tropp, and other Temple members, including Terri Buford, Johnny Jones, Michael Prokes, and Sharon Amos, impressed upon me their dismay about being represented by Charles Garry. At meetings in the room next to the radio room, and in the East House, where I stayed, they told me that Garry had sought to usurp the leadership of the organization while Jones remained in Guyana. Jones was clearly anxious to return to the United States but he, and the others in Jonestown, said that Garry strongly advised against his return. Jones said, "I sometimes think that he wants me to stay here so that he can run the Peoples Temple without any interference from me."

During Garry's visit Terri Buford had told Garry that she had read a recently published magazine article, entitled "The Party's Over," which was very critical of Newton and the Black Panther party. She expressed her feeling that the article was unfair and untrue. Garry, in the presence of Jones and others, responded that he thought the article was "excellent." According to Chaikin, Jim Jones, Harriet Tropp, and Buford, Garry added, "Huey got what was coming to him. Huey deserves everything he gets and more."

During my visit of September 15, Jones had said that they could never fire Garry because he was a "vindictive son of a bitch, and if he is talking that way about Huey now, he will talk about us much worse if we ever let him go."

After the massacre, Garry made use of his arsenal of files, selectively releasing various documents to embarrass and attack those who were critical of him. Although he suppressed many of the signed false confessions, he widely publicized tainted documents produced by Jean Brown that had

*Mazor eventually agreed to allow only Garry to search him and later said that he had smuggled in weapons which Garry missed (see chapter 1).

allegedly been signed by Terri Buford, when Buford revealed the extent of Garry's knowledge of and participation in the conduct of the Peoples Temple.

Evidently Garry even showed the documents to casual visitors to his office in an attempt to discredit his former client, Terri Buford. On December 23, 1978, he met with Mr. Eleftheris Karaoglanis, a gentleman not previously known to him. According to Karaoglanis, Garry spoke with him for more than three hours and displayed documents in an effort to prove that Buford had not spoken truthfully.

Mr. Karaoglanis later told me of Garry's unusual conduct and on December 26, 1978, he signed a letter to me regarding the meeting in Garry's office.* In that letter Karaoglanis wrote, "During the course of that meeting, Garry told me that he had destroyed all of the letters that members of the Peoples Temple had written which were, he said, signed confessions of wrongdoing on their part and were the way, Garry said, by which Jim Jones held the people hostage in the Temple. Garry's associate seemed very upset to hear Garry say that he had destroyed the evidence and he asked him why he had done such a thing. Garry said that there were three documents which he did not destroy. They were all written by Terri Buford, he said. He then showed me three documents written by Ms. Buford."

In addition, Garry attempted to publicly relieve himself of any responsibility for the actions of his client. During his speech at the University of California at Berkeley, Garry said,

> Guyana raised some very serious and very interesting not only social problems, but serious legal problems. One of the things it raises is the role of the lawyer and the extent of the lawyer's responsibility to be able to foresee and anticipate the problems that might arise as it did in Jonestown. I think that's a burden that the lawyer should not have to bear. That's not a burden the lawyer could share because the lawyer is not in the position to make policy matters.

Still later in his speech, Garry again cleared all government organizations of any wrongdoing. He said, "Jim Jones was a person who was paranoid, whereas I couldn't even see a symbol of conspiracy."

Toward the conclusion of his remarks at the University of California at Berkeley, Garry said that he never knew that there were any guns in Jonestown until the day of the massacre. No one asked him why, five months before the massacre, he had publicly claimed credit for the security

*This letter is published as Appendix I.

system in Jonestown, or why, in spite of repeated and almost desperate pleas from Jones and others, he had steadfastly refused to retract his statement about the presence of weapons in Jonestown.

When Garry was asked by reporters Pearl Stewart and Mary Ann Hogan for the Oakland *Tribune** about the role that his firm played in laundering the Temple property, he did not deny that the transfers took place. According to the reporters, the transfers had been duly recorded in Los Angeles County. Garry said that such transfers could have been made without his participation, and he contended that he was unaware of the transactions.

He said, "I don't know why they did it. It could have been because in all the work this office has done for them, we've been paid $37,500." Garry said that the property was later returned to the Temple and that he never knew why it had been turned over to the firm in the first place. He said that he never asked anyone in the Temple, although he was in contact with them daily, and he added that he did not think that his failure to inquire was "unusual." Garry's retainer with Peoples Temple called for a five-thousand-dollar monthly fee, a good portion of which had been paid. The property that had been transferred to his law firm was worth hundreds of thousands of dollars.

During the interview with the Oakland *Tribune* reporters, Garry also said that he "had no idea Jones was unstable before the massacre." He conceded that Jones was "hysterical" during the radio-telephone hookup during September 1977, and that Jones kept shouting that the members of the Temple were "all going to fight to the death." Although Jones kept shouting that all of the residents of Jonestown were going to die that day, Garry had "no idea" that Jones lacked stability. A year later, in a tape-recorded message to Jones, Garry had accused his client of being paranoid. During the intervening year, Garry observed the pressures upon his client increase, and he saw as well his concomitant deterioration.

Garry had established a relationship with Jones which frightened the client and drove him deeper into himself and his own concept of the terrors that lay ahead. During that year, Jones felt that he had no legal recourse. He believed that all possible efforts under the Freedom of Information Act had been made, and that he would never learn of the government's plans to destroy him. And he apparently believed that, although he and his aides despised Garry, and he them, that he could never discharge him.

During the fall of 1978, Jim Jones and the Temple were in a great deal of trouble. They needed a knowledgeable and principled counselor who was

*Oakland *Tribune,* 4 March, 1979.

sensitive to their problems and qualified to assist them to confront their difficulties in a legal and nonviolent fashion. Garry had urged them to secure weapons, and then broadcast that they had, thus materially increasing the pressure upon them. And this he did after he knew that Jones was capable of murdering all of his followers, as he had almost done in the fall of 1977. Garry publicly said that he knew there was a government conspiracy to destroy the Temple and Jonestown, yet he never pursued the legal remedies which might have exposed and thus defeated that effort.

If Jones had returned to the United States, as he so devoutly wished, it seems safe to assume that many of the special problems which Jones was imposing upon the community in Jonestown would have vanished, and those who resided there who wished to would have been free to leave. Yet it was Garry, who knew and often said that Jones was paranoid, who persuaded Jones that it was dangerous for him to come home, and insisted that he remain in Guyana.

To say that a paranoid personality is a paranoid, and to repeat that allegation behind his back to his friends, his aides, his supporters, and his erstwhile enemies, is not accepted treatment for the disorder. Garry exacerbated a badly deteriorating situation. With what Jones perceived to be Garry's lack of concern for the sanctity of the attorney-client privileged conversation, with Garry's physical control of the damaging Peoples Temple files, and his knowledge of the crimes they had committed, he was in a position to assist his clients out of their despair and confusion or to consign them to perdition.

Part VII

Scienter*

*SCIENTER Previous knowledge of a state of facts which it was his duty to guard against, and his omission to do which has led to the injury complained of. The term is frequently used to signify the defendant's guilty knowledge. *Black's Law Dictionary, Revised fourth edition.* (St. Paul, MN: West Publishing, 1968.)

20 What the Government Knew

Following the massacre at Jonestown, government officials within the United States apparently felt constrained to proclaim their own innocence, disingenuously stressing the unreproachable conduct of their own agencies and bureaus. The directors of the CIA and the FBI, various spokesmen for the State Department, and officials at the American embassy in Georgetown commented in self-serving declarations upon the exemplary conduct of their organizations, insisting that their escutcheons remained immaculate.

President Carter, perhaps speaking for them all, summarized the official position during a press conference held on November 30, 1978:

> In retrospect all of us can deplore what did occur. It is unconstitutional for the government of our country to investigate or to issue laws against any group, no matter how much they might depart from normal custom, which is based on religious belief. The only exception is when there are various substantive allegations that the activities of those religious groups directly violate a Federal law.
>
> I might point out that Congressman Ryan and other Congressmen did go to the Justice Department several weeks or months ago to go into the so-called brainwashing aspects of a few religious cults around the country. My understanding is that the so-called Peoples Temple was not one of those thought by them to be indulging in brainwashing. It was a recent, late development that no one, so far as I know, was able to anticipate or to assess adequately.*

The broader American societal questions raised by the unprecedented exodus of the Peoples Temple and its subsequent holocaust were rarely

*The *New York Times,* 1 December, 1978, p. A22.

addressed at home as the government and the media portrayed the deceased as little more than humanoids. Abroad it was another matter. *Pravda,* the leading newspaper in the Soviet Union, said that the available evidence shows that the victims were "People in a condition of spiritual poverty in American society" and that "they were striving for social, economic, and racial equality and justice."* The publication asserted that although religious mystics, criminal elements, and other renegades from society were among the group, the majority were unwanted people who were subjected to harassments and persecution in the United States. They lived in fear, *Pravda* continued, that even in Guyana the "punishing hand of American authorities would reach them. They were afraid for their children and they were expecting an attack upon their settlement."†

The *Pravda* analysis was basically correct in that it accurately presented the aspirations and the trepidations of the Americans who lived at Jonestown. It is not surprising that the Russian report was au courant since Russian representatives in Guyana had been in somewhat regular communication with the Americans in both Jonestown and Georgetown for much of the preceding year. The American authorities also had been regularly and intimately in contact with the Peoples Temple members, former members, supporters, and enemies of Jonestown and Georgetown as well as Ukiah, California, San Francisco, Washington, and elsewhere. One can only conclude that if President Carter truly believed, as he suggested, that only a recent surge of brainwashing in Jonestown caused the deaths there, his intelligence sources had misled him.

The Reverend Jesse Jackson, a moderate black civil rights leader whose important domestic efforts for equal education have been substantially funded by government and industry grants, offered an analysis not markedly disparate from the Soviet view. In it he said that the responsibility for the murders in Jonestown lies with the United States government "which, through rejection of people who are old and black and poor, subjected them to a search for affirmation and acceptance from any source." He added that "our following white leaders to death is not altogether new." He said "we followed them to Germany to die, to Korea, and to Vietnam," noting that the "effects of slavery are still deep in our minds."

Pravda pointed out that "the United States news media are trying to convince Americans as well as the foreign public that the deaths were the action of wild religious fanatics." That effort, however, was not entirely successful in Europe and in Asia.

*Reported in the *New York Times*, 29 November, 1978.
†Ibid.

In Stockholm, a leading newspaper, the *Dagens Nyheter,* stated, "There is a connection with the social and political development of a large generation of people."* In the Philippines, a columnist for the Manila *Daily Express* wrote, "All of the participants in this very uncivilized story are Americans, not Guyanans."† In Tokyo, *Mainichi Shimbun* reported that poor blacks who sought work and dignity in the United States were disappointed, discovered the American society to be closed to them and exclusive, and finally turned to the Peoples Temple "in search of a new world."‡

An important question remains for the United States. What responsibility must the society in general bear for the deaths of approximately one thousand of its unwanted poor? Despite efforts by the news media and the government to foreclose such a dialogue, it seems possible that those concerned with the future of this land will understand the need to carefully probe its troubled past.

A body of evidence is available that suggests responsibility for the deaths might be fixed not just generally upon the society but with telling specificity upon the government.

The evidence demonstrates that the State Department knew that if Leo Ryan conducted an investigation at Jonestown, entering the project unarmed with relevant information, and unguarded by a security force, he and others might die there. I believe it unfair to say or to suggest that State Department personnel knew or should have known that murders would occur; they must be charged with the responsibility, however, of knowing that murders might occur. That knowledge obliged them to warn Congressman Leo Ryan and his aides of the dangers inherent in the trip. That, without doubt, the State Department failed to do, according to the surviving aides and others who were present at the meeting between Ryan and the State Department.

Much of the evidence regarding what the agents of the government did to exacerbate a badly deteriorating situation in Jonestown in the months prior to the massacre remains flawed and speculative pending the declassification of the relevant data by the State Department, the American embassy in Georgetown, and the CIA and FBI. The currently available evidence is sufficiently compelling to constrain students of the matter to insist that the rest of the evidence be examined publicly. The evidence demonstrating what the government knew about the conditions in Jonestown is, however, ample and readily available. Had Ryan known what the government

*Ibid.
†Ibid.
‡Ibid.

knew, I do not believe he would have undertaken his fatal journey.

By the fall of 1977, the United States government had information which led irrefutably to the conclusion that the lives of the hundreds of Americans living at Jonestown were in jeopardy. During July 1977, the August issue of *New West Magazine* carried a long, detailed, and frightening account of Peoples Temple by Marshall Kilduff and Phil Tracy, called "Inside Peoples Temple." The allegations appeared to be sufficiently serious to warrant an official inquiry, according to one city supervisor who called for such an investigation. That month, Joseph Freitas, the district attorney of San Francisco, ordered Robert Graham, an assistant, to conduct the review. On August 28, 1977, Graham submitted a memorandum to Freitas, and to another aide containing the parameters and results of the inquiry.*

In the first paragraph, Graham reported:

> The inquiry into allegations of crimes committed in San Francisco County by Peoples Temple members began the week of July 16, 1977, after articles on the Temple appeared in the *Examiner* and *New West Magazine.* All five of the Special Prosecutions investigators have participated in the inquiry, although principal responsibility was borne by Mssrs. Reuben and Lawrence. In all, more than 70 persons have been interviewed—former PT members, current PT members, and persons reported to have knowledge of PT activities. *Little was gained from conversations with current PT members who uniformly refused much conversation with investigators on the advice of Charles Garry, PT attorney.* [Emphasis added.] After six weeks, no evidence has been developed that would warrant consideration of criminal prosecution.

The report revealed that the Special Prosecutions Unit investigated various allegations, including charges of brutality, property extortion, child abduction, kidnapping, the use of drugs against recalcitrants, and the peculiar role of Timothy Stoen. In each instance, Graham reported, there was not sufficient hard evidence of criminal conduct in San Francisco for the office to act. Regarding the use of drugs, the report said:

> *Drugs.* Some former PT members tell of the use of drugs to control recalcitrants. No one that we talked to was able to testify to observing any drugs administered at the Temple in San Francisco, however. The

*The Graham memorandum, which remained secret until December 1978, one month after the massacre, is published as Appendix B.

> commonly mentioned incident involving Danny Pietila occurred in Los Angeles.

The allegation that a recalcitrant had been involuntarily drugged in Los Angeles was dismissed for reasons of jurisdiction. A thorough look into the charges against the Temple—based in San Francisco—would have required, I believe, a closer examination of the Los Angeles incident.

Regarding the allegation that Stoen and others improperly notarized documents through which property was conveyed to the Temple, Graham wrote:

> *Notarial Violations.* The Secretary of State is looking into the possibility that PT members who were notaries committed crimes in their notarization of signatures on deeds and other documents. So far, only one of the potential crimes being investigated involves a San Francisco transaction (the Edwards deed)—and that crime, if proved, would be a misdemeanor violation of the Government Code. Continued investigations should be left to the Secretary of State.

Again the conclusion seemed to suggest shifting responsibility elsewhere. In reference to Stoen, the report stated:

> *Tim Stoen.* There are a lot of stories flying around about Tim Stoen and his role in the Temple. So far, no evidence has surfaced that would link Stoen with any criminal activity in San Francisco. The tape recording which indicated the possibility of forgery and compounding was referred to the Sheriff of Mendocino County, where the transaction occurred. We have also found no evidence to date of misconduct by Stoen as a Deputy District Attorney in San Francisco.

In the report's conclusion, Graham found that many of the practices of the Peoples Temple are "at least unsavory and raise substantial moral and non-criminal legal questions." This, when taken together with the assessment of Stoen, is the most difficult to reconcile with a sound prosecutorial approach. If Stoen had committed crimes in another county, the primary and perhaps exclusive responsibility for investigating such actions would rest with another prosecutor. Yet since virtually all of the "unsavory" actions of the Temple and its possible crimes in other counties took place while Stoen served as its attorney and one of its most prominent and inventive leaders, the lack of concern evidenced by the district attorney's report is surprising. This is particularly so in view of the fact that Joseph Freitas had hired Stoen as one of his assistants.

If Stoen had committed illegal acts in Mendocino County—possible misdemeanor violations regarding property, including property located in San Francisco; possible felonious acts, including forgery; and was an important Peoples Temple leader when other crimes and immoral acts were perpetrated—one would expect that Freitas might show a particular interest in the matter. Had Stoen confessed to Freitas his role in these actions when he applied for and subsequently secured an important position in the office of the district attorney? If so, why would Freitas have hired him? If not, did not Freitas feel that he had been euchred by Stoen when he at last discovered the odd and bizarre associations and actions of his erstwhile employee in the law enforcement business. Perhaps the final report of the San Francisco district attorney's office in this matter gives further credence to the maxim that it is unwise for officials to investigate themselves or those who are close to them. It illustrates, as well, how clever Timothy Stoen was in seeking and securing law enforcement positions while assisting his clients to avoid the provisions of the penal code.

Following the massacre, Graham conceded that neither he nor any of his five investigators had ever questioned Stoen about the serious allegations made about his conduct. Graham said that "when Stoen came back from Guyana (prior to the massacre), we asked him to talk with us about it (the charges against him) but he said it would interfere with his custody case." The prosecutors accepted that demurrer and the matter was abandoned. Had Stoen not enjoyed a close working relationship with the district attorney's office it seems doubtful that his excuse for refusing to talk with the investigators would have been accepted. The office had subpoena power; the various cases could have been submitted to the San Francisco grand jury.* Instead, the file was closed; the most important witness had not been asked a single question.

Those charged with law enforcement responsibilities declined to act during the summer of 1977 and determined to suppress the report of their own flawed investigation. Yet the record reveals that important evidence was known to them regarding the Temple some fifteen months before the massacre.

Within days after the Graham report was secreted in a file drawer in San Francisco, a telephone call was placed to a law school in that city. During the first days of September 1977, a successful and wealthy New Orleans

*Approximately one and a half years later (in December 1978), following the deaths in Guyana, Mr. Graham submitted evidence to a San Francisco grand jury regarding the violations of the law by Peoples Temple.

businessman called to speak with his daughter who was, he believed, still a student at the Golden Gate Law School. He was surprised to discover that she was no longer there.

It was Louis Gurvich, the investigator who managed to reach Jonestown to search for his daughter, Jann, after the massacre, who placed that phone call. In the past, he had assisted in locating a wayward young woman and returning her from a drug-oriented commune to her parents. When he learned that his own daughter was apparently not at law school in San Francisco, he began his inquiry in earnest. "I called contacts at Immigration," he told me, "who owned me some favors and asked if they could find out where Jann was. Two hours later they called back and said, 'Your daughter left the country on August 22, 1977.' They said they believed she had left on a charter. I knew Jann had worked with the Peoples Temple in San Francisco and I knew that group had some kind of a project in Guyana. So I called the American embassy in Georgetown and talked with Richard McCoy. He told me that he had received other calls from alarmed relatives. He knew what I was calling about. He said, 'Yes, your daughter arrived in Georgetown on August 23, and I believe that she is now in Jonestown.'

"I told McCoy that I wanted to hear from Jann or that I would be down there within a week." Gurvich then began to explore the possibility of leading a raid on Jonestown to bring his daughter back to the United States. He visited the Venezuelan Consul in New Orleans (there is no Guyanese Consul there), and secured detailed maps of the area. "I also talked with the ex-bodyguard of the shah of Iran, who was in Houston. I conferred with a combat veteran of the Vietnam war. With my own organization I could have put together twelve good men. I then began to look into the cost of renting planes. I talked with a man who knew the general area and learned that it was an intense jungle for many miles except in the proximity of deltas and the confluence of rivers.

"Then I called McCoy and I told him that I was alarmed. I said that I wanted to talk to my daughter. I did *not* tell him of my plan to go in there and try to get Jann out. He told me that he had a man going into Jonestown and he would have that man talk to my daughter immediately. He then called me back and he told me that two men had seen her and that all was well. I wanted to know if Jann could leave there if she wanted to. He said that Jann was happy there, that she liked it, that the place was fine, and that she didn't want to leave. I asked him if there was a fence or wall around the place. He said, 'No, there's no fence.' What he neglected to mention was that you don't need one. There was no way out. I did not know that then. McCoy did, but he didn't tell me.

"I told McCoy that if I did not hear from my daughter I would be coming down there. I did not say that I was coming down with support or in an effort to take her out. I felt that a threat of that nature would have been counterproductive. I loved my daughter. Of all the people in my life, I loved her the most and she loved me the most. I was determined to do anything for her. But I was going to use every conceivable method to get her out before leading a team down there. That would be buying trouble and I knew it. I knew that if I went in that way, somebody might have challenged me, and somebody might get hurt.

"After McCoy told me that his representative had seen her, and that she looked great, and that she was happy, I dropped all discussions about pricing planes and things of that nature. About two weeks later Jann called me. I didn't know that it was routed by radiotelephone through the Temple office in San Francisco and that we were being listened to from there. She told me that she was only going to be there for a year and that then she would continue her law studies. She had been at law school for two years."

Gurvich told me that he declined to move forward with the rescue operation for a number of reasons. McCoy had assured him that there were no problems at Jonestown and that Jann wanted to remain there and could leave if she wanted to. He was concerned that after mounting the operation, which would have cost, he estimated, approximately a hundred thousand dollars, it might have resulted in the wounding or killing of people if he was challenged, as he considered likely, or might have touched off a serious international incident. Worse, Jann conceivably would have declined to leave. If he had seen the San Francisco district attorney's file at that point, he might not have been so easily reassured. "I would have gone," he told me recently, "If I thought that my daughter's life was in danger.

"I began to receive letters from her. She said that she thought she could best serve humanity by teaching children and that she was going to teach history and English at both levels of primary and high school down there. The truth of the matter is, as Jann knew, that Jonestown had many virtues. At this point my fears were somewhat allayed."

Gurvich was not thoroughly convinced that his daughter could leave if she wished, although McCoy assured him that she was not being held captive and that she could return to the United States at her discretion. When Gurvich offered to send money for McCoy to hold for Jann, McCoy declined, saying that there was no need for that. Gurvich asked McCoy "to please tell me what the difficulties would be if my daughter decides to leave." McCoy responded, "I will take care of her." Gurvich told McCoy that he would send the money directly to Jann. He recalls now that "McCoy did not tell me that the mail was censored and that all the money went into Jones's trunk—maybe he didn't know."

Gurvich made one request of McCoy. He made it on more than one occasion: In telephone calls to the American embassy in Georgetown, he asked, "If ever any of the rumors about Jonestown are substantiated, will you promise me that you will call me collect, wire me collect." McCoy promised to provide him with any such information which might come his way. Gurvich, satisfied that he had done all that he could to provide for his daughter's well-being, abandoned the dangerous commando raid on the project. Yet he remained ready to reinstitute the plan upon word from McCoy that there might be a problem in Jonestown.

Within days after the move of Peoples Temple members to Guyana from San Francisco during August 1977, various relatives in the United States, motivated by the suddenness and secrecy that marked the exodus, began to inquire about conditions in Jonestown. Quickly, their concern reached the American embassy in Georgetown. In the embassy, Consul Richard McCoy had been assigned to conduct the official investigations of Jonestown for the United States government and to report back to the American ambassador, the intelligence organizations, and to the relatives who had initiated inquiries. His reports to the families were consistent. His reports to the ambassador are discussed in chapter 21 and his reports to intelligence agencies remain unavailable and shrouded in secrecy.

McCoy offered assurance to all the relatives who brought their complaints and fears to him. The conditions in Jonestown were excellent. "I just saw your daughter; she looks great and she loves it there," was his almost standard reply. He treated those who raised the questions with him as if they were suspect. McCoy assured relatives singly, in person, in telephone conversations, and in group meetings in Georgetown that he had investigated Jonestown quite thoroughly and on more than one occasion. His reports were unambiguous. The derogatory rumors were unfair, untrue, and certainly without any evidential support.

After the massacre, the State Department sought to explain away McCoy's various false statements as oversights. The department pointed out that consular employees are not, after all, FBI agents or trained investigators, and implied that McCoy was a consular official who had been playing the part of an investigator. While the general observation that many consular workers are not trained investigators may be true, the application of that principle to this situation cannot, I believe, be soundly made.

Richard McCoy was a professionally trained investigator, who had over the years been assigned to areas of conflict due to his intelligence training, skill, and background. For six years he worked for air force intelligence and, as an officer, he was given the responsibility of serving in, and helping to run, the Office of Special Investigations for the U.S. Air Force. He received a medal of commendation from the Air Force for that work. It could be said that McCoy was in fact a trained investigator playing the part of a consular official. The *New York Times* (December 8, 1978), in a puff piece, stated that after McCoy joined the State Department, "he had tours of duty in Israel, Turkey, and Yugoslavia before he was posted to Guyana in the fall of 1976." McCoy himself told a slightly different story.

When Steven Katsaris asked McCoy if it was possible that he was being fooled by Jones, who was a master at manipulation, McCoy ruled out that possibility. Katsaris later told me, "I know McCoy very well. I made three trips to Guyana and dealt with McCoy on two of them." He said that McCoy had told him that he was certain that his investigation had been thorough and that he had uncovered all of the relevant data. McCoy had offered his credentials to Katsaris, asserting that he had "spent several years in Greece while the junta was in power. 'You can't put anything over on me. I'm pretty sharp.' " Katsaris told me, "McCoy wanted to impress me that he's had some pretty difficult posts. He's worked under dictatorships. He knows how things operate and if there was anything going on sub rosa, he would know about it because he had dealt with some real manipulators."

Katsaris, who had studied the State Department's position paper, told me, "In their official document, they state that their people always saw people who they interviewed in Jonestown alone, generally walking out in the field." Since we know this is untrue, the methodology of the McCoy investigation remains a serious question—and its conclusions inaccurate.

If McCoy did his best to examine the conditions in Jonestown and to determine the desire of the residents there to remain or leave, he was a very poor investigator who was even unable to confirm allegations given to him repeatedly by many of the relatives, including Steve Katsaris. Katsaris, a former Greek Orthodox priest, who voluntarily left his position with the church to run a school for retarded children, is an impressive and determined man whose countenance is low-key and assuring. While some of the concerned relatives acted in a frenetic fashion, Katsaris was and remains a calm, controlled, and logical man even after the death of his daughter, Maria, in Jonestown. While some of the relatives were motivated by hatred, envy, political commitment, and other forces, it was clear throughout that Katsaris, like Louis Gurvich, was motivated by the love he felt for his daughter and by his concern that she was in a dangerous place. In these respects, Louis Gurvich and Steven Katsaris were very much alike. Their concern was very apparent and they did not tend to overstate the case but relied solely upon what they knew, which they carefully distinguished from what they feared and what they suspected. Katsaris and Gurvich made most compelling witnesses and sources of believable information.

During September 1977, each man communicated his fears to the relevant government agency. Each man spoke with Richard McCoy. The two men did not know each other or of each other's existence at that time.* Yet their justified fears were met with a State Department stone wall. It would be possible for a biased observer to dismiss the substance of the allegations about Jonestown, because of the manner in which some of the relatives proffered it. In the case of Gurvich and Katsaris, another approach was necessary in an effort to secure their silence and inaction. McCoy regularly assured each of them that there were no problems in Jonestown and that he and his associates had personally interviewed the residents there. That same erroneous information was later to be offered to Congressman Ryan to encourage him to embark upon his fatal journey.

During September of 1977, while the American embassy was reassuring Gurvich and Katsaris that their daughters were safe, Jim Jones was on the brink of murdering them and five hundred other Americans at Jonestown. The United States government was monitoring that near tragedy as it developed. The following May, McCoy learned through a firsthand account given to him by Debbie Blakey that many of the Jonestown residents were captives, that a number had been beaten and tortured, and that all of their lives were in danger. McCoy did not inform Gurvich or Katsaris of what he had learned. McCoy took steps to see to it that they might not learn of the evidence through any source. McCoy told Debbie Blakey not to give her evidence to the American news media.

Many mistakes in judgment and many innocent errors undoubtedly mark the road that led inexorably to the disaster on November 18. The evidence demonstrates, I believe, that the false information given to Louis Gurvich and the other relatives of the Jonestown residents by elements of the United States government was not imparted as the result of either an innocent error or a mistake in judgment.

The shadow of the eleventh-hour reprieve that prevented the murder of the five hundred Americans in Jonestown during 1977 predicted that catastrophe was closing in.

It began with a telephone call placed by Karen Layton from Georgetown to Terri Buford at the San Francisco headquarters of the Peoples Temple.

*Louis Gurvich and Steven Katsaris spoke for the first time during 1979 after I suggested to each of them that they might find some comfort in such a meeting.

Karen was desperately forwarding a message that morning which she had just received by radio from Jonestown. Terri was informed that Jones had decided that everyone in Jonestown was to die by five o'clock that evening. Stoen, Jones had said, had persuaded the courts in Georgetown that he was the lawful father of John Victor Stoen. Before he would surrender John John to the authorities, Jones said he, the child, and all five hundred residents of Jonestown would die. Sharing the proceeding hours of terror with Terri in the San Francisco office was Deborah Blakey. Radio messages from Jonestown to Terri and Debbie convinced them that the lives of the people in Jonestown were in jeopardy.

A dual strategy was adopted in an effort to forestall the mass murder. Every effort was to be made to locate Ptolemy Reid, the deputy prime minister of Guyana, who was then in the United States. Concomitantly, those leaders of leftist movements whom Jim Jones respected were to be found, briefed, and asked to tactfully urge Jones not to commit murder. Terri called Garry's assistant, Pat Richartz, who was at home in Berkeley, California. She located Garry, who was then in the Midwest. After Terri, in tears, had briefed both Garry and his aide, they understood the gravity of the situation. While Pat and Terri frantically placed telephone calls to locate Reid, Garry talked to Jones through a radiotelephone patch to urge him not to take action. Terri learned that Reid was traveling by airplane, but she was unsure of the time he was due to arrive at the airport or leave, and was not entirely sure of his ultimate destination. Pat and Terri both placed calls to local police departments at each of the possible airports in an effort to find him.

Among those who agreed to assist in calming Jones down were Huey Newton, the leader of the Black Panther party, Dennis Banks of the American Indian Movement, and leaders of the Communist party of the United States. Newton told Terri that Jones planned, not revolutionary suicide as he proclaimed, but an act of genocide against defenseless black children and elderly people. Newton was furious when he first learned of the threat. He knew, however, that righteous indignation was not called for in that sensitive moment. Both he and Dennis Banks urged Jones to hold on, to take no precipitous action, and promised to do what they could to help from their vantage point in America. A leader of the Communist party said she would begin at once to explore the possibility of an immediate move to the Soviet Union.

In a sworn statement dated June 15, 1978, Deborah Blakey stated part of her knowledge of the event. In the eleven-page affidavit,* she affirmed:

*See Appendix C.

> 17. The September, 1977 crisis concerning John Stoen reached major proportions. The radio messages from Guyana were frenzied and hysterical. One morning, Terri J. Buford, public relations advisor to Rev. Jones, and myself were instructed to place a telephone call to a high-ranking Guyanese official who was visiting the United States and deliver the following threat: Unless the government of Guyana took immediate steps to stall the Guyanese court action regarding John Stoen's custody, the entire population of Jonestown would extinguish itself in a mass suicide by 5:30 P.M. that day. I was later informed that Temple members in Guyana placed similar calls to other Guyanese officials.
>
> 18. We later received radio communication to the effect that the court case had been stalled and that the suicide threat was called off.

The Blakey affidavit was sent to Secretary of State Cyrus Vance five months before the November 18, 1978, massacre. It was also delivered at that time to the intelligence agencies, and substantial portions of the contents were published in major newspapers and were circulated by the leading news agencies.

The "suicide threat" was canceled later that day, as the Blakey affidavit states. After Deputy Prime Minister Reid was located, Marceline Jones, who had been in San Francisco, flew to a meeting with him and a member of his staff. She spoke openly of her husband's intentions. The office of the deputy prime minister was alarmed and permitted her to inform Jones that the child, John Victor Stoen, would not be taken from him. During this process Jones was persuaded that conditions had changed and at last he ended the long day of terror in Guyana.

The mechanics of how Jones planned to kill five hundred people were not known at that time, yet the participants were quite sure that the threat to do so was real. Later that year, not long before Christmas 1977, residents of the Peoples Temple in San Francisco learned of the details of Jones's plan from Jean Brown, who had just returned from a visit to Jonestown. In telling Terri Buford about her conversations with Jones, Brown said, "Jim told me that he was going to put everyone into the warehouse and burn it down with the people in it." Later, Carolyn Layton confirmed that story and offered evidence to demonstrate that Jones had been prepared to move forward with the murders. She told both Terri Buford and Debbie Blakey that "all of the babies had been given small doses of sleeping pills that day so that it would be easier to burn them to death a little later that day."

Upon Jean Brown's return from Guyana, she urged that guns be sent to Jonestown. She argued that Jones needed the weapons because death by bullets would be "more humane" than death by fire. She said that she was worried about the effects of fire upon survivors of such a disaster. She feared, she said, that people would survive only to live as vegetables. Terri, who had organized the response that prevented the deaths earlier that year, had no doubt that the death threat had been real, and that a catastrophe had been averted only at the last moment. She was adamant in opposing Jean Brown's suggestion of sending guns to Jonestown, fearing that a heavily armed Jonestown would be an even more dangerous place.

Approximately one year before the massacre, at the direction of Jim Jones, coded radio messages began to emanate from Jonestown to the Temple's headquarters in San Francisco, ordering the stateside church administrators to send weapons and ammunition to Guyana. At that time Jean Brown was employed at the Housing Authority in San Francisco, a job Jones had secured for her, and was, therefore, not present when the various Jonestown officials, including Jones himself, demanded weapons. Terri, who operated in the Temple's radio room, received the messages. In retrospect she said, "I made note of the coded words and phrases for later translation. I then pretended that the messages had been garbled and that I could not understand the request. This delaying process went on for some time. However, Debbie [Blakey] came into the radio room during one of the broadcasts. There was no way I could bar her from the room. She interpreted the order for guns accurately and then I had a very frank conversation with her."

According to Buford, she told Blakey that she strongly opposed the suggestion that Jonestown become an armed camp. She confided that she believed that Jones was irrational, that she was concerned about the safety of the people in Jonestown, and told how she had impeded the plan to send weapons out of the country. Blakey indicated her agreement.

As the demands from Jonestown for weapons became more insistent, Blakey changed her stated position and supported Jean Brown. Blakey and Brown both argued that Jones was anxious to receive the weapons and no doubt had good reasons for his stand.

At that time, according to Terri Buford, Debbie Blakey went to the room she occupied on the third floor of the Temple building and secured the funds. Blakey's room also served as the financial office. Large sums of cash, often tens of thousands of dollars, were maintained in a file cabinent in the closet in Blakey's room. Blakey gave a substantial sum to Sandy Bradshaw, who purchased some weapons and arranged for other Temple members to buy additional weapons and ammunition. Before the end of 1977, the weapons and ammunition were packed into foot lockers and duffle bags and taken to Guyana by several members of the Peoples Temple.

Toward the end of that year, soon after having made the funds available for the weapons, Debbie Blakey went to Jonestown, taking her ailing mother, Lisa Layton, with her.

Almost immediately after Debbie's arrival in Jonestown, Terri became aware that the Temple leaders there had developed a new approach to her. Regarding her radio contacts with Jones and others during that period, Terri told me, "They were cool, mistrusting, and on occasion, quite sarcastic." Early in 1978 Jones ordered Terri to return to Jonestown. Shortly after she arrived, Jones and his advisors, including Carolyn Layton, Michael Prokes, Maria Katsaris, and Harriet Tropp confronted her with a one-page typewritten letter signed by Debbie Blakey. The latter accused Terri of opposing the decision that Jones had made regarding the "mass suicide" effort the previous fall, of opposing Jim's instructions on the shipment of guns to Guyana, and of calling Jim Jones "irrational." Blakey also complained that Buford was "afraid to die."

The Blakey letter also informed Jones, quite accurately, that Buford and Eugene Chaikin had talked about getting Chaikin's children out of Jonestown so that he might be able to defect. Blakey had overheard a telephone conversation between Terri Buford and Chaikin. Jones accused Terri of "treason."

Terri, fearing for her life and knowing she might never be allowed to leave Jonestown, denied the Blakey accusations. By then Blakey was in Georgetown; she never returned to Jonestown. Weeks later she defected from Georgetown, leaving her dying mother behind in Jonestown. At the direction of Jean Brown, Blakey's brother, Larry Layton, was sent to Jonestown soon after Debbie left. He was later charged by the authorities in Guyana with murder in the deaths of Ryan and others.

After Debbie left South America with Richard McCoy, the United States Consul for Guyana, Jones gave much less credence to her charges against Buford.

The following month, when Blakey made public her sensational charges against the Jonestown community, stating that there were many weapons in the village, that people were not free to leave, and that Jones had threatened to kill the residents, she failed to disclose her own role in the events. Jones felt, not without some basis, that he had been betrayed and exposed by a former supporter.

The substance of the statements regarding the shipment of weapons to Guyana was presented by Terri Buford, under oath, to a grand jury meeting in San Francisco. Debbie Blakey and Jean Brown have been unwilling to discuss the subject with me.

While Jones favored death as the final solution of the problems that plagued him during the fall of 1977, he was, in his panic and confusion, also grasping at other straws. While overtures to the Soviet Union were being made on his behalf by the leadership in San Francisco for a full-scale and immediate exodus to Russia, Jones impetuously decided to move all five hundred residents of Jonestown to Cuba. He ordered the residents to board the *Cudjoe,* a trawler harbored near the settlement in a jungle river. Although Jones insisted that the boarding be orderly and that no one carry any extra clothing, people began to push one another and some, expecting never to return, stuffed extra clothing and other belongings under the clothes they wore. One person fell off the boat during the chaotic boarding. In a response marked by consternation, Jones, who observed that his control of the situation had slipped, and who at that moment expressed fear that the weight might exceed the limitation permitted for the freighter, called off the exodus. Later, Garry would begin to dissimilate the enormity of the entire affair by giving it the code name of Cuban shrimp-boat crisis.

In the months that followed, Jones and his aides formulated and published,* with the active participation of their attorney, Charles Garry, a philosophical foundation for what they proclaimed to be their "decision to die." Since the Temple leaders knew through threats from the Federal Communications Commission that their license would be revoked unless they conformed to standards, they further suspected that the FCC was monitoring their shortwave broadcasts from Guyana. Hence, there seemed to be no need to inform the authorities further of their commitment to die. Later, Phil Horn, chief of the Field Operations Bureau of the Federal Communications Commission, admitted that the Peoples Temple communications had been monitored over a period of eighteen months prior to November 18, 1978. During that time, numerous complaints about the abuse of the Amateur Radio Service, or shortwave ham radio, were received from hobbyists throughout the country. Even a cursory investigation of that phenomenon raises the question as to whether or not the complaints had been organized. The FCC prohibits the use of the amateur radio for business purposes except in the case of emergencies. Since there was no telephone service to Jonestown, the project relied upon the radio to conduct business

*See Appendix E.

with its San Francisco office. A very simple code was used during some broadcasts which also violated FCC regulations. Yet in this instance, as in others, the FCC did not revoke the license of the San Francisco operator, although it did harass the group with additional threats of revocation. Had the FCC revoked the license, the Temple centers would have no doubt found other acceptable means of communication. Had the FCC ignored the minor violations, the Temple would have proceeded as it did to utilize the radio to secure medical information, to permit some Jonestown relatives to communicate with their relatives, and to conduct the business of ordering food and medical supplies. The FCC chose neither of those alternatives. Rather, it issued citations and threatened to sever the group's lifeline. These acts only tended to deepen the paranoia that menaced the sanity of the leader.

During this period, according to William H. Webster, the director of the Federal Bureau of Investigation, the FBI opened a file on the Peoples Temple pursuant to a request from the office of United States Senator S. I. Hayakawa. Apparently the complaint against the Temple by Mrs. Claire Bouquet, whose son later died in Jonestown, was the basis for the FBI investigation. In a declaration before the George Washington University Law Association in early May 1979, Webster, in an attempt to exonerate his bureau, said that there had been no "intelligence error" and said that the law prohibited any restriction upon "religious groups like the Peoples Temple." He added, "We should be very, very careful about doing anything that would cause the FBI to take any action that might infringe on their freedoms, and I can't think of anything about Jonestown that causes me to think differently."

Webster's conclusion challenges one to conjure up a situation which might prompt the FBI to act. A citizen complained that she feared that her son's life was in danger. A cursory review of the evidence in the FCC file on the Peoples Temple should have confirmed her suspicions to the satisfaction of the FBI; the file should have revealed that her son may have come perilously close to having been murdered in September of 1977.

FBI agents assigned to the matter concluded only that the mother had a "very good woman's intuition" but no hard evidence that her son's life was in danger. The federal authorities, however, did have the hard evidence: They declined to share it with her and to act on it.

During the spring and early summer of 1978, the federal authorities received ample evidence that Jones might murder the members of his flock. This evidence was submitted not only to all members of the United States Senate and the House of Representatives, to the State Department, the FBI, the CIA, and the American embassy in Georgetown, but also to the United States Treasury Department, to the courts in San Francisco, and to local police forces. Ultimately, it was submitted to the American news media. The evidence took the form of affidavits, eyewitness testimony, sworn complaints filed in court, and direct statements made by witnesses who appeared to be, and in fact were, credible. It also took the form of a press conference presented from Jonestown through Charles Garry's San Francisco office via radiotelephone communication. The message was clear. The people of Jonestown would die if what they contended to be harassment continued.

On March 14, 1978, a letter was sent from the Peoples Temple on their letterhead, "TO ALL U.S. SENATORS AND MEMBERS OF CONGRESS."*

The letter stated that various government agencies, including the Treasury Department and the FCC, were "trying to initiate ways to cut off our lifelines." The letter further stated that former members of the Temple were working in concert with government agencies to destroy the Jonestown project. Cited was the improper effort by Social Security to "deny legitimate beneficiaries of their rights by cutting off all checks that were coming to Guyana." The letter stated that "lives had been saved [by the work of the Temple and the Jonestown project] that would have been meant for destruction." The specific government efforts to destroy the Jonestown project were presented together with this prologue: "We at Peoples Temple have been the subject of harassment by several agencies of the U.S. Government, and are rapidly reaching the point at which patience is exhausted."

In the event the senator or representative did not understand clearly the possible action that Jones was contemplating, the concluding sentences resolved all ambiguity:

> It seems cruel that anyone would want to escalate this type of bureaucratic harassment into an international issue, but it is equally evident that people cannot forever be continually harassed and beleaguered by such tactics without seeking alternatives that have been presented. I can say without hesitation that we are devoted to a decision that it is better even to die than to be constantly harassed from one continent to the next. I hope you can look into this matter and protect the right of over 1,000 people from the U.S. to live in peace.

The March 14, 1978, letter was subsequently distributed by Deborah Blakey and various other opponents of Jonestown, who submitted that they

*This letter is published as Appendix D.

believed the threats to be real, to the Department of State, the FBI, various courts, and to the national news media. This second circulation of the letter, together with assurances offered by his most severe critics that Jones meant what he said, took place during June 1978, five months before the massacre.

On April 11, 1978, a group of twenty-five relatives of thirty-seven children and adults residing in Jonestown submitted an accusation of "human rights violations" by Jones "against our children and relatives." The fourteen-page petition, together with several pages of supporting evidence, was delivered to a representative at the San Francisco office of the Temple on April 11.* On April 12, 1978 the San Francisco *Examiner* reported, "Led by Tim Stoen, a one-time confidant of Jones and a former assistant district attorney in San Francisco and Mendocino counties, and Steven Katsaris, a Ukiah educator, the group asked that these relatives be allowed home for a one-week visit."

The San Francisco *Chronicle* ran a brief five-paragraph story about the protest. Two of the five paragraphs were devoted to a defense of the Temple and an attack upon the concerned relatives by Charles Garry. According to the story, a "group, calling itself concerned parents, demanded that their relatives be permitted to visit the United States and cited what they claimed were violations of 'human rights' by Jones, including the prohibition of telephone calls and personal visits and censoring mail between Temple members and their families." According to the *Chronicle,* "Charles Garry of San Francisco termed the accusations 'a lot of bull—' and said the followers in Guyana named by the group 'don't want a goddam thing to do' with their relatives in this country." Garry then said "the Jonestown population has grown to 1,500 and that 'anybody who wants to leave there is free to leave.' "

The Associated Press and United Press International sent out accounts of the demonstrations. Neither the two leading San Francisco newspapers nor the wire services made mention of the most alarming allegation contained within the document they wrote about. Of the various charges made, the relatives strongly emphasized their astonishment at the Jones proclamation that he was "devoted to a decision that it is better even to die than to be constantly harassed from one continent to the next." The relatives' document focused upon that assertion in three different ways: Of the several violations complained of in the relatives' petition, the first one dealt with the decision to die. More than two pages of the petition were devoted to a discussion of the decision to die. Of the two articles of evidence submitted with the petition, one, a copy of the March 14, 1978, Peoples

*The petition and the attached documents are published as Appendix D.

Temple letter to the Congress, dealt with the decision-to-die question.

It appears that in San Francisco only the San Francisco *Progress,* a publication that does not enjoy wide circulation, printed anything at all about the most serious allegation that had been made. They quoted Stoen: "A 'collective decision to die' is not outside the realm of possibility in a completely totalitarian set-up where the leader in charge is no longer rational," the *Progress* reported.*The same story carried a reassurance by Steven Katsaris that the concerned relatives' group was "not out to break up the Temple." He was quoted as stating, "I'm not attacking Jones. We just want to see our children." The difference in approach between Stoen and Katsaris is evident. While Katsaris was indeed not attacking Jones and just trying to see his daughter, Stoen was referring to Jones as a mad dictator. If Stoen believed, as he said he did, that Jones was capable of carrying out his threat to kill the residents of Jonestown if he were harassed any further, and that it was not outside the realm of possibility, why did Stoen increase the harassment? The Katsaris approach was both pragmatic and principled. The Stoen approach, stating publicly that Jones was not rational and that he was a totalitarian leader, was both self-defeating and dangerous, given the circumstances.

The Ukiah *Daily Journal* published an editorial under the headline, "Trouble Brewing in Guyana."† The editorial revealed that "one father has even threatened to hire mercenaries to raid Jonestown and liberate his son by force. Trouble that could lead to an international incident may lie ahead."

As news stories about a planned quasi-military invasion of Jonestown were being circulated, Stoen let it be known that his close relationship with State Department officials might lead to an official U.S. government action in Guyana. In a story carrying the headline, "State Department Intervention?"‡ the Ukiah *Daily Journal* revealed, "Stoen has reportedly been moving in diplomatic channels to obtain State Department intervention in behalf of himself and his wife in securing custody of their young son." Since the evidence indicates that Stoen was not the father of the child and since Jones had told Stoen that the child and others at Jonestown would die if anyone took the child away, the use of the media to wage a psychological war against Jones seems, in retrospect, irresponsible at best, for no one knew Jones better than Stoen.

As the threats which he perceived became more menacing and more

*San Francisco *Progress*, 12 April, 1978.
†Ukiah *Daily Journal,* 26 April, 1978.
‡Ukiah *Daily Journal*, 26 April, 1978.

imminent, Jones, not unlike various national leaders, moved closer to his most militant advisors while silencing those who suggested a more moderate approach.

It is true that Jones made the ultimate decision in matters of policy, but he surrounded himself with advisors and usually listened to what they had to offer before ordering that action. However, Jones had the power, without restriction, to elevate his supporters to the position of advisor (and likewise to demote them), to heed their advice or to reject it without explanation, and to expect loyalty from them once his decision was made.

The most belligerent of his advisors was Sandra Bradshaw, stationed at the Peoples Temple office in San Francisco. The relationship between Jones and Sandy Bradshaw (she sometimes used the name Sandra Ingram and the code name Teko) was unusual even by the mores that prevailed within the Temple. She had developed a close personal relationship with Jones which was maintained for approximately nine years. Referring to herself as "Jim's hit-woman," she seemed obsessed with discussing the need to "kill traitors," and frequently talked about developing plans to carry out "assassinations" of "defectors." Bradshaw had been a probation officer in Mendocino County, and she owned weapons, including several hand guns, which she kept after she officially left her work with the police and entered the Temple. She also took with her an identification card which appeared to demonstrate a continuing relationship with police authorities and used that card, she said, to facilitate her trips in and out of the United States. She was in charge of the project of securing weapons and shipping them to Guyana, and purchased many of the weapons in her own name. Four men who worked under her supervision purchased much of the ammunition.

Jones was apparently both impressed and frightened by her dedication. It is difficult to assess his true feelings about her, especially during his last months, since his behavior patterns were so irregular. And, in order to keep his aides somewhat off balance as well as to create an aura of special concern with each of them, Jones would often speak disparagingly about the others while alone with one supporter. Yet given these restrictions, it seems likely that Jones really feared Bradshaw. While living in California, Jones would arrange to meet her approximately every six weeks in a Los Angeles motel. The meetings generally took place on a Thursday evening and were concluded by Friday morning. Jones said during that period that he thought it possible that "Sandy is trying to set me up." He regularly checked her purse to be certain that she was not carrying a tape recorder.

After Jones moved to Guyana, Sandy Bradshaw was in full charge of the gunrunning operation in the United States. During a period in which Jones was experiencing a great deal of pressure, Sandy began to request authorization from Jones to send more weapons to Guyana. This continued each evening for approximately two weeks. At that point, Jones did not want the weapons; in Jonestown he expressed his rage at Sandy for her insistence. After he unequivocally rejected her suggestion that more weapons be sent, the Georgetown office was astonished to discover that another shipment of weapons had arrived. Jones was outraged.

Another factor that made her suspect in the eyes of the Temple leadership was that despite her almost fanatical devotion to the Temple and its work, repeated public and private defenses of the Jonestown project, and an eagerness to undertake dangerous assignments, Sandy Bradshaw was reluctant to go to Jonestown. The leadership, suspecting that police agents may have been placed in their organization, often stated that such agents could be neutralized at the settlement. The great reluctance of Bradshaw to spend time in Jonestown, therefore, was seen by the leaders there as a possible clue to whom she might really be.

Jones was familiar with Bradshaw's background and viewed some of her actions since joining the Temple as counterproductive. He seemed to be concerned about her, and she remained the only Temple member whom he said he feared. Yet so enlarged was Jones's own ego that he felt it likely that whatever Sandy Bradshaw's motivation may have been when she came to the Temple, he had won her over with his personal charm, his special attention to her, and his political commitment.

Events so conspired that when Stoen, also formerly with Mendocino County law enforcement, placed threats against the Temple from the outside, Jones turned for assistance to his extremists on the inside, led by Bradshaw. At a press conference in April 1978 where Stoen charged that Jones was irrational, a dictator, and the warden of a prison camp that he had named after himself, Jones unleashed Sandy Bradshaw to respond. While Garry thundered "Bull crap," his favorite expression, Sandy Bradshaw, using the name Sandra Ingram, was quoted as stating that all of the allegations made by the Concerned Relatives were "malicious lies."* She pointed to what she said was a U.S. embassy report from Guyana, which said, "People are very happy [in Jonestown] and want to remain in Guyana." (She, herself, was still declining to go there, however.) She personally attacked the relatives, calling them "dictators" and then demanded that the press not carry the story of their charges. She concluded, "We're very concerned that nothing be printed in the press until the whole side [sic]

*Santa Rosa *Press Democrat,* 12 April, 1978.

of the story is given." Of course, one could hardly calculate a response more likely to assure press coverage than a demand to newspapers that they remain silent.

The other side of the story was presented within days by Charles Garry. A press conference over which he presided was held in his law office on April 17, 1978. The San Francisco *Progress* referred to it as a "peculiar press conference" because while it took place in Garry's office on Market Street, the news was coming from the nearby Peoples Temple at 1859 Geary Street. The news consisted of a series of statements, live from Jonestown to the Geary Street building via radio and then patched by telephone through to Garry's office. Since Garry always insisted upon presiding over all information reaching the news media about his client, he began the conference by denying all of the charges that had been made against Jonestown, assuring the reporters that each of the residents could leave if he or she wished. He said, however, that the children would not go home for a visit, explaining "they've got schools, they've got programs, and frankly we don't trust the people." The people that Garry said he did not trust were the relatives, including the parents, of the Jonestown residents. He then told the reporters that he would personally make arrangements for the parents to visit their children if they were willing to pay their own transportation. He said that he would arrange for the families to meet privately in Jonestown.

The major portion of the news conference was taken up by a statement read by Harriet Tropp. It focused on the question of the decision to die if necessary. It concluded, "We make no apologies" for having expressed that philosophy. At great length, the statement sought to defend that position. With Jones seated beside her in the radio room in Jonestown, Harriet Tropp, with rising emotion and anger, spoke to the reporters in San Francisco. She said, "If people cannot appreciate that willingness to die, if necessary, rather than to compromise the right to exist free from harassment and the kind of indignities that we have been subjected to, then they can never understand the integrity, honesty, and bravery of Peoples Temple nor the type of commitment of Jim Jones and the principles he has struggled for all his life."

Various relatives in Jonestown also read prepared statements condemning their families and praising Jim Jones.

The conference was concluded. A five-page press statement, comprised almost entirely of the words read by Harriet Tropp, was then widely distributed to the news media. Following her explanation of the decision to die, the statement contained a few words of Charles Garry's. He said of Jonestown, "I have been to Paradise. It's there for anybody to see. . . . When I returned to the States, I told my law partners in the office that I had seen Paradise."*

After the massacre, the International Relations Committee of the House of Representatives asked the State Department for a report on the affair. In a letter to Congressman Clement J. Zablocki, the chairman of the committee, the State Department reported that "The Embassy initiated a policy (not customary in normal consular practice) of scheduling periodic visits by consular officers to Jonestown to follow up on these inquiries." The State Department revealed that McCoy had himself visited Jonestown three times between August 1977 and May 1978. A fourth visit to Jonestown, the State Department said, was made by other officials on February 2, 1978, and a fifth visit by still other officials on Novedmber 7, 1978.

This official report places in jeopardy the McCoy report to Gurvich previously referred to. During September 1977, McCoy had assured Gurvich that he "had a man going into Jonestown" and that the man would talk to Jann Gurvich immediately. Subsequently McCoy telephoned Gurvich to persuade him that all was well and that there was no need for him to journey to Guyana. Gurvich told me, "McCoy called me and he told me two men have seen her and that all is well." If the State Department is correct in its letter to the congressional committee, no such visit ever took place, and McCoy may have fabricated the story to keep Gurvich from attempting to see his daughter in Jonestown.

McCoy's reports to Katsaris also bore little relationship to the facts. Katsaris told me that McCoy was sanguine about all aspects of life in Jonestown. Katsaris recalled that McCoy told him, "We have a representative that goes up there—he sees no guns, people are well fed, they seem happy." McCoy said that the representative of the embassy is "able to talk to them [Jonestown residents] in private and no one has expressed any desire to come home." It was McCoy's conclusion that "what you have is some hysterical people who are distorting reality," because they felt so strongly about their relatives having left home.

The methods McCoy employed to investigate, when he did visit Jonestown, were predictably self-defeating. He openly endangered the security of possible Jonestown dissidents and undermined the potential effectiveness of his inquiry by providing, sometimes weeks in advance of the interviews, a list of those he wished to question. This method made each person so named a suspect to Jones and his loyalist followers. Jones knew, of course, that logic required that he offer some reason to McCoy for his desire to secure

*The five-page press statement is published as Appendix E.

the names so far in advance of the interviews. Often the Peoples Temple loyalists in Georgetown told McCoy that the names were needed in advance since the residents might be "out in the bush hunting." While McCoy evidently accepted the subterfuge that the Temple organized hunting parties into the bush where dangerous animals lived, he told the relatives that he had no knowledge that any weapons were present in Jonestown.

Later, the State Department was to report in retrospect that McCoy took extraordinary precautions to ensure the integrity of his interviews and the security of any dissident Jonestown residents. These conclusions appear to conflict with the known facts.

The list of names moving from the embassy to the Temple officials adumbrated the meetings between McCoy and those he questioned in Jonestown. In an affidavit executed on June 15, 1978,* Debbie Blakey stated that ". . . the efforts made to investigate conditions in Jonestown are inadequate for the following reasons. The infrequent visits are always announced and arranged. Acting in fear for their lives, Temple members respond as they are told. The members appear to speak freely to American representatives, but in fact they are drilled thoroughly prior to each visit on what questions to expect and how to respond."

Terri Buford corroborated the sworn allegations made by Debbie Blakey. Terri told me that Sharon Amos was one of the persons assigned to drill the residents before McCoy questioned them. Sharon and others would conjure up every conceivable question that they could imagine that McCoy might think of and then brief their students on the acceptable answers. If the question was designed to determine if the residents received an adequate diet, the suspected dissidents would be informed to respond specifically: "For breakfast, it varies. Sometimes we have pancakes, other times a couple of eggs each and sometimes I don't feel like anything more than cereal and a couple of pieces of toast." The extensive and intricate drilling was, as it developed, barely necessary. McCoy rarely asked probing questions.

Although the State Department later reported that McCoy had always asked for individuals not on the list he had provided, in order to effect spontaneous meetings, we know through Debbie Blakey and other Temple members that this did not happen.

The embassy practice of affording Jones an advance look at the names might have resulted in a tragic event long before November 18. Had a relative inquired about Lovie Jean Lucas, that practice could quite possibly have resulted in her death. Jones was worried that she might be frank with

*See Appendix C.

McCoy about the weapons, the poor quality of the food, or her intermittent desire to leave the project. She was a senior citizen who was not reluctant to complain about the conditions. Jones told Jack Barron, another senior, to enter into a sexual relationship with her. Jones saw two advantages that might result from the union. Lovie Lucas might complain less with a new love in her life, and if she did continue to have reservations about Jonestown she would share them with Barron, who would waste no time in informing Jones. In that fashion, Jones learned that she was upset because the walkway in front of her house was in a state of disrepair. Jones, at once, sent a work crew to fix it. In spite of these special efforts, Lucas continued to find fault and Jones lived in fear that McCoy might talk to her.

While Jones was in the radio room with Terri Buford one day, he noticed Lucas walking down a nearby path. He terrified Buford by saying to her, "That's one woman who is going to have to die if the American Consul wants to talk to her." He said, "Tell Larry [Dr. Larry Schacht] that I want a report back tonight from him. I want him to find some way to have a person die so that it will look like natural causes." He then explained to Buford that if Lucas's name was on the list, she would have to die. Terri suggested an alternate solution. She said that if Geraldine Bailey, a senior citizen who was a fine actress, studied the mannerisms of Lovie Lucas, she could meet McCoy as Lucas if the circumstances required it. Jones appeared to accept the compromise, for he agreed with Buford that McCoy was so indifferent that in all likelihood, he would not notice a switch.

Although McCoy states, and the State Department agrees, that McCoy met with those he interviewed in private sessions, various Jonestown residents recall numerous interviews conducted by McCoy in the main pavilion with one high-ranking Jonestown aide pretending to sweep the floor in the immediate vicinity.

Since McCoy knew, and knew that the interviewee knew, that the place was an armed camp, offers by the unarmed, often unaccompanied consul officer to drive dissidents out of Jonestown were often met with a degree of healthy skepticism. No one was quite sure how the proposed trip might be accomplished, including McCoy.

During early 1978, Sharon Amos, Marceline Jones, and Terri Buford met with McCoy at his office in the American embassy in Georgetown. The three women assured him that if John Victor Stoen were taken from Jonestown, the entire community would be committed to death. Sharon said that her children would never be able to feel secure at Jonestown if a child, John John or any other child, had been taken away. She assured McCoy that the entire community had discussed the matter thoroughly, voted on the question, and had agreed to die together if the child were forced to leave. Sharon began to cry uncontrollably. Marceline sobbed. McCoy sat there watching the two women cry. He said to her, "I think that you are overreacting."

On another occasion when Peoples Temple representatives visited McCoy at his office, they initiated a discussion after McCoy had temporarily left the room. They presumed that the room was equipped with an electronic recording device. During McCoy's absence, they spoke to each other about the decision to die in the event of further harassment by Stoen, his accomplices, and those in the United States government. They chose that unusual method in a desperate effort to gain the attention of the authorities.

Early in 1978, McCoy was promoted to political officer for Guyana, Surinam, and Trinidad; he was in charge of the State Department desk in Washington, D.C., for those countries. During May 1978, shortly before he was transferred from Guyana, McCoy met with Sharon Amos and Terry Carter, Tim Carter's sister.

Jones and his followers had heard rumors that Stoen and others were planning an armed assault against them and preparing to kidnap some of the residents from the project. Several different individuals were exploring the feasibility of such an effort and one newspaper (the Ukiah *Daily Journal,* April 26, 1978) had speculated about an invasion of Jonestown by mercenaries.

It was, in fact, the tardy arrival of that newspaper article in a package along with many other news accounts that lead to an astonishing dialogue in McCoy's office. When the material arrived in Jonestown, sent there by Jean Brown, Terri Buford began to read and analyze it. When she came across the published plans for a possible invasion of Jonestown, she had called it to the attention of Jim Jones.

During that period, Gordon Lindsay, who was also preparing an exposé of the Peoples Temple for the *National Enquirer,* rented an airplane and flew low over the project several times. The plane buzzed over the people in the little village and in the fields. Elderly people became frightened. Jones and others, however, thought that the plane was likely on a reconnaissance mission and a precursor to an invasion. Later, when they discovered that the plane was not licensed in Guyana, their concern turned to panic. Jones then immediately ordered Sharon Amos and Terry Carter to meet with McCoy and tell him of their fears. When McCoy was told about the concern that there might be an armed attack on Jonestown, he thought for a moment and then urged the Temple to take action.

Regarding the plane buzzing over the compound, McCoy could not have been more blunt. This former air force intelligence officer advised the two women that if their air space was violated they should shoot down the plane. Both McCoy, for the American embassy, and Charles Garry, as counsel for Jones, had given the same advice: Secure weapons in order to fire upon intruders who might violate upon the property.

Terry Carter and Sharon Amos rushed back to the Georgetown house maintained by the Temple and immediately made radio contact with Jonestown. Karen Layton received the message from Terry Carter. Terri Buford was present in the radio room in Jonestown. Carter was excited. She said, "McCoy told us to shoot down the plane."* She continued, "Our mouths almost fell to the floor. We thought Jim should know at once. We can't figure out what it means."

Jones, who considered himself a revolutionary, was challenged by this militant advice of a bureaucrat as soon as it was relayed to him. He, too, was baffled by the event but was anxious to make sure that the evidence was beyond dispute. He asked at once, "Was McCoy's statement recorded?" When the reply was negative, he became furious.

Jones was a brilliant strategist and tactician. He felt that the reports reaching him through his intelligence apparatus were of importance and he, therefore, took precautions to ensure their accuracy. As mentioned earlier, Jones had studied the intelligence-gathering operations of organizations, such as the FBI, that relied heavily upon untrained informants. He had concluded that such sources were often suspect due to the desire of the agent to embellish the events or place a subjective interpretation upon the facts. To avoid these obvious pitfalls, Jones carefully chose those he assigned to such work. His first rule was that a minimum of two investigators be assigned to each project. To minimize the possibility of complicity between the two, he deliberately selected two people who were unfriendly toward each other; in important assignments, he chose those who despised one another.

Terry Carter and Sharon Amos hated each other. The enmity flowed from the circumstances that surrounded their lives. Terry was an attractive young woman married to Lew Jones, one of the leader's adopted sons. She had recently had a child, the first baby born to a settlement member in Guyana. She spent time with her child and with her husband. Sharon, less attractive and considerably older, did not have an ongoing relationship with a man. Her three children ranged in age from approximately eight to twenty. She constantly pointed out that she had given up her children for the movement and that Terry had not.

*This discussion, and all similar reports, were coded.

When it seemed necessary for the Temple workers to remain up all night working, Terry would suggest that they drink a cup of coffee. Sharon, a strict Temple fundamentalist, objected to that departure from the rules; Jones had suggested that the Georgetown personnel not drink it, since it was expensive. Sharon felt that five hours of sleep was sufficient for her and therefore for others at the Georgetown office. The rest of the time she insisted should be devoted to work. When Terry pointed out that many people, Sharon included, functioned more efficiently with a little more rest, Sharon accused Terry of "setting her own subjective standards" which exposed her lack of real commitment.

Terry Carter was an extremely accurate reporter. She possessed a fine memory and desire to record unadorned the events she monitored. Sharon Amos was a psychologist and had been a social worker. She tended to analyze events and to utilize her own nonobjective judgment to delve into the real meaning of occurrences. Her analysis was often accurate, always interesting, and on occasion, somewhat alarmist. The noncongenial Carter-Amos team became a fount of accurate data. If either ever offered an allegation not soundly based upon what they had learned together, the other was quick to point out the error.

When Jones heard Amos and Carter agree about McCoy's advice to arm, he was convinced that the report was accurate. But he wondered if McCoy, who had been so helpful in assisting to falsify the record and in rebutting the complaints—including the justified complaints—of relatives, was really on their side. Jones, bemused at his suggestion, also wondered if McCoy was trying to trap him into efforts to secure weapons and then use the seizure of the weapons in transit as an excuse to crack down on the Jonestown commune. Jones reasoned that in the event the latter was true, his first line of defense would be a tape-recorded statement by McCoy. Consequently, Jones ordered Carter, Amos, and Blakey to return to the embassy the following day to tape-record McCoy's advice.

The subsequent meeting was not helpful. Unknown to the Temple members, Blakey had decided to defect and had been meeting secretly with McCoy; later that evening she and McCoy left Georgetown together for the United States. During the second meeting with McCoy, Terry Carter carried the tape recorder in her purse. McCoy, delicately sidestepping all relevant questions, stared at the purse. At the time, Amos and Carter wondered how he had learned of the presence of the recorder in the purse. They thought at first that some electronic scanning device might have located it. After news reached them of Debbie's defection with McCoy, they had a better understanding of McCoy's actions.

Prior to the alarming suggestion by McCoy that the Temple should arm itself, McCoy had worked industriously to win the confidence of the Jonestown and Georgetown leadership. Jones and the more astute among his advisors puzzled over the conundrum. Why, they wondered, was the American embassy assisting them in covering up conditions at a settlement, avowedly communistic in word and—they felt—deed? Why aid a project that issued statements hostile to American foreign policy, aligned itself politically with the Soviet Union and the third world countries, and had supported voices for dissent, including the Black Panther party, the American Indian Movement, and antiwar demonstrators within the United States? The Peoples Temple was the type of organization that the CIA and FBI would target for destruction. Indeed, it was more militant and far more vulnerable than many organizations the CIA and FBI had acted against illegally and, on occasion, violently.

McCoy had presented himself as a bumbling diplomat to the Temple personnel. He gave no evidence to them of the years he had spent in intelligence for the air force or of his government work during the time of the Greek junta. They could not know that for his service in Guyana, the State Department had bestowed upon him its Superior Honor Award for "exceptional and most exemplary service" or that after the massacre, as the State Department began to obfuscate the record, its spokesman would concede that "it's been invaluable to have him [McCoy] here [in Washington] during the crisis." They saw him as he presented himself, a quiet, somewhat antigovernment career man who was so fair and so fond of the Temple that he would and did betray his commitment to the embassy to secure and report inside information correctly to them.

After the massacre, McCoy apparently was enjoined from speaking to the news media by the State Department. Nevertheless, a few of his words began to filter through. The Associated Press on December 5, 1978, reported that documents found in Jonestown after the massacre demonstrate that "Jim Jones maintained much closer relationships with United States Embassy Consular officials in Georgetown, Guyana, than has so far been officially acknowledged." The documents acquired by the Associated Press reveal that McCoy told the Temple personnel that when asked about Jonestown he "tells people that no allegations have been proven against" Jonestown and that the project is made up of "decent, law abiding citizens who are trying to help develop Guyana."

The documents also include a memorandum prepared by Sharon Amos on April 4, 1978. Here she reported that she had telephoned McCoy to complain that the American embassy was spreading rumors about Jim Jones, claiming that he was an atheist. McCoy told her that according to

John Blacken, who was the deputy chief of the mission, Jones was starting to doubt the existence of God. After sharing that confidence with Amos, McCoy said that he doubted that Blacken was distributing the story, since he was not the type of person to spread rumors. He explained, "John was very sophisticated in knowing what to say and what not to." McCoy then promised Amos that he would "discreetly find out who was the one in the embassy that was talking." Having informed on one member in the mission, McCoy had apparently agreed to locate another and betray him to the Peoples Temple as well. Little wonder that Jones was bewildered and disconcerted by McCoy's performance.

In another memorandum, Terry Carter complained that after McCoy left in May, his replacement, Douglas Ellice, was reluctant to give advance notice to the Temple of the names of the people he "had to see by request of some letters" he had received. Carter reported, "I said Dick [McCoy] always told us who he had to see. I felt he [Ellis] was reluctant about this though, it was like he would tell us when he got there so we couldn't brief them." Another memorandum made a similar complaint. "We were told by McCoy that we would never have to go through this again. It is upsetting people because in the past, Dick McCoy has always told us who."

Evidently, Ellice was properly briefed subsequently by the Temple. In the middle of September 1978, Sharon Amos showed Terri Buford the list provided by the embassy of those who were next to be interviewed. The interviews did not take place until November of that year.

Jones had concluded before May 1978 that he wanted no more weapons on the project. He continually and with growing anger rebuffed Sandy Bradshaw's entreaties to accept more weapons. However, now that the man he conceived of—not without some factual basis—as his inside contact at the embassy, was leaving the country and advising him to secure weapons, he changed his mind. He acquired additional artillery, including semiautomatic weapons, to shoot down those who encroached upon his territory and sought to destroy him.

On November 18, 1978, just six months after McCoy had advised the settlement to acquire weapons quickly, some of those weapons were utilized against people Jones believed had come to Jonestown to destroy him. Before the day was over, those weapons killed Congressman Ryan and four others at the Port Kaituma airstrip and, in addition, were responsible for hundreds of deaths at Jonestown. Within two weeks after the massacre, Thomas Reston, a State Department spokesman, issued a statement which the *New York Times* of December 2, 1978, featured on its front page. Reston said that it was "absolutely clear from the record" that the "[State Department and the American embassy in Georgetown had] discharged their responsibilities fully and conscientiously." He added, "In fact, we believe it is safe to say that more attention has been devoted by the United States government to this particular group of Americans living overseas over the past eighteen months than to any other group of Americans living abroad."

After McCoy gave his final briefing to the Temple members, he flew to the United States with Debbie Blakey on May 13, 1978. During that flight, Blakey told him in specific detail of the reasons she feared for her own safety and for the lives of those she had left in Jonestown, including her mother and her brother. Debbie had been a trusted aide to Jim Jones and she had occupied positions of importance at Jonestown and, before that, in San Francisco. She was a signatory on the foreign accounts maintained by the Temple and had, in that capacity, traveled to both Switzerland and Panama on more than one occasion. She knew where the money was banked, she knew how many weapons were in Jonestown, and she was intimately familiar with the problems which beset the community.

Blakey had planned to leave Georgetown on May 12, 1978, but the American embassy said it was unable to secure a ticket for her on the plane leaving that evening. Instead, a ticket was arranged for the next day, which was Jim Jones's birthday. It was widely known and appreciated in Jonestown that the leader's birthday was a special event. Those who knew Jones could have predicted that Blakey's departure on his birthday would be seen by him as an especially vindictive betrayal. Terry Carter and other Temple loyalists met Debbie at the airport in Georgetown and pleaded with her not to leave. She said that she had made up her mind and then turned to her traveling companion, Richard McCoy, and asked him if she should hold a press conference about conditions in Jonestown upon her return to the United States. His answer was lost on that occasion in the general confusion.

Once airborne, Blakey told McCoy that the situation in Jonestown threatened the lives of all who lived there.* She said that she believed that all of their lives were in danger. She told him that the radio messages from Guyana during the fall crisis of 1977 were frenzied and hysterical and that the entire population of Jonestown was on the edge of death, expecting to die at 5:30 P.M. that day. She told McCoy that no one was permitted to leave the settlement unless on special assignment and that the place was "swarming with armed guards." She told McCoy that the food was "woefully inadequate" and that many of the residents were ill. She said that Jones's

**State Department Report*, p. 10.

paranoia had reached a new and higher level and that he was reacting violently to media criticism.

In addition, Blakey told McCoy that "there was constant talk of death" and that in Jonestown the concept of "mass suicide" was discussed. She said that because the lives of the people in Jonestown were so difficult and because people there were afraid to contradict Jones, the concept of mass suicide was not challenged. She imparted to McCoy that a "white night," or state of emergency, was regularly declared in Jonestown. During such a crisis, she said, the population was told that mercenaries in the bush were closing in on the settlement and that death could come to them at any moment. She told McCoy that during one "white night," the people were informed that the situation was hopeless and that their response had to be a mass suicide. Approximately fifty guards, many armed with crossbows, moved from one cabin to another to make certain that everyone attended the meeting. At the meeting, she told McCoy, all of the inhabitants were required to line up, pass through a line, and drink a small glass of red liquid. They were told that they had drunk poison and would die in less than one hour. Later, Jones told the population that there had been no poison in the liquid and that he had just wished to test their loyalty. Jones added, according to Blakey, that the time was not far off, however, when it would be necessary to die by their own hands. She told McCoy that the results of all of his interviews had been predetermined, since Jones had been given advance notice of those to be questioned. Blakey told McCoy that she herself had been so worn down by the life and tension at Jonestown that she had become indifferent as to whether she lived or died.

McCoy urged Blakey *not* to tell the American press what she knew about Jonestown. When she asked him for advice about whom to brief about the situation that threatened the lives of her mother, her brother, and many of her friends, he again urged her not to reveal what she knew to the news media and suggested that instead she might talk to agents from the Federal Bureau of Investigation. A few days later, when Blakey called McCoy and asked him if she might talk to reporters about conditions at Jonestown, again he discouraged her from alerting the press. On December 1, 1978, Thomas Reston, speaking for the State Department, acknowledged that McCoy "in two conversations" had "advised Deborah Layton Blakey, a defector from Jonestown, not to 'go to the press' with her allegations of abuse and of a suicide plan at the Peoples Temple."* Reston sought to explain McCoy's conduct by stating that he had told Blakey to "contact

**New York Times,* 2 December, 1978.

Federal law-enforcement agencies." When Reston was asked what would have prevented McCoy from getting in touch with those authorities, Reston replied "nothing." Reston was then asked if McCoy's failure to contact those federal law enforcement authorities was a "lapse" on McCoy's part. Reston said that he had not heard that question discussed at the State Department. The assembled press corps evidently felt that the questions had been answered and McCoy's conduct satisfactorily explained since no other questions were directed toward that subject.

McCoy's failure to act moved Debbie Blakey into action. On June 15, 1978, she swore to an eleven-page statement that included all of the allegations she had made to McCoy on the trip to the United States.* Additional details were provided and other areas explored as well. That affidavit was sent to the Secretary of State, Cyrus Vance, and to the Federal law enforcement authorities that McCoy had neglected to brief.

In mid-June 1978, Blakey went to the press. She told Marshall Kilduff of the San Francisco *Chronicle* her view of the Jonestown settlement. Kilduff quoted Blakey as saying there were "two hundred to three hundred rifles, twenty-five pistols, and a homemade bazooka" in Jonestown. Kilduff did not reveal that Blakey had failed to mention such an extensive arsenal in her affidavit. Neither did he report McCoy's urging Blakey not to go to the press with her allegations. The sensational, one-sided Kilduff story containing both accounts, observations, and some exaggerated claims was picked up by the Associated Press and United Press International and published in a few newspapers throughout the country on June 15, 1978. The media focused on the false charge that "the Temple fields are patrolled by two rings of khaki uniformed, armed guards who have access to two hundred to three hundred rifles, twenty-five pistols, and a home made bazooka." They reported Blakey's allegation that Jones was "paranoid" and that the lives of the people in Jonestown were in jeopardy. The network television news programs did not run Blakey's account of life in Jonestown. Neither did the newspapers in New Orleans. Consequently Louis Gurvich was not warned of the trouble ahead for his daughter, Jann. He still waited for the promised telephone call from Richard McCoy, who had agreed to notify him if ever he received any evidence of potential trouble in Jonestown. The warning from McCoy never came. Months later he was notified that his daughter had perished at Jonestown.

McCoy and his superior at the State Department had routinely informed those who complained about the quality of life and the threat of death in Jonestown that they were unable to act on rumor. McCoy often said to those

*See Appendix C.

who pleaded for intervention on behalf of their relatives that "if one responsible person leaves Jonestown and gives us a firsthand account of any problem there—if any of these rumors about suicide plans or guns are confirmed by some evidence, then you will see your government act."* When Blakey left, McCoy received the evidence that he had often asserted that he was seeking. Blakey was a valuable source of data since she had been one of the most important aides to Jones. If she was inclined to exaggerate, each of her claims should have been carefully examined. McCoy and the State Department had received, in Blakey's defection, her oral statements and her unsworn written statement affidavit: enough corroboration to act. McCoy's only action, apparently, was an attempt to silence Blakey.

In California, where the Blakey allegations were published, Stephen Katsaris became even more alarmed.

Katsaris had heard members of the Concerned Relatives discuss plans for armed intervention in Jonestown. He never approved of such loose talk and reasoned that Jones, had he heard of plans for an invasion, would have reacted in a threatening manner. He told me, "I always was extremely severe on any member of the Concerned Relatives group at any meetings that talked about anything but legal ways to get our relatives out. There were always people who said, 'We ought to get some commandos and go down there.' I would always say I didn't want to hear that and 'I don't want that kind of talk here. You are playing right into Jim Jones's paranoia. We are going to put pressure on the State Department and we are going to have demonstrations and we are going to do whatever we can legally do to have our relatives come home to visit us or so that we can go down there to see them.' "

While Katsaris remained the last voice of reason and restraint, always bearing in mind the safety of his daughter, Stoen continued to speak in terms of "destroying Jonestown."

Stoen had moved to Washington, D.C., and opened a "secret office" there to urge congressional support for his custody case. When Terri Buford and Marceline Jones visited Washington to answer some of the charges that Stoen had made, they discovered how extensive and effective his lobbying effort had been. An administrative assistant to a United States senator told them that Stoen had preceded them, had been almost everywhere, and had an office in Washington. The aide said she was under orders not to reveal Stoen's office address or telephone number.

Stoen's handiwork in Washington and his personal briefing sessions with

*Various relatives, including Katsaris and Gurvich, have reported on McCoy's assurances.

Congressman Leo Ryan were successful. The congressional trip to Guyana was arranged. Steven Katsaris, Blakey, and various State Department officers briefed Ryan on the eve of his departure for South America. By then, Katsaris was determined to see to it that his daughter would be given a fair opportunity to make a most important decision in her life. He and his son, Anthony, had agreed to accompany Ryan into Jonestown. After the massacre, Katsaris told me of his plan. He and his son were going to approach Maria in Jonestown and ask her to leave with them. If she refused, they were going to use the tranquilizers they had brought. In either event, the plan called for the three members of the family to board a truck and drive down the Jonestown road into Port Kaituma. Since Steven Katsaris had not been to Jonestown, he shared the plan with Debbie Blakey and asked if she could brief him about "the security setup down there."

Debbie said, "It won't work."

Karsaris replied, "Surely I'd be able to drive faster than they could run."

Blakey told Katsaris, "When you get to the main gate you will see the chain across the road and they have a sentinel posted there."

Katsaris said, "So what the hell will they be able to do? The press will be there, a congressman will be there. What are they going to do? I'll drive right through the chain."

Debbie Blakey said, "Steve, they will shoot you."

Katsaris did not believe that shots would be fired at him.

The plan was not realized for a number of reasons. Only four relatives were chosen to accompany Ryan; Anthony was chosen, but Steve Katsaris was not. After Anthony spoke with Maria, he was satisfied that she would not have left voluntarily and that she would have resisted all efforts to remove her. Months after the events of November 18, Steven Katsaris told me that he had sought just one last opportunity to tell Maria what he believed about Jones and Jonestown. Had she accompanied him to California, he planned to tell her what he had learned and then to listen to her response. If she replied that she was familiar with the events and in fact supported the very actions which her father abhorred, he would have, he told me, been terribly saddened. "But I would have given her a first-class airplane ticket back to Georgetown and told her that she was entitled to follow her own conscience. I would have experienced a great loss if she left, but I would have felt that I had done everything I could."

Unlike Katsaris, who could not believe that the flight toward Port Kaituma might end in death, Blakey and Stoen knew that it might. They had been to Jonestown as architects of the environment there, they had each been in leadership positions with the Peoples Temple for the better part of a decade, and they had shared their knowledge with the State Department on many occasions and in many ways.

On May 3, 1979, a report commissioned by Secretary of State Cyrus R. Vance was published by the State Department. It was written by two retired senior foreign service officers. While the *Los Angeles Times* carried the news of the report as its front page feature story with the headline running across all eight columns, the *New York Times* relegated the story to page fourteen. *New York Times* readers expecting to find an in-depth analysis of the important 102-page State Department report in the Sunday issue of May 6 were met by a one-paragraph, two-sentence summation there instead.

The *New York Times* had devoted a great deal of front-page coverage to events quite peripheral to the Jonestown massacre for weeks prior to the publication of the State Department white paper. Many of those stories were designed to point the finger of suspicion away from the government agencies. The massacre was, in terms of media coverage, by far the biggest story of 1978 and one of the biggest stories of the last century. Yet the *New York Times* treated the first official report on the causes of the massacre as a matter of little concern. Perhaps that is because the report, while wrapped in layers of diplomacy, nethertheless pointed to grave errors by government personnel that might have led to the deaths in Jonestown. Since this newspaper had already concluded that such thoughts were entirely false, irresponsible, and dangerous and should be suppressed, the State Department report was hardly to be welcomed at the editorial offices of the *New York Times.*

The government knew that Jones was in control of the fate of more than one thousand Americans residing in Guyana. It had been informed that he had used drugs to control recalcitrants in his group even in the United States, where he was able to exercise less perfect authority.

The government knew that Jones and his aides had spoken publicly and often of their decision to die in the event that they perceived further government interference directed at their project. The government had been informed that Jones and his supporters had practiced suicide drills and that during September 1977, he came perilously close to murdering the five hundred residents who then comprised the village of Jonestown. The government had been informed that since that time Jones had amassed an arsenal of hundreds of weapons, including rifles, pistols, and a bazooka. The government was told by a person in a position to know the facts that the people of Jonestown had lost their liberty and were likely on the verge of losing their lives. While Jones was in almost total control of the destiny of the residents of the commune, the government discovered, on November 7,

1978, just a few days before Ryan was to visit the area, that Jones was likely drugged and no longer in control of himself.*

Thus the government knew that if Rep. Ryan and his media entourage insisted upon entering Jonestown, they and others might die. Yet the United States government took no steps to prevent the confrontation and by denying Ryan and his staff access to the relevant and crucial information in its possession, encouraged them to take that fateful trip.

*See pages 365 and 39 of this work.

21 What the Government Disclosed

About six months after the deaths in Guyana, a report of the first official study about the occurrence was released by the State Department. It was entitled, "The Performance of the Department of State and the American Embassy in Georgetown, Guyana in the Peoples Temple Case." The work was conducted by John Hugh Crimmins and Stanley S. Carpenter, both retired senior foreign service officers. The report is a serious document in that it publishes a wealth of factual data not previously available. Unfortunately, its authors interviewed only persons associated with the United States government, including State Department and embassy officers, and declined to interview others who were present at crucial meetings with government officials, and who might have broadened the findings of the report by offering both substantiating and contradictory testimony.

In addition, the report stated that the massive files of the Federal Bureau of Investigation relevant to the investigation were not examined. Even State Department and embassy "material that has been made part of the current investigation by the FBI" was "not available" to the authors of the report. No explanation was offered regarding the criteria that were established for excluding certain evidence. In spite of these flaws and apparent bias which led the authors to accept at face value, often without corroboration, the explanations offered by those who were being investigated, the report does succeed in demonstrating gross negligence within the embassy in Georgetown and the State Department in Washington, D.C.

The report makes its greatest contribution, I believe, in establishing the record as to exactly what the State Department disclosed to Congressman Ryan, his aides, and others planning to travel to Jonestown in November 1978. The State Department said that on January 11, 1978, Richard McCoy had made his second visit to Jonestown and concluded as a result of that visit and his previous visit of August 30, 1977, that "it was improbable that anyone in Jonestown was being held in bondage or against his will." On May 10, 1978, McCoy and the newly appointed Chief of Mission of the embassy, Richard Dwyer, visited Jonestown and "found no evidence of mistreatment of or individuals being held against their will." Relying upon McCoy as their only source, the authors of the report concluded that "he found it difficult to believe that the visits were stage-managed because he had free access to any place he wished to go." The report added, "On no occasion did he ever have the impression that answers to questions he put to persons he had approached unexpectedly were other than spontaneous."

Had the writers interviewed nonofficial sources, including Deborah Blakey, who, as we have seen in her affidavit, had briefed McCoy in May 1978, she would have told them that all of the visits were stage-managed, that McCoy never went anywhere on his own while in Jonestown, and that he was always escorted about. It is true that McCoy was allowed to visit each area that he requested to see. But he was incurious. He did not ask to visit the large dormitory-style buildings or the smaller cabins; he was content to allow his escorts to direct him to the buildings especially prepared for his visit. He did not ask to visit those who worked in the fields for long hours. The "spontaneous" answers came from those members of the Peoples Temple whom the leadership had delegated to be on various paths in the settlement. McCoy encountered people chewing chicken drumsticks as they passed by; they would "spontaneously" stop and say hello to him. The food had been assigned to them for that purpose.

Those who Jones thought might blurt out some unpleasant news to McCoy were sent to work at Camp One, approximately one mile away, before McCoy arrived. He never asked to visit that or similar locations.

If some ambiguity existed regarding the integrity of McCoy's interviews inside of Jonestown, the report did little to dissipate it. For example, the report reads:

"In Jonestown, the consular officers *always* conducted the interviews privately. *In most instances* they took the persons apart from other Jonestown members." (Emphasis added.)

Did McCoy give the names to Jones of those he wished to question? The report said, "In preparation for face-to-face contact in Jonestown, the Consular officers would notify the Peoples Temple of their proposed visits and provide the names of some but not all the persons they wished to interview. As a rule, the names of persons alleged to have been abused were held back so as to permit the Consul [McCoy] to determine for himself whether they had been mistreated."

Based upon my interviews with former leaders of the Peoples Temple in Jonestown who were present during McCoy's visits, such as Harriet Tropp and Mike Prokes, I do not believe that explanation to be true. I have not interviewed anyone who recalls McCoy's asking for anyone not on his previously submitted list. Indeed, those who have discussed this matter with me have assured me that McCoy never did make such requests.

Without doubt the most important evidence to reach McCoy and his superiors in the State Department and the embassy came from Blakey. It is instructive to examine their treatment of that evidence.

On May 12, 1978, according to the report, Blakey told McCoy that "all the Consular visits had been stage-managed and that there had been mass suicide rehearsals." After McCoy briefed the American ambassador to Guyana, John Burke, about Blakey's statement, Burke told McCoy that "Blakey should be asked to make a sworn statement." Accordingly, "the Consul wrote out in longhand a statement relating to mass suicide rehearsals that Blakey signed on the morning of May 13 at her hotel in the presence of the Vice Consul."

The extraordinary statement provided the very "hard evidence" that the embassy said was required for it to act. According to the report, "When he returned from the airport after seeing Blakey off, the Vice Consul placed the document in a safe in the Embassy. It remained there until early November, when it was sent to the [State] Department in connection with a freedom-of-information case." Had the Freedom of Information Act not applied, the document might even now remain secret. The report continues:

> During the flight to New York, Blakey and Consul [McCoy] had a long conversation about the activities of the Peoples Temple in Guyana. Blakey referred to the smuggling of firearms, the diversion of funds to foreign banks, and the multi-millions of assets held by the Temple. She talked of the total control that Jones seemed to have over all his followers; she said that even if some members wished to get out, they could not. When asked by the Consul why someone wishing to leave could not slip out through the jungle to Matthew's Ridge, she cited as reasons the presence of armed guards ringing Jonestown, Jones' success in convincing members that the Guyanese would return any defectors, and the isolation of the site. Blakey declared that, even when the visit of a consular officer presented an opportunity, there was not enough confidence in the ability of one individual to take them out to warrant the risks. Replying to a question about how persons allowed themselves to be brought to Guyana, Blakey said that

> a few were drugged throughout the trip, others came because of peer pressure, but most came willingly.

No doubt Blakey's faith in McCoy and the forces that he represented was diminished by the unreality of the suggestion that elderly people, children, or even adults knowledgeable about the terrors of the bush could "slip out through the jungle to Matthew's Ridge."

Blakey said that she intended to tell the American news media about the conditions in Jonestown. McCoy advised her against such actions. The reports, relying alone upon McCoy, put it a bit more gently: "Blakey asked the Consul what she should do; should she go to the press with her information? The Consul answered that he did not see why she should go to the press since previous press reports had not accomplished anything." She, of course, could have rejoined that previous reports to the embassy had accomplished nothing as well. According to the report: "He went on to say that she should go to law-enforcement agencies, mentioning the Customs Service and the Alcohol, Tobacco and Firearms Control Bureau of the Treasury Department."

Later, Blakey told McCoy that she wanted to hold a press conference. Again he discouraged her and again the State Department presented just McCoy's view: "In a telephone call to the Consul in Washington between May 16 and 18, Blakey said that she simply could not remain quiet and asked again about going to the press. Saying that in the last analysis she would have to decide for herself what was best, the Consul repeated essentially what he had told her on the plane." The State Department report noted that Blakey did go to the press during June 1978. It added, "A careful check of Federal law-enforcement and investigative agencies has established that Blakey approached none of them."

While the report was critical of Blakey for failing to go directly to the agencies in Washington, D.C.—she lived in California—it found no fault with McCoy for not informing the agencies about her statement. Indeed, the authors of the report fabricated some absurd excuses on his behalf:

> The Consul considered going himself to such agencies to report Blakey's statements. His reasons for deciding against that course were his awareness that his account would be second-hand and therefore evidentiarily weak or valueless; concerns arising from the position of the Department of Justice regarding First Amendment rights and from the Privacy Act; and his belief that Blakey's cred-

> ibility would be tested by leaving action to her. For essentially the same reasons, the Consul decided not to go to law-enforcement and investigative agencies to request that they seek out Blakey and get her story. No one in the Department and the Embassy suggested, or considered suggesting, to the Consul that he take either of these courses, a fact that indicates the embedded nature of constraints.

More likely it was Blakey who was testing the credibility of the United States government. She had made an oral statement to embassy personnel in Georgetown, on the airplane, and upon her arrival in the United States. She had signed the written statement prepared for her by the embassy in Georgetown. She persisted in notifying the news media of her concern over the objections offered by McCoy. There were obvious reasons why she might be reluctant to seek out law enforcement authorities. She had been part of the Peoples Temple leadership in Jonestown, and before that, in California. She no doubt entertained some question about her vulnerability to civil and criminal actions. In addition, her brother and mother remained in Jonestown. Less apparent are the reasons why the State Department, McCoy, and Burke did not notify the responsible agencies and why the statement that Blakey had signed remained locked away in the embassy safe in Georgetown.

The report discloses that Tim Stoen was extremely effective in his efforts to bring about a confrontation with Jonestown. He was able to enlist the State Department and the American embassy in his crusade. The report said:

> *The Effect of the Stoen Case:* The initiation in August 1977 of the bitter and crucial struggle between the Stoens and Jones for the custody of John Victor Stoen represented in a very real sense the beginning of concentrated official attention to the Peoples Temple. The custody case came to be the primary focus of the Department's and the Embassy's involvement in Temple matters for most of the period before November 18, 1978. Overall, it consumed considerably more than half the total time and effort devoted by officials to the entire array of questions revolving around the Peoples Temple. It produced two clear "penetrations" into the political and policy realms: the formal complaints in the Stoens' behalf by the Embassy to the Guyanese Foreign Ministry in September 1977 and January 1978.

The official review found that:

> The Department and the Embassy invested a great deal of time and effort, almost all of it in behalf of the Stoens and their attorneys. In the case of the Embassy, the actions covered a broad gamut of assistance: the facilitation of access by the Stoens and their American lawyer to senior Guyanese officials, including ministers; frequent consultation by Embassy officers with Guyanese officials and Guyanese attorneys for both sides about the evolution and prospects of the case; the presence of consular officers at court hearings in the terms permitted by Guyanese law and custom; formal and informal representation to the Guyanese Government when some derogation of the rights of the Stoens or their American attorney was evident or even suspected, with one such intervention bordering on an *ex parte* act (the diplomatic note of September 16, 1977); and the provision of a flow of reports on the progress of the case to the Stoens and their American counsel, either directly or via the Department.

The report concluded that the embassy and the State Department both "*went beyond the norm for custody cases involving Americans.*" (Emphasis added.)

The report listed various other assignments that the embassy carried out for the Stoens, asserting that

> . . . the Embassy Chargé in February 1978, in response to a charge by Jones of Embassy partisanship, raised with Jones the question of his alleged exercise of influence on the Guyanese Government in connection with the custody suit. (Jones denied it.) In other dealings with the Peoples Temple on the case, the Embassy, in early September 1977, stressed to representatives the importance, in Jones' own interest, of his conforming to the court order requiring his presence.

Although, as we have seen, the State Department conceded in its report that "almost all" of its "time and effort" was expanded "in behalf of the Stoens and their attorneys," the embassy constantly made false statements to Jones and his aides about that matter. The report found that: "To Temple complaints of Embassy bias favoring the Stoens, the Embassy always emphasized its impartiality and neutrality."

The State Department inquiry found that a number of officers in the department believed it possible that Stoen had ulterior motives in his campaign against Jonestown; unfortunately, this important area was not explored by the two authors. They conclude: ". . . concerning Stoen, some officers dealing with the case felt a degree of wariness and uncertainty about whether he had purposes beyond parental concerns."*

The report leaves unanswered a number of relevant questions. What led the officers to question Stoen's motives? Why did the embassy and State Department devote an admittedly abnormal amount of time and energy to one custody case, all on behalf of one or two citizens, to the possible detriment of one thousand other Americans, when there were doubts about the sincerity and motivation of the beneficiary of their acts?

While McCoy had told Jones repeatedly that the embassy was neutral in matters relating to conflicts with the Peoples Temple, he invariably assisted the Temple's adversaries. He did so in such a blatant manner that the Temple often knew about his machinations.

During May 1978, Kathy Hunter, a free-lance journalist from the United States, arrived in Georgetown. She was writing for the Ukiah *Daily Journal* a series of stories hostile to Jones, the Temple, and Jonestown. Although she had known Jones in Ukiah, she ultimately declined to visit Jonestown.† The report reveals that although her visa had expired, "the Consul was instrumental in getting her stay in Georgetown extended and in arranging for funds for her from the United States."

Then, the *National Enquirer* sent a team of two to write a horror story about Jonestown. To Temple members in May 1978, McCoy had suggested shooting down any airplane that was violating airspace over Jonestown. The report reveals, however, that the consul secretly championed the course of the two *National Enquirer* reporters: The State Department wrote, "The Consul's intercession with Guyanese authorities in July 1978 had the effect of extending the stay in Guyana of two *National Enquirer* journalists interested in doing a story on the Peoples Temple, *one* of whom was an American." (Emphasis added.) The behavior of the American consul in this episode appears to have been deliberately provocative.

The report held that: "The single most important substantive failure in the performance of the Department and the Embassy was the aborted effort by the Embassy to obtain authorization for an approach to the Guyanese Government."

*In the article about the State Department Report, published in the *New York Times* on May 4, 1979, neither this sentence nor any other statement critical of Stoen is referred to or published. Instead, Stoen is granted a status by the *New York Times* slightly short of a visionary. There he emerges as a man "trying to regain custody of his small son," who had been pleading with the secretary of state, trying to convince him that the "status in Jonestown is desperate."

†The purposes of her trip to Guyana are further explored in chapter 22.

On June 6, 1978, Ambassador Burke sent a telegram to the State Department seeking an opinion by the Office of the Legal Adviser as to whether the Guyanese government could be obliged to extend its governmental control and the protection of its legal system over an individual alien or group of aliens residing within its territory. The ambassador requested that, if the Legal Adviser's Office determined this to be the case, the embassy be authorized to approach the government of Guyana to discuss the Peoples Temple and to ask that the government exercise normal administrative control over the community. On June 26, 1978, the department concurred with the embassy's view that a host government had jurisdiction over Americans and other aliens residing in its territory. It concluded, however, that "an approach to the Government of Guyana might be construed as U.S. Government interference, unless an American citizen or family requested assistance or there was evidence of lawlessness in the Jonestown community."

Had the State Department merely asked the host government to exercise normal control over Jonestown as the ambassador had requested, and had the government of Guyana done so, the autonomous community would have enjoyed the protection of a socialist country. It might have been less vulnerable to and concerned about invasions by mercenaries and unfair treatment by the American embassy, State Department, and congressional investigators. I believe that the Guyanese government may have been reluctant to assume such a responsibility for its own reasons, and that Jones might have rejected such a proposal for reasons that seemed compelling to him at the time.

Nevertheless, the order from Washington not to explore that possibility, although the proposal seemed likely to provide some degree of security and protection for one thousand Americans, is astonishing, particularly in light of the stated reason for the order not to approach the Guyanese government with the rather obvious suggestion. United States government interference with the affairs of Guyana became a tradition with Jonestown, as we have seen; but there had been ample historical precedent before that experimental community was established. Indeed, in the foreign service clubs throughout the world, it is legend that the prime minister of Guyana was assisted into power through the not inconsiderable efforts of the Central Intelligence Agency. The former minister of foreign affairs of Guyana has said that the CIA's help was crucial and that thereafter, the prime minister asserted he had used the agency—the agency had not used him.

In a most important work about secret CIA operations in Latin America, Philip Agee disclosed some of the details of the CIA program to subvert the elections in Guyana during 1963 and 1964. Agee worked for the CIA for twelve years in three different countries. His diary shows the following entry for July 8, 1963:*

> Operations at the Georgetown station† (British Guiana) have just brought a big victory against the Marxist Prime Minister, Cheddi Jagan. Jagan has led that colony down a leftist-nationalist path since coming to power in the 1950's on the strength of Indian (Asian) predominance over blacks there. The Georgetown station operations for several years have concentrated on building up the local anti-Jagan trade-union movement, mainly through the Public Service International (PSI) which is the international Trade Secretariat for public employees. Cover is through the American Federation of State, County and Municipal Employees, the U.S. affiliate of the PSI.
>
> Last year through the PSI the Georgetown station financed an anti-Jagan campaign over the Budget that included riots and a general strike and precipitated British intervention to restore order. This past April, with station financing and direction, another crippling strike began, this one led by the Guiana civil servants union which is the local PSI affiliate, and it has taken until just now to force Jagan again to capitulate. Visitors here who have also been to the Georgetown station say eventually the Agency hopes to move the leader of the black community into power even though blacks are outnumbered by Jagan and the Indians.

The "black leader" the CIA supported is the current prime minister.

Agee's diary entry for December 18, 1964, describes the reaction at the CIA station in Georgetown, Guyana, following the election.

> A new victory for the station at Georgetown, British Guiana, in its efforts to throw out the leftist-nationalist Prime Minister and professed Marxist, Cheddi Jagan. In elections a few days ago Jagan's Indian-based party lost parliamentary control to a coalition of the black-based party and a splinter group. The new Prime Minister, Forbes Burnham, is considered to be a moderate and his ascension to power finally removes the fear that Jagan would turn British Guiana into another Cuba. The victory is largely due to CIA operations over the past five years to strengthen the anti-Jagan trade unions, principally through the Public Service International which provided the

*Philip Agee, *Inside the Company: CIA Diary* (New York: Penguin, 1975), p. 293. Hereafter referred to as *CIA Diary*.

†"Station" is the CIA base of operations.

> cover for financing public employees strikes. Jagan is protesting fraud —earlier this year he expelled Gene Meakins, one of our main labour agents in the operation, but it was no use.*

It is in this context that one must evaluate the absurd notion that the State Department ordered the ambassador not to ask the government of Guyana to consider extending its lawful jurisdiction to the American citizens residing in that country for fear of being accused of "interference."

As discussed in chapter 8, on November 6, 1978, I wrote to Congressman Leo Ryan about his proposed trip to Jonestown and urged him to return a telephone call that I had placed to him three days earlier to discuss his contemplated visit.† That same day I spoke with James Schollaert, an attorney on the staff of the International Relations Committee who was serving as an aide to Ryan. I told Schollaert that I understood Jones was quite ill and was heavily medicated, and that November 1978 was therefore, in my view, the least propitious time for an official visit. In subsequent telephone calls I made the same point.

Ryan rejected my request for a postponement of the trip, apparently because he did not believe that Jones was regularly under the influence of narcotics. I presumed that embassy personnel had checked out my allegations and determined that they were not well founded. I heard that on November 7 the embassy had visited Jonestown and met with Jones. Since my own report was not, as I had stated, based upon my own observations, I was somewhat confused by Ryan's response, but I hoped that he meant he had evidence that Jones was capable of rational conduct. This matter is clarified by the report of the State Department.

On November 7, the new American Consul, Douglas Ellice, and the political officer, Dennis Reece, visited Jonestown. They, too, gave considerable advance notice to Jones of the names of those they wished to see, in the tradition pioneered by McCoy.

This was to be the last visit by embassy personnel to Jonestown prior to Ryan's arrival. Obviously, Ryan's safety, since the embassy knew there were many weapons in Jonestown and that Jones ran the community, was directly related to the mental condition of the leader. I had already raised the question of his capability with Ryan's party, and numerous others had raised it more directly, not to say more savagely, with McCoy, with officials in the embassy in Georgetown, and with the State Department in Washing-

*Agee, *CIA Diary,* p. 406.
†The letter is published as Appendix F.

ton, as well as with the news media. The State Department report discloses that Ellice and Reece concluded on November 7 that "Jones appeared to be ill." While some Jonestown residents told them that Jones "had a fever of 105 degrees," according to the report, "the two officers were agreed that he did not have the outward signs of such a high fever." Ellice and Reece described Jones's illness: "Jones' speech was markedly slurred and he had difficulty in spelling out a word, eventually giving up the effort in confusion. He seemed to be either intoxicated, drugged, or the victim of a stroke. He did not appear to be dissembling."

One can imagine the shocked reactions of the two officials. They had learned that Jones, who was in fact deeply narcotized during that visit, was incapable of making decisions based upon judgment, lacked the capacity to speak properly, and was unable even to spell out a word. The fact that Jones was, for the first time, not unwilling to appear in that state of deterioration before officials of the United States government was further proof of his degeneration. One would have expected that the two career officers would return with alacrity to Georgetown, brief the ambassador, and send a strongly worded warning to Congressman Ryan about the dangers inherent in a visit to Jonestown. The leader who commanded a guard of armed men obviously was no longer in control of himself.

The first report filed by Ellice and Reece of their observations of November 7, 1978, was made after Ryan had been murdered. The report stated that "the joint report of the visit" was "prepared three to four weeks after the event and additional comments by them another two months later."

In Washington, Ryan was being assured at meeting after meeting with McCoy and other State Department officials that the warnings given to him by Blakey, Katsaris, and others, including me, were "nonsense" and that there was no possibility that violence might mar his visit.

The State Department report insisted that the congressional delegation "had been more fully briefed than most Congressional Delegations when the total of five structured meetings and numerous telephone conversations were considered." This approach betrayed, I submit, an inability to distinguish quality from quantity.

The congressional staff members' impression is quite different from the official version proferred by the State Department. They recall that they "instigated most of the briefing sessions."* They also point out that "very few, if any, cables or other Department documents on Jonestown were made available" to them.† McCoy and his associates did not tell Ryan and his

**State Department Report,* p. 82.
†Ibid., p. 83.

associates what they knew about the dangers that lay ahead, and in fact they suppressed the documents that would have alerted them to the dangers.

Ryan and his aides were not sufficiently familiar with the work of the embassy and the State Department regarding Jonestown to suspect that a large volume of cable traffic and other important documentary evidence existed. Yet it was clear that they were asking for all relevant information. Why did McCoy and his superiors in the State Department, who were familiar with the cables and other documents (some of them indeed were responsible for generating the traffic and other records), decide to withhold the evidence and the fact that it existed from the congressional delegation?

According to the State Department Report, there were five structured meetings for Ryan, his staff, and State Department officials, including McCoy. On September 15, 1978, Ryan and his aide Jacqueline Speier met with Assistant Secretary of the Bureau of Inter-American Affairs, Viron Vaky, and members of his staff, regarding the congressman's plans to visit Jonestown after November 10, 1978, with a party of about eight persons, including a member of the press and possibly some relatives of Temple members. Department officials assured the congressman that the embassy and the department would provide all possible assistance. McCoy outlined the embassy's past efforts concerning Jonestown, and discussed his impressions based on three visits to the community. He assured Ryan that the Jonestown community was peaceful and that he had never found any reason to suspect violence.

The second meeting took place on October 3, 1978. McCoy and Richard Belt of the Special Consular Services office met with Speier to discuss Jonestown and the proposed visit of Congressman Ryan. Neither McCoy nor Belt suggested that there might be a problem when Ryan arrived in Jonestown.

The third meeting took place on October 25. McCoy met with Speier, James Schollaert, and Thomas Smeeton, the last two of the House International Relations Committee, to discuss Congressman Ryan's trip. Speier stated that Congressman Derwinski would join Congressman Ryan, and the two, with approximately six staff members, would visit Guyana from November 14 to 18. (Congressman Derwinski subsequently decided not to go.) McCoy discussed the logistics of the trip and the necessity of obtaining the consent of the Peoples Temple.

On November 7, Ellice and Reece learned that Jones was mentally incapacitated during their visit to Jonestown. Two days later several department officials, including members of the Office of the Legal Adviser, met with Speier and Schollaert to discuss legal constraints such as the Privacy

Act and the Freedom of Information Act, as well as aspects of international law affecting dealings with Jonestown. They did not reveal that Ellice and Reece had interviewed Jones.

The last formal meeting took place on November 13. The State Department officials met with Congressman Ryan, the staff members of the delegation, and three members of the Concerned Relatives group—Blakey, Grace Stoen, and Steven Katsaris. The meeting was largely devoted to Blakey's account of conditions in Jonestown.

In addition to the various face-to-face briefings of the congressional delegation by department officials from September 14 to November 13, 1978, there were numerous telephone conversations about Jonestown and the trip preparations, largely between McCoy and Speier.

On November 14, 1978, the congressional delegation, consisting of Congressman Ryan and staff members Speier and Schollaert, departed for Guyana. Traveling on the same airplane were a number of media representatives and Concerned Relatives.

Although the State Department report documents the fact that the meetings and telephone conversations took place and when they occurred, much less information is imparted as to the substance of the meetings. On the crucial question, however, whether the State Department warned Ryan or his aides that there might be trouble ahead, the report is quite clear. It states: "On the question whether Congressman Ryan received any warning by Department officials on the possibility of violence by Temple members toward him or his party, there are no indications, either from the written record or from interviews of officers involved in the briefings, that any such warning was given."

The report acknowledges that a State Department officer, when questioned by the authors, did "recall that the Consul [McCoy] was seriously concerned by Blakey's story, which he believed could not be disregarded."

Yet when Congressman Ryan asked McCoy about possible confirmation of Blakey's disclosure of the propensity for violence in Jonestown and the mass suicide threat, McCoy repeated his previous assertion that Blakey's statement was "nonsense." The State Department report found that McCoy on two separate occasions called Blakey's evidence nonsense* after having previously told an officer of the State Department that he had assessed her allegations as credible and that he believed that she had accurately described the situation in Jonestown.

Certain facts emerge with clarity from the report. Stoen was involved in

**State Department Report,* pp. 31, 54.

a close and continuing relationship with the State Department and the American embassy in Georgetown. The United States government and its agents, knowing of Stoen's dubious conduct as counsel for the Peoples Temple, the real possibility that he was not the father of John Victor Stoen, and doubting that his motives were as he stated them, cooperated as accomplices with him in a campaign that harassed Jonestown and its leaders. This campaign surpassed normal conduct by an embassy and was blatantly biased in favor of one party against another in violation of the rules of the State Department. Ultimately the embassy convinced the leaders of Jonestown that the American government was engaged in a program to harass and destroy them.

The embassy and the State Department then intervened in the internal affairs of the government of Guyana on several occasions on behalf of those seeking to transmogrify the Jonestown community by exaggerating its weaknesses and substantial flaws and by ignoring its positive contributions. In so doing, the embassy went far beyond legal, lawful conduct—for example, when it demanded that the government of Guyana extend the visa of a non-American journalist who was preparing a substantial and hostile story about Jonestown. On another occasion, the consul also intervened with the attorney general of Guyana and the chief of immigration of Guyana on behalf of a former convict, Joseph Mazor, who later admitted that he had been on a mission to kidnap children from Jonestown and to lead an armed mercenary force against the community. McCoy must have been aware of Mazor's long criminal record when he interceded on his behalf.

When Ryan and his staff turned to the State Department and the embassy personnel for advice and information, the officers deliberately gave him bad advice and suppressed the relevant information. McCoy and his associates in Guyana, including Burke, Ellice, and Reece, and his associates in Washington, knew that Ryan might die if he went to Jonestown. I believe that had McCoy, Ellice, and Reece not denied the relevant information to Ryan and his staff but had instead divulged to them the files maintained by the State Department and the embassy, that Ryan would never have made his fatal trip.

Part VIII

Controver:* The Media and the Government

*In old English law, an inventor or deviser of false news. *Black's Law Dictionary, Revised fourth edition.* (St. Paul, MN: West Publishing, 1968).

22 Before the Massacre

In recent years the matters to which I have devoted much of my attention have been historic events in which the American intelligence agencies have been involved. I have regularly come into conflict with the interests of the police and spy organizations and, I believe, with their servants in the news media. Furthermore, I believe that it is not possible to judge fully and assess correctly these occurrences that have shaped our destiny without understanding the role of those in the news media who have often deliberately distorted the facts and attempted to discredit all who have sought to disagree with them.

Until recently I believed that these efforts were not the result of a deliberate and well-conceived plan. However, CIA documents now available under the Freedom of Information Act dispel that naïve assumption.

In 1966, a book I had written about the assassination of President Kennedy, *Rush to Judgment,* was about to be published. A CIA directive about the Kennedy assassination, Document number 1035-960 (bearing in place of a headquarters file number the legend, "Destroy When No Longer Needed") states, "Our organization is directly involved; among other facts, we contributed information to the investigation. . . . The aim of this dispatch is to provide material for countering and discrediting the claims of the conspiracy theorists." In pursuing its objective "to inhibit the circulation of such claims," and prevent the publication of my book, the CIA sent false and derogatory information about me, via their "Chiefs of Stations and Bases," throughout the world, to "friendly elite contacts, especially politicians and editors" in every country in which they operated. The CIA directed, according to its own files, that the contacts "employ propaganda assets" to "refute" my charges. They were to use "book reviews and feature articles." They told their "assets" in the news media, including the *New*

York Times and CBS-TV, that I should be attacked as "financially interested." The CIA offered arguments to be used against me. The points that the CIA said should be included in reviews of my work, including in some instances the very language, later appeared verbatim in reviews published in the *New York Times* and elsewhere.

With the assistance of the American Civil Liberties Union, these CIA documents were secured under the Freedom of Information Act. The *New York Times* (specifically John Crewdson) and other newspapers refused to publish the CIA directives when we released them to the media.

One staff reporter at the Baltimore *News-American,* Edward Colimore, thought they were of such significance that he was able to have them featured across the entire front page of that newspaper on Sunday, May 8, 1977, under the headline, "U.S. Plotted Against Warren Report Critics." However, to my knowledge, not another American newspaper published the story.

Later, when I was working on the conspiracy that shrouded Martin Luther King's death, two investigative reporters at the *New York Times,* Nicholas Horrock and Anthony Marro, entered into an illegal agreement with a contact at the House Select Committee on Assassinations to secure and publish false and derogatory information about me. This *New York Times* espionage effort included secret telephone calls from Horrock and Marro in New York to an FBI informer in Missouri to arrange for delivery of the false data. The calls were not as secret as the editors at the *Times* believed, since the FBI informant tape-recorded the conversations and later provided me with the recordings. This extraordinary *New York Times* effort was in support of the continuing FBI campaign to fix the responsibility for the murder of Dr. King upon James Earl Ray and then exonerate the bureau from complicity in the assassination.

As we examine the relationship between the American news media and the events at Jonestown, it is useful, I believe, to recall the close working relationship between the intelligence organizations and the media.

Carl Bernstein, the former *Washington Post* reporter, began to explore the relationship between the police and spy organizations (which refer to themselves as "the intelligence community" as if they were a small town in Connecticut) and the American press. His important article was not published in either the *Washington Post* or the *New York Times* and was given, upon publication,* far less attention than the subject and his conclu-

*Carl Bernstein, "The CIA and the Media," *Rolling Stone,* 20 October, 1977, pp. 55–67.

sions warranted. Bernstein's investigation revealed that there have been more than four hundred American journalists who in the past years have secretly carried out assignments for the CIA. He wrote:

> Among the executives who lent their cooperation to the Agency were William Paley of the Columbia Broadcasting System, Henry Luce of Time Inc., Arthur Hays Sulzberger of the *New York Times,* Barry Bingham, Sr., of the Louisville *Courier-Journal,* and James Copley of the Copley News Service. Other organizations which cooperated with the CIA include the American Broadcasting Company, the National Broadcasting Company, the Associated Press, United Press International, Reuters, Hearst Newspapers, Scripps-Howard, *Newsweek* magazine, the Mutual Broadcasting System, the *Miami Herald* and the old *Saturday Evening Post* and New York *Herald-Tribune.*
>
> By far the most valuable of these associations, according to CIA officials, have been with the *New York Times,* CBS and Time Inc.

Bernstein discovered, according to his article, that one of the CIA's "most valuable personal relationships in the 1960s, according to CIA officials," was with "Jerry [Jeremiah] O'Leary of the Washington *Star.*" O'Leary became the expert who regularly assured Americans that Lee Harvey Oswald was the lone assassin of President Kennedy, that James Earl Ray alone murdered Dr. King, and that Orlando Letelier was probably murdered in Washington, D.C., not by the Chilean junta but by his own commander. O'Leary also was sent to Guyana in 1978 just after the massacre and would later insist that it had been a mass suicide. O'Leary has published FBI handouts with his byline, and in each instance he has been proved wrong.

Bernstein asserted, "There are perhaps a dozen well known columnists and broadcast commentators" who are referred to by the agency as "known assets." Among them is C. L. Sulzberger of the *New York Times.* A CIA officer told Bernstein, "We gave it [an article] to Cy [Sulzberger] as a background piece and Cy gave it to the printers and put his name on it." Bernstein discovered that "the agency's relationship with the [New York] *Times* was by far its most valuable among newspapers, according to CIA officials." It was the policy of the *New York Times* "to provide assistance to the CIA whenever possible," the reporter found.

According to Bernstein, Wayne Phillips, a former *New York Times* reporter, said that the CIA tried to recruit him as an undercover operator some years ago. The agency official told him then that the CIA had a "working relationship" with Arthur Hays Sulzberger, the publisher of the *Times.* In 1976, in an effort to dissipate the impact of that story, the *Times* assigned John M. Crewdson to write about it from the viewpoint of the *New York Times.* The choice of Crewdson was consistent with the *Times'* behavior: Earlier, Crewdson had played an active role in covering up the facts about the assassination of John F. Kennedy when important information was being made available to the media in the middle 1970s, and later he would be chosen to lead the *New York Times* campaign to cover up and falsify the record about the Jonestown massacre.

Bernstein discovered that "CBS was unquestionably the CIA's most valuable broadcasting asset." CIA files also reveal a close working relationship between the agency and *Newsweek* magazine, its owner the *Washington Post,* the Associated Press, and United Press International.

The relationship between the intelligence agencies and the media becomes more pronounced and more important in matters which directly relate to the interests of the agencies. Before the Jonestown massacre, a series of newspaper-related events transpired which, in retrospect, seem to merit examination.

We have previously discussed the articles written by Lester Kinsolving. These articles, assisted and inflamed by the disclosures of Timothy Stoen, provided the foundation for subsequent assaults upon Jim Jones and the Peoples Temple from the time of their publication.

During 1977, Phil Tracy, a contributing editor to *New West,* and Marshall Kilduff, a reporter for the San Francisco *Chronicle,* published a major exposé of the Peoples Temple in *New West.* The article made no mention of the leadership role that Timothy Stoen had played in the Temple. Although Stoen had served in an important position in the district attorney's office in San Francisco and had allegedly notarized documents improperly for the Temple, no reference was made to his misconduct. Stoen had been involved in various conflicts of interest, both in Ukiah and San Francisco, and had apparently betrayed his obligation to the prosecutor's office in each city. Those matters were ignored. Although charges were made against Jones for fake faith-healing sessions, Stoen, who publicly had asserted that he had been shot and saved by Jones and that he had witnessed Jones raise the dead, was not referred to in the article. The full-fledged assault upon the Temple was marked by the care with which Kilduff and Tracy nicely extracted Stoen from the scene. Kilduff, in his role as a *Chronicle* reporter, continued this process after the massacre. He deliberately removed Stoen from the disagreeable faith-healing story to protect the lawyer.* To the

*San Francisco *Chronicle,* 21 December, 1978.

general public at the time, to whom Stoen was little known, the *New West* article appeared solely as a denunciation of the Peoples Temple. In retrospect, the Kilduff-Tracy piece seems at least as much a defense of Stoen as an attack upon the Temple.

That two reporters were very critical of a politically oriented church organization was not a major newsbreak across the country. However, Jones was predictable to those who studied him and it was not difficult to know that his fragile ego could hardly withstand the cruel assault upon him, especially one which so carefully exempted his coconspirator while it relied so heavily and openly upon Grace Stoen for its information and perhaps covertly upon Timothy Stoen as well. Jones reacted. Letters and telephone calls were sent to the publisher. Important friends were called on to request that the article be rewritten, toned down, postponed, or dropped. During that campaign, an act of violence against the office of *New West* was said to have taken place. A break-in, apparently engineered by the Peoples Temple's Diversions Department, an organization with which Stoen was familiar, was carried out to interfere with publication of the article. The headline on the front page of the San Francisco newspapers on June 17, 1977, proclaimed "New West Is Burglarized." A front-page San Francisco *Examiner* story on June 17 left little doubt as to the suspected culprits:

> *New West* magazine was burglarized last night and files on a story about the Rev. Jim Jones and his Peoples Temple were disturbed, editors of the magazine reported to police today.
>
> Police were investigating the reported break-in.
>
> It was also learned *New West*'s Northern California editor, Rosalie Muller Wright, has moved her two children from their home to an undisclosed location after receiving intimidating phone calls about the story.

The *Examiner* relied upon Tracy for the details of the break-in:

> Contributing editor Phil Tracy said a window in *New West*'s second-floor office at 325 Pacific Ave. was forced open sometime after staff members left the office last night.
>
> "Nothing was taken, but files relating to the story on Peoples Temple were disturbed," Tracy said. "The file was in a certain order and the order was not the same when I came in this morning."
>
> He said none of the other staffers had entered the unlocked file and no other files were disturbed.

The San Francisco *Chronicle* published Tracy's assertions as well as his speculations on its front page:

> Contributing editor Phil Tracy told officers it appeared to him that one of the files had been "jammed back in" the filing cabinet.
>
> Tracy speculated that a story the magazine is preparing to publish by *Chronicle* reporter Marshall Kilduff about Peoples Temple at 1859 Geary Boulevard could have been taken out of the file and photographed.*

The story of the Temple's efforts to break into the magazine, intimidate its reporters, and photograph its files was widely published throughout California and circulated by the Associated Press. More than a year later a report to the United States Congress concluded that "this anticipated publication" of the Tracy/Kilduff article in *New West* "apparently caused Jim Jones to leave the United States for Guyana."†

Terri Buford has told me that the charge that the Peoples Temple burglarized the office of *New West* also "caused Jones to conclude, just after it allegedly happened, that he could not return to the United States." In addition, Buford states, "the mass exodus of five hundred people from the United States to Jonestown during the summer of 1977 was the result of the charge that the Temple had burglarized *New West.* Jim Jones decided that some force in the government or the media or both was at work against him and that he could not prevail."

The evidence reveals that Jones was correct. The fact that he was paranoid and feared that there was a conspiracy against him does not establish that there was not such a conspiracy. If indeed there had been no burglary at the office of *New West,* then the events that destroyed the Temple in the United States, drove Jones irretrievably to Guyana, and sent five hundred others there and later five hundred more all eventually to their deaths, were events which may have been managed.

In fact, there was no burglary. The story appears to have been wholly contrived. It appears that neither Tracy nor Kilduff ever had much faith in the ability of the reported episode to withstand serious investigation. While Tracy called the press, the Peoples Temple called upon the police to investigate.

An interdepartmental memorandum to Clement De Amicis, deputy chief of Investigations of the San Francisco Police Department, dated June 29,

*San Francisco *Chronicle,* 18 June, 1977.
†*U.S. House of Representatives Report,* p. 10.

1977, reveals that the *New West* account was at best a cruel hoax. The police report discloses that officer Duffy of the central station made the initial investigation. It reads, "After inspecting the premises and interviewing Mr. Tracy, officer Duffy concluded entry had not been made."

The police report continues that "On Monday, June 20, 1977, Inspector Evans of the Burglary Detail responded to 325 Pacific [the *New West Magazine* office] and conducted the follow-up investigation. After inspecting the premises and interviewing the concerned persons, Inspector Evans also concluded that entry had not been made."

Since Tracy had speculated that a window in the office had been forced open, Captain John A. Mahoney, commanding officer of the Property Crimes division, ordered that the window be examined for prints. The police report reveals that "palm prints and fingerprints located on the outside of the lower window pane" were retrieved. Mahoney ordered an immediate search of the police fingerprint files. He also requested that all *New West* employees be fingerprinted. On June 24, 1977, Jon Carroll, an employee of *New West,* was fingerprinted at the Hall of Justice. The police report reveals that "his prints matched those found on the window."

Why Carroll had apparently maintained silence for a full week after the report of the break-in has not been explained. If there were some innocent explanation as to why his prints were found on the exterior of a window near a fire escape, it should have been forthcoming. Accusations were leveled daily at the Peoples Temple, but not after Carroll had been trapped by police work.

Making a false report to police authorities is a crime. In some jurisdictions, "where a person in committing an unlawful act not felonious or tending to great bodily harm"* nevertheless causes a death, a charge of involuntary manslaughter may result.

To the news media, the most egregious act is an apparent assault upon the press. The apocryphal burglary effectively and predictably dispatched the Temple members to Guyana.

During May 1978, as the campaign to discredit the Peoples Temple had entered into its final stage, Stoen had already begun to urge Congressman Leo Ryan to intervene, and he had also written to the secretary of state suggesting action against Jonestown.

Meanwhile, Kathy Hunter visited Guyana. Kathy Hunter is married to

**Black's Law Dictionary, Revised fourth edition* (St. Paul, MN: West Publishing, 1968), p. 1116.

George Hunter, an editor at the Ukiah *Daily Journal,* a little newspaper in a small town. Jim Jones had considered Mrs. Hunter to be a friend when the Temple was located in Ukiah. After Tim Stoen left the Temple and began to attack Jones, Kathy Hunter chose to support Stoen. Since Jones had last known her as a friend, it is more than likely that he would have welcomed her to visit Jonestown during the spring of 1978.

She told me early in October 1978, "I quite frankly expected to come back with an exclusive that would blow the hell off the thing." Her explanation of the proximate cause of her trip to Guyana is remarkable. She said that she had received a telephone call:

> A woman asked if this was Kathy Hunter and I said, "Speaking." She said, "The prime minister is calling." I laughed and said, "One of my friends is pulling my leg." I said, "Oh sure, the prime minister of what?" And she got very huffy: the prime minister of Guyana. And I said, "Forbes Burnham!" and she said, "One moment." Then you cannot mistake their way of speaking, it's impossible because I had been impressed by the Oxford accent of this tall black man and he had been educated in England because it used to be British Guyana and then they got their freedom and they called it Guyana . . . so you're in for an experience.

"Well, anyway you thought it was he," I said to her. And she responded, "There was no doubt in my mind. There was the warmth and the voice with the British accent, although softened by the Guyanese way of speaking, and he said I understand that there has been a great deal of unfavorable publicity in your country about Jonestown, would you care to come down and be my guest and see Jonestown for yourself. And I said that I would be most interested."*

Without informing the Temple of her specific plans, Kathy Hunter left for Georgetown in May 1978. According to her, she borrowed approximately two thousand dollars to cover her expenses for the trip. She said that she put some diamond rings up as collateral for a loan in order to go down there. She told me that the "assistant secretary of home ministry [in Guyana] was very sneering in his 'I understand, you pawned the family jewels to get here!' " He did not believe her, she said.

At Timehri Airport in Georgetown, she was suddenly adopted by a Guyanese woman named Pat Small, she told me. Small assisted her in securing her luggage. Hunter said:

*Interview between Mark Lane and Kathy Hunter, October 1978.

> This Guyanese woman said, "Let me help you!" and they got another bag off and then I said, "No, there is still one more," and she went back and talked to them again and I got it all. By that time the airport bus to the hotel had left and she asked if she could drive me into town, so she took me in a round-about way, showing me the things that have been accomplished in the country since the end of the colonial rule and then she asked me if I would care to come to her house for tea. Well I thought this was—would be a delightful idea to see what a Guyanese home is like.

Small also introduced her to the "right people" in Guyana, told her how terrible Jonestown was, informed her that Forbes Burnham personally made thousands of dollars from the Peoples Temple at Jonestown by leasing, not government property, but his own. Small also took her to Parliament. Small assured Hunter that the Guyanese were corrupt and communists and that she was not safe in Jonestown or even in Georgetown.

When Kathy Hunter's visa expired, Richard McCoy, the American Consul (who had not yet left for the U.S. with Debbie Blakey), intervened on her behalf with the government of Guyana to extend it just as the embassy later would on behalf of the British subject who was helping to prepare an exposé of Jonestown for the *National Enquirer.* In addition, McCoy arranged for Hunter to receive additional funds so that she could remain in the country longer.

Hunter has said that she was assisted, when she left Guyana, by Pat Small, and that when she returned to the United States she was met at the airport in the United States by Timothy Stoen. Her series of damning articles about the Peoples Temple and Jonestown, which she never did visit, were published in the Ukiah *Daily Journal* and Santa Rosa *Press Democrat* and widely accepted. They became an important part of the final and major thrust that destroyed Jonestown. Jones was enraged and furious when the pieces were published. He felt that a friend, whom he had assisted with her personal problems, had betrayed him. He was never able to understand why.

In one of her articles,* Hunter, reflecting her political awareness gleaned from Pat Small, wrote of her experience in the Parliament: "And what did I find staring at me from the wall at the right-hand side of the Prime Minister of Guyana? A near life-sized oil of China's Mao-tse Sung [sic]. Looks like it's down the road to Peking for Guyana if Burnham's referendum passes—and it looks like it will."

*Santa Rosa *Press Democrat,* 8 June, 1978.

In a series of radio reports, KCBS-AM in San Francisco relied upon Hunter's observations, assuring the listeners:

> Until recently an openly proud supporter of the Reverend Jim Jones and his energetic people-oriented programs at the Peoples Temple, she felt that Jones and the church were unfairly harassed while in Ukiah and did not believe the charges that church members were intimidated, physically beaten, and were having their properties appropriated by the Temple. She did not believe the accusations of welfare fraud and more. After Jones moved to Guyana, he allegedly talked with Miss Hunter and told her that she was welcome to visit the Guyana farm any time. Well, as soon as she was able, she hopped a plane to Guyana. It was not a pleasant trip.
>
> Not two hours after arriving, she said, Temple members phoned her at the hotel, even though she had not informed anyone of her visit. She was wined and dined and treated nicely but refused a visit to the camp with an endless series of excuses.

In fact, Kathy Hunter had gone to Guyana, as she has herself admitted, for the purpose of exposing Jonestown. While in Georgetown, she now concedes, she was invited by the Temple members to visit Jonestown, but she declined.

KCBS radio relied upon Hunter's observations in the Parliament to conclude that Guyana was moving toward a Chinese alignment.

There is no portrait of Chairman Mao in the Parliament in Georgetown. There is indeed a portrait of a Chinese gentleman, but his name is Arthur Chung. Since he is the president of Guyana, it seems not inappropriate that it be displayed there.

Following the publication of Hunter's articles, she claimed, often and very publicly, that she received threats of various types, including letters made up of words cut out from newspapers. This method of communication was one that had been employed by the Diversions Department when Stoen, according to Terri Buford, controlled its forays, but had long been abandoned before the Hunter episode for various reasons, among them that Stoen could too easily ascertain the Temple's hand.

As in the *New West* case, the Hunter articles became not the focal point in the attack but rather provided a backdrop against which the violence of the Temple might be seen.

Hunter claimed that following the threats, which my own investigation has convinced me did not emanate from Peoples Temple personnel, a window in her house was broken by an intruder. Then, she claimed that she was assaulted in her house by two black men. The press, in reporting these events, as in the *New West* break-in case, left little doubt that members of the Peoples Temple were responsible. One newspaper report widely circulated in northern California read:

> Two men allegedly broke into the home of Ukiah newspaperwoman Kathy Hunter and, capping what she described as a three-week "campaign of terror," forcibly poured a bottle of alcohol down her throat.
>
> The "campaign," according to George Hunter, executive editor of the Ukiah *Daily Journal,* began when accounts of his wife's experiences with Jim Jones' Peoples Temple in South America were published in the *Press Democrat.*
>
> "It's no put-on," he said.
>
> Mrs. Hunter was found on her kitchen floor about 9 P.M. Sunday by her 33-year-old son Michael. "She was hysterical," he said.
>
> Hospitalized after the incident, Mrs. Hunter said that two black men walked through the unlocked door to her kitchen, grabbed her, and forced her to drink the alcohol.
>
> Ukiah police are investigating the incident. "We're taking it at face value," said Sgt. Dick Perry.
>
> Detective Harold Pullins said he doesn't know if the Sunday incident is connected to a window-smashing at the Hunter home last week. Somebody broke a window late Monday night while Mrs. Hunter was sitting nearby. She cut her hand when she opened the drapes to investigate.
>
> The reporter, who tried to visit the controversial Rev. Jim Jones' outpost in Guyana, said she's been receiving threats ever since her story appeared in the *Press Democrat.*
>
> An anonymous woman caller allegedly told Hunter that "Jim knows what you're doing. If he goes down, you and all your family will go down with him."
>
> Another caller threatened to kill the Hunters, according to a police report.
>
> Michael Hunter, a legal assistant at Legal Service Foundation in Ukiah, found an ominous note at his apartment Friday night. The note, made from letters cut from a newspaper, was turned over to authorities. It reads "Hey white trash . . . we know where you live! We're watching you all the time, we know where you work, we know your home number, we know your trashy life honkey . . . you drives your dead mama's car . . . keep your ass clean and your mouth clamed [sic] up. . . ."

> The Hunter son said his wife has received threatening calls. He said he plans to move his children out of town.*

The vast majority of blacks now residing in Ukiah had originally journeyed there with Jim Jones and his Temple. When Jones, in Guyana, learned of the atmosphere that Hunter's stories had created in Ukiah, he became fearful that black Temple members still residing there might be harmed. He directed that they be taken to safety elsewhere. The charges of violence also foreclosed the possibility of Jones and his Temple's returning to Ukiah in the future. Rapidly, through the publication of manipulated articles and stories based upon arranged events, all of the options available to Jones were being eliminated.

Later, when Kathy Hunter claimed that she had been sexually abused by anonymous men, presumed to be members of the Peoples Temple, anger against Jones and his associates reached a white-hot degree. It was in this atmosphere that Leo Ryan decided to journey to Guyana.

The most significant media exposés of the Peoples Temple prior to the massacre were all tainted in some fashion. The Kinsolving-Stoen affair is interesting due to the connections of each man. The fabricated break-in of *New West*'s offices was instrumental in transforming the *New West* piece into a national event. The Hunter story is more complex. However, as in the *National Enquirer* episode, the participation of Richard McCoy is clear and important.

I do not believe that Hunter received a telephone call from Prime Minister Forbes Burnham. Either it was a hoax or she received no call at all. I also doubt very much that the Peoples Temple was involved with the "call." It is unlikely that they would trick her into coming to Guyana, particularly if they suspected her of a continuing relationship with Tim Stoen or feared she might write a series of damning articles about the Temple.

In her published diary, Hunter speaks of those who kept coming to her hotel room in Georgetown.† There she writes that "Pat came, a Richard McCoy from the U.S. Consulate came."

Since Pat Small was instrumental in directing Hunter's important work, it is useful to know who she is.

The former foreign minister of Guyana, Fred Willis, on one occasion told members of the Peoples Temple in Georgetown that Pat Small was suspected by the Guyanese government of being a foreign espionage agent. He said that she and her daughters were under surveillance as spies. Later, Pat

*Santa Rosa *Press Democrat,* 27 June, 1978.
†Ibid., 8 June, 1978.

Small was questioned by those assigned by the United States Congress to investigate the murders in Guyana. Her testimony remains classified and may not be seen by the American people. However, in describing her, the report to the congressional committee states "Ms. Pat Small, a Guyanese citizen, former self-described quasi-official receptionist for visiting VIP's to Guyana, who, together with her six children and one grandchild, is currently in the United States seeking political asylum."* In her visa application, Small states that she and the entire family will live in Ukiah, California at the house of George and Kathy Hunter. On that application, in answer to the question, "Who will furnish financial support?" Small wrote "G. Hunter."† On whose behalf and for what purpose she carried out her "duties" remain unanswered questions. Why did she flee to the United States immediately following the massacre and for what purpose has she been admitted, "seeking political asylum"?

It is not likely, I believe, that Pat Small and her family reside with the Hunters at their small home in Ukiah. I believe it unlikely as well that the Hunters are required to provide financial assistance for Small and her entire family. If the record of the congressional inquiry was made public, many of these and other questions which surround the mysterious death of one thousand Americans in Jonestown might be resolved.

On January 16, 1979, I testified before George R. Berdes, staff consultant to the Committee on Foreign Affairs of the U.S. House of Representatives in San Francisco. I told the committee's investigators:

> There is no doubt in my mind that various people sought to destroy Jonestown and that people in various government agencies manipulated Jones. Jones, himself, saw the efforts to manipulate him into an overreaction but somehow he was unable to control his own response. I believe that a responsible investigation by the Congress would seek to determine why various elements within the United States Government, including those in the State Department, withheld from Congressman Ryan and the rest of us who accompanied him to Jonestown the fact that they knew the place was an armed camp and that Jones was capable of killing the Congressman and many others.

I called upon the committee to secure the facts and to report the evidence and the findings openly to the American people. I urged that they not shroud this historic tragedy in mystery. I implored them to discover the

***U.S. House of Representatives Report*, p. 10.
†Ibid., p. 226.

facts of the conspiracy against Jim Jones and the Peoples Temple, and the reasons why Ryan was misled by the State Department and intelligence agencies.

On May 15, 1979, the committee published its final report. In its findings, the question of conspiracy against Jim Jones and the Peoples Temple is answered "in classified version only." In the findings, the question about "Awareness of danger, predicting the degree of violence" is answered "In Classified version only." The "Role and performance of the U.S. Department of State" is also found "In Classified version only."*

On May 22, 1979, I telephoned Berdes in response to his letter to me which accompanied a copy of the report. In the letter, he had written, "Every effort was made to make this investigation as comprehensive and accurate as possible. I would be pleased to receive any comments you may have."

I asked Berdes if the findings about conspiracy and all the evidence upon which those findings were based were classified. He said that both the findings and the evidence were indeed classified. Berdes told me that the material was composed of intelligence reports and information that he and his staff had secured in conducting interviews with various persons. "It is all classified," he said. I asked if I might see a copy of that classified report, and was refused. He said that it was restricted to members of the Committee and those staff employees who have received appropriate security clearance. I asked if any member of Congress had looked at the material which had been classified. To his knowledge, he said, no member of the House had looked at any of that material.

I asked him if anyone in the news media had raised any question about the classified evidence and findings, about whether or not there had been a conspiracy against Peoples Temple and to kill Congressman Ryan. He said to his knowledge, no one had asked to look at the material and no one had even asked about the evidence.

"In fact," he said "you're the first one to raise any of those questions."

**U.S. House of Representatives Report,* p. 14.

23 After the Massacre

Soon after I returned to Memphis from Guyana, I discovered that Garry, who had arrived in San Francisco a day or two earlier, had been under intensive scrutiny by some members of the press. As we have seen, Garry had been holding press conferences for the Peoples Temple at his office since the fall of 1977. At these gatherings, he had charged that he had uncovered proof of "an organized, orchestrated, premeditated government campaign" to "destroy" the Temple. This quote, signed by Garry, was displayed on Temple brochures. Upon his return to a hostile national news media following the massacre, Garry made an about-face. He protested that he had never found any evidence to support the charges that he had made, or as he put it, "I found no evidence to support any of the charges that were made by Peoples Temple."* When the media suggested that perhaps Mark Lane had initiated the concept of government conspiracy, Garry, by that time panic-stricken, was apparently quite ready to accept the idea. He also said that he had not known that there were weapons in Jonestown and pointed out that I had failed to inform him of that matter. As we have seen, in June 1978,† many months before the massacre, Garry had publicly taken credit for arming Jonestown. In addition, the well-publicized statement of Debbie Blakey, her affidavit, and sworn statements that composed the various lawsuits against the Temple, all of which Garry was defending, made the same or similar charges.

In an interview for the CBS Evening News during late November 1978, Garry repeated the assertion that he was an innocent bystander and that I had failed to warn him of the dangers. Mike Lawhead, a reporter for the

**U. S. House of Representatives Report,* p. 21.
†Santa Rosa *Press Democrat,* 22 June, 1978.

CBS-TV affiliate in Memphis, interviewed me at my home so that I might respond to the charge for the Cronkite program that evening. During that video-taped exchange with Lawhead, I observed that Garry, at the age of seventy and with his long years of experience, was no longer in a position to proclaim his virginity. I referred to the printed record of his previous and contrary positions regarding weapons in Jonestown, and the conspiracy that he had discovered more than one year before I had heard of Jones or the Temple; I suggested that there was nothing that I could tell him that he did not already know. I did not wish to focus upon Garry as the culprit, but I believed it necessary to respond to his false charges, particularly when he began to violate the attorney-client privilege by making false public statements about Terri Buford, whom he had previously represented as a member of Peoples Temple and who had acted as liaison to Garry from the Temple. Furthermore, Garry had improperly released to the news media and others tainted documents that appeared to incriminate Buford.

The forty-two minute interview with the CBS affiliate in Memphis answered each of Garry's allegations and offered documentary proof of each contention I made. That evening Cronkite ran a substantial segment of Garry making his charges. Instead of presenting my answer, which had arrived at CBS in New York early enough to be screened, edited, and used, Cronkite said, "and Mark Lane's answer is"—a still photograph of me was displayed, with Cronkite continuing, ostensibly on my behalf—"that he was not on speaking terms with Garry at that time." CBS television invented a quotation for me that seemed to confirm the accuracy of Garry's assertions, rather than permitting my own very different response to be heard. Thereafter, the CBS falsification presented by Cronkite became standard journalistic practice on the subject. At news conferences, college lectures, in numerous newspaper and magazine stories, and on radio and television programs, the charge was made that I had deliberately withheld vital information that might have saved hundreds of lives, merely because I was not on speaking terms with Charles Garry. I tried to explain that Garry had been an acquaintance for years, that I had stayed at his home on occasion, had dinner with him often, and that some months before the massacre he had spoken at a testimonial dinner in my honor and had, as was customary at such events, praised me highly. I was not only on speaking terms but enjoyed good relations with Garry. Yet Cronkite's lie prevailed. The truth, not equipped with electronic wings, was not swift enough. When this matter was brought to the attention of CBS through Mike Lawhead, it declined to allow the truthful response to be heard.

What was perhaps the most memorable episode in the bizarre media misinformation campaign about Jonestown apparently just missed becoming part of a CBS Evening News telecast.

Soon after the massacre, Terri Buford and I flew from Memphis to Los Angeles on our way to meet with United States Attorney William Hunter in San Jose. We were greeted at the Los Angeles International Airport on December 5, 1978, by a group of vociferous and aggressive newspeople who made their colleagues, the paparazzi, seem both sensitive and restrained by contrast. Among the most persistent was a CBS-TV interviewer named Linda Douglas, who continued to shout inane questions at us from the time we entered the airport until we left the area in an automobile driven by Donald Freed. She bore the unmistakable qualifications of an on-the-air television reporter; her smile and her hairdo were both in place. During our trip through the airport, Douglas pursued us with questions such as, "Do you deny that you set up a Swiss bank account for the Peoples Temple last year in Zurich, Switzerland?" Later, I asked Terri if she felt that the confused reporter had actually asked me those questions. Terri said that she had. We were both amused and surprised that CBS-TV did not yet understand that I had not even heard of the Temple last year, much less opened an account for the group. We drove to the home of a friend, Bill Stout, a serious and knowledgeable television reporter for the CBS affiliate in Los Angeles, where we spent the night. The next morning Stout told me that after we had retired, he had received a telephone call from David Fitzpatrick, a CBS-TV field producer based in New York.

Fitzpatrick had told Stout that he had uncovered in San Francisco a story of some significance: "We have proof that Lane opened a Peoples Temple bank account with Terri Buford on November 22, 1977, while they were both together in Zurich." The proof, he assured Stout, consisted of a document signed by me that day in Zurich and a witness to corroborate the written evidence. Stout cautioned Fitzpatrick about moving too quickly, since I had insisted to him that I had never heard of the Temple at that time. Fitzpatrick said that he was positive of the facts and that his story was going to be aired the next night on the Cronkite show.

The next morning, Stout told Buford and me about this call from Fitzpatrick. I telephoned Fitzpatrick, who told me that he had in his hand the document I purportedly had signed in Zurich, and that he had secured a statement from a witness who offered "absolute corroboration" as to its validity. I told Fitzpatrick that on November 22, 1977, the fourteenth anniversary of the assassination of John F. Kennedy, I was in the United States being interviewed by the news media about the assassination. I told him that I had never been to Zurich, that I had not been in Europe during 1977, that I had never been to a Swiss bank in my life, that I had not met Terri Buford until September 1978, and that until recently, when Terri gave me various papers to give to William Hunter, I had never even seen a Swiss bank document. Fitzpatrick insisted that his story was accurate and that Cronkite was going to broadcast it.

I asked Fitzpatrick to go with me to visit a document expert of his choice. I said I would pay for appropriate tests to determine the age of the paper, of the typewriter ink impressions, and of the ink used to sign my name. Fitzpatrick refused to have the document subjected to any scientific tests. I then asked him to describe my "signature" on the paper. He stammered, avoided the question, and finally said, in the face of persistent questioning, that the "signature" was "typed, not written." I asked him to read the document to me. The paper he read from described an account opened for the benefit of the Peoples Temple. It gave the code name "White Cloud," and then presented the secret number assigned by the Swiss banking authorities. I told Fitzpatrick that while my expertise in the area was severely limited—it was based upon Perry Mason and similar fare, along with a modicum of logic—it seemed clear to me that an authentic document would not reveal the name of the true depositor, in this instance, the Peoples Temple, as well as the code name and secret number. I explained that for all the security such an account would afford the Temple, the account might as well have been opened at the Chase Manhattan bank. And that, at least would avoid the expense of overseas telephone calls, cables, and trips.

I asked if there were identifying data about me on the face of the document. Fitzpatrick answered, "Yes, there's your address on it here." When pressed, he said, "Not your street address. Just your city. It says, 'Mark Lane, Memphis, Tennessee.' "

I asked Fitzpatrick to listen carefully as it was becoming clear to me that he grasped the meaning of evidence rather imperfectly. "I now live in Memphis. I did not live here before the fall of 1978. I moved here less than four months ago. I never lived in Memphis before then. Therefore, a document bearing the date November 22, 1977, and stating that my address was Memphis, Tennessee, almost a year before I had moved to there, is not just a forgery but contains on its face proof that it is a clumsy forgery."

Fitzpatrick said that he did not see how a mistake in my address proved the whole document to be invalid. I tried to explain that it was not a mistake but proof that the document had been prepared long after November 22, 1977. Since he appeared to be confused, I urged him to have someone at CBS call me who was better able to absorb and evaluate the facts. I would explain it to him, I said. I have not since heard from Fitzpatrick or any associate of his in the project. If the words "Memphis, Tennessee" had not been placed upon the forgery, very likely America would have heard the stentorian tones of Walter Cronkite treating the hoax as if it were real and then assuring us all that's the way it was.

Later, on December 21, 1978, at the press conference given by Terri Buford following her testimony the day before in front of the federal grand jury in San Francisco, a question was directed to me. A reporter asked, "Mr. Lane, what do you know about 'White Cloud'? " I told her that I believed the phrase appeared upon a forged document which I had not been allowed to see but which one of the networks possessed. I asked her if she was with the San Francisco CBS affiliate. She said that she was not. I asked how she had heard about White Cloud. Her answer was illuminating. She said, "Tim Stoen told me to ask you about it."

I accompanied Terri Buford during December 1978 when she flew to San Jose to meet with United States Attorney William Hunter, members of his staff, and FBI and Secret Service agents. We were in great fear for her life. FBI agents met us at the airport and drove us across the landing area toward a secret meeting with Hunter. When I asked our destination, the Special Agent answered only, "We'll be there shortly." We were taken to an upstairs room at a hotel to await Hunter's arrival.

After our meeting began, the telephone rang. The Assistant Special Agent in Charge of the San Francisco office answered and spoke briefly. As I asked who had called, he made no effort to conceal his anger; the caller had asked for confirmation that "Mark Lane was being interrogated" in that room. Of course, I was not being questioned—Terri Buford was. Yet the fact that the security had been penetrated meant that the secrecy promised to us had been broken. I pointed out to Hunter and the FBI agents that neither Terri nor I knew where we were being taken and that we had not been out of the presence of the agents since our arrival. I said it was logical that the leak had come from a federal source. The ranking FBI agent agreed and said he would investigate the matter. A new meeting place was found and we journeyed to it.

At that session, I suggested that we explore the possibility that Terri Buford be granted immunity since Hunter, a friend of Tim Stoen's, had previously announced that she was a "target" of investigation. Hunter suggested that he hear her statement first. After she answered all the questions put to her by the U.S. Attorney's office, the FBI, and the Secret Service, Hunter said he did not believe she required immunity since apparently she had committed no crime and would therefore not be prosecuted. He asked if she would be willing to testify before a grand jury. She agreed to do so and accepted service of a subpeona.

I asked Hunter and his aides if they wished me to make a statement. They agreed to listen while I told them about the events that occurred during the last two days at Jonestown. When I asked if they were planning to call me as a witness before the grand jury, an aide said that there probably would be no need for that. I said that I would appreciate it if I could be called to testify on the same day that Terri did, if it was decided that they wished to have my testimony. I explained that I would accompany Terri to San Francisco from Memphis when she appeared before the grand jury, and that I could save both a trip and the need to cover my own air fare if we could testify on the same day. Again they said that they doubted that I would be called and they very much appreciated my full statement and my volunteering to appear.

The next day, the *Los Angeles Times* ran a two-column story, carrying the by-line of David Johnston and Doyle McManus, in which it reported:

> Two well-placed federal law enforcement sources said Lane also broached the subject of immunity for himself both prior to Wednesday's meeting and during the conference, which began before noon and lasted late into the afternoon.
>
> It was not clear what Lane was concerned about when he raised the subject.
>
> Lane, who before the mass suicide-murder in Guyana last month was paid more than $10,000 by Peoples Temple to launch a "counter-offensive" program against the group's purported enemies, could not be reached for comment.*

To report that a lawyer familiar with the penal code and federal criminal statutes was seeking immunity for himself and to speculate about what he "was concerned about" is to imply quite clearly that the lawyer knew that he had committed a crime.

To my knowledge, the *Los Angeles Times* had made no effort to reach me for a comment. However, as soon as the story was published, I called Hunter's office. There I was assured that Hunter and the members of his staff were not responsible for the false charge and that Hunter would gladly tell the *Times,* if called, that the allegation was absurd. I called the *Los Angeles Times* and talked to one of its editors. I said that the charge was

**Los Angeles Times,* 7 December, 1978.

a lie and that I demanded an immediate retraction. I said that I would not be satisfied with a "Mark Lane denies" story in which the false allegation was repeated. I suggested, rather strongly, that an ethical publication would have called Hunter, his aides, and the FBI and Secret Service agents who were present as well as Terri Buford and myself before publishing such a serious charge. I suggested that all of these parties be called at once and their statements be published.

The next day the *Los Angeles Times* ran a story* that was less than one-third the size of the original. It said that I denied the allegation. The new story increased the unnamed federal informants from two to "a variety of federal sources" and then agreed that one of the variety had backed down.

The relevant portion of the story follows:

> Lane said there is "not one word of truth in the statement that I ever asked for immunity." He said he has done nothing for which he would need immunity.
>
> The *Times* report, which said only that Lane had broached the subject, was based upon comments by a variety of federal sources over the last week.
>
> One of those sources affirmed Thursday that Lane never asked for immunity, but did imply that federal authorities believed—however wrongly in Lane's view—that Lane was culpable in any way that immunity would be an issue in any future talks between Lane and the authorities.
>
> Other sources could not be reached.

Time magazine later picked up the libel and repeated it, stating, "Lane denies that he too is negotiating for immunity."†

Newsweek ran a similar libelous statement:

> Last week, Lane and Buford flew to San Jose, Calif., where they were hustled off by four FBI agents who met their plane. For five hours, Lane and Buford were holed up in a San Jose hotel room with the FBI, Secret Service, and U.S. District Attorney William Hunter, the man in charge of the grand jury investigation. Lane denied press reports that the trip was designed to obtain a grant of immunity for both him

**Los Angeles Times,* 9 December, 1978.
†*Time,* 18 December, 1978, p. 31.

and Buford, and he refused to reveal what information had been passed to the government.*

During early December 1978, Carol Pogash, a reporter from the San Francisco *Examiner,* conducted a lengthy and exclusive telephone interview with Terri Buford. With the advance knowledge and agreement of both parties, I listened to the interview and interjected an occasional comment. Most of the information that Terri imparted was about Timothy Stoen, and some of the information appears here in the chapter about Stoen. On December 9, 1978, Pogash's fifty-five paragraph story was published. It contained but one sentence regarding Buford's charges against Stoen: "Tim Stoen was as involved in the taped conversations and letters as anyone." This was among the least serious allegations that had been conveyed to Pogash.

Subsequently, when Terri Buford testified before the United States Grand Jury meeting in San Francisco on December 20, 1979, a number of national and local reporters surrounded me in the Federal Building to ask me what she was being interrogated about. The law prohibits the presence of observers in the grand jury room. The sacred right to counsel, protected by the law, permits a witness to leave the grand jury room after each question to confer with counsel. The attorney is free to give advice to his client and, with the client's permission, to reveal the nature of the questions to the public. Terri had conferred with me on one occasion during her testimony. In any event, the United States Attorney and the members of his staff had told me what questions would be asked of her at a meeting immediately before her testimony. I said to the reporters, "Terri Buford is being asked about guns, money, and the actions of Timothy Stoen and Charles Garry." Marshall Kilduff was standing immediately to my right in the corridor just outside the grand jury room. As he jotted down a summation of my words in his notebook, he said, "OK. Guns, money, and lawyers." I said, "Please, Marshall, not 'lawyers.' I'm a lawyer and they are not asking about me. It's 'guns, money, Stoen, and Garry.' " He looked up from his pad, smiled and said as he rewrote his notes, "OK, guns, money, Stoen, and Garry."

Later that day Carol Pogash introduced herself to me and asked if Terri might allow her to conduct a full, in-depth interview. I told her that Terri had seen her article, which contained many attacks on her by Grace Stoen and unidentified "defectors." She was not surprised that false charges against her had been published, I explained, but Buford was astonished that

**Newsweek,* 18 December, 1978, p. 30.

truthful charges against Tim Stoen had not been printed. Pogash seemed genuinely pained. She said, "Listen, I wrote what she told me. I had her statements about Stoen in the story but the editors took them out. They won't print them."

The next day Marshall Kilduff's article about Terri's testimony was prominently published in the *Chronicle.** He wrote, "She was questioned by federal officials about the illegal use of arms and weapons, according to her attorney, Mark Lane."

Later that day, Terri Buford met with approximately fifty reporters to answer questions about her testimony. I initiated the conference by asking Kilduff why he deleted the references to Stoen and Garry in the statement attributed to me. He declined to answer the question publicly, but after the news conference he told me that I had unfairly embarrassed him. He said that he had accurately quoted me in the story he had written, but that his editor had removed the names of both lawyers.

At this time, a number of events were taking place in the United States which, under other circumstances, would have captured and held my entire attention. The Select Committee on Assassinations of the House of Representatives had concluded that there had been a conspiracy to assassinate President John F. Kennedy, and that in all likelihood a conspiracy was also involved in the assassination of Dr. Martin Luther King, Jr. My work for much of the last fifteen years had finally been verified by an official inquiry. My rejoicing, however, was muted by the recent deaths of so many fine people in Jonestown and by the continuing threats made against our family in Memphis.

Immediately upon my return to the United States, a biography, in the form of a feature story was published in the *New York Times*† under the four-column headline, "Cult's Lawyers Have Long History of Controversial Cases." Many newspapers and magazines thereafter referred to me as "Cult Lawyer Mark Lane." The references to me in Pranay Gupte's *Times* story were not only pejorative but also inaccurate. My questioning of the Warren Report, the *New York Times* said, "has proven remunerative." Thus, twelve years later, the *Times* was still following the lead of the CIA in discussing my "financial interest" in the Kennedy assassination whenever the question of the murder seemed relevant. The *Times* continued, "Mr. Lane says he believes there was a right-wing conspiracy to kill the President." In fact, I do not believe that nor have I ever said that. The *Times*

*San Francisco *Chronicle,* 21 December, 1978.
†*New York Times,* 21 November, 1978.

continued: "Representing the American Indians who faced riot, arson and conspiracy charges after an incident at Wounded Knee, S.D., five years ago, he declared that the trial would be a 'major civil rights case for American Indians.' But the Indians were convicted, and legal experts do not view the case as a major civil-rights test."*

I do not recall having made the precise statement quoted, but I certainly did express that position at the time. Again, the "Indians" were not convicted. As mentioned earlier, I represented Dennis Banks, along with other lawyers; William Kuntsler and others represented Russell Means at the major federal trial. After a very lengthy trial, all of the charges against both of the defendants were dismissed, and Dennis and Russell were freed. That result was adequately reported in the *New York Times* at the time. Since this appears to be only the second time that a federal court has dismissed serious criminal charges based upon governmental misconduct (the first being the case of Daniel Ellsberg), legal experts view the case as a crucially important Indian Civil Rights case and as important in establishing the proper response to proved governmental misconduct as well. Pranay Gupte was not merely mistaken; he deliberately published a statement he knew to be untrue. I called him after the article was published and asked if he could give me the name of a single "legal expert" who told him that the Indians had been convicted and that as a result the case was not a major civil-rights test. He could not provide the name of a single source. This did not surprise me, as I understood by then that he had not talked to a legal expert. He had made up the story.

The *New York Times* article continued: "A book Mr. Lane wrote about veterans of the Vietnam War, "Conversations with Americans," was characterized by several reviewers as irresponsible. That charge was also leveled at him when, as a state Assemblyman from Manhattan's West Side in the early 1960s, Mr. Lane questioned the ethics of a former Speaker."† There

**New York Times,* 21 November, 1978.

†While I was a member of the New York State Legislature from the East Side of Manhattan, not "Manhattan's West Side," I discovered that the Speaker of the Assembly was deeply and personally involved with the only corporation able to manufacture fall-out shelters. He had also just pushed Governor Nelson Rockefeller's hundred million dollar fall-out shelter bill through the Assembly. Many thousands of people joined with me in a march on the state capitol to protest. The *New York Post* heralded our campaign and finally the *New York Times* joined in the effort. The hundred-million-dollar program was abandoned, the speaker was defeated in his reelection, and he was next heard of as a lobbyist for the race track interests at the state capitol. The newspapers in New York City had, in fact, hailed this victory over corruption. In retrospect, the *New York Times* seemingly had a different view or perhaps a different ax to grind.

were not "several reviewers" but one reviewer in the *New York Times* who seemingly relied upon Pentagon sources to condemn the book. A subsequent full-scale investigation revealed that the information fed to the *Times* reviewer, Neil Sheehan, himself a strong supporter of the war in Vietnam, was false. Thus the *New York Times* had served as a conduit for the government in condemning a book which, perhaps prematurely, exposed the war in Vietnam as an atrocity and then the *Times* relied upon its own review in a subsequent effort to discredit me.

The last paragraph of the *New York Times* article stating that my efforts to furnish evidence to the House Select Committee on Assassinations "eventually proved fruitless" and that my conclusion that "Dr. King's death was also a conspiracy" was also incorrect. Within days, the Select Committee answered that false charge as well.

Within the next ten days it became apparent that the *New York Times*'s various defenses of the State Department—its insistence upon the term "mass suicide," and its commitment to covering up the facts surrounding the tragedy—were not isolated events. The emerging pattern was brought clearly into focus in a column appearing on the Op-Ed page written by Anthony Lewis. Lewis serves as sort of minister of propaganda for the power structure at the *New York Times.* He is generally allowed to roam at the end of a rather long leash to create the illusion of independence, and to establish his liberal credentials. Yet in those matters where the truth might threaten to expose or isolate those in positions of power, Lewis is ready to squander his reputation for integrity and apparently eager to engage in unprofessional conduct.

On November 30, 1978, Lewis's all-out attack upon me, entitled, "The Mark of Zorro," directed radio and television talk-show hosts to prohibit me from speaking. It contained a directive to editors as well to refuse to publish any book I might write about Jonestown, and he further urged that colleges ban me from the campus. Lewis insisted that "it is time for the decent people of the United States to tune out Mark Lane."

I found the title that Lewis chose for his piece to be illuminating. His colleagues at the FBI, those whose crimes he has so assiduously helped to cover up over the years, had used the code name "Zorro" some years before, as Lewis undoubtedly knew, in their effort to destroy Dr. Martin Luther King Jr.; the FBI campaign against King was coordinated under the name "Zorro." The United States Senate, through its Select Committee to Study Governmental Operations with respect to the Intelligence Activities, popularly known as the Church Committee, concluded that "the sustained use of such tactics by the FBI in an attempt to destroy Dr. Martin Luther King,

Jr., violated law and fundamental human decency." Walter F. Mondale, then a member of the Church Committee, said, "I must conclude that apart from direct physical violence and apart from illegal incarceration, there is nothing in this case that distinguishes that particular action much from what the KGB does with dissenters in that country. I think it is a road map to the destruction of American democracy." Lewis, possibly amused by the FBI's campaign to destroy Dr. King, chose to defend the FBI from a serious investigation into charges of complicity, while at the same time using the FBI's own code name for character assassination as the title for his remarkable column.

Lewis then stated that I had violated the lawyers' code of professional responsibility and predicted that there would be "bar proceedings" against me as well as "civil damage suits."

For having asked relevant questions about the deaths of President Kennedy and Dr. King, he referred to me as "chief ghoul of American assassinations." Lewis, before proclaiming, "It is time for some soul-searching on the part of talk-show hosts and editors and politicians who have allowed themselves to be vehicles in his promotion of conspiracies—and of himself," called me a "pitchman," a "publicist," a "creature," and as having a "talent for preying on the gullible."

After making his series of false charges, Lewis insisted that I be denied the opportunity to respond to those allegations in the *New York Times* or elsewhere.

Perhaps it is time for readers of the *New York Times* to learn who Anthony Lewis really is, at whose feet he kneels, and whose purposes he serves. While working to create the illusion that he is a liberal, even teaching a course at Harvard Law School on freedom of the press, Lewis, unlike the enemies of democracy who a quarter of a century ago organized their tawdry blacklists in the back alleys, shamelessly proclaims his in the *New York Times* and demands that the person he has targeted for destruction be denied an opportunity to be heard.

I would not deny Lewis the right to be published. I believe that the American intelligence organizations should be supplied with a columnist who fulfills their needs, whether he does so through direction, empathy, or chance. Indeed, I think it a useful exercise for the FBI and CIA to have their positions put before us regularly so that we may better judge them and try to understand what they are trying to accomplish. I also believe, however, that a truth-in-advertising approach should be adopted. When Anthony Lewis or any other writer with access to the editorial pages of the *New York Times* wishes to present the CIA's or FBI's view of an event, the column should say so.

Lewis's career of service to the established order goes back at least a decade and a half, when I first encountered his efforts on behalf of the Warren Commission Report. He became at once a well-paid apologist for the false Report. In fact, so anxious was he to support it that he wrote a special article for Bantam Books' edition of the Report. Indeed, it appears that his service to the state in that Report propelled him into a position of prominence with his newspaper's executives. Once he embarked upon that course, hitching his own reputation and integrity to the Warren Report, he became increasingly fanatic in his efforts to defend the official document. Lawyers who had served as counsel for the Warren Commission and other initial defenders of the Report later were convinced by the evidence that they had been betrayed by the intelligence agencies; Lewis never wavered. Not for a moment did he permit the facts to interfere with judgment. And finally—when it appeared certain that even the United States Congress was about to prove the Warren Report to be valueless—Lewis, driven by an obsession, or responding to an unyielding master, apparently became somewhat unglued, rejected his liberal cover, and stated that "it is time for the decent people of the United States to tune out Mark Lane."

On June 3, 1979, The *New York Times* reported that the House Select Committee on Assassinations "has concluded that a conspiracy" was responsible for "the assassination of President Kennedy." The Committee said, "no longer are we able to accept the judgment of the Warren Commission that President Kennedy was killed by a loner who was a lone assassin."

With that conclusion established, a trip back into the stories written by Lewis, upon which his career was promulgated and his integrity resides, proves somewhat humorous.

On September 28, 1964, under a headline that covered all eight columns of the front page of the *New York Times,* Lewis wrote, "The assassination of President Kennedy was the work of one man, Lee Harvey Oswald. There was no conspiracy, foreign or domestic." Those words, as Lewis parroted the conclusions of the Warren Report, were the first paragraph of the most important story that Lewis had ever written. Each of his conclusions was wrong. Two months later, on November 23, 1964, Lewis was given an opportunity to demonstrate contrition and concern for the truth. He declined. On that date, twenty-six volumes of evidence, containing thousands of documents, hundreds of exhibits, and the testimony or other statements of 552 witnesses were publicly released. Lewis, his loyalty previously assured, was assigned to review the massive and and unindexed volume of evidence. At the same time, I secured the available material. Working many hours a day, I was able to complete the first reading approximately one year later. Lewis acted more quickly. With the evidence in his possession but a few hours, he felt prepared to write the authoritative story for the issue of the *New York Times* that went to press that very evening. He assured America that "the testimony overwhelmingly supported the conclusions of Chief Justice Earl Warren and his colleagues, as revealed in the Commission's Report Sept. 27, that the assassination was no conspiracy but the work of one unhappy man, Lee Harvey Oswald."*

It is not that Lewis's conclusion was wrong, which calls into question his lack of integrity; it was more than absurd, it was indecent, to pretend to summarize evidence he had not read. The subject matter was, after all, not the result of a baseball game or the review of a film. America was waiting to learn of the facts surrounding the death of our president. It became clear then, as it became apparent later in his efforts to shield the Federal Bureau of Investigation in the murder of Dr. King, that no matter was too sacred for Lewis to lie about.

In a companion story, published on November 24, 1964, the *New York Times* condemned me for supporting what it referred to as "a conspiracy theory" and referred to me, not as a former New York State legislator, but as one "who has lectured to paying audiences" about my view that "Oswald could not have been the assassin." In my lectures I discussed the evidence that proved that shots had been fired from at least two different directions at substantially the same time, a conclusion the United States government adopted fifteen years later. The *Times* knew, but did not report, that all of the proceeds from the lectures were given to the Citizens Commission of Inquiry, a public service organization established to investigate the facts surrounding the murder of the president.

The Lewis article appeared to open the floodgates and wave after wave of vituperation followed. False charges by CBS-TV, the *New York Times, Newsweek,* and the *Los Angeles Times* abounded and were picked up and magnified by local newspapers and compounded by a series of false assertions in *Esquire* magazine, the *National Law Journal,* and numerous other publications. I was not surprised when the attacks began, for I had been warned by two newsmen to expect the assault. The depth of the manufactured stories, the intricacies of the falsehoods, and the vehemence with which the lies were told did, however, astonish me. Les Payne, a Pulitzer Prize-winning reporter at *Newsday,* told me in Los Angeles in the presence of Donald Freed and two other witnesses that a campaign to destroy me was under way. He said that the FBI agents had been talking, presumably to the press, about the efforts to indict me. Incredulous, I said, "For what?"

**New York Times,* 24 November, 1964.

He said that they had not been specific but they had been quite emphatic. In Memphis, William Haddad, then an investigative editor for the *New York Post,* warned me that the "word was out" and that I had been targeted as the purported victim of a powerful media campaign. He, too, was certain that attacks were coming, and was unable to trace their origin.

During this period, *Newsweek* devoted two pages to a cruel and libelous attack upon me.* The headline read, "Conspiracy Addict," and stated that I had been involved in "flights and fantasy over the past fifteen years." It concluded that I would probably be unable to "persuade federal authorities" of my view of the massacre, since, in their view, "Mark Lane has simply cried wolf too often before." *Newsweek* echoed Lewis, calling me "the chief ghoul of American assassinations," and adding that I was a "vulture." The sources for these evaluations, said *Newsweek,* were "his critics," unnamed. Unnamed "legal colleagues" were offered as wondering "whether his behavior deserved disbarment." Instead of legal authorities, Harold Weisberg was brought forward and offered as an "assassination buff," to charge that I was "totally amoral." Weisberg had previously stated that he was working for the FBI, although that was omitted by *Newsweek.* The *Newsweek* reporter called Terri Buford's father and asked him how he felt about the charge that his daughter and I were engaged in sexual activity. The charge was untrue. The reporter called a Memphis practicing attorney and asked her if I had sexual relations with her. Susan Brownmiller, who formerly worked at *Newsweek,* told me that when the *Newsweek* reporter called her, the "opening question was, 'Can you confirm for us that his sex life was kinky?' "

Newsweek wrote, " 'To prove it wasn't an elitist campaign, he [Lane] turned the first crank on the Ditto machine, then the rest of us would spend the whole night finishing the chores,' complained feminist Susan Brownmiller."

I recently talked with Susan Brownmiller and asked if the answer attributed to her by *Newsweek* was accurate. She said it wasn't. "I was talking about how you were a charismatic leader, and the reporter said, 'How would you define charismatic?' I said 'Well, you know, the sort of person who turns a mimeograph machine once or twice and then you find yourself standing there for the rest of the night.' But that was a joke."

She added, "There was no 'Ditto machine' in any political campaign that I've ever been in. A Ditto machine is what they used at *Newsweek.* So you know it wasn't a real quote."†

**Newsweek,* 18 December, 1978.
†We spoke on June 8, 1979, in New York City.

Susan Brownmiller had worked for *Newsweek* for some time. She is familiar with the power of that organization and its ability to distort and destroy. She said of the interview about me, "They were terrible in what they asked me. I was frightened because I thought they were quite willing to destroy my reputation to get you. I was outraged. I was horrified that they would sacrifice me to get you."

During this period, my father, who had in the past clipped newspaper articles about my work, shared them with his friends, and then mailed them to me, was deeply upset by the widely published false charges. He continued to send me articles, now always enclosing a note demonstrating his love for me and his faith that I would be able to answer the charges. However, Cronkite's news program and various publications had refused to permit my response to be heard or seen. My father continued to support my work, but his anguish deepened. I called him during the Christmas period and he seemed worried about me. I assured him that this difficult time would pass, and that the truth would be known one day. I reminded him that Betty, his wife and my mother, who had died several years before, always urged us to keep our sense of humor no matter how hard the road. A few days later he died of a sudden heart attack.

Soon after *Newsweek* published its false accusations, the *National Law Journal* ran a front-page story about me with a colored streamer headline.* The scurrilous story, written by Martin Fox, who was not identified, republished some of the libelous material published elsewhere. It did make a unique contribution to the record, however. It quoted Russell D. Hemenway, the executive director of the Committee for an Effective Congress, as follows: "Hemenway said that Mark Lane was not his real name. He believed his surname was the anglicized version from Russian or Polish. As for the first name of Mark, Hemenway said he took it for political purposes, because the highly popular congressman in the area had been the late Vito Marcantonio, commonly known as 'Marc' in the community, and an intimate of Mayor Fiorello La Guardia. 'I think Lane even spelled his name as M-A-R-C,' Hemenway reminisced."

This bit of inventive reporting was designed, as the *National Law Journal* put it, to show that I "don't care much for the facts." These are the facts: I was born in New York City on February 24, 1927, and upon my birth given the surname Lane. My father's name was Harry Arnold Lane and my mother's name, after her marriage to my father, was Elizabeth Brown Lane. The first name given to me was Mark. The official records maintained in

**National Law Journal,* 18 December, 1978.

New York City confirm this to be true and are of course available to those interested.

The *National Law Journal* article insisted that my conclusion that there had been a conspiracy to assassinate President Kennedy was wrong and stated, "No substantial evidence has yet to be uncovered that anyone other than Oswald killed the President." The article said that my book *Rush to Judgment* "was attacked from various quarters." The article condemned me for my representation of the defendants at Wounded Knee, and said that I alleged "various nefarious deeds by the government" but failed to reveal that all of the charges against the defendants were dismissed in accordance with the motion that we had filed, charging the government with misconduct. The very allegations derided by the *National Law Journal* article were concurred in by the Federal judge who found them to be accurate, and were the basis for the historic decision. The article attacked me for having alleged that Jimmy Hoffa "might have had ties with Jack Ruby, the killer of Lee Harvey Oswald." That conclusion was subsequently reached and endorsed by the Select Committee on Assassinations of the House of Representatives as well.

As I placed that publication aside, I wondered, as I do now, how the Committee for an Effective Congress (CEC) could presume to solicit funds from the public and instruct them for whom to vote when the organization was directed by a man who served as the source for untrustworthy information. After all, the CEC offered to the public nothing more than a promise that the research was careful, unbiased, accurate, and fair.

Some weeks after the Jonestown murders, a reporter asked if I were planning to write an autobiography. I said that I had no such plans. I told him this story.

Many years ago, I was the guest of Vincent Hallinan, a venerable lawyer with a beautiful house in Marin County, not far from San Francisco. Hallinan, the father of Patrick Hallinan—Stoen's present attorney—had also asked me if I were going to write an autobiography, and urged me to do so. He said that he had written one and called it *A Lion in Court.* I laughed, struck by his candor and lack of false modesty. He asked what I might call an autobiography if I wrote one. Still laughing, I said, "*A Fly in the Ointment.*"

During January 1979, the *New York Times** solemnly reported:

**New York Times,* 24 January, 1979.

. . . President Kennedy was assassinated, and it was Mr. Lane's early, loud criticism of the Warren Commission's investigation—especially in his book "Rush to Judgment"—that propelled him to national prominence.

In the intervening years Mr. Lane has written other books about controversial events with which he has become involved, and soon there is to be one about his involvement with the Peoples Temple in Jonestown, Guyana.

In a recent interview, Mr. Lane said that he planned at least one book after that, an autobiography or a memoir. He had decided on a title, he said: "Fly in the Ointment."

I had for some time known that the editors at the *New York Times* were not parched with a thirst for the truth, that fair play was not the motivation for their work, and that no overabundance of morality in any way impaired their vision of what was to be done. Now I knew that they lacked a sense of humor as well.

John Crewdson, a burly, relatively reckless staffer who had been charged with betraying his sources in Washington, and who while there had earned the disrespect of at least one highly regarded journalist, developed character assassination into an art form. Early in January 1979, Crewdson asked to interview me about a matter of great importance. We met the next week in San Francisco. Crewdson was accompanied by a young man he said was also employed by the *Times.* I was with Cindy Giblin, who had agreed to serve as a witness to the exchange. Crewdson had suggested a very fine and expensive Chinese restaurant, pointing out his very generous expense account. I placed a tape recorder on the table and said that I intended to record the event.

I told Crewdson that an article he had written the previous month contained an inaccurate implication.* He had written, "Miss Buford, who began living with Mr. Lane in Memphis . . ." I pointed out that he knew that Terri had been living with my extended family in Memphis, including April Ferguson, her daughter, and Grace Walden, a witness to the murder of Dr. King, whose release from a mental institution I had secured the previous year. Crewdson said, "You're wrong. That's not in my piece. Anyway, what's the complaint? You afraid that people will think you're shacking up with her? Well, I've heard rumors about the two of you anyway." Crewdson was wrong. The phrase did appear in the article that carried his by-line. And judging from his response, he seemed willing to credit the false rumors he said he had heard.

**New York Times*, 22 December, 1978.

During the dinner, Crewdson asserted that I knew that cheese sandwiches served in Jonestown on November 18, 1978, had been laced with drugs, and that I had refused to eat them while watching others consume the drugged food. Crewdson said he had learned that my refusal to warn Ryan and the others might very likely lead to my disbarment.

The charge was ludicrous. During the next hours spent in the restaurant, and later in his hotel room, I recounted the events for him in the presence of two witnesses. I told him that I could not have "known" the sandwiches were drugged, when in fact they had not been tampered with in any way. No one who ate a sandwich suffered any ill effects. Rep. Ryan, I pointed out, was shot to death, as were the others at the airstrip. In Jonestown, people were forced to drink a poison potion, others were injected with it, and still others were shot to death.

I told Crewdson that I was very busy during the day on Saturday attempting to calm the confrontations that Krause and others were creating. I was not offered any lunch until my final meeting with Jones. Even then sandwiches were not offered to me, although I did see two of them on a table. By then, I told Crewdson, food occupied a very low priority. Crewdson repeated the Krause story that I had purchased cough drops to eat instead of consuming the food in Jonestown. I told him that I had eaten very heartily on Friday evening and had a substantial breakfast on Saturday morning in Jonestown, and that I drank large quantities of coffee and Flavour-Aid on both days. I told Crewdson that I had purchased the small package of cough drops because I had a cough—if I had wanted to avoid the Jonestown food I would have brought some vitamins or food supplements. But I had eaten everything that had been offered to me in Jonestown, somewhat gluttonously, I confessed. I offered numerous details, answered fully and without evasion every question that Crewdson asked.

After hours of discussion, Crewdson said he was satisfied. Cindy Giblin remembered exactly how the meeting ended. She said recently, "Mark asked Crewdson, 'Are there any other questions you wish to ask?,' and Crewdson said, 'No, you've covered it all.' Mark then said, 'Are there any about which I have not been clear?' and Crewdson replied 'No. I certainly have your position.' Mark then told Crewdson he would be in San Francisco for the next day or so and that if he had any additional questions to call him there. The *Times* reporter said that he would."

The next morning, while Crewdson and I were both in San Francisco, Crewdson called my partner, April Ferguson, in Memphis. He asked her how she felt about the possibility that I might be disbarred for knowing that the cheese sandwiches were drugged and for failing to inform Ryan and the others. He did not tell her that he had interviewed me for hours the evening before about that same matter. April suggested that he call me for an answer, observing that I was in San Francisco. Crewdson replied, "I don't want to bother him with this."

The next day the story by Crewdson ran across three columns, under the headline, "Inquiry by Legal Grievance Unit Sought on Mark Lane."* All the charges against me that Crewdson knew were untrue were printed together with his statement that "Mr. Lane was traveling today and not available for comment." April Ferguson was quoted briefly.

Even before my meeting with Crewdson in January, I had indications that he was an activist rather than an objective reporter. In December, just after the first press conference at which Terri Buford spoke in San Francisco, Crewdson approached me. He strongly advised me to move to recuse William Hunter, the United States Attorney, from conducting the investigation into the massacre; he suggested that I bring an action in the Federal District Court to force Hunter to withdraw. I was astonished that a *New York Times* reporter had suddenly become my advisor, offering a rather radical unsolicited suggestion. Since most of those who died in Jonestown were black, and since Hunter was the only black official investigating the murders, I did not follow Crewdson's advice. Yet he and others embarked upon a campaign, which was ultimately successful, to remove Hunter.

After my initial trip to Jonestown during September, 1978, I returned to Memphis with the resolve to try to assist the residents of that settlement. I had sensed that a fortress mentality prevailed among the leaders. Of course, I did not know then that my efforts at reform would be overtaken by tragic events within two months. I began at once to work to lessen tensions in Jonestown by securing information about government actions toward the community and by trying to open lines of communication between Jonestown and fair and responsible journalists within the United States. I called Art Kevin, who had been news director and national correspondent for radio station KHJ in Los Angeles. I knew him to be a serious, decent man and a fine reporter. I discovered that he had become, since last I talked with him, the news director for radio station KVI in Seattle. I told him about Jonestown and asked if he would be interested in visiting the community to make a radio documentary. We also discussed the possibility of an interview with Jones via radio hook-up through the San Francisco office of the Peoples Temple. Kevin said he would explore the technical feasibility for such a broadcast and that he was interested in doing a documentary about the community. Accordingly, on September 27, 1978, I sent

**New York Times,* 12 January, 1979.

a memorandum to the Temple advising them that such a project was a real possibility.

On January 7, 1979, Crewdson called Art Kevin and said, "I have a memo leaked to me by the FBI and it has your name on it."* The memorandum Crewdson described was apparently a copy of my note about the proposed Kevin documentary. Kevin is positive that Crewdson said it had been "leaked to him by the FBI." Kevin answered Crewdson's questions about his connection with me. He asked Crewdson to send a copy of the memorandum to him. Crewdson agreed to do so. However, he mailed no document and he failed to return any of several telephone calls that Kevin placed to him. Kevin therefore called the FBI office in San Francisco to secure a copy of the memorandum. He spoke with Joe Aaron, a Special Agent of the FBI. Then, according to Kevin, who keeps and files meticulous notes on all matters he considers important, Aaron said that neither he nor the San Francisco office of the FBI had leaked any information to Crewdson.

Aaron told him that Crewdson had made an "unethical and unlawful" proposition to him. According to Kevin, the Special Agent of the FBI told him, "Crewdson said, 'Help me dig up some dirt on Lane. I'll protect the source.' I told him that his proposition was unethical and unlawful and that I would not participate in it."

Aaron then suggested that Kevin file a request under the Freedom of Information Act with the Bureau to determine if the memorandum were available. On January 15, 1979, Kevin initiated a request with the FBI in Washington, D.C. Later Crewdson called Kevin. According to Kevin, "Crewdson was badly shaken. He seemed very upset that I revealed the FBI had 'leaked' a document to him. He said that he was very embarrassed. Then he said, 'I didn't tell you that the FBI gave me that document.' I said 'Listen, John Crewdson, I am as good a reporter as you or better. You told me that you got the document from the FBI. There is no doubt about that. You told me that. You said it clearly and without doubt. You also said you would send a copy of it to me. Since you did not send it to me I called the FBI in an effort to get the memo.' Crewdson was very upset, and he said, 'Did you tape that telephone call with me?' When I told him that I had not taped it I could almost hear an audible sigh of relief from him."

Kevin told me that he called Les Whitten, a well-known journalist who had worked with Jack Anderson for years. Kevin said, "I called Les Whitten, who I knew also, because his name was also in the memo. Whitten said

*Kevin and I talked about the matter on June 11, 1979. With his permission, I tape-recorded the conversation.

that he had a 'very low opinion' of Crewdson. He said before Crewdson left Washington for Houston he had a run-in with a source of his. Evidently Crewdson almost got his source fired at one time by revealing him in a story about an alleged FBI operation in infiltrating a newspaper. Crewdson apparently burned the source for the important story."

On February 4, 1979, the massive Crewdson story about me was published on the front page of the *New York Times.* It would be difficult to find one allegation in the story that was both truthful and relevant. Crewdson said that Kevin said " 'Although Mr. Lane invited me on the trip to Guyana with Mr. Ryan, I was too busy to go' and added: 'I didn't promise a one-hour show, I hadn't promised to do anything.' "

Kevin said the quotation attributed to him by Crewdson is totally inaccurate. In fact, I had not wanted Art Kevin or any reporter to vist Guyana with Ryan. I spoke with Kevin on September 27, 1978, more than one month before I learned that Ryan was planning a trip to Guyana. I did not speak with him again until June 1979, long after the massacre. Kevin told Crewdson that he had agreed to investigate the possibility of an interview with Jones by radio and was interested in going to Jonestown to do a documentary program.

In a series of exchanges which resulted in the publication of but two sentences in the *New York Times,* Crewdson revealed that he had unlawfully received a document from the FBI, then lied about his admission to Kevin, broke his promise to send a copy of the document to the news director, made an unethical and unlawful proposition to a special agent of the FBI, and then published a totally false statement which he attributed to Kevin.

Earlier in the article, Crewdson attributed an allegation to Donald Freed. Recently, Freed told me, "I have never spoken with John Crewdson. I would have been happy to answer his questions about Jonestown, but he never asked me any. He never called me. He apparently just made up the statement which he attributed to me."*

The Crewdson article, with a two-column headline on the front page, followed by column after column of false charges inside the newspaper, was a plea to have me disbarred. On the first page, Crewdson wrote, "A formal complaint that could lead to disbarment has been filed in New York." That charge is untrue. No formal complaint had been filed by any committee of any bar association.

Crewdson continued, "And a California psychiatrist who is suing the

*Interview with Donald Freed, June 10, 1979.

Temple said Mr. Lane posed as a magazine reporter while interviewing him, an action that apparently would violate the lawyer's code of professional responsibility." Crewdson then said there was a "judicial inquiry in New York" into my conduct. That allegation is also an outright falsehood. There is and has been no "judicial inquiry" of any nature in New York or elsewhere regarding my conduct.

Crewdson focused upon the charge that I misled the "California psychiatrist," whom he identified later in his story as "Dr. Steven Katsaris, a psychiatrist whose daughter, Maria, had become Mr. Jones' mistress." Steven Katsaris is not a doctor, he is not a psychiatrist, he never told Crewdson that he was either a doctor or a psychiatrist, and his daughter Maria had not become the mistress of Jim Jones. Also I never posed as a magazine writer and he told Crewdson the truth about that as well.

Katsaris is the director of a school in Northern California. While his daughter Maria lived in Jonestown she was not the "mistress" of Jones. Jones had been married many years to Marceline Jones. In Guyana he lived in a private room. On occasion he shared that room with Carolyn Layton (the mother of Jones's youngest son). He said that he was interested in marrying Carolyn. Maria Katsaris cared for and helped to raise John John but was not the "mistress" of Jim Jones.

Regarding the Katsaris interview, Crewdson wrote that on October 2, 1978,

> Mr. Lane travelled to Ukiah, Calif., where the Peoples Temple had been based before moving to San Francisco, to interview two other critics of the Temple, Kathy Hunter, a local newspaper reporter, and Dr. Steven Katsaris, a psychiatrist whose daughter, Maria, became Mr. Jones' mistress.
>
> Dr. Katsaris said Mr. Lane did not identify himself as a lawyer but rather as a "journalist working on an article to be printed in *Esquire* magazine."
>
> "I asked him why his name was familiar," Dr. Katsaris recalled, "and he said that maybe it was from something that he had written." Mr. Lane proceeded to question him not only about his daughter, Dr. Katsaris said, but also about a lawsuit he had brought against the Temple.
>
> Clay Felker, the editor of *Esquire,* said his magazine had never assigned Mr. Lane to write an article on the Peoples Temple or anything else. The lawyer's code of professional responsibility mandates that "in his representation of a client, a lawyer shall not knowingly make a false statement of law or fact."

There is precious little truth in Crewdson's vignette. I did not travel to Ukiah to interview Katsaris. I had an appointment to see Kathy Hunter, who, without my knowledge called Katsaris and invited him to meet me. I did not expect him to be present; in fact, he arrived at the very end of my short stay at the Hunter house and we chatted briefly. Of course, I did not identify myself as a reporter from *Esquire.*

There is no need to speculate about what I might have said to Katsaris or about what he said to Crewdson. Steven Katsaris and I agree completely about the nature of our introduction. In addition, I took the trouble to tape record the entire exchange, with his permission, and that recording confirms our recollection.

The tape recording reveals that Katsaris asked me, "Which Mark Lane are you?" I indicated that I did not know if there were others with the same name but that I was both a lawyer and a writer. Katsaris said, "What have you written that I've heard of, because your name is familiar to me?" I replied, "I wrote a book on the assassination of President Kennedy called *Rush to Judgment.* It came out in 1966."

At that point Katsaris said, "Okay, you're the Mark Lane I know. I read *Rush to Judgment.*"

After the Crewdson article appeared, *Esquire* published an article by Steven Brill that also bore false witness against me. Katsaris told Bella Stumbo, a reporter for the *Los Angeles Times,* that he did not know why Crewdson and Brill insisted on publishing statements attributed to him that were untrue. When I spoke with Katsaris later, he told me that he had never told Crewdson that I said I was working on an article for *Esquire,* but had in fact identified myself as a lawyer.

Thus the front-page story in the *New York Times* arguing for my disbarment was based upon a series of lies published by John Crewdson.

Crewdson began the story, "Last September Mark Lane was proclaiming Jonestown a socialist paradise." At the end of the first paragraph he said that three months later I was calling Mr. Jones "a paranoid murderer." He referred to this as "Mr. Lane's turnaround." Crewdson knew that Garry, not I, had called Jonestown a "paradise." While it is true that I never said that Jones had murdered anyone until after he had done so, I do not consider that to be a "turnabout," but rather a responsible comment upon the available evidence.

Crewdson is an expert at distortion. When that method does not allow him to follow slavishly the *New York Times* party line, evidently he is not above urging federal authorities to join him in violating the law. When an FBI agent demonstrates respect for the rule of law, Crewdson is willing to publish outright falsehoods. Lewis, who helps to formulate that line, and Sulzberger, who rents his integrity to the CIA and others who create policy at the *Times,* cannot be surprised by Crewdson's irresponsible conduct. For it is they more than he who disgrace the concept of a free press. Crude, rough, and unscrupulous as he is, Crewdson is but a foot soldier who has available to him the defense that he was just under orders.

Over the years I have met a small corps of intense newsmen who have dedicated a portion of their professional lives to surpressing evidence surrounding the murder of President Kennedy. George Lardner, Jr., has played that role for the *Washington Post.* A decade ago when the New Orleans District Attorney, Jim Garrison, now a judge, was investigating the Kennedy assassination, he began to focus on David Ferrie, a man he believed to be a CIA employee who had worked with Lee Harvey Oswald. Lardner flew to New Orleans and interviewed Ferrie just after Ferrie had announced that he was ready to tell Garrison everything he knew. In the morning Ferrie's body was found. Lardner, the last person known to have talked with Ferrie, claimed that he had left Ferrie's New Orleans apartment early in that morning. According to Garrison, the special examiner concluded that Ferrie had died two hours before the time that Lardner said that he left him. No doubt this discrepancy was the result of the imperfect state of the art of pathology.

Lardner became an outspoken opponent of Jim Garrison and others who worked diligently over the years to learn and publish the truth about the assassination. He published a series of cruel attacks in the *Washington Post* upon Richard Sprague, the brilliant prosecutor from Philadelphia who had solved the Yablonski murder case and who had been chosen as general counsel and staff director by the House Select Committee on Assassinations. He published a similar attack upon me. He was responsible for the suppression of a great deal of relevant information about the assassination and for the distortion of other valuable evidence. In 1975, I interviewed him briefly about his last meeting with David Ferrie. I called to his attention the coroner's report and his own statement which fixed the time of his departure from Ferrie's apartment. I then asked if he, during the last two hours with Ferrie, observed any change in Ferrie's demeanor. When he seemed puzzled by my question, I clarified it. I said "Did you notice that he was a bit more lethargic, that in fact he didn't respond at all to your questions during that latter period?" Lardner became angry and demanded to know if I was accusing him of committing some indecent act. "Nothing serious," I said, "just suppression of the facts in the *Washington Post* about the death of the president." He turned and walked away. Soon after I returned to Memphis from Guyana, Lardner was literally on my doorstep, having flown in from Washington without even making an appointment. He had been assigned by the *Washington Post* to report about me again. In his fresh attacks upon me published in the *Washington Post,* he appeared to be working in tandem with Crewdson and he displayed little regard for the facts.

Another grizzled veteran of the war upon the truth in the Kennedy and King murders is Jeremiah O'Leary, who has publicly admitted to allowing the FBI to edit his copy and said that he sees nothing wrong with the practice, particularly when the Bureau provides all of the information for the article anyway. He has consistently published the CIA and FBI lines in the Washington *Star* and has been listed by both agencies as an "asset."* He, too, participated in the unfair attacks upon Sprague, whom the intelligence agencies feared in his role as the central investigator in the two assassinations. He, too, was an important intelligence asset in the slaying of Orlando Letelier in Washington, D.C., as well.

O'Leary has threatened to sue me if I ever publicly charge that he has been paid by the intelligence agencies. I have not made such an observation either publicly or privately, for not being privy to O'Leary's financial statements I would have no evidence upon which to base an evaluation. If he had not been paid, and I for one accept his denial at face value, then at the risk of being criticized for offering unsolicited advice, I would encourage O'Leary to take the matter up with his union.

Unlike Lardner, he did not wait until I returned to Memphis to prepare his new attacks. Almost immediately after I escaped from the jungle, I was confronted by Jeremiah O'Leary standing in the brilliant sunlight of Georgetown, Guyana.

I certainly should have suspected at that moment that the old guard was gathering again.

A relatively new entry was recently introduced into the discrediting game by Clay Felker, who by then was himself an accomplished artist in the field. According to a recent *Village Voice* article,† Felker has served as the editor of a CIA-funded daily newspaper, *Helsinki Youth News*, published at the World Youth Festival in Helsinki.

When the issue of Felker's CIA connection was raised several years ago, he responded somewhat ambiguously‡ that "It was my understanding that this [the CIA funding of his newspaper] was an anti-Communist effort. I was an anti-Communist then and I remain an anti-Communist today." He

*Carl Bernstein, *Rolling Stone,* 20 October, 1977.
†*The Village Voice,* 21 May, 1979.
‡*The Village Voice*, 21 May, 1979.

claimed then that he had been duped; that he had not known the source of his funding.

Felker, who in 1978 was the editor of *Esquire* magazine, assigned his young protégé, Steven Brill, to write a feature story about me. Brill describes himself as having a "Yale Law-school trained mind." He wrote a column for *Esquire* on American law and lawyers. He is the editor of a publication called the *American Lawyer.* He wrote articles about lawyers for *New York* magazine when his sponsor, Clay Felker, was editor of that publication. He now writes for the *National Law Journal.* A glance at his publication reveals that he is "a graduate of Yale Law School." However, it is more difficult to discover that Brill is not a lawyer. He has either failed the bar examinations since his graduation or for some reason has failed to take the bar, which if passed, might permit him to practice law. Brill himself claims that he has not taken any of the examinations. His word, however, seems to be a rather slender reed upon which to base a judgment. On June 8, 1979, when I questioned Brill closely, he admitted that he had not graduated from law school until 1976.* However, he had publicly solicited funds as "a 1975 graduate of Yale Law School."†

Very likely no story about the massacre has been much less accurate and more vitriolic than the article written by Brill.‡ In San Francisco, Brill was the first reporter to tell me that he had "discovered" that I used the name "Mark Lande" and that I had claimed to be a reporter for *Esquire* magazine when I interviewed Kathy Hunter and met Steven Katsaris. I told Brill that the charge was absurd, that soon after I entered the Hunters' house in Ukiah, George Hunter asked in Kathy's presence to see my credentials. I showed him my credit cards, driver's license, and other documents, all of which bore my name. I told Brill that I had tape-recorded the interview, and offered him a copy of the transcript of the entire discussion. He said that he didn't need to look at the transcript or listen to the recording. Then he told me that "thirteen witnesses" had confirmed Hunter's story that I had posed as an *Esquire* reporter. Again I offered the evidence to him and suggested that he interview Steven Katsaris. But Brill wrote, "According to Hunter and two others who attended the subsequent meeting, Lane instead said he was Mark Lande, a reporter for *Esquire* magazine. Eight

*Telephone interview with Brill, 8 June, 1979.

†The April 1979 issue of the *American Lawyer* carried a four-page promotion solicitation letter complete with a business reply card requesting $17.50 for a subscription.

‡Steven Brill, *The Teamsters* (New York: Simon & Schuster, 1978), p. 42. For a fuller discussion of the events surrounding the publication of *The Teamsters* and the near-supression of *The Hoffa Wars* by Dan Moldea, see Appendix K.

people on the West Coast involved with Jones say Lane passed himself off as Lande of *Esquire* during that time."* However, according to another reporter, Kathy Hunter said I identified myself as "Mark Layned, spelled L-A-Y-N-E-D."† Continuing his theme, in the *Esquire* article, Brill wrote: "This masquerade may be grounds for Lane's disbarment that the Grievance Committee of the Second Judicial Department in New York City (Lane's only bar affiliation) could pursue. Disciplinary Rule 7–102 A–5 of the Lawyers Code of Professional Responsibility says that 'in his representation of a client, a lawyer shall not knowingly make a false statement of law or fact.' Lane's 'Mark Lande' act was just that."

Katsaris made it clear to those who asked him about the contrived charge that I had introduced myself at the Hunters' as Mark Lane, that he had recognized my name, and had read at least one book that I had written and was familiar with another one. That introduction took place in front of Kathy Hunter, as the tape recording reveals. Yet Brill wrote: "Worse, one of the guests interviewed at Lane's masquerade meeting with Hunter is Steven Katsaris. Katsaris was suing the Peoples Temple because he claimed that his daughter was being held hostage."

Brill's article is replete with false statements and half-truths epitomized by his treatment of my interview with Katsaris and Hunter. In addition, Brill misquoted me throughout his article and later admitted that he did not record our discussion, although in the interest of accuracy, I urged him to do so.

An example of his odd technique may be discovered from his handling of the evidence that a "Peoples Temple hit squad" may exist. The investigations for the Staff Investigative Group to the House Committee on Foreign Affairs concluded that "while the existence of a reported 'hit squad,' whose purported purpose is to eliminate Jones' staunchest opponents, cannot be concretely documented it should not be totally discounted. This group has been described as including some of Jones' most zealous adherents. There is evidence to suggest Jones and some of his key lieutenants discussed and had 'understandings' to eliminate various individuals, including national political leaders."‡

Following the massacre, Terri Buford felt obliged to give the federal authorities the evidence about a "hit squad" in the interest of preventing further violence. While the FBI, Secret Service, and U.S. attorney's office in San Francisco were impressed with the evidence offered by Buford and others, and with her conclusion that the matter might be one for continued

**Esquire,* 13 February, 1979, p. 50.
†George Carpozi, Jr., *The Suicide Cults* (New York: Manor Books, 1979), p. 225.
‡*U.S. House of Representatives Report*, p. 35.

concern, Brill ignored the evidence and wrote: "Spiced with talks about a hit squad surviving the Guyana disaster, the CIA plot is the new Lane line that we're now destined to sit through. The sole evidence that there is a hit squad, incidentally, other than Lane's client Terri Buford's statements, are the packets of Kool-Aid on his doorstep in Memphis a few days after the Guyana deaths. (The doorstep dropping of the drink mix used for the Jonestown poison is his death warning from the hit men, Lane says.) At least among law enforcement people, Lane's credibility is now such that the Memphis detectives investigating the Kool-Aid caper suspect Lane planted it himself."*

The Kool-Aid packets are not "evidence" of a hit squad and I know of no one who suggested that they were. I never offered any evidence of a hit squad, since I had none. The information that I had received came from Terri Buford. Many other former members of Peoples Temple, however, including Timothy Stoen, members of Concerned Relatives, Debbie Blakey, Elmer and Deanna Mertle, Mike Cartmell, and numerous others spoke of their fear of the Temple's "hit squad" on radio and television programs and in newspapers circulated throughout the country after the massacre. It appears that only Brill and Jean Brown denied the possibility of the existence of a hit squad. The Memphis police view of the Kool-Aid packets, which Brill, in spite of his Yale Law-trained mind, badly confused with the evidence regarding a hit squad, may well be a Brill invention.

At the conclusion of the interview, Brill asked me to comment upon the Kool-Aid incident. I told him that I did find the packets there early one morning when I opened the door looking for a newspaper. I told him that a New York literary agent, George Greenfield, was present when I found the packages. I told him that I made a full report about the matter to the FBI agents who visited my house that morning, and that I had turned the evidence over to the officers of the Memphis Police Department at their request. Brill then told me that officers of the Memphis Police Department had proof that I had planted the packages there myself. He said that the officers had given him the name of the owner of the supermarket down the block from my home. The owner, Brill said, was prepared to testify that I had purchased the Kool-Aid there the day before I claimed to have discovered it.

I told Brill that there was no supermarket "down the block" from my home. The closest market was blocks away and the closest supermarket more than a mile beyond that. I said that I had never been in any market or supermarket in Memphis, having arrived there just a short time before

***Esquire*, 13 February, 1979, p. 52.

the massacre, and that I had never purchased Kool-Aid in my life. I said that since I had made a full report to the federal and local police about the matter, he had better be sure of the facts. For to state that I had planted the Kool-Aid was tantamount to stating that I had committed crimes in making a false report of my discovery. Brill promised that he would talk to the "supermarket" owner and then give me the man's name so that I could be confronted by my accuser.

When I returned to Memphis, I met with the highest-ranking officers of the Memphis Police Department, the office of the Mayor, and various other officials to determine whether Brill or a local officer had concocted the story. The police refused to take responsibility for the story. After Brill published a very different version from the one he had developed for me, I called him. He refused to tell me the name of the Memphis police officers he had referred to in his story. When I asked him if he had talked to the supermarket owner, he refused to answer, stating "I usually don't talk more about my article than what's in them (sic)." I assured him that I understood his approach and that I appreciated that there was considerably less to his articles than met the eye.

In the months that followed, when I spoke at colleges or at press conferences, angry charges were almost invariably made against me. I was told that had I not committed crimes I would not have asked for immunity.

Bella Stumbo of the *Los Angeles Times* accompanied me as I spoke at colleges in various parts of the country. At each lecture, I described in some detail the false allegations made by the newspaper she represented;* she declined to mention this matter in her story.

I considered her to be an honest reporter, yet I was not surprised to discover that her front-page *Times* story was thoroughly dishonest. She told me that she was impressed by what I had to say and at the student support for my lecture. During our travels together she seemed inordinately depressed. I asked what troubled her and she said, "I want to do a fair job. I like you and I wanted to do a favorable article." She explained, "When I call my editor, everything positive that I tell him about you he twists around. They publish their lies and then, and this is the worst part, they actually begin to believe them."

I asked her for an example. She said, "I called my editor and said that you have a remarkable amount of energy and he said, 'Fanatics often do.' Later I told him that there was a great deal of support for you all over the

**Los Angeles Times,* 30 April, 1979.

country and he said, 'That's the most frightening thing I've heard in years.' They really believe their own lies. That's the problem."

She seemed so upset I advised her to withdraw from writing the article. Early one morning she was beaming. "I've solved it," Stumbo said, "I'm going straight home when we finish. I'm going to write the article from my notes without meeting with my editor. Then I'll just hand him the completed story. That way he will not be able to advise me or insist upon what I should write."

Bella was happy all day. The next day, as we waited for a connecting flight, she called her office and returned, she was on the verge of tears. She said, "He won't let me do it that way. He has insisted that I meet with him and discuss the entire article before I write a word. Now I don't know how to handle this."

She evidently did decide how to proceed. She wrote the article her employers wanted and suppressed her own view; she later gave me some valuable inside information about the earlier attacks made upon me in the *Los Angeles Times.*

After she returned to Los Angeles, Bella Stumbo told me that while reporters Johnston and McManus were in San Francisco covering the massacre investigation and matters peripheral to it, Johnston had written the piece that said I had requested immunity for myself.* She told me that there had been a serious brouhaha at the office after I called and the *Times* discovered that the story was completely untrue. Later, Hunter himself told the press in San Francisco that the story was absurd; even then the *Times* did not retract its story or quote Hunter. Stumbo said that Johnston was reprimanded with a punitive transfer from San Francisco to some lightweight assignment in Los Angeles. (Although both names appeared in the by-line, Johnston alone was its author.)

Bella said that Johnston had been talking to *one* federal agent (not a "variety") and that he speculated about what I might have done under other circumstances. If so, an error was responsible for the original story. However, without the prejudiced mindset at the *Los Angeles Times,* that mistake would not have been published. Had there existed at the *Times* a concern for accuracy, the article would have been retracted when the editors learned the truth from their own staff writers.

While the *Los Angeles Times* may have been willing to punish the erring reporter, apparently it drew the line at publishing the truth.

**Los Angeles Times,* 7 December, 1978.

In the unenviable record established by the national American news media regarding the tragedy in Guyana and its aftermath, the first report —that I had probably died there—was about as accurate as anything that followed.

The early misinformation was no doubt due to the primitive methods of communication then available and the predictable desire of the United States government to suppress the immediate—the government would say premature—release of any information. The disinformation that has followed evidently resulted from a deliberate plan to obfuscate the truth about the tragedy. It began, as it has so often in the past, with the *New York Times* and CBS-TV. Soon, however, it spread, as poison flowing in the bloodstream, through much of the print and electronic press. As I stood isolated and powerless, I sought to say what I had seen, but soon I was the enemy of the people, for as in Ibsen's drama, I had seen the malignancy and tried to speak of it.

In the past, as journalists pursued their careers by adhering to the guidelines enunciated years before by the CIA and FBI, I became discouraged at times. The knowledge that a similar campaign and of greater intensity had been waged against Dr. Martin Luther King, Jr., by the same subversive forces constrained me to examine the matter with some perspective. Following the massacre, the effort to discredit me and to destroy my reputation became savage. It seemed that any restraints of decency and a sense of truth had been removed. Half-truths and sly innuendos were replaced by outright falsehoods. Stories were invented, manufactured quotations were attributed to me, and fabricated law suits, nonexistent criminal complaints, and imaginary formal complaints before the bar association were widely discussed, described, and evaluated as if they had been real events.

Associates and colleagues whom I had not seen for some time tended to agree after reading the press and watching the television news broadcasts that I had "gone too far this time," although when pressed to explain the meaning of that recurrent phrase, were unable to do so. It is my belief that this practice engaged in by the *New York Times** and others have, over the

*Evidence reveals that in other matters as well, the *New York Times* did not hesitate to function as a transmission belt for CIA propaganda. E. Howard Hunt, the convicted Watergate burglar and former CIA officer, recently revealed that, acting upon orders from Director Richard Helms, he wrote a story about Soviet espionage activities during the fall of 1967. Helms had given Hunt CIA material prepared by Howard J. Osborn, the CIA's Chief of Security. Hunt told *More,* a monthly magazine dealing with journalism, "When the director calls me up and says 'I've got a couple of files here, I want you to do a story of about 800 words and I'll try it out on Cy Sulzberger,' I do it."

years, constituted a most serious threat to the concept of a free press. For that reason, among others, I will initiate multimillion-dollar lawsuits against the *New York Times,* Anthony Lewis, John Crewdson, the *Los Angeles Times,* Steven Brill, *Newsweek*, CBS-TV, and others referred to in this chapter. In those actions, I will seek to discover the sponsors of the campaign to discredit me so that they may be held accountable for their misconduct. The recent decision of the United States Supreme Court in an action brought against CBS-TV* has made it clear, I believe, that such inquiries are relevant and authorized by law. It is time, I believe, that the facade that has shielded the most insidious intrusions into the lives of Americans be torn asunder. Many of the indecent assaults upon Dr. King, Andrew Young, and their co-workers were the result of stories and photographs initiated by intelligence agencies. Many were circulated to the news media under the direct order of J. Edgar Hoover, then the director of the FBI. A similar campaign has been waged against those who have inquired into the death of Dr. King as well as the early critics of the Warren Report. No publication has been more receptive to the slander and libel and more willing to publish such false reports, I believe, than the *New York Times.* Lewis, Sulzberger, Crewdson, and their colleagues may reject an opportunity to debate these matters publicly, but they will, in the relatively near future, be given an opportunity to answer the relevant questions under oath and during a court proceeding.

There is indeed a poison in our land. It is stronger than the poison placed in the mouths of the children in Jonestown. Until we recognize it, understand its virulence and act against it, our pretensions of a free press in an open society are but a sad and painful mockery of what might have been.

Hunt said that on September 13, 1967, the *New York Times* published the CIA document on its editorial page under the by-line "C. L. Sulzberger." The article, Hunt said, was "75 percent unchanged."

According to Bill Peterson, a staff writer for the *Washington Post,* "The *New York Times* yesterday refused to comment on Hunt's allegations, and efforts to reach Sulzberger were unsuccessful."

*That matter is more fully explored in the Epilogue.

Epilogue: Blood on the First Amendment

Upon surveying the condition of the fourth estate, the federal government would be justified in rushing to assist it as a moral disaster area. In the case of *Lt. Colonel Anthony Herbert* v. *CBS-Television,* that is precisely what the United States Supreme Court did. The assistance, a ruling designed to restore some fairness to the laws of libel, and possibly even a modicum more truth to national news media reports, was accepted with almost unanimous and predictable ill grace by the royalty of the news business. The long and ritualistic editorial in the *Los Angeles Times* on April 19, 1979, which greeted the court's ruling, carried the headline, "Blood on the First Amendment." Said the article:

> By meretricious reasoning, the U.S. Supreme Court reached a meretricious decision Tuesday that bloodied the First Amendment. In a 6–3 ruling, the court held that public figures suing for libel may inquire into a journalist's "state of mind," and into the editorial process.
>
> This decision, combined with others like the ruling that granted the police the power to conduct surprise raids on the offices of news organizations, fully discloses the "state of mind" of the majority of the Burger court.
>
> That "state of mind," developing over the past decade, reveals a crabbed, narrow bias against the First Amendment as the bulwark of a free press and a free society.

The *Times* concluded:

> Not only will the decision have a chilling effect on the material that editors and reporters prepare for publication, it also will intrude deeply into the internal process behind publication by opening to discovery ideas expressed within news organizations in conversations and memoranda.
>
> Associate Justice Byron R. White, writing the majority opinion, said the 2nd U.S. Court of Appeals misconstrued the First Amendment. We believe, instead, that the Supreme Court savaged the First Amendment by this decision, and misconstrued the nature and history of the liberty that has nurtured this nation for two centuries.

James Goodale, the executive vice president of the *New York Times,* agreed. He said that the decision would "hamper the really big investigative stories" since, he reasoned, reporters would understand that if they or the publication they worked for were sued for publishing false and defamatory articles, they "in effect, are going to have to stand naked in front of the courts with respect to all their thought processes."

The president of CBS News, William A. Leonard, condemned the decision as "another dangerous invasion of the nation's newsrooms." *Broadcasting,* the industry's publication, repeated its earlier charge that the ruling would "strike to the heart of the vital human component of the editorial process."

Despite the outrageous cries of alarm by the businessmen in the industry, the decision in the *Herbert* case was but a modest effort by the court to secure or maintain some balance in actions brought by those who had been unfairly and deliberately maligned by the American news media.

Very often, when a court decision is difficult to understand, a careful review of the facts of the case may lead one to perceive that the judgment was "result-oriented." That is, the decision was based not so much on matters of law, but on the questions posed by the peculiar facts or the special status of the parties.

The special privileges that the news media had quickly assumed as a matter of right, and were most reluctant to relinquish, as we have seen, had been bestowed upon it by the Supreme Court in a case made particularly difficult due to its special circumstances. Under the leadership of Chief Justice Earl Warren, the court, during the racial confrontations of the 1950s and 1960s, issued a series of result-oriented decisions designed to redress ancient grievances. Unfortunately, some of these rulings, based less upon sound legal principles and more upon pragmatic and temporal concerns, left behind a new class of disadvantaged, and established, in libel law, an atmosphere of unanimity for the news industry even in the event of its unconscionable behavior. Neither the liberals nor the media seemed to understand the problems the court had created. Together they stood, united with the Warren Court against the clearly defined enemy. They, and consequently Warren and his colleagues, had earned for themselves and their concerns a privileged place in society.

The liberals and the national news media loved Earl Warren and the result-determined decision of his court. They were willing to ignore or attempt to explain away as youthful extravagance his excesses as a prosecuting attorney in Alameda County, California, and the crucial part he had played in the imprisonment of Japanese-Americans during World War II for reasons of race. If they were embarrassed by his report upon the death of President Kennedy, which the passage of a few short years has already found to be an historical fiction, one could hardly have detected that response, so dutifully did they rally around to defend it. Yet these shortcomings were but precursors. We are now left with the heritage of a court devoted to pragmatism and largely devoid of commitment to sound legal principles. No better example, both of this problem and the legal maxim that hard cases make bad law, can be found than in the decision of the Supreme Court in *The New York Times* v. *Sullivan.* *

The case, decided in 1964, was a landmark decision which determined that factual errors and statements which constitute defamation of a public official, as opposed to a private person, were insufficient to warrant an award of damages unless "actual malice" was present. "Actual malice" was defined as "knowledge that statements are false or in reckless disregard of the truth."†

The *New York Times* case involved a full-page advertisement, carried in March 1960 about the civil rights movement, entitled "Heed Their Rising Voices." It was signed by the "Committee to defend Martin Luther King and the Struggle for Freedom in the South," and sixty-four prominent supporters of the movement. The ad was a plea for contributions, and as part of its plea listed the efforts of the committee and the violence it had met with: ". . . they are met by those who would deny and negate that document [the Constitution and the Bill of Rights] which the whole world looks upon as setting the pattern for modern freedom. . . ." The broadside then listed some of the violences the movement had been met with: ". . . when the entire student body protested to state authorities by refusing to

**New York Times* v. *Sullivan,* 376 U.S. 254.
†Ibid., 376 U.S. 254 at 279–283.

reregister, their dining hall was padlocked in an attempt to starve them into submission." And, "They have bombed [Dr. King's] home almost killing his wife and child."

L. B. Sullivan, one of three elected commissioners of Montgomery, Alabama, and supervisor of the Police, Fire, Cemetery and Scales Departments, sued the committee, four black clergymen, and the *New York Times,* claiming that the accusations in the *Times* referred to him, although he was not named.

A Montgomery County, Alabama, court awarded Sullivan the full $500,000 he had demanded, and the Supreme Court of Alabama affirmed. The *New York Times* and the committee appealed to the United States Supreme Court.

What was the court to do? A committed movement of citizens working toward realization of promised rights was under way; blacks and whites were working together to register voters, sit in at lunch counters, ride public transportation as Freedom Riders, use public libraries, swimming pools, and amusement parks. The beginning of that groundswell was the Supreme Court case *Brown* v. *Board of Education,* * which in 1954 decided that it was harmful to black children to be denied, by state law, access to the same schools that white children attended.

It was clear, in that court presided over by Chief Justice Earl Warren, that the direction of civil rights litigation in the country was going to be for the plaintiff.

But what if the plaintiff was on the other side? Zealous members of the movement had, according to Commissioner Sullivan, falsely implied that he was responsible for these acts of violence—when in most cases the perpetrators were not known. This is libel, said Sullivan, and demanded a judgment. An Alabama jury and the Alabama courts agreed with Sullivan and granted and affirmed the judgment. Alabama was one of those states which saw itself as being invaded, once again, by the carpetbaggers from the North. Those in the power structure within the state were unhappy about the agitation and the concomitant violence, and this judgment, it surely reasoned, would serve notice to outsiders to leave Alabama at peace.

The Constitution says that rights are reserved first to the people, then to the states, and those remaining go to the federal government. Alabama, along with other southern states, felt in those days that the federal government had usurped its rights. Its only recourse, as direct defiance had proved impossible, was collateral attack. *Sullivan* was just such a device.

**Brown* v. *Board of Education*, 349 U.S. 294, 1954.

The federal court saw in that approach the renewed defiance of a state against the supreme authority of the national government. Consideration of the laws of libel was but a secondary concern. In essence, the Supreme Court dealt with the question of states' rights under the cover of amending or interpreting anew laws evolved to determine the rights of those who had been defamed.

That the statements were false, and that they could be imputed to *Sullivan,* had been proved; but this victory for Alabama over the *New York Times* and the civil rights movement could not be permitted. Thus evolved a "result-oriented" decision. Apparently it was determined at the outset that Alabama and *Sullivan* could not be allowed to prevail even though he had proved his case. Faced with that immutable conclusion, it was wrong for the Warren Court to develop and announce the rule governing libel. That rule or privilege was the finding that criticism of officials shall go unchecked, true or not, unless the official could prove something beyond carelessness. The word "malice" was used, but not, apparently, with the ordinary meaning. "Malice" in the *New York Times* seemed to mean not evil intentions but something less; not mere carelessness, but something more.

This concocted privilege, designed to help the civil rights movement and the *New York Times* out of a difficulty, has bedeviled the country ever since. "Public officials" had been extended by the progeny of *Times* v. *Sullivan* to include public figures who were not elected or appointed. As the media became a peculiarly protected species, the endangered groups grew to include those who had merely commented upon societal ills. For surely, one could reason, if the national press was sufficiently concerned to defame the individual, he must be a person of some public note. Indeed, the trouble taken by the media to falsify the record about Sullivan was itself almost proof that he was a public figure and thus devoid of rights available to all others.

Members of the court, in deciding *Times* v. *Sullivan,* saw their ruling as a means to protect the absolute right of the citizen to criticize public officials. Their concern was that those who spoke out against tyranny must not be stripped of the requisite weapons. Mr. Justice Hugo Black, in the decision, concluded that the press should be given an "absolute immunity for criticism of the way public officials do their duty." Mr. Justice Arthur Goldberg wrote that it was necessary to establish "an absolute, unconditional privilege to criticize official conduct despite the harm which may flow from excesses and abuses."

The court had reacted to the circumstances surrounding the libel action.

The Montgomery (Alabama) *Advertiser* had published a feature story with the headline "State Finds Formidable Legal Club to Swing Out-Of-State Press." That threat became a reality as another half-million-dollar libel judgment was awarded to another public commissioner based upon the same advertisement even before the Supreme Court ruled on *Times* v. *Sullivan.* In fact, by then, eleven officials in Alabama had filed suits against the *New York Times,* demanding more than $5.5 million.

The court knew that the half-million-dollar judgment was the largest in the history of the state of Alabama. The Supreme Court reacted. It agreed to review a state judgment in a libel suit for the first time in the history of the nation. Hard cases make bad law and very hard cases make very bad law.

The court ruled, "We consider this case against the background of profound national commitment to the principle that debate on public issues should be uninhibited, robust, and wide open, and that it may well include vehement, caustic, and sometimes unpleasantly sharp attacks on government and public officials."

A new legal principle had been established, drawn from, as Mr. Justice Oliver Wendell Holmes, Jr., had observed years previously, what is "understood to be convenient." The concept had been developed to guard the individual liberties of the citizens from the tyranny of the government.

The ruling, published on March 9, 1964, came at a most unsettled time for the nation. President Kennedy had been assassinated less than four months earlier. In an unprecedented action, his successor, Lyndon B. Johnson, had appointed the chief justice of the United States to head a commission assigned to investigate the murder, since so many doubts had arisen in its wake. Documents now available reveal that Warren and his colleagues on the Warren Commission were secretly meeting with American intelligence officials who were utilizing their contacts, or as they called them then, "assets," in the news media to support the false conclusions of the commission. Thus, while Earl Warren and the members of the Supreme Court were eloquently speaking out in support of a wide open, robust, and uninhibited debate on public issues, Warren and his colleagues on the commission were at work subverting the meaning of *Times* v. *Sullivan.*

While the Supreme Court, in that case, protected the rights of Dr. King and the news media, J. Edgar Hoover and his Federal Bureau of Investigation were utilizing their assets in the news media in an attempt to destroy Dr. King, and ultimately used those assets in an attempt to lure Dr. King into the Lorraine Motel in Memphis, Tennessee, during April 1965, where he was then murdered.

The court in *Times* v. *Sullivan* saw the American news media as an independent force which should be strengthened so that its contacts with government officials might be fair. The court apparently did not know that the most covert and tyrannical segments of the government, the Central Intelligence Agency and the Federal Bureau of Investigation, were manipulating, influencing, and sometimes controlling the actions of the national news media for the purpose of stifling debate and inhibiting discussion of public issues.

Recently I was able to secure various CIA documents made available under the then newly amended Freedom of Information Act. As previously mentioned, one of those documents disclosed CIA activity toward me and other Warren Commission critics. In referring to the assassination of President Kennedy, the document said, "Our investigation itself is directly involved: among other facts, we contributed information to the investigation." The dispatch, document number 1035–960, was addressed to "Chiefs, Certain Stations and Bases," and was designed, it said, "to employ propaganda assets to answer and refute the attacks of the critics [of the Warren Commission Report]." It offered "arguments" for "media discussions" and frankly proclaimed that its purpose was to "inhibit the circulation" of criticism of the Warren Commission report. Thus while the Supreme Court asserted its interest in "uninhibited" debate "on public issues," the intelligence organizations which were working with Earl Warren sought to inhibit and prevent such debate.

In *Herbert* v. *Lando et al,* decided on April 18, 1979, the Supreme Court took one small but significant step away from the protective doctrine that had been the law for a decade and a half. While it might be said, and truthfully so, that my analysis of this case and *Times* v. *Sullivan* is not that of a disinterested observer, since I am a victim of media excesses, I remind the reader that my bias, or judgment, if I may, is tempered by what might appear to be conflicting concerns. To the extent that the court sought fifteen years ago to protect Dr. King and those who marched with him, those who went to jail with him, those Freedom Riders who helped to shape our history, those who demanded the right of blacks to eat at luncheon counters, South and North, and to have access to amusement parks as well, the court sought to protect me.

Lt. Colonel Anthony Herbert is a retired army officer who served in Vietnam during the war and who received substantial media coverage during 1969 and 1970 when he accused his superior officers of covering up reports of atrocities and other war crimes. During February 1973, CBS-TV broadcasted a report about Herbert portraying him as a liar who had made up the war crimes allegations to explain why he had really been relieved of his command. The program was produced and edited by Barry Lando and narrated by Mike Wallace. Later, Lando published a related article in the *Atlantic Monthly* magazine.* Herbert sued CBS, Lando, Wallace, and the magazine, stating that the programs and articles falsely and maliciously portrayed him as a liar. In the action, Herbert conceded that he was required to prove that CBS had published damaging falsehoods due to "actual malice" as defined by the court in *Times* v. *Sullivan.* He further conceded that the court had in *Curtis Publishing Co.* v. *Butts* extended the law regarding libel from public officials to public figures. Under the rule, Herbert was obligated to demonstrate that CBS had made its false statements while knowing them to be untrue or with such a reckless disregard for the truth that it in fact entertained serious doubts about the allegations. The court had held that such "subjective awareness of probable falsety" may be found if "there are obvious reasons to doubt the veracity of the informant or the accuracy of his reports."

In view of those stringent requirements, Herbert conducted pretrial depositions in which he questioned Lando. Lando refused to answer a variety of questions on the ground that the state of mind of those who produce, edit, or publish the news is protected. The federal district court ruled that the defendant's state of mind was of "central importance" to the issue of malice in the case, and that it was obvious that the questions were relevant and "entirely appropriate to Herbert's efforts to discover whether Lando had any reason to doubt the veracity of certain of his sources, or, equally significant, to prefer the veracity of one source over another."

CBS appealed that ruling to the U.S. Court of Appeals. There, by a vote of two to one, the court found for CBS. Judge Irving R. Kaufman wrote one of the two overlapping opinions in support of the CBS contention. As was Warren, Kaufman was more than just an interested observer. He had sought to use government agencies to suppress and deter the publication of critical comments about his own actions. FBI documents now available reveal that on numerous occasions, beginning in 1965 and continuing for a decade, Kaufman sought to have J. Edgar Hoover, other officials of the FBI, the attorney general, and others intervene with the news media to suppress discussions of plays, books, and television programs about his role in the execution of Julius and Ethel Rosenberg.

For example, on April 29, 1969, Kaufman called Hoover to complain about a review of *Inquest,* a play about the Rosenberg case written by

**Atlantic Monthly,* "The Herbert Affair," May 1973.

Donald Freed. Kaufman told Hoover that the attorney general John Mitchell should be informed about the play. Subsequently, the FBI opened dossiers on each of the actors and others associated with the play. Hoover later "had an agent observe the play and furnish Kaufman and the Attorney General with brief summaries of the play." Later the FBI apparently stole a copy of the script and "furnished" it as well.

In a "Dear Edgar" letter obtained through a Freedom of Information request, Kaufman thanked Hoover for his help in suppressing a dissenting view. The FBI also arranged to prevent authors of a book about the Rosenberg case from appearing on a television program to discuss it.

Kaufman then utilized his contacts in the bar and his friendship with a former federal judge, Simon H. Rifkind, to successfully urge the American Bar Association to establish "a Special Committee of the American Bar Association" headed by Simon H. Rifkind to defend Judge Kaufman and the convictors of the Rosenbergs and Morton Sobell.

In his written opinion in the *Herbert* case, Kaufman sought to protect journalists from having to disclose the reasons they published various views to the exclusion of others. He referred to questions designed to elicit such information as "inquisitions" and said he feared for the First Amendment. In view of his own covert and unproper actions after the execution of the Rosenbergs, it seems more likely that he feared public disclosure of his own misconduct.

In reversing the court of appeals, the Supreme Court found that until *Times* v. *Sullivan,* the prevailing jurisprudence was that libel was not within the area of constitutionally protected speech. The court said that the new standard, which required that public figures prove knowing or reckless falsehood, "made it essential to proving liability that plaintiffs focus on the conduct and state of mind of the defendant." The court ruled "inevitably, unless liability is to be completely foreclosed, the thoughts and editorial processes of the alleged defenses" must be open to examination.

To the CBS contention that a decision permitting the examination of the process by which a program was produced might in the future change the nature of that process, the court responded that it hoped so. The court said that "those who publish defamatory falsehoods with the requisite culpability" are "subject to liability, the aims being not only to compensate for injury but also to deter publication of unprotected material threatening injury to individual reputations."

The court continued,

> . . . permitting plaintiffs such as Herbert to prove their cases by direct, as well as indirect, evidence is consistent with the balance struck by our prior decisions. If such proof results in liability for damages which in turn discourages the publication of erroneous information known to be false or probably false, this is no more than what our cases contemplate and does not abridge either freedom of speech or of the press.

If, hypothetically speaking, the CIA had encouraged or directed CBS to develop a program for the purpose of destroying the reputation of Col. Herbert, that communication between the agency and the network, which could well establish malice, essential as it might be to the plaintiff, would have very likely been unavailable to him prior to the recent Supreme Court ruling. The court had ruled in *Times* v. *Sullivan* that the public figure plaintiff in a libel action could recover only upon clear and convincing proof of each of the following elements which comprise the tort:

1. The statement was published by the defendant,
2. The statement defamed the plaintiff,
3. The defamation was untrue,
4. And the defendant knew the defamatory statement was untrue or published it in reckless disregard of its truth or falsity.

In *Herbert* v. *CBS,* the court ruled that that plaintiff might be allowed to inquire as to what the defendant knew. That simple ruling brought about anguished cries from the news business executives, for they knew what the Supreme Court members could only suspect. While the members of the court and of the public could only speculate about the factors that influence the national media, and guess about the impact of various forces that interfere with our right to know, the media executives could identify them readily. Their response to the Supreme Court decision was eloquent testimony to their determination to decline to identify those forces publicly.

The Warren Court reshaped the law for matters found commendable by the liberal and news media establishment, and thus earned for the chief justice of that period a reputation as a magnificent defender of the Constitution and the rights of the disadvantaged. Yet his court left behind a legacy of tortured logic, bent reasoning, and a new class of disadvantaged. Chief Justice Warren Burger and his court have adopted a very different approach and have thus earned the enmity of those who cherished Earl Warren and his work. It is for history to judge who better served the rule of law.

Appendixes

Appendix A: The Dennis Banks Declaration

DECLARATION OF DENNIS BANKS

I, Dennis Banks, declare that I am a citizen of the United States, and that I am 44 years old.

Several months ago, in May 1977, my friend Lehman Brightman was contacted on the phone by a man named George Coker. He wanted Lee to set up a meeting between myself and a man named David Conn, concerning the question of my extradition to South Dakota. Naturally I was concerned about this when I was notified of the call. In the next couple of days there were other calls. Lee called David Conn and asked him for some more information about my extradition. Conn told Lee that he wanted to talk to me about Peoples Temple and Jim Jones.

Lee asked Conn what Jim Jones had to do with my extradition. Conn wouldn't tell him. He said it was strictly confidential and that he would only talk about it with him and me personally.

So Lee set up a meeting between myself and David Conn at Lee's house in El Cerrito, for that night.

At the meeting, Conn showed up with a folder of papers. He read notes from the papers. I noticed the paper was stationery from the Standard Oil Company of California. Conn said that he was working with the U.S. Treasury Department, with an IRS agent, and with two men from the San Francisco Police Department. He told me the first name of the Treasury agent (Jim) he was working with. But Conn did not talk about my extradition problem. He read material that was disparaging to Jim Jones. He went on for some time. Finally I interrupted Conn. I asked him what all this stuff about Jim Jones had to do with my extradition. Conn asked me, "Well, you took money from the church, didn't you?" He said that my association with Peoples Temple could reflect very badly on my extradition. He then asked me to make a public denunciation of Jim Jones. He assured me that if I made such a denunciation, the rulings on my extradition would go in my favor. I asked him why a statement against Jim Jones could help my extradition.

Conn said that such a statement would be a determining factor with people like the Governor and other government agencies making decisions about my extradition. He said that if I came out with a statement against Jim Jones that a decision against my extradition could well be forthcoming.

Conn was obviously making a deal with me, and I was being blackmailed. Conn let me know that besides working with Treasury agents and other government agents, that he was already working with ex-members of Peoples Temple, such as Grace Stoen, and that he had people who would talk against Jim Jones. He said that the Treasury agents had already talked with Grace Stoen.

Conn pressed hard for me to meet with a U.S. Treasury Department agent alone that very night.

Conn also said—and he was very emphatic about this—THAT HE IN NO WAY WANTED THIS INFORMATION REVEALED FOR FEAR THAT IT WOULD "BLOW THEIR COVER" AND RUIN ANY POSSIBLE MEETING BETWEEN ME AND THE TREASURY AGENT.

I was further pressured to meet with the agent from the Treasury Department. The deal was to meet with the agent and to prepare a public statement against Jim Jones in return for some kind of immunity against my being extradited. I refused to talk with any Treasury agent without my attorney, Dennis Roberts. Conn insisted that I had to do it alone.

At this point, Lehman Brightman asked Conn to leave the house.

The next night I was called at D.Q. University by Conn. Conn told me that it was very urgent that I meet with the Treasury agent that very night, alone. I said to Conn that I had already told him I wouldn't meet with the Treasury agent without my attorney.

These agents all knew that I had a lot hanging over me. Besides the extradition (which to me is certainly a life and death matter), I also had a case in Federal Court in which the Treasury Department was involved. I have often made it clear that if I am extradited to South Dakota, that is like a sentence of death, because I am certain that I will be killed there.

So this was definitely a deal that I was being offered. Because it was not just a matter of Conn indicating that it would go well with me if I co-operated, but the implication was that if I didn't co-operate, it would go *badly* for me. This was to me a threat, and obvious blackmail. I declare, under penalty of perjury, that all of the foregoing is true and correct, executed this 6 day of September, 1977 at *Davis, California*

/s/ *Dennis J. Banks*

Appendix B: The San Francisco District Attorney's Report

MEMO TO: Joe Freitas
Danny Weinstein

DATE: August 28, 1977

FROM: Bob Graham

RE: Peoples Temple

The inquiry into allegations of crimes committed in San Francisco County by Peoples Temple members began the week of July 18, 1977 after articles on the Temple appeared in the *Examiner* and *New West* magazine. All five of the Special Prosecutions investigators have participated in the inquiry, although principal responsibility was borne by Mssrs. Reuben and Lawrence. In all, more than 70 persons have been interviewed—former PT members, current PT members, and persons reported to have knowledge of PT activities. Little was gained from conversations with current PT members, who uniformly refused much conversation with investigators on the advice of Charles Garry, PT attorney. After six weeks, no evidence has been developed that would warrant consideration of criminal prosecution.

The allegations looked into by the Special Prosecutions Unit fall into the following categories of crime:

(1) *Homicide.* Rumors of three possible murders by PT members were checked into. One alleged victim, John William Head, died in Los Angeles, and the complaining witness, Head's mother, was referred to Los Angeles authorities. The second, Anthony (Curtis) Buckley, was purportedly given a drug overdose as part of a PT discipline/control program. However, the Coroner's report shows death by natural causes (cerebral hemorrhage of

unknown etiology) and no drugs in the system. Moreover, no witness was able to place Buckley in or near the Temple within 48 hours of his death, and there is no evidence whatsoever that drugs were administered to Buckley by anyone. The third purported victim, Robert Houston, worked for Southern Pacific, and apparently fell beneath a train while on duty. Houston's widow has filed a wrongful death action against Southern Pacific, which has thoroughly investigated the death. The Southern Pacific investigators were unable to find any evidence of foul play.

(2) *Child abduction.* The allegations are that children were taken forcibly from their parents or were shipped to the PT plantation in Guyana without consent of parent or guardian. In no case in which we had the name of such a child was the allegation borne out. In the Tupper case, the father, who had legal custody, turned the child over to the mother, because he could not take care of the child; the mother went to Guyana with the child. The Biggin child was placed by the mother with the grandparents; the grandparents moved to Guyana and took the child (which they had cared for for six years) to Guyana with them. The Sly boy went to Guyana with the consent of his father, who had de facto custody. Both mother and father consented to the two Oliver boys going to Guyana. Anita Pettit delivered her two children to Temple members, when she was unable to handle them; the Mertles, who were appointed guardians of the children, returned them to the Temple when they left. Not one of the parents or guardians who consented has alleged that their consent was coerced.

The matter of Vincent Lopez arose in Alameda County and is being handled by the Superior Court of that County.

Despite puffery to that effect in PT publications, there is no evidence that any juvenile from San Francisco County was sent by the Court or probation officials to the PT plantation in Guyana.

(3) *Property extortion.* It has been alleged that PT members conveyed property to the Temple as a result of threats by members of the Temple hierarchy. We have found evidence of few property transfers to PT in San Francisco. In no case has a person who made such a transfer complained to this office. In the one case in which there is a suspicion about such a conveyance (Edwards), we have been unable to contact the alleged victims, who may be in Guyana. The press, which has been all over this aspect of the case, has also failed to produce one "victim" in San Francisco.

(4) *Arson.* On August 26, 1977, Tom Crary brought to my attention a 1974 fire at the Temple—a fire apparently predicted by Reverend Jones. Although the statute of limitations has run as to the fire, it may not have run as to any insurance proceeds collected. We will look into possible fraud.

(5) *Battery.* At the direction of Reverend Jones, Temple members were beaten with paddles, boards, and hoses for sundry infractions. These beatings were consented to by adults beaten. Parents or guardians consented to the paddling of children. In the only cases in which the names of children beaten in San Francisco were supplied to us, the children are now in Guyana, their parents consented to the discipline, and the spanking was not excessive, according to witnesses. Linda Mertle, the most famous beaten child, was paddled in Mendocino County.

(6) *Drugs.* Some former PT members tell of the use of drugs to control recalcitrants. No one that we talked to was able to testify to observing any drugs administered at the Temple in San Francisco, however. The commonly mentioned incident involving Danny Pietila occurred in Los Angeles.

(7) *Notarial violations.* The Secretary of State is looking into the possibility that PT members who were notaries committed crimes in their notarization of signatures on deeds and other documents. So far, only one of the potential crimes being investigated involves a San Francisco transaction (the Edwards deed)—and that crime, if proved, would be a misdemeanor violation of the Government Code. Continued investigation should be left to the Secretary of State.

(8) *Welfare diversion.* DSS and the City Controller are checking into the allegation that City welfare funds are being diverted to Guyana or to persons not entitled to them in San Francisco. This investigation should be left to the abovenamed agencies—as with any other welfare fraud investigation. If evidence is developed, it should be submitted to Don Didler, our welfare fraud expert.

(9) *Kidnapping.* Some former PT members and certain newspersons have contended that current members are being dragged off to Guyana against their wills. We have not been put in touch with one such person. We have been advised, through intermediaries that certain members, if they had housing possibilities within the City, would not go to Guyana. We have put these members in touch with public housing personnel, who have assured us that housing will be found. There are undoubtedly some PT members who have given everything they have to the Temple and who now want to leave the Temple but lack the resources. This is a tragic situation—but, assuming they voluntarily parted with their property, no crime has been committed.

A few people with adult children in Guyana have come to the offices for help in getting their children out of Guyana; they have been told that adult children are beyond the reach of their parents, absent incompetency.

(10) *Tim Stoen.* There are a lot of stories flying around about Tim Stoen and his role in the Temple. So far, no evidence has surfaced that would link Stoen with any criminal activity in San Francisco. The tape recording which indicated the possibility of forgery and compounding was referred to the Sheriff of Mendocino County, where the transaction occurred. We have also found no evidence to date of misconduct by Stoen as a Deputy District Attorney in San Francisco.

Except with respect to the alleged arson, the Special Prosecutions unit is converting the Peoples Temple inquiry to inactive status. We will, of course, continue to talk to anyone who can provide us with or lead us to hard evidence of criminal acts in San Francisco. Otherwise, we are moving on to more promising investigatory areas.

Obviously, nothing in this memorandum should be read as approving of the practices of People's Temple; many of which are at least unsavory and raise substantial moral and non-criminal legal questions.

Appendix C: The Deborah Blakey Affidavit

AFFIDAVIT OF DEBORAH LAYTON BLAKEY RE THE THREAT AND POSSIBILITY OF MASS SUICIDE BY MEMBERS OF THE PEOPLE'S TEMPLE

I, DEBORAH LAYTON BLAKEY, declare the following under penalty of perjury:

1. The purpose of this affidavit is to call to the attention of the United States government the existence of a situation which threatens the lives of United States citizens living in Jonestown, Guyana.

2. From August 1971, until May 13, 1978, I was a member of the People's Temple. For a substantial period of time prior to my departure for Guyana in December 1977, I held the position of Financial Secretary of the People's Temple.

3. I was 18 years old when I joined the People's Temple. I had grown up in affluent circumstances in the permissive atmosphere of Berkeley, California. By joining the People's Temple, I hoped to help others and in the process to bring structure and self-discipline to my own life.

4. During the years I was a member of the People's Temple, I watched the organization depart with increasing frequency from its professed dedica-

tion to social change and participatory democracy. The Rev. Jim Jones gradually assumed a tyrannical hold over the lives of Temple members.

5. Any disagreement with his dictates came to be regarded as "treason." The Rev. Jones labelled any person who left the organization a "traitor" and "fair game." He steadfastly and convincingly maintained that the punishment for defection was death. The fact that severe corporal punishment was frequently administered to Temple members gave the threats a frightening air of reality.

6. The Rev. Jones saw himself as the center of a conspiracy. The identity of the conspirators changed from day to day along with his erratic world vision. He induced the fear in others that, through their contact with him, they had become targets of the conspiracy. He convinced black Temple members that if they did not follow him to Guyana, they would be put into concentration camps and killed. White members were instilled with the belief that their names appeared on a secret list of enemies of the state that was kept by the C.I.A. and that they would be tracked down, tortured, imprisoned, and subsequently killed if they did not flee to Guyana.

7. Frequently, at Temple meetings, Rev. Jones would talk non-stop for hours. At various times, he claimed that he was the reincarnation of either Lenin, Jesus Christ, or one of a variety of other religious or political figures. He claimed that he had divine powers and could heal the sick. He stated that he had extrasensory perception and could tell what everyone was thinking. He said that he had powerful connections the world over, including the Mafia, Idi Amin, and the Soviet government.

8. When I first joined the Temple, Rev. Jones seemed to make clear distinctions between fantasy and reality. I believed that most of the time when he said irrational things, he was aware that they were irrational, but that they served as a tool of his leadership. His theory was that the end justified the means. At other times, he appeared to be deluded by a paranoid vision of the world. He would not sleep for days at a time and talk compulsively about the conspiracies against him. However, as time went on, he appeared to become genuinely irrational.

9. Rev. Jones insisted that Temple members work long hours and completely give up all semblance of a personal life. Proof of loyalty to Jones was confirmed by actions showing that a member had given up everything, even basic necessities. The most loyal were in the worst physical condition. Dark circles under one's eyes or extreme loss of weight were considered signs of loyalty.

10. The primary emotions I came to experience were exhaustion and fear. I knew that Rev. Jones was in some sense "sick," but that did not make me any less afraid of him.

11. Rev. Jones fled the United States in June 1977, amidst growing public criticism of the practices of the Temple. He informed members of the Temple that he would be imprisoned for life if he did not leave immediately.

12. Between June 1977, and December 1977, when I was ordered to depart for Guyana, I had access to coded radio broadcasts from Rev. Jones in Guyana to the People's Temple headquarters in San Francisco.

13. In September 1977, an event which Rev. Jones viewed as a major crisis occurred. Through listening to coded radio broadcasts and conversations with other members of the Temple staff, I learned that an attorney for former Temple member Grace Stoen had arrived in Guyana, seeking the return of her son, John Victor Stoen.

14. Rev. Jones has expressed particular bitterness toward Grace Stoen. She had been Chief Counselor, a position of great responsibility within the Temple. Her personal qualities of generosity and compassion made her very popular with the membership. Her departure posed a threat to Rev. Jones' absolute control. Rev. Jones delivered a number of public tirades against her. He said that her kindness was faked and that she was a C.I.A. agent. He swore that he would never return her son to her.

15. I am informed that Rev. Jones believed that he would be able to stop Timothy Stoen, husband of Grace Stoen and father of John Victor Stoen, from speaking against the Temple as long as the child was being held in Guyana. Timothy Stoen, a former Assistant District Attorney in Mendocino and San Francisco counties, had been one of Rev. Jones' most trusted advisors. It was rumored that Stoen was critical of the use of physical force and other forms of intimidation against Temple members. I am further informed that Rev. Jones believed that a public statement by Timothy Stoen would increase the tarnish on his public image.

16. When the Temple lost track of Timothy Stoen, I was assigned to track him down and offer him a large sum of money in return for his silence. Initially, I was to offer him $5,000. I was authorized to pay him up to $10,000. I was not able to locate him and did not see him again until on or about October 6, 1977. On that date, the Temple received information that he would be joining Grace in a San Francisco Superior Court action to determine the custody of John. I was one of a group of Temple members assigned to meet him outside the court and attempt to intimidate him to prevent him from going inside.

17. The September 1977 crisis concerning John Stoen reached major proportions. The radio messages from Guyana were frenzied and hysterical. One morning, Terry J. Buford, public relations advisor to Rev. Jones, and myself were instructed to place a telephone call to a high-ranking Guyanese official who was visiting the United States and deliver the following threat

unless the government of Guyana took immediate steps to stall the Guyanese court action regarding John Stoen's custody, the entire population of Jonestown would extinguish itself in a mass suicide by 5:30 P.M. that day. I was later informed that Temple members in Guyana placed similar calls to other Guyanese officials.

18. We later received radio communication to the effect that the court case had been stalled and that the suicide threat was called off.

19. I arrived in Guyana in December 1977. I spent a week in Georgetown and then, pursuant to orders, traveled to Jonestown.

20. Conditions at Jonestown were even worse than I had feared they would be. The settlement was swarming with armed guards. No one was permitted to leave unless on a special assignment and these assignments were given only to the most trusted. We were allowed to associate with Guyanese people only while on a "mission."

21. The vast majority of the Temple members were required to work in the fields from 7 A.M. to 6 P.M. six days per week and on Sunday from 7 A.M. to 2 P.M. We were allowed one hour for lunch. Most of this hour was spent walking back to lunch and standing in line for our food. Taking any other breaks during the workday was severely frowned upon.

22. The food was woefully inadequate. There was rice for breakfast, rice water soup for lunch, and rice and beans for dinner. On Sunday, we each received an egg and a cookie. Two or three times a week we had vegetables. Some very weak and elderly members received one egg per day. However, the food did improve markedly on the few occasions when there were outside visitors.

23. In contrast, Rev. Jones, claiming problems with his blood sugar, dined separately and ate meat regularly. He had his own refrigerator, which was stocked with food. The two women with whom he resided, Maria Katsaris and Carolyn Layton, and the two small boys who lived with him, Kimo Prokes and John Stoen, dined with the membership. However, they were in much better physical shape than everyone else since they were also allowed to eat the food in Rev. Jones' refrigerator.

24. In February 1978, conditions had become so bad that half of Jonestown was ill with severe diarrhea and high fevers. I was seriously ill for two weeks. Like most of the other sick people, I was not given any nourishing foods to help recover. I was given water and a tea drink until I was well enough to return to the basic rice and beans diet.

25. As the former financial secretary, I was aware that the Temple received over $65,000 in Social Security checks per month. It made me angry to see that only a fraction of the income of the senior citizens in the

care of the Temple was being used for their benefit. Some of the money was being used to build a settlement that would earn Rev. Jones the place in history with which he was so obsessed. The balance was being held in "reserve." Although I felt terrible about what was happening, I was afraid to say anything because I knew that anyone with a differing opinion gained the wrath of Jones and other members.

26. Rev. Jones' thoughts were made known to the population of Jonestown by means of broadcasts over the loudspeaker system. He broadcast an average of six hours per day. When the Reverend was particularly agitated, he would broadcast for hours on end. He would talk on and on while we worked in the fields or tried to sleep. In addition to the daily broadcasts, there were marathon meetings six nights per week.

27. The tenor of the broadcasts revealed that Rev. Jones' paranoia had reached an all-time high. He was irate at the light in which he had been portrayed by the media. He felt that as a consequence of having been ridiculed and maligned, he would be denied a place in history. His obsession with his place in history was maniacal. When pondering the loss of what he considered his rightful place in history, he would grow despondent and say that all was lost.

28. Visitors were infrequently permitted access to Jonestown. The entire community was required to put on a performance when a visitor arrived. Before the visitor arrived, Rev. Jones would instruct us on the image we were to project. The workday would be shortened. The food would be better. Sometimes there would be music and dancing. Aside from these performances, there was little joy or hope in any of our lives. An air of despondency prevailed.

29. There was constant talk of death. In the early days of the Peoples Temple, general rhetoric about dying for principles was sometimes heard. In Jonestown, the concept of mass suicide for socialism arose. Because our lives were so wretched anyway and because we were so afraid to contradict Rev. Jones, the concept was not challenged.

30. An event which transpired shortly after I reached Jonestown convinced me that Rev. Jones had sufficient control over the minds of the residents that it would be possible for him to effect a mass suicide.

31. At least once a week, Rev. Jones would declare a "white night," or state of emergency. The entire population of Jonestown would be awakened by blaring sirens. Designated persons, approximately fifty in number, would arm themselves with rifles, move from cabin to cabin, and make certain that all members were responding. A mass meeting would ensue. Frequently during these crises, we would be told that the jungle was swarming with

mercenaries and that death could be expected at any minute.

32. During one "white night," we were informed that our situation had become hopeless and that the only course of action open to us was a mass suicide for the glory of socialism. We were told that we would be tortured by mercenaries if we were taken alive. Everyone, including the children, was told to line up. As we passed through the line, we were given a small glass of red liquid to drink. We were told that the liquid contained poison and that we would die within 45 minutes. We all did as we were told. When the time came when we should have dropped dead, Rev. Jones explained that the poison was not real and that we had just been through a loyalty test. He warned us that the time was not far off when it would become necessary for us to die by our own hands.

33. Life at Jonestown was so miserable and the physical pain of exhaustion was so great that this event was not traumatic for me. I had become indifferent as to whether I lived or died.

34. During another "white night," I watched Carolyn Layton, my former sister-in-law, give sleeping pills to two young children in her care, John Victor Stoen and Kimo Prokes, her own son. Carolyn said to me that Rev. Jones had told her that everyone was going to have to die that night. She said that she would probably have to shoot John and Kimo and that it would be easier for them if she did it while they were asleep.

35. In April 1978, I was reassigned to Georgetown. I became determined to escape or die trying. I surreptitiously contacted my sister, who wired me a plane ticket. After I received the ticket, I sought the assistance of the United States Embassy in arranging to leave Guyana. Rev. Jones had instructed us that he had a spy working in the United States Embassy and that he would know if anyone went to the embassy for help. For this reason, I was very fearful.

36. I am most grateful to the United States government and Richard McCoy and Daniel Weber; in particular, for the assistance they gave me. However, the efforts made to investigate conditions in Jonestown are inadequate for the following reasons. The infrequent visits are always announced and arranged. Acting in fear for their lives, Temple members respond as they are told. The members appear to speak freely to American representatives, but in fact they are drilled thoroughly prior to each visit on what questions to expect and how to respond. Members are afraid of retaliation if they speak their true feelings in public.

37. On behalf of the population of Jonestown, I urge that the United States Government take adequate steps to safeguard their rights. I believe that their lives are in danger.

I declare under penalty of perjury that the foregoing is true and correct, except as to those matters stated on information and belief and as to those I believe them to be true.

Executed this *15* day of June 1978, at San Francisco, California.

/s/ *Deborah Layton Blakey*

Appendix D: Statement by the Concerned Relatives

ACCUSATION OF HUMAN RIGHTS VIOLATIONS BY REV. JAMES WARREN JONES AGAINST OUR CHILDREN AND RELATIVES AT THE PEOPLES TEMPLE JUNGLE ENCAMPMENT IN GUYANA, SOUTH AMERICA

TO: REV. JAMES WARREN JONES

From: Parents and relatives of children and adults under your control at "Jonestown," Northwest District, Cooperative Republic of Guyana

Date: April 11, 1978

I. INTRODUCTION

We, the undersigned, are the grief-stricken parents and relatives of the hereinafter-designated persons you arranged to be transported to Guyana, South America, at a jungle encampment you call "Jonestown." We are advised there are no telephones or exit roads from Jonestown, and that you now have more than 1,000 U.S. citizens living with you there.

We have allowed nine months to pass since you left the United States in June 1977. Although certain of us knew it would do no good to wait before making a group protest, others of us were willing to wait to see whether you would in fact respect the fundamental freedoms and dignity of our children and family members in Jonestown. Sadly, your conduct over the past year has shown such a flagrant and cruel disregard for human rights that we have no choice as responsible people but to make this public accusation and to demand the immediate elimination of these outrageous abuses.

II. SUMMARY OF VIOLATIONS

We hereby accuse you, Jim Jones, of the following acts violating the human rights of our family members:

1. Making the following threat calculated to cause alarm for the lives of our relatives: "I can say without hesitation that we are devoted to a decision that it is better even to die than to be constantly harrassed from one continent to the next."

2. Employing physical intimidation and psychological coercion as part of a mind-programming campaign aimed at destroying family ties, discrediting belief in God, and causing contempt for the United States of America.

3. Prohibiting our relatives from leaving Guyana by confiscating their passports and money and by stationing guards around Jonestown to prevent anyone escaping.

4. Depriving them of their right to privacy, free speech, and freedom of association by:

a. Prohibiting telephone calls;
b. Prohibiting individual contacts with "outsiders";
c. Censoring all incoming and outgoing mail;
d. Extorting silence from relatives in the U.S. by threats to stop all communication;
e. Preventing our children from seeing us when we travel to Guyana.

The aforesaid conduct by you is a violation of the human rights of our loved ones as guaranteed by Article 55 of the United Nations Charter, and as defined by the Universal Declaration of Human Rights (adopted by the U. N. General Assembly on December 10, 1948). It is also a violation of their constitutional rights as guaranteed by the Constitution of the United States, and as guaranteed by the Constitution of the Cooperative Republic of Guyana (adopted May 26, 1966).

III. THREAT OF DECISION TO DIE

On March 14, 1978 you, Jim Jones, caused to be written on Peoples Temple stationery a letter "to all U.S. Senators and Members of Congress" complaining of alleged "bureaucratic harrassment" and ending with this chilling threat:

> "[I]t is equally evident that people cannot forever be continually harrassed and beleaguered by such tactics without seeking alternatives that have been presented. I can say without hesitation that we are devoted to a decision that it is better even to die than to be constantly harrassed from one continent to the next."

A copy of your letter is attached as Exhibit A.

We know how exact you are in choosing your words, and there is little doubt that this letter was dictated by you personally since it has been your policy over the years to dictate all letters sent to governmental officials on Temple stationery. Your letter seeks to mask, by the use of irrelevant ideological rhetoric, its real purpose, which is to divert the attention of U.S. Governmental agencies towards your abuses of human rights by putting them on the defensive.

The "1,000 U.S. citizens" you claim to have brought to Guyana include our beloved relatives who are "devoted to a decision that it is better even to die." We frankly do not know if you have become so corrupted by power that you would actually allow a collective "decision" to die, or whether your letter is simply a bluff designed to deter investigations into your practices. There is supporting evidence for our concern in the affidavit of Yolanda Crawford, attached hereto as Exhibit B, which shows that you have publicly stated in Guyana that you would rather have your people dead than living in the United States, and that you have solicited people to lay down their lives for your cause. You certainly have been successful in making us fearful as to your intentions.

We hereby give you the opportunity now to publicly repudiate our interpretation of your threat. If you refuse to deny the apparent meaning of your letter, we demand that you immediately answer the following questions:

1. When you refer to "a decision that it is better even to die than to be constantly harrassed", has this "decision" already been made or is it to be made in the future? If made, when and where? Were our relatives consulted? Did anybody dissent? By what moral or legal justification could you possibly make such a decision on behalf of minor children?

2. When you say you are "devoted" to this decision, does that mean it is irreversible? If irreversible, at what point will the alleged "harrassment" have gotten so great as to make death "better"? Would it be an International Human Rights Commission investigation, or an on-premises investigation of your operations by the U. S. Government? Who besides you will decide when that point "to die" is reached?

We know your psychological coercion of the residents of Jonestown to be so "totalitarian" that nobody there, including adults, could possibly make such a decision to die freely and voluntarily. The evidence is that our relatives are in fact hostages, and we hereby serve notice that should any harm befall them, we will hold you and Peoples Temple church responsible and will employ every legal and diplomatic resource to bring you to justice.

IV. MIND-PROGRAMMING AND INTIMIDATION

The affidavit of Steven A. Katsaris, attached hereto as Exhibit C, is a personal account of his experiences in Guyana. It reveals the terrifying effect of your mind-programming on his daughter, a bright 24-year-old, which has caused her to deny belief in God, to renounce family ties, and to manifest symptoms of sleep-deprivation and a serious personality change.

Yolanda Crawford's affidavit (Exhibit B) is an eye-witness account of your activities in Guyana by someone present with you. The affidavit shows that you, Jim Jones, preach there the following doctrines: a) that you are God and there is no other God, b) that the United States is the "most evil" nation in the world, c) that allegiance to your cause must replace family loyalty and that parents should be handled at a distance for the sole purposes of collecting inheritances for the cause and of getting them not to cause trouble.

The evidence also shows that you have instituted the following practices in Guyana: a) a centralized chain of command whereby all decisions of significance are to be made by you and once made, must be followed by Temple members under threat of punishment; b) the stationing of guards around Jonestown to prevent persons from escaping; and c) the use of degrading punishments (for example, eating hot peppers), sleep-deprivation, food-deprivation, hard labor, and other coercive techniques commonly used in mind-programming.

The evidence also shows that you, Jim Jones, confiscate the passports and monies of people upon their arrival in Guyana, prohibit individual contacts with "outsiders," censor incoming and outgoing mail, prohibit telephone calls by Temple members when in Georgetown, and require Temple members to travel in groups. Ms. Crawford's affidavit also shows that you have publicly threatened that anyone who tries to leave the "cause" will be killed.

The aforesaid conduct by you is a wanton violation of the human rights of our loved ones. It is also a violation of their constitutional rights. The physical intimidation is a violation of the penal codes of the United States and the Cooperative Republic of Guyana.

V. THE HUMAN RIGHTS BEING VIOLATED

We hereby bring to your attention, Jim Jones, the particular provisions which guarantee human rights and constitutional rights that you are violating:

1. *Confiscation of Passports.* Your systematic confiscation of passports and all of the monies of Temple members upon their arrival in Guyana is for the purpose of preventing them from leaving and returning to the United States. You are thereby violating Article 13, Section 2 of the Universal Declaration of Human Rights, which reads:

> "Everyone has the right to leave any country, including his own, and to return to his country."

Your conduct is also a violation of Article 14 (1) of the Constitution of the Cooperative Republic of Guyana, which reads:

> "No person shall be deprived of his freedom of movement, that is to say, the right to move freely throughout Guyana, . . . the right to leave Guyana. . . ."

2. *Prohibiting Telephone Calls.* You systematically tell all Temple members upon their arrival in Georgetown, Guyana that they are not permitted, under threat of punishment, to make any telephone calls to family members in the United States or elsewhere, your purpose being to prevent negative information being imparted to relatives in the U. S. Your additional purpose is to overcome the bonds of family which might induce a Temple member to wish to return to his home in the U.S. This conduct is a violation of Article 19 of the Universal Declaration of Human Rights, which states:

> "Everyone has the right to freedom of opinion and expression; this right includes freedom to hold opinions without interference and to seek, receive and impart information and ideas through any media and regardless of frontiers."

This conduct is also a violation of Article 12 (1) of the Guyana Constitution, which reads:

> "Except with his own consent, no person shall be hindered in the enjoyment of his freedom of expression, that is to say, freedom to hold opinions without interference, freedom to communicate ideas and information without interference and freedom from interference with his correspondance."

3. *Prohibiting Contacts With Outsiders.* You systematically require that all Temple members, while in Georgetown, not communicate or visit with "outsiders" and not leave the communal headquarters (41 Lamaha Gardens) unless in association with other Temple members. You follow the same policy in Jonestown, enforcing your edicts with guards. Your purpose is to prevent anyone going to the U. S. Embassy and causing them to ask questions how you treat people. Your additional purpose is to discourage Temple members from being exposed to other religions or philosophies, and from viewing their lives independent of communal obligations. Your conduct is a violation of Article 20, Section 2 of the Universal Declaration of Human Rights, which states:

"No one may be compelled to belong to an association." It is also a violation of Article 18 of the same Declaration, which states:

> "Everyone has the right to freedom of thought, conscience and religion; this right includes freedom to change his religion or belief, and freedom, either alone or in community with others and in public or private, to manifest his religion or belief in teaching, practice, worship and observance."

Your conduct is also a violation of Article 13 (1) of the Guyana Constitution, which reads:

> "Except with his own consent, no person shall be hindered in the enjoyment of his freedom of assembly and association, that is to say, his right to assemble freely and associate with other persons."

4. *Censoring Mail.* You systematically require that all of the incoming mail and all of the outgoing mail of Temple members be censored by your staff. Your purpose is to discourage negative information being "leaked" to people in the U. S. and to prevent facts about the "outside" world reaching Temple members which are at variance with your "party line." This is shown by the affidavit of Ms. Crawford with respect to the Ku Klux Klan marching in the streets. Because mail is the only means of contact available to our loved ones once they are transported to Jonestown, you have thereby effectively cut off all free expression and correspondence. Your conduct is a violation of the right of our relatives to privacy, family, and correspondence under Article 12 of the Universal Declaration of Human Rights, which states:

> "No one shall be subjected to arbitrary interference with his privacy, family, home, or correspondance . . . . Everyone has the right to the protection of the law against such interference."

Your censoring of mail is also a violation of Article 12 (1) of the Guyana Constitution, which is quoted above.

5. *Extorting Silence From Relatives.* You systematically require that Temple members who write to their family members in the U. S. threaten in their letters that they will stop all further communication if any criticism is made of you or Peoples Temple. For example, Donna Ponts is a 15-year-old girl taken to Guyana in July 1977 without her father's knowledge and in violation of a court order requiring her to remain in California unless he gave permission. Attached hereto as Exhibit D is a letter from Donna to her grandmother which starts out saying: "Grandma, Hi! How are you doing? I hope you and everyone else are doing good." It ends as follows:

"I am sorry to hear that you called the radio station but since you did I will not be writing you any more."

Those of us who receive letters from our relatives in Jonestown find them standardized and unresponsive, as if written by machines. But since it is all we have, these letters are very precious to us. You have placed us in the agonizing dilemma of watching helplessly while the rights of our relatives are violated or losing all contact. We have chosen, however, not to yield to your extortion, which is a violation of Article 12 of the Universal Declaration of Human Rights, quoted above, and of Article 13 (1) of the Guyana Constitution, also quoted above.

6. *Prohibiting Our Children From Seeing Us.* Five of the parents who have signed this accusation have travelled from San Francisco some 5,000 miles in order to see their children since you took them to Guyana. The evidence is clear that you have instituted a most pernicious campaign to discredit us in our children's eyes, as can be concluded from the following experiences:

a. *Steven A. Katsaris.* On September 26, 1977 Steven A. Katsaris arrived in Guyana and attempted to meet with his daughter, Maria. She was prohibited from meeting with him, duress being employed by you to force her to lie to the U. S. Embassy that she did not wish to see her father because "he had molested" her. Mr. Katsaris had with him a letter from Maria inviting him and saying, "I love you & miss you." On November 3, 1977 Mr. Katsaris returned to Guyana to see his daughter, after first obtaining a promise of assistance from the Guyanese Ambassador to the United States. After days of waiting, Maria was allowed to see her father but only in the presence of three other Temple members. Maria gave evidence of sleep deprivation and a behavior pattern extremely hostile and different from that ever manifested before. For the details of these two visits, refer to Exhibit C.

b. *Howard and Beverly Oliver.* On December 19, 1977 Howard and Beverly Oliver, together with their attorney Roger Holmes, arrived in Guyana in order to see their two sons, William S. Oliver (age 17) and Bruce Howard Oliver (age 20). In July 1977 both boys had told their parents they were going to Guyana "for two weeks." The Olivers had a court order from a California Superior Court for the return of William. They also had in their possession letters from each son saying "I love you." After spending eight days without success trying to see their sons, they were told that "Jim Jones had a council meeting" and the decision was that "it was best that we did not see or talk to our sons." Attached as Exhibit E is a handwritten account of Beverly E. Oliver, together with a copy of a letter from each son.

c. *Timothy and Grace Stoen.* On January 4, 1978 Timothy and Grace Stoen arrived in Guyana in connection with habeas corpus proceedings commenced the preceding August. Although they had a California Superior Court order which ordered you to deliver their six-year-old child, John Victor Stoen, to them, you refused to let either parent even see their child. The evidence also shows that you have falsely accused Grace as being "unfit" (see Katsaris affidavit) and that on January 18, 1978 three Temple members surrounded Timothy at Timehri Airport in Guyana and threatened his and Grace's lives if they did not drop legal proceedings (see Crime Report made to Guyana Commissioner of Police Lloyd Barker on January 18, 1978).

The aforesaid conduct on your part constitutes a violation of Article 12 (1) of the Guyana Constitution, quoted above, and Article 12 of the Universal Declaration of Human Rights, which states as follows:

> "No one shall be subjected to arbitrary interference with his . . . family. . . ."

VI. DEMANDS FOR RELIEF

We hereby demand that you, Jim Jones, immediately cease and desist from the aforesaid conduct and that you do the following additional acts immediately:

1. Publicly answer our questions regarding your threat of a collective "decision . . . to die," and publicly promise U. S. Secretary of State Cyrus Vance and Guyana Prime Minister Forbes Burnham that you will never encourage or solicit the death of any person at Jonestown, whether individually or collectively, for any reason whatsoever;

2. Remove all guards physically preventing our relatives from leaving Jonestown;

3. Return all passports and money taken from our relatives to them for their permanent possession;

4. Permit and encourage our relatives a one-week visit home, at our expense. (Because our relatives have been in Guyana for months (and some, for years) and because it is our belief that they do not know the full Peoples Temple story and have been prejudiced against their families, we demand you demonstrate in practice your contention that they are their own agents by permitting and encouraging our relatives to visit their families in the U. S. for one week, with our guarantee that we will provide them with round trip air fare and not interfere with their return at the end of the family visit should they so choose.)

5. Permit our relatives to write letters to whomever they wish, uncensored and in private.

6. Permit our relatives to read letters sent to them in private and without censorship.

7. Abide by the orders of the courts in the United States which you have heretofore ignored.

8. Notify us within three days on your radio-phone network of your full acceptance and compliance with these demands by contacting: Steven A. Katsaris, Trinity School, 915 West Church Street, Ukiah, California 95482; telephone (707) 462-8721.

March 14, 1978

TO ALL U.S. SENATORS AND MEMBERS OF CONGRESS:

We at Peoples Temple have been the subject of harassment by several agencies of the U.S. Government, and are rapidly reaching the point at which patience is exhausted. Radical Trotskyite elements which defected from our organization when we refused to follow their violent course have been orchestrating a campaign against us. Two of these, Michael Cartmell and Jim Cobb, were actually discovered making ammunition several years ago. These same two persons have boasted about knowing persons in the IRS and FCC and using them to get back at Peoples Temple. They also vowed recently to several witnesses that they would see to it that our group of over 1,000 U.S. citizens (currently conducting a highly successful agricultural project in Guyana) were starved out by having funds cut off from the U.S. To date, several agencies have been attempting various forms of harrassment. First was the Social Security, which tried to deny legitimate, beneficiaries of their rights by cutting off all checks that were coming to Guyana. Through the intervention of various government officials, we were able to have this reinstated as it should have been.

Now, however, we see that the IRS and Treasury Dept. and even the Federal Communications Commission, are trying to initiate ways to cut off our lifelines. The FCC has suddenly decided to pursue a very minor complaint that was registered a year ago. It is clear that the intention is to disrupt our essential medium of communication, amateur radio. Each week we contact thousands of amateur radio operators; contacts and consultation with doctors in the U.S. have literally saved lives and have engendered tremendous goodwill in this part of the world. We consistently praise the U.S. over the airways and remain entirely supportive of U.S. policy in the Caribbean and around the world, especially with non-aligned nations. It seems utterly cruel to deprive such a large group of Americans of their only means of quick communication with the U.S. We cannot believe that you would want to see this, nor would you in any way condone such an organized effort to "starve out" hundreds of U.S. citizens, who are seeking to live in peace and be a credit to the U.S. elsewhere. These same agencies and elements in the press would seek to destroy any progressive thinking official.

Our cooperative project in Guyana has been cited by people the world over as an example of a new image for the U.S. This project and the efforts of Peoples Temple were recently praised in the magazine *One World,* a publication of the World Council of Churches. Even Russia's *New Times* magazine has praised this work and done so in spite of our strong support of Russian people of Jewish descent, an obvious disagreement. We receive letters weekly from Russia, as well as from people in other parts of the world who have heard of the project, offering advice and assistance. In fact, several overtures have been made from Russia, which sees our current harassment as a form of political persecution. We do not want to take assistance from any people nor do we want to become an international issue. We also do not intend to be starved out by having our legitimately earned income cut off through the efforts of Trotskyite people and embittered malcontents. We have no political aspirations whatsoever. Jim Jones has spent the last 8 months working to develop the project in Guyana. We wish to continue to do so unmolested and unhampered. This project has done a great deal of practical good for the U.S., not only in promoting a positive image in a place where many of the populace have more of a left leaning, but also in a very tangible way financially. The amount of tax dollars we have saved the U.S. by taking people off welfare and off SSI and steering some from inevitable lives of crime would total conservatively in the hundreds of thousands. More importantly than that, lives have been saved that would have been meant for destruction. It seems cruel that anyone would want to escalate this type of bureaucratic harrassment into an international issue, but it is equally evident that people cannot forever be continually harrassed and beleaguered by such tactics without seeking alternatives that have been presented. I can say without hesitation that we are devoted to a decision that it is better even to die than to be constantly harrassed from one continent to the next. I hope you can look into this matter and protect the right of over 1,000 people from the U.S. to live in peace.

/s/ Pamela C. Moton

SIGNATURES OF PETITIONERS FOR ELIMINATION OF HUMAN RIGHTS VIOLATIONS IN GUYANA BY REV. JAMES JONES

	Name of Relative at Jonestown, Guyana	*Age*	*Signature of Petitioner*	*Relationship*
1.	Charles Touchette	47	Mickey Touchette	father
2.	Joyce Touchette	45	Mickey Touchette	mother
3.	Mike Touchette	25	Mickey Touchette	brother
4.	Al Touchette	23	Mickey Touchette	brother
5.	Michelle Touchette	19	Mickey Touchette	sister
6.	Cleve Swinney	60+	Mickey Touchette	grandfather
7.	Helen Swinney	60+	Mickey Touchette	grandmother
8.	Tim Swinney	late 30s	Mickey Touchette	uncle
9.	Mary Griffith	53	Louise Blanchard	sister
10.	Marrian	14	Louise Blanchard	aunt
11.	Amonda Griffith	17	Louise Blanchard	aunt
12.	Emmith Griffith	19	Louise Blanchard	aunt
13.	Mary Griffith	52	Rose Davis	aunt
14.	Amonda Griffith	17	Rose Davis	cousin
15.	Emmit Griffith Jr	19	Rose Davis	cousin
16.	Marrian Griffith	15	Rose Davis	cousin
17.	Diana Berry	7	Rose Davis	cousin
18.	Cornellis Truss Jr.	14	Rose Davis	cousin
19.	John Victor Stoen	6	Grace L. Stoen	son
20.	Maria S. Katsaris	24	Steven A. Katsaris	daughter
21.	Mark Andrew Sly	17	Neva Jean Sly	son
22.	Donald E. Sly	42	Neva Jean Sly	husband

April 11, 1978

SUMMARY LISTING OF OUR RELATIVES IN JONESTOWN, GUYANA

Name of Relative at Jonestown	*Age*	*Signer of This Accusation*	*Relationship to Signer*
• Wagner, Mark	16	Richard Wagner (San Francisco)	Son
• Harris, Liane	21	Sherwin Harris (Lafayette)	Daughter
		Elizabeth Harris (Lafayette)	Sister

· Ponts, Donna	15	Don Ponts (Ukiah)	Daughter
· Oliver, William S.	18	Howard Oliver (San Francisco)	Son
		Beverly Oliver (San Francisco)	Son
· Oliver, Bruce H.	20	Howard Oliver & Beverly Oliver	Son
· Katsaris, Maria	24	Steven A. Katsaris (Ukiah)	Daughter
· Rozynko, Michael	20	Sandy Rozynko Mills (Oakland)	Brother
		Steven Mills (Oakland)	Bro.-in-law
· Rozynko, Chris	22	Steve Mills & Sandy Rozynko Mills	(Same)
· Stoen, John Victor	6	Grace Stoen (San Francisco)	Son
		Timothy O. Stoen (San Francisco)	Son
· Sly, Mark A.	17	Neva Jean Sly (San Francisco)	Son
· Sly, Donald E.	42	Neva Jean Sly	Husband
· Houston, Patricia	14	Robert H. Houston (San Bruno)	Grandchild
		Nadyne L. Houston (San Bruno)	Grandchild
		Carol Boyd	Niece
· Houston, Judy Lynn	13	Robert & Nadyne Houston; Carol Boyd	(Same)
· Kerns, Carol Ann	19	Ruth Reinhardt (Davis)	Sister
· Kerns, Ellen Louise	51	Ruth Reinhardt	Mother
· Harris, Magnolia	61	Sylvia White (San Francisco)	Mother
		Leinaola White (San Francisco)	Grandmother
· Lopez, Vincent	17	Walter Jones (San Francisco)	Legal Guard'n

· Simon, Marcia	22	Leon Simon (Oakland)	Daughter
· Simon, Barbara	22	Leon Simon	Daughter
· Griffith, Mary M.	52	Rose Davis (San Francisco)	Aunt
		Carnella Truss (San Francisco)	Mother
		Louise Blanchard (San Francisco)	Sister
· Cobb, John	18	James Cobb, Jr. (San Francisco)	Brother
· Cobb, Brenda	15	James Cobb, Jr.	Sister
· Cobb, Sandra	21	James Cobb, Jr.	Sister
· Cobb, Joel	12	James Cobb, Jr.	Brother
· Brown, Ava	26	James Cobb, Jr.	Sister
· Touchette, Charles	47	Mickey Touchette (San Francisco)	Father
· Touchette, Joyce	45	Mickey Touchette	Mother
· Touchette, Al	23	Mickey Touchette	Brother
· Touchette, Mike	25	Mickey Touchette	Brother
· Touchette, Michelle	19	Mickey Touchette	Sister
· Swinney, Cleve	65	Mickey Touchette	Grandfather
· Swinney, Helen	65	Mickey Touchette	Grandmother
· Swinney, Tim	39	Mickey Touchette	Uncle
· Berry, Diana	7	Carnella Truss (San Francisco)	Daughter
· Griffith, Marrian	15	Carnella Truss	Sister
· Griffith, Emmett Jr.	20	Carnella Truss	Brother
· Griffith, Amonda	17	Carnella Truss	Sister

TOTALS: 37 Relatives in Jonestown
25 Signers of Accusation (As of April 11, 1978)

Appendix E: Peoples Temple Press Release

Peoples Temple
P.O. Box 15023
San Francisco, CA 94115

April 18, 1978

FOR IMMEDIATE RELEASE

The following is a transcript of the message read to members of the press by Harriet Tropp, member of Peoples Temple Agricultural Project at Jonestown, Guyana, South America. She read the statement via amateur radio phone patch at Charles Garry's office:

"I am speaking on behalf of Peoples Temple in response to the grossly false and malicious statements that continue to be made about our community here in Guyana. Individuals participating in a self-styled group of 'Concerned Relatives' have now threatened publicly to hire mercenaries to illegally enter Guyana and use whatever means necessary, including armed attack and kidnap, to capture relatives in the Peoples Temple community. These threats were made public in a California newspaper. Peoples Temple has already alerted the President, the U.S. State Department, and appropriate government officials in Guyana. This group of 'Concerned Relatives' is a cruel hoax. If they have to send mercenaries—hired guns who will violate laws and resort to killing and mayhem to fulfill their contract—then they reveal the real nature of their efforts.

"We demand to know where the money is coming from to allow them to hire killers. We also demand that the media, which has shown such eagerness to attack our organization, show equal vehemence in condemning this criminal effort and its perpetrators. Actually, this is not a new tactic in the move against the Guyana community; armed agents have already been sent in illegally and have tried to assassinate Rev. Jim Jones and others, as well as kidnap people. Those attempts have been successfully thwarted. We hope that the public will see the cruelty and evil behind the base, nasty motives of these public liars. The people involved have been brought together and have been given assurances that they would be backed up in whatever they were trying to do against Peoples Temple. Their number is very small compared to the many relatives and parents who are coming here to visit the project.

"Our community is a dramatic expression of our deep desire to build a meaningful future for mankind through cooperation and sharing and eradication of class division. Our contribution has been recognized by many, many people who have come to visit this democratic cooperative. Teachers, workers, government officials—people from all walks of life in Guyana, as well as representatives from nations the world over have come and congratulated us for what is being accomplished. They have praised us for the example of cooperative living and diligent development of this beautiful region.

"The chairman of the Guyanese Livestock Corporation, a man who is a member of one of the most important business families in Guyana, called this project the purest egalitarian society he had ever seen, a community without elitism. Just this week 35 educators from an attending school district, together with a delegation of the most outstanding students in the entire nation, visited us unannounced and spent the entire day. They were overwhelmed with what we are doing. We are making tons of friends here. We are building good will. Providing a constructive presence, we can only enhance cooperation and counteract the negative stereotype of North American people.

"Our medical department is known far and wide for its excellent services, and many lives have been saved. We have programs in agriculture, livestock development, a complete school system and a host of community projects. Just a few days ago, representatives from one of the largest news agencies in the world spent several days with us. Representatives from other news agencies have been to the project as well, and have pronounced it a remarkable, impressive achievement. Within three to four weeks, several relatives and parents who are not members will be visiting here. They are coming even with a degree of cynicism because they have been approached by this committee. We do not ask that people who come agree with us; however, these relatives are not coming with an intention to harass, and so they are very welcome. One is the leader of another church denomination. We object to this small committee of "concerned relatives" because we have firm proof that all involved in that group have talked about kidnapping and mercenaries. That type of element is not welcome by ourselves nor by the people of Guyana.

"Young people here are finding productive, new lives, free from the pitfalls of inner city environment that would have caused a large percentage of them to become involved in one form of anti-social behavior or another —behavior which would have cost the U.S. taxpayers hundreds of thousands of dollars. We are tired of seeing people and organizations that are trying to develop constructive alternatives, to build cooperative lifestyles, being harassed unmercifully, lied about, falsely accused of crimes, and, in many cases, brought down. In recent months alone, there have been several examples of this in the Bay Area.

"Here in Guyana, we have come to build a community for a significant number of people, well over a thousand, who have been hurt, angered, alienated and victimized by adverse conditions that prevail in the declining inner cities of advanced western society. Many who were not in such desperate circumstances have also come to join us and build because of the peaceful, natural environment, ideal weather, and the chance to serve. The vast majority of our members remain in the U.S.

"Finally, we would like to address ourselves to a point that has been raised, it seems, about some statement supposedly issued officially by Peoples Temple whose contents we here are unaware of. It is supposed to have been to the effect that we prefer to resist this harassment and persecution even if it means death. Those who are lying and slandering our work here, it appears, are trying to use this statement against us. We are not surprised. However, it seems that any person with any integrity or courage would have no trouble understanding such a position. Since it is clear that the persons who are plotting so actively to destroy our organization have neither integrity nor courage, we are not at all surprised that they would find it offensive. Dr. Martin Luther King reaffirmed the validity of ultimate commitment when he told his Freedom Riders: 'We must develop the courage of dying for a cause.' He later said that he hoped no one had to die as a result of the struggle, but, 'If anyone has to, let it be me.' And we, likewise, affirm that before we will submit quietly to the interminable plotting and persecution of this politically motivated conspiracy, we will resist actively, putting our lives on the line, if it comes to that. This has been the unanimous vote of the collective community here in Guyana. We choose as our motto: not like those who marched submissively into gas ovens, but like the valiant heroes who resisted in the Warsaw ghettos. Patrick Henry captured it when he said, simply: 'Give me liberty, or give me death.'

"If people cannot appreciate that willingness to die, if necessary, rather than to compromise the right to exist free from harassment and the kind of indignities that we have been subjected to, then they can never understand the integrity, honesty, and bravery of Peoples Temple nor the type of commitment of Jim Jones and the principles he has struggled for all his life.

"It is not our purpose to die; we believe deeply in the celebration of life. It is the intention of Jim Jones, and always has been, to light candles rather than curse the darkness, to find and implement constructive solutions rather than merely complain about problems. But under these outrageous attacks, we have decided to defend the integrity of our community and our pledge to do this. We are confident that people of conscience and principle understand our position. We make no apologies for it."

QUOTES

Charles Garry, Attorney: "I have been to Paradise. It's there for anybody to see. . . . I saw a community where there is no such thing as racism. . . . There is no such thing as age-ism. . . . I have never seen so many happy faces in my life as I did in Jonestown the three days I was there. . . . Why are those people so happy? They are learning a new social order. They are learning an answer to a better life. When I returned to the States, I told my partners in the office that I had seen paradise. From what I saw there, I would say that the society that is being built in Jonestown is a credit to humanity."

Dr. Peter Fernandes, Chairman of the Guyana Livestock Corporation and world traveler: "Jonestown is the purest egalitarian society I have ever seen."

Dr. Ng-a-Fook, Guyanese Dental Surgeon: "The Peoples Temple Agricultural and Medical Mission is a first-class example of community life. I have never before seen so many people of varying races working happily side-by-side. . . . I could not help but be impressed."

Appendix F: The Mark Lane-Leo Ryan Correspondence

Nov. 6, 1978

Congressman Leo J. Ryan
1720 South Amphlett Blvd.
Suite 219
San Mateo, California 94402

Dear Congressman Ryan:

It is my understanding that you and another member of Congress and possibly two members of the staff of the International Relations Committee of the U.S. House of Representatives wish to visit Jonestown, Guyana due to complaints that have been made about the project there. It is also my understanding that you or members of the staff of the Committee have been briefed by persons hostile to the People's Temple and the project in Jonestown. It would seem to me both fair and appropriate for you to seek information from the other side as well before embarking upon a trip to Jonestown. Since I represent the People's Temple in various matters, I should be happy to meet with you and tell you of my experiences in Jonestown and with Jim Jones and with the People's Temple.

I have been informed that you wish to tour Jonestown during the middle of November. My client has asked that I be present while you make that tour. It seems entirely appropriate and proper that I should be there on that occasion. Accordingly, I placed a telephone call to your San Mateo office at 9 A.M. on Friday, November 3, 1978 to make arrangements for your trip to Jonestown and to discuss the entire matter with you. Your aide stated that you would return my telephone call but I have not as yet heard directly from you. However, I did receive a telephone call from Jim Schollaert who told me that he was a member of the Committee's staff. I informed him that I would be engaged during the middle of November in that I would be representing several witnesses who were to appear in public testimony before the House Select Committee on Assassinations in Washington, D.C.

from the middle until the end of November. I suggested to Mr. Schollaert that if you called me we could no doubt work out a date which would be satisfactory to all of us.

You should understand that Jonestown is a private community and that while they appear willing to host your visit there under certain circumstances, courtesy requires that arrangements be made in advance of your visit. For example: there are no hotels or restaurants in the area and you would be the guest of the community during your entire visit. The people of Jonestown have expressed a willingness to care for your needs and the needs of your staff and associates but they suggest, and I certainly agree, that a date which would be convenient to all of us should be arrived at through discussion.

You should be informed that various agencies of the U.S. Government have somewhat consistently oppressed the People's Temple and sought to interfere with the People's Temple, a religious institution. I am now exploring that matter fully in order to bring an action against those agencies of the U.S. Government that have violated the rights of my client. Some of the members of the People's Temple have had to flee from the U.S. in order to experience a fuller opportunity to enjoy rights which were not available to them within the U.S. You should know that two different countries, neither one of which has entirely friendly relations with the U.S., have offered refuge to the 1200 Americans now residing in Jonestown. Thus far the People's Temple has not accepted either of those offers but it is their position that if religious persecution continues and if it is furthered through a witch hunt conducted by any branch of the U.S. Government, that they will be constrained to consider accepting either of the offers. You may judge, therefore, the important consequences which may flow from further persecution of People's Temple and which might very well result in the creation of a most embarrassing situation for the U.S. Government.

I hope that this matter can be resolved in an amicable fashion and I continue to wait for a telephone call from you so that we may discuss this matter more fully.

Very truly yours,
/s/ Mark Lane
Mark Lane

ML:br
cc: Jean Brown

November 10, 1978

Mr. Mark Lane
Attorney at Law
1177 Central Ave.
Memphis, Tenn. 38104

Dear Mr. Lane:

I am in receipt of your letter regarding the proposed visit of a delegation from the House International Relations Committee to the nation of Guyana. While I am pleased to have your offer of assistance to the Committee on behalf of the People's Temple at Jonestown I must respectfully dissent from certain assumptions which were apparent in your letter.

First, the Committee and its staff, as a matter of policy and standard practice, works through our Embassy and the government of the nation which it visits. Second, it is my policy, when I am a delegation Chairman conducting inquiries at home or abroad, to deal with the principals in a given situation. To that end, I sent a telegram on November 1 to Mr. Jim Jones asking for his cooperation in a matter affecting the personal lives of an unknown but large number of U.S. citizens, who are presently residing on his property in Jonestown and in Georgetown. He has not yet replied, but I presume he is in touch with the American Embassy and Ambassador John Burke about this inquiry. It is for this reason that I asked Mr. James Schollaert, as an attorney on the staff of the Committee, to respond to your telephone inquiry, to which you make reference.

I regret that you will not be able to be in Guyana this next week, but I understand that Mr. Jones has other legal counsel available in the event he feels such counsel is necessary. In a situation where the Committee schedule does not coincide with your own personal schedule, I must obviously resolve such a conflict for the United States House of Representatives. I hope that you will understand.

I am also interested in your statement that "various agencies of the U.S. Government have somewhat consistently oppressed the People's Temple." Any such assumption with regard to our Committee is grossly in error. I am interested in locating and talking to certain persons in that community whose mothers, fathers, brothers, sisters, husbands and wives have asked me to inquire on their behalf.

It is true that most of the comments I have heard from relatives are negative, but that is precisely the purpose of this inquiry. Rather than take the word of relatives who can be presumed to be under some emotional bias, I intend to go to the source and to allow those "on the other side" the opportunity to speak in their own behalf. In this case, I have offered Mr.

Jones and his supporters the full opportunity to speak for themselves. I presume they will accept such an offer. It is made with the full intention of allowing any and all to speak for the record.

I am at a loss to understand the references on the second page of your letter to members of Mr. Jones' group who have had to "flee from the United States to enjoy their freedom." I certainly hope such persons will be available to give such testimony to support your comment.

I am even more puzzled by your further vague references to one or two other countries that have offered "refuge" to the 1200 Americans in Jonestown. Am I to understand, then, that all 1200 have already been asked if they would be willing to travel to yet another country and begin their lives, under what must already be difficult conditions at best? Perhaps we can learn more about that after we arrive.

Finally, Mr. Lane, I am truly disappointed with your use of the phrase "witch hunt" in connection with an open and honest inquiry of the United States House of Representatives into the welfare of American citizens presently living in Jonestown. The committee asks no more of Mr. Jones than any parent does whose son or daughter is away at school or whose mother or father resides in a distant convalescent home or hospital.

No "persecution", as you put it, is intended, Mr. Lane. But your vague reference to "the creation of the most embarassing situation for the American government" does not impress me at all. If the comment is intended as a threat, I believe it reveals more than may have been intended. I presume Mr. Jones would not be supportive of such a comment.

The Committee does intend to leave as scheduled. It does intend to discuss the whereabouts, living conditions and general welfare of the 1200 Americans you refer to, with our Embassy, with the officials of the nation of Guyana and of course, we hope, with Mr. Jones as the leader of the group. We ask for and hope for the cooperation of all. I, too, hope that the inquiry can move ahead in an amicable fashion.

Sincerely yours,
/s/ Leo J. Ryan
LEO J. RYAN
Member of Congress

LJR/cg

cc: Reverend Jim Jones
Foreign Minister of Guyana
Prime Minister of Guyana
Ambassador Laurence Mann of Guyana
Ambassador John Burke of the United States
Assistant Secretary of State for Latin American Affairs

Appendix G: Letter to Senator John Stennis, and Related Documents

November 16, 1976

Senator John C. Stennis
United States Senator
205 Old Senate Office Building
Washington, D.C. 20510

Dear Senator Stennis:

In the atmosphere following the debacle of the Nixon administration, the public was led to believe that the compilation of "enemy lists," the collection of dossiers, the web of intrigue and investigation surrounding private citizens that characterized those unfortunate years was coming to an end. However, a series of peculiar events last week led to a rather unusual discovery, one which seems to belie the promise of the post-Watergate climate, and one in which I am sure you will be interested. I hope that you will bear with me if this letter seems overly long, but details are necessary to fully grasp the impact of the situation.

As you are perhaps aware, Peoples Temple Christian Church, of the Disciples of Christ, a denomination numbering upwards of 2 million whose members include FBI Director Clarence Kelly and many congresspersons, is a multi-ethnic church whose theological emphasis is upon the social gospel of Jesus Christ. We stress the value of a life of human service, and to this end the church has a large variety of programs that serve the needs of people from every racial and socio-economic background. Central to our philosophy is a deep commitment to the principles of democracy as embodied in our Bill of Rights—foremost among these being freedom of speech, press, religion, and peaceful assembly. Equally important is the concomitant right to privacy. We do not believe that it is possible to maintain a viable democracy without a vigilant and spirited dedication to liberty. So it is not unusual for our congregations to invite speakers from all walks of life and every phase of the philosophical spectrum to discuss their views. John Birchers, moderate Republicans, liberals and progressives alike have spoken at our churches. We like to think of ourselves as an open forum for a free exchange of ideas.

Thus, when Ms. Unita Blackwell Wright, Mayor of Meyersville, Miss., offered to address several thousand members of our San Francisco congregation at one of our services on Sunday, November 7, the congregation gladly accepted. No doubt you are familiar with Ms. Wright, as she has been actively involved in the civil rights movement for many years, and was among the first American women to visit China with actress Shirley MacLaine in 1973. We think that an exposure to a variety of life's experiences can only serve to sharpen one's ability to separate the wheat from the chaff, and, as we have never had a speaker who could give an eyewitness view of China, we were interested in hearing her perspective.

Ms. Wright gave a humorous, down to earth, sincere talk on her ideas for peaceful, positive social change. I am basically a political moderate, cynical of all Utopian solutions. I can say that Ms. Wright at no time advocated the adoption of China's ideological structure; she merely pointed out some of the positive aspects of Chinese society, such as the absence of the need for locked doors and the safety of the streets at night, and suggested how America could emulate these characteristics to strengthen our own nation. (Even moderate members of Congress recognize that some kinds of changes are necessary within the framework of our democratic system.) She was hardly a "wild-eyed radical" and we are not starry-eyed idealists about China or any other foreign country. Certainly we would never support a dictatorial regime of whatever political label. Honestly, it is difficult for us to see how mature, responsible people can seriously believe that complex social ills can be erradicated by Utopian panaceas.

However, this innocuous exercise in one of our basic constitutional guarantees—freedom of speech—did not go by unnoticed by those who, it seems, would want to deny us this fundamental liberty.

Senator Stennis, there were other, uninvited guests that Sunday. Outside two men sat in a parked car which later proved to be rented from Sacramento. One of them reportedly had a tape recorder and was seen skulking about the side of our building eavesdropping. He was followed to the parked vehicle some distance away from the church.

Naturally, their covert interest in a Sunday church service aroused the curiosity of the over 4,000 of our members who were present for this second morning service, among them several reporters who decided to do their own investigation. It appears that the car was rented by a Mr. Thomas Dawsey. Mr. Dawsey is one of your constituents from Biloxi. Apparently, Mr. Dawsey, having been picked up at the airport Saturday by the rental agency, drove to San Francisco Sunday morning and parked some distance from our building. The car was returned Monday morning.

Some of Mr. Dawsey's relatives and friends furnished additional information that sheds a bizarre light on the picture. According to these contacts, Mr. Dawsey is an electronics expert working for a governmental agency that is guided by yourself. This particular point was told by one relative and confirmed by another source. Although we are not in agreement with your point of view, at times, nevertheless, as Chairman of the Armed Services Committee, as well as the Central Intelligence and Preparedness Subcommittees, you are a Senator who has obviously been dedicated to the interests of our country for many years. These are facts that seem to corroborate the accuracy of all that Mr. Dawsey's relatives and friends said about the nature of his work. Supposedly, Mr. Dawsey is a very high ranking member of a communications "team" (I believe that his rating is EMC 13) whose activities you are primarily responsible for. Allegedly, the activities of these select groups (one source said that there are also teams in Missouri and California) are connected with the Air Force and Kessler Base in Mississippi, near Biloxi. One relative did say that the team members were concerned with checking out possible interference with radar communication that could jeopardize our national defense, a purpose that cannot be relevant to the clandestine scrutiny of a Christian Church service, or the cloak of secrecy.

Precipitate judgments can prove faulty, of course, but when electronics experts sit outside our church, clearly trying to hear what is going on inside, we begin to wonder. After all, if their motive was innocent, why didn't they just come inside and identify the organization they represented? It would have saved them, and us, a great deal of trouble.

Latin America is alive with rumors that our government has been cooperating with efforts to introduce communications experts along the Guyanese border as part of some destabilization attempt. We have an agricultural mission on several thousand acres in that country and heretofore have not believed these rumors, passing them off as a hypersensitivity to U.S. influence in Latin America. Now we begin to wonder.

Peoples Temple is not interested in becoming enmeshed in a public campaign against mushrooming government surveillance. In fact, we are asking those who receive copies of this letter not to make its contents public, because we adhere to the principle that one is innocent of a wrong-doing until proven guilty. Moreover, we cannot see what purpose would be served either in creating further division among the American people, or presenting a false image of America as a police state to the world at large. We still have great faith in America, but in the event that it becomes evident that the First Amendment is being challenged in any segment of American life and society to an intolerable degree, several prominent journalists have been given both this letter and the supporting documentation and have agreed to go ahead with a story only upon our direct request. However, we require some clarification as to the nature of an operation that sends personnel all the way from Biloxi, Mississippi to "spy out our liberty," to quote a Scripture. One Congressman told us that it bore the earmarks of CIA involvement. Our privacy and that of Ms. Unita Wright have been grossly invaded, and we feel that to sit quietly by and tolerate its continued violation would denigrate our self-respect and moral integrity.

Sunday's incident was not the first time our church has been subjected to harassment. A brief look at just a few of the incidents we have experienced will, I think, serve to put our present concern in perspective, although they are not necessarily connected with Sunday's incident.

1. Some time ago, one of our churches was burned down. The Fire Inspector said that it was clearly the work of a professional arsonist.

2. On numerous occasions we have received harassing phone calls. One incident particularly stands out in my mind because it was so cruel. A person mimicked the voice of one of our ministers, and he said he was going to commit suicide. Another time a caller said that our Pastor had been killed. Some of the recipients of these calls were senior citizens whose health could have been jeopardized by the shock.

3. At other times, strangers have called our church offices, saying that church officials had called and insulted them rudely, and not one of our members had ever even heard of the person making the complaint!

4. We were sent what was, from outward appearances, authentic newspaper copy of a story that allegedly was to be printed about us—a very negative "article." The object was to alienate us from the paper in question, a newspaper with whom we were, and continue to be, on excellent terms. Since that time both the establishment and alternative press have been more than favorable to our work.

5. Our Pastor was sent a bouquet of flowers and a sympathy card—with his "death" given as a date in the very near future. One of his children received it.

6. A bomb was placed underneath the bus our Pastor was to ride on one night. The Bomb Squad came to dismantle the device. Many children and seniors would have been riding that bus as well.

7. Finally, several years ago we found out that some telephone operators were monitoring our office calls for days at a stretch. (This occurred in a rural community at a time when our attorney's office phones did not yet have the direct dialing system.) Having found nothing nefarious to report, they finally discontinued the activity. One operator stepped forward and told us what was happening. The telephone company investigated and said

her information appeared correct but her testimony would be required at a hearing. She told us, in tears, that if she were to testify, she would be unbearably pressured by racist elements within her department. One of the investigators said this was probably so and it was likely that the woman would lose her job. Our Pastor and the majority of the Board of Trustees felt that we had a primary obligation to see that she did not suffer for her honesty and, as our sole interest that this invasion of privacy be stopped had been achieved, we decided not to publicize the matter.

8. Just the other evening a person who refused to identify himself came by our headquarters asking information regarding our Pastor's travel schedule, specifically, what bus he regularly rode. He also was insistent about knowing the Pastor's home address.

Our aim, Senator Stennis, is not to raise a cry of "persecution." That kind of crusade is against our nature entirely. But we thought that this latest incident required a response on our part so that we can be on record as opposing this harassment, in the event we are bothered in the future. Until this time we had no concern about government interference with our privacy. As a result of these events, however, we now do intend to make disclosure requests to all appropriate government agencies under the Privacy Act of 1974 and the Freedom of Information Act.

Peoples Temple has taken youth from militant backgrounds and made them once again believe that it is possible to work for change within the system. Many conservative leaders in both the political and business spheres, together with liberals, support our church as one of the most effective deterrents to Communism or tyranny in any form. Our programs have rescued literally hundreds from lives of crime and drugs, and we know of no actively participating young person having any difficulty with the law.

We also arrange for free medical care for those in need. Just last week, in one morning alone, over 1000 people were given innoculations against several strains of influenza by doctors working in our church. (Governmental officials say these strains of flu are threatening our nation's health. Each year we always follow their guidelines and see that every member is provided with the medical care recommended.) The program of innoculations was continued daily. Peoples Temple paid the bill.

Repeated harassment can only serve to undermine the respect for our democratic system that the church has helped to foster in embittered young people. If it were not for the calm, controlled, and understanding leadership of our Pastor, no doubt many of these youths would be encouraged to return to a life of crime and militant activity by this kind of surveillance.

Peoples Temple has found that no group has a corner on truth or a franchise on reality. We have learned to listen although we may thoroughly disapprove. But we are tired of being annoyed and spied upon just because we choose to exercise our civil liberties. When relatives openly brag that government personnel are responsible to you and that you are accountable only to the President, it raises serious questions. Out of respect for you and your office, we decided to solicit your reply. One friend remarked that you are a powerful man who is organizing these groups for special undisclosed reasons that would serve the nation. Frankly, I do not see how eavesdropping on 4–5,000 people exercising their First Amendment rights in a Sunday church service will preserve the nation from destruction. Please enlighten us. In the meantime, Peoples Temple will continue to maintain our rights of freedom of speech, assembly, and religion, and we will defend these rights with our lives, if necessary.

Sincerely,
/s/ Jean F. Brown
Jean F. Brown
c/o Peoples Temple
1859 Geary Blvd.
San Francisco, California 94115

December 2, 1976

Ms. Jean Brown
Peoples Temple Staff
P.O. BOX 15157
San Francisco, Ca. 94115

Dear Ms. Brown:

I am in receipt of your recent letter regarding the survellience of Peoples Temple by persons affiliated with the Air Force.

In Order to be of assistance to you in this matter I have contacted the Department of the Air Force.

I will be in immediate contact with you upon receiving a response from the Department of the Air Force.

Kindest personal regards.

Sincerely,
/s/ Phillip Burton
PHILLIP BURTON
Member of Congress

PB:tmn

February 8, 1977

Ms. Jean Brown
People's Temple
P. O. BOX 15157
San Francisco, California 94115

Dear Ms. Brown:

In reference to your letter regarding the activities of Mr. Tommy Dawsey, I am enclosing letters I received from the Department of the Air Force in response to my inquiries on this matter.

The enclosed letters are self-explanatory and forwarded for your information.

If you have any further information, or if I can be of any further assistance, please do not hesitate to contact my office.

Kindest personal regards,

Sincerely,
/s/ Phillip Burton
PHILLIP BURTON
Member of Congress

PB:why

DEC 17 1976

Dear Mr. Burton:

This is in reply to your inquiry in behalf of Ms. Jean F. Brown of the Peoples Temple Christian Church. Ms. Brown was concerned over the actions of a Mr. Thomas Dawsey.

While a Mr. Tommy N. Dawsey is a civil service employee assigned to 1839 Electronics Installation Group at Keesler AFB, Mississippi, the commander states that his organization is not involved in any type operation as described by Ms. Brown.

Since no military law or directive appears to have been violated, the alleged activities are not within the Air Force's investigative jurisdiction.

We understand your concern and regret we cannot be of more assistance.

Sincerely,
/s/ Thomas S. Collins
THOMAS S. COLLINS,
Lt Colonel, USAF
Congressional Inquiry Division
Office of Legislative Liaison

Attachment
Honorable Phillip Burton
House of Representatives

January 10, 1977

Lt. Colonel Thomas S. Collins
Congressional Inquiry Division
Office of Legislative Liaison
Department of the Air Force
The Pentagon
Washington, D.C. 20330

Dear Colonel Collins:

I am in receipt of your letter dated December 17, 1976, in response to my inquiry on the case, Ms. Jean Brown and the People's Temple of San Francisco.

People's Temple of San Francisco has a very legitimate concern in this matter. Either Mr. Tommy N. Dawsey, or some individual using this name, was involved in the surveillance of a People's Temple gathering.

Your reply that the Commander of Keesler Air Force Base "states that his organization is not involved in any type of operation described by Ms. Brown" is not responsive.

Mr. Dawsey, or someone using his name, *was* involved in this "type of operation". My inquiry is directed at the activities of Mr. Dawsey. Mr. Dawsey was either not involved and therefore his name was used fraudulently, or else he was involved in some capacity. Even if Mr. Dawsey's involvement was in a private rather than professional capacity, this remains a serious matter.

My question still remains, was *Mr. Dawsey* involved in the surveillance of People's Temple?

Secondly, what are Mr. Dawsey's assigned duties at Keesler Air Force Base and what is the specific mission of the 1839 Electronics Installation Group at Kessler AFB.

I look forward to your early reply to these questions.

Sincerely,
/s/ Phillip Burton
PHILLIP BURTON
Member of Congress

PB:why

JAN 18 1977

Dear Mr. Burton:

This is in reply to your most recent inquiry in behalf of Ms. Jean Brown of Peoples Temple Christian Church.

We regret that we were, and still are, unable to investigate the private matters which may have involved the Peoples Temple and Mr. Tommy N. Dawsey. We are sure you can appreciate the legal aspects of the Air Force getting involved in the personal lives of private citizens.

As we previously mentioned, Mr. Dawsey is a civil service employee assigned to the 1839 Electronics Installation Group (EIG) at Keesler AFB, Mississippi. He is an electronic engineer responsible for providing electromagnetic compatability engineering services. His duties involve checking interference between communications/electronics equipment.

The mission of the 1839 EIG is to install and maintain electronic and communication systems for the Air Force, and to provide electromagnetic compatability engineering services. No aspect of that mission involves the surveillence of private citizens or organizations, except for possible commercial television or radio stations interfering with base facilities.

Thank you for your interest, and we hope this information is of assistance.

Sincerely,
/s/ John W. Farr
JOHN W. FARR, Lt Colonel,
USAF
Congressional Inquiry Division
Office of Legislative Liaison

Honorable Phillip Burton

House of Representatives

JAN 26 1977

Dear Mr. Burton:

This is in reply to your most recent inquiry in behalf of the Peoples Temple Christian Church concerning the duty status of Mr. Tommy N. Dawsey.

The Commander of the 1839th Electronics Installation Group at Keesler AFB, Mississippi, advises that official records reflect Mr. Dawsey's duty status for the period October 13 to November 22, 1976, was as follows:

October 13—Departed Keesler AFB, Mississippi, on Temporary Duty. Arrived Mather AFB, California. Purpose: Burroughs 3500 Computer Remote Terminal (CRT) Enhancement Project

October 14–15—Mather AFB

October 16–17—Non-duty

October 18–19—Mather AFB

October 20—Departed Mather AFB. Arrived Vandenberg AFB, California. Purpose: Communications Circuit Quality Improvement Task

October 21–22—Vandenberg AFB

October 23—Departed Vandenberg AFB (Non-duty)

October 24—Non-duty

October 25—Arrived March AFB (Non-duty—Veterans Day).

Purpose: Burroughs 3500 CRT Project

October 26–29—March AFB

October 30–31—Non-duty

November 1–3—March AFB

November 4—Departed March AFB. Arrived Mather AFB.

Purpose: Burroughs 3500 CRT Project

November 5—Mather AFB

November 6–7—Non-duty

November 8–12—Mather AFB

November 13–14—Non-duty

November 15–16—Mather AFB

November 17—Departed Mather AFB. Arrived Keesler AFB. (Mission Complete).

November 18–19—Keesler AFB

November 20–21—Non-duty

November 22—Keesler AFB

We understand and appreciate your personal concern over this matter and hope the foregoing information will be of assistance.

Sincerely,
/s/ John W. Farr
JOHN W. FARR, Lt Colonel, USAF
Congressional Inquiry Division
Office of Legislative Liaison

Honorable Phillip Burton

House of Representatives

Appendix H: Teresa Buford Declaration and Affidavit

DECLARATION OF TERESA BUFORD

I, TERESA BUFORD, hereby declare:

Timothy O. Stoen passed me a note, a copy of which is attached herewith and incorporated herein, one evening at Peoples Temple in the San Francisco Temple at a meeting of counselors. It was in or around the late part of 1973. I recognized the handwriting on the note as being Tim Stoen's handwriting. Tim Stoen told me to give the note to Jim Jones as Tim Stoen felt it would be a "good way to handle Jim Cobb." I wrote at the top of the note "Re: Cobb" and passed the note on.

During the conversation Tim Stoen told me that he would recommend that something be written up as a "script" that someone could read to Cobb over the telephone. He said this way he could word the "script" so as to "scare the shit out of Cobb." Tim Stoen said that when the call was made, that it should be done, if not by Annie Moore, then by some other unknown voice, and that the caller should call from a pay phone (not located near the church). Tim Stoen said that the call should not last longer than three minutes for the reason that there was a slight possibility that someone might have the call traced. Tim Stoen recommended that the caller wear gloves so that his fingerprints could not be traced. Tim Stoen suggested that the caller say something to make Cobb believe that his life was in danger.

Tim Stoen told me at the time that if Annie Moore could not do it, that I should interview other people to do the same.

The note was never acted upon.

I declare under penalty of perjury that the foregoing is true and correct.

Executed on October 10, 1978 at San Francisco, California.

/s/ Teresa Buford
Teresa Buford

STATE OF TENNESSEE
COUNTY OF SHELBY

STATEMENT OF TERESA BUFORD
REGARDING A SUM OF MONEY
PAID TO CHARLES GARRY, ESQ.

AFFIDAVIT

TERESA BUFORD, being duly sworn, deposes and says that:

ONE Shortly after Huey P. Newton returned to the United States and was put in jail I received a message from Rev. Jim Jones via ham radio to give Huey Newton five thousand dollars in cash.

TWO I went into the financial office in Peoples Temple in San Francisco and removed $5000.00 in one hundred dollar bills and drove over to Charles Garry's office.

THREE I arrived at Charles Garry's office shortly after five PM and told him that I had just received word from Jim Jones that he wanted to give Huey Newton a gift of $5000.00. I asked Charles Garry how I might deliver the money to Huey Newton. Garry then said that he would deliver it.

FOUR I gave Charles Garry the money and he closed the door and told me that he wanted to have a talk. He told me that he did not believe that Huey Newton was a free agent and that Huey was not able to call the shots in his own defense. Charles Garry then asked me if I would permit him to put the money into his safe and to hold until such time as he personally felt that Huey Newton was able to decide for himself. Since Garry felt so strongly about this I agreed.

FIVE Several months later, when I returned to San Francisco from a trip to Guyana, I asked Charles Garry if he had given the money to Huey Newton and if so what had Huey said. Garry told me that he had not done so and that Huey was still not able to really say or do what he wanted to do. I told Charles Garry that Jim Jones had wanted Huey to have that money for his defense and that that meant alot to Jim Jones. Charles Garry then said that he understood but that there were a lot of strange things going on around Huey Newton that he was checking into and that he would like for me to trust him to give Huey the money at the appropriate time. Charles Garry told me that if he were to give the money to Huey Newton just then that the money would be given to people who he felt were interested in keeping Huey Newton in jail. I thought that Charles Garry had some inside information from Huey Newton that I was not aware of.

SIX In late August or early September of this year I saw Charles Garry in Guyana. I did not want to make him think that I did not trust him by asking directly about the money so I just asked him how Huey was doing hoping that Charles Garry would mention the money. I told Charles Garry that I thought that the magazine article "The Party's Over" was a terrible piece. Charles Garry said that to the contrary that he thought that the article was "excellent" and furthermore that Huey Newton was guilty of everything that the article said about him. I was shocked to hear Charles Garry saying this. Charles Garry made no mention of the money.

SEVEN Later that day in Guyana Jim Jones was telling Garry how sorry he felt about Huey's situation and Garry said for Jim Jones not to feel sorry for Huey Newton that "Huey got what was coming to him." He said, "Huey was guilty of everything that they said and more." Jim Jones told me later that day that we could never fire Charles Garry no matter how senile we thought him to be because, said Jones, "Garry is a vindictive son of a bitch and if he is talking that way about Huey now, he will talk about us much worse if we ever let him go." Jones at that point instructed me to be sure that Charles Garry got $5,000.00 a month from that time forward without fail.

EIGHT I did not tell Jim Jones about Garry keeping the money because I did not want to upset him. Jones would have felt that he had been terribly betrayed if he thought that Garry kept money from a black man in jail. Given other pressures on Jim Jones I thought it best to drop the issue with Charles Garry rather than risk the responsibility of what would happen to Jones mentally were he to believe that his own lawyer had betrayed his wishes for personal ambition or profit.

NINE Prior to the above-related events, in October of 1977 Charles Garry talked to me on the phone about Huey Newton. This was shortly after the talk that Huey Newton had had with Jim Jones on the radio when Jim Jones was threatening "mass suicide." Charles Garry told me that Huey Newton had had to go to Cuba because he had "cracked up." He said that Huey Newton was a drunk and addicted to some type of drug and that he was not in any condition to go to court. Charles Garry said that if Huey Newton had not left the country he would have been a disgrace to the Black Panther Party.

/s/ Teresa Buford
TERESA BUFORD

Sworn to and subscribed before me this 27th day of December, 1978
(*April R. Ferguson*)
My commission expires Dec. 18, 1982.

Appendix I: Letter from Eleftheris Karaoglanis Regarding Charles Garry

December 26, 1978

Mark Lane, Esq.
1177 Central Avenue
Memphis, Tn. 38104

Dear Mr. Lane:

On December 23, 1978, a Saturday, I met in the office of Charles Garry, in San Francisco, with Garry and one of his associates. I met with Garry from approximately eleven in the morning until approximately two-thirty in the afternoon that day.

During the course of that meeting, Garry told me that he had destroyed all of the letters that members of the Peoples Temple had written which were, he said, signed confessions of wrongdoing on their part and were the way, Garry said, by which Jim Jones held the people hostage in the Temple. Garry's associate seemed very upset to hear Garry say that he had destroyed the evidence and he asked him why he had done such a thing.

Garry said that there were three documents which he did not destroy. They were all written by Terri Buford, he said. He then showed me three documents written by Ms. Buford. One was to "Jean" and at least one was to Jim Jones. Garry then told me that Ms. Buford was a liar since she has said that she was not the mistress of Jim Jones. Garry showed me a letter to Jim Jones signed by Ms. Buford to prove that she had been the mistress of Jim Jones. The other document was a one-page "confession" about smuggling one million dollars.

He also showed me a letter from Chaikin to Jones about how Garry should be eased out as the lawyer for Peoples Temple.

Garry told me that he was then sure that guns were being kept in the cellar of his law office. He said, "I know they were there." When I asked him how he knew, he said, "Believe me."

Very truly yours,
/s/ Eleftheris Karaoglanis
Eleftheris Karaoglanis

Appendix J: Mark Lane-Timothy Stoen-Patrick Hallinan Correspondence

May 7, 1979

Mr. Timothy Stoen
1 Montgomery Street
San Francisco, California 94104

Dear Mr. Stoen:

I have placed telephone calls to your attorney's office several times over the last few months but have been unable to reach him and he has failed to return any of those calls. I am, therefore, obliged to write to you directly.

As you may know, I am writing a book about the tragedy of Jonestown. I will, of course, devote some of the work to an examination of the role played by you in the events that shaped the Peoples Temple. I wish to talk with you, in the presence of your attorney and with a tape-recorder if you both desire, or send to you a series of questions or send to you a number of conclusions that I have reached with a request that you make comments about those conclusions. I agree in advance to publish in full any statement that you wish to make, each of your answers to the questions in full or any comment you may make upon my conclusions. I agree not to edit in any fashion the material that you may be willing to submit.

Some of the information I have secured has been provided by Teresa Buford with whom you worked for many years. I will be pleased to publish in full all responses to her allegations that you wish to make.

Very truly yours,
/s/ Mark Lane
Mark Lane

ML/jt

May 7, 1979

Mr. Patrick Hallinan, Esq.
345 Franklin
San Francisco, California 94102

Dear Mr. Hallinan:

I have received a sworn statement from Teresa Buford in which she affirms that she delivered to your office the sum of five thousand ($5,000.00) dollars in one hundred dollar bills. She was instructed by Jim Jones to secure that sum from the Peoples Temple larder and deliver it to you so that you could deliver it to Mr. Timothy Stoen. This was, Ms. Buford asserts, as the result of your request that Mr. Jones send the money to Mr. Stoen.

Since I will be discussing this matter in a book I am writing, I should like your answer to the following questions:

1. Did your office receive the sum from Ms. Buford?
2. Did you deliver the sum to Mr. Stoen?
3. Did you request the Peoples Temple, through their representative or representatives to pay Mr. Stoen?
4. If your office did accept the sum or if Mr. Stoen did accept the sum or if you did request a payment for him, what was the purpose behind the transfer to that sum?

I assure you that your answers to these questions will be published in full without editing on my part.

Very truly yours,
/s/ Mark Lane
Mark Lane

ML/jt

June 7, 1979

CERTIFIED/RETURN RECEIPT REQUESTED

Mark Lane, Esq.
1177 Central Avenue
Memphis, TN 38104

Dear Mr. Lane:

I have received your request that I forward on to Mr. Stoen your letter dated May 7, 1979, in which you request to interview Mr. Stoen. You couch the letter in language indicating your desire for some fairness in certain matters you intend to publish in a book by seeking to have both sides present their points of view.

I am enclosing a copy of an article which appeared in the Los Angeles Times in which you made malicious and deliberately scurrilous allegations about Tim Stoen without any basis of fact, and without any attempt to procure "the other side" of the story. Your intentions, from this article and from numerous public statements you have made, are quite clear. We do not intend to participate in any activity which will allow you to aggrandize and enrich yourself, like some eater of carrion, by way of the tragedy which claimed the lives of more than 900 people, including Timothy Stoen's child.

You have already made your position in this matter clear, and fairness and honesty have never been high on your list of priorities. You may publish what you wish, but I assure you that if your publication is libelous or invades my client's right to privacy from a sensational expose aimed at your enrichment, we will immediately file an action against your publisher and you for the relief to which we are entitled.

I remain,

Sincerely yours,
/s/ Patrick Hallinan
PATRICK SARSFIELD HALLINAN

/skc
cc: Hawthorn Books, Inc.

June 7, 1979

CERTIFIED/RETURN RECEIPT REQUESTED

Hawthorn Books, Inc.
260 Madison Avenue
New York, NY 10016

Re: *Mark Lane Book on Jonestown*

Gentlemen:

I am the attorney for Timothy Stoen and we have received information that Mark Lane intends to publish a book, and has been given an advance by Hawthorn Books, Inc., toward that purpose, on the events surrounding and leading up to the mass suicide at Jonestown, Guyana. We are also advised that Mr. Lane intends to prominently feature my client, Timothy Stoen, as the villain of the piece and as an undercover intelligence agent for the CIA or some other governmental body. These allegations are without factual basis and are defamatory and are made with malice. I am including, for your reading, an article appearing in the Los Angeles Times which sets forth the total absence of any basis for the allegations we expect to be made against Mr. Stoen. Mr. Lane has likewise made numerous public statements in which he has defamed my client, and has even gone so far as to compare him to Adolf Hitler. All of Mr. Lane's activities, including the publication of this book, are done for his personal gain.

This letter is to put you on notice that we have not given Mr. Lane, nor do we intend to give Mr. Lane, any permission to use the name of Timothy Stoen in connection with his book, nor do we extend that privilege to you. Additionally, Mr. Stoen is reasonably entitled to an expectation of privacy and freedom from the kind of exposé we expect to be forthcoming into his private life and affairs. Mr. Stoen is a practicing attorney in San Francisco and has likewise suffered the terrible loss of his child in the Jonestown massacre. For you to publish scurrilous, defamatory and unfounded accusations by Mr. Lane would cause my client to suffer severely and hold him up to scorn and ridicule in the community in which he practices law.

Should our expectations of the contents of Mr. Lane's book prove accurate, and since this letter, along with the article from the Los Angeles Times, puts you upon notice of the basis of those expected allegations, we will immediately proceed to file suit against you and Mr. Lane upon publication of his book. Minimal inquiry by you will disclose numerous other public statements made by Mr. Lane about my client, which we expect to appear in book form, and which, as pointed out in the Los Angeles Times' article, are made without "a shred of proof, with only the word of defector Terri Buford and his own suspicions . . ."

Mr. Lane has consistently made use of great tragedies to others to personally aggrandize and enrich himself. His activities surrounding the Peoples' Temple are consistent with this opportunism, an opportunism which has earned him the description of "vulture" among numerous persons who have followed his career.

I remain,

Sincerely yours,
HALLINAN AND BLUM
/s/ Patrick S. Hallinan
Patrick Sarsfield Hallinan

/skc

Enclosure

Appendix K: The Steven Brill-Simon & Schuster Effort to Postpone Publication of a Rival Book

Dan E. Moldea is an investigative reporter who worked part time as a truck driver and loader for a Teamster's local while attending school and teaching graduate school. For four years, he pursued the facts about the Teamsters Union and Jimmy Hoffa in preparation for a definitive work. The responsible work in his book, *The Hoffa Wars,** won him several grants from the Fund for Investigative Journalism. Moldea discovered an important series of connections between Jack Ruby, the murderer of Lee Harvey Oswald, and the Teamsters Union and Jimmy Hoffa. He shared that information with the investigators for the House Select Committee on Assassinations, who were looking into the assassination of President Kennedy. Moldea conceded that the evidence he had uncovered was far from conclu-

*Dan E. Moldea, *The Hoffa Wars,* (New York: Paddington, 1978).

sive; indeed, he wrote, "the subject of a possible connection of Jimmy Hoffa and the underworld to President Kennedy's assassination is of course highly speculative."*

On June 3, 1979, the news media reported that the House Select Committee on Assassination had decided that without doubt there had been a conspiracy to murder President Kennedy and that the conspiracy "perhaps involved organized crime figures."† In the first report, "to be released soon," according to the media, the Congressional Committee concluded that the conspirators "may have included organized crime figures" working together with "James R. Hoffa, former president of the International Brotherhood of Teamsters." The chief counsel for the Committee said that he would not comment upon the report, but did say "I think the mob did it." Press reports continue:‡

> The report will contend that Ruby had stalked his victim from the hours immediately after the assassination until he fired the bullet into Oswald's stomach two days later, and that he had help gaining access to the assassin, perhaps unwittingly, from Dallas policemen.
>
> The committee report maintains that Ruby also had extensive associations among organized crime figures and discloses that his telephone records indicate a small number of calls, possibly relating to criminal activity, to a variety of people connected with the underworld, including Sam Giancana, who subsequently was murdered in his home in Chicago, and strong-arm men tied to [Santos] Trafficante.
>
> The committee discounts Ruby's statement before his own death that he had killed Oswald so that the President's widow would be spared a return to Dallas, where she might be forced to relive the shattering moments of the assassination as a witness at Oswald's trial.
>
> That story was concocted by his lawyer, the committee asserts.

In supporting those conclusions, the Committee provided corroboration for the important work done by Moldea who, through interviews with government agents, gangsters, and Teamster leaders, had substantially advanced the state of the evidence. Thus Moldea's work and book became contributions to the known truth about the assassination. And therefore his book became a dangerous mechanism to those who preferred that the truth remain hidden.

Originally, Moldea had entered into a contract to publish his work with New Republic Books. Works published by that company are distributed by Simon & Schuster, which is owned by the Gulf and Western Industries conglomerate.

*Ibid., p. 169.
†*New York Times,* 3 June 1979.
‡Ibid.

Simon & Schuster, according to Brill, offered him $70,000 to write a book about the Teamsters. At that point, Brill called Moldea, and according to Moldea, tried to make a deal to postpone the publication of Moldea's book. Brill's book does not mention Jack Ruby. It ignores the evidence pointing to a possible Ruby-Teamster connection in the assassination of President Kennedy. Moldea said, "He called me up in February 1978, and said, 'I'll give you anything you want out of my book if, in turn, you come out after my book.' " Moldea rejected the bribe and said, "Let the public be the judge."

"Then," according to Moldea, "the hardball started." In March 1978, Simon & Schuster moved to suppress *The Hoffa Wars* on behalf of Brill's book. The subsidiary of the huge conglomerate informed New Republic Books that Moldea's book would not be published. Martin Peretz, the publisher of *New Republic,* was powerless. He explained to Herbert Mitgang of the *New York Times:* "We have a clause in our distribution contract with Simon & Schuster . . . saying that if a conflict arose between one of their books and ours, they could ask us to delay publication. There was no battle over it—it's there in black and white, a clear stipulation. I very much regret it because it's a powerful book."*

Moldea withdrew from the agreement with *New Republic* and the book was ultimately published by Paddington Press, a fine small house. However, Richard Snyder, the president of Simon & Schuster, was apparently angered that *New Republic* had permitted Moldea to evade the stranglehold that Simon & Schuster had so carefully arranged. Snyder told the *New York Times,* "I was surprised when I heard that *New Republic* was selling its book to Paddington. We requested them to postpone it, not to sell it."

Both books were published at the same time, in spite of the efforts by Snyder to censor the Moldea book and Brill to bribe its author.

The Book Review of the *New York Times* reviewed the books together on its front page.‡ The *Times* attacked the Moldea book, claiming that the author had indulged in "theorizing that Mr. Hoffa was plotting to assassinate President Kennedy [and that] all we have to rely upon [is] Mr. Moldea's word that 'investigators say so.' " Moldea relied upon well-established facts and, as we have seen, was quite cautious in offering a conclusion. As for the Brill book, the *New York Times* loved it, saying that "Mr. Brill, on the other hand, hews closely to the themes that really matter." Obviously, for the *New York Times,* the death of President Kennedy cannot be so characterized.

**New York Times,* 29 June, 1978.
†*New York Times,* 29 June, 1978.
‡*New York Times,* Book Review, 12 November, 1978.

Apparently the less than admirable folks who continue to operate at the Teamsters Union agreed with the *Times* that Brill did not probe into proscribed areas. They liked the book too. Brill admitted to the *Times,* "In some respects, it's a very positive story about the Teamsters. In fact, I've had an offer to go to work for the Teamsters as a public-relations consultant —which I turned down."*

Brill, according to Moldea, "portrays one labor racketeer as a quasi-reformer. Brill also is vicious in his treatment of the rank and file within the union." He added, "I spent four years being protected by and living with steel haulers, and Brill just spit upon the rank and file and the reformers among the rank and file."

Brill, who later was to say that he always had a good impression about me until after he had been assigned by *Esquire* to write about me in 1979, was apparently not telling the truth. Moldea told me that "Brill mocked me; he tried to humiliate me to sell his book and destroy mine. He was very competitive. He taunted me for being 'a conspiracy freak' and called me 'the Mark Lane of the Hoffa disappearance.' "

Moldea said that in order to publicize his book, "Brill was going around bragging to people that he had a taped conversation with one of the alleged conspirators in the Hoffa disappearance, and that he was going to reveal this information in his book." This information finally reached the FBI and naturally they asked Brill about the tape. "Then Brill wrote an article for *Esquire* about how the FBI tried to muscle him."

**New York Times,* 29 June, 1978.

Index